THE YEAR'S BEST SCIENCE FICTION AND FANTASY

2010 EDITION

THE YEAR'S BEST SCIENCE FICTION AND FANTASY

2010 EDITION

EDITED BY

RICH HORTON

PRIME BOOKS

THE YEAR'S BEST SCIENCE FICTION AND FANTASY, 2010 EDITION

Prime Books
www.prime-books.com

ISBN: 978-1-60701-218-4

For my children, Melissa and Geoffrey

TABLE OF CONTENTS

TABLE OF CONTENTS

THE YEAR IN FANTASY AND SCIENCE FICTION, 2009

RICH HORTON

In looking over the stories I chose for this year's anthology, I noticed one possible trend. Last year about 30% of the stories were from original anthologies. This year the total is about 47%, and it could have been higher—I came very close indeed to including Maureen McHugh's "Useless Things" (from **Eclipse Three**), and Andy Duncan's "The Dragaman's Bride" (from **The Dragon Book**). Does this reflect a change in the market?

Perhaps it does. In recent years, certainly, we have been gifted with a new flowering of unthemed original anthology series: George Mann's **Solaris Books of New Science Fiction**, Lou Anders's **Fast Forward**, Jonathan Strahan's **Eclipse**, and Ellen Datlow's **Del Rey Book of Science Fiction and Fantasy** (this last not yet strictly speaking a series, mind you). On the other hand, the only one of those series certain to have more entries is **Eclipse**. But themed anthologies continue to be very common. Thick books from major publishers seem to be successful, as with **The Dragon Book** (edited by Jack Dann and Gardner Dozois), **The New Space Opera 2** (edited by Dozois and Strahan), and Ellen Datlow's two fine anthologies inspired by eminent American horror writers: **Poe** and **Lovecraft Unbound**. Slimmer books from small press outfits are also thick on the ground, as with the impressive six books from Norilana this year (the best probably being Mike Allen's **Clockwork Phoenix 2**, from which I chose Ann Leckie's "The Endangered Camp" for this volume). DAW once again published an original anthology each month in 2009, and **Other Earths**, edited by Nick Gevers and Jay Lake, was one of the best anthologies of the year. And we should not forget the young adult market: I found excellent stories in both **Geektastic** (edited by Holly Black and Cecil Castellucci) and **Sideshow** (edited by Deborah Noyes).

If anthologies are (ambiguously) flourishing, how are the magazines doing? Not so well, alas. The operative word for the major magazines the past few years has been stagnation, at least in terms of circulation. And this year the news was if anything worse. One magazine (*Realms of Fantasy*) died, only to be resurrected by a new publisher after only one missed issue. Another (*The Magazine of Fantasy and Science Fiction*) switched to bimonthly publication (with thicker issues). The smaller zines remained volatile—we lost such often interesting publications as *Fictitious Force* and *Paradox*, while the beautiful little zine *Zahir* will migrate to the Web in 2010. Still, the best place to look for the best new sf and fantasy remains the top magazines: *Asimov's*, *F&SF*, *Analog*, *Realms of Fantasy*, and *Interzone*. But the smaller zines are not to be missed—they publish much less frequently than the major magazines, and they tend to publish shorter work, but their best stuff is outstanding, as I hope the stories in this book from places like *Electric Velocipede*, *Shimmer*, and the once magazine now anthology *Postscripts* will demonstrate.

The third leg in the regular source of short fiction is online magazines. (Mind you those three legs don't exhaust places to find new science fiction: for example some appear as original stories in story collections, or as chapbooks, or in non-genre magazines—this last example represented in this book by Robert Kelly's "The Logic of the World," from *Conjunctions*.) There is no doubt that the web (and other online sources) are now essential for any reader in the genre. But even as online fiction has grown in importance, its business models are still a work in progress. Perhaps the most promising subscription-model webzine, *Jim Baen's Universe*, has announced it will close after the April 2010 issue. And the always interesting site *Lone Star Stories* closed in 2009. But other webzines continue strong. *Strange Horizons* has been around for a very long time now in web years, operating on a model based on volunteer editorial work and voluntary reader contributions—and they are better than ever these days. The much newer *Clarkesworld* had a very impressive 2009. A couple of former print magazines have established excellent online presences: *Subterranean Magazine*, and *Fantasy Magazine*. *Fantasy* is even gaining an sf companion in 2010, *Lightspeed*, to be edited by John Joseph Adams. And *Tor.com*, in its second year, has consistently published truly excellent sf and fantasy. (And unlike most online sites, *Tor.com* routinely features longer stories.)

So much for the industry news. What of the content? I thought to try to organize the stories here by subcategories. Maybe this would throw some light on the concerns occupying writers in 2009. One problem is of course that stories fit into multiple categories. And some are hard to place at all.

Perhaps the most obvious recent "fad" in sf and fantasy is steampunk—unusual perhaps in that it truly straddles the sf and fantasy genres. This subgenre can be traced at least to the mid-70s and such writers as K. W. Jeter and James P. Blaylock, and arguably earlier to things like M. John Harrison's *Viriconium* stories, and even the TV series *Wild Wild West*. It's never gone away, but in the past couple of years its popularity has shot up like a Verne spaceship from a cannon. But I don't think any of the stories I've chosen this year are pure quill steampunk, though the influence of that sensibility is clear on stories like Catherynne M. Valente's "The Radiant Car Thy Sparrows

Drew," Robert Charles Wilson's "This Peaceable Land; or, The Unbearable Vision of Harriet Beecher Stowe," and John Meaney's "Necroflux Day." But all these stories fit elsewhere in the tentative categories I suggest below.

One simple category is near-future sf. This is usually Earth-bound, and focuses on plausible technological developments and the social and personal effects of these. Oddly, I think, only three of these stories fit this category—Steven Gould's "A Story, with Beans," Rachel Swirsky's "Eros, Philia, Agape," and Damien Broderick's "The Qualia Engine." And these stories are strikingly different to each other.

By contrast, quite a few stories are set in the relatively far future, generally off Earth, or if on Earth, in the context of a future in which many people live or lived off Earth. These are "The Island," by Peter Watts; "Events Preceding the Helvetican Renaissance," by John Kessel; "Glister," by Dominic Green; "On the Human Plan," by Jay Lake; "A Painter, a Sheep, and a Boa Constrictor," by Nir Yaniv; "Wife-Stealing Time," by R. Garcia y Robertson; "As Women Fight," by Sara Genge; "Mongoose," by Sarah Monette and Elizabeth Bear; and "Crimes and Glory," by Paul McAuley. Several of these are some flavor of space opera or planetary adventure. Most notable to me, considering these stories as a unit, is the way so many of them are consciously toying with the tropes of sf—Kessel is playing with space opera clichés (but rather having his cake and eating it too, as the story remains an delightful adventure), while Garcia y Robertson has fun fooling around with Edgar Rice Burroughs' models, and Monette and Bear evoke Lovecraft, Carroll, and Kipling. Genge is the outlier here—her story is a fascinating look at gender in a people who can choose theirs. Lake and Watts, in very different ways, look at the very far future.

An sf category that has seemed to be undergoing a bit of a rebirth lately is time travel, and I saw several good time travel stories this year, but only one made this book: Genevieve Valentine's "Bespoke," which takes a different angle on the subject, dealing with people who outfit time travelers appropriately.

And of course alternate history continues fairly popular. But only one of the three in this book is very traditional: Robert Charles Wilson's "This Peaceable Land; or, The Unbearable Vision of Harriett Beecher Stowe." Far stranger is "The Radiant Car Thy Sparrows Drew," by Catherynne M. Valente, with its steampunk vibes in a 1986 setting. And Ann Leckie's "The Endangered Camp" looks much farther back: to the dinosaurs. (And perhaps its "history" isn't meant to be "alternate.")

I called four stories "science fantasy," a nod to settings which combine purely fantastic notions with at least some nod to a far future or offworld setting, or with a technological grounding: Theodora Goss's "Child-Empress of Mars," Lucius Shepard's Vance hommage, "Sylgarmo's Proclamation," Holly Phillips's "The Long, Cold Goodbye," and John Meaney's "Necroflux Day."

The more clearly fantastical stories are often very hard to classify as well.

What is Eugene Mirabelli's "Catalog"? Portal fantasy, maybe? Or Paul Park's "The Persistence of Memory; or This Space for Sale"? Metafiction, at one level. One fantasy, "The Logic of the World," by Robert Kelly, is perhaps fairly standard historical fantasy (set in what seems the Middle Ages of our world, with dragons), but is hardly ordinary within that template. Also not very ordinary is Jo Walton's "Three Twilight Tales," set in an unspecified world, with hints of metafiction and hints of fable. There is one fairly clear secondary world fantasy, "Dragon's Teeth," by Alex Irvine.

And finally what may be the dominant mode in fantasy these days: fantasies set in our world in more or less the present. (Some of these might be called "urban fantasies," but not all.) Paul Park's story, already mentioned, might qualify, and also Kelly Link's "Secret Identity" (but with superheroes!), Margo Lanagan's "Living Curiousities," Toiya Kristen Finley's "The Death of Sugar Daddy," John Langan's horror-tinged and Poe-derived "Technicolor," and Nancy Kress's "Images of Anna."

What to make of all this in summary? Does it mean much that so many of the fantasies I chose are set in the fairly familiar present day, but so many of the sf stories are set on other worlds and far in the future? Perhaps it's only selection bias. Noticeable at any rate is that no matter how we choose to categorize them, stories this good tend to defy categorization—they are first and best their ownselves, individual and original creations.

A STORY, WITH BEANS

STEVEN GOULD

Kimball crouched in the shade of the mesquite trees, which, because of the spring, were trees instead of their usual ground-hugging scrub. He was answering a question asked by one of the sunburned tourists, who was sprawled by the water, leaning against his expensive carbon-framed backpack.

"It takes about a foot of dirt," Kimball said. "I mean, if there isn't anything electrical going on. Then you'll need more, depending on the current levels and the strength of the EMF. You may need to be underground a good ten feet otherwise.

"But it's a foot, minimum. Once saw a noob find a silver dollar that he'd dug up at one of the old truck stops west of Albuquerque. 'Throw it away!' we yelled at him. Why did he think they replaced his fillings before he entered the territory? But he said it was a rare coin and worth a fortune. The idiot swallowed it.

"We could have buried him. Kept his face clear but put a good foot of dirt over him. That could've worked, but there were bugs right there, eating those massive hydraulic cylinders buried in the concrete floor of the maintenance bays, the ones that drove the lifts.

"We scattered. He ran, too, but they were all around and they rose up like bees and then he stepped on one and it was all over. They went for the coin like it was a chewy caramel center."

There were three college-aged tourists—two men and a girl—a pair of Pueblo khaki-dressed mounted territorial rangers that Kimball knew, and Mendez, the spring keeper. There was also a camel caravan camped below the spring, where the livestock were allowed to drink from the runoff, but the drovers, after filling their water bags, stayed close to their camels.

There were predators out here, both animal and human.

"What happened to the noob?" the tourist asked.

"He swallowed the coin. It was in his abdomen."

"What do you mean?"

"Christ, Robert," the girl said. "Didn't you listen to the entrance briefing?

He died. The bugs would just go right through him, to the metal. There aren't any trauma centers out here, you know?"

One of the rangers, silent until now, said, "That's right, miss." He slid the sleeve of his khaki shirt up displaying a scarred furrow across the top of his forearm. "Bug did this. Was helping to dig a new kiva at Pojoaque and didn't see I'd uncovered the base of an old metal fencepost. Not until the pain hit. There weren't many bugs around, but they came buzzing after that first one tasted steel and broadcast the call. I was able to roll away, under the incoming ones."

"Why are you visiting the zone?" asked Mendez, the spring keeper. He sat apart, keeping an eye on the tourists. The woman had asked about bathing earlier and the rangers explained that you could get a bath in town and there was sometimes water in the Rio Puerco, but you didn't swim in the only drinking water between Red Cliff and the Territorial Capitol.

"You can bathe without soap in the runoff, down the hill above where the cattle drink. Wouldn't do it below," Mendez had elaborated. "You can carry a bit of water off into the brush if you want to soap 'n' rinse."

Kimball thought Mendez was still sitting there just in case she did decide to bathe. Strictly as a public service, no doubt, keeping a wary eye out for, uh, tan lines.

The woman tourist said, "We're here for Cultural Anthropology 305. Field study. We meet our prof at his camp on the Rio Puerco."

"Ah," said Kimball, "Matt Peabody."

"Oh. You know him?"

"Sure. His camp is just downstream from the Duncan ford. He likes to interview the people who pass through."

"Right. He's published some fascinating papers on the distribution of micro-cultures here in the zone."

"Micro-cultures. Huh," said Kimball. "Give me an example."

"Oh, some of the religious or political groups who form small communities out here. Do you know what I mean?"

"I do." Kimball, his face still, exchanged a glance with the two rangers.

As the woman showed no sign of imminent hygiene, Mendez climbed to his feet, groaning, and returned to his one room adobe-faced dugout, up the hill.

The woman student became more enthusiastic. "I think it's so cool how the zone has ended up being this great nursery for widely diverse ways of life! I'm so excited to be able to see it."

Kimball stood up abruptly and, taking a shallow basket off of his cart, walked downstream where the cattle watered. He filled the basket with dried dung: some camel, horse, and a bit of cow. He didn't walk back until his breathing had calmed and his face was still. When he returned to the spring, one of the rangers had a pile of dried grass and pine needles ready in the communal fire pit and the other one was skinning a long, thin desert hare.

Kimball had a crock of beans that'd been soaking in water since he'd left Red Cliff that morning. Getting it out of the cart, he added more water, a chunk of salt pork, pepper, and fresh rosemary, then wedged it in the fire with the lid, weighted down by a handy rock.

"What do you do, out here?" the woman tourist asked him. Kimball smiled lazily and, despite her earlier words, thought about offering her some beans.

"Bit of this, bit of that. Right now, I sell things."

"A peddler? Shouldn't you be in school?"

Kimball decided he wasn't going to offer her any of his beans after all. He shrugged. "I've done the required." In fact, he had his GED, but he didn't advertise that. "It's different out here."

"How old are you?" she asked.

"How old are *you*?"

She grinned. "Personal question, eh? Okay. I'm nineteen."

"I'm sixteen. Sweet, never been kissed."

She cocked her head sideways. "Yeah, right."

"Kimball," one of the rangers called from across the fire-pit. "A quarter of the hare for some beans."

"Maybe. Any *buwa*, Di-you-wi?" Kimball asked.

"Of course there's *buwa*."

"*Buwa* and a haunch."

The two rangers discussed this in Tewa, then Di-you-wi said, "*Buwa* and a haunch. Don't stint the beans."

They warmed the *buwa*, rolled up blue-corn flatbread, on a rock beside the fire. Kim added a salad of wide-leaf flame-flower and purslane that he'd harvested along the trail. The rangers spoke thanks in Tewa and Kimball didn't touch his food until they were finished.

The woman watched out of the corner of her eyes, fascinated.

The tourists ate their radiation-sterilized ration packs that didn't spoil and didn't have to be cooked and weren't likely to give them the runs. But the smell of the hare and beans wafted through the clearing and the smell of the packaged food didn't spread at all.

"That sure smells good," the girl said.

Kimball tore off a bit of *buwa* and wrapped it around a spoonful of beans and a bit of the hare. He stretched out his arm. "See what you think."

She licked her lips and hesitated.

"Christ, Jennifer, that rabbit had ticks all over it," said the sunburned man. "Who knows what parasites they—uh, it had."

The rangers exchanged glances and laughed quietly.

Jennifer frowned and stood up, stepping over sunburn boy, and crouched down on her heels by the fire, next to Kimball. With a defiant look at her two companions, she took the offered morsel and popped it into her mouth. The look of defiance melted into surprised pleasure. "Oh, wow. So *buwe* is corn bread?"

"*Buwa.* Tewa wafer bread—made with blue corn. The Hopi make it too, but they call it *piki.*"

"The beans are wonderful. Thought they'd be harder."

"I started them soaking this morning, before I started out from Red Cliff."

"Ah," she lowered her voice. "What did they call you earlier?"

"Kimball."

She blinked. "Is that your name?"

"First name. I'm Kimball. Kimball . . . Creighton."

Di-you-wi laughed. Kimball glared at him.

"I'm Jennifer Frauenfelder." She settled beside him.

"Frauenfelder." Kimball said it slowly, like he was rolling it around in his mouth. "German?"

"Yes. It means field-of-women."

Di-you-wi blinked at this and said something in Tewa to his partner, who responded, "Huh. Reminds me of someone I knew who was called Left-for-dead."

Kimball rubbed his forehead and looked at his feet but Jennifer said, "Left-for-dead? That's an odd name. Did they have it from birth or did something happen?"

"Oh," said Di-you-wi, "something happened all right." He sat up straight and spoke in a deeper voice, more formal.

"*Owei humbeyô.*"

(His partner whispered, almost as if to himself, "Once upon a time and long ago.")

"Left-for-dead came to a village in the Jornada del Muerte on the edge of the territory of the City of God, where the People of the Book reside." Di-you-wi glanced at Jennifer and added, "It was a 'nursery of diverse beliefs.'"

"Left-for-dead was selling books, Bibles mostly, but also almanacs and practical guides to gardening and the keeping of goats and sheep and cattle.

"But he had other books as well, books not approved by the Elders—the plays of Shakespeare, books of stories, health education, Darwin.

"And he stole the virtue of Sharon—"

The two male tourists sat up at that and the sunburned one smacked his lips. "The dawg!"

Di-you-wi frowned at the interruption, cleared his throat, and went on. "And Left-for-dead stole the virtue of Sharon, the daughter of a Reader of the Book by trading her a reading primer and a book on women's health."

"What did she trade?" asked the leering one.

"There was an apple pie," said Di-you-wi. "Also a kiss."

Jennifer said, "And that's how she lost her virtue?"

"It was more the primer. The women of the People of the Book are not allowed to read," added his partner.

"Ironic, that," said Kimball.

"Or kiss," said Di-you-wi said with a quelling glance. He raised his voice. "They burned his books and beat him and imprisoned him in the stocks and called on the people of the village to pelt him but Sharon, the daughter of the Reader, burned the leather hinges from the stocks in the dusk and they ran, northwest, into the malpaís where the lava is heated by the sun until you can cook *buwa* on the stones and when the rain falls in the afternoon it sizzles like water falling on coals.

"The Elders chased them on horseback but the malpaís is even harder on horses than men and they had to send the horses back and then they chased them on foot but the rocks leave no prints."

"But the water in the malpaís is scarce to none and Left-for-dead and the girl were in a bad way even though they hid by day and traveled by night. Once, in desperation, Left-for-dead snuck back and stole a water gourd from the men who chased them, while they lay sleeping, but in doing so he put them back on the trail.

"Two days later, Sharon misstepped and went down in a crack in the rock and broke both bones in her lower leg. Left-for-dead splinted the leg, made a smoke fire, and left her there. The People of the Book found her and took her back, dragged on a travois, screaming with every bump and jar.

"They discussed chasing Left-for-dead and then they prayed and the Reader said God would punish the transgressor, and they went back to their village and spread the story far and wide, to discourage the weak and the tempted.

"Left-for-dead walked another day to the north, hoping to reach the water at Marble Tanks, but he had been beaten badly in the stocks and his strength failed him. When he could go no further he rolled into a crevice in the lava where there was a bit of shade and got ready to die. His tongue began to swell and he passed in and out of darkness and death had his hand on him."

Here Di-you-wi paused dramatically, taking a moment to chase the last of his beans around the bowl with a bit of *buwa*.

Jennifer leaned forward. "And?"

"And then it rained. A short, heavy summer thunderstorm. The water dripped down onto Left-for-dead's face and he drank, and awoke drinking and coughing. And then drank some more. He crawled out onto the face of the malpaís and drank from the puddles in the rock and was able to fill the water gourd he'd stolen from the Reader's men, but he didn't have to drink from it until the next day when the last of the rain evaporated from the pockets in the lava.

"He made it to Marble Tanks, and then east to some seeps on the edge of the lava flows, and hence to the Territorial Capitol."

"Because the incident with Left-for-dead was just the latest of many, a territorial judge was sent out with a squad of rangers to hold hearings. The City of God sent their militia, one hundred strong, and killed the judge and most of the rangers.

"When the two surviving rangers reported back, the territorial governor flashed a message beyond the curtain and a single plane came in answer, flying up where the air is so thin that the bugs' wings can't catch, and they dropped the leaflets, the notice of reclamation—the revocation of the city's charter."

"That's it?" said Jennifer. "They dropped a bunch of leaflets?"

"The first day. The second day it wasn't leaflets."

Jennifer held her hand to her mouth? "Bombs?"

"Worse. Chaff pods of copper and aluminum shavings that burst five hundred feet above the ground. I heard tell that the roofs and ground glittered in the sunlight like jewels."

The sunburned man laughed. "That's it? Metal shavings?"

"I can't believe they let you through the curtain," Jennifer said to him. "Didn't you listen at all?" She turned back to Di-you-wi. "How many died?"

"Many left when they saw the leaflets. But not the most devout and not the women who couldn't read. The Speaker of the Word said that their faith would prevail. Perhaps they deserved their fate . . . but not the children.

"The last thing the plane dropped was a screamer—an electromagnetic spike trailing an antennae wire several hundred feet long. They say the bugs rose into the air and blotted the sun like locusts."

Jennifer shuddered.

Di-you-wi relented a little. "Many more got out when they saw the cloud. I mean, it was like one of the ten plagues of the first chapter of their book, after all. If they made it outside the chaff pattern and kept to the low ground, they made it. But those who stayed and prayed?" He paused dramatically. "The adobe houses of the City of God are mud and dust and weeds, and the great Cathedral is a low pile of stones and bones."

"*Owei humbeyô.*" Once upon a time and long ago.

Everyone was quiet for a moment though Jennifer's mouth worked as if to ask something, but no sound came out. Kimball added the last of the gathered fuel to the fire, banged the dust out of his basket, and flipped it, like a Frisbee, to land in his rickshaw-style handcart. He took the empty stoneware bean crock and filled it from the stream and put at the edge of the coals, to soak before he cleaned it.

"What happened to Sharon?" Jennifer finally asked into the silence.

Di-you-wi shook his head. "I don't know. You would have to ask Left-for-dead."

Jennifer: "Oh, thanks a lot. Very helpful."

Di-you-wi and his partner exchanged glances and his partner opened his mouth as if to speak, but Di-you-wi shook his head.

Kimball hadn't meant to speak, but he found the words spilling out anyway, unbidden. "I would like to say that Sharon's leg still hurts her. That it didn't heal straight, and she limps. But that she teaches others to read now down in New Roswell. That I had seen her recently and sold her school some primers just last month."

Jennifer frowned, "You would like to say that?"

"It was a bad break and I set it as best I could, but they bounced her over the lava on their way home and trusted to God for further treatment. She couldn't even walk, much less run, when the metal fell."

Jennifer's mouth was open but she couldn't speak for a moment.

"Huh," said Di-you-wi. "Hadn't heard that part, Left-for-dead."

Kimball could see him reorganizing the tale in his head, incorporating the added details. "Got it from her sister. After I recovered."

Jennifer stood and walked over to Kimball's cart and flipped up the tarp. The books were arranged spine out, paperbacks mostly, some from behind the Porcelain Wall, newish with plasticized covers, some yellowed and cracking from before the bugs came, like anything that didn't contain metal or electronics, salvaged, and a small selection of leather-bound books from New Santa Fe, the territorial capitol, hand-set with ceramic type and hand-bound—mostly practical, how-to books.

"Peddler. Book seller."

Kimball shrugged. "Varies. I've got other stuff, too. Plastic sewing-needles, ceramic blades, antibiotics, condoms. Mostly books."

Finally she asked, "And her father? The Elder who put you in the stocks?"

"He lives. His faith wasn't strong enough when it came to that final test. He lost an arm, though."

"Is he in New Roswell, too?"

"No. He's doing time in the territorial prison farm in Nuevo Belen. He preaches there, to a very small congregation. The People of the Book don't do well if they can't isolate their members—if they can't control what information they get. They're not the People of the Books, after all.

"If she'd lived, Sharon would probably have made him a part of her life . . . but he's forbidden the speaking of her name. He would've struck her name from the leaves of the family Bible, but the bugs took care of that."

Di-you-wi shook his head on hearing this. "And who does this hurt? I think he is a stupid man."

Kimball shrugged. "It's not him I feel sorry for."

Jennifer's eyes glinted brightly in the light of the fire. She said, "It's not fair, is it?"

And there was nothing to be said to that.

CHILD-EMPRESS OF MARS

THEODORA GOSS

In the month of Ind, when the flowers of the Jindal trees were in blossom and just beginning to scatter their petals on the ground like crimson rain, a messenger came to the court of the Child-Empress. He announced that a Hero had awakened in the valley of Jar.

The messenger was young and obviously nervous, at court for the first time, but when the Child-Empress said, "A Hero? What is his name?" he replied with a steady voice, "Highest blossom of the Jindal tree, his name is not yet known. He has not spoken it, for he has as yet seen no one to whom he could speak."

The Ladies in Waiting fluttered their fans, to hear him speak with such courtesy, and I said to Lady Ahira, "I think I recognize him. That is Captain Namoor, the youngest son of General Gar, who has inherited his crimson tongue," by which I meant his eloquence, for an eloquent man is said to have a tongue as sweet as the crimson nectar of the Jindal flowers.

Lady Ahira blushed blue, from her cheeks down to her knees, for she had a passion for captains, and this was surely the captain of all captains, who had already won the hearts and livers of the court.

"Let the Hero's name be Jack or Buck or Dan, one of those names that fall so strangely on our tongues, and let him be tall and pale and silent, except when he sings the songs of his people to the moons, and let him be a slayer of beasts, a master of the glain and of the double adjar." The Child-Empress clapped her hands, first two and then four, rapidly until they sounded like pebbles falling from the cliffs of the valley of Jar, or the river Noth tumbling between its banks where they narrow at Ard Ulan. And we remembered that although she was an Empress and older than our memories, she was still only a child, hatched not long after the lost island of Irdum sank beneath the sea.

"Light upon the snows of Ard Ulan, he is indeed a slayer of beasts," said the captain. The Ladies in Waiting fluttered their fans, and one sank senseless to the floor, overcome by his courtesy and eloquence. "He wounded two Garwolves who approached him, wishing to know the source of his singular odor. He wounded them with a projectile device. They are in the care of the Warden of the reed marshes of Zurdum."

"This cannot be," said the Child-Empress. "The Hero must go on his Quest, for that is the nature of Heroes, but he must not harm my creatures, neither the Garwolves singing in the morning mist, nor the Ilpin bounding over the rocky cliffs of Jar, nor the Mirimi birds that nest in the sands of Gar Kahan, nor even the Sloefrogs, whose yellow eyes blink along the banks of the river Noth. He must not bend a single wing of an Itz. Let us give him a creature to speak with, who can learn his name and where he has come from. Let us send him a Jain, and with her a Translator, so that he will perceive her as resembling his own species. Is there one of my Translators who would travel with the Jain to meet the Hero?"

All three of the court Translators stepped forward. From among them the Child-Empress chose Irman Adze, who was the oldest and most honored, and who signaled her willingness to make such an important journey by chirruping softly and nodding her head until her wattles flapped back and forth.

The Child-Empress said to Irman Adze, "Your first task is to remove his projectile device and replace it with the glain and the double adjar, so that he is suitably equipped but can cause no great harm to my creatures and the citizens of my realm." Then she turned to the court. "And let us also send an Observer, so that we may see and learn what the Hero is saying and doing." The Observers whirred and flew forward. She selected one among them and entered its instructions.

"And you, Captain," said the Child-Empress, turning to Captain Namoor, "because of the pleasure you have brought us in announcing the arrival of a Hero, you shall be permitted to wear the green feather of a Mirimi bird in your cap, and to proceed after the Chancellor on state occasions."

His training prevented Captain Namoor from blushing with the intensity of his emotions, but he must have blushed inside, for not one in a thousand receives the honor that the Child-Empress had bestowed upon him. Lady Ahira squeezed my upper left hand until it went purple and I winced from the pressure.

"What beast shall he slay, great—green feather of the Mirimi bird?" asked the Chancellor, in his ponderous way. He fancied himself a poet. The Ladies in Waiting hid their ears with their fans, and even the Pages giggled. His words were so trite, and not at all original.

"What beast indeed?" asked the Child-Empress. "Since I have said that none of our creatures must be harmed, let us send our own Poufli." Hearing his name, Poufli rose from where he had been lying at the Child-Empress's feet and licked two of her hands, while the other two stroked his filaments.

"Go, Poufli," said the Child-Empress. "Lead the Hero on his Quest, but allow him eventually to slay you, and when you have been slain, return to me, and I will think of a way to reward him that is appropriate for Heroes."

The next day, the Jain, with the Translator strutting beside her and the Observer whirring and darting around them, left for the slopes and caverns of Ard Ulan, where the Hero had awakened. Poufli bounded off in the opposite direction, to where the Child-Empress intended that the Hero should encounter his final Obstacle.

We watched, day after day, as the Hero traveled across the valley of Jar. The images transmitted by the Observer were captured in the idhar at the center of the Chamber of Audience. I preferred to watch in the mornings, when the mist still hung about the bottoms of the pillars but the dome high above was already illuminated by the rising sun, and the Mirimi birds were stirring in the branches of the Gondal trees. I would splash water on my face from one of the sublimating fountains, eat a light breakfast of Pika bread spread with Ipi berries, drink a libation made from the secretions of the Ilpin that were kept at court, and then sit on one of the cushions that the Child-Empress had provided, watching, with the other early risers, as the Hero performed his ablutions and offered his otherworldly songs to the gods of his clan.

As the Observer transmitted, the Translator interpreted for the Hero and simultaneously showed us what he saw, so we were confronted with our own landscape made strange, like the landscape of another world. The Ipi bushes, the yellow Kifli flowers that grew at the edges of the reed marshes of Zurdum, the waters of the marshes, all were flatter, as though they had lost one of their dimensions, and they lacking many colors of the spectrum. The Jain had become tall and pale, although the Translator did not disguise her undulations. The Observer had become organic. It bounded rather than flew, and was covered with a fine brown fur.

"Dog! Come here, dog!" we heard the Hero say, and "Would you like something to eat?" to the Jain, whose articulations he listened to with care, as though she were speaking a language he did not understand.

I preferred these quieter, intimate moments, although each day, in the late morning or early afternoon, the Child-Empress sent the Hero an Obstacle: once, a swarm of Itz to sting him, so that he swelled up and the Jain had to cover his arms and legs with the leaves of an Ipi bush soaked in marsh water; once, two Habira that he fought off with the glain and clever use of a flaming reed; once, a group of warriors from the town of Ard, so that he would know he was approaching the towns and cities where the citizens lived. Once, the citizens came out of a town to offer him welcome, placing a garland of pink Gondal flowers around his neck and giving him cups of the intoxicating liquor that westerners make from an iridescent fungus they call Ghram, which grows on the roots of the Gondal tree. Once, he was placed in a cage at the center of the town, and the citizens came to see him, until he said a word that was the name, they told him, of an ancient god who was still secretly reverenced.

As court Poet, it was primarily my responsibility to create the events and

Obstacles of the Quest, although the Child-Empress was an enthusiastic collaborator. After my morning viewing, I would go to her chamber. However early I went, she was always lying upon her couch, absorbed with matters of state, attending to the wellbeing of the citizens. But she would put aside her work, waving away the Chancellor and the Courtiers that were gathered around her, and say to me, "Good morning, Elah Gal. What have you thought of for my Hero today?"

The morning that the Hero reached the court of the Child-Empress, the Translators occupied themselves with interpreting us to the Hero. We looked at ourselves in the idhar, translated. We were still ourselves, yet we were no longer ourselves—Lady Ahira still blushed blue, although her knees were stiffer, and an entirely different shape. The Courtiers were stiffer as well, more angular—and silent. I must admit that I did not miss their chirring. Many of us were only partly visible, and the Translators themselves appeared only as a shiver in the air. The Pages still ran back and forth behind the cushions where we sat, but on two slender legs, like Ilpin. I had to remind myself that they would not fall—they were only translated.

The Child-Empress was still herself, still a child, still an Empress, and yet how different she was. Substantial parts of her could no longer been seen, and when she clapped, it was with only two hands.

"That must be what a child of his species looks like," whispered Lady Ahira, and would have whispered more had not the Hero walked in, with the Jain at his side and the Observer, grown positively shaggy, by his feet.

"Welcome, visitor from another land," said the Child-Empress. "Do you come from far Iranuk, or fabled Thull? Tell us what land you come from, and your name."

"No, ma'am," said the Hero. "My name is Jake Stackhouse, and as far as I can make out, unless the stars are lying to me, I'm from another planet altogether. What planet is this I've landed on?"

"Planet?" said the Child-Empress. "This is Ord, the crimson planet. Have you truly learned to travel across the darkness of space? You must be a great wizard, as well as a great warrior."

"No, ma'am," said Jake Stackhouse. "I've got no idea how I ended up on your planet, though I sure would like to find out, so I can go home again. And I'm not a warrior or a wizard, as you call them. I'm just a ranch hand, although I've had a few knocks in my life, and learned how to take care of myself."

"You do not know your way home?" said the Child-Empress. "I am sad that you are not able to return to your clan, but what is a misfortune for you may be fortunate for us. I have heard that you fought the Garwolves and defeated the warriors of the western marshes. Surely you are the most courageous man on Ord. I ask for your aid. We are threatened by a fearsome beast, called a—" I suddenly realized that when we had created this encounter, the Child-Empress and I, we had not given our beast a name "—a Poufli. This beast is ravaging our eastern cities and towns, eating and frightening our citizens. If you will defeat this beast, I will give you ten hecats of land, and one of my Ladies in Waiting to be your mate."

Captain Namoor, who stood next to the Chancellor, turned orange down to the tops of his boots. Let him, I thought. A little jealousy would do him good.

"I don't want a mate, ma'am. Just this girl here, who's traveled for the last three days, the strangest days of my life, at my side. She's saved my life a couple of times, I reckon. I don't know her name, so I call her Friday."

"You would have that female for your mate?" said the Child-Empress. "Then know, Jake Stackhouse, that she is a priestess of her people, the Jain of Ajain, from the far north, where the river Noth springs from the mountains of Ard Ulan. To mate with her, you must win her in battle with the glain and the double adjar. Are you willing to fight for her, Jake Stackhouse?"

I could not help blushing pink with surprise and appreciation. What an improvisation this was, not the words we had created together and so carefully rehearsed, but the Child-Empress's own, created at that moment. Around me I heard a scattering of applause as the court realized what had just happened. I applauded as well, pleased with her spontaneity. How honored I was that my Empress, too, was a poet.

"All right," said Jake Stackhouse, "I'll fight this Poufli for you, and then fight for the girl I love best in all the world. I never thought I'd marry a green bride, but underneath that skin of hers, she's as sweet and loyal as any woman of Earth."

"It is well," said the Child-Empress. "Defeat the Poufli for me and I will give you ten hecats of land by the upper reaches of the river Noth, where the soil is most fertile, and I will ensure that the Jain becomes your mate. Now, take some refreshment with us, Jake Stackhouse."

The Pages brought platters of the roasted fruit of the Pandam tree, and a sauce made from the sap of the Pandam, and stuffed roots, and the sweet lichen that grow on the roofs of the houses of Irum, in the south, and Ghram that had been brought from Ard for the Hero's Feast. The Hero sat on a cushion, with the Jain beside him and the Observer at his feet, and told us stories of his planet and the place he had spent his childhood, the Land of a Single Star. He spoke of towns in which warriors battled each other with projectile devices, thieves who stole from transport vehicles, and herds of creatures that stretched over the plains so you could see no end to them. He spoke of females so beautiful they were given the names of flowers. The Ladies in Waiting were so eager to hear his stories that they listened without respiring, and some of the more delicate Pages swooned or emitted the scent of marsh water. I myself, Elah Gal, the court Poet, listened and recorded, so that these stories of another planet could be placed among the Tales of the Heroes, which my ancestress Elim Dar had begun when the Child-Empress herself was only a dream of her parent's physical manifestation.

Grief and consternation spread throughout the court on the day the Observer transmitted the tragic news: the Hero was dead. His body was brought back to the palace, and three Healers examined him to determine the cause of his death. They reported their findings to the Child-Empress. Poufli was not to blame. He had played his part both enthusiastically and with care. The Hero's wounds were minor. But his dermal layer, when they examined it, had been covered with red spots. He must have had a reaction to Poufli's emissions, or perhaps to the touch of his filaments.

But Poufli was not to be consoled. He lay submerged in one of the palace fountains, beneath the translucent fish from Irum, refusing to eat, refusing to sleep, as had been his custom, at the foot of the Child-Empress's couch.

The court grieved. The Courtiers put on their white robes of death, and I myself put on the death robes that my mother had worn when her spouse of the second degree had chosen to demanifest. The Ladies in Waiting would not blush. Lady Ahira postponed the celebration of her union of the fourth degree with Captain Namoor, for which luminous mosses had already been grown on the walls of the Chamber of Audience. The Pages stood silent, neither giggling nor emitting scent. By orders of the Child-Empress, the murals on the walls of the palace were muted, until only faint outlines reminded us of their presence. The palace Guards wore mourning veils, and drifted around the halls of the palace like gibhans of the dead. The Jain was inconsolable, and filled the halls with the mourning wail of her kind. A cold wind seemed to blow through everything.

I sat beneath the Jindal tree in the palace garden and tried to create a poem about the Hero, but how can one commemorate defeat? The Child-Empress herself would not leave her chamber. I went in once a day to try to consult with her, but she simply sat by the aperture, looking out at the garden. I did not wish to interrupt her contemplations. Even the Chancellor stood by her couch without stirring, waiting for her to emerge from her grief.

On the seventh day, she came into the Chamber of Audience. She wore robes as red as the Jindal flowers, and she had adorned her arms with bracelets of small silver bells, which jingled as she moved. Poufli was at her side, pushing his noses into her robes.

"Citizens and creatures," she said, "you are sad because the Hero has died. We cannot now celebrate his victory, nor follow with fascination the story of his life here on Ord. Is this not so?"

The Ladies in Waiting, the Courtiers, the Guards, the Pages, all nodded or waved or emitted to signal their assent.

"But we should not be sad," she said. "To watch the triumph of the Hero would have been like listening to a poem by Elah Gal, or watching the blossoming of the Jindal flowers, or attending the union of Lady Ahira and Captain Namoor. It would have been most satisfying. But there is another sort of satisfaction, when Elah Gal pauses and there is silence, or the blossoms fall from the Jinhal tree, or lovers part in sorrow after their time together has ended. Do we not take satisfaction also in the passing of things, which we can no more control than we can control the way of the Mirimi bird in the air, or the way of two loves once they are mated? The death of the Hero reminds us of our own demanifestations. This too is a poem, perhaps a greater poem than the Hero's triumph would have been, because it is more difficult, and to understand it we must become more than ourselves.

"Let the Hero, whose physical manifestation our Healers have so artistically preserved, be placed on a pedestal of stone from the quarries of Gar Kahan, beneath the branches of the Jindal tree in the garden, where their blossoms will fall upon him. And let us celebrate the death of the Hero! Let us celebrate our own demanifestations, which are to come. Let the Jain be returned to her clan so that she can differentiate and deposit her eggs, and let her offspring be raised at court, in recognition of the service that she has performed for us. Let Elah Gal create a poem about the Hero, a new kind of poem for a new time, and let it be included in the Tales of the Heroes. And let us all celebrate! Come, my friends. Let song and laughter and blushes return to the palace! But I shall withdraw, for I have important work to do. Tonight, as the moons rise over Ord, I shall begin to dream, so that, in your children's children's lifetimes, another Child-Empress will be born."

For a moment, there was silence around the Chamber of Audience. Then, the murals on the walls began to glow. The Ladies in Waiting began to clap and laugh and blush. The Pages leaped into the air and landed again on their toes, emitting the scent of Kifli flowers. The Guards cast off their veils and clashed their disintegrators on their shields, so that they rang through the halls. Everywhere, there was the sound of joy and of wonder. I myself could not keep my orifices from misting. To live at a time of the dreaming! The Hero had indeed brought us something greater than we could have imagined.

I wondered, for a moment, if I would become one of those poets who are celebrated for having created what no other poet could have—if I would create the poem of the Child-Empress's dreaming, of her becoming no longer a child but the full essence of herself, until eventually she emerged in the perfection of her non-physical manifestation. But then my humility returned. Such poems were still to be created. The first of them would be about the Hero, of how he had died and yet fulfilled his Quest.

But today was a day of celebration. We sang and danced in the Chamber of Audience, celebrating the union of Lady Ahira and Captain Namoor. At the height of the festivities, the Child-Empress withdrew. But we knew now that it was not to contemplate her grief but to begin an important new event in her life. And we leaped higher and turned faster with joy, while the Musicians played their kurams and their dharms, until night fell and the mosses illuminated the ancient murals, and the moons rose, and the Jindal flowers spread their fragrance over the palace.

THE ISLAND

PETER WATTS

We are the cave men. We are the Ancients, the Progenitors, the blue-collar steel monkeys. We spin your webs and build your magic gateways, thread each needle's eye at sixty thousand kilometers a second. We never stop. We never even dare to slow down, lest the light of your coming turn us to plasma. All for you. All so you can step from star to star without dirtying your feet in these endless, empty wastes *between*.

Is it really too much to ask, that you might talk to us now and then?

I know about evolution and engineering. I know how much you've changed. I've seen these portals give birth to gods and demons and things we can't begin to comprehend, things I can't believe were ever human; alien hitchikers, maybe, riding the rails we've left behind. Alien conquerers.

Exterminators, perhaps.

But I've also seen those gates stay dark and empty until they faded from view. We've infered diebacks and dark ages, civilizations burned to the ground and others rising from their ashes—and sometimes, afterwards, the things that come out look a little like the ships *we* might have built, back in the day. They speak to each other—radio, laser, carrier neutrinos—and sometimes their voices sound something like ours. There was a time we dared to hope that they really were like us, that the circle had come round again and closed on beings we could talk to. I've lost count of the times we tried to break the ice.

I've lost count of the eons since we gave up.

All these iterations fading behind us. All these hybrids and posthumans and immortals, gods and catatonic cavemen trapped in magical chariots they can't begin to understand, and not one of them ever pointed a comm laser in our direction to say *Hey, how's it going*, or *Guess what? We cured Damascus Disease!* or even *Thanks, guys, keep up the good work*.

We're not some fucking cargo cult. We're the backbone of your goddamn empire. You wouldn't even be out here if it weren't for us.

And—and you're our *children*. Whatever you've become, you were once like this, like me. I believed in you once. There was a time, long ago, when I believed in this mission with all my heart.

Why have you forsaken us?

And so another build begins.

This time I open my eyes to a familiar face I've never seen before: only a boy, early twenties perhaps, physiologically. His face is a little lopsided, the cheekbone flatter on the left than the right. His ears are too big. He looks almost *natural*.

I haven't spoken for millennia. My voice comes out a whisper: "Who are you?" Not what I'm supposed to ask, I know. Not the first question *anyone* on *Eriophora* asks, after coming back.

"I'm yours," he says, and just like that I'm a mother.

I want to let it sink in, but he doesn't give me the chance: "You weren't scheduled, but Chimp wants extra hands on deck. Next build's got a situation."

So the chimp is still in control. The chimp is always in control. The mission goes on.

"Situation?" I ask.

"Contact scenario, maybe."

I wonder when he was born. I wonder if he ever wondered about me, before now.

He doesn't tell me. He only says, "Sun up ahead. Half lightyear. Chimp thinks, maybe it's talking to us. Anyhow . . . " My—son shrugs. "No rush. Lotsa time."

I nod, but he hesitates. He's waiting for The Question but I already see a kind of answer in his face. Our reinforcements were supposed to be *pristine*, built from perfect genes buried deep within *Eri*'s iron-basalt mantle, safe from the sleeting blueshift. And yet this boy has flaws. I see the damage in his face, I see those tiny flipped base-pairs resonating up from the microscopic and *bending* him just a little off-kilter. He looks like he grew up on a planet. He looks borne of parents who spent their whole lives hammered by raw sunlight.

How far out must we be by now, if even our own perfect building blocks have decayed so? How long has it taken us? How long have I been dead?

How long? It's the first thing everyone asks.

After all this time, I don't want to know.

He's alone at the tac tank when I arrive on the bridge, his eyes full of icons and trajectories. Perhaps I see a little of me in there, too.

"I didn't get your name," I say, although I've looked it up on the manifest. We've barely been introduced and already I'm lying to him.

"Dix." He keeps his eyes on the tank.

He's over ten thousand years old. Alive for maybe twenty of them. I wonder how much he knows, who he's met during those sparse decades: does he know Ishmael, or Connie? Does he know if Sanchez got over his brush with immortality?

I wonder, but I don't ask. There are rules.

I look around. "We're it?"

Dix nods. "For now. Bring back more if we need them. But . . . " His voice trails off.

"Yes?"

"Nothing."

I join him at the tank. Diaphanous veils hang within like frozen, color-coded smoke. We're on the edge of a molecular dust cloud. Warm, semiorganic, lots of raw materials. Formaldehyde, ethylene glycol, the usual prebiotics. A good spot for a quick build. A red dwarf glowers dimly at the center of the Tank: the chimp has named it DHF428, for reasons I've long since forgotten to care about.

"So fill me in," I say.

His glance is impatient, even irritated. "You too?"

"What do you mean?"

"Like the others. On the other builds. Chimp can just squirt the specs but they want to *talk* all the time."

Shit, his link's still active. He's *online*.

I force a smile. "Just a—a cultural tradition, I guess. We talk about a lot of things, it helps us—reconnect. After being down for so long."

"But it's *slow*," Dix complains.

He doesn't know. Why doesn't he know?

"We've got half a lightyear," I point out. "There's some rush?"

The corner of his mouth twitches. "Vons went out on schedule." On cue a cluster of violet pinpricks sparkle in the Tank, five trillion klicks ahead of us. "Still sucking dust mostly, but got lucky with a couple of big asteroids and the refineries came online early. First components already extruded. Then Chimp sees these fluctuations in solar output—mainly infra, but extends into visible." The tank blinks at us: the dwarf goes into time-lapse.

Sure enough, it's *flickering*.

"Nonrandom, I take it."

Dix inclines his head a little to the side, not quite nodding.

"Plot the time-series." I've never been able to break the habit of raising my voice, just a bit, when addressing the chimp. Obediently (*obediently*. Now *there's* a laugh-and-a-half) the AI wipes the spacescape and replaces it with

. . . .

"Repeating sequence," Dix tells me. "Blips don't change, but spacing's a log-linear increase cycling every 92.5 corsecs Each cycle starts at 13.2 clicks/corsec, degrades over time."

"No chance this could be natural? A little black hole wobbling around in the center of the star, maybe?"

Dix shakes his head, or something like that: a diagonal dip of the chin that somehow conveys the negative. "But way too simple to contain much info. Not like an actual conversation. More—well, a shout."

He's partly right. There may not be much information, but there's enough. *We're here. We're smart. We're powerful enough to hook a whole damn star up to a dimmer switch.*

Maybe not such a good spot for a build after all.

I purse my lips. "The sun's hailing us. That's what you're saying."

"Maybe. Hailing *someone*. But too simple for a rosetta signal. It's not an archive, can't self-extract. Not a bonferroni or fibonacci seq, not pi. Not even a multiplication table. Nothing to base a pidgin on."

Still. An intelligent signal.

"Need more info," Dix says, proving himself master of the blindingly obvious.

I nod. "The vons."

"Uh, what about them?"

"We set up an array. Use a bunch of bad eyes to fake a good one. It'd be faster than high-geeing an observatory from this end or retooling one of the on-site factories."

His eyes go wide. For a moment he almost looks frightened for some reason. But the moment passes and he does that weird head-shake thing again. "Bleed too many resources away from the build, wouldn't it?"

"It would," the chimp agrees.

I suppress a snort. "If you're so worried about meeting our construction benchmarks, Chimp, factor in the potential risk posed by an intelligence powerful enough to control the energy output of an entire sun."

"I can't," it admits. "I don't have enough information."

"You don't have *any* information. About something that could probably stop this mission dead in its tracks if it wanted to. So maybe we should get some."

"Okay. Vons reassigned."

Confirmation glows from a convenient bulkhead, a complex sequence of dance instructions fired into the void. Six months from now a hundred self-replicating robots will waltz into a makeshift surveillance grid; four months after that, we might have something more than vacuum to debate in.

Dix eyes me as though I've just cast some kind of magic spell.

"It may run the ship," I tell him, "but it's pretty fucking stupid. Sometimes you've just got to spell things out."

He looks vaguely affronted, but there's no mistaking the surprise beneath. He didn't know that. He *didn't know.*

Who the hell's been raising him all this time? Whose problem is this?

Not mine.

"Call me in ten months," I say. "I'm going back to bed."

It's as though he never left. I climb back into the bridge and there he is, staring into tac. DHF428 fills the tank, a swollen red orb that turns my son's face into a devil mask.

He spares me the briefest glance, eyes wide, fingers twitching as if electrified. "Vons don't see it."

I'm still a bit groggy from the thaw. "See wh—"

"The *sequence!*" His voice borders on panic. He sways back and forth, shifting his weight from foot to foot.

"Show me."

Tac splits down the middle. Cloned dwarves burn before me now, each perhaps twice the size of my fist. On the left, an *Eri*'s-eye view: DHF428 stutters as it did before, as it presumably has these past ten months. On the right, a compound-eye composite: an interferometry grid built by a myriad precisely-spaced vons, their rudimentary eyes layered and parallaxed into something approaching high resolution. Contrast on both sides has been conveniently cranked up to highlight the dwarf's endless winking for merely human eyes.

Except it's only winking from the left side of the display. On the right, 428 glowers steady as a standard candle.

"Chimp: any chance the grid just isn't sensitive enough to see the fluctuations?"

"No."

"Huh." I try to think of some reason it would lie about this.

"Doesn't make *sense*," my son complains.

"It does," I murmur, "if it's not the sun that's flickering."

"But *is* flickering—" He sucks his teeth. "You can *see* it fl—wait, you mean something *behind* the vons? Between, between them and us?"

"Mmmm."

"Some kind of *filter*." Dix relaxes a bit. "Wouldn't we've seen it, though? Wouldn't the vons've hit it going down?"

I put my voice back into ChimpComm mode. "What's the current field-of-view for *Eri*'s forward scope?"

"Eighteen mikes," the chimp reports. "At 428's range, the cone is three point three four lightsecs across."

"Increase to a hundred lightsecs."

The *Eri*'s-eye partition swells, obliterating the dissenting viewpoint. For a moment the sun fills the tank again, paints the whole bridge crimson. Then it dwindles as if devoured from within.

I notice some fuzz in the display. "Can you clear that noise?"

"It's not noise," the chimp reports. "It's dust and molecular gas."

I blink. "What's the density?"

"Estimated hundred thousand atoms per cubic meter."

Two orders of magnitude too high, even for a nebula. "Why so heavy?" Surely we'd have detected any gravity well strong enough to keep *that* much material in the neighborhood.

"I don't know," the chimp says.

I get the queasy feeling that I might. "Set field-of-view to five hundred lightsecs. Peak false-color at near-infrared."

Space grows ominously murky in the tank. The tiny sun at its center, thumbnail-sized now, glows with increased brilliance: an incandescent pearl in muddy water.

"A thousand lightsecs," I command.

"There," Dix whispers: real space reclaims the edges of the tank, dark, clear, pristine. 428 nestles at the heart of a dim spherical shroud. You find those sometimes, discarded cast-offs from companion stars whose convulsions spew gas and rads across light years. But 428 is no nova remnant. It's a *red dwarf*, placid, middle-aged. Unremarkable.

Except for the fact that it sits dead center of a tenuous gas bubble 1.4 AUs across. And for the fact that this bubble does not *attenuate* or *diffuse* or *fade* gradually into that good night. No, unless there is something seriously wrong with the display, this small, spherical nebula extends about 350 lightsecs from its primary and then just *stops*, its boundary far more knife-edged than nature has any right to be.

For the first time in millennia, I miss my cortical pipe. It takes forever to saccade search terms onto the keyboard in my head, to get the answers I already know.

Numbers come back. "Chimp. I want false-color peaks at 335, 500 and 800 nanometers."

The shroud around 428 lights up like a dragonfly's wing, like an iridescent soap bubble.

"It's *beautiful*," whispers my awestruck son.

"It's photosynthetic," I tell him.

Phaeophytin and eumelanin, according to spectro. There are even hints of some kind of lead-based Keipper pigment, soaking up X-rays in the picometer range. Chimp hypothesizes something called a *chromatophore*: branching cells with little aliquots of pigment inside, like particles of charcoal dust. Keep those particles clumped together and the cell's effectively transparent; spread them out through the cytoplasm and the whole structure *darkens*, dims whatever EM passes through from behind. Apparently there were animals back on Earth with cells like that. They could change color, pattern-match to their background, all sorts of things.

"So there's a membrane of—of *living tissue* around that star," I say, trying to wrap my head around the concept. "A, a meat balloon. Around the whole damn *star*."

"Yes," the chimp says.

"But that's—Jesus, how thick would it be?"

"No more than two millimeters. Probably less."

"How so?"

"If it was much thicker, it would be more obvious in the visible spectrum. It would have had a detectable effect on the von Neumanns when they hit it."

"That's assuming that its—cells, I guess—are like ours."

"The pigments are familiar; the rest might be too."

It can't be *too* familiar. Nothing like a conventional gene would last two seconds in that environment. Not to mention whatever miracle solvent that thing must use as antifreeze . . .

"Okay, let's be conservative, then. Say, mean thickness of a millimeter. Assume a density of water at STP. How much mass in the whole thing?"

"1.4 yottagrams," Dix and the chimp reply, almost in unison.

"That's, uh . . . "

"Half the mass of Mercury," the chimp adds helpfully.

I whistle through my teeth. "And that's *one* organism?"

"I don't know yet."

"It's got organic pigments. Fuck, it's *talking*. It's intelligent."

"Most cyclic emanations from living sources are simple biorhythms," the chimp points out. "Not intelligent signals."

I ignore it and turn to Dix. "Assume it's a signal."

He frowns. "Chimp says—"

"*Assume*. Use your imagination."

I'm not getting through to him. He looks nervous.

He looks like that a lot, I realize.

"*If* someone were signaling you," I say, "*then* what would you do?"

"Signal . . ." Confusion on that face, and a fuzzy circuit closing somewhere " . . . back?"

My son is an idiot.

"And if the incoming signal takes the form of systematic changes in light intensity, how—"

"Use the BI lasers, alternated to pulse between 700 and 3000 nanometers. Can boost an interlaced signal into the exawatt range without compromising our fenders; gives over a thousand Watts per square meter after diffraction. Way past detection threshold for anything that can sense thermal output from a red dwarf. And content doesn't matter if it's just a shout. Shout back. Test for echo."

Okay, so my son is an idiot *savant*.

And he still looks unhappy—"But Chimp, he says no real *information* there, right?"—and that whole other set of misgivings edges to the fore again: *He.*

Dix takes my silence for amnesia. "Too simple, remember? Simple click train."

I shake my head. There's more information in that signal than the chimp can imagine. There are so many things the chimp doesn't know. And the last thing I need is for this, this *child* to start deferring to it, to start looking to it as an equal or, God forbid, a *mentor*.

Oh, it's smart enough to steer us between the stars. Smart enough to calculate million-digit primes in the blink of an eye. Even smart enough for a little crude improvisation should the crew go too far off-mission.

Not smart enough to know a distress call when it sees one.

"It's a deceleration curve," I tell them both. "It keeps *slowing down*. Over and over again. *That's* the message."

Stop. Stop. Stop. Stop.

And I think it's meant for no one but us.

We shout back. No reason not to. And now we die again, because what's the point of staying up late? Whether or not this vast entity harbors real intelligence, our echo won't reach it for ten million corsecs. Another seven million, at the earliest, before we receive any reply it might send.

Might as well hit the crypt in the meantime. Shut down all desires and misgivings, conserve whatever life I have left for moments that matter. Remove myself from this sparse tactical intelligence, from this wet-eyed pup watching me as though I'm some kind of sorcerer about to vanish in a puff of smoke. He opens his mouth to speak, and I turn away and hurry down to oblivion.

But I set my alarm to wake up alone.

I linger in the coffin for a while, grateful for small and ancient victories. The chimp's dead, blackened eye gazes down from the ceiling; in all these millions of years nobody's scrubbed off the carbon scoring. It's a trophy of sorts, a memento from the early incendiery days of our Great Struggle.

There's still something—comforting, I guess—about that blind, endless stare. I'm reluctant to venture out where the chimp's nerves have not been so thoroughly cauterised. Childish, I know. The damn thing already knows I'm up; it may be blind, deaf, and impotent in here, but there's no way to mask the power the crypt sucks in during a thaw. And it's not as though a bunch of club-wielding teleops are waiting to pounce on me the moment I step outside. These are the days of détente, after all. The struggle continues but the war has gone cold; we just go through the motions now, rattling our chains like an old married multiplet resigned to hating each other to the end of time.

After all the moves and countermoves, the truth is we need each other.

So I wash the rotten-egg stench from my hair and step into *Eri's* silent cathedral hallways. Sure enough the enemy waits in the darkness, turns the lights on as I approach, shuts them off behind me—but it does not break the silence.

Dix.

A strange one, that. Not that you'd expect anyone born and raised on *Eriophora* to be an archetype of mental health, but Dix doesn't even know what side he's on. He doesn't even seem to know he has to *choose* a side. It's almost as though he read the original mission statements and took them *seriously*, believed in the literal truth of the ancient scrolls: Mammals and Machinery, working together across the ages to explore the Universe! United! Strong! Forward the Frontier!

Rah.

Whoever raised him didn't do a great job. Not that I blame them; it can't have been much fun having a child underfoot during a build, and none of us were selected for our parenting skills. Even if bots changed the diapers and VR handled the infodumps, socialising a toddler couldn't have been anyone's idea of a good time. I'd have probably just chucked the little bastard out an airlock.

But even I would've brought him up to speed.

Something changed while I was away. Maybe the war's heated up again, entered some new phase. That twitchy kid is out of the loop for a reason. I wonder what it is.

I wonder if I care.

I arrive at my suite, treat myself to a gratuitous meal, jill off. Three hours after coming back to life I'm relaxing in the starbow commons. "Chimp."

"You're up early," it says at last, and I am; our answering shout hasn't even arrived at its destination yet. No real chance of new data for another two months, at least.

"Show me the forward feeds," I command.

DHF428 blinks at me from the center of the lounge: *Stop. Stop. Stop.*

Maybe. Or maybe the chimp's right, maybe it's pure physiology. Maybe this endless cycle carries no more intelligence than the beating of a heart. But there's a pattern inside the pattern, some kind of *flicker* in the blink. It makes my brain itch.

"Slow the time-series," I command. "By a hundred."

It *is* a blink. 428's disk isn't darkening uniformly, it's *eclipsing*. As though a great eyelid were being drawn across the surface of the sun, from right to left.

"By a thousand."

Chromatophores, the chimp called them. But they're not all opening and closing at once. The darkness moves across the membrane in *waves*.

A word pops into my head: *latency*.

"Chimp. Those waves of pigment. How fast are they moving?"

"About fifty-nine thousand kilometers per second."

The speed of a passing thought.

And if this thing *does* think, it'll have logic gates, synapses—it's going to be a *net* of some kind. And if the net's big enough, there's an *I* in the middle of it. Just like me, just like Dix. Just like the chimp. (Which is why I educated myself on the subject, back in the early tumultuous days of our relationship. Know your enemy and all that.)

The thing about *I* is, it only exists within a tenth-of-a-second of all its parts. When we get spread too thin—when someone splits your brain down the middle, say, chops the fat pipe so the halves have to talk the long way around; when the neural architecture *diffuses* past some critical point and signals take just that much longer to pass from A to B—the system, well, *decoheres*. The two sides of your brain become different people with different tastes, different agendas, different senses of themselves.

I shatters into *we*.

It's not just a human rule, or a mammal rule, or even an Earthly one. It's a rule for any circuit that processes information, and it applies as much to the things we've yet to meet as it did to those we left behind.

Fifty-nine thousand kilometers per second, the chimp says. How far can the signal move through that membrane in a tenth of a corsec? How thinly does *I* spread itself across the heavens?

The flesh is huge, the flesh is inconceivable. But the spirit, the spirit is—

Shit.

"Chimp. Assuming the mean neuron density of a human brain, what's the synapse count on a circular sheet of neurons one millimeter thick with a diameter of five thousand eight hundred ninety-two kilometers?"

"Two times ten to the twenty-seventh."

I saccade the database for some perspective on a mind stretched across thirty million square kilometers: the equivalent of two quadrillion human brains.

Of course, whatever this thing uses for neurons have to be packed a lot less tightly than ours; we can see through them, after all. Let's be superconservative, say it's only got a thousandth the computational density of a human brain. That's—

Okay, let's say it's only got a *ten*-thousandth the synaptic density, that's still—

A *hundred* thousandth. The merest mist of thinking meat. Any more conservative and I'd hypothesize it right out of existence.

Still twenty billion human brains. Twenty *billion*.

I don't know how to feel about that. This is no mere alien.

But I'm not quite ready to believe in gods.

I round the corner and run smack into Dix, standing like a golem in the middle of my living room. I jump about a meter straight up.

"*What the hell are you doing here?*"

He seems surprised by my reaction. "Wanted to—talk," he says after a moment.

"You *never* come into someone's home uninvited!"

He retreats a step, stammers: "Wanted, wanted—"

"To talk. And you do that in *public*. On the bridge, or in the commons, or—for that matter, you could just *comm* me."

He hesitates. "Said you—*wanted* face to face. You said, *cultural tradition*."

I did, at that. But not *here*. This is *my* place, these are my *private quarters*. The lack of locks on these doors is a safety protocol, not an invitation to walk into my home and *lie in wait*, and stand there like part of the fucking *furniture* . . .

"Why are you even *up*?" I snarl. "We're not even supposed to come online for another two months."

"Asked Chimp to get me up when you did."

That fucking machine.

"Why are *you* up?" he asks, not leaving.

I sigh, defeated, and fall into a convenient pseudopod. "I just wanted to go over the preliminary data." The implicit *alone* should be obvious.

"Anything?"

Evidently it isn't. I decide to play along for a while. "Looks like we're talking to an, an island. Almost six thousand klicks across. That's the thinking part, anyway. The surrounding membrane's pretty much empty. I mean, it's all *alive*. It all photosynthesizes, or something like that. It eats, I guess. Not sure what."

"Molecular cloud," Dix says. "Organic compounds everywhere. Plus it's concentrating stuff inside the envelope."

I shrug. "Point is, there's a size limit for the brain but it's *huge*, it's . . . "

"Unlikely," he murmurs, almost to himself.

I turn to look at him; the pseudopod reshapes itself around me. "What do you mean?"

"Island's twenty-eight million square kilometers? Whole sphere's seven quintillion. Island just happens to be between us and 428, that's—one in fifty-billion odds."

"Go on."

He can't. "Uh, just . . . just *unlikely*."

I close my eyes. "How can you be smart enough to run those numbers in your head without missing a beat, and stupid enough to miss the obvious conclusion?"

That panicked, slaughterhouse look again. "Don't—I'm not—"

"It *is* unlikely. It's *astronomically* unlikely that we just happen to be aiming at the one intelligent spot on a sphere one-and-a-half AUs across. Which means . . . "

He says nothing. The perplexity in his face mocks me. I want to punch it.

But finally, the lights flicker on: "There's, uh, more than one island? Oh! A *lot* of islands!"

This creature is part of the crew. My life will almost certainly depend on him some day. That is a very scary thought.

I try to set it aside for the moment. "There's probably a whole population of the things, sprinkled though the membrane like, like cysts I guess. The chimp doesn't know how many, but we're only picking up this one so far so they might be pretty sparse."

There's a different kind of frown on his face now. "Why *Chimp*?"

"What do you mean?"

"Why call him Chimp?"

"We call it *the* chimp." Because the first step to humanising something is to give it a name.

"Looked it up. Short for *chimpanzee*. Stupid animal."

"Actually, I think chimps were supposed to be pretty smart," I remember.

"Not like us. Couldn't even *talk*. Chimp can talk. *Way* smarter than those things. That name—it's an insult."

"What do you care?"

He just looks at me.

I spread my hands. "Okay, it's not a chimp. We just call it that because it's got roughly the same synapse count."

"So gave him a small brain, then complain that he's stupid all the time."

My patience is just about drained. "Do you have a point or are you just blowing CO_2 in—"

"Why not make him smarter?"

"Because you can never predict the behavior of a system more complex than you. And if you want a project to stay on track after you're gone, you don't hand the reins to anything that's guaranteed to develop its own agenda." Sweet smoking Jesus, you'd think *someone* would have told him about Ashby's Law.

"So they lobotomized him," Dix says after a moment.

"No. They didn't *turn* it stupid, they *built* it stupid."

"Maybe smarter than you think. You're so much smarter, got *your* agenda, how come *he's* still in control?"

"Don't flatter yourself," I say.

"What?"

I let a grim smile peek through. "You're only following orders from a bunch of other systems *way* more complex than you are." You've got to hand it to them, too; dead for stellar lifetimes and those damn project admins are *still* pulling the strings.

"I don't—*I'm* following?—"

"I'm sorry, dear." I smile sweetly at my idiot offspring. "I wasn't talking to you. I was talking to the thing that's making all those sounds come out of your mouth."

Dix turns whiter than my panties.

I drop all pretense. "What were you thinking, chimp? That you could send this sock-puppet to invade my home and I wouldn't notice?"

"Not—I'm not—it's *me*," Dix stammers. "*Me* talking."

"It's *coaching* you. Do you even know what 'lobotomised' *means*?" I shake my head, disgusted. "You think I've forgotten how the interface works just because we all burned ours out?" A caricature of surprise begins to form on his face. "Oh, don't even fucking *try*. You've been up for other builds, there's no way you couldn't have known. And you know we shut down our domestic links too. And there's nothing your lord and master can do about that because it *needs* us, and so we have reached what you might call an *accommodation*."

I am not shouting. My tone is icy, but my voice is dead level. And yet Dix almost *cringes* before me.

There is an opportunity here, I realize.

I thaw my voice a little. I speak gently: "You can do that too, you know. Burn out your link. I'll even let you come back here afterwards, if you still want to. Just to—talk. But not with that thing in your head."

There is panic in his face, and against all expectation it almost breaks my heart. "*Can't*," he pleads. "How I *learn* things, how I *train*. The *mission* . . . "

I honestly don't know which of them is speaking, so I answer them both: "There is more than one way to carry out the mission. We have more than enough time to try them all. Dix is welcome to come back when he's alone."

They take a step towards me. Another. One hand, twitching, rises from their side as if to reach out, and there's something on that lopsided face that I can't quite recognize.

"But I'm your *son*," they say.

I don't even dignify it with a denial.

"Get out of my home."

A human periscope. The Trojan Dix. That's a new one.

The chimp's never tried such overt infiltration while we were up and about before. Usually it waits until we're all undead before invading our territories. I imagine custom-made drones never seen by human eyes, cobbled together during the long dark eons between builds; I see them sniffing through drawers and peeking behind mirrors, strafing the bulkheads with X-rays and ultrasound, patiently searching *Eriophora*'s catacombs millimeter by endless millimeter for whatever secret messages we might be sending each other down through time.

There's no proof to speak of. We've left tripwires and telltales to alert us to intrusion after the fact, but there's never been any evidence they've been disturbed. Means nothing, of course. The chimp may be stupid but it's also cunning, and a million years is more than enough time to iterate through every possibility using simpleminded brute force. Document every dust mote; commit your unspeakable acts; put everything back the way it was afterwards.

We're too smart to risk talking across the eons. No encrypted strategies, no long-distance love letters, no chatty postcards showing ancient vistas long lost in the red shift. We keep all that in our heads, where the enemy will never find it. The unspoken rule is that we do not speak, unless it is face to face.

Endless idiotic games. Sometimes I almost forget what we're squabbling over. It seems so trivial now, with an immortal in my sights.

Maybe that means nothing to you. Immortality must be ancient news from whatever peaks you've ascended by now. But I can't even imagine it, although I've outlived worlds. All I have are moments: two or three hundred years, to ration across the lifespan of a universe. I could bear witness to any point in time, or any hundred-thousand if I slice my life thinly enough—but I will never see *everything*. I will never see even a fraction.

My life will end. I have to *choose*.

When you come to fully appreciate the deal you've made—ten or fifteen builds out, when the trade-off leaves the realm of mere *knowledge* and sinks deep as cancer into your bones—you become a miser. You can't help it. You ration out your waking moments to the barest minimum: just enough to manage the build, to plan your latest countermove against the chimp, just enough (if you haven't yet moved beyond the need for Human contact) for sex and snuggles and a bit of warm mammalian comfort against the endless dark. And then you hurry back to the crypt, to hoard the remains of a human lifespan against the unwinding of the cosmos.

There's been time for education. Time for a hundred postgraduate degrees, thanks to the best caveman learning tech. I've never bothered. Why burn down my tiny candle for a litany of mere fact, fritter away my precious, endless, finite life? Only a fool would trade book-learning for a ringside view of the Cassiopeia Remnant, even if you *do* need false-color enhancement to see the fucking thing.

Now, though. Now, I want to *know*. This creature crying out across the gulf, massive as a moon, wide as a solar system, tenuous and fragile as an insect's wing: I'd gladly cash in some of my life to learn its secrets. How does it work? How can it even *live* here at the edge of absolute zero, much less think? What vast, unfathomable intellect must it possess to see us coming from over half a lightyear away, to deduce the nature of our eyes and our instruments, to send a signal we can even *detect*, much less understand?

And what happens when we punch through it at a fifth the speed of light?

I call up the latest findings on my way to bed, and the answer hasn't changed: not much. The damn thing's already full of holes. Comets, asteroids, the usual protoplanetary junk careens through this system as it does through every other. Infra picks up diffuse pockets of slow outgassing here and there around the perimeter, where the soft vaporous vacuum of the interior bleeds into the harder stuff outside. Even if we were going to tear through the dead center of the thinking part, I can't imagine this vast creature feeling so much as a pinprick. At the speed we're going we'd be through and gone far too fast to overcome even the feeble inertia of a millimeter membrane.

And yet. *Stop. Stop. Stop.*

It's not us, of course. It's what we're building. The birth of a gate is a violent, painful thing, a spacetime rape that puts out almost as much gamma and X as a microquasar. Any meat within the white zone turns to ash in an instant, shielded or not. It's why *we* never slow down to take pictures.

One of the reasons, anyway.

We can't stop, of course. Even changing course isn't an option except by the barest increments. *Eri* soars like an eagle between the stars but she steers like a pig on the short haul; tweak our heading by even a tenth of a degree and you've got some serious damage at twenty percent lightspeed. Half a degree would tear us apart: the ship might torque onto the new heading but the collapsed mass in her belly would keep right on going, rip through all this surrounding superstructure without even feeling it.

Even tame singularities get set in their ways. They do not take well to change.

We resurrect again, and the Island has changed its tune.

It gave up asking us to *stop stop stop* the moment our laser hit its leading edge. Now it's saying something else entirely: dark hyphens flow across its skin, arrows of pigment converging towards some offstage focus like spokes pointing towards the hub of a wheel. The bullseye itself is offstage and implicit, far removed from 428's bright backdrop, but it's easy enough to extrapolate to the point of convergence six lightsecs to starboard. There's something else, too: a shadow, roughly circular, moving along one of the spokes like a bead running along a string. It too migrates to starboard, falls off the edge of the Island's makeshift display, is endlessly reborn at the same initial coordinates to repeat its journey.

Those coordinates: exactly where our current trajectory will punch through the membrane in another four months. A squinting God would be able to see the gnats and girders of ongoing construction on the other side, the great piecemeal torus of the Hawking Hoop already taking shape.

The message is so obvious that even Dix sees it. "Wants us to move the gate . . . " and there is something like confusion in his voice. "But how's it know we're *building* one?"

"The vons punctured it en route," the chimp points out. "It could have sensed that. It has photopigments. It can probably see."

"Probably sees better than we do," I say. Even something as simple as a pinhole camera gets hi-res fast if you stipple a bunch of them across thirty million square kilometers.

But Dix scrunches his face, unconvinced. "So sees a bunch of vons bumping around. Loose parts—not that much even *assembled* yet. How's it know we're building something *hot*?"

Because it is very, very, smart, you stupid child. Is it so hard to believe that this, this—*organism* seems far too limiting a word—can just *imagine* how those half-built pieces fit together, glance at our sticks and stones and see exactly where this is going?

"Maybe's not the first gate it's seen," Dix suggests. "Think there's maybe another gate out here?"

I shake my head. "We'd have seen the lensing artefacts by now."

"You ever run into anyone before?"

"No." We have always been alone, through all these epochs. We have only ever run *away*.

And then always from our own children.

I crunch some numbers. "Hundred eighty two days to insemination. If we move now we've only got to tweak our bearing by a few mikes to redirect to the new coordinates. Well within the green. Angles get dicey the longer we wait, of course."

"We can't do that," the chimp says. "We would miss the gate by two million kilometers."

"Move the gate. Move the whole damn site. Move the refineries, move the factories, move the damn rocks. A couple hundred meters a second would be more than fast enough if we send the order now. We don't even have to suspend construction, we can keep building on the fly."

"Every one of those vectors widens the nested confidence limits of the build. It would increase the risk of error beyond allowable margins, for no payoff."

"And what about the fact that there's an intelligent being in our path?"

"I'm already allowing for the potential presence of intelligent alien life."

"Okay, first off, there's nothing *potential* about it. It's *right fucking there*. And on our current heading we run the damn thing over."

"We're staying clear of all planetary bodies in Goldilocks orbits. We've seen no local evidence of spacefaring technology. The current location of the build meets all conservation criteria."

"That's because the people who drew up your criteria *never anticipated a live Dyson sphere*!" But I'm wasting my breath, and I know it. The chimp can run its equations a million times but if there's nowhere to put the variable, what can it do?

There was a time, back before things turned ugly, when we had clearance to reprogram those parameters. Before we discovered that one of the things the admins *had* anticipated was mutiny.

I try another tack. "Consider the threat potential."

"There's no evidence of any."

"Look at the synapse estimate! That thing's got order of mag more processing power than the whole civilization that sent us out here. You think something can be that smart, live that long, without learning how to defend itself? We're assuming it's *asking* us to move the gate. What if that's not a *request*? What if it's just giving us the chance to back off before it takes matters into its own hands?"

"Doesn't *have* hands," Dix says from the other side of the tank, and he's not even being flippant. He's just being so stupid I want to bash his face in.

I try to keep my voice level. "Maybe it doesn't *need* any."

"What could it do, *blink* us to death? No weapons. Doesn't even control the whole membrane. Signal propagation's too slow."

"We *don't know*. That's my *point*. We haven't even tried to find out. We're a goddamn road crew; our onsite presence is a bunch of construction vons press-ganged into scientific research. We can figure out some basic physical parameters but we don't know how this thing thinks, what kind of natural defenses it might have—"

"What do you need to find out?" the chimp asks, the very voice of calm reason.

We can't find out! I want to scream. *We're stuck with what we've got! By the time the onsite vons could build what we need we're already past the point of no return! You stupid fucking machine, we're on track to kill a being smarter than all of human history and you can't even be bothered to move our highway to the vacant lot next door?*

But of course if I say that, the Island's chances of survival go from low to zero. So I grasp at the only straw that remains: maybe the data we've got in hand is enough. If acquisition is off the table, maybe analysis will do.

"I need time," I say.

"Of course," the chimp tells me. "Take all the time you need."

The chimp is not content to kill this creature. The chimp has to spit on it as well.

Under the pretense of assisting in my research it tries to *deconstruct* the island, break it apart and force it to conform to grubby earthbound precedents. It tells me about earthly bacteria that thrived at 1.5 million rads and laughed at hard vacuum. It shows me pictures of unkillable little tardigrades that could curl up and snooze on the edge of absolute zero, felt equally at home in deep ocean trenches and deeper space. Given time, opportunity, a boot off the planet, who knows how far those cute little invertebrates might have gone? Might they have survived the very death of the homeworld, clung together, grown somehow colonial?

What utter bullshit.

I learn what I can. I study the alchemy by which photosynthesis transforms light and gas and electrons into living tissue. I learn the physics of the solar wind that blows the bubble taut, calculate lower metabolic limits for a life-form that filters organics from the ether. I marvel at the speed of this creature's thoughts: almost as fast as *Eri* flies, orders of mag faster than any mammalian nerve impulse. Some kind of organic superconductor perhaps, something that passes chilled electrons almost resistance-free out here in the freezing void.

I acquaint myself with phenotypic plasticity and sloppy fitness, that fortuitous evolutionary soft-focus that lets species exist in alien environments and express novel traits they never needed at home. Perhaps this is how a lifeform with no natural enemies could acquire teeth and claws and the willingness to use them. The Island's life hinges on its ability to kill us; I have to find *something* that makes it a threat.

But all I uncover is a growing suspicion that I am doomed to fail—for violence, I begin to see, is a *planetary* phenomenon.

Planets are the abusive parents of evolution. Their very surfaces promote warfare, concentrate resources into dense defensible patches that can be fought over. Gravity forces you to squander energy on vascular systems and skeletal support, stand endless watch against an endless sadistic campaign to squash you flat. Take one wrong step, off a perch too high, and all your pricey architecture shatters in an instant. And even if you beat those odds, cobble together some lumbering armored chassis to withstand the slow crawl onto land—how long before the world draws in some asteroid or comet to crash down from the heavens and reset your clock to zero? Is it any wonder we grew up believing life was a struggle, that zero-sum was God's own law and the future belonged to those who crushed the competition?

The rules are so different out here. Most of space is *tranquil*: no diel or seasonal cycles, no ice ages or global tropics, no wild pendulum swings between hot and cold, calm and tempestuous. Life's precursors abound: on comets, clinging to asteroids, suffusing nebulae a hundred lightyears across. Molecular clouds glow with organic chemistry and life-giving radiation. Their vast dusty wings grow warm with infrared, filter out the hard stuff, give rise to stellar nurseries that only some stunted refugee from the bottom of a gravity well could ever call *lethal*.

Darwin's an abstraction here, an irrelevant curiosity. This Island puts the lie to everything we were ever told about the machinery of life. Sun-powered, perfectly adapted, immortal, it won no struggle for survival: where are the predators, the competitors, the parasites? All of life around 428 is one vast continuum, one grand act of symbiosis. Nature here is not red in tooth and claw. Nature, out here, is the helping hand.

Lacking the capacity for violence, the Island has outlasted worlds. Unencumbered by technology, it has out-thought civilizations. It is intelligent beyond our measure, and—

—and it is *benign*. It must be. I grow more certain of that with each passing hour. How can it even *conceive* of an enemy?

I think of the things I called it, before I knew better. *Meat balloon. Cyst.* Looking back, those words verge on blasphemy. I will not use them again.

Besides, there's another word that would fit better, if the chimp has its way: Roadkill. And the longer I look, to more I fear that that hateful machine is right.

If the Island can defend itself, I sure as shit can't see how.

"*Eriophora*'s impossible, you know. Violates the laws of physics."

We're in one of the social alcoves off the ventral notochord, taking a break from the library. I have decided to start again from first principles. Dix eyes me with an understandable mix of confusion and mistrust; my claim is almost too stupid to deny.

"It's true," I assure him. "Takes way too much energy to accelerate a ship with *Eri*'s mass, especially at relativistic speeds. You'd need the energy output of a whole sun. People figured if we made it to the stars at all, we'd have to do it with ships maybe the size of your thumb. Crew them with virtual personalities downloaded onto chips."

That's too nonsensical even for Dix. "*Wrong.* Don't have mass, can't fall towards anything. *Eri* wouldn't even *work* if it was that small."

"But suppose you can't displace any of that mass. No wormholes, no Higgs conduits, nothing to throw your gravitational field in the direction of travel. Your center of mass just *sits* there in, well, the center of your mass."

A spastic Dixian head-shake. "*Do* have those things!"

"Sure we do. But for the longest time, we didn't *know* it."

His foot taps an agitated tattoo on the deck.

"It's the history of the species," I explain. "We think we've worked everything out, we think we've solved all the mysteries and then someone finds some niggling little data point that doesn't fit the paradigm. Every time we try to paper over the crack it gets bigger, and before you know it our whole worldview unravels. It's happened time and again. One day mass is a constraint; the next it's a requirement. The things we think we know—they *change*, Dix. And we have to change with them."

"But—"

"The chimp can't change. The rules it's following are ten billion years old and it's got no fucking imagination and really that's not anyone's fault, that's just people who didn't know how else to keep the mission stable across deep time. They wanted to keep us on-track so they built something that couldn't go off it; but they also knew that things *change*, and that's why *we're* out here, Dix. To deal with things the chimp can't."

"The alien," Dix says.

"The alien."

"Chimp deals with it just fine."

"How? By killing it?"

"Not our fault it's in the way. It's no threat—"

"I don't care whether it's a *threat* or not! It's alive, and it's intelligent, and killing it just to expand some alien empire—"

"*Human* empire. *Our* empire." Suddenly Dix's hands have stopped twitching. Suddenly he stands still as stone.

I snort. "What do you know about humans?"

"*Am* one."

"You're a fucking trilobite. You ever see what comes *out* of those gates once they're online?"

"Mostly nothing." He pauses, thinking back. "Couple of—ships once, maybe."

"Well, I've seen a lot more than that, and believe me, if those things were *ever* human it was a passing phase. "

"But—"

"Dix—" I take a deep breath, try to get back on message. "Look, it's not your fault. You've been getting all your info from a moron stuck on a rail. But we're not doing this for Humanity, we're not doing it for Earth. Earth is *gone*, don't you understand that? The sun scorched it black a billion years after we left. Whatever we're working for, it—it won't even *talk* to us."

"Yeah? Then why do this? Why not just, just *quit*?"

He really doesn't know.

"We tried," I say.

"And?"

"And your *chimp* shut off our life support."

For once, he has nothing to say.

"It's a *machine*, Dix. Why can't you get that? It's *programmed*. It can't change."

"*We're* machines, just built from different things. *We* change."

"Yeah? Last time I checked, you were sucking so hard on that thing's tit you couldn't even kill your cortical link."

"How I *learn*. No *reason* to change."

"How about acting like a damn *human* once in a while? How about developing a little rapport with the folks who might have to save your miserable life next time you go EVA? That enough of a *reason* for you? Because I don't mind telling you, right now I don't trust you as far as I could throw the tac tank. I don't even know for sure who I'm talking to right now."

"*Not my fault.*" For the first time I see something outside the usual gamut of fear, confusion, and simpleminded computation playing across his face. "That's *you*, that's *all* of you. You talk—*sideways*. *Think* sideways. You all do, and it *hurts*." Something hardens in his face. "Didn't even need you online for this," he growls. "Didn't *want* you. Could have managed the whole build myself, *told* Chimp I could do it—"

"But the chimp thought you should wake me up anyway, and you always roll over for the chimp, don't you? Because the chimp always knows best, the chimp's your *boss*, the chimp's your fucking *god*. Which is why I have to get out of bed to nursemaid some idiot savant who can't even answer a hail without being led by the nose." Something clicks in the back of my mind but I'm on a roll. "You want a *real* role model? You want something to look up to? Forget the chimp. Forget the mission. Look out the forward scope, why don't you? Look at what your precious chimp wants to run over because it happens to be in the way. That thing is better than any of us. It's smarter, it's peaceful, it doesn't wish us any harm at—"

"How can you know that? Can't know that!"

"No, *you* can't know that, because you're fucking *stunted*. Any normal caveman would see it in a second, but *you*—"

"That's crazy," Dix hisses at me. "*You're* crazy. You're *bad*."

"*I'm* bad?" Some distant part of me hears the giddy squeak in my voice, the borderline hysteria.

"For the mission." Dix turns his back and stalks away.

My hands are hurting. I look down, surprised: my fists are clenched so tightly that my nails cut into the flesh of my palms. It takes a real effort to open them again.

I almost remember how this feels. I used to feel this way all the time. Way back when everything *mattered*; before passion faded to ritual, before rage cooled to disdain. Before Sunday Ahzmundin, eternity's warrior, settled for heaping insults on stunted children.

We were incandescent back then. Parts of this ship are still scorched and uninhabitable, even now. I remember this feeling.

This is how it feels to be awake.

I am awake, and I am alone, and I am sick of being outnumbered by morons. There are rules and there are risks and you don't wake the dead on a whim, but fuck it. I'm calling reinforcements.

Dix has got to have other parents, a father at least, he didn't get that Y chromo from me. I swallow my own disquiet and check the manifest; bring up the gene sequences; cross-reference.

Huh. Only one other parent: Kai. I wonder if that's just coincidence, or if the chimp drew too many conclusions from our torrid little fuckfest back in the Cyg Rift. Doesn't matter. He's as much yours as mine, Kai, time to step up to the plate, time to—

Oh shit. Oh no. Please no.

(There are rules. And there are risks.)

Three builds back, it says. Kai and Connie. Both of them. One airlock jammed, the next too far away along *Eri*'s hull, a hail-Mary emergency crawl between. They made it back inside but not before the blue-shifted background cooked them in their suits. They kept breathing for hours afterwards, talked and moved and cried as if they were still alive, while their insides broke down and bled out.

There were two others awake that shift, two others left to clean up the mess. Ishmael, and—

"Um, you said—"

"*You fucker!*" I leap up and hit my son hard in the face, ten seconds' heartbreak with ten million years' denial raging behind it. I feel teeth give way behind his lips. He goes over backwards, eyes wide as telescopes, the blood already blooming on his mouth.

"*Said* I could come back—!" he squeals, scrambling backwards along the deck.

"He was your fucking *father*! You *knew*, you were *there*! He died right in *front* of you and you didn't even *tell* me!"

"I—I—"

"Why didn't you tell me, you asshole? The chimp told you to lie, is that it? Did you—"

"*Thought you knew!*" he cries, "Why *wouldn't* you know?"

My rage vanishes like air through a breach. I sag back into the 'pod, face in hands.

"Right there in the log," he whimpers. "All along. Nobody hid it. How could you not know?"

"I did," I admit dully. "Or I—I mean . . . "

I mean I *didn't* know, but it's not a surprise, not really, not down deep. You just—stop looking, after a while.

There are *rules.*

"Never even *asked*," my son says softly. "How they were doing."

I raise my eyes. Dix regards me wide-eyed from across the room, backed up against the wall, too scared to risk bolting past me to the door. "What are you doing here?" I ask tiredly.

His voice catches. He has to try twice: "You said I could come back. If I burned out my link . . . "

"You burned out your link."

He gulps and nods. He wipes blood with the back of his hand.

"What did the chimp say about that?"

"He said—*it* said it was okay," Dix says, in such a transparent attempt to suck up that I actually believe, in that instant, that he might really be on his own.

"So you asked its permission." He begins to nod, but I can see the tell in his face: "Don't bullshit me, Dix."

"He—actually suggested it."

"I see."

"So we could talk," Dix adds.

"What do you want to talk about?"

He looks at the floor and shrugs.

I stand and walk towards him. He tenses but I shake my head, spread my hands. "It's okay. It's okay." I lean back against the wall and slide down until I'm beside him on the deck.

We just sit there for a while.

"It's been so long," I say at last.

He looks at me, uncomprehending. What does *long* even mean, out here?

I try again. "They say there's no such thing as altruism, you know?"

His eyes blank for an instant, and grow panicky, and I know that he's just tried to ping his link for a definition and come up blank. So we *are* alone. "Altruism," I explain. "Unselfishness. Doing something that costs you but helps someone else." He seems to get it. "They say every selfless act ultimately comes down to manipulation or kin-selection or reciprocity or something, but they're wrong. I could—"

I close my eyes. This is harder than I expected.

"I could have been happy just *knowing* that Kai was okay, that Connie was happy. Even if it didn't benefit me one whit, even if it *cost* me, even if there was no chance I'd ever see either of them again. Almost any price would be worth it, just to know they were okay.

"Just to *believe* they were . . . "

So you haven't seen her for the past five builds. So he hasn't drawn your shift since Sagittarius. They're just sleeping. Maybe next time.

"So you don't check," Dix says slowly. Blood bubbles on his lower lip; he doesn't seem to notice.

"We don't check." Only I did, and now they're gone. They're both gone. Except for those little cannibalized nucleotides the chimp recycled into this defective and maladapted son of mine. We're the only warm-blooded creatures for a thousand lightyears, and I am so very lonely.

"I'm sorry," I whisper, and lean forward, and lick the gore from his bruised and bloody lips.

Back on Earth—back when there *was* an Earth—there were these little animals called cats. I had one for a while. Sometimes I'd watch him sleep for hours: paws and whiskers and ears all twitching madly as he chased imaginary prey across whatever landscapes his sleeping brain conjured up.

My son looks like that when the chimp worms its way into his dreams.

It's almost too literal for metaphor: the cable runs into his head like some kind of parasite, feeding through old-fashioned fiberop now that the wireless option's been burned away. Or *force*-feeding, I suppose; the poison flows into Dix's head, not out of it.

I shouldn't be here. Didn't I just throw a tantrum over the violation of my own privacy? (Just. Twelve lightdays ago. Everything's relative.) And yet I can see no privacy here for Dix to lose: no decorations on the walls, no artwork or hobbies, no wraparound console. The sex toys ubiquitous in every suite sit unused on their shelves; I'd have assumed he was on antilibinals if recent experience hadn't proven otherwise.

What am I doing? Is this some kind of perverted mothering instinct, some vestigial expression of a Pleistocene maternal subroutine? Am I that much of a robot, has my brain stem sent me here to guard my child?

To guard my *mate*?

Lover or larva, it hardly matters: his quarters are an empty shell, there's nothing of Dix in here. That's just his abandoned body lying there in the pseudopod, fingers twitching, eyes flickering beneath closed lids in vicarious response to wherever his mind has gone.

They don't know I'm here. The chimp doesn't know because we burned out its prying eyes a billion years ago, and my son doesn't know I'm here because—well, because for him, right now, there *is* no here.

What am I supposed to make of you, Dix? None of this makes sense. Even your body language looks like you grew it in a vat—but I'm far from the first human being you've seen. You grew up in good company, with people I *know*, people I trust. Trusted. How did you end up on the other side? How did they let you slip away?

And why didn't they warn me about you?

Yes, there are rules. There is the threat of enemy surveillance during long dead nights, the threat of—other losses. But this is unprecedented. Surely someone could have left something, some clue buried in a metaphor too subtle for the simpleminded to decode . . .

I'd give a lot to tap into that pipe, to see what you're seeing now. Can't risk it, of course; I'd give myself away the moment I tried to sample anything except the basic baud, and—

—Wait a second—

That baud rate's way too low. That's not even enough for hi-res graphics, let alone tactile and olfac. You're embedded in a wireframe world at best.

And yet, look at you go. The fingers, the eyes—like a cat, dreaming of mice and apple pies. Like *me*, replaying the long-lost oceans and mountaintops of Earth before I learned that living in the past was just another way of dying in the present. The bit rate says this is barely even a test pattern; the body says you're immersed in a whole other world. How has that machine tricked you into treating such thin gruel as a feast?

Why would it even want to? Data are better grasped when they *can* be grasped, and tasted, and heard; our brains are built for far richer nuance than splines and scatterplots. The driest technical briefings are more sensual than this. Why settle for stick-figures when you can paint in oils and holograms?

Why does anyone simplify anything? To reduce the variable set. To manage the unmanageable.

Kai and Connie. Now *there* were a couple of tangled, unmanageable data-sets. Before the accident. Before the scenario *simplified*.

Someone should have warned me about you, Dix.

Maybe someone tried.

And so it comes to pass that my son leaves the nest, encases himself in a beetle carapace and goes walkabout. He is not alone; one of the chimp's teleops accompanies him out on *Eri*'s hull, lest he lose his footing and fall back into the starry past.

Maybe this will never be more than a drill, maybe this scenario—catastrophic control-systems failure, the chimp and its backups offline, all maintenance tasks suddenly thrown onto shoulders of flesh and blood—is a dress rehearsal for a crisis that never happens. But even the unlikeliest scenario approaches certainty over the life of a universe; so we go through the motions. We practice. We hold our breath and dip outside. We're on a tight deadline: even armored, moving at this speed the blueshifted background rad would cook us in hours.

Worlds have lived and died since I last used the pickup in my suite. "Chimp."

"Here as always, Sunday." Smooth, and glib, and friendly. The easy rhythm of the practiced psychopath.

"I know what you're doing."

"I don't understand."

"You think I don't see what's going on? You're building the next release. You're getting too much grief from the old guard so you're starting from scratch with people who don't remember the old days. People you've, you've *simplified*."

The chimp says nothing. The drone's feed shows Dix clambering across a jumbled terrain of basalt and metal matrix composites.

"But you can't raise a human child, not on your own." I know it tried: there's no record of Dix anywhere on the crew manifest until his mid-teens, when he just *showed up* one day and nobody asked about it because nobody ever . . .

"Look what you've made of him. He's great at conditional If/Thens. Can't be beat on number-crunching and Do loops. But he can't *think*. Can't make the simplest intuitive jumps. You're like one of those—" I remember an Earthly myth, from the days when *reading* did not seem like such an obscene waste of lifespan—"one of those wolves, trying to raise a Human child. You can teach him how to move around on hands and knees, you can teach him about pack dynamics, but you can't teach him how to walk on his hind legs or talk or be *human* because you're *too fucking stupid*, Chimp, and you finally realized it. And that's why you threw him at me. You think I can fix him for you."

I take a breath, and a gambit.

"But he's nothing to me. You understand? He's *worse* than nothing, he's a liability. He's a spy, he's a spastic waste of O_2. Give me one reason why I shouldn't just lock him out there until he cooks."

"You're his mother," the chimp says, because the chimp has read all about kin selection and is too stupid for nuance.

"You're an idiot."

"You love him."

"No." An icy lump forms in my chest. My mouth makes words; they come out measured and inflectionless. "I can't love anyone, you brain-dead machine. That's why I'm out here. Do you really think they'd gamble your precious never-ending mission on little glass dolls that needed to bond?"

"You love him."

"I can kill him any time I want. And that's exactly what I'll do if you don't move the gate."

"I'd stop you," the chimp says mildly.

"That's easy enough. Just move the gate and we both get what we want. Or you can dig in your heels and try to reconcile your need for a mother's touch with my sworn intention of breaking the little fucker's neck. We've got a long trip ahead of us, chimp. And you might find I'm not quite as easy to cut out of the equation as Kai and Connie."

"You cannot end the mission," it says, almost gently. "You tried that already."

"This isn't about ending the mission. This is only about slowing it down a little. Your optimal scenario's off the table. The only way that gate's going to get finished now is by saving the Island, or killing your prototype. Your call."

The cost-benefit's pretty simple. The chimp could solve it in an instant. But still it says nothing. The silence stretches. It's looking for some other option, I bet. It's trying to find a workaround. It's questioning the very premises of the scenario, trying to decide if I mean what I'm saying, if all its book-learning about mother love could really be so far off-base. Maybe it's plumbing historical intrafamilial murder rates, looking for a loophole. And there may be one, for all I know. But the chimp isn't me, it's a simpler system trying to figure out a smarter one, and that gives me the edge.

"You would owe me," it says at last.

I almost burst out laughing. "*What*?"

"Or I will tell Dixon that you threatened to kill him."

"Go ahead."

"You don't want him to know."

"I don't care whether he knows or not. What, you think he'll try and kill me back? You think I'll lose his *love*?" I linger on the last word, stretch it out to show how ludicrous it is.

"You'll lose his trust. You need to trust each other out here."

"Oh, right. *Trust*. The very fucking foundation of this mission."

The chimp says nothing.

"For the sake of argument," I say after a while, "suppose I go along with it. What would I *owe* you, exactly?"

"A favor," the chimp replies. "To be repaid in future."

My son floats innocently against the stars, his life in balance.

We sleep. The chimp makes grudging corrections to a myriad small trajectories. I set the alarm to wake me every couple of weeks, burn a little more of my candle in case the enemy tries to pull another fast one; but for now it seems to be behaving itself. DHF428 jumps towards us in the stop-motion increments of a life's moments, strung like beads along an infinite string. The factory floor slews to starboard in our sights: refineries, reservoirs, and nanofab plants, swarms of von Neumanns breeding and cannibalizing and recycling each other into shielding and circuitry, tugboats and spare parts. The very finest Cro Magnon technology mutates and metastasizes across the universe like armor-plated cancer.

And hanging like a curtain between *it* and *us* shimmers an iridescent life form, fragile and immortal and unthinkably alien, that reduces everything my species ever accomplished to mud and shit by the simple transcendent fact of its existence. I have never believed in gods, in universal good or absolute evil. I have only ever believed that there is what works, and what doesn't. All the rest is smoke and mirrors, trickery to manipulate grunts like me.

But I believe in the Island, because I don't *have* to. It does not need to be taken on faith: it looms ahead of us, its existence an empirical fact. I will never know its mind, I will never know the details of its origin and evolution. But I can *see* it: massive, mind boggling, so utterly inhuman that it can't *help* but be better than us, better than anything we could ever become.

I believe in the Island. I've gambled my own son to save its life. I would kill him to avenge its death.

I may yet.

In all these millions of wasted years, I have finally done something worthwhile.

Final approach.

Reticles within reticles line up before me, a mesmerising infinite regress of bullseyes centering on target. Even now, mere minutes from ignition, distance reduces the unborn gate to invisibility. There will be no moment when the naked eye can trap our destination. We thread the needle far too quickly: it will be behind us before we know it.

Or, if our course corrections are off by even a hair—if our trillion-kilometer curve drifts by as much as a thousand meters—we will be dead. Before we know it.

Our instruments report that we are precisely on target. The chimp tells me that we are precisely on target. *Eriophora* falls forward, pulled endlessly through the void by her own magically-displaced mass.

I turn to the drone's-eye view relayed from up ahead. It's a window into history—even now, there's a timelag of several minutes—but past and present race closer to convergence with every corsec. The newly-minted gate looms dark and ominous against the stars, a great gaping mouth built to devour reality itself. The vons, the refineries, the assembly lines: parked to the side in vertical columns, their jobs done, their usefulness outlived, their collateral annihilation imminent. I pity them, for some reason. I always do. I wish we could scoop them up and take them with us, re-enlist them for the next build—but the rules of economics reach everywhere, and they say it's cheaper to use our tools once and throw them away.

A rule that the chimp seems to be taking more to heart than anyone expected.

At least we've spared the Island. I wish we could have stayed awhile. First contact with a truly alien intelligence, and what do we exchange? Traffic signals. What does the Island dwell upon, when not pleading for its life?

I thought of asking. I thought of waking myself when the time-lag dropped from prohibitive to merely inconvenient, of working out some pidgin that could encompass the truths and philosophies of a mind vaster than all humanity. What a childish fantasy. The Island exists too far beyond the grotesque Darwinian processes that shaped my own flesh. There can be no communion here, no meeting of minds. Angels do not speak to ants.

Less than three minutes to ignition. I see light at the end of the tunnel. *Eri's* incidental time machine barely looks into the past any more, I could almost hold my breath across the whole span of seconds that *then* needs to overtake *now*. Still on target, according to all sources.

Tactical beeps at us. "Getting a signal," Dix reports, and yes: in the heart of the Tank, the sun is flickering again. My heart leaps: does the angel speak to us after all? A thank-you, perhaps? A cure for heat death? But—

"It's *ahead* of us," Dix murmurs, as sudden realization catches in my throat.

Two minutes.

"Miscalculated somehow," Dix whispers. "Didn't move the gate far enough."

"We did," I say. We moved it exactly as far as the Island told us to.

"*Still in front of us!* Look at the *sun*!"

"Look at the *signal*," I tell him.

Because it's nothing like the painstaking traffic signs we've followed over the past three trillion kilometers. It's almost—random, somehow. It's spur-of-the-moment, it's *panicky*. It's the sudden, startled cry of something caught utterly by surprise with mere seconds left to act. And even though I have never seen this pattern of dots and swirls before, I know exactly what it must be saying.

Stop. Stop. Stop. Stop.

We do not stop. There is no force in the universe that can even slow us down. Past equals present; *Eriophora* dives through the center of the gate in a nanosecond. The unimaginable mass of her cold black heart snags some distant dimension, drags it screaming to the here and now. The booted portal erupts behind us, blossoms into a great blinding corona, every wavelength lethal to every living thing. Our aft filters clamp down tight.

The scorching wavefront chases us into the darkness as it has a thousand times before. In time, as always, the birth pangs will subside. The wormhole will settle in its collar. And just maybe, we will still be close enough to glimpse some new transcendent monstrosity emerging from that magic doorway.

I wonder if you'll notice the corpse we left behind.

"Maybe we're missing something," Dix says.

"We miss almost everything," I tell him.

DHF428 shifts red behind us. Lensing artifacts wink in our rearview; the gate has stabilized and the wormhole's online, blowing light and space and time in an iridescent bubble from its great metal mouth. We'll keep looking over our shoulders right up until we pass the Rayleigh Limit, far past the point it'll do any good.

So far, though, nothing's come out.

"Maybe our numbers were wrong," he says. "Maybe we made a mistake."

Our numbers were right. An hour doesn't pass when I don't check them again. The Island just had—enemies, I guess. Victims, anyway.

I was right about one thing, though. That fucker was *smart*. To see us coming, to figure out how to talk to us; to use us as a *weapon*, to turn a threat to its very existence into a, a . . .

I guess *flyswatter* is as good a word as any.

"Maybe there was a war," I mumble. "Maybe it wanted the real estate. Or maybe it was just some—family squabble."

"Maybe didn't *know*," Dix suggests. "Maybe thought those coordinates were empty."

Why would you think that? I wonder. *Why would you even care?* And then it dawns on me: he doesn't, not about the Island, anyway. No more than he ever did. He's not inventing these rosy alternatives for himself.

My son is trying to comfort me.

I don't need to be coddled, though. I was a fool: I let myself believe in life without conflict, in sentience without sin. For a little while I dwelt in a dream world where life was unselfish and unmanipulative, where every living thing did not struggle to exist at the expense of other life. I deified that which I could not understand, when in the end it was all too easily understood.

But I'm better now.

It's over: another build, another benchmark, another irreplaceable slice of life that brings our task no closer to completion. It doesn't matter how successful we are. It doesn't matter how well we do our job. *Mission accomplished* is a meaningless phrase on *Eriophora*, an ironic oxymoron at best. There may one day be failure, but there is no finish line. We go on forever, crawling across the universe like ants, dragging your goddamned superhighway behind us.

I still have so much to learn.

At least my son is here to teach me.

THE LOGIC OF THE WORLD

ROBERT KELLY

Easter was long past. It was the quiet time of year when nothing was happening but the slow dawning of grain and fruit, the green shoots thickening to stems, stems beginning to round out toward what, months later, in the quietest time, would be ripe for harvest. Deep earth was asleep. Only her skin was lively, the powers and forms she had been dreaming all winter long were off on their own now, and she could sleep.

So that even here, where there was no sowing and no reaping, reigned the incessant uprising of tree and fern and toadstool, the everupward life of the forest itself, in the quiet heat of afternoon. The lilies rosy speckled like swift river fish had faded now, but the Pentecost roses were getting ready to blossom.

The knight cared about such things, though he didn't know much about their names. He noticed, though, and cared about the thickening, the coming of color into the plant, lifting some pale or vivid hue magically right out of the green, how did it happen, how could the brown twig and green leaf suddenly start to yield scarlet, yellow, or the rare of blue? Where do colors come from? He remembered, though he couldn't see it right now, the way sometimes the moisture caught in his eyelashes caught the sun so that tiny rainbows formed and scattered. What are colors?

He let himself think about such things. It was good to have a keen eye, to keep his vision whetted by noticing the slight difference between today and tomorrow, as the plant shows it, so subtly but so clearly, by its changes. Keep vision whetted by noticing the patterns that insects make in the air, or how certain tamped-down foliage means a deer has slept here with her fawn. He was good at watching.

And on the old track through the dark woods there was much to watch, evidence of people before him come and gone, and others whose presence, neither friendly nor hostile, he could feel nearby, unseen, ever present. They were people who did not concern themselves with travelers: a knight like himself, a monk or two, or even a company of pilgrims, they just amounted to weather in the woods, passing, not really there.

The knight felt almost comforted by their presence, at peace with their indifference. Just as he felt indifferent but alert to the trees and herbs he passed by, or slept beneath, or nibbled in the morning, when he knew this leaf was safe, to wake his breath and shape the waking air.

It was still morning as he rode, and he was beginning to feel the first stirrings of hunger. He had plenty of bread in his saddlebag, and sweet water in his leather bottle, but he was a well-reared young man, and knew that one should not eat while doing some other thing, in this case riding, watching, understanding the world he passed through. Eating takes the soul inside, to survey the food's journey to the center—that is how he had been taught. And taught too that doing things while eating sapped the nourishment from the food, and also drained the soul from the other thing he might be doing. He had seen other people, some of them knights or priests even, munching while they walked or worked wood or read in a book—he shook his head to think of such folly, that people should live on the earth and not understand the simplest things about their bodies' relations with the place they lived in.

The track he followed was narrow but clear. He rode cautiously, frequently having to duck beneath a heavy branch, or gently lift a younger one aside—do not break the tree that shelters the path, that was another thing he knew.

Just ahead now he could see, in something of a clearing where more sun came through, another traveler on the path. He was seated on a fallen log, it seemed, and the knight could see a big bag slumped beside the man. As the knight drew closer, he saw that the seated man was a leper, his walking staff with rattle top lying beside him, his shabby old tunic still showing clear enough the huge rough heart shape painted on it in rust. The leper was eating, but dropped his loaf and went to pick up the staff and rattle it, to warn the knight.

"Good morning, Sir Leper," the knight called out in a friendly way. The leper let the staff fall, and smiled up. His face was mostly still there, and the smile was easy enough to look at.

"Good morning, Lord Knight," the leper replied, each man courteously elevating the social status of the other. Perhaps the leper had been a man of better station once upon a time.

There was not much to say. But the knight lingered, of a mind to share and inquire.

"Have you food enough, Sir Leper? I have a bit in my satchel."

"Thank you kindly, my lord, but I have some meat in mine too. And there is good water in a spring a little way beyond; you'll pass it in five minutes, if you need. It breaks out of a single rock upright among cool ferns. I like the place, but do not linger there, because I am as you see me."

The knight knew no easy way to respond to that, and turned his words aside.

"What is this place we're in? Whose forest is this?"

"I don't know its name, or it may not have one, and I have lived near at hand most of my life, apart from the years I wandered in the Holy Land that taught me to wear such clothes as these," said the leper, sweeping one hand down along his tunic, which was blazoned with the Heart of Pity, as they called it, that all lepers in this land must wear. "They say the woods are owned by the Abbey of Saint Ulfric, but no one lives in that abbey any longer, and the last abbot died when I was a child. Whoever may own the land, there is no doubt who controls it. For this whole forest is in the clutches of a dragon who lives in a gorge only a mile or a mile and a half, depending on what path you take to reach it, from where we are sitting."

"A dragon!" exclaimed the knight. "Does he do great mischief in the woods?"

"Not to the trees, but you will have noticed, perhaps, that no animals have crossed your path, and few are the birds that flew over you."

"I had not noticed. Why is that?"

"Most have been consumed by the dragon," said the leper. "My uncleanness must spoil his appetite, since he has never bothered me, though I have seen him half a dozen times, and I am sure he's seen me more often than that, since little does he miss in what goes forward."

"What does he look like, when you see him, this dragon?"

"Much as you suppose. Vast and sinuous and mostly green, with flakes of bony stuff atop his spine that would slice a man in half. Wings he has as well, of a pale bluish color, translucent like the wings of a bat, and very long. His face is an interesting one: He has the fangs you'd expect, but set in a muzzle of some nobility, more lion than snake, more eagle than lion. Hard to be sure, since his face seems to change its bones with his mood."

"That is very odd," said the knight. He was silent for a while, thinking of what he had heard. Then asked: "If the dragon has eaten up all the deer and boars and hares in these woods, what does he live on, do you think?"

"I know the answer to that," said the leper. "He leaves the woods and raids the towns and granges all about, on the far side of the forest, away from the side from which you came. He is a plague and a bother to them, but strange to say, though he breathes fire like any dragon, he never burns down a house or croft or mill. Mostly he'll seize cattle or sheep, a goat or a dog, and that will sate him. But sometimes he has been known to snatch a maiden, wrap her in his coils, and fly away with her to his gorge. At least that is what people think. The bones of the girls are never found."

"That is a sad and shameful thing, that a young woman be carried off at all, let alone by such a beast."

"Beast he may be, though I'm not sure of that, since I have heard him talk."

"Talk!"

"Yes, and not the way crows talk, for example, where you have to hold your heart and mind a certain way to understand what they're saying. No, this dragon talks as you and I are talking now, using words, most of which I recognize."

"Have you spoken with him then?" asked the knight, a little doubtful all at once of the character of this leper.

"Never, but I have heard him speaking. Whether to himself or to another I could not tell. Out of fear I kept my distance. Damaged and distressed as it is, this body is still precious to me, and I would fain keep it a while longer."

"What does he say, this dragon? What is there for him to speak about, I wonder."

The leper closed his eye and thought a bit before he answered.

"You know, lord, I am not sure. While he was speaking, I understood perfectly what he said and what he meant. But afterward, and now, all I can do is remember understanding. But what I understood, that I can't remember."

"It seems to me," said the knight, "that I should go and see what this dragon has to say for himself. And if he does not give a good account, I suppose I must seek with God's help to slay him, and rid the forest and the farms of his harm. This seems then to be an adventure that has come to me. Thank you, Sir Leper."

"That is gracious of you, Lord Knight, but better to thank me later, when you see whether or not this is a good thing you undertake."

"How could it, with God's help, fail to be good?"

"I could not say, Lord Knight, but the dragon may not be of a mind to be slain. Or he may speak with such wiles as to dissuade you. Or even win you to his cause, whatever that might be."

"Speaking of that, you speak well, Sir Leper, if I may say so. Your words are intelligent and suave and well chosen, dare I say it, and much wittier than mine. You remind me of certain clerics who had the kindness to instruct me when I was very young."

"Yes, Lord Knight, I was a priest once upon a time, and went with the Jerusalem Farers on their crusades, to give them counsel and keep them honest along the way, much good it did."

A leper priest is a scary thing indeed, the young knight thought, but wasn't sure why it should be so. Why scarier than a leper farmer or a leper soldier? Yet it was, almost as if it meant that something was wrong in the way the world was made. That a priest should give up women and begetting and owning and amassing, and yet be subject to this degrading disease. And all a priest's learning went for naught. Not naught, though, since here he was being instructed by this wise priest.

"I grieve for your distress," said the knight, and the other knew he meant not just the leprosy but also his sadness at the human condition, where rutting soldiers would not listen to their priests, and stole and spoiled and ravened.

"Bless you for your understanding," said the leper, and said no more.

The knight sat a while longer and thought about what he had learned. Now it is a knight's business to balance the iniquity in the moral world and the imperfections in the natural order with his own virtue and prowess and that special quality of responsible loving-kindness called honesty. It would appear, and so it seemed to him, that the activities of the dragon, as reported, constituted an imperfection in this forest in particular, and the scheme of things in general, one that should be mended. And the code of Holy Adventure, by which knights have always lived, and still do live, calls for the knight who discovers the flaw in the pattern to be the one who heals it.

The leper was sitting quietly, and the knight supposed the man wanted to get on with his meal—the sun was straight overhead now. But the leper made no gesture one way or another, just sat.

"Sir Leper," asked the knight, "could you show me the way to the dragon's gorge?"

The leper smiled, and gently thrust his rear leg forward. Only now did the knight see that there was scarcely a foot at the end of the leg, just a mass of clotted cloths tied round a stump that did not bear thinking about.

"My lord will see that I am not skilled at walking these days, and will forgive me for not keeping him company. I walk little as I can, and on the softest places, where the pine needles let fall the soft, safe road that is my bed as well. I will tell you, though, how to meet your dragon."

How strange, the knight thought, that the priest had already made the dragon the knight's own.

"From this place keep onward as you were going. As I said before, you will soon come to a spring among the ferns—it will be on your right side as you go. Pause and drink—the water is healthy and bracing. Just past the spring you will see, on the same side, a thickety place, all rustling aspen leaves and shadow. In the thicket you will soon find, God willing, a little path, evident, wide enough for your horse, I think. Take this and follow it. It rises slowly through trees to a bare hill, climbs the hill—it is no more than a mile from the spring—and from the top, you will look down into the gorge of the one of whom we have spoken. God be with you, Lord Knight."

"And with you, Sir Priest, and thank you."

The knight made a civil gesture, which was returned. Then he urged his horse onward. In a few minutes man and rider came to the rock among ferns. The knight dismounted and drank, and drank again. And felt again the hunger he'd been feeling before the leper. Why not eat his midday meal here?

He did so. And as he chewed on the good grainy bread, he thought a little about priest and dragon, maiden and duty, then drew his mind back to the bread. Because thinking about things while eating is no better than riding or plowing a field while eating. Eat while eating, ride while riding, sleep while sleeping. But thinking has a way of creeping in, the way dream creeps into blameless sleep and tells its incoherent stories. Not easy not to think. Best to think about bread, his jaws chewing, his body dark with waiting.

When he swallowed as much of his bread as he'd let himself eat this summery day with supper far away, he packed up his things, drank again from the spring, and remounted. Soon enough he spied a little track off through the aspens, and veered that way, hoping it was the right one. A dark way indeed, and the leaves on their slender branches had a way of being mobile, moving before him, beside him, behind him, as if they were opening the curtain of themselves and leading him further in.

Now that the leper had alerted him to the absence of beast and fowl, the knight kept an ear open for any bird cry he might hear. It was true, the forest was quiet, very quiet, apart from the noises he made brushing through the trees. A few times there did come the clear call of a crow from up ahead, a sound he liked hearing. It made him easier about his choice of path. He trusted crows, and any place where they gathered.

A mile or so, the leper priest had said. Ambling though the horse was, and the leaves thick around them, he expected he'd find himself at the hill in no great while, and indeed the ground was gradually, perceptibly rising before him. Soon the aspens gave way to a treeless slope close covered with heather, and he spurred his horse up. Again the crows called ahead of him, more than one—three, he guessed, from the timbre of their cries. At the top of what seemed not a hill but a ridge, the knight looked down into the gorge he expected to see.

Deep it was, and running arrow-straight from south to north (it seemed) through the forest. Seventy or eighty feet down, a feeble stream winked along the narrow valley. On the far side of the gorge, tall pines stood, and two or three crows seemed tossed from branch to branch, but no longer did they cry. He had come, he thought, to where he was supposed to be, so no more directions were needed. Here it is. The steep slopes of the gorge fell away—walking back and forth along the rim, he could spy no trail, and it was too steep for any horse. Where was the dragon?

The slope in front of him was densely matted with juniper and cedar and heather, while the slope on the far side seemed crusted with a low, thick ground cover, a row of spiky bushes running along it halfway down. What he saw was quiet, and gave him no sense of awe or fear. As a good and honest knight, he knew fear, knew it well, and knew how to deal with it most times. Without fear there could be no courage—his teachers had taught him that. Without fear there can only be a creeping uneasiness, a draining, enervating malaise. Fear is brilliant, though, and summons even cowards to be brave. These were good thoughts to be having, he thought, when looking for dragons. But where was the dragon? No smell, no sound, no glimpse of his presence. Or of what he might have done. In earlier encounters with dragons he had heard about, the knight had always found near the caverns scattered bones, garments stripped from poor travelers devoured, bracelets, pieces of gold even, though most of those were buried deep within some cave or burrow. The knight looked for such evidence now, and found nothing. Was this the right place? He wondered about the leper, whether a man like that, however well spoken and kindly acting, might not have, in his own despair, come to take pleasure in leading other men astray, as once he had tried vainly to lead them toward the good. Where was the dragon?

The knight slipped off his horse, tethered the creature to a sturdy, thick old juniper bush, and plucked off a few of those cloudy blue berries. He mashed them in his fingers, inhaled the heady smell of them—they smelled like a rain shower on a hot, sunny day. He dropped the seedy pulp but licked his fingers. The taste was nothing at all like the smell. That is how things are. The knight sat down crosslegged, and waited, staring into the ravine.

It was pleasant being where he was. The horse found nourishment in deep, unvisited grasses among the shrubs. A quiet wind was moving, and it dawned on the knight that it was because the wind was coming from over his shoulder that he smelled none of the stench people had told him to expect anywhere that dragons had stayed a while.

He wondered what manner of dragon this might be. The description the priest had given could, depending on just how faithful a describer he had been, suit several sorts of dragon: the Cloud Worm (and the blue wings suggested it) ,who nests in earth but spends most of his day aloft; or the Diggon Nail, who burrows straight down in the earth and (it seems an evil miracle) turns himself inside out to shoot out again, arrow swift, from the earth to seize its prey; or the Riverlord, who lived mostly in streams and lakes to keep his fires banked against the moment of need. But the nobility the priest had noted in the dragon's face, "more lion than snake, more eagle than lion," did not match any of those three kinds. None of the other dragons he knew about had wings at all, or tall scales on their backbones. So he would await the encounter, and learn.

As he sat there, reviewing his knowledge of such matters as might be useful to recall in the next while, he grew sleepy. He knew well enough that sleep is not to be fought off—only enemies are to be fought, but not to be indulged either; only bad friends need to be indulged. No, sleep was a good friend, and should be met candidly, and only when the time was right. The time seemed right, nothing asked itself of him, he let his eyelids close, and let himself drift toward sleep.

A breath of air tickled along his neck, and his eyes opened. And before he let them close again he noticed, or thought he noticed, that there was some subtle difference in the slope on the far side of the ravine. It had changed, its contour was not what it had been, but the knight could not tell just how. He decided to experiment: He closed his eyes, drifted almost away, then quickly opened them. Yes, there was a change; the curve of the bushes was different.

Then, as he watched, eyes wide, the change happened—a ripple ran through the shrubs and grasses over there, and then a stronger one. He could feel no wind to account for it, or for the next, even heftier, ripple. Then the whole hillside lifted up and looked at him.

For it was the dragon himself, stretched out and likely asleep, that he had been watching all this while, the tough green scales and hairy interweaves of the great body now clearly discernible, the huge head (he had thought it a distant tree) now reared halfway up the sky turned round to gaze at the knight, who felt awe and fear, states of feeling he had been trained to turn into thinking. He thought, calmly and quickly, taking and holding and releasing his breaths in the rhythm he had been taught by a monk when he was still in the hands of his master.

The dragon's head swung nearer, balancing gently halfway across the gorge. The eyes of this dragon, which was in fact the first of any kind that the knight had seen with his own eyes, these eyes that looked at him were many colored. They did not glitter like the eyes of a snake or glisten like those of a frog. They were more catlike, he thought, in that they seemed to go very deep into themselves and open up in there onto some other space. The hall in an ancient castle they all are coming from, he thought.

Smoke drifted out of the dragon's nostrils. Watching the smoke curl away into emptiness made him feel strange, so he concentrated on his breathing, and on letting his eyes do their work with the eyes of the animal.

Though it didn't much look like an animal.

"Can you with all your seeing see who I am?" asked the dragon. The voice was smaller than you'd imagine, deep enough, but seeming to come from nowhere. In fact, the knight looked around to see if someone else had spoken.

"No," said the dragon, "it is I who spoke. Do you feel fit to answer my question? Can you see who I am?"

"Truth to tell, I can't. I have been looking, maybe even staring, forgive me, I know that isn't polite, but somehow I imagined an animal would not mind being stared at. I mean, animals—cats, for instance, or deer, or owls—are always staring."

"That is logical, Sir Parsival. But animals do mind being stared at as if they were not worth any other mode of discourse. Seeing can be very distancing. The object you look at so intently can be rendered into a mere thing by your beholding. Instead, you should try to use all of your senses, mental senses at least, to observe."

"How do you know my name?"

"I know all the names, Sir Parsival. And I know which name belongs to whom, and what everybody's real name is."

But Parsival doubted suddenly. In his mind's eye he could see the leper hobbling through the aspen grove, hurrying along a shortcut to the dragon's lair, and whispering to the dragon the name of his soon-to-be assailant. And once the knight started thinking that way, he soon imagined that the leper had deliberately lured him, for no decent reason, into this encounter with the dragon. The leper was some sort of agent or tool of the dragon. No wonder he stank and had scaly skin. The knight didn't blurt out all that, of course, but only said, suspiciously enough: "I think the leper came secretly to you and told you my name."

And even as he said so, he realized that he had not told the leper his name.

"Not so, Sir Parsival, I would not need a priest to tell me what I can read from your heart."

"How did you know the leper was a priest? He wears no sign of his former glory."

"I know what everybody is, and everybody was, and some part of what everybody will be—but not all," explained the dragon, "so do not ask much about what is to come. What is to come is written in what has been. You think I am a monster (you haven't said so, but I can tell), whereas I think I myself am nothing but the logic of the world."

The dragon paused, more as if to reflect than to give the knight a chance to speak, then went on: "And the logic of the world is frightening enough, God knows."

"You dare to speak of God!"

"Everybody talks about God. Be closer!"

At that command, abruptly spoken, Parsival drew back, and his hand began to coax his sword out of its scabbard. Yet suddenly he was closer, much closer, right in front of the dragon's face, but he had not moved. The great head had swung further toward him. He could feel the warmth of the dragon's breath on his face. He had been holding his breath, for fear of the evil smell of that breath, and perhaps a righteous fear of inhaling evil itself into his innocent body. But he had to breathe, and snatched a quick inhalation. To his surprise, the smell was far from unpleasant. It reminded him of many things—the skin beside his mother's earlobe when he had kissed her goodbye, a birchbark box he had once opened and found full of old rose petals, most of their color gone but still a rosy scent left for him.

"See," said the dragon, "you are beginning to stare with other senses now."

Bravely, the knight inhaled deeply. And now he found other fragrances mingling too, more enigmatic—sun on hot slate, a cucumber stung by a wasp and turned a little brown around the bite, a door slammed by the wind and the dust on the threshold whirled up by its motion, tickle in the nostrils, could moonlight have a smell? And wasn't that the smell of the place in the woods where he'd seen a stag rubbing itself against a beech tree? He sneezed.

Instantly the huge membranous wings of the dragon whirled and came to rest a few feet above the knight's head.

"Why? What?" gasped the knight.

"I am shielding you from the noontime; the sun is greedy for the part of a man's soul that flies out when he sneezes and looks around and soon comes back unless it's snatched by some power. I shield you from that power."

"Thank you," said the knight, still a little breathless from his big sneeze.

"That is the first word or sign of courtesy you have shown me, Sir Parsival.

Thank you for it, though someday you'll grasp that it does you more good than it does me. Now tell me, why have you come to slay me?"

"Not easy to explain, now that you ask me. At this moment, I don't feel very much like killing you. Or anything else."

"Those words are good to hear. (Even better that you speak them.) But before this very moment on the porches of my house, in pleasant sunlight, and no birds shouting, why did you think to come slay me?"

"I suppose I didn't 'think to' slay you. I really didn't think at all. I have been raised in a tradition that tells me that virtue lies in smiting or slaying the enemy. The same tradition recognizes enemies of all kinds—wolves and bears, snakes and spiders, foreigners and bandits, demons, bad neighbors, dragons, monsters, devils, and the Devil himself. All of them are against us, and we must be quick to flee them or slay them, whichever is in our power. And many of the great older brethren in my company have distinguished themselves by slaying dragons. Or so it is said. I have never seen it done. To be truthful, you are the first dragon I have ever seen."

The dragon's head drew even closer, and turned slowly from side to side as if to give the knight a chance to see him whole. Poised now a foot or two above, the dragon spoke.

"Do I seem to you to belong to the class of enemies you have listed? Is it enough just for me to be a dragon to make you slay me, or must I first be guilty of bad behavior? And if so, what wrong have I done you?"

The knight edged back a little to get some distance from that all-too-observant face, the broad nostrils carved in the shapely muzzle, the all-color eyes resting, always resting, calmly on him.

"No wrong, Sir Dragon. But the leper told me of your depredations on the farmlands and houses outside the woods, and the maidens you have carried off. It seemed from what he said that you were behaving exactly as dragons are said to behave. Therefore it fell to me to remedy the evil—the one who learns about it must do something about it, that is the rule."

"A good rule," said the dragon. "But what it means to 'do something,' ah, that's another matter. We should one day have a talk about that."

"Do you deny that you have raided and ravened in the plains round about?"

"Come into my house deeper, sir, and you will find no plunder. There are no maidens here."

"Did the leper lie?"

"Perhaps the priest in him made him do it. They are creatures of books and ceremonies, priests. He, like you, has learned how dragons make nuisances of themselves, and, like you, assumes that since I am a dragon, I have done what the dragons in his books are said to do."

"So I should not be afraid of you?"

"You have done very well so far in hiding your fear, or perhaps distracting us both from it. But on the contrary, you should be very afraid of me. I told you that I am logical. Now I tell you that I am wise. The two flanks of the mind are deployed, and there is no room for stupidity or hatred or indifference. And not much room for love—just enough to keep the world at work."

"But how can I slay wisdom?"

The dragon looked very sad a moment, unless the knight deceived himself by interpreting a certain wetness of the eye.

"Slay wisdom? The priests do it all day long, and what they leave still breathing the schoolmasters and the merchants soon make away with. Wisdom, being eternal, is the easiest thing to slay."

"That's too deep for me," said the knight. And he stood up, tugging the sword loose at last from the sheath. The dragon did not move.

"O little one, o little knight, my little son! Don't you know you have already slain me? Don't you know that you'll come back tomorrow morning and there will be no dragon here, just an empty gorge, with a trickle of reddish water in it, rusty from the iron sills in this old rock. No dragon, no hoard, no maiden. But your mind will be different. You will listen to me in your head again. You will realize that, just like the cowardly creature your traditions claim I am, I have rushed into hiding. You will slowly realize that I have hidden myself in the snuggest cavern of all, deep inside your mind, and that you will never altogether silence me. Because once you have slain someone or something, you take into yourself everything they are and know and do."

Parsival did not raise his sword, but let it fall. He began to cry. Wisdom is so cruel, so tender, what can he do but cry? He is young, after all, not yet seventeen, and his mother is dead.

He blinks tears out of his eyes and says, "I'm sorry, I'm sorry, I meant no harm."

"And none was done," said the voice of the dragon.

"What shall I do?"

"Do what you have done. Be quick to listen, slow to lift the sword. Learn from everything you see and everyone you meet. Even lepers. Even priests. Even me."

Then there was no dragon. The air was just the same, the gorge was as it had been before; perhaps the far slope was a little more barren, perhaps not. Memory is not reliable.

The knight stowed away his sword, untethered his horse, mounted, and went back down the way he had come. He wiped his eyes on his sleeve. Perhaps he should seek out the leper and disabuse him of his false ideas about the dragon. And yet, he thought, it was those wrong ideas that had brought him to this meeting. The meeting seemed important, very important, but Sir Parsival could not exactly say how or why. He left it to work itself out in his mind, the way things do. No need to bother the poor leper, let him think as he pleased.

Then Parsival attended to his path, the calm demeanor of his horse. Strange, now he thought about it, that his horse had not shied from the dragon, had not even whinnied or shifted. All through the conversation, the horse had gone on browsing. He began to think about the horse, what it must have felt. What an animal must know.

THE LONG, COLD GOODBYE

HOLLY PHILLIPS

Berd was late and she knew Sele would not wait for her, not even if it weren't cold enough to freeze a standing man's feet in his shoes. She hurried anyway, head down, as if she hauled a sled heavy with anxiety. She did not look up from the icy pavement until she arrived at the esplanade, and was just in time to see the diver balanced atop the railing. Sele! she thought, her voice frozen in her throat. The diver was no more than a silhouette, faceless, anonymous in winter clothes. Stop, she thought. Don't, she thought, still unable to speak. He spread his arms. He was an ink sketch, an albatross, a flying cross. Below him, the ice on the bay shone with the apricot-gold of the sunset, a gorgeous summer nectar of a color that lied in the face of the ferocious cold. The light erased the boundary between frozen sea and icy sky; from where Berd stood across the boulevard, there was no horizon but the black line of the railing, sky above and below, the cliff an edge on eternity. And the absence the diver made when he had flown was as bright as all the rest within the blazing death of the sun.

Berd crossed the boulevard, huddled deep within the man's overcoat she wore over all her winter clothes. Brightness brought tears to her eyes and the tears froze on her lashes. She was alone on the esplanade now. It was so quiet she could hear the groan of tide-locked ice floes, the tick and ping of the iron railing threatening to shatter in the cold. She looked over, careful not to touch the metal even with her sleeve, and saw the shape the suicide made against the ice. No longer a cross: an asterisk bent to angles on the frozen waves and ice-sheeted rocks. He was not alone there. There was a whole uneven line of corpses lying along the foot of the cliff, like a line of unreadable type, the final sentence in a historical tome, unburied until the next storm swept in with its erasure of snow. Berd's diver steamed, giving up the last ghost of warmth to the blue shadow of the land. He was still faceless. He might have been anyone, dead. The shadow grew. The sun spread itself into a spindle, a line; dwindled to a green spark and was gone. It was all shadow now, luminous dusk the color of longing, a blue to break your heart, ice's consolation for the blazing death of the sky. Berd's breath steamed like the broken man, dusting her scarf with frost. She turned and picked her way across the boulevard, its pavement broken by frost heaves, her eyes still dazzled by the last of the day. It was spring, the 30th of April, May Day Eve. The end.

Sele. That was not, could never have been him, Berd decided. Suicide had become a commonplace this spring, this non-spring, but Sele would never think of it. He was too curious, perhaps too fatalistic, certainly too engaged in the new scramble for survival and bliss. (But if he did, *if* he did, he would call on Berd to witness it. There was no one left but her.) No. She shook her head to herself in the collar of her coat. Not Sele. She was late. He had come and gone. The diver had come and gone. Finally she felt the shock of it, witness to a man's sudden death, and flinched to a stop in the empty street. Gaslights stood unlit in the blue dusk, and the windows of the buildings flanking the street were mostly dark, so that the few cracks of light struck a note of loneliness. Lonely Berd, witness to too much, standing with her feet freezing inside her shoes. She leaned forward, her sled of woe a little heavier now, and started walking. *She* would not go that way, not *that* way, she would *not*. She would find Sele, who had simply declined to wait for her in the cold, and get what he had promised her, and then she would be free.

But where, in all the dying city, would he be?

Sele had never held one address for long. Even when they were children Berd could never be sure of finding him in the same park or alley or briefly favored dock for more than a week or two. Then she would have to hunt him down, her search spirals widening as he grew older and dared to roam further afield. Sometimes she grew disheartened or angry that he never sought her out, that she was always the one who had to look for him, and then she refused. Abstained, as she came to think of it in more recent years. She had her own friends, her own curiosities, her own pursuits. But she found that even when she was pursuing them she would run across Sele following the same trail. Were they so much alike? It came of growing up together, she supposed. Each had come too much under the other's influence. She had not seen him for more than a year when they found each other again at the lecture on ancient ways.

"Oh, hello," he said, as if it had been a week.

"Hello." She bumped shoulders with him, standing at the back of the crowded room—crowded, it must be said, only because the room was so small. And she had felt the currents of amusement, impatience, offense, disdain, running through him, as if together they had closed a circuit, because she felt the same things herself, listening to the distinguished professor talk about the "first inhabitants," the "lost people," as if there were not two of them standing in the very room.

"We lost all right," Sele had said, more rueful than bitter, and Berd had laughed. So that was where it had begun, with a shrug and a laugh—if it had not begun in their childhood, growing up poor and invisible in the city built on their native ground—if it had not begun long before they were born.

Berd trudged on, worried now about the impending darkness. The spring dusk would linger for a long while, but there were no lamplighters out to spark the lamps. In this cold, if men didn't lose fingers to the iron posts, the brass fittings shattered like rotten ice. So there would be no light but the stars already piercing the blue. *Find Sele, find Sele.* It was like spiraling back into childhood, spiraling through the city in search of him. Every spiral had a beginning point. Hers would be his apartment, a long way from the old neighborhood, not so far from the esplanade. *He won't be there*, she warned herself, and as if she were tending a child, she turned her mind from the sight of the dead man lying with the others on the ice.

Dear Berd,

I cannot tell you how happy your news has made me. You are coming! You are coming at last! It seems as though I have been waiting for a lifetime, and now that I know I'll only have to wait a few short weeks more they stretch out before me like an eternity. Your letters are all my consolation, and the memory I hold so vividly in my mind is better than any photograph: your sweet face and your eyes that smile when you look sad and yet hold such a melancholy when you smile. My heart knows you so well, and you are still mysterious to me, as if every thought, every emotion you share (and you are so open you shame me for my reserve) casts a shadow that keeps the inner Berd safely hidden from prying eyes. Oh, I won't pry! But come soon, as soon as you can, because one lifetime of waiting is long enough for any man . . .

Sele's apartment was in a tall old wooden house that creaked and groaned even in lesser colds than this. Wooden houses had once been grand, back when the lumber was brought north in wooden ships and the natives lived in squat stone huts like ice-bound caves, and Sele's building still showed a ghost of its old beauty in its ornate gables and window frames. But it had been a long time since it had seen paint, and the weathered siding looked like driftwood in the dying light. The porch steps moaned under Berd's feet as she climbed to the door. An old bell pull hung there. She pulled it and heard the bell ring as if it were a ship's bell a hundred miles out to sea. The house was empty, she needed no other sign. All the same she tried the handle, fingers wincing from the cold brass even inside her mitten. The handle fell away from its broken mechanism with a clunk on the stoop and the door sighed open a crack, as if the house inhaled. It was dark inside; there was no breath of warmth. All the same, thought Berd, all the same. She stepped, anxious and hopeful, inside.

Dark, and cold, and for an instant Berd had the illusion that she was stepping into one of the stone barrow-houses of her ancestors, windowless and buried deep under the winter's snow. She wanted immediately to be out in the blue dusk again, out of this tomb-like confinement. Sele wasn't here.

And beyond that, with the suicide fresh in her mind and the line of death scribbled across her inner vision, Berd had the sense of dreadful discoveries waiting for her, as if the house really were a tomb. *Go. Go before you see . . .* But suppose she didn't find Sele elsewhere and hadn't checked here? Intuition was not infallible—her many searches for Sele had not always borne fruit—she had to be sure. Her eyes were adjusting to the darkness. She found the stairs and began to climb.

There was more light upstairs, filtering down like a fine gray-blue dust from unshuttered windows. Ghost light. The stairs, the whole building, creaked and ticked and groaned like every ghost story every told. Yet she was not precisely afraid. Desolate, yes, and abandoned, as if she were haunted by the empty house itself; as if, having entered here, she would never regain the realm of the living; as if the entire world had become a tomb. *As if.*

It was the enthusiasm she remembered, when memory took her like a sudden faint, a shaft of pain. They had been playing a game of make-believe, and the game had been all the more fun for being secreted within the sophisticated city. Like children constructing the elaborate edifice of Let's Pretend in the interstices of the adult world, they had played under the noses of the conquerors who had long since forgotten they had ever conquered, the foreigners who considered themselves native born. Berd and Sele, and later Berd's cousins and Sele's half-sister, Isse. They had had everything to hide and had hidden nothing. The forgotten, the ignored, the perpetually overlooked. Like children, playing. And for a time Sele had been easy to find, always here, welcoming them in with their bits of research, their inventions, their portentous dreams. His apartment warm with lamplight, no modern gaslights for them, and voices weaving a spell in point and counterpoint. *Why don't we . . . ? Is there any way . . . ? What if . . . ?*

What if we could change the world?

The upper landing was empty in the gloom that filtered through the icy window at the end of the hall. Berd's boots thumped on the bare boards, her layered clothes rustled together, the wooden building went on complaining in the cold, and mysteriously, the tangible emptiness of the house was transmuted into an ominous kind of inhabitation. It was as if she had let the cold dusk in behind her, as if she had been followed by the wisp of steam rising from the suicide's broken head. She moved in a final rush down the hall to Sele's door, knocked inaudibly with her mittened fist, tried the handle. Unlocked. She pushed open the door.

"Sele?" She might have been asking him to comfort her for some recent hurt. Her voice broke, her chest ached, hot tears welled into her eyes. "Sele?"

But he wasn't there, dead or alive.

Well, at least she was freed from this gruesome place. She made a fast tour of the three rooms, feeling neurotic for her diligence (but she did have to make sure all the same), and opened the hall door with all her momentum carrying her forward to a fast departure.

And cried aloud with the shock of discovering herself no longer alone.

They were oddly placed down the length of the hall, and oddly immobile, as if she had just yelled *Freeze!* in a game of statues. Yes, they stood like a frieze of statues: Three People Walking. Yet they must have been moving seconds before; she had not spent a full minute in Sele's empty rooms. Berd stood in the doorway with her heart knocking against her breastbone, her eyes watering as she stared without blinking in the dead light. Soon they would laugh at the joke they had played on her. Soon they would move.

Berd was all heartbeat and hollow fear as she crept down the hallway, hugging the wall for fear of brushing a sleeve. Her cousin Wael was first, one shoulder dropped lower than the other as if he was on the verge of turning to look back. His head was lowered, his uncut hair fell ragged across his face, his clothes were far too thin for the cold. The cold. Even through all her winter layers, Berd could feel the impossible chill emanating from her cousin's still form. Cold, so cold. But as she passed she would have sworn he swayed, ever so slightly, keeping his balance, keeping still while she passed. Keeping still until her back was turned. Wael. Wael! It was wrong to be so afraid of him. She breathed his name as she crept by, and saw her breath as a cloud.

If any of them breathed, their breath was as cold as the outer air.

Behind Wael was Isse, Sele's beautiful half-sister. Her head was raised and her white face—was it only the dusk that dusted her skin with blue?—looked ahead, eyes dark as shadows. She might have been seeing another place entirely, walking through another landscape, as if this statue of a woman in a summer dress had been stolen from a garden and put down all out of its place and time. Where did she walk to so intently? What landscape did she see with those lightless eyes?

And Baer was behind her, Berd's other cousin. He had been her childhood enemy, a plague on her friendship with Sele, and somehow because of it her most intimate friend, the one who knew her too well. His name jumped in Berd's throat. He stood too close to the wall for Berd to sidle by. She had to cross in front of him to the other wall and he *had* to see her, though his head, like Wael's, was lowered. He might have been walking alone, brooding a little, perhaps following Isse's footsteps or looking for something he had lost. Berd stopped in front of him, trembling, caught between his cold and Isse's as if she stood between two impossible fires.

"Baer?" She hugged herself, maybe because that was as close as she dared come to sharing her warmth with him. "Oh, Baer."

But grief did not lessen her fear. It only made her fear—made *them*—more terrible. She had come too close. Baer could reach out, he only had to reach out . . . She fled, her sleeve scraping the wall, her boots battering the stairs. Down, down, moving too fast to be stopped by the terror of what else, what worse, the dark lobby might hold. Berd's breath gasped out, white even in the darkest spot by the door. It was very dark, and the dark was full of reaching hands. The door had no handle. It had swung closed. She was trapped. No.

No. But all she could whisper, propitiation or farewell, was her cousin's name. "Baer . . . " *please don't forget you loved me.* "Baer . . . " *please don't do me harm.* Until in an access of terror she somehow wrenched open the door and sobbed out, feeling the cold of them at her back, "I'm sorry!" But even then she could not get away.

There was no street, no building across the way. There was no way, only a vast field of blue . . . blue . . . Berd might have been stricken blind for that long moment it took her mind to make sense of what her eyes saw. It was ice, the great ocean of ice that encircled the pole, as great an ocean as any in the world. Ice bluer than any water, as blue as the depthless sky. If death were a color it might be this blue, oh! exquisite and full of dread. Berd hung there, hands braced on the doorframe, as though to keep her from being forced off the step. She forgot the cold ones upstairs; remembered them with a new jolt of fear; forgot them again as the bears came into view. The great white bears, denizens of the frozen sea, exiles on land when the spring drove the ice away. Exiles no more. They walked, slow and patient and seeming sad with their long heads nodding above the surface of the snow; and it seemed to Berd, standing in her impossible doorway—if she turned would she find the house gone and nothing left but this lintel, this doorstep, and these two jambs beneath her hands?—it seemed to her, watching the slow bears walk from horizon to blue horizon, that other figures walked with them, as white-furred as the bears, but two-legged and slight. She peered. She leaned out, her arms stretched behind her as she kept tight hold of her wooden anchors, not knowing anymore if it was fear that ached within her.

And then she felt on her shoulder the touch of a hand.

She fell back against the left-hand doorjamb, hung there, her feet clumsy as they found their new position. It was Baer, with Wael and Isse and others—yes, others!—crowding behind him in the lobby. The house was not empty and never had been, no more than a tomb is empty after the mourners have gone.

"Baer . . . "

Did he see her? He stood as if he would never move again, his hand outstretched as though to hail the bears, stop them, call them to come. He did not move, but in the moment that Berd stared at him, her heart failing and breath gone, the others had come closer. Or were they moved, like chess pieces by a player's hand? They were only *there*, close, close, so close the cold of them ate into Berd's flesh, threatening her bones with ice. Her throat clenched. A breath would have frozen her lungs. A tear would have frozen her eyes. At least the bears were warm inside their fur. She fell outside, onto the ice—

—onto the stoop, the first stair, her feet carrying her in an upright fall to the street. Yes: street, stairs, house. The door was swinging closed on the dark lobby, and there was nothing to see but the tall, shabby driftwood house and the brass doorknob rolling slowly, slowly to the edge of the stair. It did not fall. Shuddering with cold, Berd scoured her mittens across her ice-streaked face and fled, feeling the weight of the coming dark closing in behind her.

> *Dear Berd,*
>
> *I am lonely here. Recent years have robbed me of too many friends. Do I seem older to you? I feel old sometimes, watching so many slip away from me, some through travel, some through death, some through simple, inevitable change. I feel that I have not changed, myself, yet that does not make me feel young. Older, if anything, as if I have stopped growing and have nothing left to me but to begin to die. I'm sorry. I am not morbid, only sad. But your coming is a great consolation to me. At last! Someone dear to me—someone dearer to me than anyone in the world—is coming towards me instead of leaving me behind. You are my cure for sorrow. Come soon . . .*

Berd was too cold, she could not bear the prospect of canvassing the rest of Sele's old haunts. Old haunts! Her being rebelled. She ran until the air was like knives in her lungs, walked until the sweat threatened to freeze against her skin. She looked back as she turned corner after corner—no one, no one—but the fear and the grief never left her. Oh, Baer! Oh, Wael, and beautiful Isse! It was worse than being dead. Was it? Was it worse than being left behind? But Berd had not earned the grief of abandonment, no matter how close she was to stopping in the street and sobbing, bird-like, open-mouthed. She had no right. She was the one who was leaving.

At least, she was if she could find Sele. If she could only find him this once. This one last time.

She had known early on that it was love, on her part at least, but had been frequently bewildered as to what kind of love it was. Friendship, yes, but there was that lightness of heart at the first sight of him, the deep physical contentment in his rare embrace. She had envied his lovers, but had not been jealous of them. Had never minded sharing him with others, but had always been hurt when he vanished and would not be found. Love. She knew his lovers were often jealous of her. And Baer had often been jealous of Sele.

That had been love as well, Berd supposed. It was not indifference that made Berd look up in the midst of their scheming to see Baer watching her from across the room; but perhaps that was Baer's love, not hers. Baer's jealousy, that was not hers, and that frightened her, and bored her, and nagged at her until she felt sometimes he could pull her away from Sele, and from the warm candlelit conspiracy the five of them made, with a single skeptical glance. He had done it in their childhood, voicing the doubting realism that spoiled the game of make-believe. "You can't ride an ice bear," he had said—not even crushingly, but as flat and off-hand as a government form. "It would eat you," he said, and one of Berd and Isse's favorite games died bloody and broken-backed, leaving Baer to wonder in scowling misery why they never invited him to play.

Yet there he was, curled, it seemed deliberately, in Sele's most uncomfortable chair, watching, watching, as Sele, bright and quick by the fire, said, "Stories never die. You can't forget a story, not a real story, a living story. People forget, they die, but stories are always reborn. They're real. They're more real than we are."

"You can't live in a story," Baer said, and it seemed he was talking to Berd rather than Sele.

Berd said, "You can if you make the story real."

"That's right," Baer said, but as though he disagreed. "The story is ours. It only becomes real when we make it happen, and there has to be a way, a practical way—"

"We live in the story," Sele said. "Don't you see? *This* is a story. The story *is*."

"This is real life!" Baer mimed exasperation, but his voice was strained. "This story of yours is a *story*, you're just making it up. It's pure invention!"

"So is life," Sele said patiently. "That doesn't mean it isn't real."

Which was true; was, in fact, something Berd and Sele had argued into truth together, the two of them, alone. But Berd was dragged aside as she always was by Baer's resentful skepticism—resentful because of how badly he wanted to be convinced—but Berd could never find the words to include them in their private, perfect world, the world that would be perfect without him—and so somehow she could not perfectly immerse herself and was left on the margins, angry and unwilling in her sympathy for Baer. How many times had Berd lost Sele's attention, how many times had she lost her place in their schemes, because Baer was too afraid to commit himself and too afraid to abstain alone? Poor Baer! Unwilling, grudging, angry, but there it was: poor Baer.

And there he was, poor Baer, inside a cold, strange story, leaving Berd, for once, alone on the outside with Sele. With Sele. If only she were. *Oh Sele, where are you now?*

It seemed that the whole city, what was left of it, had moved into the outskirts where the aerodrome sprawled near the snow-blanked hills. There had been a few weeks last summer when the harbor was clear of ice and a great convoy of ships had docked all at once, creating a black cloud of smoke and a frantic holiday as supplies were unloaded and passengers loaded into the holds where the grain had been—loaded, it must be said, after the furs and ores that paid for their passage. Since then there had been nothing but the great silver airships drifting in on the southern wind, and now, as the cold only deepened with the passage of equinoctial spring, they would come no more. *Until*, it was said, *the present emergency has passed*. Why are some lies even told? Everyone knew this was the end of the city, the end of the north, perhaps the beginning of the end of the world. The last airships were sailing soon, too few to evacuate the city, too beautiful not to be given a gorgeous goodbye. So the city swelled against the landlocked shore of the aeroport like the Arctic's last living tide.

The first Berd knew of it—it had been an endless walk through the empty streets, the blue dusk hardly seeming to change, as if the whole city were locked in ice—was the glint and firefly glimmer of yellow light at the end of the wide suburban street. She had complained, they all had, about the brilliance of modern times, the constant blaze of gaslight that was challenged, these last few years, not by darkness but by the soulless glare of electricity. But now, tonight, Berd might have been an explorer lost for long months, drawing an empty sled and an empty belly into civilization with the very last of her strength. How beautiful it was, this yellow light. Alive with movement and color, it was an anodyne to grief, an antidote to blue. Her legs aching with her haste, Berd fled toward, yearning, rather than away, guilty and afraid. And then the light, and the noise, and the quicksilver movement of the crowd pulled her under.

It was a rare kind of carnival. More than a farewell, it was a hunt, every citizen a quarry that had turned on its hunter, Death, determined to take Him down with the hot blood bursting across its tongue. Strange how living and dying could be so hard to tell apart in the end. Berd entered into it at first like a swimmer resting on the swells, her relief at the lights that made the blue sky black, and at the warm-blooded people all around her steaming in the cold, made her buoyant, as light as an airship with a near approximation of joy. *This* was escape, oh yes it was. The big houses on their acre gardens spilled out into the open, as if the carpets and chandeliers of the rich had spawned tents and booths and roofless rooms. Lamps burned everywhere, and so did bonfires in which the shapes of furniture and books could still be discerned as they were consumed. The smells wafting in great clouds of steam from food carts and al fresco bistros made the sweet fluid burst into Berd's mouth, just as the music beating from all sides made her feet move to an easier rhythm than fear. They were alive here; she took warmth from them all. But what storerooms were emptied for this feast? Whose hands would survive playing an instrument in this cold?

The aerodrome's lights blazed up into the sky. Entranced, enchanted, Berd drifted through the crowds, stumbling over the broken walls that had once divided one mansion from the next. (The native-born foreigners had made gardens, as if tundra could be forced to become a lawn. No more. No more.) That glow was always before her, but never within reach. She stumbled again, and when she had stopped to be sure of her balance, she felt the weight of her exhaustion dragging her down.

"Don't stop." A hand grasped her arm above the elbow. "It's best to keep moving here."

Here? She looked to see what the voice meant before she looked to see to whom the voice belonged. "Here" was the empty stretch between the suburb and the aerodrome, still empty even now. Or perhaps even emptier, for there were men and dogs patrolling, and great lamps magnified by the lenses that had once equipped the lighthouses guarding the ice-locked coast. This was the glow of freedom. Berd stared, even as the hand drew her back into the celebrating, grieving, furious, abandoned, raucous crowd. She looked around at last, when the perimeter was out of view.

"Randolph!" she said, astonished at being able to put a name to the face. She was afraid—for one stopped breath she was helpless with fear—but he was alive and steaming with warmth, his pale eyes bright and his long nose scarlet with drink and cold. The combination was deadly, but Berd could believe he would not care.

"Little Berd," he said, and tucked her close against his side. With all their layers of clothing between them it was hardly presumptuous, though she did not know him well. He was, however, a crony of Sele's.

"You look like you've been through the wars," he said. "You need a drink and a bite of food."

And he needed a companion in his fin de siècle farewell, she supposed.

"The city's so empty," she said, and shuddered. "I'm looking for Sele. Randolph, do you know where he might be?"

"Not there," he said with a nod toward the aerodrome lights. "Not our Sele."

"No," Berd said, her eyes downcast. "But he'll be nearby. Won't he? Do you know?"

"Oh, he's around." Randolph laughed. "Looking for Sele! If only you knew how many women have come to me, wondering where he was! But maybe it's better you don't know, eh, little Berd?"

"I know," said little Berd. "I've known him longer that you."

"That's true!" Randolph said with huge surprise. He was drunker than she had realized. "You were pups together, weren't you, not so long ago. Funny to think . . . . Funny to think, no more children, and the docks all empty where they used to play."

A maudlin drunk. Berd laughed, to think of the difference between what she had fled from and what had rescued her. All the differences. Yet Randolph had been born here, just the same as Wael and Isse and Baer.

"Do you know where I can find him, Randolph?"

"Sele?" He pondered, his narrow face drunken-sad. "Old Sele . . . "

"Only I need to find him tonight, Randolph. He has something for me, something I need. So if you can tell me . . . or you can help me look . . . "

"I know he's around. I know!" This with the tone of a great idea. "I know! We'll ask the Painter. Good ol' Painter! He knows where everyone is. Anyone who owes him money! And Sele's on that list, when was he ever not? We'll go find Painter, he'll set us right. Painter'll set us right."

So she followed the drunk who seemed to be getting drunker on the deepening darkness and the sharpening cold. The sky was indigo now, alight with stars above the field of lamps and fires and human lives. Fear receded. Anxiety came back all the sharper. Her last search, and she had only this one night, this one night, even if it had barely begun. And the thought came to her with a shock as physical as Baer's touch: it was spring: the nights were short, regardless of the cold.

She searched faces as they passed through fields of light. Strange how happy they were. Music everywhere, bottles warming near the fires, a burst of fireworks like a fiery garden above the tents and shacks and mansions abandoned to the poor. Carnival time.

Berd had never known this neighborhood, it was too far afield even for the wandering Sele and her sometimes-faithful self. All she knew of it was this night, with the gardens invaded and the tents thrown open and spilling light and music and steam onto the trampled weeds and frozen mud of the new alleyways. They made small stages, their lamplit interiors as vivid as scenes from a play. Act IV, scene i: the Carouse. They were all of a piece, the Flirtation, the Argument, the Philosophical Debate. And yet, every face was peculiarly distinct, no one could be mistaken for another. Berd ached for them, these strangers camped at the end of the world. For that moment she was one of them, belonged to them and with them—belonged to everything that was not the cold ones left behind in the empty city beside the frozen sea. Or so she felt, before she saw Isse's face, round and cold and beautiful as the moon.

No. Berd's breath fled, but . . . no. There was only the firelit crowd outside, the lamplit crowd within the tent Randolph led her to, oblivious to her sudden stillness, the drag she made at the end of his arm. No cold Isse, no Wael or Baer. No. But the warmth of the tent was stifling, and the noise of music and voices and the clatter of bottle against glass shivered the bones of her skull.

The Painter held court, one of a hundred festival kings, in a tent that sagged like a circus elephant that has gone too long without food. He had been an artist once, and had earned the irony of his sobriquet by turning critic and making a fortune writing for twenty journals under six different names. He had traveled widely, of course, there wasn't enough art in the north to keep a man with half his appetites, but Berd didn't find it strange that he stayed when all his readers escaped on the last ships that fled before the ice. He had been a prince here, and some princes did prefer to die than become paupers in exile. Randolph was hard-pressed to force himself close enough to bellow in King Painter's ear, and before he made it—he was delayed more than once by an offered glass—Berd had freed her arm and drifted back to the wide-open door.

It seemed very dark outside. Faces passed on another stage, a promenade of drunks and madmen. A man dressed in the old fashioned furs of an explorer passed by, his beard and the fur lining of his hood matted with vomit. A woman followed him wearing a gorgeous rug like a poncho, a hole cut in the middle of its flower-garden pattern, and another followed her with her party clothes torn all down her front, too drunk or mad to fold the cloth together, so that her breasts flashed in the lamplight from the tent. She would be dead before morning. So many would be, Berd thought, and her weariness came down on her with redoubled weight. A stage before her, a stage behind her, and she—less audience than stagehand, since these performers in no wise performed for her—stood in a thin margin of nowhere, a threshold between two dreams. She let her arms dangle and her head fall back, as if she could give up, not completely, but just for a heartbeat or two, enough to snatch one moment of rest. The stars glittered like chips of ice, blue-white, colder than the air. There was some comfort in the thought that they would still shine long after the human world was done. There would still be sun and moon, snow and ice, and perhaps the seals and the whales and the bears. Berd sighed and shifted her numb feet, thinking she should find something hot to drink, talk to the Painter herself. She looked down, and yes, there was Isse standing like a rock in the stream of the passing crowd.

She might have been a statue for all the notice anyone took of her. Passersby passed by without a glance or a flinch from Isse's radiating cold. It made Berd question herself, doubt everything she had seen and felt back at the house. She lifted her hand in a half-finished wave and felt an ache in her shoulder where Baer had touched her, the frightening pain of cold that has penetrated to the bone. Isse did not respond to Berd's gesture. She was turned a little from where Berd stood, her feet frozen at the end of a stride, her body leaning toward the next step that never came. Still walking in that summer garden, her arms bare and as blue-white as the stars. Berd rubbed her shoulder, less afraid in the midst of carnival, though the ache of cold touched her heart. Dear Isse, where do you walk to? Is it beautiful there?

Something cold touched Berd's eye. Weeping ice? She blinked, and discovered a snow flake caught in her eyelashes. She looked up again. Stars, stars, more stars than she had seen moments ago, more stars than she thought she would see even if every gaslight and oil lamp and bonfire in the north were extinguished. Stars so thick there was hardly any black left in the sky, no matter how many fell. Falling stars, snow from a cloudless sky. Small flakes prickled against Berd's face, so much colder than her cold skin they felt hot. She looked down and saw that Baer and Wael had joined Isse, motionless, three statues walking down the impromptu street. How lonely they looked! Berd had been terrified in the house with them. Now she hurt for their loneliness, and felt an instant's powerful impulse to go to them, join them in their pilgrimage in whatever time and place they were. The impulse frightened her more than their presence did, and yet . . . And yet. She didn't move from the threshold of the tent, but the impulse still lived in her body, making her lean even as Isse leaned, on the verge of another step.

Snow fell more thickly, glittering in the firelight. It was strange that no one seemed to notice it, even as it dusted their heads and shoulders and whitened the ground. It fell more thickly, a windless blizzard that drew a curtain between Berd and the stage of the promenade, and more thickly still, until it was impossible that so much snow could fall—and from a starlit sky!—and yet she was still able to see Wael and Baer and Isse. It was as though they stood not in the street but in her mind. She was shivering, her mouth was dry. Snow fell and fell, an entire winter of snow pouring into the street, the soft hiss of the snowflakes deafening Berd to the voices, music, clatter and bustle of the tent behind her. It was the hiss of silence, no louder than the sigh of blood in her ears. And Isse, Wael, and Baer walked and walked, unmoving while the snow piled up in great drifts, filling the street, burying it, disappearing it from view. There were only the three cold ones and the snow.

And then the snow began to generate ghosts. Berd knew this trick from her childhood, when the autumn winds would drive fogbanks and snowstorms onto the northern shore. The hiss and the monotonous whiteness gave birth to muttered voices and distant calls, and to the shapes of things barely visible behind the veil of mist or snow. People, yes, and animals like white bears and caribou and the musk oxen Berd only knew from the books they read in school; and sometimes stranger things, ice gnomes like white foxes walking on hind legs and carrying spears, and wolves drawing sleds ridden by naked giants, and witches perched backwards on white caribou made of old bones and snow. Those ghosts teased Berd's vision as they passed down the street of snow, a promenade of the north that came clearer and clearer as she watched, until the diamond points of the gnomes' spears glittered in the lamplight pouring out of the tent and the giants with their eyes as black as the sky stared down at her as they passed. Cold filled her, the chill of wonder, making her shudder. And now she saw there were others walking with the snow ghosts, people as real as the woman who wore the beautiful carpet, as solid as the woman who bared her breasts to the cold. They walked in their carnival madness, as if they had found their way through the curtain that had hidden them from view. Still they paid no notice to the three cold ones, the statues of Baer and Isse and Wael, but they walked there, fearless, oblivious, keeping pace with the witches, the oxen, the bears.

And then Randolph grasped Berd's sore shoulder with his warm hand and said, "Painter says Sele's been sleeping with some woman in one of the empty houses . . . Hey, where'd everybody go?"

For at his touch the snow had been wiped away like steam from a window, and all the ghosts, all the cold ones, and all the passersby were gone, leaving Berd standing at the edge of an empty stage.

"Hey," Randolph said softly. "Hey."

It was perfectly silent for a moment, but only for a moment. A fire burning up the street sent up a rush of sparks as a new log went on. A woman in the tent behind them screamed with laughter. A gang of children ran past, intent in their pursuit of some game. And then the promenade was full again, as varied and lively as a parade.

Berd could feel Randolph's shrug and his forgetting through the hand resting on her shoulder. She could feel his warmth, his gin-soaked breath past her cheek, his constant swaying as he sought an elusive equilibrium. She should not feel so alone, so perfectly, utterly, dreadfully alone. They had gone, leaving her behind.

"No." No. *She* was the one who was leaving.

"Eh?" Randolph said.

"Which house?" Berd said, turning at last from the door.

"Eh?" He swayed more violently, his eyes dead, lost in some alcoholic fugue.

"Sele." She shook him, and was surprised by the stridency in her voice. "Sele! You said he was in a house with some woman. Which house?" Randolph focused with a tangible effort. "That's right. Some rich woman who didn't want to go with her husband. Took Sele up. Lives somewhere near here. One of the big houses. Some rich woman. Bitch. If I'd been her I'd've gone. I'd've been dead by now. Gone. I'd've been gone by now . . ."

Berd forced her icy hands to close around both his arms, holding him against his swaying. "Which house? Randolph! *Which house?*"

> *My dearest Berd,*
>
> *I'm embarrassed by the last letter I wrote. It must have given you a vision of me all alone in a dusty room, growing old before my time. Not true! Or, if it is, it isn't the only truth. I should warn you that I have been extolling your virtues to everyone I know, until all of my acquaintance is agog to meet the woman, the mysterious northerner, the angel whose coming has turned me into a boy again. You are my birthday and my school holiday and my summer all rolled into one, and I cannot wait to parade you on my arm. Will it embarrass you if I buy you beautiful things to wear? I hope it won't. I want shamelessly to show you off. I want you to become the new star of my almost-respectable circle as you are the star that lights the dark night of my heart . . .*

4198 Goldport Avenue.

There *were* no avenues, just the haphazard lanes of the carnival town, but the Painter (Berd had given up on Randolph in the end) had added directions that took into account new landmarks and gave Berd some hope of finding her way. Please, oh please, let Sele be there.

"It's a monstrous place," the Painter had said. His eyes were greedy, unsated by the city's desperation, hungry for hers. "A bloody great Romantic pile with gargoyles like puking birds and pillars carved like tree nymphs. You can't miss it. Last time I was there it was lit up like an opera house with a red carpet spilling down the stairs. Vulgar! My god, the woman has no taste at all except for whiskey and men. Your Sele will be lucky if she's held onto him this long."

His eyes had roved all over Berd, but there was nothing to see except her weary face and frightened eyes. He dismissed her, too lazy to follow her if she wouldn't oblige by bringing her drama to him, and Randolph was so drunk by then that he stared with sober dread into the far distance, watching the approach of death. Berd went alone into the carnival, feeling the cold all the more bitterly for the brief warmth of the Painter's tent. Her hands and feet felt as if they were being bitten by invisible dogs, her ears burned with wasp-fire, her shoulder ached with a chill that grew roots down her arm and into the hollow of her ribs. Cold, cold. Oh, how she longed for warmth! Warmth and sunshine and smooth pavement that didn't trip her hurting feet, and the proper sounds of spring, waves and laughter and shouting gulls, rather than the shouting crowd, yelping as though laughter were only a poor disguise for a howl of despair. She stumbled, buffeted by strangers, and wished she could only *see*, if she could only *see*. But Wael and Isse and Baer were near. She knew that, even in the darkness; heard their silence in the gaps and blank spaces of the noisy crowd, felt their cold. And oh, she was frightened. She missed them terribly, grieved for them, longed for them, and was terrified that longing would bring them back to her, as cold and strange and wrong as the walking dead.

But she would not go that way, not that way, she would not.

Berd stumbled again. Under her feet, barely visible in the light of a bonfire ringed by dancers there lay a street sign that said in ornate script Goldport Ave. She looked up, past the dancers and their fire—and what was that in the flames? A chair stood upright in the coals and on the chair an effigy, please let it be an effigy, burning down to a charcoal grin—she dragged her gaze up above the fire where the hot air shivered like a watery veil, and saw the pillared house with all its curtains open to expose the shapes dancing beneath the blazing chandeliers. Bears and giants and witches, and air pilots and buccaneers and queens. Fancy dress, as if the dancers had already died and moved on to a different form. Berd climbed the stairs, the vulgar carpet more black than red after the passage of many feet, and passed through the wide-open door.

She gave up on the reception rooms very soon. They were so hot, and crowded by so many reckless dancing drunks, and the music was a noisy shambles played by more drunks who seemed to have only a nodding acquaintance with their instruments. Perhaps the dancers and the musicians had traded places for a lark. Berd thought that even were she drunk and in the company of friends it would still seem like a foretaste of hell, and she could feel a panic coming on before she had forced a way through a single room. Sele. Sele! Why wouldn't he come and rescue her? She fought her way back into the grand foyer and climbed the wide marble stairs until she was above the heads of the crowd. Hot air mingled with cold. Lamps dimmed as the oil in the reservoirs ran low, candles guttered in ornate pools of wax; no one seemed to care. They would all die here, a mad party frozen in place like a story between the pages of a book. Berd sat on a step halfway above the first landing and put her head in her hands.

"There you are. Do you know, I thought I'd missed you for good."

Berd burst into tears. Sele sat down beside her and rocked her, greatcoat and all, in his arms.

He told her he had waited on the esplanade until his feet went numb. She told him about the suicide. She wanted to tell him about his sister, Isse, and her cousins, but could not find the words to begin.

"I saw," she said, "I saw," and spilled more tears.

"It isn't a tragedy," Sele said, meaning the suicide. "We all die, soon or late. It's just an anticipation, that's all."

"I know."

"There are worse things."

"I know."

He drew back to look at her. She looked at him, and saw that he knew, and that he saw that she knew, too.

"Oh, Sele . . ."

His round brown face was solemn, but also serene. "Are you still going?"

"Yes!" She shifted so she could grasp him too. "Sele, you have to come with me. You must, now, you have no choice."

He laughed at her with surprise. "What do you mean? Why don't I have a choice?"

"They—" She stammered, not wanting to know what she was trying to say. "Th-they have been following me, Wael and Baer and Isse. They've been following. They want—They'll come for you, too."

"I know. I've seen them. I expect they'll come soon."

"I'm sorry. I know it's wrong, but they frighten me so much. How can you be so calm?"

"We did this," he said. "We wanted change, didn't we? We asked for it. We should take what we get."

"Oh, Sele." Berd hid her face against his shoulder. He was only wearing a shirt, she realized. She could feel this chill of his flesh against her cheek. She whispered, "I can't. It's too dreadful. I can't bear to always be so cold."

"Oh, little Berd." He stroked her hair. "You don't have to. I've made my choice, that's all, and you've made yours. I don't think, by now, there's any right or wrong either way. We've gone too far for that."

She shook her head against him. She wanted very much to plead with him, to make her case, to spin for him all her dreams of the south, but she was too ashamed, and knew that it would do no good. They had already spun their dreams into nothing, into cold and ice, into the land beyond death. Anyway, Sele had never, ever, in all their lives, followed her lead. And at the last, she could not follow his.

They pulled apart.

"Come on," Sele said. "I have your things in my room."

The gas jet would not light, so Berd stood by the door while Sele fumbled for candle and match. Two candles burning on a branch meant for four barely carved the shape of the room out of the darkness. It seemed very grand to Berd, with heavy curtains round the bed and thick carpets on the floor.

"A strange place to end up," she said.

Sele glanced at her, his dark eyes big and bright with candlelight. "It's warm," he said, and then added ruefully, "It was warm. Anyway, I needed to be around to meet some of the right people. It's such a good address, don't you know."

"Better than your old one." Berd couldn't smile, remembering his old house, remembering the street sign under her feet and the shape in the bonfire outside.

"Anyway." Sele knelt and turned up a corner of the carpet. "My hostess is nosy but not good at finding things. And she's been good to me. I owe her a lot. She helped me get you what you'll need."

"The ticket?" Berd did not have enough room for air in her chest.

"Ticket." Sele handed her the items one at a time. "Travel papers. Letters."

"Letters?" She was slow to take the last packet. Whose letters? Letters from whom?

"From your sponsor. There's a rumor that even with a ticket and papers they won't let you on board unless you can prove you aren't going south only to end up a beggar. Your sponsor is supposed to give you a place to stay, help you find work. He's my own invention, but he's a good one. No," he said as she turned the packet over in her hands, "don't read them now. You'll have time on the ship."

It was strange to see her name on the top envelope in Sele's familiar hand. He had never written her a letter in her life. She stowed them away in her pocket with the other papers and then checked, once, twice, that she had everything secure. *I can't go.* The words lodged in her throat. She looked at Sele, all her despair—at going? at staying?—in her eyes.

"You're right to go," Sele said. "Little Berd, flying south away from the cold."

"I don't want to leave you." Not *I can't,* just *I don't want to.*

"But you will."

She shivered, doubting, torn, and yet knowing as well as he that he was right. She would go, and he would go too, on a different journey with Isse and Wael and Baer. So cold. She hugged him fiercely, trying to give him her heat, wanting to borrow his. He kissed her, and then she was going, going, her hand in her pocket, keeping her ticket safe. Running down the stairs. Finding the beacon of the aerodrome even before she was out the door.

Out the door. On the very threshold she looked out and saw what she had not thought to look for from the window of Sele's room. Inside, the masquerade party was in full swing, hot and bright and loud with voices and music and smashing glass. Outside . . .

Outside the ice had come.

It was as clear as it can be only at the bottom of a glacier, where the weight of a mile of ice has pressed out all the impurities of water and air. It was as clear as glass, as clear as the sky, so that the stars shone through hardly dimmed, though their glittering was stilled. Berd could see everything, the carnival town frozen with every detail preserved: the tents still upright, though their canvas sagged; the shanties with the soot still crusted around their makeshift chimneys. Even the bonfires, with their half-burnt logs intact, their charcoal facsimiles of chairs and books and mannequins burned almost to the bone. In the glassy starlight Berd could even see all the little things strewn across the ground, all the ugly detritus of the end of the world, the bottles and discarded shoes, the dead cats and dead dogs and turds. And she could see the people, all the people abandoned at the last, caught in their celebratory despair. The whole crowd of them, men and women and children, young and old and ugly and fair, frozen as they danced, stumbled, fucked, puked, and died. And, yes, there were her own three, her own dears, the brothers and sister of her heart, standing at the foot of the steps as if they had been caught, too, captured by the ice just as they began to climb. Isse, and Wael, and Baer.

The warmth of the house behind Berd could not combat the dreadful cold of the ice. The music faltered as the cold bit the musicians hands. Laughter died. And yet, and yet, and yet in the distance, beyond the frozen tents and the frozen people, a light still bloomed. Cold electricity, as cold as the unrisen moon and as bright, so that it cast the shadows of Baer and Wael and Isse before them up the stairs. The aerodrome, yes, the aerodrome, where the silver airships still hung from their tethers like great whales hanging in the depths of the clear ocean blue. Yes, and there was room at the right-hand edge of the stairs where Berd could slip between the balustrade and the still summer statue of Wael, her cousin Wael, with his hair shaken back and his dark eyes raised to where Berd still stood with her hand in her pocket, her ticket and travel pass and letters clutched in her cold but not yet frozen fist. The party was dying. There was a quiet weeping. The lights were growing dim. *Now or never*, Berd thought, and she took all her courage in her hands and stepped through the door.

My darling, my beloved Berd,

I wish I had the words to tell you how much I love you. It's no good to say "like a sister" or "like a lover" or "like myself." It's closer to say like the sun that warms me, like the earth that supports me, like the air I breathe. And I have been suffering these past few days with the regret (I know I swore long ago to regret nothing, even to remember *nothing I might regret, but it finds me all the same) that I have never come to be with you, your lover or your husband, in your beloved north. It's as though I have consigned myself to some sunless, airless world. How have I let all this time pass without ever coming to you? And now it is too late, far too late for me. But I am paid with this interminable waiting. Come to me soon, I beg you. Save me from my folly. Forgive me. Tell me you love me as much as I love you . . .*

THE ENDANGERED CAMP

ANN LECKIE

After the terrible push to be free of the Earth was past, we could stand again. In a while, the engineers had said, everything would float, but for now we were still accelerating. We were eight in the small, round room, though there were others on the sky-boat—engineers, and nest-guardians examining the eggs we had brought to see how many had been lost in the crushing, upward flight. But we eight stood watching the world recede.

The floor and walls of the room were of smooth, gold metal. Around the low ceiling was a pattern of cycad fronds and under this scenes from the histories. There was the first mother, ancestor of us all, who broke the shell of the original egg. The picture showed the egg, a single claw of the mother piercing that boundary between Inside and Outside. With her was the tiny figure of her mate. If you are from the mountains, you know that he ventured forth and fed on the carcass of the world-beast, slain by the mother, and in due time found the mother and mated with her. If you are a lowlander, he waited in the shell until she brought the liver to him, giving him the strength to come out into the open. Neither was pictured—the building of the sky-boat had taken the resources of both mountains and lowlands.

On another panel was Strong Claw, her sharp-toothed snout open in a triumphant call. She stood tall on powerful legs, each foot with its arced killing claw, sharp and deadly. Her arms stretched out before her, claws spread, and her long, stiff tail stretched behind. The artists had worked with such skill that every feather could be distinguished. Behind her was the great tree that had carried her across the sea, and in the water were pictured its inhabitants: coiled ammonites, hungry sharks, and a giant mososaur, huge-mouthed enough to swallow a person down at a gulp. Before Strong Claw was forested land, full of food for the hunting, new territory for her and her daughters yet unhatched.

A third panel showed the first sky-boat departing for the moon that had turned out to be farther away than our ancestors ever imagined. That voyage had been a triumph—the sky-boat (designed, all were ceaselessly told, by lowlander engineers) had achieved a seemingly impossible goal. But it had also been a disaster—as the mountain engineers had predicted, and the lowlanders refused to believe until the last, irrefutable moment, there had been no air on the moon. But as we had now set our sights on Mars, the artist had left off the end of the tale, to avoid ill-omen.

The engineers had used mirrors to cast an image of the Earth on the last, blank panel of the curved wall. It was this that held our attention.

As we watched, disaster struck. A sudden, brilliant flash whited out the image for an instant, and after that an expanding ring began to spread across the face of the world, as though a pebble had been dropped into a pond. Almost instantly a ball of fire rose up from the center of the ripple and expanded outward, obscuring it. I blinked, slowly, deliberately, sure that my vision was at fault. Still the fire grew until finally it dissipated, leaving a slowly-expanding veil of smoke.

There was silence in the sky-boat for some time.

Out of the speaking tube came the quiet voice of an engineer in the chamber below us. "A great stone from the void." There are many such, it seems, but no song speaks of them, no history tells us what happens when one strikes the Earth. This would not hinder the engineers, who are full of predictions and calculations.

"I was not informed," said White Ring into the tube. She was facing the image, her back to us. "Why?"

"We did not know," came the faint voice of the engineer.

"Do we not watch the skies?"

"The skies are vast. The stones are dark. We might have seen it if we looked in precisely the right place, at the right time. Or perhaps not."

"And now?"

Around me, not a feather stirred. "The cloud will continue to expand. The impact will leave a crater." Here the voice hesitated. "My colleague thinks perhaps twenty-five to thirty-five leagues wide, though I believe she has miscalculated the object's size. Perhaps forty-five to sixty leagues." White Ring's killing claw clicked on the floor. "I have not calculated how long it will take the cloud to disperse," the engineer continued. "I fear it will grow to cover the whole world. There may be fires as rocks fall back down to the ground. It hit water, so—"

"Silence!" ordered White Ring. "How far will the damage reach?"

A moment of silence from the tube. "It depends," came the voice, slowly, carefully. "On how thick the cloud is, and how long it stands between the Earth and the Sun. And if there are fires. And other things we haven't calculated yet."

For just a moment White Ring's feathers ruffled as though a breeze had stirred them. Nearly every other face was turned towards the view of Earth, but I looked at her, sidelong, without moving my snout. I felt the muscles in my back and my legs tense, and I forced them to relax lest the click of my largest claw on the deck betray my thoughts.

"We must go back," White Ring said. Snouts turned towards her in surprise. She turned her head to look behind her, and then turned fully, her daughter ducking low to avoid her tail. Others in the ring ducked and turned so that all who had faced forward could face the center of the circle. "We can stay above until the cloud disperses, and then land."

"*Can* we go back?" One of the younger females.

"We must," said White Ring, her tone admitting no dispute. "This venture was risk enough with the world safe behind us. If we are the only ones left alive . . . ."

White Ring's daughter called through the speaking tube, and an answer came back. "We might be able to, if we act soon enough. We will have to make some calculations. But . . . "

"Make them," said White Ring. Her daughter eyed the rest of us, watching.

They had told us that leaving the Earth would be difficult. Three of our number had died in the punishing climb. But all of us standing here had survived it. Could those so silent and still around me be willing to throw that away, to throw away everything we had worked for? It seemed so.

The engineer had said *If we act soon enough*. A question of fuel, no doubt. If I did not speak up now, the time would be gone.

But here was my difficulty: every other person in the room was a lowlander. The superiority of mountain optics had ensured that some of the engineers aboard were highlanders, but I was one of only two surviving who was not either an engineer or an egg tender. If I spoke now, no one else would speak in support of me, unless they were completely convinced of my argument. Or unless I killed White Ring, in which case they would likely follow me out of fear if nothing else. But as things stood, I would not be allowed even to strike.

But I am no coward. "We must *not* go back," I said.

My neighbors sidled away, as far as they could in the cramped space, claws clicking on the metal floor. I stood face to face with White Ring.

"I hear nothing," said White Ring. Her killing claw tapped once, twice.

"This ship won't be built again," I said, "not in our lifetimes. Look!" I gestured at the picture with one clawed finger, at the still-spreading smoke. "Will we reach Mars, or will we die having made all this effort and accomplished nothing?"

White Ring looked around the circle, watching the faces and the demeanor of the others. I did not dare take my eyes off her to make the same survey. "I hear nothing," she said again.

"Coward! You disgrace our ancestors!"

Instantly White Ring's neck snaked forward and she snapped her teeth together a breath from my neck. I stood still as stone.

"Will you challenge me?" White Ring hissed. "At this time? Is your ambition so great?"

I would not allow my feathers to lift, or flutter. I would not allow a single twitch that I did not intend. "Did Strong Claw turn back?" I asked. I would have pointed to the picture, but I did not wish to move.

"She knew all was well behind her," said White Ring. "If none survive on Earth, and we die attempting Mars, what then?"

"We don't know there's air to breathe where we're going," said the daughter beside White Ring, when I didn't answer. "There was none on the moon."

"What a wonder this is! You lowlanders disbelieved when the engineers from the mountains said there was no air on the moon. Now you disbelieve when you are told that Mars certainly has an atmosphere."

"Bent light," White Ring began, her voice scornful.

"There is more than just the bending of light to prove it. There are plants, the astronomers have said so. We see them wax and wane with the seasons. There is no reason to think that Mars will not be much like Earth."

"The astronomers are not all agreed. Not even those from the mountains."

"But you have staked your life on it," I pointed out.

"While other lives were sure to continue," said White Ring. "What if everyone else is dead?"

"Then they are dead because Earth is now unlivable," I said. "And in that case, why turn back?"

"I know your ambition of old," said White Ring. "I had not thought you would exercise it at a time like this."

My feathers twitched then, I couldn't avoid it. I allowed them to tremble and rise. White Ring and her daughter watched me with malice, the other five with fear, or perhaps something else.

The moment stretched out. Time—time might be an enemy or an ally. Prolong the contention, and the moment to turn back would have passed. Allow the return to begin, and there would be only a short space, if any at all, in which it would be possible to correct our course.

"You call me ambitious," I said, "and I am. I would reach Mars! Did any of us embark without a similar ambition? But now you abandon what we have all worked so hard to attain! And when I point this out, I am threatened. Why is this? If one of you," and here I pointed around the circle, "had spoken, would this have been the response?" Had I seen movement among the others? Someone about to speak, some thoughtful twitch of feathers? "You may kill me if you like, as I am clearly outnumbered. But it will not change the truth."

One of those who had been silent spoke. "There is something in what she says."

White Ring was silent a moment. "It would be best not to fight," she said. "I would not lose more of us. Bring out the histories."

"Bring out the histories," I agreed.

She scratched at the unyielding metal ground with her foot, never taking her eyes off me. Then she barked a short order to her daughter, who repeated White Ring's word into the speaking tube.

The ladder well was behind me. I did not look as I heard the singer climbing into the room, or move as he squeezed past into the center of the circle in front of White Ring. I never moved my eyes from her, and let the others shift to let him by.

He was shorter even than most males, and his feathers were a dull brown, specked with black. He was an unprepossessing thing until he opened his mouth, as I well knew. He was my son.

He lowered his head in front of White Ring. "You choose first," she said to me. I should have been daunted—if I chose first, hers would be the last word. But I was not.

"I choose *Strong Claw's Voyage*," I said.

We are all susceptible to the power of song. The songs you've known since hatching, in the mouth of a great singer, will quicken your pulse and stop your breath. As my son called out the opening lines to the history I had chosen, all in the room were compelled by his voice to listen. Feathers ruffled and then settled, and all were still and there was no sound but his song.

There is no need to give the details here. The story is told, in its essentials, in the picture on the wall of the sky-boat, and in any event I might have chosen anything from the histories I wished, so long as White Ring would feel safe making the obvious choice when her turn came.

No, the song, and its argument, is already clear to you. Instead, I will tell you about my son.

When I was younger, and looking for a mate, I had resolved to have only the strongest, wiliest male I could find. I wanted large, strong daughters. I wanted children who would distinguish themselves on a hunt. I turned down suitors who were stupid, or weak, or too short. Some I killed. I would have killed the little brown-feathered thing that approached me last, but he opened his mouth and sang.

His voice! I lost all reason.

When the first clutch of eggs hatched, I had five daughters and six sons. Three of the daughters seemed strong enough. Three of the males were small and weak, and I thought they might die. But one of those, as I bent near to it, a tiny, naked-looking thing, let out one barely audible peep.

I ate the four weaklings and fed them to him. His health was all my care in the coming months, and he grew strong.

He was undersized, but he was clever. I taught him what I could, and when the day came, that comes for all male children, the day to leave his mother and sisters behind forever, I instructed him to seek out the singers guild.

For most mothers, when that day comes it is as though they never had male children. The boys go off to other territories, and if they're seen again the sight raises no sentiment in the breast of the formerly doting mother.

Your daughters are yours for life; your sons cease to exist when they leave the nest. But I took what steps I could to ensure that my son would be mine, no less than my daughters, even after he had gone to the singers guild.

I didn't know then that I would be on the sky-boat, or that a giant rock would hurtle out of the heavens and destroy the Earth. And even had I known, I could not have predicted that the lowlander singer would die during the launch, leaving my boy the only historian on the ship. But I knew that a singer's voice has a power entirely different from claws and teeth. White Ring had said she knew my ambition of old, but she did not realize its true extent.

The song ended. Strong Claw, victorious through all dangers, never turning back though she knew not what the end of her voyage would be, stood at last on the shore of the land she had discovered. Every listener sighed to hear it. It is an old song, and a pleasing one, with a clear lesson—the strong and resolute prevail.

It was no more than I had already said. And as I had hoped—expected!— White Ring answered with *The Endangered Camp*.

It is a story older even than Strong Claw's. It begins when a party of hunters goes out looking for iguanadon. (I myself have never seen an iguanadon, but they thunder through the oldest stories in vast herds.) They leave behind them in the woods their camp, a nursery. "Mounds of earth and leaves," the singer sang, "the infants waiting their time to come forth, and the guardians of the nests watchful."

An idyllic scene! But while the hunters are gone, the camp is attacked. The beast's tearing claws and rending teeth kill one guardian, and the others circle the nests as well as they can, and cry out together, *Let the hunting party return!*

Close around me, the listeners were rapt and their eyes wide, and they barely breathed, such was the power of the singer's voice.

The hunting party did return, of course. They heard the cries of the guardians, and ran with desperate speed back to the camp. Three guardians were killed, and four hunters, but they drove off the beast, saved the eggs, saved the pack. So the history tells us.

Now, this is the strange thing about history. When we are in doubt as to what course to take, or there is some debate, we examine the histories, we say, "So our ancestors did then, and so we should do now." And we think of the past as a solid, unbreakable rock that will always have the same form. But by accident or design, the rock is shaped. A singer drops a line here, a verse there, knowing or unknowing. And if you change the past, you change the future.

Stop with the beast defeated, and the eggs safe, and the salutary moral is clear. The lowlander singers I had heard had always stopped there. But it's not the end of the story. The four dead hunters had been among the most experienced, many of the others were injured, and food was scarce that year anyway. The seven dead from the attack fed the pack for a while, but after that they plundered the nests to survive, and no children were born that year.

I did not think White Ring would expect the singer to continue, even if she knew of the ending. The ill-omen of it would be too strong. Any singer would know what she meant by requesting it, and know, if he knew the end, to leave it off. But oh, my clever boy! He sang the rest of the song.

For a moment, as he continued where she had expected him to stop, she stood paralyzed. The others blinked in surprise, but his voice transfixed them and they were silent. White Ring drew her head back, and I saw her killing claws twitch. Even so she waited until he had finished.

"You made that up," accused White Ring's daughter when he fell silent. White Ring still held her threatening pose, ready to strike. But she dared not touch the singer; there was no other on board.

"You're very young," I said, my leg muscles tense with the desire to jump. "It's fashionable these days to leave that verse off, but anyone of any experience and education knows that's how the story ends." I swiveled my snout towards White Ring, and bared my teeth. "Isn't that so?"

"I have never heard it," said White Ring, still poised to strike. Her gaze was fixed on the boy, a small, brown-specked shape in the middle of the circle. "You have violated your obligation as a singer. Why? There can have been no collusion. Can you have done such a terrible thing merely from a hatred of lowlanders?"

Even if I had told her he was mine she would not have been able to imagine why such a thing would matter. And besides, he had sung truly. I might have laughed, but I did not; this was a dangerous moment.

"I have heard it," said a quiet voice. The others turned their heads but I never took my eyes off White Ring. She never took her eyes off my son.

"My great-aunt's mate was a singer," the voice continued. I placed it—a sturdy, handsome male, gray and black feathered, still young. He had kept quiet before now, as was proper. "He died when I was still a chick, but I remember he sang it in just that way." Silence. And then, even more timidly than before, "I was surprised to hear it requested. I wondered if you would signal the singer to leave the ending off. But then I thought, *he won't sing the ending, no one ever has except my uncle.*"

White Ring and her daughter would have no qualms about killing the black and gray male. They drew their heads back, hissing.

In that instant, a voice came from the speaking tube. "We have completed our calculations."

The low ceiling made it impossible to jump. Instead I drew my head back and then struck forward with all the force I could muster, hoping the boy would be quick enough to move out of the way.

The room erupted in screams and shouts. My teeth snapped together where White Ring's neck had been an instant before. I grabbed her shoulder and as she raked me with her claws I brought my foot up with its deadly killing claw.

White Ring grabbed me and sank her teeth into my shoulder, but she was too late. My foot came up, and I drove my claw into her belly, and pulled my leg convulsively back.

Her jaws opened in a scream, and I let go of her and stepped back. The black and gray male was locked with the daughter. No one else was in the room—they must have fled down the ladder well.

"You are dead, White Ring," I said. Pink entrails sagged out of the bleeding slash in her belly. "I need only keep out of reach for a while."

"Return to Earth," she said. "What if we're all that's left?"

I wanted to take a step back and lean against the wall, but I wasn't sure if she still had strength for a last charge, and I didn't want to show any weakness.

"You have doomed us," she said, and fell to her knees, and then onto her side, guts squirting out with the force of her fall. Still I did not approach. Until she was reliably dead she was a danger.

Instead I looked over at the black and gray male, who stood now over the daughter's corpse. His feathers drooped, and he was covered in blood, whose it was impossible to tell. "Are you hurt?" I asked. I hoped he wasn't. He was handsome, and obviously strong.

"Yes," he said.

"Go down to the doctor. On your way, inform the engineers of the change in command." He bowed his head low and limped to the ladder well. My son had climbed up, and made way for him.

I stepped over to the daughter and pushed her with my foot. She was dead. Carefully, tentatively, I did the same for her mother.

Dead.

"Well, my chick," I said. "There will be new songs, and they will be yours." I turned to see him standing at the well. He bobbed his head. We had always understood each other.

My shoulder hurt, and my neck, where I had been clawed. I would have to see the doctor soon enough myself, but not this very moment. I turned around to see the image of the smoking, burning Earth. "Earth is dead, or if not it may as well be. Mars will be ours." If anyone still lived on the Earth, perhaps one day they would venture away from the world and find, on Mars, the evidence of our triumph.

Let cowards retreat. We go forward. We live!

DRAGON'S TEETH

ALEX IRVINE

I: The Tomb

They brought the singer to the obsidian gate and waited. A sandstorm began to boil in the valley that split the mountains to their west. Across the miles of desert, they watched it rear and approach. Still the singer did not sing. She was blind, and had the way of blind singers. They were as much at the mercy of the song as anyone else.

All of them were going to die in the sandstorm. At least the guard captain, Paulus, hoped so. If the sandstorm did not kill them, whatever was in the tomb would. Of the two deaths, he much preferred the storm. Two fingers of his right hand touched his throat and he hummed the creed of his god, learned from the Book at the feet of a mother he had not seen since his eighth year. The reflex was all that mattered. The first moon, still low over the mountains, vanished in the storm a moment after the mountains themselves.

The singer began to sing. Paulus hated her for it, but with the song begun, even killing her would not stop it. In one of the libraries hung the severed head of a singer, in a cage made of her bones. No one living could remember who she was, or understand the language of the song. The scholars of the court believed that whoever deciphered the song would know immortality.

They were at the mouth of a valley that snaked down from the mountains and spilled into a flat plain that once had been a marsh, a resting place for migrating birds. The tomb's architect, according to the scholars, had believed that the soul's migration was eased by placing the tomb in such a place. In the centuries since the death of the king, his world had also died. The river that fed the marshes shifted course to the south; the desert swept in. Paulus scanned the sky and saw no birds.

At first he found the song pleasing. The melody was unfamiliar to him, in a mode that jarred against the songs he remembered from his boyhood. Then all the gates in his mind boomed shut again. He was not a boy taken into the king's service who remembered the songs his mother might have sung. He was the guard captain Paulus and he was here in the desert to have the singer sing her song, and then to die.

Why, they had not been told. The tomb was to be opened. Paulus was a soldier. He would open the tomb. In doing so, he would die, but Paulus did not fear death. He had faced it in forms seen by few other men, had survived its proximity often enough that it had grown familiar. Fatalism was an old friend. The song made his teeth hurt; no, not the song, but some effect of the song. In this place, it was awakening something that had slumbered since The Fells was a scattering of huts on the riverbank. This king had died so long ago that his name was lost. At his death the desert had been green. The world changed, aged with the rest of them. In the desert, you breathed the air of a world where everything had happened already, and it made you feel that you could never have existed.

The obsidian gate shifted with a groan and the wind rose. Sand cascaded down the walls, revealing worked stone, as the singer's song began the work of undoing a burial that had taken the desert centuries to complete. The dozen soldiers with Paulus shifted on their feet, casting glances back and forth between the gate and the approaching storm. They rested hands on sword hilts, gauged the distance to their horses; Paulus could see each of them running through a delicate personal calculation, with the storm on one side and a deserter's crucifixion on the other.

At the mouth of the tomb, at the end of his life, Paulus had only gossip to steer by. Someone important, a merchant named Jan who had the king's ear, wanted to free the spirit that inhabited the tomb. The king had agreed. Paulus wondered what favor he owed that made him willing to cast away the lives of a dozen men. Perhaps they would not die. Still, they had ridden nine days across the desert, to a tomb so old and feared that it existed on maps only through inference; the desert road bent sharply away from it, cutting upward to run along the spine of a line of hills to the north before coming back down into the valley and following the ancient riverbed up to the Salt Pass, from which a traveler could see the ocean on a clear day. Paulus wondered what in the tomb had convinced the road builders believe that three days' extra ride was worth it.

The singer wept, whether in ecstasy or sorrow Paulus could not tell. Swirls of sand reared in the figures of snakes all around them, striking away in the rising wind. The obsidian gate was open an inch. The wind scoured sand away from the front of the tomb, revealing a path of flat stones. Another inch of darkness opened up. The singer's vibrato shook slivers from the gate that swept away over their heads like slashes of ink inscribed on the sky. Slowly the gate shivered open, grinding across the stones as the singer began to scream. The soldiers broke and ran; Paulus let them go, to die in whatever way they found best. A sound came from the tomb, answering the singer, and the harmony of voices living and dead burst Paulus' eardrums. Deaf, he felt the wind beat his face. Darkness fell as the storm swallowed the sky. The air grew thick as saliva. The sand undulated like a tongue. From the open gate of the tomb, Paulus smelled the exhalation of an undead spirit. He drew his sword, and then the sandstorm overtook them.

When it had passed, Paulus fumbled for the canteen at his belt. He rinsed his eyes, swished water around in his mouth and spat thick black gunk . . . onto a floor of even stones. He was in the tomb, without memory of having entered. Water dripped from his beard and he felt the scrape and grind of sand all over his body. He was still deaf. Hhis eardrums throbbed. Where was the rest of the guard? He turned in a slow circle, orienting himself, and stopped when he was facing the open doorway. A featureless sandscape, brushed smooth by the storm and suffused with violet moonlight, stretched to an invisible horizon. The skin on the back of Paulus' neck crawled. He turned back to face into the tomb, growing curious. He enough oil for a torch. Its light seemed a protective circle to him as he ventured into the tomb to see what might have been left behind when the spirit emerged into the world. What it might do was no concern of his. He had been sent to free it; it was free. The merchant in The Fells had what he had paid for.

Torch held off to his left, sword in his right hand, Paulus walked down the narrow entry hall. He went down a stairway and at the bottom found the open sepulcher. The ancient king's bones lay as they had been left. His hair wisped over a mail coat that caught the torchlight.

Am I to be a graverobber? Paulus thought. The spirit was fled. Why not?

He took a cutting of the king's hair, binding it with a bit of leather from the laces of his jerkin. Arrayed about the king's body were ceremonial articles: a sword pitted and brittle with age, jars which had once held spices and perfumes, the skeletons of a dog and a child. Paulus went through it all, keeping what he knew he could sell and ignoring anything that looked as if it might be infected with magic. He worked methodically, feeling distanced from himself by his deafness. After an hour's search through the main room of the tomb and an antechamber knee-deep in sand from the storm, he had a double handful of gold coins. Everything else he saw—a sandstone figurine with obsidian eyes, a jeweled torc obscured by the king's beard, a filigreed scroll case laid diagonally into a wall alcove just inside the door—made him leery of enchantment. The gold would do.

Leaving the tomb, he stumbled over the body of the singer, buried in a drift of sand just inside the shattered gate. There was no sign of the rest of his men. It disturbed Paulus that he had no memory of entering the tomb as the storm broke over them, but memory was a blade with no handle. When it failed, best to live with the failure and live to accumulate new memories. He took another drink, scanned the desert for sign of the horses, and gave up. Either he would walk back, or he could cross the mountains and sail around the Cape of Thirst from the city of Averon. The boat would be quicker and the coastal waters less treacherous than the desert sands. Paulus turned west.

II: The Fells

In three days, he was coming down the other side of the pass. Two days after that, he was sleeping in the shadow of wine casks on the deck of a ship called *Furioso*. On the twelfth day after walking out of the tomb, Paulus stepped off the gangplank into the dockside chaos of The Fells, and wound his way through the city toward the Ridge of the Keep. He wondered how the merchant Jan would know that the spirit was freed, and also how Mikal, the marshal of the king's guard, would react to the loss of his men.

To be the sole survivor of a battle, or of an expedition, was to be assumed a liar. Paulus knew this. He could do nothing about it except tell what portion of the truth would serve him. Any soldier learned that truths told to superiors were necessarily partial.

Mikal received his report without surprise, in fact without much reaction at all. "Understood," he said at the end of Paulus' tale. "His Majesty anticipated the possibility of such losses. You have done well to return." Mikal wrote in the log of the guard. Paulus waited. When he was done writing, Mikal said, "You will return to regular duties once you have repeated your story for Jan Destrier."

So Paulus walked back through The Fells, from the Ridge of the Keep down into the market known as the Jingle and then upriver past the quay where he had disembarked from *Furioso*, to tell his story to a man named for a horse. In the Jingle he remembered where as a boy he performed acrobatics for pennies, and where his brother Piero had saved his life by changing him into a dog and then saved it again by trading one of his eyes for a spell. Paulus had not seen his brother in years. So much in one life, he thought. I was a boy, feeding chickens and playing at being a pirate. Then I was in The Fells, rejected from the King's service. Then I did serve the King, and still do. I have fought in his wars, and killed the men he wanted killed, and now I have released the spirit of a dead king into the world to satisfy an arrangement whose details I will never know.

But whom have I ever stood for the way Piero stood for me?

Jan Destrier's shopfront faced the river across a cobblestoned expanse that was part street and part quay. There was no sign, but Paulus had been told to look for a stuffed heron in the doorway. He could not remember who had told him. Mikal? Unease roiled his stomach, but his step was sure and steady as he crossed the threshold into Jan Destrier's shop. The merchant was behind a counter through whose glass top Paulus could see bottles of cut crystal in every shape, holding liquids and pooled gases that caught the light of a lantern hung over Jan Destrier's head. He was a large man, taller than Paulus and fat in the way men allowed themselves to get fat when their lives permitted it. At first Paulus assumed the bottles held perfume; then he saw the alchemical array on a second table behind the merchant and he understood. Jan Destrier sold magic.

At once Paulus wanted to run, but he was not the kind of man who ran, perhaps because he did not value his life highly enough to abase himself for its sake. He hated magic, hated its unpredictability and the supercilious unction of the men who brokered its sale, hated even more the wizards of the Agate Tower who bound the lives of unknowing men to their own and from the binding drew their power. Once, drunk, Paulus and a groom in the castle stables named Andrew had found themselves arguing over the single best thing a king could do upon ascending the throne. Andrew, hardheaded and practical, wanted a decisive war with the agitating brigands in the mountains to the north; Paulus wanted every wizard and spell broker in The Fells put to the sword. The conversation had started off stupid and gotten worse as the bottle got lighter.

Now here he was in the shop of a broker, sent by a superior on business that concerned the king. Paulus could spit the broker on his sword and watch him die in the facets of his crystal bottles, but he himself would die shortly after. It was not his kingdom and never would be. He was obligated to carry out the orders he had been given.

"Jan Destrier," he said. "Mikal the king's marshal sent me to you."

"You must have something terribly important to tell me, then," Destrier said. "Tell it."

"I led a detachment of the guard out into the desert, where the Salt Pass Road bends away from the dry riverbed," Paulus said. "We had a singer with us. She opened a tomb, and the spirit of the king buried there was freed." He felt like he should add something about the deaths of the singer and his men, but Jan Destrier would not care. "As you requested," he finished.

"There has been a misunderstanding," Destrier said. "I did not wish the spirit to escape."

Paulus inclined his head. "Beg pardon, that was the order I received."

"As may be." Destrier beckoned Paulus around the counter. "Come here." Paulus did, and the merchant stopped him when he had cleared the counter. "What I wanted was for the spirit to come here. That was what the singer was for. Well, partly."

"Then permit me to convey my regrets at the failure of the King's Guard," Paulus said. "The spirit came out of the tomb, but I did not see it after that. There was a storm."

"I'm sure there was," Destrier said. "There almost always is. Never fear, the spirit arrived just as I had hoped." He held up a brass instrument, all curls and notched edges. Paulus had never seen its like before. "You were kind enough to bring it along with you. Or, perhaps I should say that it was kind enough to bring you along with it."

No, Paulus thought. If the spirit was there, then it saw me robbing the tomb. He closed his fingers around the cutting of the king's hair, thinking that if he could destroy the fetish—crisp it in one of the candle flames that burned along the edges of the merchant's table—that perhaps the spirit would no longer be able to find him. Already he was too late. The spirit, enlivened by some magnetism of the merchant's, drained the strength from his hands. Paulus felt the whisper of its soul in his brain, like the echo of wind in the black silence of a tomb. His legs were the next to go. His arms jerked out looking for something to hold onto, but nothing was there, and when the numbness crept past his knees, Paulus crumpled to the floor. He felt the paralysis like a drug, spinning his mind away from his body until at last he lost touch even with his senses and fell into a dream that was like dying.

"I thought it would ride the singer," Jan Destrier said. "How odd that it chose you instead."

He did not know how long the stupor lasted. When he regained his senses, everything about him was as it had been before: the table littered with alchemical vessels and curling parchment, the border of pinprick candle flames, the batwing eyebrows of the merchant shadowing his eyes. The merchant looked up as Paulus stirred. "You have performed admirably," he said. "It's not every man who would have survived the initial possession, and even fewer live to tell of the extraction."

There would be nothing to tell, Paulus thought. He had no memory of it.

"Where has the spirit gone, then?" he asked. It would come for him, of that he was sure. It had ridden him back to The Fells and now that it was free it would exact some revenge for his spoliation of its tomb. Perhaps it would ride him back, if by coming it had fulfilled whatever geas the merchant had laid on it. Then it would abandon him in the sands to die, the way he had thought he would die when the first notes of the singer's song had begun to resonate in the stones of the tomb.

"I have it here." Destrier produced a cucurbit stoppered with wax, and filled with a swirling fluid. "The stopper is made from the catalyst. When I apply heat, it will melt into the impure spirit, and the reaction will precipitate the spirit into another glass. This essence is my stock in trade. You are familiar with the magic market?"

"I know of it," Paulus said. "I have never made use of it." This was a lie, but Paulus had no compunction about lying to merchants, who were in his experience congenital liars. Twice in his life, his brother had spent magic on him.

"Well, do keep me in mind if you ever find yourself in need," the merchant said.

Paulus' curiosity got the better of him. He framed his question carefully, already outlining a strategy for evading and defeating the spirit. But first he had to know as much as possible about its nature. "Is there magic in the spirit because it died having not used its own? How do you know it has any?"

"Magic is more complicated than the nursery rhymes and old wives' tales would have it," the merchant said. "Yes, every human is born with a spark, and may use it. But other forms of enchantment and power inhere in the world. In stones, in articles touched by great men or tainted by proximity to unexpected death. These can be refined, their magic distilled and used. This is what I do. In the case of spirits, and whether their magic results from unused mortal power or something else," he went on, "it is not what the mathematicians would call a zero-sum endeavor. By trapping the spirit, I trap the potential for its magic that it has brought back from the other world. Distilled and processed, this magic can be sold just as any other. Although the nature of the spirit makes such magics unsuitable for certain uses."

The echoes of the possession still sounded in the hollows of Paulus' mind. He heard the merchant without active understanding. "We are finished here?" he asked.

"Quite," the merchant said. "Do convey my commendation of your performance to your superior officers."

"A commendation would carry more weight coming from yourself," Paulus said.

The merchant scribbled on a parchment, folded it, and sealed it. "Then let us hope the weight of it does not overburden you," he said. Paulus left him setting small fires under the alembic that would purify the spirit's essence into a salable bit of magic.

He delivered the merchant's commendation to Mikal because not to do so would have been stupid. Then he set about shaping a plan to get that distilled element of magic back from the merchant before he sold it, and in its use an unsuspecting client became a tool for the spirit's vengeance on Paulus. He did not have enough money to buy the magic and knew that he could not trade his own; the essence of the undead spirit was doubtless more powerful. He could take it by force, but he would have to kill the merchant, and then leave The Fells—and the King's service—forever. The cowardice of this path repelled him. He owed the King his life. Twice over. He did not love the King, but Paulus understood obligation.

It was obligation that brought him to the seneschal's chamber after word of the merchant's commendation circulated through the court. Mario Tremano had once been the king's tutor. Now much of the court's business was quietly transacted by means of his approval. He was a careful man, an educated man, and a cruel man. Paulus feared him the way he feared all men who loved subtlety. It was tradition in The Fells for scholars to wield influence, but it was also tradition for them to overreach; as Piero often joked, the scholar's stooped posture cried out for straightening on the gallows. Paulus went to Mario Tremano's chamber wondering if Jan Destrier's commendation had made him useful, or doomed him. The only way to find out was to go.

Nearing seventy years of age, Mario cultivated the appearance of a scholar despite his wealth and the raw unspoken fact of his power. He wore a scholar's simple gown and black cap, and did not braid his beard or hair. "Paulus," he said as his footman escorted Paulus into his study. "You have attracted attention from powerful friends of the King."

"I have always tried to serve the King," Paulus said.

"And serve the King you have," Mario said with a smirk. Paulus noted the insult and folded into his understanding of his situation. It was hardly the first time he had heard cutting remarks about the part of his life he'd spent as a dog. The more venomous ladies of the court still occasionally yipped when they passed him in the castle's corridors. Eleven years had done little to dull the appeal of the joke. The seneschal paused, as if waiting for Paulus to react to the slight. "Now, in our monarch's autumn years, you have a glorious chance to perform a most unusual service," he went on.

"However I may," Paulus said. He had heard that the king was unwell, but Mario's open acknowledgment suggested that the royal health was on unsteadier footing than Paulus had known. He was ten years older than Paulus, and should still have been in the graying end of his prime.

"Your willingness speaks well of you, Captain." Mario spread a map on a table below a window that faced out over The Fells and weighted its edges with candlesticks. Paulus saw the broad estuary of the Black River, with The Fells on its western side. The great Cape of Thirst swept away to the southwest, ending in a curl sheltering Averon. To the north and west, Paulus saw names of places where he had fought in the king's wars: Kiriano, Ie Fure, the Valley of Caves. This was the first time he had ever seen such a map. It made the world seem at once larger, because so much of it Paulus had never seen, and smaller, because it could be encompassed on a sheet of vellum.

The seneschal tapped a location far to the north. *Mare Ultima*, Paulus read. "How long do you think it would take you to get there?"

Paulus looked at the distance between The Fells and Averon, which was twelve days on horse. Then he gauged the distance from The Fells to Mario's fingertip, taking into account the two ranges of mountains. "Six weeks," he guessed. "Or as much as eight if the weather is bad."

"The weather will be bad," Mario said. "Of that you can be sure. Winter falls in September in that country."

It was late in June. Paulus waited for the seneschal to continue his geography lesson, but a sharp question from the chamber door interrupted them. "What have you told him?"

Paulus was kneeling as he turned, the rich tones of the queen's voice acting on his muscles before his brain registered what had been said. He dared not look at her, for fear that he would fall in love as his brother had. This fear had accompanied him for the past eleven years, since he had reawakened into humanity. She had done it, bought the magic to restore his human form, as a reward to his brother for his long service as the king's fool. His brother was blind now, and loved the queen for her voice and her scent and the sound of her gown sweeping along the stone floors. Paulus carried a mosaic of her in his head: the fall of her hair, caught in a thin shaft of sunlight; a line at the corner of her mouth, which had taught Paulus much about the passage of years; a time when an ermine stole slipped from her shoulder and Paulus caught his breath at the sight of her pulse in the hollow of her throat. He believed that if he ever looked her full in the face, and held her gaze for a heartbeat, that love would consume him.

"Your Majesty," Mario said. "He has as yet only heard a bit about the seasons in the north."

"Rise, Captain," the queen said. Paulus did, keeping his eyes low. To the seneschal, the queen said, "Well. Perhaps you should tell him what we are about to ask him to do."

"Of course, Your Majesty. Captain, what stories have you heard about dragons?"

Paulus looked up at the seneschal. "Of dragons? The same stories as any child, Excellency. I think."

Mario retrieved a book from a shelf behind his desk. He set it on the map and opened it. "A natural history," he said. "Written by the only man I know who has ever seen a dragon. A source we can trust. Can you write?"

Paulus nodded.

"Then you must copy this," Mario said, "while we instruct you in the details of your task."

Paulus took up a quill and began to write. *Dragons are solitary beasts, powerful as whales and cunning as an ape. They mate in flight only, and the females are never seen except at these moments. Where they nest and brood, no man knows . . .* At some point during the lesson that followed, the queen touched Paulus on the shoulder. It felt like a blessing, an expression of faith. His unattainable lady who had given him back the shape of a man was now setting him a quest, and though he would probably die, he would undertake the quest feeling that she had offered him a destiny.

His task was this: in the broken hills between the northernmost range of mountains and the icy Mare Ultima, there lived a dragon. *Extremes of heat and cold are the dragon's love. In caves of ice and on the shoulders of volcanoes, there may they be found in numbers.* Once, before ascending the throne, the king had hunted it, and survived the failure of the hunt. It was the queen's wish that before he died, her husband should know that he had outlived the dragon. *A dragon might live hundreds of years. No man can be certain, because no man lives as long as a dragon.* It was to be her death-gift to him, in thanks for the years they had spent as man and wife. "He has lived a life as full as mortal might wish," she said. "Yet this memory hounds him, and I would not have it hound him when he is in his grave."

"Your Majesty, it will not," Paulus said. Whether he meant that he believed he would kill the dragon, or meant only that worldly desires did not accompany spirits, he could not have said. *Many tales and falsehoods exist regarding magical properties of the dragon's blood. These include . . .*

"How are we to know it is done?" the seneschal said.

"What token would His Majesty wish, as proof of the deed?" Paulus asked the queen. He kept his eyes on the page, and the nib of the quill wet. . . . *language of birds, which some believe to derive their origin from a lost race of smaller dragons quite gone from the world.*

"On the king's thigh is a scar from the dragon's teeth," she said, "and under his hair a scar from its tail. I would have its long teeth and the tip of its tail. The rest you may keep. I care not for whatever treasure it might hoard."

In fact, according to the seneschal's book, dragons did not hoard treasure. *They care not for gold or jewels, but such may be found in their dens if left by those who try to kill a dragon and fail. It is said that such treasure grows cursed from being in the dragon's presence, but place no faith in this superstition.* Paulus copied this information down without relaying it to the queen. "Captain," Mario said. "Jan Destrier spoke well enough of you that you perhaps should visit him before you embark. He certainly would have something to assist you."

"Many thanks, Excellency," Paulus said. "Would it be possible to put something in writing, that there is no confusion on the merchant's part?"

"I hope you do not express doubt as to my word," the seneschal said.

Although the dragon is said to speak, it does not. Some are said to mimic sounds made in their presence, as do parrots and other talking birds, but I do not know if this is true. Paulus was almost done copying the pages. His hand hurt. He could not remember ever having written three pages at once. "Beg pardon, no, Excellency," he said. "I doubt only the merchant's memory and attachment to his wares, and I have no gold to buy what he refuses to give."

This was a carefully shaded truth. Gold Paulus had; whether it was enough to buy any useful magic, he did not know.

"Well said, Captain," the queen commented.

The seneschal was silent. Out of the corner of his eye, Paulus could see that he was absolutely still. Paulus' soldier instinct began to prickle on the back of his neck and he hesitated in his copying as his hand reflexively began to reach for his sword. There was bad blood in the room. *It is said that a dragon recognizes the man who will kill it, and this is the only man it will flee. Contrary to this saying, I have never observed a fleeing dragon, nor expect to.* Paulus would never be able to prove it, but in that instant he knew that when the king passed from this world, Mario Tremano would attempt to send his widow quickly after. He resolved without a second thought to kill the seneschal when he returned from his errand to the Mare Ultima. *The dragon's scale is fearsome strong, and will deflect nearly any blade or bolt, but its weaknesses are: inside the joints of the legs, near the anus, the eyes, under the hinges of the jaw.*

"Yes. Apparently being around the court has taught you some tricks, Captain. You must leave immediately," Mario said when Paulus finished copying. He handed Paulus a folded and sealed letter. It could have been a death warrant for all Paulus knew. "Our king must know that this is done, and his time is short."

Paulus rose to leave, rolling the copied pages into a tight scroll that he slid under his belt. Twice now, the seneschal had slighted him. "You may choose any horse," the queen said. "And the armory is yours."

"Your Majesty's generosity humbles me," Paulus said.

"Apparently so much that you act the peasant in my presence," she said, a bit archly. "Will you not look me in the face, Captain Paulus of the King's Guard?"

I would, Paulus thought. How I would. "Your Majesty," he said, "I fear that if I did, I would be unable to go from you, and would prove myself unworthy of your faith in me."

"He certainly is loyal," said Mario the seneschal. Paulus took his leave, right hand throbbing, slighted a third time in front of his queen. One day it would come to blades between him and the seneschal.

That was a battle that could not yet be fought. First, he must survive a long trip to the north and a battle with a dragon. It was said that only a king or a hero could kill a dragon. Paulus was not a king and he did not know if he was a hero. He had fought eleven years of wars, had killed men of every color in every territorial hinterland and provincial capital claimed by The Fells, had survived wounds that he had seen kill other men. Perhaps he had performed heroic deeds. If he survived the encounter with the dragon, the question would be put to rest.

He chose a steel-gray stallion from the stable, young but proven in the Ie Fure campaign the summer before. Andrew, emerging from the workshop where he repaired tack, said, "Paulus, you can't mean it. That one's Mikal's favorite."

"Andrew, friend, if the horse doesn't come back, I won't be coming, either. And if both of us do come back, I'll have the court at my feet. So I have nothing to worry about from Mikal either way."

"Court at your feet," Andrew repeated. "How's that?"

"The queen has sent me to kill a dragon." Paulus said.

"There's no such thing as dragons," Andrew said.

"The queen thinks there are, and she wants me to kill one of them." Paulus swung up onto the horse. "So I will. Now come with me to the armory."

Paulus had never fought with a lance, but he had thrown his share of spears. He took three, and a great sword with a blade twice as wide and a foot longer than the long sword he'd carried these past six years. He added a short butchering knife with a curve near the tip of its blade, which he imagined to be a better tool for digging out a dragon's teeth than his dagger. A sling, for hunting along the way, and a helmet, greaves, and gauntlets to go over the suit of mail that lay oiled and wrapped in canvas in one of Paulus' saddlebags. The book had said nothing about whether dragons could breathe fire. If they could, none of his preparations would make any difference.

"Two swords, spears, knives," Andrew said. "I'll wager a bottle you can kill it just with the sling."

"That's not a bet you make with a man you think is going to survive," Paulus said. Andrew didn't argue the point.

"If I'm not back by the first of November, I won't be back," Paulus said. He clasped hands with Andrew and rode out of the keep into the stinking bustle of The Fells. The sun was sinking toward the desert that began a half-day's ride west from the Black River's banks. Paulus thought of the tomb, and the spirit, and grew uncertain about the plan that was already forming in his head. Twenty minutes' ride through the city brought him to Jan Destrier's door. He tied the horse and went inside.

The spell broker was cleaning a tightly curled copper tube. "Ah, the bearer of spirits is returned," he said. "To purchase, no doubt."

Paulus held out the letter from Mario Tremano. After reading it, the broker said, "I see. I am to assist you."

"I am leaving on a quest given by the queen Herself," Paulus said.

"A quest. Oh my," Destrier said. "For what?"

"For something I will not be able to get without help from your stores."

"Specificity, O Captain of the Guard," Destrier said. "What is it you want? Luck? Do you wish not to feel cold, or fire? Thirst? Do you wish to be invisible, or to go nine days without sleep?"

"I wish the essence of the spirit I brought back to you," Paulus said.

Destrier laughed. "I might as well wish the queen's ankles locked around the back of my neck," he said. "We're both going to be disappointed."

It was not Paulus' life that mattered. Not his success or failure at killing the dragon. It was the murderous guile he had sensed in the presence of Mario Tremano and what that meant for the life of the queen after her husband was no longer there to be a useful asset to the seneschal. For her, Paulus would do anything. He stole nothing after killing Jan Destrier; he used the fetish of the dead king's hair to find the essence of the spirit, which was an inch of clear fluid in a brass bulb the size of a fig. He tied it around his neck with a piece of leather, threading the binding of the fetish into the knot that held the bulb.

There would be consequences. If Paulus brought back the teeth and tail of the dragon, he would survive them; if he did not, it would not matter. On the street, he made no effort to hurry. Most of those who had heard Jan Destrier die would be more interested in plundering his expensive wares than in reporting that the killer was dressed in the livery of the King's Guard. He rode for the North River Gate and out into the world beyond The Fells.

He did not know how much power was in the spirit's essence, or of what kind. He did not know whether any of its soul survived inside the brass bulb. But he had a token of the body it had once animated, and he had six weeks to find out.

III: The Quest

With ten days left in August, Paulus came down out of the mountains into the land that on Mario Tremano's map looked like a thin layer of fat between the mountains and the Mare Ultima. He had seen snow three times in the mountains already and heard an avalanche on a warm day after a heavy storm. He had been traveling fifty days. Twice he had cut his beard with the butchering knife. He had killed one man so far, for trying to steal his horse. Mikal's horse. He had hunted well, and so eaten well, and even traded some of his game for cheese and bread and the occasional piece of fruit at farmsteads and villages along the way.

He had also learned something of the nature of the spirit in the brass bulb that hung next to the fetish around his neck. If there was anything Paulus mistrusted more than magic, it was dreams, but nevertheless it was through dreams that he had begun to learn. He was sitting in front of a campfire built in the ribcage of a dragon, listening to the bones speak, telling him he knew nothing of dragons. Your book is full of lies, the voice said.

The Book is about faith and learning, Paulus replied, touching two fingers to his throat. The Journey and the Lesson. It was what his mother had taught him.

Idiot, the voice said. Your book about dragons is what I mean.

It may be, Paulus said.

It is.

He awoke from that first dream with the brass bulb unstoppered and held to his lips. "No," he said, and stoppered it again. "So you do know me."

He would have to be careful, he thought. Something of the spirit remained and he could not know whether it wished him good or ill. He would learn, and when the time came to face the dragon, he would hope he had learned enough.

The second dream took him after he rose in the night to piss into a creek in the foothills of the first mountain range that lay between him and the Mare Ultima. As he drifted back into sleep, he dreamed of walking out into that creek, trying to wash something from his skin that burned and sickened him. This is what you will feel, said the voice of the water over the rocks. This and much worse.

Paulus stopped and stood, dripping and naked, letting the feeling inhabit him, imagining what it would be like to withstand it and fight through it. How much worse? he asked . . . and woke screaming in a predawn fog, with the gray stallion a shadow rearing at the agony in his voice.

The night of the first snow, as he crested the first pass and descended into a valley bounded by canyons and glaciers that curved like ribs into sparkling tarns, he was reminded of the first dream. He cut a lean-to from tree branches and packed the snow over and around it, then huddled under his blanket with a small fire at the mouth of the lean-to. When he slept, the voice was the sound of tree branches cracking under the weight of snow. I have killed dragons.

What does that matter to me? You cannot kill this one for me, and even if you could, it would shame me to permit it.

Shame, the voice cackled. It looks very different when you are dead.

Someday I will know that, Paulus said. But not soon.

Sooner than you wish, unless you listen.

Then talk, so I can decide if what you say is worth listening to.

You cut hair from my body, and took gold from my tomb, the voice said.

All the more reason to be suspicious of you.

With a cackle, the voice said How much you think you know. Who guided you to the broker's? And when you came back to the broker's—do you think you found me? No, mortal man. I brought you to me. I would kill a dragon again.

A cold, shameful fear made Paulus moan in his sleep. The queen—

No. Her mind is her own. I was a king, and would not meddle with others of my station. You, on the other hand . . .

Paulus woke up. In the pages he had copied from Mario Tremano's book, it was said that kings of old had killed dragons, and driven them to the wastes of the north and west. He rolled the brass bulb in his palms. The spirit had said that the book was full of lies. If the spirit told the truth, then kings of old had not killed dragons, which meant that the spirit was lying.

That is man's logic, he thought, remembering a story from the Book in which a man tried to reason with lightning. Yes, the lightning had said. There is no flaw in your thought, save that it is man's thought, and I am lightning.

Shaking out the blanket and refolding it over the horse's back, Paulus found himself in the same position. In a week, or perhaps ten days, he would find the dragon. Then he would discover which lies the spirit was telling.

With ten days left in August, he came down out of the mountains and began asking the questions. The people who hunted seals and caribou along the shores of Mare Ultima spoke a language he knew only from a few words picked up on campaigns, when mercenary companies had come down from this land of black rock and blue ice, bringing their spears and an indifference to suffering bred at the end of the world. He pieced together, over days, that there was a dragon, and that it slept in a cave formed after the eruption and collapse of a volcano. He worked his way across the country, eating white rabbits and salmon and the dried blubber of seals, building his strength, until he found the dragon's cave.

The mountain still smoked. Standing on a ridge that paralleled the shore, some miles distant, Paulus looked south. The mountains, already whitening. North: water the color of his stallion, broken by ice floes all the way to a misty horizon. East: coastal hills, green and gray speckled with snow. West: more mountains, their peaks shrouded in clouds. The people he had spoken to said that in the west, mountains burned.

This was as good a place as any to find a dragon, Paulus thought. As good a place as any to die.

The dragon's cave was a sleepy eye perhaps a half-mile up the ruined side of a mountain. The top of the mountain was scooped out, ringed with sharp spires; a waterfall drained what must have been an immense lake in the crater, carving a canyon down the mountainside and a new river through the hills to the Mare Ultima. Paulus could smell some kind of flower, and the ocean, and from somewhere far to the west the tang of smoke. He dismounted and began to prepare. First, the mail shirt, still slick with oil. Gauntlets, their knuckles squealing like the hinges of a door not hung true. Greaves buckled over his boots. The great sword across his back. Shield firm on his left forearm, spear in his right hand, long sword on his hip. The butchering knife sheathed behind his left hip.

Then he thought, No. This is man's thinking, and I am going to fight the lightning.

He stabbed the spear into the ground, and let the great sword fall from his back. Setting his shield down, Paulus took off the gauntlets. He snapped the leather thong around his neck and unwound the binding of the fetish. With the butchering knife, he cut a tangled lock of his own hair. There was more gray in it than he remembered from the last time he had looked in a mirror, but he was forty-five years old now. He twisted the two locks of hair together into a tangle of black and gray long enough that he could wind it around the base of the middle finger on his right hand, and then in a figure-eight around his thumb. He bound it in place, and unstoppered the bulb. As he tipped a few drops of the fluid onto the place where the figure-eight crossed itself, he heard the voices of ice and snow, rocks and water, bones of dragons. He put a gauntlet on his right hand over the charm and tipped a few more drops into its palm. The rest he sprinkled over the blade of the sword. Then he cast the bulb away clinking among the stones.

It would work or it would not. Picking up his shield and holding his sword before him, Paulus picked his way at an angle up the slope toward the dragon's cave. A voice in his head said, *Now you know why I did not ride the singer.*

Afterward, he was screaming, and when she came to him, he thought he was being guided out of his life. She spoke, and soothed him, and left him there in his own blood, writhing as the dragon's poison ate its way under his skin. The spirit was gone. In the echoes of its departure Paulus felt the slash of the dragon's claws, shredding his mail shirt and the muscle underneath. When his body spasmed with each fresh wave of poisoned agony, the grating of the mail links on the stone floor of the cave was the sound of the dragon's scales as it uncoiled and raised its head to meet him. The white of his femur and his ribs was the white of its bared fangs crushing his shield and snapping the bones in his wrist. And when he arched his back in seizure, as the poison worked deeper into his body, the impact of his head on the ground was the blinding slap of its tail and then the shock of his blade, driven home and snapped off in the hollow underneath its front leg. The dragon was dead and Paulus soon would be. He thrashed his right arm, flinging the bloody gauntlet away, and caught the fetish in his teeth. His face was slick with the dragon's blood and his own tears. Gnawing the fetish loose, he spat it out. Free, he thought. Free to die my own death. O my queen . . .

And she was back, with a sledge freshly cut and smelling of sap. Paulus recognized the language she spoke, but couldn't pick out the words. When she dragged him over the stones at the mouth of the cave, pain blew him out like a candle.

The next thing he could remember was the sound of wind, and the weight of a fur blanket, and the rank sweat of his body. He was inside, in a warm place. A creeping icy draft chilled his face. Paulus opened his eyes. The woman was stirring something in a pot over a fire. He tried to sit up and his wounds reawakened. The sound that came out of him was the sound wounded enemies made when the camp women went around the battlefield to kill them. The woman laid her bone spoon across the lip of the pot and came over to squat next to him. "Shhhhh," she said. Black, black hair, Paulus thought. And black, black eyes. Then he was gone again.

It was quiet and dark when next he awoke. He heard the woman breathing nearby. He flexed his fingers, wondering that he could still feel all ten. Under the blanket, he began to explore his body. His left wrist was bound and splinted, and radiated the familiar pain of a healing broken bone. Heavy scabs covered the right side of his body from just below his shoulder all the way down to the knee. He wiggled his toes. Something was sticking out of the scabs, and after puzzling over it Paulus realized that the woman—or someone—had stitched the worst of his wounds, with what he could not tell. He was going to live. He knew the smell of infection and his nose could not find it. He had clean wounds. Bad wounds, but clean. They would heal. He would walk, and he would live. He saw details in the near-perfect darkness of the room: the last embers in the fire pit, the swell of the woman under her blankets. His fingers roamed over his body, feeling the pebbled scars where the dragon's poison had burned him and the strangely smooth expanses that were without wounds. He flexed the muscles of his arms, and they hurt, but they worked. When he moved his legs, the deep tears in his right thigh cried out. Not healed yet, then. Putting that together with the way his wrist felt, Paulus guessed that it had been two weeks since the woman had found him in the mouth of the dragon's cave.

The teeth, he thought. And the tail.

He must not fail the queen.

"The dragon," he said to the woman the next morning. She shushed him. "I have to—"

Again she shushed him. Paulus sank back into the pile of furs and skins. He still had no strength. He watched her move around, taking in the details of her home. It was made of stone and wood, the spaces between the stones stuffed with moss and earth. One wall was a single slab of stone; a hillside, with three manmade walls completing the enclosure. Timbers slanted from the opposite wall to rest against the natural wall, covered with densely woven branches. Paulus couldn't believe it could contain warmth, but it did. He threw his covers off, suddenly sweating in the fur cocoon. The woman did not react to Paulus' nakedness. She opened a door he hadn't noticed and the interior of the house lit up with sunlight reflected from deep drifts of snow. The snow must be waist-deep, Paulus thought. Perhaps the dragon's cave was buried. Perhaps no one here wanted trophies from its carcass. Exhausted again, he did not resist when the woman settled covers back over him and went about her business. "Why did you save me?" Paulus asked her.

She shushed him, and again he fell asleep.

Gradually over the winter he learned more of her language, and she bits and pieces of his. From this he learned that she had hauled him to her home, put him on the pile of furs, and tended his wounds with skill that few surgeons in The Fells possessed. Or she was fortunate, and Paulus was strong. Perhaps he would have lived in any case, given shelter and food. He would never know.

His horse was outside, kept in an overhung spot along the bluffs that also made up the fourth wall of the house. As soon as he was strong enough, he went out to see it and found that someone in this icy wilderness knew something about horses; it was brushed, its hooves were trimmed. If these people had mastered ironworking, Paulus thought, the horse would have new shoes. The hospitality was humbling. He thanked her and asked her to thank whoever had taken care of the horse. About the dragon, she appeared confused when he finally made her understand that he had traveled for two months just to get pieces of it to take home. "For my queen," he said. Though she understood the words, the concept made no sense to her. Arguing with lightning, Paulus thought. Her name meant Joy in her language. She lived alone. Her mother and father were dead, and this was their house. In the good weather months, she fished and wove and tanned hides; in the winter, she kept to herself and wove cloth to sell the next summer. There was a village twenty minutes' walk away. A man there wanted to marry her, but she would not have him. He was the one who had cared for the stallion.

Paulus thanked her again. She shrugged. What else would she have done?

Growing stronger, he went out into the snow dressed in clothes Joy made. He met a few of the villagers, who lost interest in him as soon as they confirmed that he had not made Joy his wife. The dragon, it seemed, had made little difference in their lives. It ate caribou and sea lions. There were plenty of both to go around. In The Fells, should he survive to return there, Paulus would be celebrated; here, he was a curiosity.

On one of the first spring days, smells of the earth heavy in his nose, Paulus went out from Joy's house with the butchering knife tucked in his belt. He found his way to the dragon's cave and went inside. It lay more or less as he had left it. His broken sword blade, its edges now rusted, protruded from behind its left front leg. Marveling, Paulus paced off the length of its body. Fifty feet. It was mostly still frozen. He laid out the canvas sheet he'd used to protect his armor and set to work hacking into the carcass with the butchering knife. Four fangs for the queen, and the tip of the tail. Then he gouged out most of the rest of its teeth, leaving those that broke as he worked them free of the jawbone. In the pages he had copied from Mario Tremano's book were recipes for alchemical uses of the dragon's eyes, as well as a notation that its heart was said to confer the strength of giants. The eyes came out easily enough; the heart was another matter. Paulus went to work prying loose the scales on its breast until he could crack through its ribs. The heart, larger than his head, was pierced six inches deep by the blade of his sword. Sweating in the cold, he cut it out and put it with the eyes. Then he added several dozen of its scales, each the size of his spread hand.

When he was done, he walked back to Joy, who was outside bartering a roll of cloth for the haunch of a moose killed by a villager who would have gladly given her the haunch, and anything else, if she would accept him. That night, Joy and Paulus ate moose near the fire. When they were done, she got up to put the bowls in water. He handed her his dagger, slick with grease, and she looked at it for a moment before slashing it across his right forearm.

Paulus sprang away from her, hand instinctively dropping toward a sword hilt that wasn't there. "Joy!" he shouted, squaring off against her, glancing around for something he could use as a weapon. He had no doubt that he could overpower her, even weak as he still was, but no man ever went unarmed against an opponent with a knife if there was even a stick nearby that could improve the odds.

She pointed at his forearm. Unable to help himself, he looked. The skin was unmarked. Paulus looked back at her. She made no move to approach him; after a moment, she turned and dropped the knife into the pot of water with the bowls.

It is said of the dragon's blood that washing in it renders human flesh invulnerable to blade or arrow, the seneschal's book had said. Paulus had read over those lines the way he had the rest of the more fanciful passages, skeptically and with no effort to keep them in mind. But it was true. He had felt the blade hit his arm. It should have opened him up to the bone.

"Dragon," Joy said, and began to wash the dishes.

She knew, Paulus thought. She was showing him. Not just the transformation of his skin wetted with the dragon's lifeblood; she was showing him that he had survived.

"How," he began, and stopped when he realized he had too many questions to ask, and no words to ask them, and that she had no words to answer. He watched her dry his dagger and set it aside on the table. Before she could pick up another dish, he caught her wrist and drew her toward him. Her expression changed and he thought she would pull away, but she let him draw her down into the furs. She kept her eyes locked on his. Paulus—who had once been a dog, and who had spoken to the dead, and who had winterlong danced on the line between life and death—knew that when she looked into his eyes, she was seeing a dead man she had once loved.

For him, too, she was someone else. The spill of her hair across his chest was the queen's hair, caught in sunlight. Her body moving against his was the queen's body, pledged to another. Her eyes shining in the last light of the fire were the queen's eyes Paulus never dared to meet.

"He died out on the ice," she said when he asked, a few days later. "Hunting whales."

How long since he had had a woman? Nearly a year, Paulus thought. And he did not want to let this woman go. For her, perhaps longer. She said that her man who died hunting whales was her first, and only. The way she spoke of him made Paulus conscious that he had never felt that way about any woman but the queen, whom he could never have. The queen, with her dying husband and the seneschal Mario Tremano plotting against her. He had come to the ends of the earth, slain a dragon, to realize the futility of his desire. If he could not have her, he could at least save her. This, too, Joy had taught him. Paulus was stronger now. The time was coming when he would have to leave. The dragon's heart and eyes were almost dried. He had carefully cleaned the bits of gum and blood from its teeth, for presentation to his queen. But he was not ready to leave yet. He started obliquely, and over the early weeks of spring more directly, gauging her reactions to the idea of coming south. He described the city, the Keep on the Ridge, the queen, his brother the fool. Subtlety never came easy to him and was impossible to maintain; on the first day in May, he told her that his errand was not yet complete. He must return to The Fells.

"I would have you come with me," he said. They were tangled in a blanket and in each other's scents. Night was falling. She would never know what it had cost him to speak the words. Having Joy meant acquiescing to the caprice of Fate that kept him apart from the queen he would love. Having Joy meant being a curiosity at court, the guard captain who had once been a dog and now had a wife with callused hands from a distant land, who had never seen silk. But he was willing. He would take her if she said yes.

"I would have you stay here," Joy said. "But I know you will not. Go."

"In a little while," Paulus said.

Joy shook her head. "If you know that you are going, go," she said. "Go to your queen. Go."

"You saved my life," he said. Meaning that he felt an obligation to her, but also that he believed she too was obligated, that once she had held his life in her hands, she was no longer able to stand back from him and watch him go. Man logic, he thought. And she is lightning.

"I am from this place," Joy answered. "Someday when I am done mourning, I will take a man from the village, and there will be children in this house. I would take you if you would stay; but if you will not, go to your queen."

There was nothing to say to this. Paulus was not going to stay and Joy was not going to go. She had nursed him back to health, but she did not want him. She wanted a fisherman, a black-haired hunter of moose and caribou, a second chance at her man who had died on the ice. Not a soldier from a foreign land, entering his forty-seventh year, determined to finish a quest he had begun in honor of a woman he could never have. They both knew what it was to find solace for a little while and then reawaken into the desire for what they could never have, or never have again.

The next morning, Paulus saddled the horse and packed into its saddlebags the teeth and tail of the dragon, the scales, the heart, and the eyes. His sword and shield were broken, his armor shredded, his spear taken to hunt seals, the great sword ruined by a winter under snow. He had a thousand miles to cover with a knife and the sling, and a good horse. Mikal would be glad to see it, but not at all glad to see Paulus.

Perhaps the queen would be glad to see him. Perhaps.

Joy came out from the house with jerky and a fish. "I caught it this morning before you woke up. Your first meal when you ride away from the ocean should always be a fish," she said. Paulus thought he understood. He swung up onto the horse and did not look back as he rode south, up the hill track toward the mountains.

AS WOMEN FIGHT

SARA GENGE

Merthe stands next to the felled doe and casts a worried look at the sky. He's aching to train for Fight. Between hunting and setting traps, he hasn't trained for a fortnight, but it's too late and he's too far from home. He hoists the doe on his shoulder and heads back. Snow crunches like starch under his boots, reminding him of when he was a young woman and knew a dozen names for snow, all stolen from the dessert section of a cookbook. Whipped cream, soufflé, eggnog with a crisp burnt crust . . .

The doe is small and Ita will complain. She trusts Merthe only when she can see what he's accomplished in a day's work. She'll want proof that he hasn't been lazing around, or worse, training for Fight. As if he's ever neglected to feed the family. As if he'd ever put his own future before theirs. He swears under his breath. Five years as a man is too much to bear and he vows he will not lose the Fight again even if it means training every waking hour that he isn't hunting.

When he gets home, the children run to him shouting. He lets them tug at his beard, tries to hug them all at once. He senses them drifting away. No matter that he can still feel them tugging at his breasts. He is either the figure of authority, or the gentle giant. The clown. They come to him to play, but if the wound is deep, it is their mother that they run to.

"Did you hunt at all?" Ita asks.

He nods but says no more. He's been a man so long that this flesh has imprinted its own ways into his mind. Male silence comes easy these days; he revels in communication by grunts—or kisses. He knows how much it enrages her; he sometimes tries to be more verbal. But not now. Anything that'll annoy her may throw her off her game. She's won five years in a row. He needs all the help he can get.

He winks at the children and nods towards the shed. They run off, bringing back the doe between the six of them, the toddlers contributing by getting in the way. Serga doesn't go with them; shei is the eldest, almost ten. Merthe sometimes wonders if shei still remembers heir first mother, still remembers Merthe in Ita's body. He fears shei doesn't: shei was so young when Ita and he swapped places. And yet, Serga stares at him with understanding, a look of pity even. Merthe shivers.

Ita hurries about and Merthe lets her serve him. In the warmth of the winter hut, the children quickly lose their wraps. Merthe's clothes crack open like a husk, revealing thawing feet and a wide chest that has lost its summer tan. He looks upon Ita to do the same and, finally, she obliges. She's gained some weight since she took over that body. Her arms are rich and soft but Merthe isn't fooled: he knows first hand the damage they can inflict in combat. She bounces about, all hips and breasts, and the toddlers stare at her as if she were food, following her with eyes and mouths round as Os. Merthe lets his eyes roam her body, disguising one desire for the other. Ah, to be in those hips again. Yeah gods, to inhabit them! There's bounce to her skin and the marks of pregnancy stretch proud across her tummy. Some of them, Merthe put there when he bore Serga and Ramir.

She serves him and leans forward to whisper in his ear.

"Like what you see? Enjoy. You're not getting back in here any time soon."

He grabs her by the waist and tumbles her, eats her mouth, lets her feel the weight of his body on hers. The strength. She gasps in surprise and the children laugh. They're still androgens, and too young to read beneath the surface and into the hidden struggle between man and wife.

She giggles with them, making Merthe's ribs jiggle against hers. He lets her sit up—the children are awake—and nibbles her ear.

"I'll be in there in no time, darling," he says. He doesn't specify what exactly he means by that.

The weeks before Fight come and go so fast that Merthe wonders if he's growing old. Time always seems to speed up the further along you go. Three days before the match, Elgir walks up to the hut at dawn. He's their closest neighbor but Merthe doesn't know him that well. The People don't gather too close. Hunters need their space and the gender arrangement makes for frequent domestic fighting. Nobody likes to live close to noisy neighbors.

Merthe crawls out to meet him without disturbing Ita. The two men step inside the shed, neither knowing what to say.

Merthe offers Elgir a cup of tea.

"You'd make a good woman," Elgir says.

Merthe grunts at the compliment. "Yes, I did make a good wife."

"Ah yes, I forgot. The first two are yours, aren't they?"

It takes Merthe a second to realize Elgir means the children. Merthe nods to hide his shame. It seems impossible that he can't reclaim that body. And the whole village knows how much he wants it. He damns himself. It would not matter so much if he could appear not to care.

"Don't beat yourself up. She's so good she's scary," Elgir says.

Elgir himself has little to fear. He can easily defeat his partner, Samo. She's a small woman and not too fast. She's only been in a woman's body for a year and relied so much on muscle when she was a man that she never mastered technique. Looking at Elgir, Merthe understands how someone inhabiting that body could grow complacent. The man could fell a tree with a backhand cuff.

"How are things at home?" Merthe asks. It must be hard on Samo, knowing that she's going to lose. Elgir made a stunning fighter as a woman. The litheness that is Samo's bane was an advantage when Elgir was in control. Merthe remembers a particularly impressive kick roll in which a female Elgir was too fast for the eye. Merthe misses that lightness. Some days, he trudges around with the grace of a bear.

"Samo doesn't want to lose," Elgir replies.

"Who does?" says Merthe.

Elgir's eyes hold Merthe's for a second. "Some do. Some like being men. Some don't care either way," Elgir says.

Merthe blushes; nobody can judge another person's likes or dislikes, but some things are rarely said in public. Both men look down.

"The moss is thick this winter," Elgir says.

"Yes. It'll get cold fast."

It is so quiet that Merthe can hear the snow fall.

"Say, how about we hunt together. If we get something big, we can split. We can keep the women happy and still have time to train," Elgir suggests.

Merthe knows Ita will disapprove, so he grabs his things and goes with Elgir before she can object.

They spot a squirrelee wallowing up the dikes to get from pond to pond. It digs the snow with its front paws for nuts hidden the previous season. It's only as big as Eme, Merthe's youngest, but Merthe knows that most of its flesh is fat, good for thickening stews. It's a worthy catch, even if the women will complain about getting only half.

But when the time comes to cast his spear, Elgir freezes up. It's no time for questions, so Merthe shoots his arrow through air that tastes like sugared ice. The squirrelee falls.

Elgir goes ahead to retrieve it. Merthe wonders at the man's hesitation.

"Nice shot," Elgir says. He punches Merthe on the shoulder. "They say you cannot forget how to be a man anymore than you can forget how to suckle," Elgir says, "but I seem to forget every single time. One year is not enough to relearn it all. I was female for so long before that . . . "

Merthe remembers. Elgir only lost last season because she caught the bluing cold. She barely escaped with her life—losing the Fight was a small thing compared to that. Everyone still wonders why Samo and Elgir didn't postpone their fight until after her recovery. Was Samo really that desperate to win?

"Then why is it that you wish to remain a man?" Merthe asks. It is a bold question and he hopes he is not mistaken. But intuition isn't just a woman's gift.

"It's not that . . . " Elgir says. Silence rings off the dusted pines. The men find a clearing and unpack their cheese-and-bread. The cheese has no smell. Merthe sniffs it, licks it.

"It's good," Elgir says.

"Yes. I wish I could taste it like she . . . like they . . . like the women do," Merthe says.

"Wouldn't make much difference. Smell's all that counts towards taste. This cheese tastes good because it has a hot bite to it, but the smell is rather bland. Trust me. I remember."

"But Ita says—"

"Ita is pulling your leg. This cheese has no smell."

Merthe curses Ita and tucks in. Sometimes he wonders why he wants to be a woman so much, since he can't even remember what it was like. But he's kidding himself. Even if he can't remember the particulars the overall impression remains. He recalls that first year after he defeated his first partner. Smells so much more vivid, skin so fine that it could feel the gentlest summer breeze, the touch of the sun . . . He knows of men and women down south who never change bodies. They are content to live their whole lives as one sex. Sometimes, in his darkest moments, Merthe wants to do likewise. If those men manage, why can't he?

But those men have the blessing of ignorance. They do not know what it is like to feel their bellies grow full. They do not understand the transforming pain of childbirth, the draining of milk from the nipple. The real smell of onion as it cooks.

"What is it then?" he asks. He's suddenly angry at Elgir, for taking this so lightly. "I like being a woman," Elgir concedes. "I also like being a man. I like changing from one to the other. If you think about it, that's how all of this started, right? We swap bodies the better to understand each other's minds. We were meant to be balanced, equal. That's why our women are faster than the eye and stronger than the ones down South. It makes us even. Swapping bodies was never meant to cause strife."

"Interesting theological argument. Maybe if we pray hard enough, we can all be women. What do you think?"

Elgir snorts half-frozen milk up his nose. His eyes tear and he laughs, but Merthe wonders if he's not also crying.

"It doesn't matter which body you're in. Sure, it's great to be a woman for the first few months after a transition, but after a while you simply get used to it and you don't make use of all those fantastic senses you're supposed to have. Senses work by comparison—if all of your passions are strong, they fade against each other as certainly as if they're all weak. That's why swapping frequently makes sense. That way you can renew the strong feelings often and spend enough time as a man to learn to appreciate the subtler pleasures too."

"What does Samo think of that?"

"She thinks I'm full of worm shit," Elgir says.

They burst out laughing.

Suddenly, Elgir stops laughing and starts crying. Men's tears, quiet, no fuss. But he doesn't try to hide them. Merthe wishes they were women so that they could hug each other and cry and then laugh at their silliness. He loves the way Ita's tears are unapologetic and arbitrary. They come and go like a morning sprinkle over nothing or they storm out and make him wish he'd never been born. Women have practice with crying. They communicate with tears. Men just sit there and cry.

But Elgir seeks him out to finish the last shudders in his arms.

"What is it?" Merthe asks.

"Samo doesn't like being a man."

"Neither do I. She'll just have to get used to—"

Elgir shuts his eyes and shakes his head.

"What is it? What is it?" Merthe asks.

"She doesn't take well to being a man. Not at all. She . . . he . . . is angry . . . all the time."

It sounds worse than just an argument. Merthe doesn't understand. "Why didn't you leave?" he asks.

But Merthe knows why he hasn't left. He hasn't left for the same reasons that Merthe hasn't divorced Ita. He thought things would get better. He hoped for change. The children stay with the mother . . .

"What exactly is it that she . . . he . . . does?"

"He's violent." Elgir bursts out crying and Merthe is confused. Even in a man's body, Samo is no match for Elgir. It makes no sense that Samo could batter Elgir. "It's not me she hurts," Elgir wails and, now, Merthe realizes he's crying from shame.

"The children. As a man, he hit Tine and Vis," Merthe says.

"That's why I let him win last winter. I thought once she was a woman again, it would all be over. It helped, at first. But last night, I saw a bruise on Tine's arm. The kid swears shei fell off a tree, but both of them are awfully quiet when their mother is around. Maybe I'm imagining things."

"She's still hitting them?" Merthe asks. "What are you doing here? What are you doing leaving them alone with her!" He stands up and paces, trying to decide whether to hit Elgir or run back towards his neighbor's house to save those children from their mother.

Elgir grabs Merthe's arm but Merthe wrenches it away. "How could you let that happen?" Merthe shouts. "You could have gone to the elders. Left without their approval, even. Stolen the children—whatever it took! How could you? How could you?"

He hoists his bag on his back and heads home, forgetting the squirrelee. Elgir runs after him. When Merthe doesn't stop, Elgir tackles him to the ground.

"Stop. Listen." Merthe stops struggling, less from the command than from the finality of a man twice his side pinning him to the ground.

"I'll save those kids, I promise you. I'll keep them safe from Samo if it's the last thing I do! But I'd rather do it smart. You know how the elders are, they'll argue and fret for months before reaching a decision and in the meantime, the kids will be alone with Samo. An angry Samo. A Samo who's been humiliated in public. I have failed them as a father and as a mother, but I won't compound one mistake with another."

Elgir stops pressing down quite so hard, but he doesn't let go. Both men sit up, hands on each other's arms. It's not a fight grip but it would take no effort to turn it into one.

"What are you going to do, then?" Merthe asks.

"I will win. I will win and leave, and I'll take the children with me."

Merthe lets go, sits back on the snow. As much as he hates the idea of Tine and Vis spending the next week alone at home with Samo, he realizes Elgir's way is best. As soon as he takes back his woman body, he'll be entitled to take the children where he pleases. Merthe tries not to feel sorry for Samo: she birthed them both.

"Do you know where you're going to go? Do you have family to help you out?" he asks.

"I'll worry about that later."

Merthe promises himself that he'll take food from his own mouth before Elgir's children go hungry. He's a strong hunter; he can hunt for two households. Ita will just have to accept it.

It's only later, back at home, that he realizes that he doesn't plan on being the hunter for the coming year.

Serga comes out to meet him at the door and it takes Merthe a moment to figure out why this surprises him. Serga hasn't been at the door with the other children for a while. The kid is too old to puppy around heir father.

Serga wants something. Heir eyes are impatient for Merthe to dispose of his hunting gear and head towards the shed to clean the squirrelee. Shei doesn't even cast a sidelong glance at the half-carcass, even though heir scathing looks are usually as incisive (and effective) as heir mother's.

Merthe takes off his coat and starts skinning. Serga stares on until Merthe motions towards the belly of the animal. There's enough work for two.

Serga hesitates and Merthe wonders if he has insulted the child by offering heir man's work. After all, no woman will touch an animal until it's clean and adolescents like to pretend they're women. But Serga takes heir own blade from heir apron and settles down in front of Merthe.

"It's happened," Serga whispers. "It's arrived."

Merthe hides his surprise and looks Serga up and down discreetly. Yes, there's an adult's budding body under the wraps. He hadn't expected it to happen so soon, but he'd always known his children would have to grow up. Serga isn't too young for her first bleeding.

"Have you told your mother?" Merthe asks, and regrets it. Serga has come to him, not Ita. He mustn't push heir away.

Shei shakes heir head.

"The other thing too? Or is it just your period?" Some adolescents don't have erections until a couple of years after their first bleeding.

Serga winces; Merthe is too blunt. He tries not to smile.

"The other thing . . . I think so."

Merthe grunts his understanding and waits.

"What do I do now?" Serga throws the knife to the ground. It rattles against the floorboards and shei looks up, scared. You don't treat a good knife like that. But Merthe gets up, wipes the knife on his pants and hands it back to Serga without scolding.

"You don't have to Fight this season, or even the next. You can still be our child for a little longer, if that's all right with you," he whispers and places his hand on heir shoulder.

Serga nods and clasps heir apron.

"But why do I have to Fight at all? Why can't I just stay like this always?"

"Fighting is fun. You'll come to enjoy it," he says.

"What if I can't? What if I'm really bad? What if—"

"It's okay to lose."

"Mother says—"

"Your mother is a very gifted woman, but in some things, she acts like an idiot." Merthe wonders if those words are his, or Elgir's. "She's so proud of winning that she pretends that losing is a big deal. You're going to win some years and lose some years and, either way, you're going to be happy. You're going to love your children and your spouse. You're going to enjoy good food and soft clothes. The differences are there, but the things that matter remain the same."

It's a white lie, but the words spring from his mouth with such a force that Merthe wonders if they aren't true.

Elgir and Samo are the first to Fight each season and their combat casts a long shadow on everyone else's match. Merthe wonders what Fight will be like when Elgir and Samo are no longer the item leading the way.

Their combat is short; Elgir seems too sad to care about putting on a good show. Samo comes at him in a blur and the men in the crowd gasp, always surprised at how fast a woman can move.

Samo has learned from previous failures. She never sits still and blows punctuate her every motion. Elgir stands still and takes them, face flat as granite. Merthe wonders if he plans to win through attrition.

Suddenly, his arm shoots out and he catches Samo across the chest. They crash down, Elgir breaking their fall so that Samo lands almost softly, cocooned inside his arms.

He holds her much longer than necessary, after the bell has rung, after the cheering is over. He holds her after Samo has stopped thrashing in anger and frustration, after the children stop hollering. It is their final embrace and Elgir makes it last. This is how Elgir loves, fervently. Even after the unthinkable, he cannot bear to let go.

When the crowd is no longer interested, Elgir presses his palm against Samo's and Merthe can feel his own pores opening up in sympathy, the clever little soul-holes through which bodies are exchanged. It only lasts a second but Merthe knows that those two feel their minds entwined into eternity.

And then it's done, and Samo in his new male body pushes Elgir away so hard that Merthe winces. Elgir stands up, wearing that body with a grace Samo could never muster. She nods her head, a last goodbye, and whistles for the children. By now, even Samo must know they won't be coming home tonight.

That evening, Merthe arrives home with half a nme bird. There's hardly any meat on it and Ita will have to add some sausage to thicken the stew, but nobody will go hungry, not Ita and the children, not Elgir and hers. Sometimes you're lucky, sometimes you aren't. That's the way hunting goes.

When Ita sees the bird she blanches, and Merthe braces for a harangue on hunting and responsibility. But Ita is too angry to bait or mock. Merthe has never seen her like this. She storms back into the house while Merthe goes to the shed to clean the bird.

Dinner is silent and Ita hustles the children to bed long before their bedtime. One of the younger ones whimpers, but Serga cuts heir short with a pinch which Merthe pretends not to see. He's too exhausted to fight heir too.

"Who is she?" Ita whispers after the children are in their bunks.

"What?"

"Don't play games with me, Merthe, who's the woman you keep bringing meat to. Taking it from your children's mouths!"

Merthe laughs "It's not . . . I'm not . . ."

"Don't go telling me you hunted with Elgir again! She's a woman now, Samo can hunt for her. I don't know why I believed you the first time, men hunt alone, but I was so trusting—"

"What is it that really bothers you, Ita? Me with another woman or your stupid pantry? It's bursting at the edges, for every god's sake. You give food away else it rot before we can eat it! Is that what I am to you? The oaf who keeps your stomach full?"

Ita opens her mouth, but manages only a gurgle. She grabs her coat. Polar winter sweeps into the house as she opens the door. The cold steals the breath from his mouth; the sharpness from his brain. It takes him a second to react and take off after her, wrapped only in his sleeping blanket.

The snow outside is knee deep and she isn't wearing shoes. He scoops her up from a drift and drapes her across his shoulders. She doesn't resist.

"You idiot, don't you see I do it for you?" she wails in his ear over the wind. "Everyone knows you're such a good hunter that I have food to spare. My mother, the neighbors . . . As long as my pantry is full, nobody can question us or our marriage. Whenever those hags at the market start gossiping about how I should find a stronger Fighter, I give them meat, pelts. That shuts them up. They don't talk, at least not to my face."

Merthe pushes the door open and stomps his feet until he feels them. He doesn't know what to think, much less what to say. He puts Ita down and goes to fetch the liquor. More than half the bottle is missing. He stares pointedly at Ita.

"Don't look at me. I think Serga has started drinking behind my back." She sounds annoyed, but not terribly worried. Adolescents will be adolescents. It's hard to figure out one's body when one is so new to it, especially when one is neither a man nor a woman, but a compendium of impulses with no way to work them off. Merthe's lips twitch as he remembers his own childhood.

"There is no woman, Ita." He sits next to her by the hearth. "Samo and Elgir have broken up. I promised Elgir that her children wouldn't starve. I'm hunting for them for now, at least until Elgir finds a man. That shouldn't take long."

"Can't Samo hunt for them? He has a responsibility towards those children!"

"Samo isn't going to be hunting. Elgir can hunt small game by herself, but not with the children tagging along."

"Really? You must be exaggerating. I can't think of a man who'll visit his children and not bring something . . ."

"Samo isn't setting foot in Elgir's house."

"Well, that's just wrong! I can understand being angry, but keeping a man from his children—"

"You don't know the half of it!" Merthe sets the glass down and frowns: he hadn't intended to shout. "It's bad, Ita, it's really bad."

"Then tell me," she says. *You never tell me anything.* After so long, Merthe hears the words even when she doesn't utter them.

"Samo hits the kids." That gets her attention. He explains in as few words as he can, glad that she's finally decided to shut up and listen.

"Those poor kids. Those poor poor kids," she says.

Merthe tries to explain how angry he is at Elgir for letting it happen.

"You can't judge. You don't know what Elgir was going through at the time . . ."

"And you do?" Surely, this isn't about him!

"Of course not." She puts a cool hand on his forehead. Despite how angry he is, she soothes him. Ita and he work best together when they do not speak. He wonders why it can't always be like that. A life in silence. Sometimes, his reticence to speak is just that, a desire for this quiet companionship. It is only with words that they hate each other.

When his time to Fight comes, Merthe tells himself the outcome doesn't really matter. He tells himself the same lies he told Serga, trying to believe them with a child's fervor. He fastens his boots and sets out.

A crowd is waiting for him. As he approaches, Elgir joins him, arriving at the square from the left. They walk the last stretch together, Elgir's children trailing from her skirt.

"How are things going?" Merthe asks.

"I should be the one asking that!" Elgir laughs. "Are you afraid?"

"No." Surprisingly, it's the truth. He's too wound up to be scared. "Do you still believe what you said in the forest the other day? Do you still think it's such a good idea to swap bodies from time to time? Or has that precious woman's body changed your mind?"

Elgir laughs. "Oh, yes, I believe it. We are trapped inside these bodies. We've learned since childhood that women do this or that and we never dare to break free of that mold. We're as pitiful as the men and women down South, who only know one way of living, except that we don't have the excuse of ignorance. But hell, it does feel good to sniff my children with this nose again. I'll grant you that." She turns sharply and her children squeal and take off. Obviously, "smelling the children" is a game with them.

They turn into the square where a dozen men cheer when they see Merthe. Merthe turns around but she nods at him to go. She's got her arms full of toddler.

"Do your best." Her face looks pinched. Merthe realizes that if he wins, she will lose her hunter.

He salutes each of the four metallic pillars that mark the Fighting ground. They are made from the remnants of a ship that brought the People here from the sky. Or so the elders say. It seems impossible that people should sail through air. It is true, however, that bodies may only be exchanged within their embrace and only after Fight. Years ago, Merthe and Ita, like all newlyweds, spent some time trying to game the rules and learned that the only result was temporary impotence and a headache that lasted for hours.

On a whim, he jumps into the Fighting square and seeks out Ita before combat begins. He stares at the judge, dares him to object, and takes Ita to the side.

"Are you nervous?" he asks.

She looks at him suspiciously. He sighs, takes her hand and brings the palm to his lips. Her eyes lighten up.

"It's just a game, Ita."

"Maybe it is to you. That's why you always lose."

He lets go of her hand, turns to the crowd. People are coming from villages that he hasn't even been to. He wishes he could confide in Ita, but everything he says will be used against him.

"I'm worried about Elgir," he blurts. "Who will hunt for her when I'm a woman?"

Ita smiles. She thinks it's banter. "I think you'll be able to keep her in meat and gravy for a while yet."

"Really? You would not object?"

"Are you serious?"

It's no use. He heads towards his corner and starts preparing.

Roll of drums; the combatants step up to the judge. Merthe wonders whether he should try to imitate Elgir. Maybe he can just take Ita's hits and try to snatch an advantage when he sees it. Surely, it would be a lot less tiresome that fighting. He is so tired of fighting all the time.

But then he realizes that this is Fight, not just any fight. His verbal skills do not matter and since combatants must remain silent, Ita's wit cannot hurt him inside the ring. Suddenly, he feels protected by those four pillars. He has a good half hour of silence ahead of him, maybe an hour if he can make the fight last. He yearns for intimacy without the burden of words. And there is nothing more intimate than violence.

The drums are still and the crowd holds their breaths. Ita starts bouncing and jabbing, trying to circle around him and hit him when he blinks. She moves fast—al-ways a good strategy for a woman—and attempts to bring him down with repeated blows.

Her first hit catches him unawares and he staggers back. No, Elgir's strategy won't work. There is blood in his mouth. He's supposed to hold still, he knows. Maybe feint a bit, watch for patterns and fell her with one decisive blow. Those same muscles that lend force to his blows suck up his energy. Unlike Ita, he cannot jump around forever. He is supposed to preserve his strength, not to commit, strike only when he can win.

But he is so tired of doing what he's supposed to and maybe Elgir is right and we get caught up in patterns, live life within patterns, pushing ourselves beyond our limits because a man should lift that much, throw that far. And maybe, just maybe, Merthe realizes, we do the opposite and fall pitifully short because we've been told our bodies have less endurance that our wife's.

Merthe starts bouncing. His feet know the way. Women fight like they dance, his mother taught him, and he was always such a good dancer.

Ita's rhythm lets up in surprise and he jabs, but she ducks in time and starts bouncing again. He loves her technique and mirrors her as they spin round and round. Merthe is the ugly sibling, echoing heir elder's every move, struggling to copy what can only be born of natural grace.

Ita doesn't know how to hit a moving target. She hasn't fought with a mobile partner for a long time.

His breath is labored; she hardly breaks a sweat. She starts sweating; the pain in his chest won't let up. She pants and swerves; his vision clouds but he sees the gap in her defense and punches through.

She crashes down and he falls right after. For a second, he wonders if she's all right. He put himself in that blow, his loves, his wants, his strengths and weaknesses. He wonders if it was too much for her. But she groans and sits up, spits blood and, of all things, laughs.

"Well, you got me there."

"I'm sorry," he says.

"Oh no, you're not. You won."

He lies back, head spinning. Yes, he won.

His chest still hurts and he wonders how bad it is.

The bell rings. She crawls up against him, sets her palm against his and they're off into the limbo of joy. Her mind rises up to him. For a second, both of them are in his body and hers hangs, limp, behind. He creeps in, wondering if the beams still hold in this castle which he's left so long ago. Merthe draws a breath which is oh, so sweet. She smells the male sweat of Ita next to her.

But no. Two women need a hunter and a young androgen needs to learn that being a man isn't so bad. She pushes back into the old body. He regains control and shoves Ita into hers. She was so fond of her female form that it seems a pity to tear her from it. Plus, she made a terrible husband.

Ita tumbles away from him and he sees disbelief in her eyes.

"Really?"

"Really."

"You're leaving me! You're leaving with her!"

It takes a moment for him to understand what she's saying. But, of course, she cannot fathom why anyone would want to be a man. The only explanation that she will consider is that Merthe plans to start a new life with Elgir and that he needs a man's body for that.

"I'm not going with her." He doesn't say he's not leaving, though, because he's not quite sure what he'll do. He can support both women, but he doesn't have the strength for either. He needs time, alone, in silence. He knows just the place for that.

The judge walks up and hesitates before signaling the end of the transition. The elders squirm, then shrug their shoulders. Merthe has won: he may do as he likes. That night, there's scratching at the door of the shed. "Does your mother know you're here?" he asks a trembling Serga standing by the doorway. "No. I think. I don't think so, she was asleep." Merthe lets heir in, moves his quilts to a corner and places a stack of blankets next to the fire for heir to sleep in. Shei stomps heir feet all the way to bed, and Merthe stays awake until the shivering melts into regular breathing and only soft childish hairs peek out from beneath the covers. He'll wake heir before sunrise and make heir go back to bed inside the house. Ita mustn't know that shei's fled to him for comfort after their separation. Merthe may be too confused to know what he wants just yet, but he doesn't want to hurt Ita. Whether he can live with her or not is a different matter.

SYLGARMO'S PROCLAMATION

LUCIUS SHEPARD

From a second-story window of the Kampaw Inn, near the center of Kaspara Viatatus, Thiago Alves watched the rising of the sun, a habit to which many had become obsessively devoted in these, the last of the last days. A faltering pink ray initiated the event, probing the plum-colored sky above the Mountains of Magnatz; then a slice of crimson light, resembling the bloody fingernail of someone attempting to climb forth from a deep pit, found purchase in a rocky cleft. Finally the solar orb heaved aloft, appearing to settle between two peaks, shuddering and bulging and listing like a balloon half-filled with water, its hue dimming to a wan magenta.

Thiago grimaced to see such a pitiful display and turned his back on the window. He was a powerfully constructed man, his arms and chest and thighs strapped with muscle, yet he went with a light step and could move with startling agility. Though he presented a formidable (even a threatening) image, he had a kindly, forthright air that the less perceptive sometimes mistook for simple-mindedness. Salted with gray, his black hair came down in a peak over his forehead, receding sharply above the eyes—a family trait. Vanity had persuaded him to repair his cauliflower ears, but he had left the remainder of his features battered abd lumped by long years in the fighting cage. Heavy scar tissue thickened his orbital ridges, and his nose, broken several times during his career, had acquired the look of a peculiar root vegetable; children were prone to pull on it and giggle.

He dressed in leather trousers and a forest green singlet, and went downstairs and out onto the Avenue of Dynasties, passing beneath several of the vast monuments that spanned it; a side street led him through a gate in the city wall. Swifts made curving flights over the River Chaing and a tall two-master ran with the tide, heading for the estuary. He walked briskly along the riverbank, stopping now and again to do stretching exercises; once his aches and pains had been mastered by the glow of physical exertion, he turned back toward the gate. The city's eccentric spires—some capped by

cupolas of gold and onyx, with decorative finials atop them; others by turrets
of tinted glass patterned in swirls and stripes; and others yet by flames, mists,
and blurred dimensional disturbances, each signaling the primary attribute
of the magician who dwelled beneath—reduced the backdrop of lilac-colored
clouds to insignificance.

In the Green Star common room of the Kampaw, a lamplit, dust-hung
space all but empty at that early hour, with carved wainscoting, benches and
boards, and painted-over windows depicting scenes of golden days and merry-
making through which the weak sun barely penetrated, Thiago breakfasted
on griddlecakes and stridleberry conserve, and was contemplating an order
of fried glace[1] to fill in the crevices, when the door swung open and four men
in robes and intricately tiered caps crowded inside and hobbled toward his
table. Magicians, he assumed, judging by the distinctive ornaments affixed to
their headgear. Apart from their clothing, they were alike as beans, short and
stringy, with pale, round faces, somber expressions and close-cropped black
hair, varying in height no more than an inch or two. After an interval a fifth
man entered, closed the door and leaned against it, a maneuver that struck
Thiago as tactical and put him on the alert. This man differed from his fellows
in that he walked without a limp, moving with the supple vigor of youth, and
wore loose-fitting black trousers and a high-collared jacket; a rakish, wide-
brimmed hat, also black, shadowed his features.

"Have I the pleasure of addressing Thiago Alves?" asked one of the
magicians, a man whose eyes darted about with such an inconstancy of focus,
they appeared on the verge of leaping out of his head.

"I am he," Thiago said. "As to whether it will be a pleasure, much depends
on the intent of your youthful associate. Does he mean to block my means of
egress?"

"Certainly not!"

The magican made a shooing gesture and the youth stepped away from
the door. Thiago caught sight of several knives belted to his hip and remained
wary.

"I am Vasker," the magician said. "And this worthy on my left is
Disserl." He indicated a gentleman whose hands roamed restlessly over his
body, as if searching for his wallet. "Here is Archimbaust." Archimbaust
nodded, then busied himself with a furious scratching at his thigh. "And
here Pelasias." Pelasias emitted a humming noise that grew louder and
louder until, by dint of considerable head-shaking and dry-swallowing, he
managed to suppress it.

[1] A variety of mollusc valued for their succulent flesh. It was once proposed that glace
possessed a form of intelligence, this based on the fact that many who consumed
them raw reported experiencing poignant emotional states and hearing what seemed
to be pleas in an unknown tongue. For this reason, they are now served either fried
or broiled. As to the question of their sentience, their severely depleted population
prevents a comprehensive study.

"If we may sit," Vasker went on, "I believe we have a proposal that will profit you."

"Sit if you like," said Thiago. "I was preparing to order glace and perhaps a pot of mint tea. You have my ear for as long as it will take to consume them. But I am embarked upon a mission of some urgency and cannot listen to distractions, no matter how profitable."

"And would it distract you to learn . . . " Archimbaust paused in his delivery to scratch at his elbow. " . . . that our proposal involves your cousin. The very one for whom you are searching?"

"Cugel?" Thiago wiped his mouth. "What of him?"

"You seek him, do you not?" asked Disserl. "As do we."

"Yet we have an advantage," said Vasker. "We have divined his whereabouts." Thiago wiped his mouth with a napkin and glared at him. "Where is he?"

"Deep within the Great Erm. A village called Joko Anwar. We would travel there ourselves and secure him, but as you see we lack the physical resources for such a task. It requires a robust individual like yourself."

The young man made a sound—of disgust, thought Thiago—and looked away.

"It is possible to dispatch you to the vicinity of Joko Anwar within minutes," said Archimbaust. "Why risk a crossing of the Wild Waste and endure the discomfort and danger of a voyage across the Xardoon Sea?"

"Should you travel by conventional means, you may not achieve your goal," Disserl said. "If Sylgarmo's recent projections are correct, we might have as little as a handful of days before the sun quits the sky."

The wizards began debating the merits of Sylgarmo's Proclamation. Vasker adhered to the optimistic estimate of two and a half centuries, saying the implications of Sylgarmo's equations were that there would soon be a solar event of some significance, yet not necessarily a terminal one. Archimbaust challenged Sylgarmo's methods of divination, Disserl held to the pessimistic view, and Pelasias offered a vocabulary of dolorous hums and moans.

To silence them, Thiago banged on the table—this also had the effect of summoning the serving girl and, once he had given her his order, he asked the magicians why they sought Cugel.

"It is a complex issue and not easily distilled," said Vasker. "In brief, Iucounu the Laughing Magician stole certain of our limbs and organs. We set Cugel to retrieve them, armed with knowledge that would put an end to Iucounu for all time. Our limbs and organs were restored, but they were returned to us in less than perfect condition. Thus we limp and scratch and shake, and poor Pelasias is forced to communicate his dismay as might a sick hound."

It seemed to Thiago that Vasker had summarized the matter quite neatly. "And you blame Cugel? Why not Iucounu or one of his servants? Perhaps the manner in which the limbs and organs were stored is at fault. It may be that an impure concentrate was used. Your explanation does not ring true."

"You fail to comprehend the full scope of Cugel's iniquity. I can . . . "

"I know him as well as any man," said Thiago. "He is spiteful, greedy, and uses people without conscience or concern. Yet never has he acted without reason. You must have done him a grievous injury to warrant such vindictiveness."

Led by Pelasias' groaning commentary, the magicians vehemently protested this judgment. Archimbaust was eloquent in their defence. "Our last night together we toasted one another with Iucounu's wine and feasted on roast fowl from his pantry," he said. "We sang ribald tunes and exchanged amusing anecdotes. Indeed, Pelasias performed the Five Amiable Assertions, thus consecrating the moment and binding us to friendship."

"If that is the case, I would counsel you to think well before you dissemble further." The serving girl set down his tea and Thiago inhaled the pungent steam rising from the pot. "I have little tolerance for ordinary liars and none whatsoever for duplicitous magicians."

The four men withdrew to the doorway and talked agitatedly among themselves (Pelasias giving forth with plaintive whimpers). After listening for a minute or so, the young man hissed in apparent dissatisfaction. He doffed his hat, releasing a cloud of dark hair, and revealed himself to be a young woman with comely features: a pointy chin and lustrous dark eyes and cunning little mouth arranged in a sullen pout. She would have been beautiful, but her face was so etched with scars, she resembled a patchwork thing. The largest scar ran from the hinge of her jaw down her neck and was wider than the rest, looking as though the intent had been not to disfigure, but to kill. She came toward Thiago and spoke in an effortful hoarse whisper that he assumed to be a byproduct of that wound.

"They claim that while taking inventory of Iucounu's manse, Cugel happened upon a map made by the magician Pandelume, who dwells on a planet orbiting a distant star," she said. "The map marks the location of a tower. Within the tower are spells that will permit all who can master them to survive the sun's death."

"Cugel's behavior becomes comprehensible," said Thiago. "He wished to disable his pursuit."

The magicians hobbled over from the door. Vasker cast a sour glance at the young woman. "This, then, is our offer," he said to Thiago. "We will convey you and Derwe to a spot near Joko Anwar, the site of Pandelume's tower. There you wil . . . "

"Who is this Derwe?"

"Derwe Coreme of the House of Domber," the woman said. "I ruled in Cil until I ran afoul of your *cousin*." She gave the word a loathing emphasis.

"Was it Cugel who marked you so?"

"He did not wield the knives. That was the fancy of the Busacios, a race vile both in form and disposition who inhabit the Great Erm. Yet Cugel is responsible for my scars and more besides. In exchange for information, he handed me over to the Busacios as if I were a bag of tiffle."

"To continue," said Vasker in a peremptory tone. "Once there you will enter the tower and immobilize Cugel. He must be kept alive until we have questioned him. Do this and you will share in all we learn."

The serving girl brought the glace—Thiago inspected his plate with satisfaction.

"When we have done with him," Vasker went on, "you may extract whatever pleasure you can derive from his torment." He paused. "Can we consider the bargain sealed?"

"Sealed?" Thiago hitched his shoulders, generating a series of gratifying pops. "Our negotiation has just begun. Is that a spell sniffer I observe about Archimbaust's neck? And that amulet dangling from Disserl's hat, it is one that induces a sudden sleep, is it not? Such trinkets would prove invaluable on a journey such as you propose. Then there is the question of my fee. Sit, gentlemen. You may pick at my glace if you wish. Let us hope by the time the meal is done, you will have succeeded in satisfying my requirements."

The forest known as the Great Erm had the feeling and aspect of an immense cathedral in ruins. Enormous trees swept up into the darkness of the canopy like flying buttresses and from that ceiling depended masses of foliage that might have been shattered roof beams shrouded in tapestries ripped from the walls, the result of an ancient catyclysm. Occasionally Derwe Coreme and Thiago heard faint obsessive tappings and cries that could have issued from no human throat; once they saw an ungainly white shape drop from the canopy and flap off into the gloom, dwindling and dwindling, becoming a point of whiteness, seeming to vanish ultimately into a distance impossible to achieve in so dense a wood, as if it had burrowed into the substance of the real and was making its way toward a destination that lay beyond the borders of the world. The hummocky ground they trod broke into steep defiles and hollows, and every surface was sheathed in moss and lichen, transforming a tallish stump into an ogre's castle of orange and black, and a fallen trunk into a fairy bridge that bridged between a phosphorescent green boulder and a ferny embankment beneath which long-legged spiders with doorknob-sized bodies wove almost invisible webs wherein they trapped the irlyx, gray man-shaped creatures no bigger than a clothespin that struggled madly against the strands of silk and squeaked and thrust with tiny spears as the hairy abdomens of their captors, stingers extruded, lowered to strike.

It was Derwe who first sighted Pandelume's tower, a slender needle of yellowish stone showing the middle third of its height through a gap in the foliage. From atop a rise, they saw that beyond the tower, the land declined into a serpentine valley, barely a notch between hills, where several dozen huts with red conical roofs were situated on a bend in a river; beyond the valley, the Great Erm resumed. They hastened toward the tower, but their path was impeded by a deep gorge that had been hidden from their eyes by vegetation. They walked beside it for half-an-hour but found no spot sufficiently narrow to risk jumping across. The walls of the gorge were virtually concave and the bottom was lost in darkness, thus they had no hope of climbing down and then up the opposite side.

"Those fools have sent us here for nothing!" Derwe Coreme rasped.

"Patience finds a way," Thiago said. "Soon it will be dark. I suggest we camp by the stream we crossed some minutes ago and wait out the night."

"Are you aware what night brings in the Great Erm? Bargebeetles. Gids and thyremes. Monstrosities of every stamp. A Deodand has been trailing us for the past hour. Do you wish to share your blanket with him?"

"Where is he? Point him out!"

She gazed at him quizzically. "He stands there, in back of the oak with the barren lower limb."

Thiago strode directly toward the oak.

Not having anticipated so bold an approach, the Deodand, upon seeing Thiago, took a backward step, his silver eyes widening with surprise. His handsome black devil's face gaped, exposing an inch more of the fangs that protruded from the corners of his mouth. Thiago gave him a two-handed push, adding to his momentum, and sent him sprawling. He caught one of his legs, stepped over it, dropped to his back and, holding the foot to his belly, he braced against the creature's body and rolled, wrenching the knee from its socket and—though the flesh felt like petrified wood—fracturing the ankle. The Deodand emitted a throaty scream and screamed again as Thiago stood and drove a heel into his other knee. He repeated the action and heard a crack. Unable to stand, the Deodand crawled after him, his breath hissing. Thiago nimbly eluded his grasp and snapped the elbow joints with deft heel-stomps. He kicked him in the head, to no visible affect. However, he kept on kicking and at last a silver eye burst, cracks spreading across it as they might in a sheet of ice, and fluid spilled forth.

The Deodand thrashed about, keening in frustration.

"How can this be? That you, a human, could have bested me?"

He spoke no more, for Derwe Coreme kneeled at his side and pricked his throat with a thin-bladed knife, causing him to gag, whereupon she sliced off his carmine tongue and stuffed it into his mouth. Within seconds, he had drowned, choking on the blood pouring into his throat.

"I could have dealt with the Deodand," Derwe Coreme said as they retraced their steps toward the stream. "And with far greater efficiency."

Thiago made an impertinent sound with his tongue. "Yet you gave no sign of doing so."

"An auspicious moment had not offered itself."

"Nor would it have until the Deodand pounced."

She stopped walking and her hand went to the hilt of a hunting knife. "You fight well, but your style is not one that will allow you to survive long in the Great Erm. I, on the other hand, survived here for three years."

"Under the protection of the Busacios."

Her hand tightened on the hilt. "Not so. I escaped after eight months. The remainder of those years I spent hunting Busacios." She shifted her stance the slightest bit, easing back her left foot and resting her full weight upon it. "Do you know why Vasker hired you? They expect you to control me. They are afraid I will be so inflamed by the sight of Cugel, I may not be able to restrain myself from killing him and all the knowledge that can save them will go glimmering."

"Are they correct in that assumption?"

"Only in that I will not be controlled." With her left hand, she brushed a stray hair from her eyes, carefully laying it in place behind her ear. "It is impossible to discern the depths of one's own heart. My reaction to meeting Cugel again is thus unknowable. If you intend to thwart me, however, perhaps now would be the time."

Thiago felt the push of her anger; her pulse seemed to fill the air. "I will await a more auspicious moment."

He began walking again and after a second or two she ran to catch up.

"What are your intentions toward Cugel?" she asked. "I must be the one to kill him."

"A seer of peerless reputation in Kaiin has assured me that Cugel will not die by my hand, but by his own."

"He said that? Then he is a fool. Cugel would never take his own life! He defends it as a pig his last truffle."

Thiago shrugged. "The seer is not often wrong."

A frown notched Derwe Coreme's brow. "Of course, if I were to force suicide upon him, if I were to torture him and then offer a choice of more pain, unbearable pain, or the use of one of my knives to end his suffering . . . That would be delicious, would it not? To watch him slice into his body, seeking the source of his life's blood, his hands trembling, almost too weak to make the final cut?"

"It would serve a purpose," said Thiago.

She went with her head down for a few paces and then said, "Yes, the longer I think about it, the more certain I become of your seer's acumen."

At twilight Thiago built a fire that illumined a ragged clearing some fifteen yards in diameter. The stream cut through the edge of the lighted area and, after staring at it yearningly for several minutes, Derwe Coreme stood and removed her jacket.

"I intend to bathe while the warmth of day still lingers," she said. "There are scars on my body as well as my face, but if the urge to see me at my bath persists, I cannot prevent you from watching. I would caution you, however, against acting upon whatever attendant urges may spring to mind. My knives are never far from hand."

Thiago, who was eating parched corn and dried apples, grunted to signal his indifference. Yet though he determined not to watch, he could not resist. At that distance the scars resembled tattoos. Kneeling in the stream, the water running about her waist, she was lovely and clean-limbed, an image from legend, the nymph unmindful of a spying ogre, and he wondered at the alchemy that had transformed her into such a hate-filled creature . . . though he had witnessed such a human result on many previous occasions. Cupping her hand, she sluiced water across her shoulders. He imagined that a woman's back must be the purest shape in all the world.

Darkness fell. She stepped from the stream, dried herself, probing him with glances as though to know his mind, and then, wrapping herself in a blanket, came to sit by the fire. He maintained a stoic reserve and thought to detect irritation in her manner, as if she were annoyed by his lack of reaction to her nudity. Her scars were livid from the cold water, but now he saw them as designs and irrelevant to her beauty. The fire spoke in a language of snaps and crackles, and a night thing quarreled with itself, its ornate chortling echoing above a backdrop of lesser hoots and trills. She asked why he had chosen fighting as a profession.

"I liked to fight," he said. "I like it still. In Kaiin there is always a call for fighters to fill Shins Stadium. I did not enjoy hurting my opponents as much as some of the others. Not in the beginning, anyway. Later . . . perhaps I did. I became First Champion of Kaiin for six years."

"Did something happen?" she asked. "To make you better or more fierce?"

"Cugel."

She waited for him to go on.

"It's an old story." He spat into the fire. "A woman was at issue."

When he did not elaborate, she asked why he had waited so long to even the score.

"I lost sight of the matter," he said. "There were other women. I had money and a large house and friends with which to fill it. Then Sylgarmo's Proclamation alerted me to the fact that time was growing short. I began to miss the woman again and I recalled the debt I owed my cousin."

They were silent a while, each absorbed in their own thoughts. Something stirred in the bushes; then a feral outcry, the leaves and branches shook violently; then all was quiet. Derwe Coreme shifted closer to Thiago, reached out tentatively and touched the tip of her finger to a scar that transected his eyebrow, turning a portion of it gray.

"Mine are deeper, but you have more scars than I," she said wonderingly.

She seemed animated by something other than her usual sullen fury. Her hand lingered near his cheek and in the unsteady light of the fire her expression was open and expectant; but she snatched back her hand and, like an old sun restored for an instant to youthful radiance, its burst of energy spent, she lapsed once again into a funereal glow.

Thiago's imagination peopled the avenues among the trees with sinister ebony figures whose eyes were the color of fire. Dark spotches the size of a water-shadow filtered down through the canopy. He blinked them away and fought off fatigue. Some time later Derwe Coreme shook him awake. He was dazed, mortified, sputtering apologies for having fallen asleep.

"Keep quiet!" she said.

He continued to apologize and she flicked her hand at his cheek, not quite a slap, and said, "Listen!"

A sound came from the direction of the gorge. He thought initially it was that of a large beast munching greenery, smacking its lips and making pleased rumbles between bites; but as it grew louder and more distinct, he decided this impression had been counterfeited by many voices speaking at once. It grew more distinct yet and he became less certain of its nature.

The gorge brimmed with a night mist. Three pale lights, halated by the mist, rode atop an immense shape that moved ponderously, sluggishly, surging forward one plodding step after another, as though mired in mud. Peering into the murk, Thiago heard laughter and chatter, such as might be uttered by a great assemblage; then a piercing whistle came to his ears. The beast rumbled in apparent distress and flung up its head so that it surfaced from the mist. The sight of its coppery sphinx-like face, bland and empty of all human emotion, struck terror into his heart. A gid![2] Beside him, Derwe Coreme let out a shriek. The gid halted its progress, its cavernous bleak eyes fixed on the thicket where they were hiding. Its nose, the merest bump perforated by two gaping nostrils, lent it a vaguely amphibian aspect, and the lights (globes affixed to its temples and forehead) added a touch of the surreal. Mist obscured its wings and sloping, muscular body.

"Show yourselves!" a booming voice sang out. "It is I, Melorious, who speaks! I offer safe passage through the Great Erm."

This pronouncement stilled the babble of voices, but soon they returned, directing merry insults and impudent remarks toward Melorious. The gid surged forward and again lifted its head, trying to wedge it through the break in the earth, but failed in the attempt—it was too wide by half. Thiago was now

---

[2] The gid is a hybrid of man, gargoyle, whorl, and leaping insect. In their "newt" stage they are relatively harmless, yet they inspire an atavistic fear. Once they have tasted human blood a metamorphosis occurs within minutes and they acquire mental powers that permit them to dominate lesser minds with ease. The physical changes are, reputedly, also extreme, but this is unproven, since a mere handful of men and women have survived the sight of an adult gid and none have capable of reporting coherently on the particulars. The "newt" gid is copper in color, with black facial markings. As to the adult's coloration, we have only the word of Cotuim Justo, blind since birth, who claimed that the beast's colors "burned my eyes."

situated directly above the gid's back and through the mist he saw what looked to be steel panniers strapped to its side. The panniers were each divided into four segments and each segment served as a cage in which forty or fifty men and women were kept. Thiago estimated there were several hundred people so encaged, yet none exhibited the attitude of captives, but rather acted like the passengers on a pleasure barge. Amorous couples lay intertwined on the floor. In another of the panniers, a band consisting of lutes, quintajells and nose-trumpets began tuning their instruments.

"You need not fear the gid," boomed Melorious. "I have bound it with a potent spell that renders it as docile as a pet thrail. Travel the Great Erm in complete security! Enjoy the companonship of beautiful women lacking all moral rectitude! Come away to Cil and Saskervoy . . . with first a stop at my subterranean palace for a feast to end all feasts."

The gid rumbled again, attempting to push the top of its head up through the gorge; a piercing whistle caused it to cease. Thiago perceived an opportunity. He sketched out his scheme with whispers and hand signals. Derwe Coreme looked at him aghast, shook her head vigorously, and shaped the word, no, with her mouth.

"Conscience will not permit me to leave you to the perils of the forest." A bald, honey-colored man clad in a jacket and trousers of dark blue silk worked with gilt designs, ostensibly Melorious, appeared on the gid's neck, tethered by a line; he spoke into a small hand-held device. Several other figures, untethered, cowered at his side, clinging to folds of the skin. "Make yourself known at once or I will have to send my minions after you. Wood gaunts and Deodands, beware! The flesh of my men bears a fatal taint that causes demon mites to breed in the belly of whatever consumes it."

Thiago burst from the thicket, half-dragging Derwe Coreme. She resisted, but upon realizing there was no going back, she outsped him to the edge and leaped, landing atop the gid's head, now a few feet beneath the lip of the gorge, and sprinted across his brow for the opposite side. Thiago also leaped, but did not land where he had intended. The gid, alarmed by Derwe's impact, trying to learn what had struck it, tipped its face to the sky, and Thiago came down feet-first near the center of its left eye. He expected to penetrate the membrane, to drown in the humor, but instead he slid along the clammy surface of the eye, fighting for purchase. The gid roared in anguish and tossed its head violently, sending Thiago hurtling through the air and crashing into a ragthorn bush. Screams from the men and women in the panniers stabbed at the air, but he could scarcely distinguish them from the ringing in his ears. Stunned, not knowing where he was, he peeked out and discovered that the ragthorn bush overhung the gorge. A little honey-colored bug in dark blue silks, Melorious dangled from his tether, hanging in front of the gid's vast, empty face. As Thiago looked on, he managed to set himself aswing by kicking at the gid's monstrous cheek, but every swing carried him back to the creature, nearer its unsmiling mouth. He had lost the hand-held device and thus his voice (and his whistles) went unheard. It seemed to Thiago that the gid stared at Melorious with a certain melancholy, as though it realized its youth was about to end and was made reluctant by the idea, by the grisly requirements demanded by this rite of passage. Melorious bumped against the creature's nose and, as he swung out wide again, the gid extended its neck and lazily snapped him up.

Ignoring his hurts, Thiago scrambled to his feet and ran, beating aside branches, tripping over roots, half-falling, intent on putting distance between himself and the gid. Behind him, the creature roared and, though no less loud, it seemed a narrower throat had shaped it—a snarly, grating sound with an odd buzzing quality. There was no sign of Derwe Coreme. He tried to recall if he had seen her clamber up onto the far side (this side) of the gorge, but without success. His lungs began to labor and, after a passage of seconds, he threw himself down under the snakelike roots of a mandouar and burrowed furiously until he was covered with black dirt. A minute or so later he felt a discharge of heat as if something on fire had passed close overhead. He put his head down and lay still for quite some time. When at length he sat up, he kept watch on the sky, picking thorns from his flesh, ill at ease and alert for the slightest sound.

A torrential shower dowsed the first of daylight, a pulsating redness in the east, and thereafter the overcast held. Wind herded black and silver clouds across the sky, accompanied by fitful thunder. Thiago felt around for his pack. It was gone, along with their supply of food and the various runes and devices he had coerced Vasker into giving him. The tower's summit was visible above a high hill and as he went toward it the rain started up again, blowing sideways into his face, drenching him to the bone. Just below the crest of the hill stood the ruins of a shrine. Its stone porch was more or less intact and beneath it a figure dressed in black sat cross-legged beside a crackling fire. Derwe Coreme. The carcass of small animal, its bones picked clean, lay beside her. She looked at him incuriously and licked grease from her fingers.

He sat facing her, miserable as mud. A thorn he had been unable to dig out of his back gave him a fresh jab. "Do you have anything to eat?" he asked.

"Where is your pack? Is our food then at the bottom of the gorge." She gave a rueful sigh, dug into a pocket and handed him a cloth in which a few edible roots and nuts were wrapped.

The roots yielded a bitter juice and, as he gnawed on one, he experienced a sharp pain in his jaw.

She watched him probe the inside of his gum with a forefinger and said, "When we met in Kaspara Viatatus, I worried that you were much like Cugel. The manner in which you dealt with Vasker and the rest reminded me of him. After you crippled the Deodand, I understood you were nothing like Cugel. He does not have your courage and, though your fighting style is not optimal, it reflects a directness of personality. A type of honesty, I thought. Now, having seen you destroy hundreds of lives by means of a foolhardy act, I wonder if what I assumed to be honesty was simply brute stupidity. And I ask myself, is moral incompetence any different from outright iniquity? The result is the same. Innocents die."

"Are you so naïve that you believe Melorious had a festive weekend planned for those in his cages? His spells had bedizened them—they were dead already. Or perhaps it is for Melorious you grieve?"

She seemed about to speak, but bit back the words. Finally she said, "You forced me to jump into the gorge and race across the forehead of a gid. Does this not, in retrospect, seem ill-considered?"

"Risky, yes. But we have reached our objective, so it can hardly be countenanced ill-considered."

" 'Patience finds a way', you said. I suppose this is exemplary of the quality of your patience?"

"One must recognize when the time for patience has passed. I made a decision."

She brushed dirt from her trousers. "Kindly consult me in detail as to all your future decisions."

The sky cleared by mid-morning and the sun struck shifting black crescents of shadow from the field of boulders that lay beneath the tower; but the tower itself cast no shadow, a fact that gave Thiago pause, as did the presence of a pelgrane that flapped up from the summit and briefly circled above them before returning to her perch. A female and, judging by her clumsy and erratic flight, gravid—a condition that would render her especially vicious and unpredictable. None of this had a discernable effect upon Derwe Coreme, whose eagerness increased with every step. As they drew near, she could no longer contain her enthusiasm and broke into a trot. By the time Thiago reached the base of the tower, however, she was the picture of dismay, darting about, sliding her hands along the walls and making noises of frustration.

"There's no door!" she said. "Nothing. There's nothing!"

The tower was a seamless flow of stone, a single unbroken piece more than a hundred feet high, evolving at its top into a bulbous shape—this had been cut into an intricate filigree pattern of windows that would allow someone inside to scan the area below without revealing themselves. Leaving Derwe Coreme to vent her anger, Thiago began a circumnavigation of the base, testing each slight declivity and projection in hopes that pressing upon one of them would cause a hidden door to open. After an hour or thereabouts, his circuit less than a third complete, he heard bellicose voices coming from the opposite side of the tower, Derwe Coreme's hoarse outcries loudest of all. She had struck a defensive pose, knives in both her hands, and was fending off five men who encircled her. A sixth lay upon the ground, bleeding from slashes on his arm and chest. On seeing Thiago, the men fell back and their menacing talk subsided. They were a motley group, ranging in age from a mere lad to an elderly, weather-beaten individual with a conical red hat, identical to the roofs of the village below, jammed low onto his brow so that wisps of gray hair stuck out beneath it like bent wires. They were armed with rakes and clad in coarse white garments that were belted about their waists with green sashes. Lead amulets bearing the image of a crude anthropomorphic figure hung from their necks.

"Ho! What's this?" Thiago gestured with his fist and this served to drive the men farther from Derwe Coreme. "Explain yourselves at once."

The elderly man was pushed to the fore. "I am Ido, the spiritual chargeman of Joko Anwar. We sought only to inquire of the woman in the name of Yando and she rasped at us in a demon's voice and attacked. Poor Stellig has suffered a dreadful wound."

"Lies! They laid hands on me!" Derwe Coreme surged toward the men and Thiago side-stepped to block her way.

"Enlighten me as to the nature of this Yando," he said.

"He is the god of Joko Anwar," Ido said. "Indeed, it is said he is the god of all forlorn places."

"By whom is this said?"

"Why, by Yando himself."

A portly man with a patchy beard whispered in his ear and Ido said, "To clarify. Yando often appears as a man of burning silver and in this guise he does not speak. But of late he sends his avatar, who confides in us Yando's truth."

Derwe Coreme, who had relaxed from her defensive posture, laughed derisively and started to speak, but Thiago intervened.

"Lately, you say? Did the appearance of the avatar predate Sylgarmo's Proclamation?"

"On the contrary," said Ido. "It was not long after the Proclamation that Yando sent him to instruct us so we might be saved by the instrumentality of his disciple, Pandelume."

Thiago gave the matter a turn or two. "This avatar . . . does he bear some resemblance to me? Does, for instance, his hair come down in peak over his forehead? Like so?"

Ido examined Thiago's hair. "There is a passing similarity, but the avatar's hair is black and of a supreme gloss."

Derwe Coreme hissed a curse. Thiago laid a hand on her arm. "What form did the avatar's instruction take?"

All the men whispered together and after they had done, Ido said, "Am I to understand that you wish to undergo purification?"

Thiago hesitated, and Derwe Coreme sprang forward, putting her knife to Ido's throat.

"We wish access to the tower," she said.

"Sacrilege!" cried the portly man. "The Red Hat is assaulted! Alert the village!"

Two men ran back toward the village, giving shouts of alarm. Derwe Coreme pressed on the blade and blood trickled from its edge.

"Grant us immediate access," she said. "Or die."

Ido closed his eyes. "Only through purification can one gain entrance to the tower and the salvation that lies beyond."

Derwe Coreme might have sliced him open then and there, but Thiago caught her wrist and squeezed, forcing her to relinquish the knife. Ido stumbled away, rubbing his neck.

Thiago sought to pacify Ido and the portly man, but they refused to listen to his entreaties—they huddled together, lips moving silently, offering ornate gestures of unknown significance to the heavens. At length, giving up on reason, he asked Derwe Coreme, "Can you persuade them to instruct us in the rite of purification?" She had retrieved her knife and was testing the edge with her thumb, contemplating him with a brooding stare.

Well," he said. "Can you do so? Preferably without a fatality? I would consider it a personal favor if we could avoid a pitched battle with the villagers."

She walked over to Ido and held up the blade stained with his blood to his eyes. He loosed a pitiable wail and clutched the portly man more tightly.

"Without interference, I can work wonders," she said.

At darkest dusk, Derwe Coreme and Thiago stood alone and shivering in the boulder-strewn field beneath the tower. They wore a twin harness of wood and withe that culminated in a great loop above their heads—this, Ido explained, would allow Yando's winged servant to lift them on high and bring them to salvation. Except for a kind of diaper, designed so as to prevent the harness from cutting into their skin, they were naked and their bodies were festooned with painted symbols, the purpose of which had also been explained in excruciating detail.

Though no more risible than the tenets of other religions, the rites and doctrines of Yando as dictated by the avatar revealed the workings of a dry, sardonic wit. Thiago had no doubt they were his cousin's creation.

"Consider the green blotch currently being applied," Ido had said. "By no means is its placement arbitrary. When Yando was summoned from the Uncreate to protect us, he woke to discover that he had inadvertently crushed a litter of copiropith whelps beneath his left thigh. The blotch replicates the stain left by those gentle creatures.[3]"

---

[3] It is something of a euphemism to describe the behavior of the copiropith whelp or imp (the term more commonly used) as "gentle." After devouring their mother and a majority of their siblings, the litter typically invade the nasal cavities of humans and attach themselves to certain nodes of the nervous system, provoking the victim to grin broadly and to hop and caper about in dervish fashion, all while experiencing terrible pain that results, after some weeks, in death. As adults, however, the whelps acquire an affectionate personality, soft, bluish gray fur, and a pleasing, cuddlesome look. In this form they are greatly prized as pets and believed by some (particularly residents of the Cloudy Isles) to house the souls of the men and women they have killed, and thus are treated as family members.

A last blush of purple faded from the sky. Thiago could barely make out Derwe Coreme beside him, hugging herself against the chill. He cleared his throat and launched into a hymn of praise to Yando, stopping when he noticed that Derwe Coreme remained silent.

"Come," he said. "We must sing."

"No, I will not," she said sullenly.

"The winged servant may not appear."

"If by 'winged servant' you refer to the pelgrane, hunger will bring her to us. I refuse to play the fool for Cugel."

"In the first place, that the pelgrane and the winged servant are one is merely my hypothesis. Granted, it seems the most likely possibility, but the winged servant may prove to be another agency, one with a discriminating ear. Secondly, if the pelgrane is the winged servant and notices that we are less than enthusiastic in our obedience to ritual, this may arouse its suspicions and cause it to deviate from its routine. I feel such a deviation would not be in interests."

Derwe Coreme was silent.

"Do you agree?" Thiago asked.

"I agree," she said grudgingly.

"Very well. On the count of three, may I suggest you join me in rendering with brio, "At Yando's Whim, So We Ascend In Gladness'."

They had just begun the second chorus when the oily reek of a pelgrane filled Thiago's nostrils. Great wings buffeted the air and they were dragged aloft. The harness swayed like a drunken bell, making it difficult to sustain the vocal, yet they persevered even when the pelgrane spoke.

"Ah, my lunchkins!" it said merrily. "Soon one of you will rest in my belly. But who, who, who shall it be?"

Thiago sang with greater fervor. The pelgrane's egg sac, a vague white shape, depended from its globular abdomen. He pointed this out to Derwe Coreme and she reached into her diaper. He shook his head violently and added urgency to his delivery of the words "not yet" in the line, " . . . though not yet do we glimpse the heights . . . " Scowling, she withdrew her hand.

A pale nimbus of light bulged from the sloping summit of the tower. As they were about to land, Derwe Coreme unhitched herself from the harness. She clung to the loop by one hand, slashed open the sac with the knife that had been hidden in herd diaper, and spilled the eggs into the dark below, drawing an agonized shriek from the pelgrane. Thiago also unhitched. The moment his feet touched stone, he made a leap, grabbed a wing strut and sawed at it with one of Derwe Coreme's knives. With a wing nearly severed from its body, the pelgrane lost its balance, toppled onto its side and slid toward the abyss, gnashing its tusks and tossing its great stag-beetle head in pain. It hung at the edge, frantically beating its good wing and clawing at the stone.

Breathing heavily, Thiago sat down amongst the bones that littered the summit and watched it struggle. "Why only one of us?" he asked.

The pelgrane continued to struggle.

"You are doomed," Thiago said. "Your arms will not long support your weight and you will fall. Why not answer my question? You said that soon one of us would be in your belly? Why just one?"

The pelgrane achieved an uneasy equilibrium, a claw hooked on an imperfection in the stone. "He only wanted the women. The men provided me with sustenance."

"By 'he', do you mean Cugel?"

Drool fettered the pelgrane's tusks. "My time was near and it was onerous for me to hunt. I struck a bargain with the devil!"

"Was it Cugel? Tell me!"

The pelgrane glared at him, loosed its hold on the edge and slipped away into the darkness without a sound.

At the apex of the summit, pale light that emanated from no apparent source spilled from a shaft enclosing a spiral staircase. With her prey close at hand, Derwe Coreme lost all regard for modesty. She ripped off the diaper and, a knife in each hand, began her descent. Thiago's diaper caught on the railing and he, too, rid himself of the garment.

The shaft opened onto a circular room into whose walls the windows Thiago had seen from the ground were cut. It was absent all furnishings and lit by the same pale sourceless light. A second stairway led down to an even larger room, pentagonal in shape, its gray marble walls resplendent with intricate volutes and a fantastic bestiary carved in bas relief. The air retained a faint sourness, as of dried sweat. Cut into the floor, also of gray marble, was a complicated abstract design. Five curving corridors angled off from the room, receding to a depth Thiago would have believed impossible, given the dimensions of the tower; but this, he reminded himself, was a magician's tower that cast no shadow and likely was governed by laws other than those to which he was accustomed.

They went cautiously along the first of the corridors, passing a number of doors, all locked, and came at last to a door at the corridor's end that stood open and admitted to a room, a laboratory of sorts. Derwe Coreme made to enter, but Thiago barred her way with his arm.

"Look first," he said.

She frowned, yet raised no objection.

Many-colored light penetrated the room from panels in a domed ceiling, shifting from dull orange to peach to lavender. Volumes of obvious antiquity lined the walls. Upon a long table, vials bubbled over low flames and the components of a mysterious device, a puzzle of glittering steel and crystal, lay scattered about. An immense bell jar contained dark objects suspended in what looked to be a red fluid. Several more such jars held items that Thiago could not identify, a few of which appeared to be moving. Then the scene changed. Their view was still of the same room, yet they were considerably closer to the table. The objects submerged in red fluid were fragments of a sunken ship. Gray creatures with sucker mouths, elongated hands and paddle feet crawled over the wreck, as if searching for something. Another jar enclosed a miniature city with a strange geometric uniformity to its architecture whose two tallest towers were aflame. Beneath the largest glass bell, a herd of four-legged beasts with flowing blond hair and womanly breasts fled across a mossy plain, pursued by an army of trees (or a single multi-trunked tree) that extended root-like tentacles to haul itself along.

Unsettled, Thiago and Derwe Coreme returned to the room of gray marble and entered a second corridor, passing along it until they reached a door at its nether end. Through it they saw a valley of golden grasses lorded over by hills with promontories of corroded-looking black rock that might have been the ruins of colossal statuary rendered unrecognizable by time. They could discern no signs of life, no movement whatsoever. The absence of all kinetic value bred a sense of foreboding in Thiago. At the end of a third corridor they stood overlooking a vista that could have been part of the Sousanese Coast south of Val Ombrio: a high reddish sun, barren hills, a stretch of forest, and then a lowland declining to water that glowed a rich pthalocyanine blue. All seemed normal until a flight of winged serpents the size of barges soared low along the coast and in the eye of one that flew straight at the door, veering aside at the last second, Thiago glimpsed their terrified reflection.

They had quit trying the doors, but as they retreated toward the marble room, Thiago idly turned a doorknob and thought to hear a gasp issue from the other side.

"Who's there?" Thiago gave the door a shake.

He received no answer. Again he rattled the door and said, "We have come to free you. Let me in!"

After an interval, a woman's voice cried out, "Please help us! We have no key."

Derwe Coreme pressed on; when Thiago called to her, she said, "Whoever she is, she can wait. I have two more corridors to inspect."

Before he could speak further, she passed beyond the bend in the corridor. He felt diminished by her absence and this both surprised and iritated him.

He examined the hinges of the door. The bolts were flush to the metal and he did not think he could loosen them with a knife. He set his shoulder to the planking and gave it a test blow. Solid. The corridor, however, was narrow enough that he could brace his back against the opposite wall and put all his strength into a kick. He did so and felt the lock give way the slightest bit. The sound of the kick was startlingly loud, but he drove his foot into the lock again and again until the wood splintered. A few more blows and the door swung open. Two beautiful dark-haired women attired in gauzy costumes that left little to the imagination stood gaping at him in the center of a room furnished with a bed, an armoire, and a mirror. In reflex, Thiago covered himself as best he could.

The younger of the women, scarcely more than a girl, prostrated herself.

The older woman regarded him with a mix of hauteur and suspicion; then she stepped forward, standing almost eye-to-eye. She had the well-tended look and fine bone structure of the patrician women with whom he had consorted in Kaiin. Her hair was bound with an ivory and emerald clip. He could not picture her ladling dumplings onto a farmer's plate in Joko Anwar.

"Who are you?" she asked in a firm voice.

"Thiago Alves of Kaiin."

"My name is Diletta Orday. I was traveling in . . . "

"We have no time to exchange personal histories. Is there somewhere you can hide? I cannot fight and watch over you both."

Diletta's eyes darted to the side. "There is no hiding place for us so long as the avatar lives."

The girl on the floor moaned and Diletta said in a challenging tone, "Ruskana believes you will rape us."

"That is not my intent." He cast about in the corners of the room. "There were more of you, were there not?"

"We were nineteen in all. The avatar led seventeen along the corridors. None returned. He claims they are with Yando."

Cugel, Thiago told himself, must have been testing the open doorways, sending the women through and observing what happened. Chances were, he had not liked the results.

"He is no avatar," Thiago said.

"I am not a fool. I know what he is." She pointed to the armoire and said archly, "If your intent is to fight, you may need your hands. His clothes are there. Perhaps something will fit."

Within the armoire was an assortment of men's clothing. The shirts fit too snugly, hampering his freedom of movement; but he found a pair of trousers that he could squeeze into.

"Can you tell me where he is?" he asked.

"Oh, you will see him shortly."

As he turned, made curious by the lilt in her voice, he felt a sharp sting in his neck and saw Diletta pulling back from him, wearing a look of triumph. He staggered and, suddenly dizzy, went to one knee. Something struck him in the back and he toppled on his side. A second strike rolled him onto his back. The girl, Ruskana, was engaged in kicking him, grinning like a madwoman. He tried to focus on Diletta, but his vision clouded. Her voice echoed and faded, losing all hint of meaning and tone, becoming an ambient effect, and the kicks, too, became a kind of effect, no longer causing pain, each one seeming to drive him farther from the world.

Voices, too, ushered Thiago back to consciousness. A woman's voice complaining . . . Ruskana? Another woman, lower-pitched, asking what she should do. Diletta. Then a familiar man's voice that brought Thiago fully awake. He lay on his back, his hands bound beneath him, and began to work at loosening his bonds even before he opened his eyes.

"There must have been a woman with him," said Cugel from a distance. "The pelgrane would not have flown him to the summit, otherwise."

"Hunger may have overwhelmed its sense of duty," said Ruskana.

"I attribute no sense of duty to the pelgrane," said Cugel peevishly. "I suggest that if Thiago had come alone to the field, it would have gained nothing by flying to the summit. It would have eaten him where he stood."

"We have searched most of the night," Diletta said. "If a woman *was* here, she is not here now. Perhaps she took refuge at the end of one of the corridors. If that is the case, we have no need to worry."

Thiago could not make out Cugel's response. He slitted his eyes and saw he was lying in a small featureless room with gray marble walls close beside a bluish metal egg some fifteen feet high and ten feet wide, supported by six struts. Beyond lay a stair on the bottom step of which Ruskana stood. It led upward to a ceiling of gray marble. Thiago assumed there was a concealed exit and this would open onto the room with the five branching corridors. He redoubled his efforts at loosening his bonds.

"Is it ready?" Diletta asked, moving into view.

"I must refer to Iucounu's notes. Minor adjustments may be required."

Cugel came out from behind the egg. He wore a high-collared black cape, gray trousers, and a velvet tunic of striped mauve and black. On his right thumb was a ring of black stone. His sharp features seemed a perversion of Thiago's own. What had once manifested as a roguish quality, the product of a quick wit and a penchant for irreverence, seemed to have been eroded by the years, resolving into an imprint of cruelty and capriciousness. The sight of him captivated Thiago. It was as if his view of the world had lacked only this lean figure to complete it. Now, seeing him in the flesh, his loathing for Cugel was given such weight and substance that he understood what he had felt before was a shadow of his true hatred of the man. He was so overwhelmed with revulsion that he could not even make a pretense of being unconscious; he stared at his cousin like a hawk watching supper emerge from a hole until Cugel directed a cursory glance his way.

"Cousin!" A smile sliced Cugel's features, but did not touch his eyes. "I would not have recognized you if you hadn't declared yourself to Diletta. You've grown so formidable. You have been exercising, have you not? All those scars, so much gray in your hair! I trust life has not treated you unkindly."

Thiago was unable to muster speech.

"What has led you to seek me out after all these years?" Cugel asked. "A desire to rekindle our childhood bond? Judging by your expression, I think not. An old enmity, perhaps. But what? I cannot recall ever having done you injury. Certainly none to warrant so desperate a journey as you must have made."

Thiago managed to croak a single word: "Ciel."

Cugel squatted beside him, tipped his head to one side. "Ciel? It has a ring, I admit, but . . . " He smacked his forehead. "Not that blond poppet you were smitten with during our formative years? A sweet bite of the apple, that one. By now, she must be a grandmother. Is she well?"

"You know she is not." Thiago worked at his bonds.

"Ah, yes. I remember. A pity you weren't there to save her, but you had your priorities in those days, always busy at your brutish sport and your revels. Blaming me for Ciel's death . . . you would do as well to blame a bee for sipping from a flower."

Thiago tried to sweep his legs out from beneath him with a kick, but Cugel, agile as ever, avoided it and caught his ankle. He dragged him forward and left him in front of the machine.

"I have better to do than listen to you whine about a girl dead a quarter of a century." Cugel flung open a transparent door in the face of the machine and indicated the ovoid chamber within—it contained two padded seats. "In moments, we will be away to a pleasant world far from this moribund planet and its dead sun."

"Sylgarmo's Proclamation has yet to be proven," Thiago said.

"Has it now?"

Smirking, Cugel went to the wall and pressed an indentation. With a grating noise, a portion of the wall retracted, creating as it did a large circular window.

"Welcome to the last morning of the world," said Cugel.

The sky as revealed by window was black. Not pitch black, but black pervaded by a sickly glow, the source of which hung nearly dead-center of the window: the sun. Though it was at ten o'clock high, he could look directly at it and for a long moment he could do nothing else. Pale orange plasma filmed across the surface of a sphere that resembled an ember left over from a blaze, a great round ball of crusted carbon cracked and seamed with fire. From points on opposite sides of the sphere there arose enormous crimson effulgences, plumes of solar flame with the aspect of two mismatched horns, flares flung out into space that seemed as though they would eventually form into pinchers that would pluck the earth from its orbit. It was a ghastly, soul-shriveling thing to see. A dread weakness invaded Thiago's limbs. Ruskana clapped a hand to her mouth and Diletta put a hand on the wall for support. For his part, Cugel appeared enlivened by the sight.

"Ruskana! Take a last look around," he said, rubbing his hands together. "We want no interruptions. Quickly, girl! Diletta! See to the provisions."

The sound of Cugel's voice enlisted Thiago's hatred once again. He had made progress with his bonds, but needed more time.

"Ruskana!" he shouted as the girl mounted the stair. "There are only two seats inside the machine. Do you believe he will be here when you return? Every woman he has ever known, he has played her false."

"Ruskana is to ride astride my lap," said Cugel. "This has been discussed. Now go!" He waved her on.

"There have been a thousand Ruskanas before you," Thiago said. "Beginning with my Ciel. We quarreled, she and I. Cugel lured her to a solitary place on the outskirts of Kaiin, under the guise of offering advice on how she might repair the relationship. There he drugged her and she died . . . whereupon he fled. Do not expect better of him, I caution you."

Ruskana hovered near the top of the stair, the picture of uncertainty.

"Did you expect me stand my ground while you raised a mob?" Cugel made a derisive noise. "That was ever your way. To choose someone you believed was weak for a scapegoat and excite the public temper. But there is no mob here, only these two devoted women. I have come too far and endured too much to be thwarted by the likes of you." He held his fisted right hand to Thiago's face, showing him the ring of black ring. "This is Iucounu's ring. I bested him with his own magic. I have bested demons, giants, creatures that would leave you trembling. What did you hope to achieve against me?"

Cugel stood over Thiago, his face a neutral mask. He reached into the folds of his cape, produced a parchment scroll and tossed it onto Thiago's chest.

"A gift, cousin," he said. "The Spell of Forlorn Encystment. It is an option you may wish to exercise. Ask yourself if life is worth living imprisoned within the earth when there is no other choice, and act according to your answer." He turned to the stair. "Quickly now, Ruskana!"

The girl darted up the last few steps and pressed a stud in the ceiling; a section of the ceiling began to lift.

"She was done with you, Thiago," Cugel said. "She complied with my every desire."

Ruskana shrilled a warning. Derwe Coreme had slipped through the opening and stood at the top of the stair, wearing a man's shirt and trousers. The two women grappled briefly and Ruskana fell, cracking her head on the marble floor. Derwe Coreme spied Cugel and came toward him, knife in hand, face twisted with rage. Cugel darted for the egg and she screamed—it seemed ripped from her chest, furious like a raptor's scream. She hurled the knife, but Diletta pushed Cugel aside. The knife took her in the throat, penetrating both sides of her neck, and she collapsed. Derwe Coreme hurled a second knife, but it clanged off the door of the egg, with Cugel safe inside. Spatters of Diletta's blood dappled his cheek, lending him a clownish aspect.

Derwe Coreme sprinted down the steps and pounded on the door, screaming all the while. Cugel's expression was one of bewilderment. It was as though he were asking, Who is this scarred termagant? He busied himself with final preparations, ignoring her screams . . . if, indeed, he heard them.

Thiago burst the cords that constrained him.

A humming proceeded from the egg as Cugel, eyes closed in concentration, spoke the activating spell. Thiago got to his feet, and, standing beside Derwe Coreme, confronted him through the door. His spell complete, Cugel opened his eyes and smiled at them with the sweet tranquility of a man gone beyond judgment. The humming rose in pitch.

Thiago gave the egg a tentative push. He cleared Derwe Coreme away from the door, backed off several paces, and ran at it, striking it with his shoulder.

Cugel's smile faltered. Thiago had another run at the egg, and this time moved it slightly. His shoulder ached, but he made a third run. Concern was written on Cugel's face, but then the humming evolved into a keening and the egg appeared to be covered in sparkling silt, a film that vibrated over the metal surfaces. Cugel's smile returned. Thiago charged again, but was repulsed violently and thrown onto his back. The egg rippled, winking bright to dark. Soon it grew insubstantial and vanished, leaving a translucent afterimage in the air.

Thiago studied the afterimage as it faded. Was there a trace of desperation in Cugel's smile? The beginnings of fear? Was it a true smile or a rictus leer, a sign that his cousin was at the end *in extremis*? Perhaps Thiago's bull-rushes had taken a toll, or perhaps Pandelume's egg had borne Cugel to a less pleasant world than he had imagined and his expression was the initial register of that place. It was useless to speculate. One could but hope. He sank to the floor beside Derwe Coreme, who sat with head in hands.

"He did not know me," she said mournfully.

Thiago thought to reassure her, but had not the energy to do so. After a bit, he put a hand on her shoulder. She stiffened, but permitted the contact.

"What happened to you?" he asked. "You were gone the entire night."

"It was strange," she said. "They searched for me carrying tubes of blue concentrate. I might have killed one, but not both, so I hid in the room at the end of the corridor we first explored."

"The study . . . the laboratory?"

"Yes. I met someone there. I . . . It was an old man, I think. He gave me these clothes and spoke to me of many things. Yet I cannot picture him, nor do I recall a word he said."

"Pandelume," said Thiago.

"If it was he, I cannot remember."

A curious white flickering, a discharge of some type, passed across the face of the sun. They stared hopefully, but it remained a molten horror, like an emblem on an evil flag. Some of the cracks in the black crust were sealing over and the coating of orange plasma looked to have thinned; but it was otherwise unchanged.

"We have to go!" Derwe Coreme sprang to her feet.

"It is a fine notion, but how?"

She went to the wall, pressed an indentation next to the one Cugel had pressed. A wide section of the floor retracted with an accompanying grinding noise. Light streamed upward from a hole. Another staircase spiraled downward. Thiago asked how she had known about the stair. She shook her head and set about retrieving her knives. To remove the blade from Diletta's neck, she was forced to wrench and tug, her foot pinning the corpse's shoulder in place, until it came free with a sucking noise. She wiped it clean on her trousers and started down the stairs. Thiago could find no reason to stir himself. One death was like another.

A whisper, one that seemed shaped by the tower itself, as if it were a vast throat enclosing them, said, "Go. Goooo . . . ." The walls of the room wavered like smoke and Thiago had an apprehension that Pandelume was all around them, that the voice was his, and that his substance *was* the stuff of the walls, the floors, that this was not merely his place . . . it was *him*. Deciding that the prospect of a bottomless stair was less fearful than what he might face were he to remain, Thiago came wearily to his feet and began his descent.

It was a long way to the bottom of the stair, longer than would accord with tower's height, and they stopped to rest on several occasions. During one such rest period, Derwe Coreme said, "How could those women stay with him?"

"You were with him once."

"Yes, but I would have left at the earliest opportunity. Our association was based solely on necessity."

"The women may have been no different from you at the outset. Cugel has a knack for bending people to his will, even when they do not care for him."

"Do you think he is alive?"

Thiago shrugged. "Who can say?"

At the bottom of the tower was a partly open door. They passed through it and into the field of boulders. The sun was at meridian, shining down a reddish light that, though a shade dimmer than usual, was well within its normal range of brightness. They gazed at it, silent and uncomprehending, shielding their eyes against the glare.

"I am afraid," said Derwe Coreme as they walked toward the edge of the Great Erm. "Did the sun rekindle as we descended? Have we crossed over to another plane of existence? Did Pandelume intercede for us? Life offered few certainties, but now there are even fewer."

The high sun burnished the massy dark green crowns of the trees, causing them to seem drenched with blood. Derwe Coreme passed beneath the first of them and along an avenue that ran between two mandouars. Thiago glanced back and saw the tower dissolve into a swirling mist; from the mist another image materialized, that of a gigantic figure who looked to be no more than emptiness dressed in a hooded robe, the features invisible, the body apparent yet unreal. For an instant, something sparkled against the caliginous blackness within the cowl, a blue oval no bigger than a firefly. The same blue, Thiago noted, as the egg in which Cugel had escaped, pulsing with the same vital energy, twinkling like a distant star. It winked dark to bright to dark and then vanished, swallowed by the void.

Intially, Thiago was distressed to think that Cugel might be alive, but when he considered the possibilities, that Cugel might travel on forever in that void, or that he might be bound for some hell of Pandelume's device, or for one of the worlds they had glimpsed at the ends of the corridors, for the table in the workshop, say, where he would be imprisoned beneath a glass bell and subject to exotic predation . . . though a clear judgment on the matter was impossible, these notions dispelled his gloom.

Pandelume's figure dispersed, fading and fading until only the feeble red sun and some puffs of cloud were left in the sky. Thiago broke into a jog in order to catch up with Derwe Coreme. Following her trim figure into the shadows, he recognized that though nothing had changed, everything had changed. The sun or something like it lived on, and the world below was still ruled by magicians and magic, and they themselves were ruled by the magic of doubt and uncertainty; yet knowing this no longer felt oppressive, rather it envigorated him. He was free for the moment of gloom, lighter at heart by one hatred, and the next time Derwe Coreme asked one of her imponderable questions, some matter concerning fate or destiny or the like, he thought he might be inclined, if he deemed the occasion auspicious, to provide her with a definitive answer.

THREE TWILIGHT TALES

JO WALTON

Once upon a time, a courting couple were walking down the lane at twilight, squabbling. "Useless, that's what you are," the girl said. "Why, I could make a man every bit as good as you out of two rhymes and a handful of moonshine."

"I'd like to see you try," said the man.

So the girl reached up to where the bright silver moon had just risen above the hills and she drew together a handful of moonshine. Then she twisted together two rhymes to run right through it and let it go. There stood a man, in a jacket as violet as the twilight, with buttons as silver as the moon. He didn't stand there long for them to marvel at him. Off he went down the lane ahead of them, walking and dancing and skipping as he went, off between the hedgerows, far ahead, until he came to the village.

It had been a mild afternoon, for spring, and the sun had been kind, so a number of people were sitting outside the old inn. The door was open, and a stream of gold light and gentle noise was spilling out from inside. The man made of moonshine stopped and watched this awhile, and then an old widower man began to talk to him. He didn't notice that the moonshine man didn't reply, because he'd been lonely for talking since his wife died, and he thought the moonshine man's smiles and nods and attention made him quite the best conversationalist in the village. After a little while sitting on the wooden bench outside the inn, the old widower noticed the wistful glances the moonshine man kept casting at the doorway. "Won't you step inside with me?" he asked, politely. So in they went together, the man made of moonshine smiling widely now, because a moonshine man can never go under a roof until he's been invited.

Inside, there was much merriment and laughter. A fire was burning in the grate and the lamps were lit. People were sitting drinking ale, and the light was glinting off their pewter tankards. They were sitting on the hearthside, and on big benches set around the tables, and on wooden stools along the bar.

The inn was full of villagers, out celebrating because it was a pretty day and the end of their work week. The man made of moonshine didn't stop to look around, he went straight over to the fireplace.

Over the fireplace was a mantelpiece, and that mantelpiece was full of the most extraordinary things. There was a horn reputed to have belonged to a unicorn, and an old sword from the old wars, and a dragon carved out of oak wood, and a candle in the shape of a skull, which people said had once belonged to a wizard, though what a wizard would have wanted with such a thing I can't tell you. There was a pot the landlord's daughter had made, and a silver cup the landlord's father had won for his brewing. There were eggs made of stone and a puzzle carved of wood that looked like an apple and came apart in pieces, a little pink slipper said to have belonged to a princess, and an iron-headed hammer the carpenter had set down there by mistake and had been looking for all week.

From in between a lucky horseshoe and a chipped blue mug, souvenir of a distant port, brought back by a sailor years ago, the moonshine man drew out an old fiddle. This violin had been made long ago in a great city by a master craftsman, but it had come down in the world until it belonged to a gypsy fiddler who had visited the inn every spring. At last he had grown old and died on his last visit. His violin had been kept carefully in case his kin ever claimed it, but nobody had ever asked for it, or his body either, which rested peacefully enough under the grass beside the river among the village dead.

As soon as the man made of moonshine had the violin in his hands he began to play. The violin may have remembered being played like that long ago, in its glory days, but none of the villagers had ever heard music like it, so heart-lifting you couldn't help but smile, and so toe-tapping you could hardly keep still. Some of the young people jumped up at once and began to dance, and plenty of the older ones joined them, and the rest clapped along in time. None of them thought anything strange about the man in the coat like a violet evening.

It happened that in the village, the lord of the manor's daughter had been going about with the blacksmith's apprentice. The lord of the manor had heard about it and tried to put a stop to it, and knowing his daughter only too well, he had spoken first to the young man. Then the young man had wondered aloud if he was good enough for the girl, and as soon as he doubted, she doubted too, and the end of the matter was that the match was broken off.

Plenty of people in the village were sorry to see it end, but sorriest was a sentimental old woman who had never married. In her youth, she had fallen in love with a sailor. He had promised to come back, but he never did. She didn't know if he'd been drowned, or if he'd met some prettier girl in some faraway land, and in the end the not knowing was sadder than the fact of never seeing him again. She kept busy, and while she was waiting, she had fallen into the habit of weaving a rose wreath for every bride in the village. She had the best roses for miles around in the garden in front of her cottage, and she had a way with weaving wreaths too, twining in daisies and forget-me-nots so that each one was different. They were much valued, and often dried and cherished by the couples afterward. People said they brought luck, and everyone agreed they were very pretty. Making them was her great delight. She'd been looking forward to making a wreath for such a love match as the lord of the manor's daughter and the blacksmith's apprentice; it tickled her sentimental soul.

The little man made of moonshine played the violin, and the lord of the manor's daughter felt her foot tap, and with her toe tapping, she couldn't help looking across the room at the blacksmith's apprentice, who was standing by the bar, a mug in his hand, looking back at her. When he saw her looking he couldn't help smiling, and once he smiled, she smiled, and before you knew it, they were dancing. The old woman who had never married smiled wistfully to see them, and the lonely widower who had invited the little man in looked at her smiling and wondered. He knew he would never forget his wife, but that didn't mean he could never take another. He saw that smile and remembered when he and the old woman were young. He had never taken much notice of her before, but now he thought that maybe they could be friends.

All this time nobody had been taking much notice of the moonshine man, though they noticed his music well enough. But now a girl came in through the back door, dressed all in grey. She had lived alone for five years, since her parents died of the fever. She was twenty-two years old and kept three white cows. Nobody took much notice of her. She made cheese from her cows, and people said yes, the girl who makes cheese, as if that was all there was to her. She was plain and lonely in her solitary life, but she couldn't see how to change it, for she didn't have the trick of making friends. She always saw too much, and said what she saw. She came in, bringing cheese to the inn for their ploughman's lunches, and she stopped at the bar, holding the cheese in her bag, looking across the room at the violinist. Her eyes met his, and as she saw him, he saw her. She began to walk across the room through the dancers, coming toward him.

Just as she had reached him and was opening her mouth to speak, the door slammed back and in walked the couple who had been quarrelling in the lane, their quarrel all made up and their arms around each other's waists. The moonshine man stopped playing as soon as he saw them, and his face, which had been so merry, became grave. The inn fell quiet, and those who had been dancing were still.

"Oh," said the girl, "here's the man I made out of two rhymes and a handful of moonshine! It was so irresponsible of me to let him go wandering off into the world! Who knows what might have come of it? But never mind, no harm done." Before anyone could say a word, she reached toward him, whipped out the two rhymes, then rubbed her hands to dust off the moonshine, which vanished immediately in the firelight and lamplight of the bright inn parlour.

2

It was at just that time of twilight when the last of the rose has faded into the west, and the amethyst of the sky, which was so luminous, is beginning to ravel away into night and let the first stars rub through. The hares were running along the bank of the stream, and the great owl, the one they call the white shadow, swept silently by above them. In the latticework of branches at the edge of the forest, buds were beginning to show. It was the end of an early spring day, and the pedlar pulled his coat close around him as he walked over the low arch of the bridge where the road crossed the stream, swollen and rapid with the weight of melted snow.

He was glad to see the shapes of roof-gables ahead of him instead of more forest stretching out. He had spent two cold nights recently, wrapped in his blankets, and he looked forward to warmth and fire and human comfort. Best of all, he looked forward to plying his trade on the simple villagers, selling his wares and spinning his stories. When he saw the inn sign swinging above one of the doors, he grinned to himself in pure delight. He pushed the door open and blinked a little as he stepped inside. There was firelight and lamplight and the sound of merry voices. One diamond-paned window stood ajar to let out the smoke of fire and pipes, but the room was warm with the warmth of good fellowship. The pedlar went up to the bar and ordered himself a tankard of ale. He took a long draft and wiped his mouth with the back of his hand.

"That's the best ale I've had since I was in the Golden City," he said.

"That's high praise if you like," the innkeeper said. "Hear this, friends, this stranger says my ale is the best he's tasted since the Golden City. Is that your home, traveller?"

The pedlar looked around to see that the most part of the customers of the busy inn were paying attention to him now, and not to each other. There were a pair of lovers in the corner who were staring into each other's eyes, and an old man with a dog who seemed to be in a world of his own, and a girl in grey who was waiting impatiently for the innkeeper's attention, but all the other eyes in the place were fixed on the pedlar.

"I don't have a home," he said, casually. "I'm a pedlar, and my calling gives me a home wherever I go. I roam the world, buying the best and most curious and useful things I can find, then selling them to those elsewhere who are not fortunate enough to travel and take their choice of the world's goods. I have been to the Golden City, and along the Silver Coast; I've been in the east where the dragons are; I've been north to the ice; I've come lately through the very heart of the Great Forest; and I'm heading south where I've never been, to the lands of Eversun."

At this, a little ripple of delight ran through the listening villagers, and that moment was worth more than wealth to the pedlar, worth more than the pleasure of selling for gold what he had bought for silver. His words were ever truths shot through with sparkling lies, but his joy in their effect was as real as hot crusty bread on a cold morning.

"Can we see what you have?" a woman asked shyly.

The pedlar feigned reluctance. "I wasn't intending to sell anything here," he said. "My wares are for the lands of Eversun; I want to arrive there with good things to sell them, to give me enough coin to buy their specialities. I'm not expecting much chance to replenish my stock between here and there." The woman's face fell. "But since you look so sad, my dear, and since the beer here is so good and the faces so friendly, I'll open my pack if mine host here will throw in a bed for the night."

The landlord didn't look half as friendly now, in fact he was frowning, but the clamour among the customers was so great that he nodded reluctantly. "You can sleep in the corner of the taproom, by the fire," he said, grudgingly.

At that a cheer went up from the crowd, and the pedlar took his pack off his back and began to unfold it on a table, rapidly cleared of tankards and goblets by their owners. The outside of the pack was faded by the sun to the hue of twilight, but the inside was a rich purple that made the people gasp.

Now some of the pedlar's goods were those any pedlar would carry—ribbons, laces, yarn in different colours, packets of salt, nutmegs, packets of spices, scents in vials, combs, mirrors and little knives. He had none of the heavier, clattering goods, no pans or pots or pails that would weigh him down or cause him to need a packhorse to carry the burden. These ordinary goods he displayed with a flourish. "This lace," he said, "you can see at a glance how fine it is. That is because it is woven by the veiled men of the Silver Coast, whose hands can do such delicate work because they never step out into the sun. See, there is a pattern of peonies, which are the delight of the coastal people, and here, a pattern of sea waves."

When those who wanted lace had bought lace, he held up in each hand sachets of salt and pepper. "This salt, too, comes from the Silver Coast, and is in such large clear crystals because of a secret the women of that coast learned from the mermaids of making it dry so. The pepper comes from the Golden City, where it grows on trees and is dried on the flat rooftops so that all the streets of the city have the spicy smell of drying peppercorns."

"Does it never rain?" asked an old woman, taking out her coin to pay twice what the pepper would have been worth, except that it would spice her food with such a savour of story.

"In the Golden City, it rains only once every seven years," the pedlar said solemnly. "It is a great occasion, a great festival. Everyone runs into the streets and dances through the puddles. The children love it, as you can imagine, and splash as hard as they can. There are special songs, and the great gongs are rung in the temples. The pepper trees burst into huge flowers of red and gold, and the priests make a dye out of them which colours these ribbons. It is an expensive dye, of course, because the flowers bloom so rarely. They say it makes the wearers lucky, and that the dye doesn't fade with washing, but

I can't promise anything but what you can see for yourselves, which is how good a colour it makes." He lifted handfuls of red and yellow and orange ribbons in demonstration, which were hastily snapped up by the girls, who all crowded around.

The whole company was clustered around the pedlar now, even the lovers, but the landlord was not displeased. Every so often, when he grew hoarse, or claimed he did, the pedlar would put down his perfumes or lengths of yarn and say it was time for them all to drink together, and there would be a rush for the bar. The landlord had already sold more ale and wine than on an ordinary night, and if the pedlar was having his drinks bought for him, what of it? The landlord had bought some spices for his winter wines, and a silver sieve for straining his hops. He no longer grudged the pedlar his corner by the fire.

The pedlar went on now to his more unusual items. He showed them dragon scales, very highly polished on the inside, like mirrors, and rough on the outside. He asked a very high price for them. "These are highly prized in the cities of Eversun for their rarity, and the young ladies there believe, though I can't swear it is the truth, that looking at your face in such a mirror makes it grow more beautiful." Only a few of the village maidens could afford the price he asked, but they bought eagerly.

The grey girl had been standing among the others for some time, but she had bought nothing. The pedlar had noticed her particularly, because she had not paid attention to him at first, and when she had come to watch, he had smiled inwardly. As the display went on and she stood silent, smiling to herself aside from time to time, he grew aware of her again, and wanted to bring her to put her hand into her pocket and buy. He had thought the ribbons might tempt her, or then again the dragon scales, or the comb made from the ivory of heart trees, but though he had sold to almost everyone present, she had made no move.

Now he turned to her. "Here is something you will like," he said, "I do not mean to sell this here, but I thought it might interest you to look at it, for it is your colour." He handed her a little grey bird, small enough to fit into the palm of the hand, carved very realistically so you could feel each feather.

The grey girl turned it over in her hands and smiled, then handed it back. "I do not need a carven bird," she said.

"Why, no more does anyone else, but I see it fooled your eye, and even your hand. This bird, friends, is not carved. It comes from the Great North, from the lands of ice, and the bird flew too far into the cold and fell to the ground senseless. If you hold it to your lips and breathe, it will sing the song it sang in life, and they say in the north that sometimes such a bird will warm again and fly, but I have never seen it happen." He put the bird's tail to his lips and blew gently, and a trill rang out, for the bird was cleverly carved into a whistle. They were a commonplace of the Silver Coast, where every fishergirl had such a bird-whistle, but nobody in the village had ever seen one before.

The grey girl raised her eyebrows. "You say that was a living bird of the Great North that froze and turned to wood?"

"It has the feel of wood, but it is not wood," the pedlar insisted.

"Let me hold it a moment again," she asked. The pedlar handed it over. The grey girl held it out on the palm of her hand where everyone could see it. "No, it is wood," she said, very definitely. "But it's a pretty enough lie to make true." She folded her fingers over the bird and blew over it. Then she unfolded her fingers, and the bird was there, to all appearances the same as before.

The pedlar drew breath to speak, but before he could, the carved bird ruffled its feathers, trilled, took one step from the girl's hand onto her grey sleeve, then took wing, flew twice around over the heads of all the company, and disappeared through the open crack of the window.

3

As the leaves were turning bronze and gold and copper, the king came into the forest to hunt. One morning he set off to follow a white hart. They say such beasts are magical and cannot be caught, so the king was eager. Nevertheless, as often happens to such parties, they were led on through the trees with glimpses of the beast and wild rides in pursuit until the setting sun found them too far from their hunting lodge to return that night. This was no great hardship, for while the king was young and impetuous and had a curling black beard, he had many counsellors whose beards were long and white and combed smooth. Most of them had, to the king's secret relief, been left behind in the palace, but he had brought along one such counsellor, who was believed to be indispensable. This counsellor had thought to order the king's silken pavilions brought on the hunt, along with plenty of provisions. When the master of the hunt discovered this cheering news, he rode forward through the company, which had halted in a little glade, and brought it to the king, who laughed and complimented his counsellor.

"Thanks to you," he said, "the worst we have to fear is a cold night under canvas! What an adventure! How glad I am that I came out hunting, and how sorry I feel for those of the court who stayed behind in the Golden City with nothing to stir their blood." For the king was a young man, and he was bored by the weighty affairs of state.

The indispensable counsellor inclined his head modestly. "I was but taking thought for your majesty's comfort," he said.

Before he or the king could say more, the king's bard, who was looking off through the trees, caught sight of a gleam of light far off among them. "What's that?" he asked, pointing.

The company all turned to look, with much champing of bits but not many stamped hooves, for the horses were tired at the end of such a day. "It is a light, and that means there must be habitation," the king said, with a little less confidence than he might have said it in any other part of the kingdom. The Great Forest had a certain reputation for unchanciness.

"I don't know of any habitation in this direction," said the master of the hunt, squinting at the light.

"It will be some rude peasant dwelling, rat ridden and flea infested, far less comfortable than your own pavilions," the counsellor said, stroking his fine white beard. "Let us set them up here and pay no attention to it."

"Why, where's your spirit of adventure?" the bard asked the counsellor. The king smiled, for the bard's question was much after his own heart.

The king raised his voice. "We will ride on to discover what that gleam of light might be." In a lower tone, as the company prepared to ride off, he added to the counsellor, "Even if you are right, and no doubt you are, at the very least we will be able to borrow fire from them, which will make our camp less cold."

"Very wise, your majesty," the counsellor said.

They rode off through the twilight forest. They were a fine company, all dressed for hunting, not for court, but in silks and satins and velvets and rare furs, with enough gold and silver about them and their horses to show that they were no ordinary hunters. The ladies among them rode astride, like the men, and all of them, men and women, were beautiful, for the king was young and as yet unmarried and would have nobody about him who did not please his eye. Their horses were fine beasts, with arching necks and smooth coats, though too tired now to make the show they had made when they had ridden out that morning. The last rays of the sun had gilded them in the clearing, touching the golden circlet the king wore about his dark unruly locks; now they went forward into deepening night. The sky above them was violet, and a crescent moon shone silver like a sword blade. The first stars were beginning to pierce the sky when they splashed across a brook and saw a little village.

"What place is this?" the king asked the master of the hunt.

"I don't know, sire. Unless we have come sadly astray it isn't marked on my map," the master of the hunt said.

"We must have come astray then," the king said, laughing. "I don't think the worse of you for it, for we were following a hart through the forest, and though we didn't kill it, I can't think when I had a better day's sport. But look, man, this is a stone-built village with a mill and a blacksmith's forge, and an inn. This is a snug little manor. A road runs through it. Why, it must pay quite five pounds of gold in taxes."

The counsellor smiled to himself, for he had been the king's tutor when he was a prince, and was glad to see he remembered the detail of such matters.

The master of the hunt shook his head. "I am sure your majesty is right, but I can't find it on my map."

"Let us go on and investigate," the bard said.

It had been the red gleam of the forge they had seen from far off, but it was the lamplight spilling out of the windows of the inn that the bard waved toward.

"Such a place will not hold all of us," the king said. "Have the tents set up for us to sleep, but let us see if we can get a hot supper from this place, whatever it is."

"A hot supper and some country ale," the bard said.

"There are three white cows in the water meadow beside the stream," the master of the hunt pointed out. "The country cheese in these parts is said to be very good."

"If you knew what parts these were, no doubt my counsellor could tell us all about their cheeses," the king said.

They dismounted and left the horses to the care of those who were to set up the tents. The four of them strode into the village to investigate. The bard brought his little harp, the counsellor brought his purse, the master of the hunt brought a shortsword on his belt, but the king brought nothing.

The inn was warm and friendly and seemed to contain the whole population of the village. Those who were not there came in as soon as the news came to them of the king's arrival. The counsellor negotiated with the innkeeper and soon arranged that food and drink could be provided for the whole company, and beds for the king and the ladies, if the ladies did not mind crowding in together. The master of the hunt pronounced the ale excellent, and the villagers began to beg the bard to play. The rest of the company, having set up the tents and rubbed down the horses, began to trickle into the inn, and the place became very full.

The king wandered around the inn, looking at everything. He examined the row of strange objects that sat on the mantelpiece, he peered out through the diamond-paned windows, he picked up the scuttle beside the fire and ran his hand along the wood of the chair backs, worn smooth by countless customers. The villagers felt a little shy of him, with his crown and his curling black beard, and did not dare to strike up conversation. For his own part he felt restless and was not sure why. He felt as if something was about to happen. Until the bard started to play, he thought he was waiting for music, and until he was served a plate of cold pork and hot cabbage he thought he was waiting for his dinner, but neither of these things satisfied him. Neither the villagers nor his own company delighted him. The villagers seemed simple, humble, rustic; their homespun clothes and country accents grated on him. In contrast, the gorgeous raiment and noble tones of his company, which were well enough in the palace or even his hunting lodge, seemed here overrefined to the point of decadence.

At length the door at the back opened and a girl came in, clad all in grey and carrying a basket. The master of the hunt had called for cheese, and she was the girl who kept the cows and made the cheese. She was plain almost to severity, with her hair drawn back from her face, but she was young and dignified, and when the king saw her he knew that she was what he had been waiting for, not just that night but for a long time. He had been picking at his dinner, but he stood when he saw her. There was a little circle of quiet around the corner where he sat, for his own people had seen that he did not want conversation. The girl glanced at him and nodded, as if to tell him to wait, and went with her basket to the innkeeper and began to negotiate a price for her cheese. The king sat down and waited meekly.

When she had disposed of her cheeses, the girl in grey picked her way through the room and sat down opposite the king. "I have been waiting for you all my life. I will marry you and make you my queen," he said. He had been thinking all the time she was at the bar what he would say when she came up to him, and getting the words right in his mind. For the first time he was glad he was king, that he was young and handsome, that he had so much to offer her.

"Oh, I know that story," she said. She took his ale tankard and breathed on it, and passed it back to him. He looked into it and saw the two of them tiny and distant, in the palace, quarrelling. "You'd pile me with jewels and I'd wither in that palace. You'd want me to be something I'm not. I'm no queen. I'm no beauty, no diplomat. I speak too bluntly. You'd grow tired of me and want a proper queen. I'd go into a decline and die after I had a daughter, and you'd marry again and give her a stepmother who'd persecute her."

"But I have loved you since I first saw you," the king insisted, although her words and the vision had shaken him. He took a deep draft of the ale to drive them away.

"Love? Well now. You feel what you feel, and I feel what I feel, but that doesn't mean you have to fit us into a story and wreck both our lives."

"Then you . . ." the king hesitated. "I know that story. You're the goddess Sovranty, whom the king meets disguised in a village, who spends one night with him and confirms his sacred kingship."

She laughed. "You still don't see me. I'm no goddess. I know that story though. We'd have our one night of passion, which would confirm you in your crown, and you'd go back to your palace, and nine months later I'd have a baby boy. Twenty years after that he'd come questing for the father he never had." She took up a twist of straw that was on the table and set it walking. The king saw the shape of a hero hidden among the people, then the straw touched his hand and fell back to the table in separate strands.

"Tell me who you are," the king said.

"I'm the girl who keeps the cows and makes the cheeses," she said. "I've lived in this village all my life, and in this village we don't have stories, not real stories, just things that come to us out of the twilight now and then. My parents died five years ago when the fever came, and since then I've lived alone. I'm plain, and plainspoken. I don't have many friends. I always see too much, and say what I see."

"And you wear grey, always," the king said, looking at her.

She met his eyes. "Yes, I do, I wear grey always, but how did you know?"

"When you're a king, it's hard to get away from being part of a story," he said. "Those stories you mentioned aren't about us. They're about a king and a village girl and a next generation of stories. I'd like to make a new story that was about you and me, the people we really are, getting to know each other." He put out his hand to her.

"Oh, that's hard," she said, ignoring his hand. "That's very hard. Would I have to give up being a silver salmon leaping in the stream at twilight?"

"Not if that's who you are," he said, his green eyes steady on hers.

"Would I have to stop being a grey cat slipping through the dusky shadows, seeing what's to be seen?"

"Not if that's who you are," he said, unwavering.

"Would I have to stop being a grey girl who lives alone and makes the cheeses, who walks along the edges of stories but never steps into them?"

"Not if that's who you are," said the king. "But I'm asking you to step into a new story, a story that's never been before, to shape it with me."

"Oh, that's hard," she said, but she put her hand on the king's hand where it lay on the rough wooden table. "You've no sons, have you?"

"No sons, but I have two younger brothers," he said, exhilaration sweeping through him.

She looked around the room. "Your fine bard is singing a song, and your master of the hunt is eating cheese. Your counsellor is taking counsel with the innkeeper, and no doubt hearing all about the affairs of the village. Your lords and ladies are drinking and eating and patronising the villagers. If you really want to give up being a king and step into a new story with me, now is the time."

"What do I have to do?" he asked, very quietly, then she pulled his hand and for a moment he felt himself falling.

It was a little while before anyone noticed he had gone, and by then nobody remembered seeing the two cats slipping away between the tables, one grey and one a long-haired black with big green eyes.

NECROFLUX DAY

JOHN MEANEY

For Dad's sake, Carl tried to pretend that supper at Shadbolt's Halt was terrific, but they both know otherwise. Last year, on Carl's eleventh birthday, they'd truly had a great time. Tonight, exactly a year later, the atmosphere was quieter, a reflection of the greater tension enveloping the city.

The food *was* good: komodo steak and buttery mashed tubers, then squealberry pie and ice cream, washed down with hot blue chocolate. But no waiters came out to sing Happy Birthday, and Carl and Dad were seated behind a heavy pillar, where entirely human diners could not see the hint of otherness in father and son as they ate.

Even the flamewraiths, dancing (in their minimized aspect) inside wall-mounted crystalline bowls, seemed to have caught the tension. How a flame could appear angular or edgy was beyond Carl, but he knew what he sensed—and while he could never be a Bone Listener like Dad, he knew how to perceive deeply.

Last night, he'd overheard Dad talking to their neighbour, Mr. Varlin. One of the words had been unfamiliar to him, so he'd pulled down the old Fortinium Dictionary that smelled of dust, and now he wondered at the implications of "pogrom" appearing in an old man's description of the way Tristopolis was changing.

"Er, Dad?" Carl wanted to change the mood, and thinking of Tristopolis had reminded him of something. "Do you know much about the city's founding?"

"Has Sister Stephanie-Charon set you some homework about the Tri-Millennial?"

"We have to write an essay for next week."

"So you know I can't help you."

Dad—Jamie Thargulis to the adult world—had access to the Lattice, which was out of the reach of most Bone Listeners, never mind standard humans. Now, as Dad blinked his dark-brown bulbous eyes, Carl wondered what it truly meant to work as an Archivist, to immerse oneself in the centuries-old flow of understanding.

"I wasn't trying to cheat, Dad."

"Sorry, son. I know. So do you want to take a swing past Möbius Park? I hear they're testing the parade balloons tonight."

The celebration was three months away. Carl had watched the St Lazlo Day parade last year. He and Dad had stood next to a group of true believers, their foreheads marked with the cobalt-pigment Sign of the Holy Reaver, which they would not erase until the Feast of Magnus.

"Will we see the parade?"

"I don't know, son. This year, things are . . . Well. Maybe we'll just stay at home."

"OK."

"You're finished?"

Carl nodded, and Dad turned to gesture towards a waiter. The man came with the bill in hand, already written, as though he had known that Dad would not be ordering anything more.

Dad counted out three nine-florin coins, then looked up at the waiter.

"Thank you for the service."

He added a thirteen-sided coin to the amount.

"Goodbye, sir," said the waiter.

Dad, still seated, swallowed.

The street, wide and bordered with centuries-old architecture, looked dim beneath the eternally deep-purple sky. Carl and Dad stood in a patch of orange light thrown by the restaurant windows, buttoning up their overcoats. Wearing his fedora, Dad looked standard human. He waved to a purple taxi. The cab slowed, then accelerated, and was past them.

"Sharp eyesight," muttered Dad.

A stone gargoyle glided overhead, high up.

"I'd like to walk," said Carl.

"All right, son. Let's do that."

They strolled to Illbeck Pentangle, where the traffic was heavy and it took a while to cross, then continued to the high stone walls of Möbius Park. They followed the road outside the walls, keeping to the other side of the road. At school, some older boys had scorned the stories of lone pedestrians disappearing forever—not just intruders, who deserved whatever happened—but Dad was always careful here, and he was an Archivist who worked for the city.

"The South-South-East Gate," he said. "Looks like it's open."

Tall and formed of black iron, the gates were closed whenever possible. Now, Carl could see along the gentle curved of Actualisation Arc, bordered by dark parkland, and the black-grass clearing where half-inflated balloons were rising.

"There's a Leviathan." He pointed. "See?"

But what he really noticed was the faint silver glimmer of the force-shield that contained ravenous ectoplasma wraiths among the trees. Beyond, deep inside Möbius Park, reared the great skull outline of City Hall.

"I thought," muttered Dad, "there'd be more to see."

"No, this is great."

"We could get some juice at—"

"It would be nice to go home."

"We'll take the hypotube, in that case."

A floating amber P-sign indicated a Pneumetro station, two blocks along a street that headed away from the park. It took a few minutes to walk the distance, before descending to a Magenta Line platform just as a train slid in.

"Good timing," said Dad.

They boarded the last ovoid carriage, which would split off at the next branch line, Magenta 7. As they sat, Carl noticed a scaly-skinned man who was watching a group of standard-human youths. They waved red beer-bottles, foul-mouthing each other and the world.

A percussive wave kicked the train into motion. Then necromagnetic windings in the tunnel walls—Sister Stef had explained it to the class—boosted the acceleration. Carl turned to ask Dad about it; but Dad, too, was observing the youths.

When the train stopped at Wailmore Twist, the youths got off. The scaly-skinned man glanced at Dad, then opened a copy of the Tristopolitan Gazette, and held it up as a shield. He didn't lower the paper even when the train rattled going through Shadebourne Depths. Here, the station was disused; but the slum tenements up above (where Carl was not supposed to wander) included the boarding house where Sister Stef had stayed as a newly arrived immigrant, before coming to the school and joining the Order of Thanatos. She'd told her story to the class.

Dad and Carl got off at Bitterwell Keys, and climbed the winding stairs to street level. A fine quicksilver rain was falling as they crossed Blamechurch Avenue, and reached the purplestone house that they called home.

"Happy Birthday, son."

"Yes. Thanks, Dad."

In his bedroom, Carl leaned against the iron frame, knowing what Dad was doing downstairs. In the parlour, dark and polished, he was holding his favourite blue-and-white photograph of his dead wife, Mareela. For Carl, she—Mother—existed only as blurred images of warmth, dark hair and a smile.

He'd been two years old when she died.

Mareela Thargulis had been standard human, and pretty. From her, Carl inherited his green eyes, so incongruous in a face that otherwise marked him as of Bone Listener stock. It was a sign that, while he might carry his father's blood, hearing the resonance of bones, living or dead, would be forever beyond him.

"*He's neither one thing nor the other,*" old Mrs. Scragg had muttered to one of her friends on the street, as Carl had passed them by. "*Shouldn't be allowed.*"

Now, he stared at himself in the rust-splotched mirror.

It's not fair.

Tonight had been terrible. He was a dreamer, never the brightest in class, but he'd wanted Sister Stef to say something nice to Dad tomorrow, during Parents' Evening. Somehow, thoughts of the Tri-Millennial essay had become mixed up with the heaviness of hatred he felt on the air, the increasing hostility of ordinary citizens to freewraiths and boundwraiths, and even to those who were almost human.

Even in the schoolyard, things were changing. He'd been bullied because of his slight size before, but now it was worse.

I've had enough.

He wanted to be different, to have some kind of strength, even if it manifested in a way no ordinary human could appreciate. And he wanted to write an essay to prove Sister Stef's intuition—that he knew she had—that Carl Thargulis had a spark of originality in him, that he was a dreamer with ability.

Because I can do it.

Never the cleverest, never the strongest . . . but this was in his power.

I know I can.

And he was twelve years old, after all. It was time for him to try.

Now.

Was that it? At the inner corner of his left eye?

Right now.

Was there a twitch of scarlet movement?

Yes! Try . . .

A slender red, hair-thin articulated limb extended—for sure—from inside his lower eyelid. It waved, it really waved—

Yes!

—then withdrew inside his eye socket.

Oh no.

He strained, but knew he'd lost it.

Hades.

It was too much. He was too weak, or just not good enough.

Try again.

But Dad called from the landing outside: "Go to bed, son."

"All right, Dad."

Then Carl undressed, folded his clothes, and climbed into bed, beneath the old, comfortable-smelling blankets. The iron frame creaked. He closed his eyes.

Happy Birthday, me.
Sleep curled up maternally around him.

In the early morning, after prayers she didn't believe in, Sister Stephanie-Charon Mors straightened her dark-burgundy habit before going out into the schoolyard. There, she stared up at the featureless indigo sky, wondering whether it would ever seem natural to her.

She had been born a Lightsider (as only Reverend Mother knew) in TalonClaw Port, where everything was bright, and heating (along with motive power) came from lava conduits in which fire-daemons controlled the magma flow. Tristopolis had seemed so different when she arrived here, and in many ways it remained strange.

The dark sky allowed her to think of her childhood bedroom with the heavy drapes drawn, while she waited wide-eyed in shadows, knowing Mam was down in the kitchen while Pop was inside the corner bar. Soon, he would be home, drunk, and that was when it would start—the awfulness, the smack of knuckles on flesh, and then the yelling.

She had such a fine understanding of the troubled lives of the poorer kids here in school, the ones who lived in Shadebourne Depths. It was why Reverend Mother had said, during her last appraisal: *"You're the worst nun in the Order of Thanatos, and probably the finest teacher."*

In reply, she'd apologized, not knowing what else to say.

Here in the yard, on her first day, she'd stood during morning break while the kids played snatchball and tag, filling the place with chaos. A small group, holding hands, had danced in a ring chanting a traditional rhyme that she, as a new immigrant, had never heard.

Verdigris butterfly,
Spider so cute.
Snip out their tongues,
And then they are mute.

The children had released hands and twirled on the spot, then continued:
Worms in their eyeballs,
No one can see
Beetles devour
My true love and me.

And they had crouched down in a gesture that Stef had recognized immediately as symbolic of death. So easy to remember the way that Pop had—

Sister Zarly Umbra was ringing the bell.

—unlocked the front door, and taken the steps—

It was time for lessons.

—nearly always seven steps, before he—

No.

This was *time for lessons* and the children came first, as they always would. Yet Parents' Evening was scheduled for tonight, meaning that Bone Listener Jamie Thargulis would be here, with those dark-brown eyes that held intelligence, and implied insight with an overlay of sorrow it was hard for Stef to resist, though she had never revealed her feelings. The Order of Thanatos demanded chastity. While she might not hold to the order's beliefs, still it formed her only sanctuary,

The kids were entering the yard, and it was time for her to do what she was good at.

But she wondered, as she saw the smirk on burly Ralen O'Dowd's face, and the way that young Carl Thargulis followed him, rubbing at the dirt on his own shirt—Ralen's footprint?—whether she would ever make the kind of difference that could erase the memory of the sacrifice it took to come here, halfway around the world, just a daydream away from the past.

Carl's stomach ached from Ralen's kick, but he tried to follow the lesson. If he concentrated, he could forget the anticipation of more beatings to follow—every day this week, Ralen had promised, for no reason except that he could.

"Starting with the inner planets," said Sister Stef from beside the blueboard. "Does anyone remember, which is closest to the sun?"

Carl could name them all, and in the right order—but Ralen was watching. Carl said nothing.

"All right. I'll start." Sister Stef picked up a stick of yellow chalk. "Prometheus, Venus, then Earth."

Rubbing at his stomach, Carl felt despair. He stared at the steel punishment ruler that hung on the wall, the ruler that Sister Stef so rarely used. He wished he could see Ralen suffer.

"And the next planet? Anyone?"

Angela, her skin pale-blue, held up her hand.

"Is it Mars, Sister?"

"Very good, Angela." Sister Stef wrote it up. "Next?"

"Please, Sister," said Roger, thin and nervous. "Is it Hel?"

"Good answer, Roger. That *is* a planet, just not the next one."

Ralen guffawed.

"And do you know the correct answer, Master O'Dowd? No? Anyone?"

She looked around the room. Carl stared at his desktop, defaced by the pens and penknives of previous generations.

"Oberon, then." Sister Stef wrote. "Followed by Jupiter, Saturn, Poseidon and Roger's favourite, Hel."

Roger blushed.

"As it happens," added Sister Stef, pointing to the board, "Earth and Mars are close enough to have mixed up dust in space, swapping little particles of life, just as Oberon swapped dust with Mars."

Carl wished Sister Stef would talk more about this kind of thing, but he knew this diversion would be short-lived.

"You have things called mitochondria in your body, Ralen O'Dowd, that used to be germs with their own genetic material."

Some of the other children sniggered.

"And the zodules of sages and witches are particularly rich in thaumacules derived from Oberon's—Well, never mind. Let's carry on with what we're supposed to be learning, shall we?"

In her notebook, Angela was writing the word 'sages'. Carl knew it was a Lightsider's slip of the tongue: the name of a profession that did not exist in the Federation. Dad had told him so.

And he'd also told Carl not to share his speculation, because Lightsiders were so rarely believers, and that held implications for Sister Stef's position here. Carl had agreed without understanding.

He spent the midmorning break and lunchtime staying out of Ralen's sight. But just as the afternoon session was about to start, two burgundy-clad nuns swept down on Ralen—Sister Zarly Umbra and an older, dour Sister whose name Carl didn't know—and led him into the building.

When the lesson began in Sister Stef's classroom, Ralen's desk was unoccupied.

Part of Carl hoped that Ralen was in Reverend Mother's study, experiencing the hook-and-whip that some pupils whispered about. But when Sister Stef announced that she had some dreadful news, her words poured sickness into him.

"Poor Ralen's father passed away at work today. An accident."

From next door, through the thick classroom wall, came the sound of children chanting the Final Litany of St Magnus the Slayer. Sister Stef scowled, before rubbing her face and instructing everyone to open their history books.

That evening, the walk home was devoid of the fear of ambush by Ralen, of threatened pain or taunting humiliation.

It was a disappointing kind of freedom.

Two hours later, Parents' Evening was in progress, and Jamie Thargulis was sitting on a small chair—designed for kids—trying to keep calm, staring at Sister Stephanie-Charon.

"I'm sorry if Carl's a dreamer."

"That's not a criticism." Sister Stef's smile was nice. "He's not ready to flourish just yet."

"In the kind of school I went to, dreaming wasn't exactly encouraged."

"That would be a Bone Listener academy?"

"Yes. Thank Fate that Carl isn't eligible to—You know."

"Hmm." Sister Stef looked at the blank blueboard. "Reverend Mother sent some UP supporters packing. They were on the street corner handing out leaflets."

"Things are getting worse."

In Fortinium, the now-discredited Senator Blanz had tried to push his Vital Renewal Bill through the Senate, to pass a bill removing the civil rights of freewraiths and near-humans. It had failed, yet the Tristopolitan city council had power to pass their own regulations, and public mood had turned in a dark direction.

"So long as Mayor Dancy remains in office," said Sister Stef, "we're all right."

Jamie appreciated the solidarity. Sister Stef was standard human.

"I suppose I can't comment. As an Archivist."

"Oh. You must have access to all sorts of fascinating Lattice information."

To Jamie, information was inscribed with pain and stored in bones, yet Sister Stef's words were true. His vocation remained fascinating.

The classroom door swung inwards.

"Hello," said a nun. She glanced at the iron wall-mounted skull-clock. Steel cogs moved within its eye sockets. "Just checking you were still with Mr. Thargulis."

"Finishing up. Thank you, Sister Zarly."

Jamie struggled to get out of the too-small chair, wondering whether he'd embarrassed Sister Stef by taking up too much time. Her face was perhaps the tiniest bit pink.

"Um," said Jamie. "Carl's pretty taken with your essay theme."

"The Tri-Millennial? He's got a whole week to do it in."

The iron skull-clock ticked. Its pendulum was a swinging scythe; its housing was a long-preserved cranium; the slow-rotating hands were carved knucklebones of long-dead nuns.

"Yes," said Jamie. "He'll enjoy it."

"Good."

They were standing very close.

"Um . . . Goodnight, Sister."

"Goodnight, Mr. Thargulis."

Alone in his room, Carl strained and squeezed.

"Ugh—"

Squeezed harder.

Come on.

Being at home by himself, this late, was unusual. It meant he could try it without Dad sensing he was—

Yes.

A faint hair-width of red struggled from the inside corner of his right eye. It wriggled and hurt, but it was growing bigger.

For the first time, he knew he could do it.

Yes.

Another slender arachnid leg extruded itself, then another. In seconds a tiny red spider was dragging itself out from Carl's eyeball, scrabbling an inch down his cheekbone, then stopping to rest.

Another.

He focused, and squeezed again. It was still hard, but he continued, and in only a few seconds a second scarlet spider clambered from the slickness of his eye.

Again.

This time, tiny legs appeared from beneath his left lower eyelid. It took longer, but finally the third spider hauled itself free. Carl knew now that he could manifest with either eye, however much it burned.

"I knew I could," he said to the rust-flecked mirror.

He was no Bone Listener; but Dad was an Archivist, and in that much at least, Carl carried his father's blood.

"I knew it."

By the time Dad got home, Carl had squeezed a total of eight spiders into existence, and hidden them inside his shirt drawer, and commanded them to sleep.

In the washroom, Sister Stef wiped her face, still feeling sick. It was a reaction to the fear she'd sensed in Angela Haxten's parents, for while Angela's skin was just faintly blue, her parents' colouring was more pronounced. Mr. Haxten had moved with the kind of difficulty Stef associated with a bad beating.

This she knew from childhood memory, of Mam and Pop and the sound of—

No. The past is behind me.

Just now she had told the Haxtens how strong and confident their daughter was growing. It was a form of lie that the nuns called a Benedictory Confabulation. Perhaps Angela *would* develop the strength she would need, just as Stef had finally left that world where she had listened so often for the key turning in the front-door lock, for the sound of drunken footsteps across the old linoleum floor, and the rattle of the glass door handle as Pop reached the—

Behind me.

—kitchen where Mam was waiting for the—

Gone.

—waiting for the—

No.

She stopped herself. Turning on the cold water tap, she rinsed her mouth. Then she went out to meet the next set of parents.

"Mr. and Mrs. Blackhall? Lovely to see you again."

Later that night, Jamie lay in bed—in his own half of the bed, a decade after Mareela's death—rolling first one way and then the other, trying not to think of the way Sister Stef might look without that formal burgundy habit, or how long her hair would be if it were hanging loose.

"Go to sleep," he told the darkness.

And he would not think about the slenderness of her waist, or how her skin might feel if he pressed his hand against it . . . He would *not* think of it.

Despite the tricks of meditation and prayer that the order had taught her, Stef lay with her eyes open, staring into the darkness of her private sleeping-cell beneath the school. The childhood memories of TalonClaw Port were behind her, but they would *stay* there only if she constantly forced them back.

Meanwhile the thought of dark-brown eyes with such depth, such insight into arcane knowledge . . . that thought was forbidden.

Jamie Thargulis.

Totally forbidden.

Carl slept deeply. At some point, he dreamed of entering the consciousness of his eight spiders, of the octet formed from his computational blood. The spiders climbed down from the drawer, across the floor, and beneath the door—the gap was a vast opening to his eight new viewpoints—and then began the great trek downstairs, before ascending the coatstand.

There was something peaceful and secure about the way he, through his spiders, was able to nestle in the folds of Dad's overcoat, to slip inside the small tears in the old thick fabric, to hide inside the lining, and grow quiescent once more.

Inside his dream, the dream he knew was true, Carl smiled, and commanded his spiders to wait.

The first part of the morning was tough. Carl tried to concentrate on Sister Stef's words, fighting down the attraction of linking to his spiders, and managed to wait until first break. Then, he established contact, just long enough for the spiders to clamber out of Dad's overcoat and find places to hide behind Dad's adding-machine.

The device was intricate, formed from interlocking bones and beetle wing cases. The rattling calculations did not disturb his hidden arachnid observers.

During the longer lunch break, he ate his grilled cicadas too fast. Afterwards, crouched in a corner of the yard away from the other kids, he closed his eyes.

"—to see you, Brixham." This was Dad's voice, as heard by Carl's spiders. "Why is the OCML visiting this time?"

"Just some queries. If you could pre-process and then pass back to us . . . "

"I'll do it this afternoon."

One of the spiders (under Carl's direction) crept from behind the adding-machine, stopped, then continued to the black shoe that looked like a pitted cliff face. The man—the Bone Listener—looked massive, like a geological feature more than a person.

The spider moved quickly, climbing up the tangled grey fibres of the trouser leg, into the turn-up, then settling inside.

"*Thank you, Archivist Thargulis. I'll—*"

"Carl?"

It was Sister Zarly Umbra calling from across the yard.

"Yes, Sister?"

"Are you all right?"

"Um. Yes, Sister."

"Then line up with the others, ready to go back inside."

"Yes, Sister."

During the afternoon's algebra, Carl's awareness slipped away to Dad's office from time to time, just the lightest of touches. Tonight, late, he would link in fully to explore the Archives, manipulating computational blood, though deaf to the music of the bones.

". . . And I hope you're doing good work on your essays at home, everyone," said Sister Stef. "Not just because the Tri-Millennial celebration is important. We're going to try something new in class next week. Now turn to—"

Was it for the essay, to please Sister Stef, or for the joy of working with the power he'd always hoped he had? Either way, think of what he might learn! Such arcana . . . a word most of the other kids would not understand.

And splitting his consciousness across eight spiders was so . . . fascinating . . . in a way he could not have explained to anyone, not even Dad.

Tonight.

To be alone. To link properly with his spiders.

Tonight, I'll learn everything!

This was going to be difficult. Fear and regret and anger—strange, undirected anger at the past, at events that were no longer real—swirled and roiled inside Stef's head. A sleepless night and the realization that she was no longer a new immigrant, scared and broke and confused by the oddities of a new culture, and some core of honesty that perhaps she had always possessed . . . all of these had tipped her into a state where she needed to decide, or so it seemed. Then she'd realized the decision was already formed in her mind, hard and complete.

She walked along the familiar, shadow-filled bonestone corridor that led to Reverend Mother's study. It was a contrast to the airy, quartz-walled tunnel lit by rivulets of magma that she had walked through as a schoolgirl, in trouble again, on her way to see the principal.

An unseen boundwraith dragged the ceramic door into its cavity in the wall, and Stef entered the room, hands folded like any penitent nun, knowing that this would be a transgression that could not be washed away by entering Contrition Trance or enacting the Seven Steps of Regret.

"Sister Stephanie-Charon Mors. Do you need to talk? That *is* unusual."

This was the hour when, without appointment, any nun could enter. Usually it was the weaker ones with some pedantic difficulty that was problematic only because they made it so.

"Yes, Reverend Mother."

"Come in, and sit."

Reverend Mother was narrow with age, but straight-backed on her hard, cushionless bonestone stool. The whites of her eyes were clear as a girl's.

Stef sat in the comfortable visitor's chair. In contrast to Reverend Mother's stool, it was designed to make a point. The intended message was the power of humility. Stef had always thought it meant Reverend Mother was a tough old bitch who needed nothing but her own certainty.

"Would you prefer helebore tea," added Reverend Mother, "or to come to the point?"

"You said"—Stef consciously tightened her stomach to exhale, calming herself—"I was the worst nun in the order."

"You'll remember I qualified that sentence. You're one Hades of a teacher, Sister Stephanie-Charon."

Stef was blinking. Then she focused on Reverend Mother, knowing that this was the moment.

"I don't believe."

"What don't you believe?" asked Reverend Mother.

Behind her was a private altar, a worn block of pale-grey stone on which worn icons, chiselled in millennia gone by, were barely visible. It was a fragment of a titanic human knuckle, perhaps belonging to the same long-dead person whose petrified skull now formed City Hall's central building. Whether huge people had once walked the earth, or whether mages had caused the transformation (either fatally or post mortem) no one knew, and only scholars cared.

The Order of Thanatos had myths to explain everything, but few of them were rational.

"Any of it," said Stef. "I don't believe any of your stories."

"You mean the Teachings Thanatical."

"Yes. I *do* love teaching, just teaching the children. You were right in that."

Reverend Mother's eyes were shining. Stef tightened her jaw muscles, knowing that the old woman could use mesmeric language to induce compliance, but not in someone who remained alert and sure of her position.

This was not a time to think of Bone Listener Jamie Thargulis and his dark eyes, because dreaminess would open the door for Reverend Mother to use her verbal skills.

"You're a logical thinker, Sister, but there's a clear boundary"—softly—"between faith and logic."

"Yes, Reverend Mother. And we probably agree on where the boundary lies."

"But you don't have the desire to leap over it?"

"That's not the way I think of it."

"I see."

Reverend Mother's eyes were shining like ice. Again, Stef tightened her muscles, pulling her attention back into the moment.

"I'm sorry," she said. "For deceiving you, when you gave me a home here."

"No."

Ice was in Reverend Mother's voice as well.

"I'm sorry?"

"It's yourself, Stephanie, that you have deceived."

This time, Stef's diaphragm tightened by itself.

"You didn't call me Sister."

"No. I did not."

"I'm really—"

Reverend Mother held out her hand, palm down.

"Leave me now, Stephanie."

Stef stood up, fighting back the stinging in her tear ducts. Then she nodded, because to make the usual Sign of Thanatos would be an insult now, and turned away.

She went out into the corridor, and walked on, aware of the grinding noise behind her—the door rolling back into place, dragged by the bound-wraith—and of the chill draught and ancient smell, and the way that she had just severed a major lifeline, for the second time in her life.

Alone in his bed, grinning, Carl descended into ecstasy. One by one, he merged with seven of his spiders, while allowing the remaining spider to remain quiescent, hidden in a turn-up of Bone Listener Brixhan Somebody-or-Other's trousers.

But those seven, what they saw!

First, they climbed from behind the bone-and-scarab-carapace adding-machine, then crawled from Dad's office, out into the corridors of the Archives. Security scanwraiths passed over them, ignoring their presence, for Carl's spiders were formed from computational blood and so belonged here.

They explored.

From the ceiling of a vast hall, all seven spiders watched (from disparate viewpoints) as lines and rivers of their own kind—thousands, maybe millions of blood-spiders—streamed across floors and walls and ceilings, into and out of ducts, carrying their fragments of data and logic around the organized Archivists, merging the Bone Listeners' investigations.

It was wonderful. It was a place of ecstasy.

And this was not even the Lattice, which his spiders had yet to explore.

Three words, so far, had come to her.

I deeply regret . . .

Stef was alone in her dorm-cell, seated at the small stone table, holding her carved-bone fountain-pen, without any idea what she should write with it. Then she pushed aside her notepaper, as a tear dripped downwards, softly forming a wet disk on stone.

This was heartrending, but she had to continue.

It occupied vast pits, extending its massive volume into areas of stone cells, threading through them, granting tiny insignificant men and women—the Archivists, all of them Bone Listeners with an aptitude for pain—access to its arcs and nodes of bone. Information and inference, learning and logic, coexisted in its vastness . . . without self-conscious awareness. Had it been alive, capable of sensing itself, it would have been a godlike being, ruling or destroying or ignoring the Earth, whatever it saw fit. As it was, it formed a repository of more than facts—it held the emotions and satori-bliss of insight, the nirvana of information-merging, the dreams and pain of wisdom.

Its struts were of bone. It was vast and three-dimensional.

This was the Lattice.

And through his seven spiders, even without Bone Listener awareness, Carl could sense its power. He watched as guardian-moths of living copper, their wings razor-edged, flitted among the struts, while spiders crawled and flowed, conjoining the Lattice with the tiny frail Archivists who used it.

Carl, via his spiders, followed one such flow of spiders as it split into smaller and smaller tributaries, eventually leading to a single stone couch (one among dozens, maybe hundreds involved in this information quest) on which an Archivist-Scribe lay with eyes wide open, allowing exit and entry of blood-spiders to his own self.

Scarlet spiders danced across his staring eyeballs, and pulled themselves down into the sockets, merging with his thoughts, before dragging themselves back out. The Archivist-Scribe's gaze was fixed, for he could not blink, but the smile on his mouth was wide. He was merged with the flow whose medium was computational blood, manifested as a sea of spiders.

But Carl was observing, not using the Lattice.

Now it was time to hunt for facts, to prove to himself that while he could not hear the bones, his spiders could resonate with others of their kind, allowing him to sense information currently in the flow, though he could never initiate investigation himself.

Perhaps that limitation hid an advantage, for he would never feel the depths of pain that every Archivist experienced, during each moment inside the Lattice.

It took a long time.

Later, both Carl and his spiders slept exhausted, and his dreams were strange.

Jamie Thargulis dreamed of Stephanie-Charon Mors in another guise, as if she were divested of her nun's habit—a fantasy—to live as an ordinary woman. Her ordinary name would be Stephanie, but Stephanie what?

Even asleep, he dared not hope she might be Stephanie Thargulis someday. After a time, the dream dissipated, and he came awake, his cheekbones chilled by evaporating tears.

Next evening, Carl began to write the essay, knowing this was going to be something special.

He began by rhetorically asking what it meant to assign an age to a city. Was there an official founding date? Should one begin with the date the first stone was laid? Or with the completion of its first tower, or the flight of its first gargoyle?

In quick, brief paragraphs, he laid out his reasons for agreeing that this year, 6607, was a good year to consider the Tri-Millennial Anniversary (three thousand three hundred and thirty-three years, in the official terminology) of the founding of Tristopolis. In that first year, City Hall was inaugurated, and seventeen of its greatest towers were completed.

But while I agree with the founding year, he continued, *the date within that year is contentious.*

He stopped, found his old dictionary, and checked the spelling of "contentious." Yawning, he nodded, then decided this was enough for the first night. Besides, he had facts but not what you might call a theme. He wanted this essay to shine, to excel, to amaze Sister Stef. Thank Hades he had until Sepday to finish.

Lying down on the bed, he thought about linking to his spiders, but drifted into ordinary sleep.

Next morning, in the schoolyard, Carl stared up at the indigo sky, allowing his eyes to defocus. His spiders were in Dad's office and—Dad was at work.

He broke contact.

Any Archivist was sensitive to resonance, and if Dad sensed computational blood that was not quite his own . . . Carl, blinking, thought he saw someone draw back inside an upper window of the school. Had Sister Stef been watching him?

A game of snatchball was starting up, but Carl had no interest, except that it meant no one was looking his way. Eyelids fluttering, he sank inside his awareness, linking to his other spider, which remained hidden inside the turn-up of a Bone Listener's trouser leg.

Now, Carl caused the spider to clamber out of hiding, and scuttle across a wide-seeming floor to hide beneath a filing-cabinet formed of bone. This must be the subterranean OCML—the Office of the Chief Medical Listener. Here, forensic Bone Listeners carried out autopsies on suspicious deaths. There might be police officers in attendance.

I could be in big trouble.

He checked his spider was out of sight, then broke the link. In the school-yard, the snatchball game swirled in joyful chaos, a communal celebration of physicality and energy that had nothing to do with him.

Alone in her cell, Stef stared at the wall, seeing the memory of nightmare: shuffling men and women on the docks of TalonClaw Port, heading for the gangways that led downwards, into the great dockside holds.

At the time, as a girl, she had noticed only the well-dressed passengers on the overhead bridges, boarding the vast teardrop-shaped suboceanic liners, with their shining rear propellers. If she thought at all about the devastated, hopeless individuals who would board via the hidden tubes beneath the waves, it was with a snooty superiority: she would never travel third-class.

"I didn't know."

Her eyes, so animated in class, now held only loss.

"Oh, Pop. I loved you."

No other sound entered the cold stone cell.

In the evening, once more alone in his room, Carl resumed the link. His lone spider traversed several ceilings until he came to a room in which postmortems took place. There, he was sickened to watch a Bone Listener drive platinum divining forks into a corpse that could never feel pain.

During life, microstructures laid down in bone resonated with the neural patterns and neuropeptide flow of thought and emotion and memory. The bones stored interference patterns that could scatter or concentrate necroflux in ways Carl did not understand.

He felt awful as he withdrew.

But later, when he should have been asleep, he could not help himself. He re-formed the link and rode the spider as it dropped to a uniformed porter's shoulder, and hid beneath the epaulette. The man assisted in moving a body onto a gurney, and then along corridors to an underground garage.

A black ambulance was waiting with its wings furled, but the porter and his colleagues rolled the gurney past it. They stopped at the rear of an ordinary-looking indigo van. On its side shone the Skull-and-Ouroboros logo of the Energy Authority. The porters loaded the corpse into the back, beside two other pale bodies; then they sat down on metal benches inside the van.

Someone closed the doors, and soon the van was in motion. No one sensed the scarlet spider clinging to the porter's shoulder, beneath his epaulette.

An hour later (during which Carl had broken the link only twice, to go to the bathroom and to make himself a cup of helebore tea), the porter was in the Westside Energy Complex. Here the air seemed awash with half-glimpsed black waves, as if necroflux were visible to arachnid sight. The spider's form was suffering in this environment, so Carl caused it to move quickly, wanting to see as much as possible before the spider disintegrated.

For a time he watched workers direct quicksilver shrikes—a flock of living metal birds—to strip away the flesh from corpses on biers. The shrikes, as if in payment for their sustenance, dragged thin dark threads from the bodies, and dropped them on the floor. Afterwards, when the bones were stripped and the flock was nesting overhead once more, the human workers coiled the dark threads around spools of bone. The threads were nerves, and Carl had no idea why they might be useful to keep.

But his spider had limited time, so it scuttled fast across the ceiling, following his sense of energy in the air, heading for the greater concentration.

Soon, it was perched high on the external cladding of a reactor pile, one of many that stood in long rows inside the cavern complex. This was a huge place, immense to human eyes, impossible for Carl to comprehend through his spider.

More workers (these in heavy protective suits with gauntlets) were loading bones into an opened reactor, stacking them in careful alignment inside the resonance cavity. Once filled, the reactor would contain the bones of two thousand dead people. Waves of necroflux would pulse back and forth, building intensity until the energy could be used to deliver warmth and lighting and motive power to the city overhead.

No one intended the side effect, as the sweeping necroflux replayed a tangled burning chaos of thoughts and emotions, the mashed-together pain of two thousand lives, forced into one tortured whole. That awful crescendo was playing out now in each reactor pile, over and over, until the bones were used up, and more fuel was required.

Oh, Hades.

It was terrible. It was impossible to look away.

I knew it, but I didn't understand.

Everyone knew, and everyone ignored the reality.

I can't look.

But he did look, remaining linked with his spider until the spillover resonance finally shook it apart. Then its body began slopping away into liquid blood, thickening and denaturing into stickiness, and the link was gone.

In his room, Carl sat with his mouth open, breathing fast, wishing he'd severed the link earlier.

But I've got it.

He had needed a theme. He'd read the dates, but the history had been far removed, listing events that seemed unreal.

I wish I didn't.

But he had his essay now.

Finally, it was Sepday and the beginning of class.

The essay was inside Carl's desk. He felt its presence like a glow from beneath the ancient, defaced desktop. He had written something special, and he knew it.

"I mentioned we would try something new." Sister Stef spoke without smiling. She'd looked serious for days. "We're going to read our essays aloud, one at a time."

Normally, the thought of such a thing would have terrified Carl. But with an essay like the one he'd written, a feeling of unstoppable triumph was rising inside him.

"We'll take turns, but I'll ask for volunteers to start—"

Carl's hand was up, as if it had risen by itself.

"—so it'll be Carl first, then Angela."

He felt warm, energised.

"Of course," continued Sister Stef, "Ralen can just relax. Welcome back, from all of us."

That was when Carl realized that Ralen had been sitting in his normal desk all along, so subdued—his gaze directed down at his desktop—that the usual signals of dissatisfaction and potential violence had been absent.

Oh, no.

Poor Ralen was devastated, as Carl knew Dad had been when Mother died, when his world was ripped away from him. And that was awful.

I can't read it. Not aloud.

Because the cleverness of his essay was also shocking, depending on the listeners' ignorance—if Carl read it aloud—of the reality of life and death. He'd thought he was being smart, writing about things that people didn't want to know, but now—

"So, Carl. Will you start?"

"I . . . I didn't do it, Sister. I . . . forgot."

"You forgot."

"Yes, Sister." He felt a whirlpool of sickness inside. "Sorry."

"Then"—Sister Stef breathed out, and looked at the steel punishment ruler on its hook—"you'll step forward to the front of the class."

Blurred, the classroom seemed to recede as Carl stood, and shakily walked to Sister Stef.

"Hold out your hand."

He raised it, palm upwards, wishing he didn't know what was about to come.

"I'm disappointed, Carl Thargulis." Sister Stef made no move towards the ruler. "There are so many things I don't believe in, including the teaching power of violence. But *you*, you I did have faith in. Sit down."

Carl returned to his desk, feeling worse than if pain had cut into his soft palm. Taking his seat, he only half-noticed the sympathy on Ralen's face.

This was awful.

Now it was her final day. Stef moved in a trance, teaching mechanically, scarcely responsive to questions for fear the emotional dam might give way. Sister Zarly Umbra avoided her for the same reason, being the only other nun, besides Reverend Mother, to know that Stef's packed bags already waited atop the cot in her cell, that a room in a hostel was already booked.

Tonight Stef would slip out through the iron gates forever.

At the end of the last lesson—the last lesson *ever*—she watched her pupils file out, hoping Angela would thrive, that the city would somehow change back to the way it had been, tolerating near-humans. And there went Carl, such a disappointment. Even Ralen, the bully, had suffered such trauma, and she hoped his life would turn around, and regretted that she was unlikely to learn how things worked out for any of them, her boys and girls.

But this was not her home, not any longer.

The classroom was empty. She felt insubstantial, like a wraith who could slip through floor or wall to disappear. Soon enough, in an ordinary human way, that was what she had to do.

"Damn it," she said. "Damn it all to Hades."

How would the children feel tomorrow, when a new teacher greeted them?

"They'll forget me. So what?"

Her gaze descended to Carl's desk. Yes, he had disappointed her, particularly since she had been so sure he was excited by the essay theme.

She walked to Carl's desk and raised the lid. Perhaps an intuitive part of her already knew what she would find inside. The lace-bound pages lay on top of his textbooks.

There was a title page, and it read:

TRI-MILLENNIUM
THE DATE'S TRUE MEANING
by Carl Thargulis, aged 12

She lifted the essay out of the desk.

An hour later, she was hammering on Bone Listener Jamie Thargulis' door, with Carl's essay in hand. Jamie opened the door.

"I'd like a word," she said.

"Er . . . All right." Jamie Thargulis stepped back. "Have you been crying?"

Stef ran a hand through her hair, then adjusted her unfamiliar coat. Jamie Thargulis was staring.

"Where's Carl, Mr. Thargulis?"

"Upstairs in his room. I'll just—"

"No. There's something I need to talk about. To a . . . friend."

"You'd better come in. And call me Jamie, if you'd like."

"Yes. Please."

She followed him—Jamie—to a small sitting-room. There he gestured to an old, overstuffed armchair, and she sat down. The room was cluttered and cosy, comforting.

"I've left the order."

But that wasn't what was overwhelming her. It was Carl's doing, truly, but it wasn't his *fault*, that was the thing. He'd written something wonderful, but now she was hurting.

"You've . . . what?"

"So I can't talk to Reverend Mother, not now, and I need to. Talk. To someone."

"All right." Jamie closed the door, and crossed to the other armchair. "Tell me."

"My mother—please don't laugh."

"Why should I?" Jamie's voice sounded so gentle. "Just talk."

"She was a big woman, and an alcoholic. She used to wait for my father, for Pop to come home, and then she'd . . . beat him. With empty bottles, or a roller from the wringer."

"Oh, Thanatos."

"Yes. Pop was small, and never fought back. He got drunk to numb the pain. He—"

"It's OK. You don't need to tell me."

"I do. It's just—Sometimes, as a girl, I'd go down to the docks. You know I lived in TalonClaw Port?"

"Carry on."

"I used to see . . . people. Shuffling to the docks. I didn't realize—"

"What was that?"

"I thought they were passengers, you see. I didn't realize. Because I was young, and we all of us ignore the realities."

Jamie's fingertips touched the back of her hand.

"Tell me."

"My father," she said aloud, after all these years, "sold himself. He became one of them. The shuffling horde. The doomed."

"I don't understand."

She passed over the pages she'd been holding.

"Your son would. He's not afraid to look."

"Carl?"

Jamie stared at the essay, then returned his gaze to her, focusing those incredible dark eyes on *her*.

"It's not like the necroflux piles," she said, "but it's close enough. Except in the suboceanic liners, they don't extract bones from corpses. They use entire human beings. Alive. I can't begin to imagine the agony."

Jamie shook his head.

"The money," Stef continued, "was enough to buy me passage, away from TalonClaw Port, and to enrol in college. It was hidden in my bed, the whole roll of cash. But I blew the lot on airfare, because I couldn't bear to travel by ship. Not after—"

"Tell me," said Jamie once more.

"Pop wasn't a passenger," she said. "He was *fuel*, along with all the others. He sold himself to set me free."

It was another Sepday, three months later, when they stood together, the three of them amid a crowd of over a million people, thronging the heart of Tristopolis. They stood on the sidewalk at the northern end of Avenue of the Basilisks, watching the great parade pass by.

"Hey," said Dad. "There's the Leviathan that Carl and I saw."

"The balloons at Möbius Park?" asked Stef. "That's terrific."

She leaned close and kissed him, hard. Keeping her arm around Dad, she ruffled Carl's hair, and he grinned up at her.

"It was neat," he said.

" 'Neat,' huh? You have a better command of the language than that, young man."

"I know."

Dad smiled.

"You two," he said.

A clown floated past, borne by freewraiths whose half-materialized forms glowed festive orange and yellow.

"It's not just a Tri-Millennial we're celebrating, is it?" said Stef.

During the past three months, there had been two changes of mayor, and a turnaround in public mood. The Trueblood Bill had passed, then been revoked. Now the city was returning to its previous cosmopolitan acceptance of everyone.

"No." Dad kissed her. "It's our celebration too, thanks to this young miscreant."

He winked, and Carl grinned.

"The interview," said Stef, "at Tech tomorrow?"

She meant the secular college she'd applied to for a teaching post.

"Uh-huh?"

"Reverend Mother rang while you were at work. She said if Bill—that's the principal—didn't offer me the position on the spot, I was to say that some people remember what he got up to behind the bike sheds thirty years ago."

"Some other kind of anniversary?"

"Shh." Stef's hand was gentle as she touched Carl's head. "Not in front of our boy."

On that night she'd shown up at the door, the night she left the Order of Thanatos for good, she'd had sat in the old armchair for a long time. Finally, after the tears were done, she had asked Jamie to hand back Carl's essay. Then she'd read the beginning aloud.

"*And the date, Sepday 37th of Unodecember 6608,*" she'd recited, "*confuses two anniversaries. While it is 3333 years since the inauguration of City Hall, the date of Unodecember 37th is remarkable for something else, dating back only six centuries.*

"*It is hard to imagine what a city would be like without heat and lighting. But it is impossible to know where the power comes from, if you can't imagine how the bones hurt and scream. When a person dies, what happens is—*"

She stopped, then continued to the end, forcing her way through the step-by-step description that Carl had provided, and the revelation that six hundred years ago, on Unodecember 37th, the first necroflux reactor pile had gone online, delivering its power to the city.

"You're a Bone Listener," she said then. "Do you realize how hard that is for a person to read?"

"Yes," Jamie said, before doing something strange: taking hold of the blue-and-white photo of Mareela, and placing it face down on a table. "Carry on, please."

"That's it. Fine writing."

"Disturbing," said Jamie, for reasons that became clear only later, when he and Stef quizzed Carl about his Archive-derived knowledge, and his observation of the inner workings of the Energy Authority.

"Yes. I remember my first day at the school"—Stef put down the essay—"when I stood in the yard, watching the children play a game called Ring-Around-A-Rhyme. You know it? They didn't have it where I came from."

She pointed to the essay, where Carl had written the second verse of the rhyme.

> *Worms in their eyeballs,*
> *No one can see*
> *Beetles devour*
> *My true love and me.*

Jamie nodded.

"It's about burial," he said. "Back when we used to bury the dead, instead of turn them into fuel."

"I realized that immediately, and I knew that the kids had no idea. But it's propaganda, isn't it? Old propaganda, from six centuries back, and still required. To make the idea of burial repulsive."

"And get people to forget what's waiting."

They looked at each other.

"What *is* waiting, Jamie?"

"I don't know, Sister . . . "

"Call me Stef."

The three of them watched until the final float of the parade had passed by.

"How about Shadbolt's Halt?" said Dad. "We could have an ice-cream."

"I'd rather go home," said Carl.

"Me too," murmured Stef.

Dad took her hand.

"Then that's what we'll do," he said.

THE PERSISTENCE OF MEMORY; OR, THIS SPACE FOR SALE

PAUL PARK

Stuck, facing a deadline, I decided to sell some of my things on eBay, not objects so much as ideas. Or rather, lack of ideas: I thought I could kill two birds with one stone. I auctioned off the pieces of a story I am trying to write, the location, the characters, the theme, the devices, even the title. I had seven auctions running simultaneously. I bid on a few things myself, to drive up the price. And I was rewarded by a spasm of activity the last few hours which brought in pledges totaling several hundred dollars, enough to double the money I would likely make from some anthology.

Not every auction made the minimum reserve. And there was a downside: the story had to take place in Philadelphia. A love story: fine, whatever. I'm not so jaded that I can't remember what that's like. But the treatment had to involve some use of meta-fiction, some recursive pattern. For example, the story could be about writing a story. Or else more particularly, it could be about itself. Regardless, these are techniques I've increasingly hated, because they tend to involve a lot of stupid fooling around. They are always reminding you that what you're reading is a construct, just some marks on paper. But the whole point of writing is creating an illusion that something really happened. That's why people read. That's what they want.

Here are the directions I received:

Dear Paul Park,

I really liked your last story in F&SF. I appreciate the thought that ordinary problems have miraculous solutions. If you're right, then maybe you could do something for me and the girl I love. We're coming up on our fourth anniversary, and I was hoping to find some kind of special way to tell her how I still feel, even after some time. Her name

*is Sarah Kettle, and she is 26 years old. She works as a counselor for
soldiers with traumatic injuries. She plays the guitar and enjoys poetry.
And I think she might trust you or value what you have to say, because
she liked your story too, with reservations, after I'd explained it—she
never would have read it on her own. I'm sending you some jpegs, so
you can see how beautiful she is. Try to do something with her smile.
You can see how it lights up the whole room. Thanks.*

It was true—Sarah Kettle had a lot of teeth. There she was, cross-legged on
the floor of a cozy grad-student apartment, posing dutifully with her guitar.
She was dressed in jeans and a white shirt, unbuttoned a few buttons, but you
couldn't see much. In the next photograph she had a more serious expression
on her face. Her straight black hair, cut to the line of her jaw, obscured one
eye, most of her big nose.

You must know, true love never does run smooth. Our hero had submitted
bids in three separate categories and won two of them. In his eagerness to
work his girlfriend into the story, he had exceeded my reserve by more than
ninety dollars. But in the final auction he had undervalued himself by one
dollar and twenty-seven cents or thereabouts, and only found out when it was
too late. This often happens. It has happened to me.

It meant our hero had allowed himself to be out-bid at the last second
by someone else, a fellow named Benjamin Burgis. He also forwarded an
image—only one, out of focus, taken in a group with some of his co-workers
in their white coats. He said he didn't care how he appeared to me, not that
it mattered, because he didn't require a very complicated treatment. I got the
impression he wanted to be represented as some kind of monstrous version of
himself, a sniveling zombie, perhaps a psychopath.

I didn't say anything about that to our hero. He was traumatized enough
already, and it was only by promising him a cameo that I was able to convince
him not to withdraw his bid. I wanted to buck up his courage, and so I told
him what I'd do. He would come in at the last second and snipe his rival in
return. Nor would I abandon Sarah Kettle to a fate worse than death. I would
do everything in my power not to let the zombie touch her with his long,
hairy, filthy, suppurating hands.

Ben Burgis hadn't pledged very much, certainly not enough to allow him to
take any sexual liberties. I felt I didn't owe him anything at all. And of course
our hero, because of his stupidity, had all but written himself out of his own
story. What an idiot, perhaps, but the least I could do was offer him a sensitive
portrayal of the woman he loved. Perhaps, as a result of my efforts, she would
put her guitar aside, brush the hair out of her face, stand up and put her arms
around his waist and then his neck. Maybe she would reconsider.

Frankly, I was of two minds about the whole thing. And I felt I needed
more information to achieve whatever it was he wanted, to guarantee his
satisfaction. A couple of pictures weren't enough to do her justice. Was that a

gold chain around her neck under her shirt? What did her voice sound like? Where was she from? Where had she gone to school? What did her parents do? I had to think about all that. And I couldn't just choose things at random, or to please myself. Sarah Kettle was a real person, not just my creation. She had her own needs, her own stubbornness. I couldn't just manipulate her however I wanted. I googled her and didn't find much, a few stray pieces of co-authorship, mostly papers on veterans' affairs.

So I made the following request:

> . . . I feel I want to make this work for you. She looks like a really nice young woman, and as you say she has a killer smile. If you have a cv, you can forward it, but what I really want to know are things that are more personal, things that will enable me to bring her to an independent life. Maybe stories of you two together, or else things that have happened to her. Fears. Dreams. Opinions. I want you to feel you can speak to her through me. Do you have a sample of her handwriting? Give me any photographs you have. Also anything to show me the inside of her apartment—pictures on the wall. Furniture. Layout. Any favorite things. You can tell a lot about people from the objects they choose to live with. Under the circumstances, this story isn't going to involve other characters. Just at the end, as I said. Most of it is going to be a kind of portrait. So the more you can give me, the better it will be.

And in a couple of days I had a little package in my hands. I confess I was nervous when I opened it. As I hoped, there were some letters, and also a small brick of snapshots, meticulously tied in a black ribbon. There was a cd.

In my New York apartment, I slipped the disk into the machine, then sat down on the couch with a glass of scotch. I heard a woman's voice: "This is just something I'm working on." And then a mixture of songs, some traditional, some original, I guessed—Sarah Kettle accompanying herself on the guitar. In between, a few serious, breathy, self-conscious comments: a shy person speaking for posterity. "This isn't really ready yet." "This is a song about my mother." "Because we weren't religious, Thanksgiving was always a big deal around our house . . . "

The voice itself was unexceptional. But I found myself affected nonetheless, as I untied the ribbon, held it up to my nose. Then I leafed through the photographs. They weren't all of her. As I'd hoped, there were some pictures of the bedroom, the double bed with its white frame, its patchwork quilt, its orange gooseneck lamp on the bedside cabinet. A poster of Salvador Dali's "The Persistence of Memory" on the wall above the computer. Framed photos of her family in Lafayette Hill.

" . . . I remember those times when my brother came home from college and we were all together again. We'd sing songs and then go out into the neighborhood, visiting people I'd known all my life. Sometimes I'd feel annoyed by the routine. But it took me a long time to realize how lucky I was." Then the song began. It was about a Thanksgiving party at the VA hospital. Nothing earth-shattering.

Always you look for patterns, and then things that don't fit. In her bedroom there was one expensive piece of furniture, a drop-leaf table from Connecticut. I saw parts of it a couple of times. Then in one photograph it had been pushed against the wall and loaded down with bottles and vases that would wreck its surface, I thought. It looked like a piece from the 1820s. Didn't she know how much it was worth?

I sat on my new couch, listening to the cd. I had arranged the pictures on my coffee table, and now I pulled out the ones that showed my actual subject, her face, her body. I put the rest aside. But the portraits I also separated into groups, according to whether they were candid or posed, or according to what mood they captured, or according to whether I could fit them into an imagined narrative. Then I gathered them at random, squared them face down like a tarot deck, turned them over one by one.

There was one I thought had been included by mistake, a nude. It had been stuck to the back of something more innocuous. I pulled it free, set it aside, didn't look at it.

And now I tried to arrange the photographs into chronological order. Four years of a relationship. In fact I could see different hair-styles, different events—birthdays, perhaps. And Thanksgiving. Sarah Kettle liked candle-light. She liked to pose next to the spread table, a turkey baster in her hand. I counted three of those. Time had gone by. I tried to see it in her face.

I put my glass down on the stone coaster. I ran my finger along the table's soft mahogany. Finally, I wiped my hands on my bathrobe and picked up the last photograph, the nude. Again, I don't think it had been forwarded intentionally. Part of the surface of the Polaroid was marred, where it had stuck to the back of another print.

By this time I was used to the several expressions of Sarah Kettle— aggressive, embarrassed, goofy, pensive, anxious, even angry, when she had not, I gathered, wished or consented to be photographed. Because of that, and because I was listening to a prissy, self-conscious little rendering of "It Ain't Me, Babe," I expected to see some sign of irritation in her face. But there was nothing close. Almost for the first time she stared straight at the camera. High cheekbones, thick lips, delicate, long jaw. One hand was on her hip, one knee was bent. Dark skin, dark eyes. Her head was cocked to one side, so that her hair fell away from her small ear.

She had a long scar along the outside of one leg, the remains of a sports injury, I thought. And she was a beautiful young woman, as it turned out. Beautifully formed. She had a small, delicate tuft of pubic hair. And because her expression was so indistinct (Boredom? Cold? Happiness? Desire?), it served to emphasize by contrast the peculiar clarity of the rest of the photographs, how each one seemed to show a single unmixed mood. How strange it was, I thought, always to know what someone else was thinking.

Perhaps I shouldn't have looked at that last photograph. Perhaps I should have thrown it away, because it wasn't useful to the story I was trying to write. I had pretended to myself it couldn't hurt and probably might help, the way a painter might want to look at a model's naked body, even if the finished portrait shows no skin at all—I have no idea how painters think. What I know is, once I saw that final photograph there was no going back, not so much because of the body but because of the face—those sleepy, almond eyes.

I gathered the pictures and laid them all aside, except for that one. I turned on my laptop. I had some ideas, and I scratched at them for a few hours. I thought I'd try to invent some stories, a series of interlocking sketches with her in the middle—a mystery, a fantasy, a joke. Like for example, I thought about her walking back and forth, back and forth, scratching her bare arms. She was wearing something blue—very sweet, with little embroidered flowers. "I'm really, really sorry," she said, looking really, really sorry. Tears in her eyes: "I never wanted to hurt you. We saw each other every day. He works on the floor above me, for God's sake. We didn't plan on this."

Or else outside in the cold, dressed in a wool jacket and a scarf. We were walking along Kelly Drive by the art museum. She was laughing. "What are you looking at?" she said to me. "Old man—wipe that grin off your face." Then she came up and put her mittened hand against my chest.

Or else something less literal, something more symbolic. Maybe if there was something that was threatening her. Some beast at the door, and there was some way to protect her. I thought of a gray journey through the cold, a lighted window at the end.

But all that was too murky, too sequential, with too much of an implied plot. And she herself was out of sight: In each of these scenes, I wanted to present her in one single mood. And the idea was, I would lay these stories out around an empty center, which in my mind I would fill with the image from the final photograph. So: unstated, undescribed, and yet, now that I thought about it, the key to the whole thing—I couldn't get it out of my head. This was partly because I needed more exposition and saw no way to get it. I wanted a better sense of the woman's attitude toward the person taking the photograph. I wanted clarification, perhaps other exposures from the same session, dozens of them, each one presenting a different version of that mixed, nuanced expression. And the body, of course—our hero would fixate on my interest in the body. He'd never send me anything else. He wouldn't pay me. I might as well ask for something that smelled like her, a yellow t-shirt from the University of Pennsylvania, where I used to have a real job, not like now. Or as long as I was dreaming, maybe something more intimate, a pair of underpants or a brassiere. Yes, something like that might definitely help me out.

"Sometimes I feel like I've spent too long in this room," she sang. Etc.,

etc., and that was the end of the cd. I picked up one of her letters, typed, no scent:

> . . . *I want to show myself to you, but I can't. I want to talk to you in just a normal way like before. At least I remember it being normal, but maybe that's what memory does. I can't believe it was always like this. Would we have gotten to know each other like we have?*

What was she talking about? My correspondent, the person who had commissioned the story in the first place, I wondered if he had a chance in hell. But he deserved nothing, because of his stupidity. I turned off my machines and went to bed.

I had other projects going, so I didn't think about Sarah Kettle for a few days. I put all the pictures and letters in a drawer. Maybe I'd let some sort of plot develop without paying attention. Or I could try to get some outside help. I was teaching a class at the New School, and I thought I'd try a new form of triple-dipping. This was in the context of a general discussion about how writing something or describing something could enrich an experience, and also about whether memory could function more like photographs or like the movies. As an example, I showed my students one of the Thanksgiving scenes and asked them to invent stories about Sarah Kettle. It was interesting what they perceived, what they distorted. Then I revealed part of how I intended to use this image and the others. I also revealed part of the problem I'd been having. As a solution, a couple of students recommended a technique that we'd discussed, a "sling-shot" ending, which would break the story off before the conflict was resolved. Someone else suggested that in the final struggle I shouldn't necessarily reveal who was the hero, who was the monster. This intrigued me, though I didn't see at first how I could use both ideas at once. I have several engaging students in that class. One in particular, although she doesn't say much.

It so happened that I had some independent business that brought me to Philadelphia later that week. I took the train. And when after ninety minutes I got out at 30th Street Station, I decided to walk to my appointment on Washington Square, even though my memories of the city were complicated, and as recently as November I had promised never to return if I could help it. Those feelings had faded, but as I walked through the gray streets (it was an overcast March day), I found them coming back. I plodded over the bridge, down JFK past City Hall, and headed on down Market Street. I had some time to kill, but even so, what was I doing here? I could have taken the subway. Then I remembered Sarah Kettle's address from her cv, and realized where she lived was on the way—why not? Added value, if I described the house. Maybe just the sight of it would jar something loose—I'd thought about her briefly on the train. It wasn't yet four o'clock, but I knew she kept irregular hours. I played with the idea of knocking on the door, but I was afraid of scaring her, or else inspiring one of those angry looks I'd seen in the photographs. I felt I knew everything about her and at the same time nothing at all, the kind of simultaneous impression usually reserved for lovers or family members, and a little creepy in this case. I wouldn't want her to think I was stalking her. That wouldn't help her idiotic boyfriend's (or former boyfriend's) idiotic proposal. I cut over to Spruce Street, and up a street of row houses with alleyways between them. I was glancing at the numbers, and I crossed the street to the wrong side, so I could get a look at the entire house. She lived on the first floor, and the light was on.

After a few minutes, I slipped down the alleyway around to the back. As I suspected, there was a sequence of three long fire-escapes that doubled as back porches, one on top of the other. I saw the light on in Sarah Kettle's bedroom. I glanced at my watch, wondering if I had time to stay here long enough to see Ben Burgis slouch home from his job at the hospital, crash through the front door, try to grab her in his horrible embrace.

As I thought about this, I found I had climbed up the first steps of the fire-escape, onto the back porch. I could see the kitchen door above me. There was the lighted window.

But then I checked my watch again, and as I turned I saw Annie Mertz come up the alleyway, a bag of groceries balanced on one hip. She was Sarah Kettle's neighbor on the third floor. I tried to avoid her, but she'd reached the bottom of the steps. She put her hand on the railing. "Paul," she said, "Paul, is that you?"

Then after a moment: "What are you doing here? You'd better not let Ben see you. Is this about your stupid table?"

After another moment: "Paul, you're crying. Please—are you okay? Does Sarah even know you're here?"

THIS PEACEABLE LAND; OR, THE UNBEARABLE VISION OF HARRIET BEECHER STOWE

ROBERT CHARLES WILSON

"It's worth your life to go up there," the tavernkeeper's wife said. "What do you want to go up there for, anyway?"

"The property is for sale," I said.

"Property!" The landlady of the roadside tavern nearly spat out the word. "There's nothing up there but sand hills and saggy old sheds. That, and a family of crazy colored people. Someone claims they sold you that? You ought to check with the bank, Mister, see about getting your money back."

She smiled at her own joke, showing tobacco-stained teeth. In this part of the country there were spittoons in every taproom and Bull Durham advertisements on every wall. It was 1895. It was August. It was hot, and we were in the South.

I was only posing as an investor. I had no money in all the baggage I was carrying—very little, anyhow. I had photographic equipment instead.

"You go up those hills," the tavernkeeper's wife said more soberly, "you carry a gun, and you keep it handy. I mean that."

I had no gun.

I wasn't worried about what I might find up in the pine barrens.

I was worried about what I would tell my daughter.

I paid the lady for the meal she had served me and for a second meal she had put up in neat small box. I asked her whether a room was available for the night. There was. We discussed the arrangements and came to an agreement. Then I went out to where Percy was waiting in the carriage.

"You'll have to sleep outside," I said. "But I got this for you." I gave him the wrapped dinner. "And the landlady says she'll bring you a box breakfast in the morning, as long as there's nobody around to see her."

Percy nodded. None of this came as a surprise to him. He knew where he was, and who he was, and what was expected of him. "And then," he said, "we'll drive up to the place, weather permitting."

To Percy it was always "the place"—each place we found.

Storm-clouds had dallied along this river valley all the hot day but no rain had come. If it came tonight, and if it was torrential, the dirt roads would quickly become useless creeks of mud. We would be stuck here for days.

And Percy would get wet, sleeping in the carriage as he did. But he preferred the carriage to the stable where our horses were put up. The carriage was covered with rubberized cloth, and there was a big sheet of mosquito netting he stretched over the open places during the night. But a truly stiff rain was bound to get in the cracks and make him miserable.

Percy Camber was an educated black man. He wrote columns and articles for the *Tocsin*, a Negro paper published out of Windsor, Canada. Three years ago a Boston press had put out a book he'd written, though he admitted the sales had been slight.

I wondered what the landlady would say if I told her Percy was a book-writer. Most likely she would have denied the possibility of an educated black man. Except perhaps as a circus act, like that Barnum horse that counts to ten with its hoof.

"Make sure your gear is ready first thing," Percy said, keeping his voice low although there was nobody else about—this was a poor tavern on a poor road in an undeveloped county. "And don't drink too much tonight, Tom, if you can help it."

"That's sound advice," I agreed, by way of not pledging an answer. "Oh, and the keeper's wife tells me we ought to carry a gun. Wild men up there, she says."

"I don't go armed."

"Nor do I."

"Then I guess we'll be prey for the wild men," said Percy, smiling.

The room where I spent the night was not fancy, which made me feel better about leaving my employer to sleep out-of-doors. It was debatable which of us was better off. The carriage seat where Percy curled up was not infested with fleas, as was the mattress on which I lay. Percy customarily slept on a folded jacket, while my pillow was a sugar sack stuffed with corn huskings, which rattled beneath my ear as if the beetles inside were putting on a musical show.

I slept a little, woke up, scratched myself, lit the lamp, took a drink.

I will not drink, I told myself as I poured the liquor. I will not drink "to excess." I will not become drunk. I will only calm the noise in my head.

My companion in this campaign was a bottle of rye whisky. Mister Whisky-Bottle, unfortunately, was only half full, and not up to the task assigned him. I drank but kept on thinking unwelcome thoughts, while the night simmered and creaked with insect noises.

"Why do you have to go away for so long?" Elsebeth asked me.

In this incarnation she wore a white dress. It looked like a confirmation dress. She was thirteen years old.

"Taking pictures," I told her. "Same as always."

"Why can't you take pictures at the portrait studio?"

"These are different pictures, Elsie. The kind you have to travel for."

Her flawless young face took on an accusatory cast. "Mama says you're stirring up old trouble. She says you're poking into things nobody wants to hear about any more, much less see photographs of."

"She may be right. But I'm being paid money, and money buys pretty dresses, among other good things."

"Why make such trouble, though? Why do you want to make people feel bad?"

Elsie was a phantom. I blinked her away. These were questions she had not yet actually posed, though our last conversation, before I left Detroit, had come uncomfortably close. But they were questions I would sooner or later have to answer.

I slept very little, despite the drink. I woke up before dawn.

I inventoried my photographic equipment by lamplight, just to make sure everything was ready.

It had not rained during the night. I settled up with the landlady and removed my baggage from the room. Percy had already hitched the horses to the carriage. The sky was drab under high cloud, the sun a spot of light like a candle-flame burning through a linen handkerchief.

The landlady's husband was nowhere to be seen. He had gone down to Crib Lake for supplies, she said, as she packed up the two box lunches, cold cuts of beef with pickles and bread, which I had requested of her. She had two adult sons living with her, one of whom I had met in the stables, and she felt safe enough, she told me, even with her husband absent. "But we're a long way from anywhere," she added, "and the traffic along this road has been light ever since—well, ever since the Lodge closed down. I wasn't kidding about those sand hills, Mister. Be careful up there."

"We mean to be back by nightfall," I said.

My daughter Elsebeth had met Percy Camber just once, when he came to the house in Detroit to discuss his plans with me. Elsie had been meticulously polite to him. Percy had offered her his hand, and she, wide-eyed, had taken it. "You're very neatly dressed," she had said.

She was not used to well-dressed black men. The only blacks Elsebeth had seen were the day laborers who gathered on the wharves. Detroit housed a small community of Negroes who had come north with the decline of slavery, before Congress passed the Labor Protection Act. They did "the jobs white men won't do," for wages to which white men would not submit.

"You're very prettily dressed yourself," Percy Camber had said, ignoring the unintended insult.

Maggie, my wife, had simply refused to see him.

"I'm not some radical old Congregationalist," she told me, "eager to socialize with every tawny Moor who comes down the pike. That's your side of the family, Tom, not mine."

True enough. Maggie's people were Episcopalians who had prospered in Michigan since before it was a State—sturdy, reliable folks. They ran a string of warehouses that catered to the lake trade. Whereas my father was a disappointed Whig who had spent a single term in the Massachusetts legislature pursuing the chimera of Free Education before he died at an early age, and my mother's bookshelves still groaned under the weight of faded tomes on the subjects of Enlightened Marriage and Women's Suffrage. I came from a genteel family of radical tendencies and modest means. I was never sure Maggie's people understood that poverty and gentility could truly co-exist.

"Maggie's indisposed today," I had told Percy, who may or may not have believed me, and then we had settled down to the business of planning our three-month tour of the South, according to the maps he had made.

"There ought to be photographs," Percy said, "before it's all gone."

We traveled several miles from the tavern, sweating in the airless heat of the morning, following directions Percy had deduced from bills-of-transfer, railway records, and old advertisements placed in the Richmond and Atlanta papers.

The locality to which we were headed had been called Pilgassi Acres. It had been chartered as a business by two brothers, Marcus and Benjamin Pilgassi of South Carolina, in 1879, and it had operated for five years before the Ritter Inquiry shut it down.

There were no existing photographs of Pilgassi Acres, or any of the institutions like it, unless the Ritter Inquiry had commissioned them. And the Final Report of the Ritter Inquiry had been sealed from the public by consent of Congress, not to be re-opened until some time in the twentieth century.

Percy Camber intended to shed some light into that officially ordained darkness.

He sat with me on the driver's board of the carriage as I coaxed the team over the rutted and runneled trail. This had once been a wider road, much-used, but it had been bypassed by a Federal turnpike in 1887. Since then nature and the seasons had mauled it. So the ride was tedious and slow. We subdued the boredom by swapping stories: Percy of his home in Canada, me of my time in the army.

Percy "talked white." That was the verdict Elsebeth had passed after meeting him. It was a condescending thing to say, excusable only from the lips of a child, but I knew what she meant. Percy was two generations out of slavery. If I closed my eyes and listened to his voice I could imagine that I had been hired by some soft-spoken Harvard graduate. He was articulate, even for a newspaper man. And we had learned, over the course of this lengthy expedition, to make allowance for our differences. We had some common ground. We were both the offspring of radical parents, for example. The "madness of the fifties" had touched us both, in different ways.

"You suppose we'll find anything substantial at the end of this road?" Percy asked.

"The landlady mentioned some old sheds."

"Sheds would be acceptable," Percy said, his weariness showing. "It's been a long haul for you, Tom. And not much substantial work. Maybe this time?"

"Maybe."

"Documents, oral accounts, that's all useful, but a photograph—just one—just to show that something remains—well, that would be important."

"I'll photograph any old shed you like, Percy, if it pleases you." Though on this trip I had seen more open fields—long since burned over and regrown—than anything worthy of being immortalized. Places edited from history. Absences constructed as carefully as architecture. I had no reason to think Pilgassi Acres would be different.

Percy seldom spoke aloud about the deeper purpose of his quest or the book he was currently writing. Fair enough, I thought—it was a sensitive subject. Like the way I don't talk much about Cuba, though I had served a year and a half there under Lee. The spot is too tender to touch.

These hills were low and covered with stunted pines and other rude vegetation. The road soon grew even more rough, but we began to encounter evidence of a prior human presence. A few fenceposts. Scraps of rusted barbwire. The traces of an old narrow-gauge rail bed. Then we passed under a wooden sign suspended between two lodge-poles, on which the words *PILGASSI ACRES*, in an ornate script, were still legible, though the seasons had bleached the letters to ghosts.

There was also the remnant of a wire fence, tangled over with brambles.

"Stop here," Percy said.

"Might be more ahead," I suggested.

"This is already more than we've seen elsewhere. I want a picture of that sign."

"I can't guarantee it'll be legible," I said, given the way the sun was striking it, and the faint color of the letters, pale as chalk on the white wood.

"Well, try," Percy said shortly.

So I set up my equipment and did that. For the first time in a long while I felt like I was earning my keep.

The first book Percy had written was called *Every Measure Short of War*, and it was a history of Abolitionism from the Negro point of view.

The one he was writing now was to be called *Where are the Three Million?*

I made a dozen or so exposures and put my gear back in the carriage. Percy took the reins this time and urged the horses farther up the trail. Scrub grass and runt pines closed in on both sides of us, and I found myself watching the undergrowth for motion. The landlady's warning had come back to haunt me.

But the woods were empty. An old stray dog paced us for a few minutes, then fell behind.

My mother had once corresponded with Mrs. Harriet Beecher Stowe, who was well-known abolitionist at one time, though the name is now mostly forgotten. Percy had contacted my parents in order to obtain copies of that correspondence, which he had quoted in an article for the *Tocsin*.

My mother, of course, was flattered by his interest, and she continued her correspondence with Percy on an occasional basis. In one of his replies Percy happened to remark that he was looking for a reliable photographer to hire for the new project he had in mind. My mother sent him to me. Perhaps she thought she was doing me a favor.

Thus it was not money but conscience that had propelled me on this journey. Conscience, that crabbed and ecclesiastical nag, which inevitably spoke, whether I heeded it or not, in a voice much like my mother's.

The remains of Pilgassi Acres became visible as we rounded a final bend, and I was frankly astonished that so much of it remained intact. Percy Camber drew in his breath.

Here were the administrators' quarters (a small building with pretensions to the Colonial style), as well as five huge barnlike buildings and fragments of paving-stones and mortared brick where more substantial structures had been demolished.

All silent, all empty. No glass in the small windows. A breeze like the breath from a hard-coal stove seeped around the buildings and tousled the meadow weeds that lapped at them. There was the smell of old wood that had stood in the sunlight for a long time. There was, beneath that, the smell of something less pleasant, like an abandoned latrine doused with lime and left to simmer in the heat.

Percy was working to conceal his excitement. He pretended to be casual, but I could see that every muscle in him had gone taut.

"Your camera, Tom," he said, as if the scene were in some danger of evaporating before our eyes.

"You don't want to explore the place a little first?"

"Not yet. I want to capture it as we see it now—from a distance, all the buildings all together."

And I did that. The sun, though masked by light high clouds, was a feverish nuisance over my right shoulder.

I thought of my daughter Elsebeth. She would see these pictures some day. "What place is this?" she would ask.

But what would I say in return?

Any answer I could think of amounted to drilling a hole in her innocence and pouring poison in.

Every Measure Short of War—the title of Percy's first book—implied that there might have been one—a war over Abolition, that is; a war between the States. My mother agreed. "Though it was not the North that would have brought it on," she insisted. (A conversation we had had on the eve of my marriage to Maggie.) "People forget how sullen the South was in the years before the Douglas Compromise. How fierce in their defense of slavery. The 'Peculiar Institution!' Strange, isn't it, how people cling most desperately to a thing when it becomes least useful to them?"

My mother's dream, and Mrs. Stowe's for that matter, had never been achieved. No Abolition by federal statute had ever been legislated. Slavery had simply become unprofitable, as its milder opponents and apologists used to insist it inevitably would. Scientific farming killed it. Crop rotation killed it. Deep plowing killed it, mechanized harvesters killed it, soil fertilization killed it.

Embarrassment killed it, once Southern farmers began to take seriously the condescension and disapproval of the European powers whose textile and tobacco markets they craved. Organized labor killed it.

Ultimately, the expense and absurdity of maintaining human beings as farm chattel killed it.

A few slaves were still held under permissive state laws (in Virginia and South Carolina for example), but they tended to be the pets of the old Planter Aristocracy—kept, as pets might be kept, because the children of the household had grown fond of them and objected to their eviction.

I walked with Percy Camber through the abandoned administration building at Pilgassi Acres. It had been stripped of everything—all furniture, every document, any scrap that might have testified to its human utility. Even the wallpaper had peeled or rotted away. One well-placed lightning strike would have burned the whole thing to the ground.

Its decomposing stairs were too hazardous to attempt. Animals had covered the floorboards with dung, and birds lofted out of every room we opened. Our progress could have been charted by the uprisings of the swallows and the indignation of the owls.

"It's just an empty building," I said to Percy, who had been silent throughout the visit, his features knotted and tense.

"Empty of what, though?" he asked.

I took a few more exposures on the outside. The crumbling pillars. The worm-tunneled verandah casting a sinister shade. A chimney leaning sideways like a drunken man.

I did not believe, could not bring myself to believe, that a war within the boundaries of the Union could ever have been fought, though historians still worry that question like a loose tooth. If the years after '55 had been less prosperous, if Douglas had not been elected President, if the terrorist John Brown had not been tried in a Northern court and hanged on a Northern gallows . . . *if, if,* and *if ad infinitum.*

All nonsense, it seemed to me. Whatever Harriet Beecher Stowe might have dreamt, whatever Percy Camber might have uncovered, this was fundamentally a peaceable land.

This is a peaceable land, I imagined myself telling my daughter Elsebeth; but my imagination would extend itself no farther.

"Now the barracks," Percy said.

It had been even hotter in the administration building than it was outside, and Percy's clothes were drenched through. So were mine. "You mean those barns?"

"Barracks," Percy repeated.

Barracks or barns—they were a little of both, as it turned out. The one we inspected was a cavernous wooden box, held up by mildew and inertia. Percy wanted photographs of the rusted iron brackets which had supported rows of wooden platforms—a few of these remained—on which men and women had once slept. There were a great many of these brackets, and I estimated that a single barracks-barn might have housed as many as two hundred persons in its day. An even larger number, if mattresses had been laid on the floors.

I took the pictures he wanted, by the light that came through fallen boards. The air in the barn was stale, despite all the holes in the walls, and it was a relief to finish my work and step out into the relentless dull sunshine.

The presence of so many people must have necessitated a dining hall, a communal kitchen, sanitary facilities at Pilgassi Acres. Those structures had not survived, however, except as barren patches among the weeds. Dig down a little—Percy had learned this technique in his research—and you would find a layer of charcoal for each burned building or outhouse. Not every structure in Pilgassi Acres had survived the years, but each had left its subtle mark.

One of the five barns was not like the others, and I made this observation to Percy Camber as soon as I noticed it. "The rest of these barracks, the doors and windows are open to the breeze. The far one in the north quarter has been boarded up—d'you see?"

"That's the one we should inspect next, then," Percy said.

We were on our way there when the first bullet struck.

My mother had always been an embarrassment to me, with her faded enthusiasms, her Bible verses and Congregationalist poetry, her missionary zeal on behalf of people whose lives were so tangential to mine that I could barely imagine them.

She didn't like it when I volunteered for Cuba in 1880. It wasn't a proper war, she said. She said it was yet another concession to the South, to the aristocracy's greed for expansion toward the equator. "A war engineered at the Virginia Military Institute," she called it, "fought for no good reason."

But it blended Northerners and Southerners on a neutral field of battle, where we were all just American soldiers. It was the glue that repaired many ancient sectional rifts. Out of it emerged great leaders, like old Robert E. Lee, who transcended regional loyalties (though when he spoke of "America" I often suspected he used the word as a synonym for "Virginia"), and his son, also a talented commander. In Cuba we all wore a common uniform, and we all learned, rich and poor, North and South, to duck the Spaniards' bullets.

The bullet hit a shed wall just above Percy Camber's skull. Splinters flew through the air like a cloud of mosquitos. The sound of the gunshot arrived a split-second later, damped by the humid afternoon to a harmless-sounding *pop*. The rifleman was some distance away. But he was accurate.

I dropped to the ground—or rather discovered that I had already dropped to the ground, obeying an instinct swifter than reason.

Percy, who had never been to war, lacked that ingrained impulse. I'm not sure he understood what had happened. He stood there in the rising heat, bewildered.

"Get down," I said.

"What is it, Tom?"

"Your doom, if you don't get down. *Get down!*"

He understood then. But it was as if the excitement had loosened all the strings of his body. He couldn't decide which way to fold. He was the picture of confusion.

Then a second bullet struck him in the shoulder.

"Liberty Lodges," they had been called at first.

I mean the places like Pilgassi Acres, back when they were allowed to flourish.

They were a response to a difficult time. Slavery had died, but the slaves had not. That was the dilemma of the South. Black men without skills, along with their families and countless unaccompanied children, crowded the roads—more of them every day, as "free-labor cotton" became a rallying cry for progressive French and English buyers.

Who were Marcus and Benjamin Pilgassi? Probably nothing more than a pair of Richmond investors jumping on a bandwagon. The Liberty Lodges bore no onus then. The appeal of the business was explicit: Don't put your slaves on the road and risk prosecution or fines for "abandonment of property." We will take your aging and unprofitable chattel and house them. The men will be kept separate from the women, to prevent any reckless reproduction. They will live out their lives with their basic needs attended to, for an annual fee only a fraction of what it would cost to keep them privately.

What the Pilgassi brothers (and businessmen like them) did not say directly (but implied in every line of their advertisements) was that the Liberty Lodge movement aimed to achieve an absolute and irreversible decline in the Negro population in the South.

In time, Percy had told me, the clients of these businesses came to include entire State governments, which had tired of the expense and notoriety incurred by the existence of temporary camps in which tens of thousands of "intramural refugees" could neither be fed economically nor be allowed to starve. It had been less onerous for them to subsidize the Lodges, which tended to be built in isolated places, away from casual observation.

Percy's grandfather had escaped slavery in the 1830s and settled in Boston, where he picked up enough education to make himself prominent in the Abolition movement. Percy's father, an ordained minister, had spoken at Lyman Beecher's famous church, in the days before he founded the journal that became the *Tocsin*.

Percy had taken up the moral burden of his forebears in a way I had not, but there was still a similarity between us. We were the children of crusaders. We had inherited their disappointments and drunk the lees of their bitterness.

I was not a medical man, but I had witnessed bullet wounds in Cuba. Percy had been shot in the shoulder. He lay on the ground with his eyes open, blinking, his left hand pressed against the wound. I pried his hand away so that I could examine his injury.

The wound was bleeding badly, but the blood did not spurt out, a good sign. I took a handkerchief from my pocket, folded it and pressed it against the hole.

"Am I dying?" Percy asked. "I don't feel like I'm dying."

"You're not all that badly hurt or you wouldn't be talking. You need attention, though."

A third shot rang out—I couldn't tell where the bullet went.

"And we need to get under cover," I added.

The nearest building was the boarded-up barracks. I told Percy to hold the handkerchief in place. His right arm didn't seem to work correctly, perhaps because the bullet had damaged some bundle of muscles or nerves. But I got him crouching, and we hurried toward shelter.

We came into the shadow of the building and stumbled to the side of it away from the direction from which the shots had come. Grasshoppers buzzed out of the weeds in fierce brown flurries, some of them lighting on our clothes. There was the sound of dry thunder down the valley. This barracks had a door—a wooden door on a rail, large enough to admit dozens of people at once. But it was closed, and there was a brass latch and a padlock on it.

So we had no real shelter—just some shade and a moment's peace.

I used the time to put a fresh handkerchief on Percy's wound and to bind it with a strip of cloth torn from my own shirt.

"Thank you," Percy said breathlessly.

"Welcome. The problem now is how to get back to the carriage." We had no weapons, and we could hardly withstand a siege, no matter where we hid. Our only hope was escape, and I could not discern any likely way of achieving it.

Then the question became moot, for the man who had tried to kill us came around the corner of the barracks.

"Why do you want to make these pictures?" Elsie asked yet again, from a dim cavern at the back of my mind.

In an adjoining chamber of my skull a different voice reminded me that I wanted a drink, a strong one, immediately.

The ancient Greeks (I imagined myself telling Elsebeth) believed that vision is a force which flies out from the eyes when directed by the human will. They were wrong. There is no force or will in vision. There is only light. Light direct or light reflected. Light which behaves in predictable ways. Put a prism in front of it and it breaks into colors. Open a shuttered lens and some fraction of it can be trapped in nitrocellulose or collodion as neatly as a bug in a killing jar.

A man with a camera is like a naturalist, I told Elsebeth. Where one man might catch butterflies, another catches wasps.

I did not make these pictures.

I only caught them.

The man with the rifle stood five or six yards away, at the corner of the barracks. He was a black man in threadbare coveralls. He was sweating in the heat. For the while there was silence, the three of us blinking at each other.

Then, "I didn't mean to shoot him," the black man said.

"In that case you shouldn't have aimed a rifle at him and pulled the trigger," I said back, recklessly.

Our assailant made no immediate response. He seemed to be thinking it over. Grasshoppers lit on the cuffs of his ragged pants. His head was large, his hair cut crudely close to the skull. His eyes were narrow and suspicious. He was barefoot.

"It was not my intention to hurt anyone," he said again. "I was shooting from a distance, sir."

Percy by this time had managed to sit up. He seemed less afraid of the rifleman than he ought to have been. Less afraid, at any rate, than I was. "What *did* you intend?"

He gave his attention to Percy. "To warn you away, is all."

"Away from what?"

"This building."

"Why? What's in this building?"

"My son."

The "three million" in Percy's title were the men, women and children of African descent held in bondage in the South in the year 1860. For obvious reasons, the number is approximate. Percy always tried to be conservative in his estimates, for he did not want to be vulnerable to accusations of sensationalizing history.

Given that number to begin with, what Percy had done was to tally up census polls, where they existed, alongside the archived reports of various state and local governments, tax and business statements, Federal surveys, rail records, etc., over the years between then and now.

What befell the three million?

A great many—as many as one third of them—emigrated North, before changes in the law made that difficult. Some of those who migrated continued on up to Canada. Others made lives for themselves in the big cities, in so far as they were allowed to. A smaller number were taken up against their will and shipped to certain inhospitable "colonies" in Africa, until the excesses and horrors of repatriation became notorious and the whole enterprise was outlawed.

Some found a place among the freemen of New Orleans, or worked boats, largely unmolested, along the Gulf Coast. A great many went West, where they were received with varying degrees of hostility. Five thousand "irredeemably criminal" black prisoners were taken from Southern jails and deposited in a Utah desert, where they died not long after.

Certain jobs remained open to black men and women—as servants, rail porters, and so forth—and many did well enough in these professions.

But add the numbers, Percy said, even with a generous allowance for error, and it still comes up shy of the requisite three million.

How many were delivered into the Liberty Lodges?No one can answer that question with any certainty, at least not until the evidence sealed by the Ritter Inquiry is opened to the public. Percy's estimate was somewhere in the neighborhood of 50,000. But as I said, he tended to be conservative in his figures.

"We were warned there was a family of wild men up here," I said.

"I'm no wilder than I have to be," the gunman said. "I didn't ask you to come visit."

"You hurt Percy bad enough, whether you're wild or not. Look at him. He needs a medic."

"I see him all right, sir."

"Then, unless you mean to shoot us both to death, will you help me get him back to our carriage?"

There was another lengthy pause.

"I don't like to do that," the black man said finally. "There won't be any end to the trouble. But I don't suppose I have a choice, except, as you say, sir, to kill you. And that I cannot bring myself to do."

He said these words calmly enough, but he had a way of forming his vowels, and pronouncing them deep in his throat, that defies transcription. It was like listening to a volcano rumble.

"Take his right arm, then," I said. "I'll get on his left. The carriage is beyond that ridge."

"I know where your carriage is. But, sir, I won't put down this rifle. I don't think that would be wise. You can help him yourself."

I went to where Percy sat and began to lift him up. Percy startled me by saying, "No, Tom, I don't want to go to the carriage."

"What do you mean?" the assailant asked, before I could pose the same question.

"Do you have a name?" Percy asked him.

"Ephraim," the man said, reluctantly.

"Ephraim, my name is Percy Camber. What did you mean when you said your son was inside this barracks?"

"I don't like to tell you that," Ephraim said, shifting his gaze between Percy and me.

"Percy," I said, "you need a doctor. We're wasting time."

He looked at me sharply. "I'll live a while longer. Let me talk to Ephraim, please, Tom."

"Stand off there where I can see you, sir," Ephraim directed. "I know this man needs a doctor. I'm not stupid. This won't take long."

I concluded from all this that the family of wild Negroes the landlady had warned me about was real, and that they were living in the sealed barn.

Why they should want to inhabit such a place I could not say.

I stood apart while Percy, wounded as he was, held a hushed conversation with Ephraim, who had shot him.

I understood that they could talk more freely without me as an auditor. I was a white man. It was true that I worked for Percy, and that Percy was my employer—but that fact would not have been obvious to Ephraim any more than it had been obvious to the dozens of hotel-keepers who had assumed without asking that I was the master and Percy was the servant. My closeness to Percy was unique and all but invisible.

After a while Ephraim allowed me to gather up my photographic gear, which had been scattered in the crisis.

I had been fascinated by photography even as a child. It had seemed like such patent magic! The magic of stopped time, places and persons rescued from their ephemeral natures. My parents had given me books containing photographs of Indian elephants, of the pyramids of Egypt, of the natural wonders of Florida.

I put my gear together and waited for Percy to finish his talk with the armed lunatic who had shot him.

The high cloud that had polluted the sky all morning had dissipated during the afternoon. The air was still scaldingly hot, but a touch less humid. A certain brittle clarity had set in. The light was hard, crystalline. A fine light for photography, though it was beginning to grow long.

"Percy," I called out.

"What is it, Tom?"

"We have to leave now, before the sun gets any lower. It's a long journey to Crib Lake." There was a doctor at Crib Lake. I remembered seeing his shingle when we passed through that town. Some rural bonesetter, probably. A doughty relic of the mustard-plaster era. But better than no doctor at all.

Percy's voice sounded weak; but what he said was, "We're not finished here yet."

"What do you mean, not finished?"

"We've been invited inside," he said. "To see Ephraim's son."

Some bird, perhaps a mourning dove, called out from the gathering shadows among the trees where the meadow ended.

I did not want to meet Ephraim's son. There was a dreadful aspect to the whole affair. If Ephraim's son was in the barn, why had he not come out at the sound of gunshots and voices? (Ephraim, as far as I could tell, was an old man, and his son wasn't likely to be an infant.) Why, for that matter, was the barracks closed and locked? To keep the world away from Ephraim's son? Or to keep Ephraim's son away from the world?

"What's his name?" I asked. "This son of yours."

"Jordan," he said.

I had married Maggie not long after I got back from Cuba. I had been trying to set up my photography business at the time. I was far from wealthy, and what resources I possessed I had put into my business. But there was a vogue among young women of the better type for manly veterans. I was manly enough, I suppose, or at least presentable, and I was authentically a veteran. I met Maggie when she came to my shop to sit for a portrait. I escorted her to dinner. Maggie was fond of me; and I was fond of Maggie, in part because she had no political convictions or fierce unorthodox ideals. She took the world as she found it.

Elsebeth came along a year or so after the wedding. It was a difficult birth. I remember the sound of Maggie's screams. I remember Elsebeth as a newborn, bloody in a towel, handed to me by the doctor. I wiped the remnant blood and fluid from her tiny body. She had been unspeakably beautiful.

Ephraim wore the key to the barn on a string around his neck. He applied it to the massive lock, still giving me suspicious glances. He kept his rifle in the crook of his arm as he did this. He slid the huge door open. Inside, the barn was dark. The air that wafted out was a degree or two cooler than outside, and it carried a sour tang, as of long-rotten hay or clover.

Ephraim did not call out to his son, and there was no sound inside the abandoned barracks.

Had Ephraim once held his newborn son in his arms, as I had once held Elsebeth?

The last of the Liberty Lodges were closed down in 1888. Scandal had swirled around them for years, but no sweeping legal action had been taken. In part this was because the Lodges were not a monolithic enterprise: A hundred independent companies held title to them. In part it was because various state legislatures were afraid of disclosing their own involvement. The Lodges had not proved as profitable as their founders expected—the plans had not anticipated, for instance, all the ancillary costs of keeping human beings confined in what amounted to a jail (guards, walls, fences, discipline, etc.) for life. But the *utility* of the Lodges was undisputed, and several states had quietly subsidized them. A "full accounting," as Percy called it, would have tainted every government south of the Mason Dixon Line, and not a few above it. Old wounds might have been reopened.

The Ritter Inquiry was called by Congress when the abuses inherent in the Lodge system began to come to light, inch by inch. By that time, though, there had been many other scandals, many other inquests, and the public had grown weary of all such issues. Newspapers—apart from papers like the *Tocsin*—hardly touched the story. The Inquiry sealed its own evidence, the surviving Lodges were hastily dismantled, and the general population (apart from a handful of aged reformers) paid no significant attention.

"Why dredge up all that ugliness?" Maggie had asked me.

Nobody wants to see those pictures, Elsebeth whispered.

Nobody but a few old scolds.

It was too dark in the immense barracks to be certain, but it seemed to me there was nobody inside but the three of us.

"I came here with Jordan in '78," Ephraim said. "Jordan was twelve year old at the time. I don't know what happened to his mama. We got separated at the Federal camp on the Kansas border. Jordan and I were housed in different buildings."

He looked around, his eyes abstracted, and seemed to see more than an old and ruined barracks. Perhaps he could see in the dark—it was dark in here, the only light coming through the fractionally open door. All I could see was a board floor, immaculately swept, picked out in that wedge of sun. All else was shadow.

He found an old crate for Percy to sit on. The crate was the only thing like furniture I could see. There was nothing to suggest a family resided here, apart from the neatness, the sealed entrances and windows, the absence of bird dung. I began to feel impatient.

"You said your son was here," I prompted him.

"Oh yes sir. Jordan's here."

"Where? I don't see him."

Percy shot me an angry look.

"He's everywhere in here," the madman said.

Oh, I thought, it's not Jordan, then, it's the spirit of Jordan, or some conceit like that. This barn is a shrine the man has been keeping. I had the unpleasant idea that Jordan's body might be tucked away in one of its shadowed corners, dry and lifeless as an old Egyptian king.

"Or at least," Ephraim said, "from about eight foot down."

He found and lit a lantern.

One evening in the midst of our journey through the South I had got drunk and shared with Percy, too ebulliently, my idea that we were really very much alike.

This was in Atlanta, in one of the hotels that provides separate quarters for colored servants traveling with their employers. That was good because it meant Percy could sleep in relative comfort. I had snuck down to his room, which was little more than a cubicle, and I had brought a bottle with me, although Percy refused to share it. He was an Abstinence man.

I talked freely about my mother's fervent abolitionism and how it had hovered over my childhood like a stormcloud stitched with lightning. I told Percy how we were both the children of idealists, and so forth.

He listened patiently but at the end, when I had finally run down, or my jaw was too weary to continue, he rummaged through the papers he carried with him and drew out a letter that had been written to him by Mrs. Harriet Beecher Stowe.

Mrs. Stowe is best remembered for her work on behalf of the China Inland Mission, but she came from an abolitionist family. Her father was the first president of the famous Lane Theological Seminary. At one point in her life she had attempted a novel meant to expose the evils of slavery, but she could not find a publisher.

Percy handed me the woman's letter.

I have received your book "Every Measure Short of War," the letter began, *and it brings back terrible memories and forebodings. I remember all too distinctly what it meant to love my country in those troubled years, and to tremble at the coming day of wrath.*

"You want me to read this?" I asked drunkenly.

"Just that next part," Percy said.

Perhaps because of your book, Mr. Camber, Mrs. Stowe wrote, *or because of the memories it aroused, I suffered an unbearable dream last night.*

It was about that war. I mean the war that was so much discussed but which never took place, the war from which both North and South stepped back as from the brink of a terrible abyss.

In my dream that precipice loomed again, and this time there was no Stephen Douglas to call us away with concessions and compromises and his disgusting deference to the Slave Aristocracy. In my dream, the war took place. And it was an awful war, Mr. Camber. It seemed to flow before my eyes in a series of bloody tableaux. A half a million dead. Battlefields too awful to contemplate, North and South. Industries crippled, both the print and the cotton presses silenced, thriving cities reduced to smoldering ruins—all this I saw, or knew, as one sees or knows in dreams.

But that was not the unbearable part of it.

Let me say that I have known death altogether too intimately. I have suffered the loss of children. I love peace just as fervently as I despise injustice. I would not wish grief or heartbreak on any mother of any section of this country, or any other country. And yet—!

And yet, in light of what I have inferred from recent numbers of your publication, and from the letters you have written me, and from what old friends and acquaintances have said or written about the camps, the deportations, the Lodges, etc.,—because of all that, a part of me wishes that that war had indeed been fought!—if only because it might have ended Slavery. Ended it cleanly, I mean, with a sane and straightforward liberation, or even a liberation partial and incomplete; a declaration, at least, of the immorality and unacceptability of human bondage—anything but this sickening decline by extinction, this surreptitious (as you so bitterly describe it) "cleansing."

I suppose this makes me sound like a monster, a sort of female John Brown, confusing righteousness with violence, and murder with redemption.

I am not such a monster. I confess a certain admiration for those who, like President Douglas, worked so very hard to prevent the apocalypse of which I dreamed last night, even if I distrust their motives and condemn their means. The instinct for peace is the most honorable of all Christian impulses. My conscience rebels at a single death, much less one million.

But if a War could have ended Slavery . . . would I have wished it? Welcomed it?

What is unbearable, Mr. Camber, is that I don't know that I can answer my own horrifying question either honestly or decently. And so I have to ask: Can you?

I puzzled it out. Then I gave Percy a blank stare. "Why are you showing me this?"

"We're alike in many ways, as you say, Tom. But not all ways. Not all ways. Mrs. Stowe asks an interesting question. Answering it isn't easy. I don't know your mind, but fundamentally, Tom, despite all the sympathies between us, the fact is, I suspect that in the end you might give the *wrong* answer to that question—and I expect you think the same of me."

There was another difference, which I did not mention to Percy, and that was that every time I remarked on our similarities I could hear my wife's scornful voice saying (as she had said when I first shared the idea of this project with her), "Oh, Tom, don't be ridiculous. You're nothing like that Percy Camber. That's your mother talking—all that abolitionist guilt she burdened you with. As if you need to prove you haven't betrayed the *cause*, whatever the *cause* is, exactly."

Maggie failed to change my mind, though what she said was true.

"From about eight foot down," Ephraim said cryptically, lifting the lantern.

Eight feet is as high an average man can reach without standing on something. Between eight feet and the floor is the span of a man's reach.

"You see, sir," Ephraim said, "my son and I were held in separate barracks. The idea behind that was that a man might be less eager to escape if it meant leaving behind a son or father or uncle. The overseers said, if you run, your people will suffer for it. But when my chance come I took it. I don't know if that's a sin. I think about it often." He walked toward the nearest wall, the lantern breaking up the darkness as it swayed in his grip. "This barracks here was my son's barracks."

"Were there many escapes?" Percy asked.

I began to see that something might have been written on the wall, though at first it looked more like an *idea* of writing: a text as crabbed and indecipherable as the scratchings of the Persians or the Medes.

"Yes, many," Ephraim said, "though not many successful. At first there was fewer guards on the gates. They built the walls up, too, over time. Problem is, you get away, where is there to go? Even if you get past these sandy hills, the country's not welcoming. And the guards had rifles, sir, the guards had dogs."

"But you got away, Ephraim."

"Not far away. When I escaped it was very near the last days of Pilgassi Acres." (He pronounced it *Pigassi*, with a reflexive curl of contempt on his lips.) "Company men coming in from Richmond to the overseer's house, you could hear the shouting some nights. Rations went from meat twice a week to a handful of cornmeal a day and green bacon on Sundays. They fired the little Dutch doctor who used to tend to us. Sickness come to us. They let the old ones die in place, took the bodies away to bury or burn. Pretty soon we knew what was meant to happen next. They could not keep us, sir, nor could they set us free."

"That was when you escaped?"

"Very near the end, sir, yes, that's when. I did not want to go without Jordan. But if I waited I knew I'd be too weak to run. I told myself I could live in the woods and get stronger, that I would come back for Jordan when I was more myself."

He held the lantern close to the board wall of this abandoned barracks.

Percy was suffering more from his wound now than he had seemed to when he received it, and he grimaced as I helped him follow Ephraim. We stood close to the wild man and his circle of light, though not too close—I was still conscious of his rifle and of his willingness to use it, even if he was not in a killing mood right now.

The writing on the wall consisted of names. Hundreds of names. They chased each other around the whole of the barn in tight horizontal bands.

"I expect the overseers would have let us starve if they had the time. But they were afraid federal men would come digging around. There ought to be nothing of us left to find, I think was the reasoning. By that time the cholera had taken many of us anyhow, weak and hungry as we were, and the rest . . . well, death is a house, Mr. Camber, with many doorways. This is my son's name right here."

Jordan Nash was picked out by the yellow lantern light.

"Dear God," said Percy Camber, softly.

"I don't think God come into it, sir."

"Did he write his own name?"

"Oh, yes, sir. A northern lady taught us both to read, back in the Missouri camp. I had a Bible and a copy book from her. I still read that Bible to this day. Jordan was proud of his letters." Ephraim turned to me as if I, not Percy, had asked the question: "Most of these men couldn't write nor read. Jordan didn't just write his own name. He wrote *all* these names. Each and every one. A new man came in, he would ask the name and put it down as best he could. The list grew as we came and went. Many years' worth, sir. All the prisoners talked about it, how he did that. He had no pencil or chalk, you know. He made a kind of pen or brush by chewing down sapling twigs to soften their ends. Ink he made all kind of ways. He was very clever about that. Riverbottom clay, soot, blood even. In the autumns the work crews drawing water from the river might find mushrooms which turn black when you picked them, and they brought them back to Jordan—those made fine ink, he said."

The pride in Ephraim's voice was unmistakable. He marched along the wall with his lantern held high so we could see his son's work in all its complexity. All those names, written in the space between a man's reach and the floor. The letters were meticulously formed, the lines as level as the sea. Some of the names were whole names, some were single names, some were the kind of whimsical names given to house servants. They all ran together, to conserve space, so that in places you had to guess whether the names represented one person or two.

. . . John Kincaid Tom Abel Fortune Bob Swift Pompey Atticus Joseph Wilson Elijah Elijah Jim Jim's Son Rufus Moses Deerborn Moses Raffity . . .

"I don't know altogether why he did it," Ephraim said. "I think it made him feel better to see the men's names written down. Just so somebody might know we passed this way, he said."

Jordan lived in this barracks from eight foot down. And so did shockingly many others.

"This is why you shot at us," Percy whispered, a kind of awe or dread constricting his throat.

"I make it seem dangerous up here, yes, sir, so that nobody won't come back and take it down or burn it. And yet I suppose they will sooner or later whether I scare anybody or not. Or if not that then the weather will wear it down. I keep it best I can against the rain, sir. I don't let birds or animals inside. Or even the daylight, sir, because the daylight fades things, that ink of Jordan's is sensitive to it. All be gone one day I suppose, but I will too, by and by, and yourselves as well, of course."

"Perhaps we can make it last a little longer," Percy said.

Of course I knew what he meant.

"I'll need light," I said.

The fierce hot light of the fading day.

Ephraim was anxious to help, once Percy explained the notion to him. He threw open the barracks door. He took down the wood he had tacked over the south-facing windows. There were iron bars in the window frames.

In the corners the light was not adequate despite our best efforts. Ephraim said he had a sheet of polished tin he used for a mirror, which might help reflect the sunlight in. He went to his encampment to get it. By that time he trusted us enough to leave us alone for a short time.

Once again I suggested escape. But Percy refused to leave. So I kept about my work.

There were only so many exposures I could make, and I wanted the names to be legible. In the end I could not capture everything. But I did my best.

Ephraim told us about the end of Pilgassi Acres. He had been nearby, hidden half-starving in a grove of dwarf pines, when he heard the initial volley of gunshots. It was the first of many over the several hours that followed. Gunfire in waves, and then the cries of the dying. By that sound he knew he would never see his son Jordan again.

Trenches were dug in the ground. Smoke from the chimneys lay over the low country for days. But the owners had been hasty to finish their work, Ephraim said. They had not bothered to burn the empty barracks before they rode off in their trucks and carriages.

Ever since that time Ephraim had sheltered in the barn of a poor white farmer who was sympathetic to him. Ephraim trapped game in exchange for this modest shelter. Eventually the farmer lent him his rifle, so that Ephraim could bring back an occasional deer as well as rabbits and birds. The farmer didn't talk much, Ephraim said, but there were age-browned copies of

Garrison's *Liberator* stored in the barn; and Ephraim read these with interest, and improved his vocabulary and his understanding of the world.

Hardly anyone came up to Pilgassi Acres nowadays except hunters following game trails. He scared them off with his rifle if they got too close to Jordan's barracks.

There was no point leaving the barracks after dark, since we could not safely travel in the carriage until sunrise. Percy's condition worsened during the night. He came down with a fever, and as he shivered his wound began to seep. I made him as comfortable as possible with blankets from the carriage, and Ephraim brought him water in a cracked clay jug.

Percy was lucid, but his ideas began to run in whimsical directions as midnight passed. He insisted that I take Mrs. Stowe's letter from where he kept it in his satchel and read it aloud by lamplight. It was this letter, he said, that had been the genesis of the book he was writing now, about the three million. He wanted to know what Ephraim would make of it.

I kept my voice neutral as I read, so that Mrs. Stowe's stark words might speak for themselves.

"That is a decent white woman," Ephraim said when had heard the letter and given it some thought. "A Christian woman. She reminds me of the woman that taught me and Jordan to read. But I don't know what she's so troubled about, Mr. Camber. This idea there was no war. I suppose there wasn't, if by war you mean the children of white men fighting the children of white men. But, sir, I have seen the guns, sir, and I have seen them used, sir, all my life—*all* my life. And in my father's time and before him. Isn't that war? And if it *is* war, how can she say war was avoided? There were many casualties, sir, though their names are not generally recorded; many graves, though not marked; and many battlefields, though not admitted to the history books."

"I will pass that thought on to Mrs. Stowe," Percy whispered, smiling in his discomfort, "although she's very old now and might not live to receive it."

And I decided I would pass it on to Elsebeth, my daughter.

I packed up my gear very carefully, come morning.

This is Jordan's name, I imagined myself telling Elsie, pointing to a picture in a book, the book Percy Camber would write.

This photograph, I would tell her, represents light cast in a dark place. Like an old cellar gone musty for lack of sun. Sunlight has a cleansing property, I would tell her. See: I caught a little of it here.

I supposed there was enough of her grandmother in her that Elsebeth might understand.

I began to feel hopeful about the prospect.

Ephraim was less talkative in the morning light. I helped poor shivering Percy into the carriage. I told Ephraim my mother had once published a poem in the *Liberator*, years ago. I couldn't remember which issue.

"I may not have seen that number," Ephraim said. "But I'm sure it was a fine poem."

I drove Percy to the doctor in Crib Lake. The doctor was an old man with pinch-nose glasses and dirty fingernails. I told him I had shot my servant accidentally, while hunting. The doctor said he did not usually work on colored men, but an extra ten dollars on top of his fee changed his mind.

He told me there was a good chance Percy would pull through, if the fever didn't worsen.

I thanked him, and went off to buy myself a drink.

ON THE HUMAN PLAN

JAY LAKE

I am called Dog the Digger. I am not mighty, neither am I fearsome. Should you require bravos, there are muscle-boys aplenty among the rat-bars of any lowtown on this raddled world. If it is a wizard you want, follow the powder-trails of crushed silicon and wolf's blood to their dark and winking lairs. Scholars can be found in their libraries, taikonauts in their launch bunkers and ship foundries, priests amid the tallow-gleaming depths of their bone-ribbed cathedrals.

What I do is dig. For bodies, for treasure, for the rust-pocked hulks of history, for the sheer pleasure of moving what cannot be moved and finding what rots beneath. You may hire me for an afternoon or a month or the entire turning of the year. It makes me no mind whatsoever.

As for you, I know what you want. You want a *story*.

Oh, you say you want the truth, but no one ever really wants the truth. And stories are the greatest of the things for which I dig. Mightier even than the steel-bound femurs of the deinotheria bred by the Viridian Republic, which I can show you in vast necropolii beneath the Stone-Doored Hills. More treasured than the golden wires to be pulled by the fistful from the thinking heads which line the Cumaean Caves, screaming as the lights of their eyes flash and die.

Anyone with a bit of talent and the right set of bones to throw can foretell the future. It's written in fat-bellied red across every morning sky. But to aftertell the past, that is another trick entirely.

They say death is the door that never opens twice. At least, not until it does. Sorrow is usually the first child of such a birthing, though just as often the last to be recognized.

People die. Cities die. Nations die. In time the sun itself will die, though already it grows red and obese, a louche, glowering presence fat on the midsummer horizon. When the daystar opens up its arms, all graves will be swallowed in fire, but for now, the bones of men lie atop older bones beneath the friable earth.

Likewise the skins of cities. All our places are built on other places. A man might dig down until the very heat of the earth wells up from the bottom of his shaft, and still there will be floors and streets and wooden frames pressed to stone fossils to greet him there.

You know that the first woman to greet the morning had gone to sleep the night before as an ape. Some angel stirred her dreams with God's long spoon, and the next day she remembered the past. The past was young then, not even thirty hours old, but it had *begun*.

That woman bred with an ape who didn't yet know he was man, then birthed a hairy little baby who learned she was another woman, and so the world unfolded into history. That woman died, too, laid herself down into the earth and let herself be covered with mud which turned to rock.

If I dig down far enough, someday I'll find that grandmother of us all. But this story you've come for is about another time, when I only dug down to death's doorstep.

It was an exogen come to me, in the twenty-seventh hour of the day. My visitor was taller than a pike-pole, with skin translucent as the slime of a slug. Still, it was on the human plan, with two arms, two legs, and a knobby bit at the top that glittered. The ropes and nodules of its guts shimmered inside that slick, smooth, shiny skin. Its scent-map was strange, the expected story of starships and time's slow decay mixed in with spices and a sweat which could have gotten a rock-crusher drunk.

Dangerous, this one. But they always were. The safe ones stayed home.

"Digger," the exogen said. It used a voder which could have come from before the dawn of technology. Believe me, I *know*.

I'm not one for judging a man by his shape. Metatron knows I find myself judged enough. Still, I'm cautious around one who comes from too far away, for a man distant from his home has no need of scruples. "Aye, and that's me."

Something flashed pale, pallid blue in the exogen's middle gut. "Compensation."

One of them types. I could handle this. Like talking to a Taurian. All syntax implied inside a hyperlimited morphemic constellation. Like playing a game of two hundred questions. "Compensation in what cause?"

"Seeking."

"That's what I do. I seek. By digging. What do you seek?"

"Death."

That one required some careful thought. I didn't reckon this exogen had come all the way across the Deep Dark between the stars just for me to dig him a grave. Not that I hadn't dug a grave or four in my day. It was just that no one spent the kind of energy budget this exogen had dedicated to being here on Earth simply to lay themselves down.

"Anyone's death in particular?"

"Death." My visitor flashed a series of colors, then manipulated its voder. "Thanatos."

"Oh, Death his own self." I considered that. "You must be aware that death isn't really anywhere to be found. Mythic personification doesn't leave behind calling cards for me to dig up. Entropic decay does, but *everything* is evidence of that."

I knew from experience that it would take the exogen a while to assemble my loose stream of lexemes into a meaningful morph that fit its own mind. I'd been working on my sun-altar when it had found me among the dunes of rusted bolts where I make my home. So I returned to my labors, confident that my visitor would speak again when it was ready.

Exogens work on their own timescale. Some are sped up so fast they can experience a standard-year in a few hours, others move so slowly they speak to rocks, and perceive trees as fast-moving weeds. In time, this one would answer.

Two days later, it did.

"Secrets," the exogen said, as if no time had passed at all.

"You want me to dig for the secrets of death?" I laughed. "There's no secret to death. It finds us all. Death is the least secret thing in the universe. I can open any grave and show you."

The traveler's hand brushed down its translucent front, trailing tiny colored flares. "Undying." The voder somehow sounded wistful.

I picked up a ritual axe from the Second Archaean Interregnum, traced a claw tip down the blade edge. "That's easy enough to take care of. Dying is simple. It's living that's hard."

For an awful moment, I wondered if the exogen was going to dip its head and dare me into trying that pulsing neck. Instead it just stared a while. I thought the exogen had slipped back into slow-time, until it spoke again. "Door."

"Door." Death's door? That was a figure of speech as old as architecture. This exogen must have something more literal in mind.

"Door." This time the voder's tones implied an emphatic conclusion. The exogen shut down, sinking into a quietude that took it across the border from life into art. The sense of light and life which had skimmed across it like yellow fog on a sulfuritic lake was gone.

I had acquired my very own statue. Walking, talking, likely intelligent, and certainly fantastically wealthy.

For a test, I poked one tip of the Achaean axe into its chest. About where the sternum would be on the human plan. It was like poking a boulder. The exogen's skin had no give, and the sense of weightiness was downright planetary.

Door. What in all the baroque hells of the Mbazi Renaissance did it mean by *door*?

You know perfectly well that while the Earth is dying, it's nowhere near dead. Even a corpse on the forest floor isn't dead. Intestinal flora bloom in the madness of a sudden, fatal spring. Ants swarm the massive pile of loosening protein. Patient beetles wait to polish bones until they gleam like little fragments of lost Luna embedded in the soil.

So it is with this world. I can tell by the cut of your suit that you're from offworld, but I can tell by the quality that you didn't ship in from across the Deep Dark. A patient man with an unlimited air supply and a wealth of millennia in his hand can almost walk from here to Proxima Centauri by station-hopping, but anyone terrestrial planning to move between the stars on anything like the scale of a human standard lifetime is very, very wealthy. And you are plainly terrestrial in origins, and just as plainly from those boots are not so wealthy.

I'm sorry. Did I offend? Take it from me, after you've riven open the graves of a million generations, you find your sense of tact has evaporated with all the rest of time's detritus. *I'm* poor, poor as a chuck moose, so I see no shame in anyone else's poverty.

Besides, this story I'm telling you may save your life some day. Surely that's worth an unintentional insult or two. Not that I'm planning another, mind you, but Dog the Digger is famously plainspoken as any of his kind, for all that he's not on the human plan.

Here we are, a collection of mortally wounded peoples on a mortally wounded planet, but we yet live. No matter the elevation of our estate. I may be a beetle polishing the bones of the world rather than a bright explorer at the morning of all civilizations, but still I draw breath. (Metaphorically speaking, of course.)

And so it fell to me to search for meaning in the exogen's request. After a month had gone by, his skin was cooled to the color of cold iron, and no one might ever have believed him to be alive. He stood like a man marking his own grave and stared sightlessly at the spot where I happened to have been positioned that night.

At least I understood now how he passed between the stars. The exogen had no life support requirements, and was immune to boredom. He wasn't so much undying as unliving.

I went to my friend Pater Nostrum. A man very nearly on the human plan, as so few of us were in these terribly late days, Pater Nostrum lived in a cathedral he'd built himself as an agglutination of debris, donations and some downright thievery. He dowsed for his cathedral one shard at a time, using a rod made of Gerrine Empire hullmetal wrapped in sable manskin. A time or ten I'd dug and hauled great, broad-beamed members for him, fetched by some unseen-to-me holy mandate from the dank rust-grained soil.

The genetics in that rod's leather grip were worth more than all of Pater Nostrum's earthly accumulations, but as a priest, he was beyond caring of such things. Or so he told himself, me, and everyone else who would listen.

This day I claimed back from him one of the favors owed.

"Pater," I said. It was the season for my third body, which was generally the most comfortable for those with whom I spoke. Not that the exogen would have cared, or truly, even Pater Nostrum.

He smiled, resplendent in his robes of rich vinyl trimmed with donkey fur. "Digger, my . . . son. Welcome."

We met in his cathedral's Second Sanctuary, a round-walled room with a ceiling line that very nearly described a hyperbolic curve. Armor cladding off some ancient starship, with a look like that. The walls were relieved with 10,432 notches (I am incapable of not counting such things in my first glance), and each notch held a little oil lamp wrought from some old insulator or reservoir or other electromechanical part. They all burned, which argued for some extremely retarded combustion characteristics. The scent map of the room confirmed that well enough.

"I would ask something of you, Pater Nostrum. I cannot yet say whether it is a remembering or a scrying or just some keyword research in the deep data layers."

Information flows everywhere on this earth. It is encoded in every grain of sand, in the movements of the tumbling constellations of micro-satellites and space junk above our heads, in the very branching of the twigs on the trees. Knowing how to *reach* that information, how to query it and extract something useful—well, that was one reason why the world had priests.

Prayer and sacrifice invoked lines of communication which remained obdurately shut to most of us most of the time.

"I will do this thing for you gladly," Pater Nostrum said. "But you must first cross my palm with slivers, to make our bargain whole and place you under my hieratic seal."

This I knew as well, and so had brought a cluster of shattered beast-ivory from a sand-filled sea cave recently explored beneath the Hayük Desert. I scattered it over his open hand in a brittle mist.

Pater Nostrum closed his fist and grimaced. I knew with skin like his that the ivory would cut, burn, slice. When he opened his hand, the usual small miracle had occurred. A tooth with four twisted roots lay whole on the bloody palm.

"Well brought, Digger," the priest said. He smiled. "And of course my debt to you is long-incurred. So speak plainly and tell me what you seek."

I closed my eyes a moment and let my skin tell me the story of the point-source warmth of ten thousand little flames. The framing of this question had been much on my mind of late, with me working at great length to tease it out. Still, no matter what I said, I'd be wrong. Clearly enough the only choice was to address the moment and trust my friendship with this old priest.

"There is a client. A difficult one. It has charged me with finding the door into death. I would know if ever there was such a thing outside the sliding walls of metaphor. If so, where might I find this door, or evidence of its former existence?"

"A door into death." The priest stared up at his hyperbolic ceiling, his eyes following the receding curve into some dark infinity. "I will scry," Pater Nostrum muttered. The air began to swirl around him, dust motes orbiting his upturned face like swallows around a charnel house chimney. His eyes rolled inward until nothing remained within his lids but a silvery glowing sliver. One by one, the flames on the wall niches began going out in tiny pops as the priest drew from their energy in some pattern known only to him.

I settled to watch. The brilliant dust of a thousand millennia of nanotechnology meant the world could describe *itself*, if like any competent priest one only knew how to ask the questions.

So he scried. The flames carried Pater Nostrum inward on a wave of information, a palimpsest of infinitely successive and fractal functional languages, protocols, handshakes, field-gestalts and far stranger, more curious engineering dead ends. I knew there had once been information systems which stored data in the probabilistic matrices of quantum foam, extracting it again in a fractional femtosecond as observational dynamics collapsed the informational field to null. Likewise I knew there had once been information systems which relied upon the death of trees to transmit data at a bit rate so low it could be measured in packets per century.

Pater Nostrum could reach them all. At least on his best days. Each little lamp was a channel into some dead language, some time-hoared data protocol, some methodology which had once swept the world so hard that its fingerprints remained in the noösphere.

One by one, 10,432 flames went out. Slowly we passed through shadow before being cast into darkness. I don't measure time on the human plan myself, and so hunger, micturation, joint fatigue and the like tend not to impinge overmuch on my situational experience, but Pater Nostrum experienced all those and more, until blood ran gelid-dark from his nose and ears as the last of the lights winked away to leave the two of us alone in lightless splendor demarcated only by the priest's breathing and my scent map of his body's sudden advancement into further decay.

Finally he came back to me.

"Well." Pater Nostrum picked his way through his words with an exaggerated care. "It has not been so in more decades than I care to admit to."

"You scry well, Father," I said politely.

"I should not think to scry so well again. Not as I value my own health."

"Surely the gods forfend."

"Gods." He snorted. "I am a *priest*. What does my work have to do with gods?"

"I can't say, Father." After that I waited for him to find the thread of his thoughts.

Finally Pater Nostrum spoke. "There was a movement during the era of the Viridian Republic. Religious, scientific, cultural."

A long pause ensued, but that did not seem to require an answer, so I did not answer him.

He gathered himself and continued. "They called themselves Lux Transitum. This movement believed that life is a waveform. So long as you do not collapse the waveform, life continues. Death was viewed not as a biological process but as an unfortunate event within the realm of some very specialized physics."

"Life is . . . life," I replied. "Antientropic organization in chemical or electromechanical systems which, when left unattended, tends to metastatize into computers, people, starships, catfish and what have you."

Lighting a candle from the inner pocket of his vinyl robes, Pater Nostrum shook his head. "As the case may be. I only reflect what I have been told. I do not believe it. Sooner argue with the dead that contend with the noösphere."

"Wise policy, every bit of it."

"At least for those of us on the human plan." He tried another grin, but this one failed.

More silence followed, as if Pater Nostrum was now determined to subdivide his attention into short tranches interspersed by gaps of inertia.

Finally I stepped into the conversation again. "Did Lux Transitum have a laboratory or a temple? Is there some place where they addressed this uncollapsed waveform?"

"Hmm?" Pater Nostrum looked at me as if noticing me for the first time. "Oh, well, yes."

"Father." I imbued my voice with infinite patience, something this body was fairly good at. "Where might I find their holy place?"

He woke to my question with a non sequitur. "How long have you been alive, Digger?"

"Me?" I stopped and considered that. "At least 7,313 years, by the most conservative view. Counting since the last cold restart of my cognitive processes."

"How long have I been alive?"

"I shouldn't know with any certainty," I said, "but we met shortly after the Andromachus strike. Which was 4,402 years ago the second Thursday of next month."

"You are not on the human plan, but I am." He leaned close, almost touching me. "Do you think the human plan called for four thousand year old priests? When was the last time you saw a child?"

I tried to remember when I'd last encountered a juvenile of *any* species. Not just human. "Surely people must breed somewhere."

"Surely," said Pater Nostrum. "But not here on Earth, it seems."

"This would not come naturally to my attention," I pointed out. "But you might have noticed it somewhere along the way."

"You know," the priest said vaguely. "The days are bathed in almost endless red light. There is always something to do. So few people roam the world . . ."

"A thought-block," I said sympathetically.

He seemed shocked. "On the entire human race?"

"What human race?"

We walked outside under the dying sun and argued long over whether Lux Transitum had the right of it, and what *had* been done with people. Most of all, whether to wake them up.

You're wondering now, aren't you? How long ago did this happen? What did Dog the Digger do next? Did I wake the exogen and what did I tell him when I did?

Look around you. What do you see? Quiet place we've got. That line of hills over there is a linear city from the Vitalist Era. Bury it in a quarter million years of rain and three major eruptions due west of here, and there's nothing left but low hills covered with scrub. Until you go digging.

Now beneath your feet. The red sand dusting your boots is rust accumulation from when teratons of asteroidal iron were brought down by the Wolfram Bund to clad the world in an impermeable metal shell.

Feel how the air tickles your throat when you breathe? You'd be appalled at how much processing power goes into your lungs, and what percentage of that crosses through the alveoli into your bloodstream. There's a *reason* that access to this damned planet is so heavily restricted.

So we live here in our lowtowns and our cathedrals and our shanties and caverns and buried mansions, and nothing ever changes. That was the big secret the exogen was searching for. You can transcend death, but only through stasis. The whole point and purpose of life on the human plan is death. Otherwise you are *us*, grubbing in the ruins of a million years of dreaming.

And you are us, now. Check in with your shuttle. I can promise you it's not going back up in this lifetime. My fourth and sixth bodies have already disassembled the engines and control surfaces. You will live forever, too, my friends, trapped in the same story as the rest of us.

The exogen?

He'll wake up eventually. We're letting him sleep. He's already found the answer. He just doesn't have to dig holes under a bloodred sky to earn it every day.

I am called Dog the Digger. I am not mighty, neither am I fearsome. But I am all you will ever know now.

Or maybe this is just a story, like you asked for. Under the crimson light of a dying sun, is there any real difference between a story and the truth?

Welcome to my Earth.

TECHNICOLOR

JOHN LANGAN

Come on, say it out loud with me: "And Darkness and Decay and the Red Death held illimitable dominion over all." Look at that sentence. Who says Edgar Allan Poe was a lousy stylist? Thirteen words—good number for a horror story, right? Although it's not so much a story as a masque. Yes, it's about a masque, but it is a masque, too. Of course, you all know what a masque is. If you didn't, you looked it up in your dictionaries, because that's what you do in a senior seminar. Anyone?

No, not a play, not exactly. Yes? Good, okay, "masquerade" is one sense of the word, a ball whose guests attend in costume. Anyone else?

Yes, very nice, nicely put. The masque does begin in the sixteenth century. It's the entertainment of the elite, and originally, it's a combination of pantomime and dance. Pantomime? Right—think "mime." The idea is to perform without words, gesturally, to let the movements of your body tell the story. You do that, and you dance, and there's your show. Later on, there's dialogue and other additions, but I think it's this older sense of the word the story intends. Remember that tall, silent figure at the end.

I'm sorry? Yes, good point. The two kinds of masque converge.

Back to that sentence, though. Twenty-two syllables that break almost perfectly in half, ten and twelve, "And Darkness and Decay and the Red Death" and "held illimitable dominion over all." A group of short words, one and two syllables each, takes you through the first part of the sentence, then they give way to these long, almost luxurious words, "illimitable dominion." The rhythm—you see how complex it is? You ride along on these short words, bouncing up and down, alliterating from one "d" to the next, and suddenly you're mired in those Latinate polysyllables. All the momentum goes out of your reading; there's just enough time for the final pair of words, which are short, which is good, and you're done.

Wait, just let me—no, all right, what was it you wanted to say?

Exactly, yes, you took the words out of my mouth. The sentence does what the story does, carries you along through the revelry until you run smack-dab into that tall figure in the funeral clothes. Great job.

One more observation about the sentence, then I promise it's on to the story itself. I know you want to talk about Prospero's castle, all those colored rooms. Before we do, however, the four "d"s. We've mentioned already, there are a lot of "d" sounds in these thirteen words. They thread through the line, help tie it together. They also draw our attention to four words in particular. The first three are easy to recognize: they're capitalized, as well. Darkness, Decay, Death. The fourth? Right, dominion. Anyone want to take a stab at why they're capitalized?

Yes? Well . . . okay, sure it makes them into proper nouns. Can you take that a step farther? What kind of proper nouns does it make them? What's happened to the Red Death in the story? It's gone from an infection you can't see to a tall figure wandering around the party. Personification, good. Darkness, Decay, (the Red) Death: the sentence personifies them; they're its trinity, its unholy trinity, so to speak. And this godhead holds dominion, what the dictionary defines as "sovereign authority" over all. Not only the prince's castle, not only the world of the story, but all, you and me.

In fact, in a weird sort of way, this is the story of the incarnation of one of the persons of this awful trinity.

All right, moving on, now. How about those rooms? Actually, how about the building those rooms are in, first? I've been calling it a castle, but it isn't, is it? It's "castellated," which is to say, castle-like, but it's an abbey, a monastery. I suppose it makes sense to want to wait out the Red Death in a place like an abbey. After all, it's both removed from the rest of society and well-fortified. And we shouldn't be too hard on the prince and his followers for retreating there. It's not the first time this has happened, in literature or life. Anyone read *The Decameron*? Boccaccio? It's a collection of one hundred stories told by ten people, five women and five men, who have sequestered themselves in, I'm pretty sure it's a convent, to wait out the plague ravaging Florence. The Black Death, that one.

If you consider that the place in which we find the seven rooms is a monastery, a place where men are supposed to withdraw from this world to meditate on the next, its rooms appear even stranger. What's the set-up? Seven rooms, yes, thank you, I believe I just said that. Running east to west, good. In a straight line? No. There's a sharp turn every twenty or thirty yards, so that you can see only one room at a time. So long as they follow that east to west course, you can lay the rooms out in any form you like. I favor steps, like the ones that lead the condemned man to the chopping block, but that's just me.

Hang on, hang on, we'll get to the colors in a second. We need to stay with the design of the rooms for a little longer. Not everybody gets this the first time through. There are a pair of windows, Gothic windows, which means what? That they're long and pointed at the top. The windows are opposite one another, and they look out on, anybody? Not exactly: a chandelier hangs down from the ceiling. It is a kind of light, though. No, a candelabra holds candles. Anyone else? A brazier, yes, there's a brazier sitting on a tripod outside either window. They're, how would you describe a brazier? Like a big metal cup, a bowl, that you fill with some kind of fuel and ignite. Wood, charcoal, oil. To be honest, I'm not as interested in the braziers as I am in where they're located. Outside the windows, right, but where outside the windows? Maybe I should say, What is outside the windows? Corridors, yes, there are corridors to either side of the rooms, and it's along these that the braziers are stationed. Just like our classroom. Not the tripods, of course, and I guess what's outside our windows is more a gallery than a corridor, since it's open to the parking lot on the other side. All right, all right, so I'm stretching a bit, here, but have you noticed, the room has seven windows? One for each color in Prospero's Abbey. Go ahead, count them.

So here we are in this strange abbey, one that has a crazy zig-zag suite of rooms with corridors running beside them. You could chalk the location's details up to anti-Catholic sentiment; there are critics who have argued that anti-Catholic prejudice is the secret engine driving Gothic literature. No, I don't buy it, not in this case. Sure, there are stained-glass windows, but they're basically tinted glass. There's none of the iconography you'd expect if this were anti-Catholic propaganda, no statues or paintings. All we have is that enormous clock in the last room, the mother of all grandfather clocks. Wait a minute . . .

What about those colors, then? Each of the seven rooms is decorated in a single color that matches the stained glass of its windows. From east to west, we go from blue to purple to green to orange to white to violet to—to the last room, where there's a slight change. The windows are red, but the room itself is done in black. There seems to be some significance to the color sequence, but what that is—well, this is why we have literature professors, right? (No snickering.) Not to mention, literature students. I've read through your responses to the homework assignment, and there were a few interesting ideas as to what those colors might mean. Of course, most of you connected them to times of the day, blue as dawn, black as night, the colors in between morning, noon, early afternoon, that kind of thing. Given the east-west layout, it makes a certain amount of sense. A few more of you picked up on that connection to time in a slightly different way, and related the colors to times of the year, or the stages in a person's life. In the process, some clever arguments were made. Clever, but not, I'm afraid, too convincing.

What! What's wrong! What is it! Are you all—oh, them. Oh for God's sake. When you screamed like that, I thought—I don't know what I thought. I thought I'd need a new pair of trousers. Those are a couple of graduate students I've enlisted to help me with a little presentation I'll be putting up shortly. Yes, I can understand how the masks could startle you. They're just generic white masks; I think they found them downtown somewhere.

It was their idea: once I told them what story we would be discussing, they immediately hit on wearing the masks. To tell the truth, I half-expected they'd show up sporting the heads of enormous fanged monsters. Those are relatively benign.

Yes, I suppose they do resemble the face the Red Death assumes for its costume. No blood splattered on them, though.

If I could have your attention up here, again. Pay no attention to that man behind the curtain. Where was I? Your homework, yes, thank you. Right, right. Let's see . . . oh—I know. A couple of you read the colors in more original ways. I made a note of them somewhere—here they are. One person interpreted the colors as different states of mind, beginning with blue as tranquil and ending with black as despair, with stops for jealousy—green, naturally—and passion—white, as in white-hot—along the way. Someone else made the case for the colors as, let me make sure I have the phrasing right, "phases of being."

Actually, that last one's not bad. Although the writer could be less obtuse; clarity, people, academic writing needs to be clear. Anyway, the gist of the writer's argument is that each color is supposed to take you through a different state of existence, blue at one end of the spectrum representing innocence, black at the other representing death. Death as a state of being, that's . . . provocative. Which is not to say it's correct, but it's headed in the right direction.

I know, I know: Which is? The answer requires some explanation. Scratch that. It requires a boatload of explanation. That's why I have Tweedledee and Tweedledum setting up outside. (Don't look! They're almost done.) It's also why I lowered the screen behind me for the first time this semester. There are some images I want to show you, and they're best seen in as much detail as possible. If I can remember what the Media Center people told me . . . click this . . . then this . . .

Voila!

Matthew Brady's *Portrait* of Edgar, taken 1848, his last full year alive. It's the best-known picture of him; were I to ask you to visualize him, this is what your minds' eyes would see. That forehead, that marble expanse—yes, his hair does make the top of his head look misshapen, truncated. As far as I know, it wasn't. The eyes—I suppose everyone comments on the eyes, slightly shadowed under those brows, the lids lowered just enough to suggest a certain detachment, even dreaminess. It's the mouth I notice, how it tilts up ever-so-slightly at the right corner. It's hard to see; you have to look closely. A strange mixture of arrogance, even contempt, and something else, something that might be humor, albeit of the bitter variety. It wouldn't be that much of a challenge to suggest colors for the picture, but somehow, black and white is more fitting, isn't it? Odd, considering how much color there is in the fiction. I've often thought all those old Roger Corman adaptations, the ones Vincent Price starred in—whatever their other faults, one thing they got exactly right was Technicolor, which was the perfect way to film these stories, just saturate the screen with the most vibrant colors you could find.

I begin with the *Portrait* as a reminder. This is the man. His hand scraped the pen across the paper, brought the story we've been discussing into existence word by word. Not creation *ex nihilo*, out of nothing, creation . . . if my Latin were better, or existent, I'd have a fancier way to say out of the self, or out of the depths of the self, or—hey—out of the depth that is the self.

Moving on to my next portrait . . . Anyone?

I'm impressed. Not many people know this picture. Look closely, though. See it?

That's right: it isn't a painting. It's a photograph that's been tweaked to resemble a painting. The portrait it imitates is a posthumous representation of Virginia Clemm, Edgar's sweetheart and child bride. The girl in the photo? She'll be happy you called her a girl. That's my wife, Anna. Yes, I'm married. Why is that so hard to believe? We met many years ago, in a kingdom by the sea. From? "Annabel Lee," good. No, just Anna; although we did meet in the King of the Sea Arcade, on the Jersey shore. Seriously. She is slightly younger than I am. Four years, thank you very much. You people. For Halloween one year, we dressed up as Edgar and Virginia—pretty much from the start, it's been a running joke between us. In her case, the resemblance is striking.

As it so happened, yes we did attend a masquerade as the happy couple. That was where this photo was taken. One of the other guests was a professional photographer. I arranged the shot; he took it, then used a program on his computer to transform it into a painting. The guy was quite pleased with it; apparently it's on his website. I'm showing it to you because . . . well, because I want to. There's probably a connection I could draws between masquerade, the suppression of one identity in order to invoke and inhabit another, that displacement, and the events of our story, but that's putting the car about a mile before the horse. She'll like that you thought she was a girl, though; that'll make her night. Those were her cookies, by the way. Are there any left? Not even the sugar cookies? Figures.

Okay, image number three. If you can name this one, you get an "A" for the class and an autographed picture of the Pope. Put your hand down, you don't know. How about the rest of you?

Just us crickets . . .

It's just as well; I don't have that picture of the Pope anymore. This gentleman is Prosper Vauglais. Or so he claimed. There's a lot about this guy no one's exactly sure of, like when he was born, or where, or when and where he died. He showed up in Paris in the late eighteen-teens and caused something of a stir. For one winter, he appeared at several of the less reputable *salons* and a couple of the, I wouldn't go so far as to say more reputable— maybe less disreputable ones.

His "deal?" His deal, as you put it, was that he claimed to have been among the quarter of a million soldiers under Napoleon Bonaparte's personal command when, in June of 1812, the Emperor decided to invade Russia. Some of you may remember from your European history classes, this was a very bad idea. The worst. Roughly a tenth of Napoleon's forces survived the campaign; I want to say the number who limped back into France was something like twenty-two thousand. In and of itself, being a member of that group is nothing to sneeze at. For Vauglais, though, it was only the beginning. During the more-or-less running battles the French army fought as it retreated from what had been Moscow, Vauglais was separated from his fellows, struck on the head by a Cossack's sword and left for dead in a snow bank. When he came to, he was alone, and a storm had blown up. Prosper had no idea where he was; he assumed still Russia, which wasn't too encouraging. Any Russian peasants or what have you who came across French soldiers, even those trying to surrender, tended to hack them to death with farm implements first and ask questions later. So when Prosper strikes out in what he hopes is the approximate direction of France, he isn't what you'd call terribly optimistic.

Nor is his pessimism misplaced. Within a day, he's lost, frozen and starving, wandering around the inside of a blizzard like you read about, white-out conditions, shrieking wind, unbearable cold. The blow to his head isn't helping matters, either. His vision keeps going in and out of focus. Sometimes he feels so nauseated he can barely stand, let alone continue walking. Once in a while, he'll see a light shining in the window of a farmhouse, but he gives these a wide berth. Another day, and he'll be closer to death than he was even at the worst battles he saw—than he was when that saber connected with his skull. His skin, which has been numb since not long after he started his trek, has gone from pale to white to this kind of blue-gray, and it's hardened, as if there's a crust of ice on it. He can't feel his pulse through it. His breath, which had been venting from his nose and mouth in long white clouds, seems to have slowed to a trickle, if that. He can't see anything; although, with the storm continuing around him, maybe that isn't so strange. He's not cold anymore—or, it's not that he isn't cold so much as it is that the cold isn't torturing him the way it was. At some point, the cold moved inside him, took up residence just beneath his heart, and once that happened, that transition was accomplished, the temperature outside became of much less concern.

There's a moment—while Vauglais is staggering around like you do when you're trying to walk in knee-high snow without snowshoes, pulling each foot free, swiveling it forward, crashing it through the snow in front of you, then repeating the process with your other foot—there's a moment when he realizes he's dead. He isn't sure when it happened. Some time in the last day or so. It isn't that he thinks he's in some kind of afterlife, that he's wandering around a frozen hell. No, he know he's still stuck somewhere in western Russia. It's just that, now he's dead. He isn't sure why he's stopped moving. He considers doing so, giving his body a chance to catch up to his apprehension of it, but decides against it. For one thing, he isn't sure it would work, and suppose while he's standing in place, waiting to fall over, someone finds him, one of those peasants, or a group of Russian soldiers? Granted, if he's already dead, they can't hurt him, but the prospect of being cut to pieces while still conscious is rather horrifying. And for another thing, Prosper isn't ready to quit walking. So he keeps moving forward. Dimly, the way you might hear a noise when you're fast asleep, he's aware that he isn't particularly upset at finding himself dead and yet moving, but after recent events, maybe that isn't so surprising.

Time passes; how much, he can't say. The blizzard doesn't lift, but it thins, enough for Vauglais to make out trees, evergreens. He's in a forest, a pretty dense one, from what he can see, which may explain why the storm has lessened. The trees are—there's something odd about the trees. For as close together as they are, they seem to be in almost perfect rows, running away into the snow on either side of him. In and of itself, maybe that isn't strange. Could be, he's wandered into some kind of huge formal garden. But there's more to it. When he looks at any particular tree, he sees, not so much bark and needles as black, black lines like the strokes of a paintbrush, or the scratches of a pen, forming the approximation of an evergreen. It's as if he's seeing a sketch of a tree, an artist's estimate. The black lines appear to be moving, almost too quickly for him to notice; it's as if he's witnessing them being drawn and re-drawn. Prosper has a sudden vision of himself from high above, a small, dark spot in the midst of long rows of black on white, a stray bit of punctuation loose among the lines of an unimaginable text.

Eventually, Vauglais reaches the edge of the forest. Ahead, there's a building, the title to this page he's been traversing. The blizzard has kicked up again, so he can't see much, but he has the impression of a long, low structure, possibly stone. It could be a stable, could be something else. Although there are no religious symbols evident, Prosper has an intuition the place is a monastery. He should turn right or left, avoid the building—the Russian clergy haven't taken any more kindly to the French invaders than the Russian people—instead, he raises one stiff leg and strikes off towards it. It isn't that he's compelled to do so, that he's in the grip of a power that he can't resist, or that he's decided to embrace the inevitable, surrender to death. He isn't even especially curious about the stone structure. Forward is just a way to go, and he does.

As he draws closer, Vauglais notices that the building isn't becoming any easier to distinguish. If anything, it's more indistinct, harder to make out. If the trees behind him were rough drawing, this place is little more than a scribble, a jumble of lines whose form is as much in the eye of the beholder as anything. When a figure in a heavy coat and hat separates from the structure and begins to trudge in his direction, it's as if a piece of the place has broken off. Prosper can't see the man's face, all of which except the eyes is hidden by the folds of a heavy scarf, but he lifts one mittened hand and gestures for Vauglais to follow him inside, which the Frenchman does.

And . . . no one knows what happens next.

What do I mean? I'm sorry: wasn't I speaking English? No one knows what happened inside the stone monastery. Prosper writes a fairly detailed account of the events leading up to that point, which is where the story I'm telling you comes from, but when the narrative reaches this moment, it breaks off with Vauglais's declaration that he's told us as much as he can. End of story.

All right, yes, there are hints of what took place during the five years he was at the Abbey. That was what he called the building, the Abbey. Every so often, Prosper would allude to his experiences in it, and sometimes, someone would note his remarks in a letter or diary. From combing through these kinds of documents, it's possible to assemble and collate Vauglais's comments into a glimpse of his life with the Fraternity. Again, his name. There were maybe seven of them, or seven after he arrived, or there were supposed to be seven. He referred to "Brother Red," once; to "The White Brother" at another time. Were the others named Blue, Purple, Green, Orange, and Violet? We can't say; although, as an assumption, it isn't completely unreasonable. They spent their days in pursuit of something Vauglais called The Great Work; he also referred to it as The Transumption. This seems to have involved generous amounts of quiet meditation combined with the study of certain religious texts—Prosper doesn't name them, but they may have included some Gnostic writings.

The Gnostics? I don't suppose you would have heard of them. How many of you actually got to church? As I feared. What would Sr. Mary Mary say? The Gnostics were a religious sect who sprang up around the same time as the early Christians. I guess they would have described themselves as the true Christians, the ones who understood what Jesus's teachings were really about. They shared sacred writings with the more orthodox Christians, but they had their own books, too. They were all about *gnosis*, knowledge, especially of the self. For them, the secret to what lay outside the self was what lay inside the self. The physical world was evil, a wellspring of illusions and delusions. Gnostics tended to retreat to the desert, lead lives of contemplation. Unlike the mainstream Christians, they weren't much on formal organization; that, and the fact that those Christians did everything in their power to shunt the Gnostics and their teachings to the margins and beyond, branding some of their ideas as heretical, helps explain why they pretty much vanished from the religious scene.

"Pretty much," though, isn't the same thing as "completely." (I know: such precise, scientific terminology.) Once in a while, Gnostic ideas would resurface, usually in the writings of some fringe figure or another. Rumors persist of Gnostic secret societies, occasionally as part of established groups like the Jesuits or the Masons. Which begs the question, Was Vauglais's Fraternity one of these societies, a kind of order of Gnostic monks? The answer to which is—

Right: no one knows. There's no record of any official, which is to say, Russian Orthodox religious establishment: no monastery, no church, in the

general vicinity of where we think Prosper was. Of course, a bunch of Gnostic monastics would hardly constitute anything resembling an official body, and so might very well fly under the radar. That said, the lack of proof against something does not count as evidence for it.

That's true. He could have been making the whole thing up.

Transumption? It's a term from classical rhetoric. It refers to the elision of a chain of associations. Sorry—sometimes I like to watch your heads explode. Let's say you're writing your epic poem about the fall of Troy, and you describe one of the Trojans being felled by an arrow. Let's say that arrow was made from the wood of a tree in a sacred grove; let's say, too, that that grove was planted by Hercules, who scattered some acorns there by accident. Now let's say that, when your Trojan hero sinks to the ground, drowning in his own blood, one of his friends shouts, "Curse the careless hand of Hercules!" That statement is an example of transumption. You've jumped from one link in a chain of associations back several. Make sense?

Yes, well, what does a figure of speech have to do with what was going on inside that Abbey?

Oh wait—hold on for a moment. My two assistants are done with their set up. Let me give them a signa . . . Five more minutes? All right, good, yes. I have no idea if they understood me. Graduate students.

Don't worry about what's on the windows. Yes, yes, those are lamps. Can I have your attention up here, please? Thank you. Let me worry about Campus Security. Or my masked friends out there will.

Okay—let's skip ahead a little. We were talking about The Transumption, a.k.a. The Great Work. There's nothing in his other references to the Abbey that offers any clue as to what he may have meant by it. However, there is an event that may shed some light on things.

It occurs in Paris, towards the end of February. An especially fierce winter scours the streets, sends people scurrying from the shelter of one building to another. Snow piles on top of snow, all of it turning dirty gray. Where there isn't snow, there's ice, inches thick in places. The sky is gray, the sun a pale blur that puts in a token appearance for a few hours a day. Out into this glacial landscape, Prosper leads half a dozen men and women from one of the city's less-disreputable *salons*. Their destination, the catacombs, the long tunnels that run under Paris. They're quite old, the catacombs. In some places, the walls are stacked with bones, from when they were used as a huge ossuary. (That's a place to hold the bones of the dead.) They're also fairly crowded, full of beggars, the poor, searching for shelter from the ravages of the season. Vauglais has to take his party deep underground before they can find a location that's suitably empty. It's a kind of side-chamber, roughly circular, lined with shelves full of skull piled on skull. The skulls make a clicking sound, from the rats shuffling through them. Oh yes, there are plenty of rats down here.

Prosper fetches seven skulls off the shelves and piles them in the center of the room. He opens a large flask he's carried with him, and pours its contents over the bones. It's lamp oil, which he immediately ignites with his torch. He sets the torch down, and gathers the members of the *salon* around the skulls. They join hands.

It does sound as if he's leading a séance, doesn't it? The only difference is, he isn't asking the men and women with him to think of a beloved one who's passed beyond. Nor does he request they focus on a famous ghost. Instead, Vauglais tells them to look at the flames licking the bones in front of them. Study those flames, he says, watch them as they trace the contours of the skulls. Follow the flames over the cheeks, around the eyes, up the brows. Gaze into those eyes, into the emptiness inside the fire. Fall through the flames; fall into that blackness.

He's hypnotizing them, of course—Mesmerizing would be the more historically-accurate term. Under the sway of his voice, the members of the *salon* enter a kind of vacancy. They're still conscious—well, they're still perceiving, still aware of that heap of bones burning in front of them, the heavy odor of the oil, the quiet roar of the flames—but their sense of their selves, the accumulation of memory and inclination that defines each from the other, is gone.

Now Prosper is telling them to think of something new. Picture the flesh that used to clothe these skulls, he says. Warm and smooth, flushed with life. Look closely—it glows, doesn't it? It shines with its living. Watch! watch—it's dying. It's growing cold, pale. The glow, that dim light floating at the very limit of the skin—it's changing, drifting up, losing its radiance. See—there!—ah, it's dead. Cool as a cut of meat. Gray. The light is gone. Or is it? Is that another light? Yes, yes it is; but it is not the one we have watched dissipate. This is a darker glow. Indigo, that most elusive of the rainbow's hues. It curls over the dull skin like fog, and the flesh opens for it, first in little cracks, then in long windows, and then in wide doorways. As the skin peels away, the light thickens, until it is as if the bone is submerged in a bath of indigo. The light is not done moving; it pours into the air above the skull, over all the skulls. Dark light is rising from them, twisting up in thick streams that seek each other, that wrap around one another, that braid a shape. It is the form of a man, a tall man dressed in black robes, his face void as a corpse's, his head crowned with black flame—

Afterwards, when the half-dozen members of the *salon* compare notes, none of them can agree on what, if anything, they saw while under Vauglais's sway. One of them insists that nothing appeared. Three admit to what might have been a cloud of smoke, or a trick of the light. Of the remaining pair, one states flat-out that she saw the Devil. The other balks at any statement more elaborate than, "Monsieur Vauglais has shown me terrible joy." Whatever they do or don't see, it doesn't last very long. The oil Prosper doused the skulls with has been consumed. The fire dies away; darkness rushes in to fill the gap.

The trance in which Vauglais has held the *salon* breaks. There's a sound like wind rushing, then quiet.

A month after that expedition, Prosper disappeared from Paris. He had attempted to lead that same *salon* back into the catacombs for a second—well, whatever you'd call what he'd done. A summoning? (But what was he summoning?) Not surprisingly, the men and women of the *salon* declined his request. In a huff, Vauglais left them and tried to insert himself into a couple of even-less-disreputable *salons*, attempting to use gossip about his former associates as his price of admission. But either the secrets he knew weren't juicy enough—possible, but I suspect unlikely—or those other *salons* had heard about his underground investigations and decided they preferred the comfort of their drawing rooms. Then one of the men from that original *salon* raised questions about Prosper's military service—he claimed to have found a sailor who swore that he and Vauglais had been on an extended debauch in Morocco at the very time he was supposed to have been marching towards Moscow. That's the problem with being the flavor of the month: before you know it, the calendar's turned, and no one can remember what they found so appealing about you in the first place. In short order, there's talk about an official inquiry into Prosper's service record—probably more rumor than fact, but it's enough for Vauglais, and he departs Paris for parts unknown. No one sees him leave, just as no one saw him arrive. In the weeks that follow, there are reports of Prosper in Libya, Madagascar, but they don't disturb a single eyebrow. Years—decades later, when Gauguin's in Tahiti, he'll hear a story about a strange white man who came to the island a long time ago and vanished into its interior, and Vauglais's name will occur to him, but you can't even call that a legend. It's . . . a momentary association. Prosper Vauglais vanishes.

Well, not all of him. That's right: there's the account he wrote of his discovery of the Abbey.

I beg your pardon? Dead? Oh, right, yes. It's interesting—apparently, Prosper permitted a physician connected to the first *salon* he frequented to conduct a pretty thorough examination of him. According to Dr. Zumachin, Vauglais's skin was stubbornly pallid. No matter how much the doctor pinched or slapped it, Prosper's flesh remained the same gray-white. Not only that, it was cold, cold and hard, as if it were packed with ice. Although Vauglais had to inhale in order to speak, his regular respiration was so slight as to be undetectable. It wouldn't fog the doctor's pocket mirror. And try as Zumachin might, he could not locate a pulse.

Sure, Prosper could have paid him off; aside from his part in this story, there isn't that much information on the good doctor. For what it's worth, most of the people who met Vauglais commented on his skin, its pallor, and, if they touched it, its coldness. No one else noted his breathing, or lack thereof, but a couple of the members of that last *salon* described him as extraordinarily still.

Okay, back to that book. Actually, wait. Before we do, let me bring this up on the screen . . .

I know—talk about something completely different. No, it's not a Rorschach test. It does look like it, though, doesn't it? Now if my friends outside will oblige me . . . and there we go. Amazing what a sheet of blue plastic and a high-power lamp can do. We might as well be in the east room of Prospero's Abbey.

Yes, the blue light makes it appear deeper—it transforms it from ink-spill to opening. Prosper calls it "*La Bouche*," the Mouth. Some mouth, eh?

That's where the design comes from, Vauglais's book. The year after his disappearance, a small Parisian press whose biggest claim to fame was its unauthorized edition of the Marquis de Sade's *Justine* publishes Prosper's *L'Histoire de Mes Aventures dans L'Etendu Russe*, which translates something like, "The History of My Adventures in the Russian," either "Wilderness" or "Vastness." Not that anyone calls it by its title. The publisher, one Denis Prebend, binds Vauglais's essay between covers the color of a bruise after three or four days. Yes, that sickly, yellowy-green. Of course that's what catches everyone's attention, not the less-than-inspired title, and it isn't long before customers are asking for "*le livre verte*," the green book. It's funny—it's one of those books that no one will admit to reading, but that goes through ten printings the first year after its appears.

Some of those copies do find their way across the Atlantic, very good. In fact, within a couple of months of its publication, there are at least three pirated translations of the green book circulating the booksellers of London, and a month after that, they're available in Boston, New York, and Baltimore.

To return to the book itself for a moment—after that frustrating ending, there's a blank page, which is followed by seven more pages, each showing a separate design. What's above me on the screen is the first of them. The rest—well, let's not get ahead of ourselves. Suffice it to say, the initial verdict was that something had gone awry in the printing process, with the result that the *bouche* had become *bouché*, cloudy. A few scholars have even gone so far as to attempt to reconstruct what Prosper's original images must have been. Prebend, though—the publisher—swore that he'd presented the book exactly as he had been instructed.

For those of us familiar with abstract art, I doubt there's any great difficulty in seeing the black blot on the screen as a mouth. The effect—there used to be these books; they were full of what looked like random designs. If you held them the right distance from your face and let your eyes relax, almost to the point of going cross-eyed, all of sudden, a picture would leap out of the page at you. You know what I'm talking about? Good. I don't know what the name for that effect is, but it's the nearest analogue I can come up with for what happens when you look at the Mouth under blue light—except that the image doesn't jump forward so much as sink back. The way it recedes—it's as if it extends, not just through the screen, or the wall behind it, but beyond all that, to the very substratum of things.

To tell the truth, I have no idea what's responsible for the effect. If you find this impressive, however . . .

Look at that: a new image and a fresh color. How's that for coordination? Good work, nameless minions. Vauglais named this "*Le Gardien*," the Guardian. What's that? I suppose you could make an octopus out of it; although aren't there a few too many tentacles? True, it's close enough; it's certainly more octopus than squid. Do you notice . . . right. The tentacles, loops, whatever we call them, appear to be moving. Focus on any one in particular, and it stands still—but you can see movement out of the corner of your eye, can't you? Try to take in the whole, and you swear its arms are performing an intricate dance.

So the Mouth leads to the Guardian, which is waving its appendages in front of . . .

That green is bright after the purple, isn't it? Voila "*Le Récif*," the Reef. Makes sense, a cuttlefish protecting a reef. I don't know: it's angular enough. Personally, I suspect this one is based on some kind of pun or word play. "*Récif*" is one letter away from "*récit*," story, and this reef comes to us as the result of a story; in some weird way, the reef may be the story. I realize that doesn't make any sense; I'm still working through it.

This image is a bit different from the previous two. Anyone notice how?

Exactly: instead of the picture appearing to move, the light itself seems to—I like your word, "shimmer." You could believe we're gazing through water. It's—not hypnotic, that's too strong, but it is soothing. Don't you think?

I'll take your yawn as a "yes." Very nice. What a way to preface a question. All right, all right. What is it that's keeping you awake?

Isn't it obvious? Apparently not.

Yes! Edgar read Prosper's book!

When. The best evidence is sometime in the early eighteen thirties, after he'd relocated to Baltimore. He mentions hearing about the green book from one of his fellow cadets at West Point, but he doesn't secure his own copy until he literally stumbles upon one in a bookshop near Baltimore's inner harbor. He wrote a fairly amusing account of it in a letter to Virginia. The store was this long, narrow space located halfway down an alley; its shelves were stuffed past capacity with all sizes of books jammed together with no regard for their subject. Occasionally, one of the shelves would disgorge its contents without warning. If you were underneath or to the side of it, you ran the risk of substantial injury. Not to mention, the single aisle snaking into the shop's recesses was occupied at irregular intervals by stacks of books that looked as if a strong sneeze would send them tumbling down.

It's as he's attempting to maneuver around an especially tall tower of

books, simultaneously trying to avoid jostling a nearby shelf, that Edgar's
foot catches on a single volume he hadn't seen, sending him—and all books
in the immediate vicinity—to the floor. There's a huge puff of dust; half a
dozen books essentially disintegrate. Edgar's sense of humor is such that he
appreciates the comic aspect of a poet—as he styled himself—buried beneath
a deluge of books. However, he insists on excavating the book that undid
him.

The copy of Vauglais's essay he found was a fourth translation that had
been done by a Boston publisher hoping to cash in on the popularity of the
other editions. Unfortunately for him, he the edition took longer to prepare
than he'd anticipated—his translator was a Harvard professor who insisted on
translating Prosper as accurately as he could. This meant an English version
of Vauglais's essay that was a model of fidelity to the original French, but that
wasn't ready until Prosper's story was last week's news. The publisher went
ahead with what he titled *The Green Book of M. Prosper Vauglais* anyway, but
he pretty much lost his shirt over the whole thing.

Edgar was so struck at having fallen over this book that he bought it on
the spot. He spent the next couple of days reading and re-reading it, puzzling
over its contents. As we've seen in "The Gold Bug" and "The Purloined Letter,"
this was a guy who liked a puzzle. He spent a good deal of time on the seven
designs at the back of the book, convinced that their significance was right
in front of him.

Speaking of those pictures, let's have another one. Assistants, if you
please—

Hey, it's Halloween! Isn't that what you associate orange with? And
especially an orange like this—this is the sun spilling the last of its late
light, right before all the gaudier colors, the violets and pinks, splash out.
You don't think of orange as dark, do you? I know I don't. Yet it is, isn't it?
Is it the darkest of the bright colors? To be sure, it's difficult to distinguish
the design at its center; the orange is filmy, translucent. There are a few too
many curves for it to be the symbol for infinity; at least, I think there are.
I want to say I see a pair of snakes wrapped around one another, but the
coils don't connect in quite the right way. Vauglais's name for this was "*Le
Coeur*," the Heart, and also the Core, as well as the Height or the Depth,
depending on usage. Obviously, we're cycling through the seven rooms
from "The Masque of the Red Death;" obviously, too, I'm arguing that
Edgar takes their colors from Prosper's book. In that schema, orange is at
the center, three colors to either side of it; in that sense, we have reached
the heart, the core, the height or the depth. Of course, that core obscure
the other one—or maybe not.

While you try to decide, let's return to Edgar. It's an overstatement to
say that Vauglais obsesses him. When his initial attempt at deciphering the
designs fails, he puts the book aside. Remember, he's a working writer at a
time when the American economy really won't support one—especially one

with Edgar's predilections—so there are always more things to be written in the effort to keep the wolf a safe distance from the door. Not to mention, he's falling in love with the girl who will become his wife. At odd moments over the next decade, though, he retrieves Prosper's essay and spends a few hours poring over it. He stares at its images until they're grooved into the folds of his brain. During one long afternoon in 1840, he's sitting with the book open to the Mouth, a glass of water on the table to his right. The sunlight streaming in the windows splinters on the waterglass, throwing a rainbow across the page in front of him. The arc of the images that's under the blue strip of the bow looks different; it's as if that portion of the paper has sunk into the book—behind the book. A missing and apparently lost piece of the puzzle snaps into place, and Edgar starts up from the table, knocking over his chair in the process. He races through the house, searching for a piece of blue glass. The best he can do is a heavy blue jug, which he almost drops in his excitement. He returns to the book, angles the jug to catch the light, and watches as the Mouth opens. He doesn't waste any time staring at it; shifting the jug to his right hand, he flips to the next image with his left, positions the glass jug over the Guardian, and . . . nothing. For a moment, he's afraid he's imagined the whole thing, had an especially vivid waking dream. But when he pages back to the Mouth and directs the blue light onto it, it clearly recedes. Edgar wonders if the effect he's observed is unique to the first image, then his eye lights on the glass of water, still casting its rainbow. He sets the jug on the floor, turns the page, and slides the book closer to the glass.

That's how Edgar spends the rest of the afternoon, matching the designs in the back of Vauglais's book to the colors that activate them. The first four come relatively quickly; the last three take longer. Once he has all seven, Edgar re-reads Prosper's essay and reproaches himself as a dunce for not having hit on the colors sooner. It's all there in Vauglais's prose, he declares, plain as day. (He's being much too hard on himself. I've read the green book a dozen times and I have yet to find the passage where Prosper hints at the colors.)

How about a look at the most difficult designs? Gentlemen, if you please . . .

There's nothing there. I know—that's what I said, the first time I saw the fifth image. "*Le Silence*," the Silence. Compared to the designs that precede it, this one is so faint as to be barely detectable. And when you shine a bright, white light onto it, it practically disappears. There is something in there, though; you have to stare at it for a while. Moreso than with the previous images, what you see here varies dramatically from viewer to viewer.

Edgar never records his response to the Silence, which is a pity. Having cracked the secret of Vauglais's designs, he studies the essay more carefully, attempting to discern the use to which the images were to be put, the nature of Prosper's Great Work, his Transumption. (There's that word again. I never clarified its meaning vis à vis Vauglais's ideas, did I?) The following year, when Edgar sits down to write "The Masque of the Red Death," it is no small part as an answer to the question of what Prosper was up to. That answer shares features with some of the stories he had written prior to his 1840 revelation; although, interestingly, they came after he had obtained his copy of the green book.

From the looks on your faces, I'd say you've seen what the Silence contains. I don't suppose anyone wants to share?

I'll take that as a, "No." It's all right: what you find there can be rather ... disconcerting.

We're almost at the end of our little display. What do you say we proceed to number six? Here we go . . .

Violet's such a nice color, isn't it? You have to admit, some of those other colors are pretty intense. Not this one, though; even the image—"L'Arbre," the Tree—looks more or less like a collection of lines trying to be a tree. Granted, if you study the design, you'll notice that each individual line seems to fade and then re-inscribe itself, but compared to the effect of the previous image, this is fairly benign. Does it remind you of anything? Anything we were discussing, say, in the last hour or so?

Oh never mind, I'll just tell you. Remember those trees Vauglais saw outside the Abbey? Remember the way that, when he tried to focus on any of them, he saw a mass of black lines? Hmmm. Maybe there's more to this pleasant design than we'd thought. Maybe it's, not the key to all this, but the key trope, or figure.

I know: which means what, exactly? Let's return to Edgar's story. You have a group of people who are sequestered together, made to disguise their outer identities, encouraged to debauch themselves, to abandon their inner identities, all the while passing from one end of this color schema to the other. They put their selves aside, become a massive blank, a kind of psychic space. That opening allows what is otherwise an abstraction, a personification, to change states, to manifest itself physically. Of course, the Red Death doesn't appear of its own volition; it's called into being by Prince Prospero, who can't stop thinking about the reason he's retreated into his abbey.

This is what happened—what started to happen to the members of the *salon* Prosper took into the Parisian catacombs. He attempted to implement what he'd learned during his years at the Abbey, what he first had perceived through the snow twirling in front of his eyes in that Russian forest. To manipulate—to mold—to . . .

Suppose that the real—what we take to be the real—imagine that world outside the self, all this out here, is like a kind of writing. We write it together; we're continuously writing it together, onto the surface of things, the paper, as it were. It isn't something we do consciously, or that we exercise any conscious control over. We might glimpse it in moments of extremity, as Vauglais did, but that's about as close to it as most of us will come. What if, though, what if it were possible to do something more than simply look? What if you could clear a space on that paper and write something *else*? What might you bring into being?

Edgar tries to find out. Long after "The Masque," which is as much caution as it is field guide, he decides to apply Prosper's ideas for real. He does so during that famous lost week at the end of his life, that gap in the biographical record that has prompted so much speculation. Since Virginia succumbed to tuberculosis some two years prior, Edgar's been on a long downward slide, a protracted effort at joining his beloved wife. You know, extensive forests have been harvested for the production of critical studies of Edgar's "bizarre" relationship with Virginia; rarely, if ever, does it occur to anyone that Edgar and Virginia might honestly have been in love, and that the difference in their ages might have been incidental. Yet what is that final couple of years but a man grieving himself to death? Yes, Edgar approaches other women about possible marriage, but why do you think none of those proposals work out?

Not only is Edgar actively chasing his death, paddling furiously towards it on a river of alcohol; little known to him, death has noticed his pursuit, and responded by planting a black seed deep within his brain, a gift that is blossoming into a tumor. Most biographers have remained ignorant of this disease, but years after his death, Edgar's body is exhumed—it doesn't matter why; given who Edgar was, of course this was going to happen to him. During the examination of his remains, it's noted that his brain is shrunken and hard. Anyone who knows about these things will tell you that the brain is one of the first organs to decay, which means that what those investigators found rattling around old Edgar's cranium would not have been petrified gray matter. Cancer, however, is a much more durable beast; long after it's killed you, a tumor hangs around to testify to its crime. Your guess is as good as mine when it comes to how long he'd had it, but by the time I'm talking about, Edgar is in a pretty bad way. He's having trouble controlling the movements of his body, his speech; half the time he seems drunk, he's stone cold sober.

There's something else. Increasingly, wherever he turns his gaze, whatever he looks at flickers, and instead of, say, an orange resting on a plate, he sees a jumble of black lines approximating a sphere on a circle. It takes him longer to recall Vauglais's experience in that Russian forest than you'd expect; the cancer, no doubt, devouring his memory. Sometimes the confusion of lines that's replaced the streetlamp in front of him is itself replaced by blankness, by an absence that registers as a dull white space in the middle of things. It's as if a painter took a palette knife and scraped the oils from a portion of their picture until all that remained was the canvas, slightly stained. At first, Edgar thinks there's something wrong with his vision; when he understands what he's experiencing, he speculates that the blank might be the result of his eyes' inability to endure their own perception, that he might be undergoing some degree of what we would call hysterical blindness. As he's continued to see that whiteness, though, he's realized that he isn't seeing less, but more. He's seeing through to the surface those black lines are written on.

In the days immediately prior to his disappearance, Edgar's perception undergoes one final change. For the slightest instant after that space has uncovered itself to him, something appears on it, a figure—a woman. Virginia, yes, as he saw her last, ravaged by tuberculosis, skeletally thin, dark hair in disarray, mouth and chin scarlet with the blood she'd hacked out of her lungs. She appears barefoot, wrapped in a shroud stained with dirt. Almost before he sees her, she's gone, her place taken by whatever he'd been looking at to begin with.

Is it any surprise that, presented with this dull white surface, Edgar should fill it with Virginia? Her death has polarized him; she's the lodestone that draws his thoughts irresistibly in her direction. With each glimpse of her he has, Edgar apprehends that he's standing at the threshold of what could be an extraordinary chance. Although he's discovered the secret of Prosper's designs, discerned the nature of the Great Work, never once has it occurred to him that he might put that knowledge to use. Maybe he hasn't really believed in it; maybe he's suspected that, underneath it all, the effect of the various colors on Vauglais's designs is some type of clever optical illusion. Now, though, now that there's the possibility of gaining his beloved back—

Edgar spends that last week sequestered in a room in a boarding house a few streets up from that alley where he tripped over Prosper's book. He's arranged for his meals to be left outside his door; half the time, however, he leaves them untouched, and even when he takes the dishes into his room, he eats the bare minimum to sustain him. About midway through his stay, the landlady, a Mrs. Foster, catches sight of him as he withdraws into his room. His face is flushed, his skin slick with sweat, his clothes disheveled; he might be in the grip of a fever whose fingers are tightening around him with each degree it climbs. As his door closes, Mrs. Foster considers running up to it and demanding to speak to this man. The last thing she wants is for her boarding house to be known as a den of sickness. She has taken two steps forward when she stops, turns, and bolts downstairs as if the Devil himself were tugging her apron strings. For the remainder of the time this lodger is in his room, she will send one of the serving girls to deliver his meals, no matter their protests. Once the room stands unoccupied, she will direct a pair of those same girls to remove its contents—including the cheap bed—carry them out back, and burn them until nothing remains but a heap of ashes. The empty room is closed, locked, and removed from use for the rest of her time running that house, some twenty-two years.

I know: what did she see? What could she have seen, with the door shut? Perhaps it wasn't what she saw; perhaps it was what she felt: the surface of things yielding, peeling away to what was beneath, beyond—the strain of a will struggling to score its vision onto that surface—the waver of the brick and mortar, of the very air around her, as it strained against this newness coming into being. How would the body respond to what could only register as a profound wrongness? Panic, you have to imagine, maybe accompanied by sudden nausea, a fear so intense as to guarantee a lifetime's aversion to anything associated with its cause.

Had she opened that door, though, what sight would have confronted her? What would we see?

Nothing much—at least, that's likely to have been our initial response. Edgar seated on the narrow bed, staring at the wall opposite him. Depending on which day it was, we would have noticed his shirt and pants looking more or less clean. Like Mrs. Foster, we would have remarked his flushed face, the sweat soaking his shirt; we would have heard his breathing, deep and hoarse. We might have caught his lips moving, might have guessed he was repeating Virginia's name over and over again, but been unable to say for sure. Were we to guess he was in a trance, caught in an opium dream, aside from the complete and total lack of opium-related paraphernalia, we could be forgiven.

If we were to remain in that room with him—if we could stand the same sensation that sent Mrs. Foster running—it wouldn't take us long to turn our eyes in the direction of Edgar's stare. His first day there, we wouldn't have noticed much if anything out of the ordinary. Maybe we would have wondered if the patch of bricks he was so focused on didn't look just the slightest shade paler than its surroundings, before dismissing it as a trick of the light. Return two, three days later, and we would find that what we had attributed to mid-afternoon light blanching already-faded masonry is a phenomenon of an entirely different order. Those bricks are blinking in and out of sight. One moment, there's a worn red rectangle, the next, there isn't. What takes its place is difficult to say, because it's back almost as fast as it was gone; although, after its return, the brick looks a bit less solid . . . less certain, you might say. Ragged around the edges, though not in any way you could put words to. All over that stretch of wall, bricks are going and coming and going. It almost looks as if some kind of code is spelling itself out using the stuff of Edgar's wall as its pen and paper.

Were we to find ourselves in that same room, studying that same spot, a day later, we would be startled to discover a small area of the wall, four bricks up, four down, vanished. Where it was—let's call what's there—or what isn't there—white. To tell the truth, it's difficult to look at that spot—the eye glances away automatically, the way it does from a bright light. Should you try to force the issue, tears dilute your vision.

Return to Edgar's room over the next twenty-four hours, and you would find that gap exponentially larger—from four bricks by four bricks to sixteen by sixteen, then from sixteen by sixteen to—basically, the entire wall. Standing in the doorway, you would have to raise your hand, shield your eyes from the dull whiteness in front of you. Blink furiously, squint, and you might distinguish Edgar in his familiar position, staring straight into that blank. Strain your gaze through the narrowest opening your fingers can make, and for the half a second until your head jerks to the side, you see a figure, deep within the white. Later, at a safe remove from Edgar's room, you may attempt to reconstruct that form, make sense of your less-than-momentary vision. All you'll be able to retrieve, however, is a pair of impressions, the one of something coalescing, like smoke filling up a jar, the other of thinness, like a child's stick-drawing grown life-sized. For the next several months, not only your dreams, but your waking hours will be plagued by what you saw between your fingers. Working late at night, you will be overwhelmed by the sense that whatever you saw in that room is standing just outside the cone of light your lamp throws. Unable to help yourself, you'll reach for the shade, tilt it back, and find . . . nothing, your bookcases. Yet the sensation won't pass; although you can read the spines of the hardcovers ranked on your bookshelves, your skin won't stop bristling at what you can't see there.

What about Edgar, though? What image do his eyes find at the heart of that space? I suppose we should ask, What image of Virginia?

It—she changes. She's thirteen, wearing the modest dress she married him in. She's nine, wide-eyed as she listens to him reciting his poetry to her mother and her. She's dead, wrapped in a white shroud. So much concentration is required to pierce through to the undersurface in the first place—and then there's the matter of maintaining the aperture—that it's difficult to find, let alone summon, the energy necessary to focus on a single image of Virginia. So the figure in front of him brushes a lock of dark hair out of her eyes, then giggles in a child's high-pitched tones, then coughs and sprays scarlet blood over her lips and chin. Her mouth is pursed in thought; she turns to a knock on the front door; she thrashes in the heat of the disease that is consuming her. The more time that passes, the more Edgar struggles to keep his memories of his late wife separate from one another. She's nine, standing beside her mother, wound in her burial cloth. She's in her coffin, laughing merrily. She's saying she takes him as her lawful husband, her mouth smeared with blood.

Edgar can't help himself—he's written, and read, too many stories about exactly this kind of situation for him not to be aware of all the ways it could go hideously wrong. Of course, the moment such a possibility occurs to him, it's manifest in front of him. You know how it is: the harder you try to keep a pink elephant out of your thoughts, the more that animal cavorts center-stage. Virginia is obscured by white linen smeared with mud; where her mouth is, the shroud is red. Virginia is naked, her skin drawn to her skeleton, her hair loose and floating around her head as if she's under water. Virginia is wearing the dress she was buried in, the garment and the pale flesh beneath it opened by rats. Her eyes—or the sockets that used to cradle them—are full of her death, of all she has seen as she was dragged out of the light down into the dark.

With each new monstrous image of his wife, Edgar strives not to panic. He bends what is left of his will toward summoning Virginia as she was at sixteen, when they held a second, public wedding. For an instant, she's there, holding out her hand to him with that simple grace she's displayed as long as he's known her—and then she's gone, replaced by a figure whose black eyes have seen the silent halls of the dead, whose ruined mouth has tasted delicacies unknown this side of the grave. This image does not flicker; it does not yield to other, happier pictures. Instead, it grows more solid, more definite. It takes a step towards Edgar, who is frantic, his heart thudding in his chest, his mouth dry. He's trying to stop the process, trying to close the door he's spent so much time and effort prying open, to erase what he's written on that blankness. The figure takes another step forwards, and already, is at the edge of the opening. His attempts at stopping it are useless—what he's started has accrued sufficient momentum for it to continue regardless of him. His lips are still repeating, "Virginia."

When the—we might as well say, when Virginia places one gray foot onto the floor of Edgar's room, a kind of ripple runs through the entire room, as if every last bit of it is registering the intrusion. How Edgar wishes he could look away as she crosses the floor to him. In a far corner of his brain that is capable of such judgments, he knows that this is the price for his *hubris*—really, it's almost depressingly formulaic. He could almost accept the irony if he did not have to watch those hands dragging their nails back and forth over one another, leaving the skin hanging in pale strips; if he could avoid the sight of whatever is seething in the folds of the bosom of her dress; if he could shut his eyes to that mouth and its dark contents as they descend to his. But he can't; he cannot turn away from his Proserpine as she rejoins him at last.

Four days prior to his death, Edgar is found on the street, delirious, barely-conscious. He never recovers. Right at the end, he rallies long enough to dictate a highly-abbreviated version of the story I've told you to a Methodist minister, who finds what he records so disturbing he sews it into the binding of the family Bible, where it will remain concealed for a century and a half.

As for what Edgar called forth—she walks out of our narrative and is not seen again.

It's a crazy story. It makes the events of Vauglais's life seem almost reasonable in comparison. If you were so inclined, I suppose you could ascribe Edgar's experience in that rented room to an extreme form of auto-hypnosis which, combined with the stress on his body from his drinking and the brain tumor, precipitates a fatal collapse. In which case, the story I've told you is little more than an elaborate symptom. It's the kind of reading a literary critic prefers; it keep the more . . . outré elements safely quarantined within the writer's psyche.

Suppose, though, suppose. Suppose that all this insanity I've been feeding you isn't a quaint example of early-nineteenth-century pseudoscience. Suppose that its interest extends well beyond any insights it might offer in interpreting "The Masque of the Red Death." Suppose—let's say the catastrophe that overtakes Edgar is the result of—we could call it poor planning. Had he paid closer attention to the details of Prosper's history, especially to that sojourn in the catacombs, he would have recognized the difficulty—to the point of impossibility—of making his attempt alone. Granted, he was desperate. But there was a reason Vauglais took the members of his *salon* underground with him—to use as a source of power, a battery, as it were. They provided the energy; he directed it. Edgar's story is a testament to what must have been a tremendous—an almost unearthly will. In the end, though, it wasn't enough.

Of course, how could he have brought together a sufficient number of individuals, and where? By the close of his life, he wasn't the most popular of fellows. Not to mention, he would have needed to expose the members of this hypothetical group to Prosper's designs and their corresponding colors.

Speaking of which: pleasant as this violet has been, what do you say we proceed to the *piece de resistance*? Faceless lackeys, on my mark—

Ahh. I don't usually talk about these things, but you have no idea how much trouble this final color combination gave me. I mean, red and black gives you dark red, right? Right, except that for the design to achieve its full effect, putting up a dark red light won't do. You need red layered over black—and a true black light, not ultraviolet. The result, though—I'm sure you'll agree, it was worth sweating over. It's like a picture painted in red on a black canvas, wouldn't you say? And look what it does for the final image. It seems to be reaching right out of the screen for you, doesn't it? Strictly speaking, Vauglais's name for it, "*Le Dessous*," the Underneath, isn't quite grammatical French, but we needn't worry ourselves over such details. There are times I think another name would be more appropriate: the Maw, perhaps, and then there are moments I find the Underneath perfect. You can see why I might lean towards calling it a mouth—the Cave would do, as well—except that the perspective's all wrong. If this is a mouth, or a cave, we aren't looking into it; we're already inside, looking out.

Back to Edgar. As we've said, even had he succeeded in gathering a group to assist him in his pursuit, he would have had to find a way to introduce them Prosper's images and their colors. If he could have, he would have . . . reoriented them, their minds, the channels of their thoughts. Vauglais's designs would have brought them closer to where they needed to be; they would have made available certain dormant faculties within his associates.

Even that would have left him with challenges, to be sure. Mesmerism, hypnosis, as Prosper himself discovered, is a delicate affair, one subject to such external variables as running out of lamp oil too soon. It would have been better if he could have employed some type of pharmacological agent, something that would have deposited them into a more useful state, something sufficiently concentrated to be delivered via a few bites of an innocuous food—a cookie, say, whose sweetness would mask any unpleasant taste, and which he could cajole his assistants to sample by claiming that his wife had baked them.

Then, if Edgar had been able to keep this group distracted while the cookies did their work—perhaps by talking to them about his writing—about the genesis of one of his stories, say, "The Masque of the Red Death"—if he had managed this far, he might have been in a position to make something happen, to perform the Great Work.

There's just one more thing, and that's the object for which Edgar would have put himself to all this supposed trouble: Virginia. I like to think I'm as romantic as the next guy, but honestly—you have the opportunity to rescript reality, and the best you can come up with is returning your dead wife to you? Talk about a failure to grasp the possibilities . . .

What's strange—and frustrating—is that it's all right there in "The Masque," in Edgar's own words. The whole idea of the Great Work, of Transumption, is to draw one of the powers that our constant, collective writing of the real consigns to abstraction across the barrier into physicality. Ideally, one of the members of that trinity Edgar named so well, Darkness and Decay and the Red Death, those who hold illimitable dominion over all. The goal is to accomplish something momentous, to shake the world to its foundations, not play out some hackneyed romantic fantasy. That was what Vauglais was up to, trying to draw into form the force that strips the flesh from our bones, that crumbles those bones to dust.

No matter. Edgar's mistake still has its uses as a distraction, and a lesson. Not that it'll do any of you much good. By now, I suspect few of you can hear what I'm saying, let alone understand it. I'd like to tell you the name of what I stirred into that cookie dough, but it's rather lengthy and wouldn't do you much good, anyway. I'd also like to tell you it won't leave you permanently impaired, but that wouldn't exactly be true. One of the consequences of its efficacy, I fear. If it's any consolation, I doubt most of you will survive what's about to follow. By my reckoning, the power I'm about to bring into our midst will require a good deal of . . . sustenance in order to establish a more permanent foothold here. I suspect this is of even less consolation, but I do regret this aspect of the plan I'm enacting. It's just—once you come into possession of such knowledge, how can you not make use—full use of it?

You see, I'm starting at the top. Or at the beginning—before the beginning, really, before light burst across the perfect formlessness that was everything. I'm starting with Darkness, with something that was already so old at that moment of creation that it had long forgotten its identity. I plan to restore it. I will give myself to it for a guide, let it envelop me and consume you and run out from here in a flood that will wash this world away. I will give to Darkness a dominion more complete than it has known since it was split asunder.

Look—in the air—can you see it?

CATALOG

EUGENE MIRABELLI

One minute he was there, the same as ever, and the next—**Wham!**—he was in this other place where everything had lost its thickness, was deflated, flat. For a moment he wondered if maybe the world was as solid as ever but his mind had collapsed—a thought that made his head spin, or would have if a young woman hadn't turned up just then, saying, "Here we are."

"Oh! I. Yes! Here we are," he said, trying to gather his wits.

The young woman had her hand on the door of a life-size photograph of a glossy black sports car, a cut-out photo backed with wood or stiff cardboard so it stood there looking as if it were real.

"As you can see, the Alfa Romeo Spider is a beautiful two-seater convertible," she told him, smiling. "It replaces an older version, the Spider 916 model, which was introduced back in 1995."

His head had cleared and he saw it wasn't a photo but the thing itself, a gleaming black sports car, a two-seater with golden brown leather seats. The woman was in a skimpy white dress, more like a stretched T-shirt than a dress.

"Where am I? What's happening?" he said.

"What's happening nowadays is a Type 939 with front-wheel drive and six-speed manual transmission." She had leaned into the cockpit and, still looking at John, placed her hand gently, caressingly, on the knob of the erect shift. "As you can imagine, it has power and lots of it!"

"I'm not interested in cars," he cried. "I don't know what I'm doing here or how I got—."

Her smile vanished for a moment, but then she brightened. "I know what you're wondering. And the answer is 9.4 miles per gallon," she told him, smiling once more.

"Listen, maybe you can tell me—," he started to say.

But she was walking away, her high heels making a brisk tap-tap-tap on the shiny showroom floor. Her back was bare just to the cleft of her buttocks and her dress appeared not filled by her body but merely held against it by the slender white ribbon tied in a bow knot at the nape of her neck.

"This is impossible," he muttered, following her toward the big glass door.

"Impossible?" she said, turning to him with a smile. "Almost impossible. But, *yes*, this is a 1963 Ferrari, a 250 GT Lusso." She trailed her hand up the rear of a dazzling red car. "One of the most sought after classic Ferrari vehicles. Beautifully restored, the black leather interior is as soft as glove—."

John had shoved open the glass door, stepped outside and was looking around. He didn't recognize any of the buildings. He discovered he didn't have his cell phone with him; he jammed his hands into his pockets, felt his wallet and his apartment keys—all there. He walked to the end of the block, stopped at the cross street and saw that the sign was missing—no surprise— then he turned around and began walking to the other end. The block was composed of expensive shops selling men's shirts, electronic gear, wine, sun glasses, fancy driving gloves, and sports equipment.

He was standing on the curb, wondering if this was a part of Manhattan he didn't know, when she said, "Here we are again." Now she was wearing a yellow swim-top and a short brown suede skirt.

"You've changed, but you look familiar," he said, puzzled.

She laughed. "We were in the auto showroom, remember?"

"No, no, no. I mean from before then." He had closed his eyes and was rubbing his forehead with his fist. "I don't understand—."

"I do photo shoots. Not as many as I'd like, but maybe you saw one of my spreads."

He looked at her. "You know this part of the city?"

"Not really.—Oh, look!" She had abruptly squatted, half kneeling to display a dazzling white inner thigh, and was now scratching the curly head of a friendly terrier. "Oh, you cute, cute doggy!" She rubbed her cheek against the dog's muzzle. The terrier wagged its tail, jumped backward and dashed off. "Bouncy little dog."

"A Jack Russell terrier," he said. "Not my favorite breed."

"Can you imagine meeting a fun dog like that? So cute and friendly! That's why I *love* the city."

"What city?" he asked, intending to find out what city this was. "What city do you love?"

"I love San Francisco for its wonderful views. I love Boston for its historical sites. I love New York for its great museums. And also Washington, DC, for its historical sites and great museums, I think."

"I'm sure we've met someplace before," he murmured. "You live around here?" he asked her, still hoping to learn where he was.

"Certainly." She stepped off the curb into street traffic and hailed an onrushing cab. "Let's go."

In the cab he asked her name. "Veronica London," she said. "What's your's?"

"John Mousse."

"Moose? You mean like the animal? The one like the reindeer?"

He peered out the cab window at the building façade sweeping past, flat as a photo. "Yeah, the one like the reindeer."

"Now it's your turn, John, so what's your favorite city?"

"I don't like cities."

2

In her apartment Veronica asked, "Can I get you something to drink?"

John looked around. "I don't know what I'm doing here," he told her.

She smiled as if they were about to have fun. "Oh, I think you do. I think we both know what you're doing here. Or going to be doing."

"I'm just lonely," he protested. "That's all I am, and confused."

"Forget about that," she told him. "Let me get you something to drink."

"It's too early in the day for me to start drinking."

"I have an ex-presso machine. I can make you some presso," she said.

"Presso?"

"It's European coffee."

"It is? Oh, *that*! Yes. Espresso. I'll have that," he said.

She smiled. "Make yourself comfortable. I'll get things started."

Veronica returned carrying a small tray with two diminutive cups of coffee. She was in a semi-transparent slip or nightgown or breakfast robe or peignoir or something—John didn't know what it was called—a loose white garment that flowed in a cataract from her shoulders to her breasts, to her hips, knees and ankles, allowing the ivory-rose color her flesh to show through. She set the tray on a marble-topped café table by the window where a gauze curtain was filled with blurred sunlight. John couldn't take his eyes off her.

"Here's to you," she said, raising her cup in a toast.

"I'm positive we've met," he told her. "I just can't place you. I recognize you but I can't quite recall where."

"A lot of people think they know me," she said.

3

The bed upon which she waited was covered with thick rumpled folds of crushed amber velvet and as she unfolded herself in the rosy half-light the silver jewelry in her navel gleamed and winked, catching his eye. "Hey," he said. "That's a staple! *You've got a silver staple in your navel.* And—Yes!—*Now* I remember. You're Miss November! In the magazine! Yes, yes, yes!"

"That was two years and seven months ago," she said, her voice husky with desire. "And you've kept it all that time. Come," She stretched, opening her arms to him.

"A magazine! Oh, God, what's happening," he cried.

The usual was happening.

Afterward he told her, "I don't know why I did that. I don't even know what I'm doing here. We have nothing in common, absolutely nothing, you and me."

"Don't worry," she said languidly, but with an edge to her voice. "That wasn't a marriage ceremony we performed."

"I'm sure you're a very nice person," he hastened to add. "But you're not my type."

She didn't say anything for a moment. "You kept my magazine so long it must be a collector's item. I'm flattered."

"I was using it to hide a different magazine," he explained.

They were lying side by side on the big disheveled velvet bed and now she turned her head to look at him. "Just who *is* your type?" she asked.

"You'd laugh if I told you."

"Try me."

He hesitated. "You know the L. L. Bean catalog?" he asked tentatively.

"Nope."

"They sell regular clothes, mostly, but also canoes and tents—camping equipment."

"So?" She sat up, pulling her knees to her chin.

"So there's a woman in the Christmas issue two years ago and she's my type."

She glanced at him. "A woman in some outdoor clothing and camping catalog?"

"Yes."

"You want her for *this*?" she said, incredulous. "She's your type?"

He felt his face getting hot, flushing. "Yes," he confessed.

Veronica looked at him a moment, then let herself flop backward onto the velvet bed cover. "You see, I didn't laugh."

When he awoke at noon she was gone and a note lay on his clothes which he'd tossed onto a bed chair last night. *Good Morning John—Don't forget to leave the door so it locks when you exit. Make sure you try it after you've shut it. And I've set the Ex-Presso machine so it will make regular American coffee.*

Bye-bye,

Veronica (a very nice person)!!!

4

If there had been a park across the street yesterday, John hadn't seen it, but that morning he went into it because the greenery—the long view of the grassy field, the pond and grove of trees, the promise of rural life—was so inviting. Inside the park, nature looked too simplified. A bright yellow sun was shining, the sky was blue, the grass smoothly green on both sides of the nicely curved path. The man seated on the bench up ahead had folded his newspaper, had put it beside his briefcase and was smoking a pipe. A little dog dashed up from nowhere, paused to look at John, then scooted back across the grass. A moment later the mutt dashed across the gravel path, barking happily, a little girl in a yellow dress chasing it. The man with the pipe stood up. "See Spot run. Run, Spot, run!" he cried. A little boy in a crisp white jersey and neat blue shorts had come running. "See Jane run. Run, Jane, run!" he shouted. When he saw John, the boy shouted, "Jane runs fast. Can Jane catch Spot?" John walked as briskly as he could and watched the kid out of the corner of his eye. The boy trotted beside him, saying in bold face type, "**Jane plays catch. I play catch. Do you play catch? Jane plays catch**." John thrust his foot out, sent the kid sprawling onto the grass. The walkway branched ahead and John took the path that he saw led out of the park, letting the brat's wild "Run, Jane, run!" diminish far behind him.

5

Shutting up the kid made John feel better but the world still felt weird. Veronica's apartment house was nowhere in sight. In fact, the street he crossed on his way out of the park didn't look to him to be any part of the street he would have crossed on his way in, and now he noticed the city skyline had shrunk, as if from the cold. The automobile traffic and the people along the sidewalk looked all right. A rust-rotted minivan pulled away from the curb, its dented rear hatch springing open just enough for a thick snake of electric cord to slide out dragging a guitar which John grabbed just before it hit the pavement. The van drove off, a whirlwind of advertising posters billowing up from the open hatch, then abruptly halted. A thin guy with a bone-white face got out and began to gather up the loose posters, jamming them under his arm while making his way, head down, toward the curb—then he saw John standing there with the guitar cradled in his arms. "It's safe," John told him.

"Holy crap! Thanks, man. I owe you."

"You're in a band?"

The thin guy took the guitar and handed him a poster.

ROD & ANNABEL LEE.
Crushed Rock
!We're Getting Louder!
One week starting Friday
at Witt's End

"Good name, sounds like a good band," John said, just to be polite. "Maybe the poster needs a little work," he added.

The guy laughed. "Yeah, the poster's shit. We need a re-write and a design or something."

Apparently his face was that white by nature. He had deep socketed eyes, hadn't shaved in three days and his hair stuck out as if electrified. John had the uneasy feeling that he knew this face from someplace.

"You're Rod?" John asked him.

"Right. And if I didn't have my hands full I'd shake your hand. This guitar's worth more than I am."

"How do I get out of here?" John asked in a rush.

"What do you mean?" Rod asked.

"One minute I was in my apartment and—," he broke off, fearing he'd sound crazy. "What I mean is—My name's John Mousse and I'm a graphic artist," he blurted. "In my other life."

"In your other life," Rod echoed. "Hey, I like that." He laughed. They stood there talking a while, then Rod said, "I got to get going. Hop in if you want. Got to drive around putting up these lousy posters. You can help."

So John climbed into the van and they drove around putting up the lousy posters, wrapping them around lamp posts, tacking them to newspaper kiosks, pasting them to the front of brownstone townhouses. "Keep an eye out for the cops. They're fussy-fussy about where we put these things," Rod had told him. So John patrolled as lookout while Rod pasted another to the back panel of a pickup truck, a station wagon, a bus, and two posters side-by-side on the front door of the library.

Some hours later they were at a community bulletin board in a parking lot when Rod asked him, "You don't like being a graphic artist?"

"I like it most of the time. I can do it alone. A couple of months ago I quit the group I worked for. I work from my apartment now."

"Could you design us a poster? Special lettering or a logo or something?" he asked, all the while searching for an open space on the crowded bulletin board. The cork was covered with loose sheets of paper—bus schedules, café menus, local events, part-time jobs, puppies and second-hand cars—each note tacked over the other, like roof shingles.

"Sure. I can do that," John said.

Rod had a cigarette lighter in his hand. "Anybody around?" he asked, flicking the lighter with his thumb.

"Two old ladies. A mother pushing a stroller with a kid in it." John told him. "No cops."

John had already run the small flame along the bottom edge of the bottom row, setting the papers ablaze. "All those missing kitty-cats," he muttered, patting out the last scraps of fire. "They just want to be free." He tacked his poster in the scorched center of the bulletin board. "I'll take you to the house," he said, turning to John. "You can meet my sister and Annabel. And if we're lucky one of them will feed us."

6

The house was a three-story yellowish stucco building with patches of moss growing on it. The façade looked oddly flat, as if it were a giant sheet of paper upon which somebody had meticulously painted windows and a door and greenish splotches of moss. And the sky in back, a shade of greenish gray, looked painted too. A young woman in black jeans and a black jersey was sitting on the front steps, peeling a peach. "Welcome to the low-rent area," Rod told him. A long crack had opened down the front of the house and a stretch of stucco had fallen off. "It still needs a lot of fixing up, but it's all ours. We own it.—Watch out for the ditch!"

John stood looking at the house. "I feel weird. I have the feeling I've been here before," he said. "I mean, I've seen this before. Even all these dead leaves."

"That's called déjà vu," the young woman said.

"This is my sister Madeline," Rod told him.

"I've seen this in a book," John said. "It's an illustration for a story."

"I'd shake your hand except it's sticky," Madeline said. "My hand I mean, sticky." Like her brother, she had dazzlingly white skin, and hers was emphasized by black eye-shadow, black lipstick and black nail polish. Her black hair was pulled not to the back but to one side of her head and held there with a sliver clasp.

"John's a graphic artist, in another life," Rod told her. And turning to John, he said, "Madeline's a part-time waitress, but in real life she's a song writer, and a good one."

"Come on in," Madeline said. She swallowed the last chunk of peach, licked her fingers and looked around for a place to throw the pit, but kept it in her hand. "I'll give you the tour."

In the kitchen she tossed the peach pit into a crock labeled COMPOST, washed her hands and showed John room after room, up and down the house, then arrived back in the kitchen where Rod was looking into the refrigerator.

"It's the middle of the afternoon," she told Rod, "So I guess you're ready for breakfast, right?"

"We're artists, Madeline, we get up late."

"I can make you a good salad. If you want the cold cuts you'll have to fix them yourselves."

"Maddy's a vegetarian," Rod told John. "She won't touch meat, won't handle it."

"I don't eat flesh," Madeline said.

"Salad is *fine*," John said, hoping to sound agreeable.

Sometime after lunch the second guitarist drove up with the drummer, and a while later Annabel Lee showed up (short platinum blond hair floating over her head like a halo) then everyone climbed the stairs to the third floor where they rehearsed. The band had echoes of 1970s rock, which surprised John who had expected something bizarre, and Annabel Lee had a good voice. Madeline was on the keyboard for one piece but, as she told him, she preferred writing music to playing it. There wasn't anything for John to do, so when Madeline went downstairs he went with her. Madeline made a pot of coffee and John steered conversation away from himself as much as possible. Madeline said she and her brother came from a place in Philadelphia. "But it's no longer extant," she said, meaning, as far as John could tell, that it had been paved over. At first he had been distracted by the black eye shadow and black lipstick, but he found he was getting used to it. "Are you religious?" he asked her.

"Spiritual maybe, but not religious. Why do you ask?" she said.

He said he couldn't help but notice she was wearing earrings with big dangling crosses. "Oh, these." She smiled. "It's just a style," she said. Sometime later they heard the clatter on the stairway which meant the rehearsal had broken up and a minute later everyone was in the kitchen talking at once.

The second guitarist and the drummer drove off, but Annabel stayed and Rod volunteered to drive out to get pizza. "Let me come along, I want to pay," John told him. So Madeline phoned the order in to Mama Mia's Pizza while Rod and John drove out to get it. "Annabel comes from Boston," Rod told him, "That's why she says cah for car, and pahk for park, unless it's in a lyric."

"She seems nice."

"Yeah. She is," Rod said, thinking about it. "We used to be married. Actually, we still are, except we don't live together much. We separated to get a divorce, but it turned out we got along much better that way, so that's the way it is. The sex is hotter, too."

John slumped down a bit. "Everybody I know is married. Some of them twice."

"Ever been married?"

"No," John murmured. He remained silent for a while. "That reminds me," he began, then broke off. "I know this sounds strange, but I haven't got a place—."

"You can stay at the house. We got room."

"Thanks."

They stopped at an ATM machine. John put in his card, tapped in his number and waited. Nothing happened. Rod kicked the machine; it buzzed to life and slid out the money. "I know this lousy machine," Rod told him. "It cheats. Count the cash."

"It's *real* bills!" John said, delighted.

"What were you expecting, Monopoly money?"

John laughed. "Yes, but it doesn't matter." He paid for the pizzas, two six-packs of beer, a bottle of bourbon, a cheap razor and a tooth brush.

7

They sat around the kitchen table, devoured the pizza and washed it down with beer, then scrubbed the dishes and stacked them on the shelf. Everyone was tired. Rod and Annabel Lee shared a joint, and John leaned back against the wall, contented. The world didn't seem quite so weird or, to be precise, the weirdness didn't matter so much. When Madeline turned to him and said, "Name your opiate," he said, "I'll have what you're having."

She smiled, showing her teeth, and poured a big glass of bourbon for him. "It's refreshing to have someone sane in this house."

"You flatter me," he told her.

"Sanity is way over-rated," Rod said, sweet smoke drifting from his mouth with each word.

John knew he was drinking too much, but it didn't seem to matter to anyone else, so he decided it didn't matter to him either. It was becoming clear where he was and why everyone was so familiar here. It was coming back to him, or maybe coming forward; anyway, it was on the tip of his tongue to tell everybody that he knew. And he would have, but the weirdness, or whatever it was, didn't bother him any longer. Rod's deep socketed eyes and electrified hair, and Annabel's platinum blond halo, didn't seem so odd. Furthermore, he could see that Madeline's work on herself—painting her eyelids and her lips black, the way she had swept her hair sideways across her head and down one side, even the silver crosses swinging from her ears—was a kind of art, a visual presentation, something like his own graphic work. Maybe that's why he turned to Rod and said, "I like your sister. I'm glad she doesn't eat flesh."

"I guess she's likeable in her own weird way," Rod conceded. "Listen to this—." He turned to the CD player that somebody had brought to the table. "This is a recording we made last year. Didn't do much, but it's good, really good."

"For Christ'sake, Rod, he was at the rehearsal, isn't that enough?" Madeline said.

"Rod has found a new audience," Annabel said.

Then there was a gap and Rod told him how when he was a kid there was this nice bit from "Hotel California" that fascinated him and he still thought it was one of the best guitar performances ever. In fact, they were playing the "Hotel California" now and the music was in the air all around them, and the lyrics were resonating in John's head or, yes, in his heart, and the last thing he remembered he was running for the door, thinking he had to find the passage back to the place he was before, but the chorus said, Chill out, we are destined to receive, you can check-out any time you want, *But you can never leave!*

At which point John put his cheek to the kitchen table and wept while the guitars played on and on.

8

When John awoke the next morning his head throbbed and he felt dizzy or nauseated, he couldn't tell which. He climbed out of bed—the bed being a folded army blanket thrown over a mattress on the floor—and went down the hall to the bathroom. He was standing at the toilet in his under-shorts and t-shirt when the memory came back to him of Rod holding his head while John knelt, vomiting into the bowl. He took a shower, went downstairs and found Rod at the kitchen table, buttering toast. "How you feeling?" Rod asked him, his electrified hair glowing in the mid-day sunlight.

"Not good," he croaked.

"Want coffee, toast?"

"I don't think so.—I'm sorry about last night."

"Shit happens," Rod said, dismissing it.

"Where's Madeline?"

"She waitresses mornings."

"What's good for a hangover?" John asked, seating himself cautiously at the table. "My head feels like a big, big bell."

"Try the toast and coffee."

John cleared his throat and announced, "Your full name is Roderick Usher. And your sister's name is Madeline. And." His speech was rather slow this morning.

"Right," Roderick said. He paused, his toast half way to his mouth, waiting for John to conclude the sentence.

"And you two are characters in a short story by Edgar Allen Poe."

"Not really," Rod said. He bit into his toast which gave a satisfying crunching sound. "We're real and the story is make-believe."

"In the story you accidentally put your sister into a tomb alive because you think she's dead."

"That's what I mean. I've done a lot of crazy things but I've never buried Maddy alive. Or dead, for that matter."

Half an hour later Madeline arrived back from her job at the café and Rod told her, "John thinks we're escapees from a short story by Edgar Allan Poe."

"I can't blame him," Madeline said. "Hi, John."

John was washing out his cup at the sink and he said hi.

"He says I buried you alive," Rod reported.

"I only look that way sometimes when I'm tired," she told John.

"No, no! All I meant was that I recognized this house," John explained hurriedly, turning to her. "It's the house in 'The Fall of the House of Usher,' I remember the illustration."

"I read the story where somebody gets walled up in a wine cellar," Rod said. "He gets buried alive that way, behind a wall. That was in Poe."

"There's something weird going on," John said, shutting his eyes, rubbing his temples.

"When you have déjà vu you feel weird." Madeline said. "You feel like, oh, I've seen this before, like, oh, everything is happening like it happened before. It feels eerie. It happens to everybody at one time or another."

"It feels like I come from—I don't know—another space or time."

"You come from California?" Rod asked.

"I live in New York."

"Well, you're in Connecticut now," he said. "A wholly different state."

"I've go to get back. I can't live off you guys."

Rod laughed. "Hey, man, you're not living off us. You've been here *one* night and you paid for our dinner and drinks. We owe you. So relax," Rod told him. "Relax."

That evening Rod and Annabel Lee shared some low grade smokes—"True ditch weed," Rod called it—Madeline had half a glass of Jack Daniels and John drank coffee. Rod had told Annabel about John's weird feelings and she had looked concerned. Later, when Rod and Annabel were getting ready to go out to a club, she turned to John and said, "Maybe you came in from a parallel universe, an alternate world."

"Oh, sure," Rod muttered. "Make it complicated."

"It's a respectable theory among physicists," Annabel said defensively.

"Leave the poor man alone. He's had a hard day," Rod said.

"The idea is that when you look at a quantum wave it turns into only one of its possible states," she told John. "But the others continue to exist, and those are the alternate worlds."

"Do you want to see that singer or not?" Rod asked her.

"What singer?" Madeline asked.

"Some twenty-year-old who puts on a black leather corset and fishnet stockings and thinks that makes her a singer. She's at the DownTown."

Rod and Annabel Lee left. John re-heated the coffee and poured himself another cup. "Well, that clears *that* up. This is an alternate world." He gave a brief laugh. "What I don't understand is why you don't think I'm crazy."

9

But they didn't think he was crazy. It was clear to them that he came from an alternative world and was quite sane. The next day at breakfast when he told Rod about walking through a park that looked like an old-fashioned first-grade reader, all Rod said was, "You did right to trip the little bastard." And that night at dinner when he told everyone about his meeting the centerfold girl, they all accepted that, too. "Centerfold women do exist," Madeline said. "They're models or actresses."

"But I didn't meet a model or actress, I met the sex pot she was pretending to be in the photo. She even had a staple in her navel where it holds the magazine pages together."

Rod refilled John's wine glass, saying, "What was she like, you know, in bed? What happened next?"

"Hey!" Annabel cut in. "Maybe he likes his privacy."

"The only reason I had the magazine was to hide my L. L. Bean catalog inside it," John said. "In the catalog there were photos of people skiing or buying Christmas wreaths and things like that, and one of the woman was, well, I was attracted to her. It's that simple. Crazy about her, actually. Obsessed, you might say. For the past two years." He felt out of breath.

"What did she look like?" Madeline asked him.

"She was just *nice*, that's all. She looked—. I could tell she—. She was authentic, *real*. She was beautiful, but that's not important. She was—she was what you want when you want to marry someone. I want to marry her."

There was silence around the table. John felt his face getting hot, his hand darted out for his wine glass but knocked it over—"Sorry!"—and he jumped up and got a paper towel to mop up the spilled wine.

The next day Annabel Lee drove over to Providence to visit a widowed aunt whose husband used to buy sporting gear from L. L. Bean; the uncle had died over a year ago and, sure enough, Annabel found the Christmas catalog from two years past and brought it back with her. That night she slid it across the kitchen table and asked him, "Which one is she?"

John opened the catalog, flipped a couple of pages, then turned the magazine around so the others could see it. "Look, the man with the string of Christmas tree lights in his hand is married to the woman who is about to hand him the cup of eggnog, and the woman off by the fireplace—that's the one I told you about.

"Nice sweater," Rod said. "Looks warm."

"How do you know who's married to who?" Annabel asked.

"He's decorating the family Christmas tree, right? Then the person bringing eggnog from the kitchen would be his wife. And there's other scenes, too." He swept three pages back. "Look. They're outside in the snow and, see, the father is pulling the sled with the little girl on it and the woman next to the sled, looking down at her daughter, is the same one who made the eggnog. And this other woman—I wish I had her name—is looking at them and smiling. And there's the farmhouse in the background."

"Oh, yes," Madeline said.

"There's other indoor photos," John said, sweeping several pages aside. "Look. Here she is alone. This is a bedroom, an old-fashioned bedroom. See the edge of the bed quilt? And the braided rug? She has no wedding ring."

"Nice bathrobe," Rod said.

"And this is one of my favorite photos," John said, turning to the front of the catalog. "See. It's the farm house, the wreath on the big front door, and the light from the window shining on the snow outside, and through the window you can see the people inside, standing by the fire, talking. –What do you think?"

"I think you should look for her," Annabel told him. "Don't go back to your other life in that parallel universe." Rod and Madeline agreed with Annabel. "Stay in this one," they said.

And that's what John did. He stayed and got an outdoor job with a landscape company in Stamford, Connecticut. He insisted on paying Rod and Madeline for his room, despite their objections, and he contributed his share for food and other household expenses and, of course, he designed a new poster for the band, as well as helping to set up the lights and amplifiers when they played. He bought blue jeans, chinos, and a few shirts from—you guessed it—L. L. Bean. He had always had friends or, to be exact, friendly acquaintances at work, one or two anyway, one for sure, but he had never felt so at home in his life as he did now.

From time to time he thought about phoning his number in Brooklyn Heights, but a certain uneasiness or superstitious dread had always made him hesitate and he'd forget about it. Early in December he bought himself a cheap pay-as-you-go cell phone and on a whim he did phone his old apartment. It rang and rang and just as he was about to hang up there was a *click* and a woman's voice said Hello. John fumbled for words, told her his name and asked about his furniture. "What furniture do you mean?" the woman asked, clearly baffled by the question. He asked was there furniture in the apartment. "No, it's quite empty and ready to rent. If you'd like to see it, we can set up an appointment and—." He told her he had his graphics studio there and the woman said, "Yes, it would make an excellent graphics studio." She was still talking when John hung up, finished with his old life. Anyway, by then he'd bought a green twelve-year-old third-hand Chevy pickup truck and was ready to go looking for the young woman in the catalog.

"Where you going to look?" Rod asked him.

"From the appearance of the white clapboard farm house and the depth of the snow, I figure Maine," John said.

"Good, that narrows it down."

On December 10 John Mousse said good-bye to Roderick Usher and his sister Madeline Usher and to Annabel Lee. He knew they were an odd looking bunch but, frankly, he liked them and they made him feel good. He had never asked Annabel Lee about her name, which was the same as the title of a poem by Edgar Allan Poe, but he guessed she would have a good explanation for it. Pale Madeline had previously kept her hair dyed black to match her punk-Goth style, but last night she'd changed it to an electric blue. When he said good-bye he stroked her hair, saying, "It's beautiful, Madeline, really beautiful." Rod, his eyes looking even more deeply socketed than ever, gave him an envelope with all the money John had paid to rent the bedroom. Then John hopped into his rattle-trap pickup truck and drove off, hammering his horn and waving to them. Way down the road he turned on the windshield wipers because it had begun to snow in very fine little flakes.

10

Ordinarily it isn't a hard drive from western Connecticut to Maine. You take 91 North to Hartford, then branch North East on 84 into Massachusetts and onto the Mass Pike going North East until you cross 495. Then you make a big curve North and East around Boston and when you reach 95, the coastal highway, you go across a bit of New Hampshire and North, North East into Maine. But John was driving straight into a North Easter, a New England blizzard. More and more of the world was being erased and by the time he reached Maine everything outside the pickup was blank. He drove into the night, his headlights filled with a dense whirling white confetti, as if a deranged artist had torn the world to a zillion bits and was hurling them at the pickup truck. John must have turned off the highway, because when the storm passed and the sky cleared he was on a narrow freshly plowed road, driving between high banks of snow.

At the crest of a hill he pulled to a stop. In the moonlight he could see for miles over gentle white hills and dark pine woods. He got out, astonished at the quiet and the pure deep, deep space. He climbed the snow bank and saw lighted windows at the other end of a nearby snowfield, and lights down in the valley. He parked the pickup as far to the side as he could, then he climbed the snow bank and plodded through the dreamy deep snow to the house. Lamplight from a big front window spilled onto the snow, and he could see a man and two women decorating a Christmas tree. He knocked at the door and the man opened it. "Hi," John said. "My name is John Mousse and I'm lost."

"It's a bad night to get lost in," the man said, an easy-going guy wearing an L. L. Bean blue canvas shirt. "But it looks like it's over. Come in, give us your coat, tell us where you want to get to."

John stepped inside and, dizzy with anxiety, held the edge of the door frame while he took off his coat and knocked the snow from his boots. A woman in a new forest-green wool jacket handed him a mug of steaming cocoa and the young woman coming across the room asked him, "Did you say you were John Mousse?"

"Yes," John said.

"You're not lost. My name is Kate Greenway. I'm the woman you spoke to a couple of days ago about renting a place. You asked if it was furnished." She was in the China blue heather ribbed merino wool sweater from two years ago. "The phone got cut off and I was so afraid you hadn't heard the directions on how to get here."

"I recognize you," John said, his heart banging so hard he was afraid she'd hear it. "Recognize your voice, I mean. For the apartment. Yes."

"It's just up the road about a mile, a refinished barn next to my house. Completely modern appliances inside. It's small, but I think you'll like it."

The easy-going guy and the woman in the dark jacket had turned away to help a little girl hang an ornament on the tree.

"I'm sure I'll like it," John said. "I've wanted to live in a place like this for years. Away from the city, out in the country."

"And here you are at last," Kate said. "Because I've been waiting—I mean, the apartment's been waiting—I mean, the apartment, it's really nice."

"So this is Maine, the real Maine," John said, happy to be here. And Kate smiled, and it was a warm smile, and "Yes," she said. "Yes."

CRIMES AND GLORY

PAUL McAULEY

" 'Where are they?' "

"They? Who's this 'they,' Niles?" I say, wondering if he's finally flipped. "There's nobody out here but us chickens. And we're where we've always been. Right behind you and catching up fast."

"It's a famous question, Emma. Even though I know your training wasn't all it could have been, I'm surprised and more than a little shocked that you don't recognise it."

At the beginning of this long chase, Niles Sarkka maintained an imperial silence, week after week, month after month. He didn't answer my calls, and after a while I gave up trying to call him. Then, after turnover, after we switched off our motor and flipped end for end and switched it back on and began to decelerate, applying the brakes as we slid down the steepening slope of the warm yellow star's gravity well, he called me. He wanted to know why we'd left it so late; I told him that a smart fellow like him should be able to work it out for himself.

But he hasn't, not yet, although he's been nagging away at it ever since. As our ship has grown closer to his, as both have grown closer to our final destination, the calls have begun to increase in frequency. And like most people living on their own, Niles has developed eccentric habits. He calls without any regard for time of day, so I have to carry the q-phone everywhere, and it's a big old heavy thing the size of a briefcase, one of the first models. This call, the second in three days, has fetched me out of my weekly bath, and baths are a big deal on the ship. It's not just a question of scrubbing off a week's worth of grime; it's also an escape from the 1.6 g pull. Sinking into buoyant water and resting sore joints and swollen legs and aching backs. Forgetting for a little while how far we've come from all that's known, and the possibility we might not be able to get back. So, standing dripping wet on an ice-cold floor, grappling with the q-phone and trying to knot a towel around me while the other women slosh and wallow in hot dark water in the big bamboo tub, I'm annoyed and resentful, and having a hard time hiding it.

Saying, "As far as I'm concerned, my training was good enough to catch you."

Fortunately, Niles Sarkka ignores my sarcasm. He's in one of his pedagogical moods, behaving as if he's back in front of the TV camera, delivering a solemn lecturette to his adoring audience.

" 'Where are they?' " he says. "A famous question famously asked by the physicist Enrico Fermi when he and his colleagues were discussing flying saucers and likelihood of faster-than-light travel. 'Where are they?' Fermi exclaimed. Given the age and size of the Galaxy, given that it was likely that life had evolved more than once, the Earth should have been visited many times over. If aliens existed, they should already be here. And since they weren't, Fermi argued, they did not exist. Many scientists and philosophers challenged his paradox with a variety of ingenious solutions, or tried to explain the absence of aliens with a variety of equally ingenious scenarios. But we are privileged to know the answer. We know that they were there all along. We know that the Jackaroo have been watching us for centuries, and chose to reveal themselves in our hour of greatest need. But their appearance provoked many other questions. Where did they come from? Why were they watching us, and why have they intervened? Why have they survived for so long, when we know that other intelligent species have not? Are they outliers, or something different? Are we like them, or are we like the other so-called Elder Cultures—doomed to a finite span, doomed to die out, or to evolve into something beyond our present comprehension? Or are we doomed by our association with the Jackaroo, who set us free from the cage of Earth, yes, but only to let us move into a slightly larger cage. Where we can be studied or played with until they grow tired of us. And so on, and so on. The Jackaroo provided a kind of answer to Fermi's question, Emma, but it generated a host of new mysteries. Soon, we will discover the answers to some of them. Doesn't it excite you? It should. *I* am excited. Excited, and amazed, and more than a little afraid. If you and your farmer friends have even the slightest hint of imagination, you should feel excited and amazed and afraid too. For we are fast approaching the threshold of a new chapter of human history."

Like every criminal who knows the game is up, Niles Sarkka is trying to justify actions that can't be justified. Trying to climb a ladder of words towards that last little chink of light high above the dungeon of his plight. I let him talk, of course. It's always easier to let the guilty talk. They give so much away it isn't even funny. Niles Sarkka is responsible for the deaths of three people and stole code that could, yes, this is about our only point of agreement, radically change our understanding of our place in the Universe and our relationship with the Jackaroo. So of course I let him talk, but I'm getting cold, standing there in only a towel, my vertebrae are grinding together, blood is pooling in my tired and swollen legs, and I'm growing more impatient than usual with his discursions and bluster, his condescending lesson on the history of the search for extraterrestrial life. So when at last he says that he doesn't care what people think of him now, that history will judge him and that's all that counts, I can't help myself.

"I'll tell you who will judge you, Niles. A jury of your peers, in Court One of the Justice Centre in Port of Plenty."

He hangs up. Affronted and offended no doubt, the pompous fool. Anxiety nips at me, I wonder if this time I've gone too far, but it soon passes. I know he will call back. Because he wants to convince me that, despite all the bad things he's done, he will be vindicated by what he expects to discover. Because he has only one q-phone, and I have its twin. Because he has no one else to talk to, out here in the deep and lonely dark between the stars.

As far as I was concerned, it began with a call from one of our contacts in the Port of Plenty Police Department, telling me that the two code jockeys I was looking for, Everett Hughes and Jason Singleton, had been traced to a motel.

It was a little past eight in the evening. As usual, I'd been writing up notes on the day's work with half an eye on the news channel. I found the remote and switched off the TV and said, "Are they in custody?"

"It looks like they're dead. The room they rented is burned out, and there are two crispy critters inside. I hate to be the bearer of bad news, but there it is. And info is info, good or bad, right?"

I didn't bother to reassure him that he would get paid in due course. "Who's the attending?"

"Zacarias. August Zacarias. He's good police, closes more than his fair share of cases. A prince of the city, too."

"Where can I find him?"

"He's still at the scene. From what I hear, it's a mess out there."

The motel was at the outer edge of the city, close to an off-ramp on the orbital freeway and an access road that climbed a slope of thorn scrub to an industrial park. The streetlights along the road were out, the long low sheds of the park squatted in darkness, and the lights were out in the motel office and its string of rooms, too. A transformer on top of a power-line pole fizzed and sparked. I parked behind a clutch of police cruisers and the satellite van of the local TV news team, and badged my way past the patrol officers who were keeping a small crowd on the right side of crime scene tape strung between a couple of saw horses. The TV reporter and her camerawoman tried to zero in on me, but I ducked away. I was excited and apprehensive: this had brought three months of careful investigative work to a sudden and unwelcome crux, and I had no idea how it would play out.

The warm night air stank of charred wood, smoke, and a sharp tang like freshly-cut metal. The headlamps of a pair of fire trucks patchily lit an L-shaped string of rooms that enclosed two sides of the parking lot; their flashers sent flickers of orange light racing over wet tarmac and the roofs of angle-parked cars and pickup trucks. Firefighters in heavy slickers and yellow helmets were rolling up hoses. A chicken was perched on the cab of a pickup and several more strutted and pecked amongst a couple of picnic tables set on a strip of grass by a derelict swimming pool. The room at the end of the short arm of the L was lit by portable floods, light falling strong and stark on blackened walls, smoke curling from the broken door and the smashed, soot-stained window. Jason Singleton's car, an ancient Volkswagen Faraday, stood in front of this ruin. The windshield was shattered and its hood was scorched clean of paint and its plastic fender was half-melted.

The homicide detective who had caught the call, August Zacarias, was a tall man in his fifties, with matt black skin and wooly hair clipped short and brushed with grey at the temples, dressed in a brown suit with a windowpane check and polished brown Oxford loafers, a white shirt and a buttercup yellow silk tie. A micropore mask hung under his chin and he stripped off soot-stained vinyl gloves as he came towards me, saying that he understood I wanted to take his case away from him. He had a signet ring on the index finger of his right hand: the kind of ring, faced with a chunk of opal, worn by male members of the Fortunate Five Hundred.

"As far as I'm concerned, you've walked into *my* case," I said.

"You're English."

"Yes. Obviously."

"Were you in the police before you came here?"

"Ten years in the Met."

"The London police? Scotland Yard?"

"New Scotland Yard."

"And then you came here, and joined the geek police."

"I joined the UN police, Detective Zacarias, and currently I'm working with the Technology Control Unit. Now we've bonded, perhaps you can tell me what happened here."

August Zacarias had a friendly smile and possessed the imperturbable calm of someone with absolute confidence in his authority, but from bitter experience I knew exactly what he was thinking: that I was a meddling, boot-faced bureaucrat with a humour bypass and a spreadsheet for a soul who was about to steal a perfectly good double murder from him and cause him all kinds of grief besides. And I couldn't help wondering how he paid for his tailored suit, handmade loafers and expensive cologne, whether the gold Rolex on his left wrist was real or a street-market fake, whether he was just a working stiff who wanted nothing more than to put down this case and move on to the next, or whether he had a private agenda. Aside from the usual rivalry between our two branches of law enforcement, the plain fact of the matter is that the PPPD is riddled with corruption. Most of its patrol officers take kickbacks and bribes; many of its detectives and senior officers are in the pockets of politicians, gangsters, or business people.

"Myself, I am from Lagos," he said. "I was in the army there, and now I am a homicide detective here. And that's what this is. Homicide. Two men died in that room, Inspector Davies. Someone has to answer for that."

"Have the bodies been identified?"

"You want to know if they are the two young men you are looking for. I'm afraid I can't confirm that yet. They are very badly burned."

"This is Jason Singleton's car," I said.

"It is certainly registered to him. And according to several of the residents it was used by a man answering Mr. Singleton's description. Tall and blond, in his twenties, possibly English. His friend was heavyset, with long black hair, tattoos, and an American accent. Also in his twenties. That sounds like your other missing coder, Everett Hughes, yes? Although they signed the register as Mr. Gates and Mr. Jobs."

"Geek humour."

"I wondered if it was supposed to be funny. You posted an APB for both men. May I ask why?"

"I believe they stole Elder Culture technology from their employer."

"That would be Mayer Lansky."

"You work fast, Detective Zacarias."

"Out of necessity, Inspector. We had two hundred and forty-one straight-up murders in this city last year, not to mention a significant number of suspicious deaths, fatal accidents, and kidnaps. We put down just thirty-three per cent of those murders. The municipal council and the police commissioner want us to improve our success rate, we already have ninety-eight names on the board, and it's only April. If I don't close this in a day or two, it will be pushed aside by a fresh case. So, these boys stole something from their employer and hid out here while they looked for a buyer, is that it?"

"We're being frank with each other, detective."

"I hope so."

"Frankly, I want you to stay away from Meyer Lansky. He's important to us."

"I don't suppose you can tell me why."

"I'm afraid not. Has the car been searched yet?"

"We didn't find anything in it. We are waiting for a tow truck. The crime scene people will examine it back at the police garage, under sterile conditions. Unless you want to take charge of it."

"We don't have the facilities. But someone will observe and advise your crime scene techs while they work on it. Did you find a computer or a phone in the room?"

"Not yet. Things are very much melted together."

"Or something like a fat thermos flask?"

"You are welcome to examine the crime scene, Inspector. I'll even let you pat down the bodies before the ME takes them away."

I ignored his impertinence. "I want your people to maintain a perimeter until my people arrive. Until they do, nothing should be touched. The bodies will remain where they are. I will need you to turn over all witness statements. And please, don't say a word to the TV people, or anyone else."

"Those bodies are cooked all the way through, and something fried every electrical device in the immediate vicinity. What they stole, was it some kind of Elder Culture energy weapon?"

"Everett Hughes owns motorcycle. A 125cc Honda. I don't see it."

"Then it's probably not here," August Zacarias said. He was smiling, enjoying our little to and fro. Having fun. "Perhaps the killer took it. Or perhaps these two young men tried to sell whatever it was they stole, the deal went wrong, and they killed the would-be buyers and fled. Or perhaps we're looking at a case of spontaneous combustion, and in the confusion one of the residents in the motel stole Mr. Hughes's motorcycle."

"Anything is possible."

"You do not care to speculate. Or you know more than I."

"I don't know enough to speculate."

August Zacarias liked that answer. "How long have you been watching Meyer Lansky?"

"Long enough."

"And now the roof has fallen in on you."

"We rarely choose where to fight our battles, detective. If we are finished here, I have some phone calls to make. And you could help me by maintaining the perimeter until my people arrive."

"My boss will be pleased that we can hand over the responsibility for these deaths to you. It means that we have two fewer cases to investigate, a microscopic improvement to our statistics. Myself, I do not think that numbers are so very important. I don't care about stolen alien ju-ju either. What is important for me is that the dead are given a voice. That someone speaks for them, makes sure that they are not forgotten, and that whoever is responsible for what happened to them is brought to justice."

August Zacarias looked straight at me when he said this, and I could see that he meant it. Perhaps he was in someone's pocket, perhaps not, but he took his work seriously.

"I'll do my best by them," I said. "If there's anything that I need to know, now is the time to tell me."

"I can tell you that this is a good place to hide," August Zacarias said. "When the city was very young, VIPs stayed here. The freeway wasn't built then, or very little else, for that matter. There were splendid views across fern forests to the bay. Now, half the rooms are rented by the hour, with the kind of traffic that implies. Most of the others were occupied by semi-permanent residents who can't afford anywhere else. An old Chinese woman who keeps chickens and will put curses on people, or remove them, for a small fee. A Ukranian poet who is drinking himself to death. A small gang of Indonesians who work as day labourers on various construction sites. They trap the giant lizards that live in the brush and roast them over fires in the empty swimming pool. Last year, two of them fought with parangs in the parking lot. One lost most of an arm, and bled to death before his friends could get him to hospital. I worked the case. The winner of that little set-to went away for two years, manslaughter."

"You know the place."

August Zacarias smiled and made a sweeping gesture. "Welcome to my world, Ms Davies."

"Luckily, I'm just visiting."

"That's what Everett Hughes and Jason Singleton thought. And look what happened to them."

I phoned Varneek Sehra and told him to bring his crew to the scene as soon as possible. Then I phoned my boss, Marc Godin, and told him what had happened. Marc wasn't happy about being called late at night, and he wasn't happy about the mess the double murder might cause, but he was already ahead of me when it came to discussing what to do next.

"We can't contain the story. The local TV news is already onto it. And if the Koreans aren't already involved, they soon will be. Pak Young-Min will want to have some hard words with his man Lansky."

"Words will be the least of it, sir."

"In any case, if he has not already done so, Lansky may try to scrub his records of incriminating evidence. I'll draw up stop and seizure papers and we'll visit Judge Provenzano and get them made official. Then you can visit Mr. Lansky and ask him to come in and talk to us."

"I already have papers drawn up," I said, and told him where to find them.

"Always prepared, Emma."

"I must have had a premonition."

"Meet me at the office in . . . how long will it take, out there?"

"I'm just waiting for Varneek to take over," I said.

"A shame about those two kids," Marc said. "But perhaps this will give us something to use against Monsieurs Lansky and Pak."

"Yes, we should always look on the bright side," I said.

Let me speak about the dead for a moment. Let me do the right thing by them, as Detective August Zacarias would say.

Like most people who won the emigration lottery and didn't sell their prize to one of the big corporations or to a redistribution agency, or give it away to a relative who either deserved it or wanted it more than they did, or have it stolen by a jealous neighbour, a spouse or a child or a random stranger (UN statistics show that more than four per cent of emigration lottery winners are murdered or disappeared), or simply put it away for a day that never came and meanwhile got on with their lives in the ruins of Earth (and it was still possible to live a life more or less ordinary after the economic collapses, wars, radical climate events, and all the other mess and madness: even after the Jackaroo pitched up and gave us access to a wormhole network linking some fifteen M class red dwarf stars in exchange for rights to the outer planets of the Solar System, for the most part, for most people, life went on as it always did, the ordinary little human joys and tragedies, people falling in love or out of love, marrying, having children, burying their parents, worrying about being passed over for promotion, or losing their job, or the lump in their breast, or the blood in the toilet bowl)—like everyone, in other words, who won the emigration lottery and believed that it was their chance to get out from under whatever muddle or plight they were in and start over (more UN statistics: thirty-six per cent of married lottery winners divorce within two months), Jason Singleton and Everett Hughes wanted to change their lives for the better. They wanted more than the same old same old, although that's what most people get. People think that by relocating themselves to another planet, the ultimate in exoticism, they can radically change their lives, but they always forget that they bring their lives with them. Accountants ship out dreaming of adventure and find work as accountants; police become police, or bodyguards to high-end businesspeople or wealthy gangsters; farmers settle down on some patch of land on coastal plain west of Port of Plenty or on one of the thousands of worldlets in the various reefs that orbit various stars in the network, and so on, and so forth. But Everett Hughes and Jason Singleton were both in their early twenties, and as far as they were concerned anything was possible. They wanted to get rich. They wanted to be famous. Why not? They'd already been touched by stupendous good fortune when they'd won tickets to new and better lives amongst the stars. After that, anything seemed possible.

They met aboard the shuttle that took them out of Low Earth Orbit to the wormhole throat anchored at the L5 point between the Earth and the Moon, and plunged through the wormhole and crossed more than five thousand light years in the blink of an eye and emerged at the leading Lagrangian point of a Mars-sized moon of a blue-green methane gas giant that orbited an undistinguished M0 red dwarf star, and travelled inward to the planet of First Foot and landfall at the spaceport outside the city of Port of Plenty.

It was a journey I had made twenty-two years ago, after I'd divorced my first husband and two weeks later won a place on the emigration lottery. At the time, it had seemed like a message from fate's hotline: pack up what was left of my life, travel to a new world, start afresh. When I arrived on First Foot, Port of Plenty had been a shanty town amongst alien ruins. I worked for the PPPD for three years, then signed up with the UN Security Agency, working in the spaceport to begin with, then joining what was then the brand-new Technology Control Unit. A year after that I met my second husband and we married and it all went wrong very quickly, but that's another story and besides, the man is dead.

And all this time Port of Plenty was growing around me, extending along the shoreline of Discovery Bay, climbing through the semi-arid hills that circled it, spreading into the outer margins of the Great Central desert. It's a sprawling megalopolis now, a nascent Los Angeles or Mexico City. A whole generation has grown up on First Foot, they're having children of their own, and still the shuttles keep coming, loaded with lottery winners and those who can afford to buy the tickets of winners and those who have had their ticket bought for them by corporations, or by the city authority, or by the UN or some other sponsor. Our original settlement, an ugly unplanned patchwork of favelas and shantytowns, has grown into a clean, modern city. Big office blocks in the centre where the corporations and private finance companies work. A marina, and parks, and restaurants and shopping malls. Suburbs. Oh, we've made ourselves at home, all right. But it isn't our home. It's an alien world with a deep history. And settlers have spread out through the wormhole network, discovering Sargassos of ancient ships and refurbishing them, making homes on moons and reefs of worldlets previously settled by countless other races of sentient beings, Elder Cultures who died out or moved on, leaving behind ruins and all kinds of artifacts, some of them functional.

That's where the UN Technology Control Unit, a.k.a. the geek police, comes in. Some Elder Culture technology, like the room-temperature super-conductors and paired virtual particles that enabled us to develop q-phones, hypercomputers, and much else, is useful. Some of it, like grasers and other particle and beam weapons, is both useful and dangerous. And some of it is simply dangerous. Stuff that could give an individual the power to hold worlds to ransom. Stuff that could change the human race so radically that it would either die out or become something other than human. That's why UN created a legislative apparatus to clamp down on illegal trading of Elder Culture technology, to make sure that new technologies developed by legiti-mate companies can't be licensed until they have passed strict tests, and so on and so forth.

The Technology Control Unit is at the sharp end of this legislation. I believed then and still believe now, despite everything, that it is important work. At any time, someone could stumble over something that could change the way we live, how we think of ourselves, how we *think*. In the end, that's what the UN is trying to protect. The right to continue to be human. We have been given a great gift by the Jackaroo. A chance to start over after a terrible war and two centuries of uncontrolled industrialisation and population growth almost ruined our home planet. It is up to us to make the best of that, and make sure that we don't destroy ourselves by greedy or foolish appropriation of technologies so advanced they are, as the old saying goes, indistinguishable from magic.

Fortunately, anyone who wants to make any kind of money from a functional and potentially useful scrap of Elder Culture technology has to come to First Foot, and the city of Port of Plenty. Port of Plenty has a research and manufacturing base that can spin product from Elder Culture artifacts, and it also regulates traffic between the fifteen systems and Earth—and Earth is still the biggest and best market, the only place where real fortunes can be made. But there are also people who want to exploit dangerous Elder Culture artifacts and technologies regardless of the consequences. Some are genuine explorers and scientists; some, like Niles Sarkka, belong to the tinfoil hat brigade. Crackpot theorists. Green ink merchants. Monomaniacs. And some, like Meyer Lansky, are crooks, plain and simple.

At first glance, Meyer Lansky's code farm was a genuine business, one of more than a dozen that dealt in the stuff prospectors pulled from the shells of ships abandoned by the previous tenants of the wormhole network, the Ghajar. They had been some kind of gypsy species that like all the other Elder Cultures had died out or vanished, and had left behind almost no trace of its civilisation or culture apart from its ships. Most had been left parked in orbital junkyard Sargassos, some dead hulks, others slumbering in deep hibernation; a few lay wrecked on the various planets and moons and worldlets of the fifteen stars. Some archaeologists believed that the crashed ships were casualties of a war between factions of the Ghajar; others that they had beached their ships much as whales and smaller cetaceans on Earth, because of disease or panic or confusion or suicidal ennui, had sometimes swum into shallow waters and become stranded by retreating tides. In any case, whether dead or alive or smashed to flinders, all the ships were to some degree or another infested with code. It was quantum stuff, hardware and software embedded in the spin properties of fundamental particles in the molecular matrices of the ships' hulls, raw and fragmented, and crufty with errors and necrotic patches that had accumulated during millennia of disuse and exposure to cosmic radiation.

Coders working in farms like Meyer Lansky's analysed and catalogued this junk and stitched together viable fragments and spent hours and days trying to get them to run in virtual partitions on the farm's hypercomputer cloud. Code approved by the licensing board was bought by software developers who used it to patch controls ships reclaimed from the vast Sargassos, manipulate exotic matter, refine the front ends of quantum technology, and so on and so forth. There were theoretical applications, too—four of the so-called hard mathematical problems had been solved using code reclaimed by the farms.

Meyer Lansky's code farm had been licensed, regulated, and entirely legitimate until he'd run up huge gambling debts and sold control of his business to a shell company owned by a family of Korean gangsters. Now, its legitimate work was a front for black market trade in chunks of viable code too hot and dangerous to ever win a research and development license, and for wholesaling viral fragments to dealers who supplied codeheads with tickets to strange places of the mind, a trade that was growing to be as troublesome as crack cocaine.

Everett Hughes and Jason Singleton had been working in Meyer Lansky's code farm until they'd suddenly quit without warning and dropped clean out of sight. Ten days later, everything blew up at the motel room. We'd been researching the farm for three months, patiently accumulating dossiers on everyone who worked there, but the grisly double murder ripped our clandestine investigation wide open. We shut down the place before Lansky or the Koreans could destroy evidence of wrongdoing, and brought Singleton's and Hughes's co-workers in for interview. Towards the end, I knew more about the two young men than I did about some of my friends. Singleton was from my home town, London, England; Hughes was from Anchorage, Alaska; both were young, white, English-speaking males who were serious computer freaks. They'd bonded when they'd met on the shuttle, stuck together after the shuttle touched down and they were set adrift in the raw hypercapitalism of Port of Plenty. Neither had much in the way of stake money, or any kind of plan. They were flying by the seats of their pants, driven by a mix of arrogant optimism and naivete, confident that because they were young and energetic and talented they were bound to spot some opportunity ripe for exploitation.

At first, they did agency work in the IT department of one of the big multinationals that had set up in Port of Plenty, but the pay was rotten, with no benefits whatsoever apart from vouchers for the subsidised canteen, and it was the kind of boring and frustrating work they'd both been doing back on Earth—Singleton in a university; Hughes for the Russian company that had purchased Alaska from the US government after a failed attempt at secession. In short, it was everything they'd hoped to escape, and after only four weeks they quit and went to work on Meyer Lansky's code farm.

The pay wasn't much better than the agency work and the benefits were equally exiguous, but as far as Singleton and Hughes were concerned it was far more romantic than writing object location routines for suits who didn't really know what they wanted. And his fellow coders agreed that Everett Hughes had a talent for the work. A weird ability to instantly assess the viability of any kind of code, the way some people saw colours in words, or music in numbers. Either it looked good or it didn't, he said. Meaning that the code should conform to a kind of symmetry or beauty, although he found it hard to explain exactly what that was, and if pressed he would grow surly, hunch his shoulders, sneer that it wasn't worth trying to explain it because either you had the righteous gift or you didn't. He had the gift, and he was usually right. Jay Singleton got by through determination and hard work, but Everett Hughes flew.

Apparently, they had been planning to stash away a good percentage of their pay until they had accumulated enough to buy themselves berths on a code-hunting jaunt. They'd have to buy their own equipment, and front the gangmaster fees for transport plus a thirty per cent kickback on anything they made, but they were confident that they would strike a hot lode that would set them up for life. But it seemed that the two of them had grown bored with working and saving and saving and working, and had taken a short-cut. They'd stolen something from Meyer Lansky, and either Lansky or the Koreans had found them and killed them and taken the stuff back, or they'd tried to sell it to the wrong people. Those were my working hypotheses, but I was worried that the code itself might have had something to do with the two bodies in the burnt-out motel room—we were running a pool in the TCU on when someone would stumble across true AI, and who knew what else someone might find out there? In any case, Hughes and Singleton must have stolen the code because they'd though it valuable. And if it was valuable, it must be functional: unknown code with unknown capabilities, out there in the world. Recapturing it was suddenly my main priority, and the first thing I needed to do was to shut down Meyer Lansky's operation and find out what Hughes and Singleton had been working on before they'd bugged out.

Like all the ships we humans use, the reef farmers' ship is a shell retrieved from one of the vast Sargassos that orbit almost every one of the fifteen stars. Many ships are frozen relics no more functional or repairable than a watch that's spent a thousand years at the bottom of the ocean; others are merely quiescent, systems ticking over in a sleep deeper than any hibernation, but fully functional once awakened: all are ancient, handed down from Elder Culture to Elder Culture, modified and rebuilt and modified again until scarcely a trace of the original remains.

The farmers bolted the usual translation interface to the ship's control systems, but weren't able to customise the lifesystem for human occupation because the ship possesses fierce self-repairing mechanisms that resist any alterations (which was why the farmers could buy it at a knock-down price: few people want a ship with a mind of its own). The lifesystem supplies food that is both unpalatable and toxic to humans, the light is actinic, and the air like the air of a high altitude steel refinery: not enough oxygen or water, desert-dry and hot, stinking of tholines and sulphur dioxide.

The ships' crew and its single passenger—me—live in a series of pressure tents bolted to the bulkhead near the pool of nannodust that serves as an airlock. The maintenance system treats us as cargo and leaves us alone as long as we do not interfere with other areas of the ship. There is a large commons and a series of smaller rooms, including sleeping niches partioned by fibreboard like the cells of a wasp's nest, a communal bathroom, and the small red-lit space, crowded with racks of electronic gear, that serves as the bridge. The commons is cozy enough, carpeted with overlapping rugs and cushions and beanbags and lit by small lamps and strings of fairylights, but even so we live like refugees, the rest of the ship's chambers looming above us like so many chimney shafts, walls pitted with cells of various sizes, lit by the pitless glare of the lights, scoured by hot, random winds.

It's a perfect example of the human experience after First Contact—men and women living like mice in the walls of worlds they barely understand. The ship's fusion motors, for instance, are sealed mysteries. Very simple things that have been working for a hundred times longer than the existence of human agriculture on Earth, fuelled by deuterium and tritium mined by ancient ramscoop factories that swim through the atmospheres of certain ice giants.

Fuel is the key to the end of the chase.

Ours is a big ship, as ships go: an A3-Class heavy lifter. Even so, it can't carry enough fuel for a round trip out to Terminus's neighbouring star, so a drone has been sent after us, loaded with a cargo of deuterium and tritium. A major investment by the farmers that I hope the UN will defray, although the chair of the farmers' council, Rajo Hiranand, is sanguine about it. Telling me that her people made a huge gamble when they settled the worldlets of Terminus's inner belt, and so far it has paid off more handsomely than they ever expected. They've laid claim to several hundred planoformed rocks where they grow crops and ranch sky sheep, and share the profits from exploitation of artifacts and code unearthed by prospectors—the abundance and variety of artifacts found on Terminus's worldlets is second only to that of the fifteen stars' the solitary habitable planet, First Foot. And now they have invested in this, a prospecting expedition of their own.

Rajo and I agree that Niles Sarkka may be crazy, but he is not stupid. That he must have good and convincing reasons for heading out Terminus's neighbour. It isn't likely that he will find what he expects to find there, of course. But the fact that the navigation code points to a location close to the star must mean something is there, or was once there, in the long ago when the Ghajar were the tenants of the fifteen stars.

The rational part of me hopes that Niles Sarkka won't find anything useful, let alone prove that his wild idea is right. But I'm also caught up in this crazy chase: I want to believe—I *have* to believe—that there's a pot of gold around that star, something that will justify my refusal to obey a direct order. Something that will redeem me.

Now that we are slowly but surely catching up with Sarkka, I've told him several times that we are prepared to rescue him as long as he cooperates. I'm trying to get him used to the idea that, after he reaches his goal, we'll come alongside his ship and take him off and bring him home. So far, though, he's having none of it. Sometimes he rants at me; sometimes he's cool and reasonable, like a patient teacher correcting the error of a particularly stupid but wilful pupil.

He has no intention of returning, he says. He will spend the rest of his life with the Elder Culture that lurks somewhere around that star. Either they'll take him in, or he'll settle close by and found an institute or research centre.

"And if you're wrong?" I say.

"I am not wrong," he says.

"If there's nothing there. Just suppose."

"I do not intend to return."

And meanwhile the star grows brighter as both ships fall towards it, fusion motors blazing with a pull of a shade over 1.6 g, the maximum acceleration of every ship so far reburbished.

It is the brightest star in the sky now. Blue-white as a chip of ice. There's a thin ring of rocks close in, but none of them are cased in an atmosphere or are more massive that they should be, and in any case all of them are far too hot to be habitable. And there's a single planet, a gas giant about the size of Saturn, orbiting beyond the star's snowline. A somber world whose atmosphere is darkened by vast belts of carbon dust, as if polluted by some vast industrial process. It has multiple rings of sooty ice, and a retinue of moons, the larger ones balls of ice wrapped around silicate cores, the smaller ones captured chunks of carbonaceous chondrite in eccentric and mostly retrograde orbits. Somewhere amongst them, Niles Sarkka believes, is proof that his theory is correct, vindication for every bad thing he's ever done. Somewhere out there, he thinks, aliens have been hiding for tens of thousands of years.

Although Marc and I did our very best, it wasn't possible to make Meyer Lansky understand that we were prepared to do a deal with him rather than throw him in jail. Or maybe he understood, and didn't care. He was angry that his business had been shut down, and he was scared that his boss, Pak Young-Min, would find out that he'd been rolled by a couple of his code monkeys and conclude that he wasn't up to the job—the usual retirement plan for the Pak family's gangland employees and associates was a bullet in the back of the head and a short ride down the river to the sea. So Lansky refused my offer of protection when I served papers on him at his house around midnight, and he refused again when he was brought in for questioning. A broad-shouldered man dressed in a white suit, neatly barbered hair dyed the colour of tarnished aluminium, he sat in my office with a grim, shuttered expression and his arms folded across his chest, giving Marc and me the dead eye while his lawyer explained why he couldn't answer any of our questions.

One of the assistant city attorneys was there, too, and Marc and I knew things had taken a turn for the worse when she asked for a break and stepped out of the interrogation room with Lansky's lawyer. Marc took the opportunity to tell Lansky all over again why he would be doing the city and the UN a service by telling us where the stolen code was and what had happened to the two coders, repeating the scenario he'd already painted, with Lansky as the innocent party, first robbed by two of his employees, and then involuntarily involved in their murder by his boss.

"You had to tell Pak Young-Min about the theft because otherwise it would come down on your head. I understand that. But after that it was out of your hands and things got out of control," Marc said. He had taken off his jacket and hung it on the back of his chair at the beginning of the session; now, in white shirt and red braces, he leaned forward and stared straight at Lansky. "You are a smart man. You know how much trouble you are in. And you know what Pak Young-Min is capable of. But we're here to help. We can make your troubles disappear. All you have to do is tell us exactly what happened. What was stolen. What happened to the two foolish kids who stole it. Where it is now."

Meyer Lansky shook his head, eyes half-closed, lips pressed tight. He looked as if he was trying by sheer mental effort to teleport himself to some more congenial place.

Marc looked up at me, and I told Lansky that the UN would settle him anywhere he chose. That we'd even take him back to Earth, if he cooperated with us. That he would have a chance to start over, and meanwhile the men he feared would be put away for the rest of their lives.

Lansky shook his head. "Nothing was stolen. Those two kids, they just left. It happens all the time."

"It's time to tell the truth," Marc said. "Lying about what Pak Young-Min did won't save you. He'll go down anyway, and you'll go with him. But you can save yourself. All you have to do is tell the truth. It seems hard, I know. But once you start, you will feel so much better. It will be like a great weight lifting from your back."

Marc was good, and I did my best to back him up, but we couldn't get through to Lansky. "Talk to my lawyer," he said, and wouldn't say anything else.

At last his lawyer and the assistant CA came back. The assistant shaking her head, the lawyer telling Lansky that he was good to go.

"Hardshelled son of bitch," Marc said, after they had left.

"He's scared."

"Of course. But not of us, unfortunately."

"I suppose we'll have to wait for the forensic results," I said. I was tired and empty. It was two in the morning, my investigation had been broken open, and I had nothing to show for it.

"We will rest and tomorrow begin again," Marc said, as he shrugged into his jacket. "You are my best investigator, Emma. I trust you to deliver what we need."

But our first break wasn't anything to do with me, or with Varneek Sehra's forensic crew, either. It was all due to one of our technical staff, Prem Gurung.

Prem was a modest young man who attributed his find to luck, but I knew better. His cubicle was as messy the bedroom of as an undisciplined teenager—desk stacked with folders, papers, fabbed trinkets, and littered with every kind of electronic junk, walls tiled with photographs, postcards, print-outs, cartoons and coasters in defiance of every regulation—but he was a skilled, intelligent, and hard-working investigator. He had been examining the work logs of Everett and Singleton, and chunks of the mirrored code they had been working on, and had quickly found something of interest in one particular piece, an incomplete variant of the navigation package used to control refurbished ships retrieved from the Sargassos.

"It isn't is so much what's there as what isn't," Prem said.

He was eager to show me, and I reluctantly agreed to take a look. Code is usually explored and manipulated via virtual simulations disneyed up by interface ware: dreamscapes that look a little like coral reefs, their exotic beauty haunted by sharks and moray eels and riptides that can fry synapses or burn permanent hallucinations in optic nerves. Coders, exposed to the stuff eight or ten hours a day, commonly suffer all kinds of transient hallucinations and risk permanent neurological damage—psychosis, blindsight, loss of motor control, death. But they are like deep sea divers working in the chthonic depths, while I was a snorkelling tourist dipping in for a brief peek, gliding over a garden of colourful geometric shapes, complex fractal packages of self-engulfing information that branched like bushes or were packed as tightly as human brains or formed shelves or fans or spires, everything receding into deep shadow in every direction, under a flexing silvery sky. Still, I couldn't shake off the sense of things unseen and fey lurking at the edges, where steep cliffs plunged into the unknown.

Prem guided me to a spot carpeted with intricate spires, and asked me if I saw it.

"I'm not very technical, Prem."

"It's a patch, copied from another part of the code," he said, turning the viewpoint through three hundred and sixty degrees. Spires of every size and shape, glowing with purples and greens and golds, flowed around us in a three-dimensional tapestry. "It isn't easy to see at first, which is of course the point. But when you do see it, it's obvious. I have written a little executable. Here . . ."

A ghostly scape descended from the silvery sky, spires in wirework outline sitting askew the spires that stood around us.

"It does not seem to match at all, until you perform a simple geometric transformation," Prem said.

The wirework outline spun and stretched and merged with every contour of the spires around us, gleaming like frost on their complex and colourful surfaces.

"I think someone deleted something and wanted to cover it up," Prem said. "Fortunately for us, he was skilled, but lazy. Instead of designing something from scratch, he copied and distorted another part of the code and stitched it in. It is on the surface a seamless illusion. It even runs several processing cycles, although they are of course all futile. Like code that has gone bad, as much code does."

The strange shapes and colours of the code reef, hallucinatory bright, crammed with thorny details that repeated at every level of magnification, were aggravating my headache. I hadn't had much sleep and was running on coffee and fumes. I stripped off my VR and asked Prem if he had any idea about what had been deleted; he told me that despite the fractal nature of the code, little or nothing of the excised portion could be reconstructed. He started to witter on about working up a rough contour grid by extrapolation from the boundaries, using edge-crossing-detection, random-walk searches, and vertex-pruning mutators, blah blah blah. Like every tech, he was more interested in playing with a problem than actually solving it. I cut him off and said, "Bottom line, you don't know what it is, and there's no way of finding out."

"I'm afraid so. The deletion is too thorough for reconstruction, and catalogue comparisons have proven to be of no use."

"They stole something. We don't know what it is, but Hughes and Jackson definitely stole something. They mirrored the code and deleted the original, did their best to cover up what they'd done, and made off with the copy."

"That's certainly one scenario," Prem said. "Although there is a problem. How did they smuggle the stolen code past the farm's security?"

It was a good point. Code is stored in specific quantum states of electrons and other fundamental particles, so it can't be copied and stored as easily as the vast binary strings of ordinary software; to prevent decay into quantum noise, mirrored code has to be kept in cold traps, and these are cooled with liquid helium. Archive traps are as big as trucks; the smallest portable trap is somewhat larger than an ordinary domestic thermos flask. And like all coding farms, Meyer Lansky's business possessed an insanely paranoid level of security. Coders had step through scanning frames when entering or leaving, and they were subject to continuous scrutiny by CCTV cameras and random searches.

"Perhaps they had bribed a guard, or secreted the cold trap in some other piece of equipment sent out for servicing," I said. "Or perhaps Lansky himself might have been in on it."

"Or perhaps they didn't smuggle anything out," Prem said. "Perhaps they hacked into the farm's records and found out where the code came from, then deleted the code and altered the records. Perhaps they did not sell the code, but the location of the original."

I liked the idea—it would certainly explain why Hughes had left with Sarkka—but there was no way of proving or disproving it unless we caught up with them. Meanwhile, Varneek Sehra's crew had come up blank on DNA analysis because the two bodies had been thoroughly cooked, but they had identified one body as Jason Singleton's from its English dental work, and the second wasn't Everett Hughes, but a male in his forties. He had an old, healed bullet wound in his left shoulder, and examination of his burnt skin under uv light had revealed a blood group tattoo on his right ankle, suggesting that he'd been a soldier at some point. Varneek's crew had also retrieved a partial thumbprint from a stolen SUV in the motel's parking lot, and that had yielded a hit on the US military database: Abuelo Baez, who'd served as a sergeant in the Special Forces of the US Army until two years ago. The name did not appear on the emigration records, so he must have arrived on First Foot under an alias, either working for one of the corporations, or on the dark side. Varneek was planning to work up a facial reconstruction and use it to track down the dead man's emigration file; I hoped that once I knew Abuelo Baez's alias, I would be able to discover what he had been doing in Port of Plenty, perhaps even link him to Meyer Lansky or to the Pak family. Varneek also told me that there was a small discrepancy between the two bodies. Jason Singleton's body had smoke particles in its lungs, consistent with someone who had burned to death; Abuelo Baez's didn't. Either the ex-soldier had been killed outright by the blast, or he'd been dead before the room had been set on fire, it wasn't possible to tell.

All of this was useful, but it was my hunch about the missing motorcycle that yielded the most significant advance in the case. It had been discovered in the parking lot of a mini-mall a kilometre south of the motel; security camera footage showed that it had arrived some thirty minutes before the fire in the motel had been started. Everett Hughes had been riding it, and loitered near a rank of vending machines for some forty minutes until a white Honda Adagio pulled up.

I showed Marc the footage of Hughes getting into the Adagio, pulled down an enhanced freeze-frame of the moment when the courtesy light in the car came on as Hughes opened the door, briefly illuminating a bearded man wearing a baseball cap pulled low enough to obscure half his face. I explained that the driver had not yet been identified, but the car had been traced to the Hertz branch at the spaceport, where it had been rented using a snide credit card, and it had been retrieved for trace analysis.

"After Hughes and the driver returned the Adagio to the rental company, they took the shuttle bus to a ship that departed two hours later. A standard J-class cruiser registered in Libertaria. It dropped through Wormhole #2 six hours ago, and I've asked our offices in every port it could reach from that part of the network to look out for it. That's the bad news. The good news is that the Varneek and the PPPD's forensic people retrieved fibres and hair from the seats, and fingerprints from the steering wheel and elsewhere. Hughes's friend is Niles Sarkka."

Without missing a beat, Marc said, "I am not sure that I would classify that as good news."

Niles Sarkka was one of the Fortunate Five Hundred, the self-styled elite who'd ridden the first emigration lottery shuttle to First Foot. Before his downfall, he'd been a leading expert on Elder Cultures with a chair at the

University of Port of Plenty, and the star of a TV show popular in Port of Plenty and exported to almost every country back on Earth. In each episode, he led his crew of prospectors to a new site in search of strange and valuable Elder Culture artifacts, surviving dangers and hardships, exploring weird landscapes and worldlets, unearthing wonders. Most of it was faked and exaggerated, of course, but Sarkka was a handsome and charismatic man with an infective enthusiasm for his work. Also, to the disgust of his fellow academics and the delight of his TV audience, he recklessly embraced crackpot ideas about the fates of the Elder Cultures, and conspiracy theories that suggested that the Jackaroo had influenced human history by dropping meteorites or manipulating the climate or starting the world war that, just before they'd turned up as saviours, had almost destroyed us. He was a leading exponent of the belief that the fifteen stars were not a chance to start afresh, but a trap. A cage in which we would be the involuntary participants in some vast and strange experiment, as had the Elder Cultures which had preceeded us. And he had worked up a crazy theory of his very own, which he talked up on every episode of his show. All of this made him rich and famous and notorious, but in the end his hubris was clobbered by nemesis. In the end he took one risk too many, and other people paid for his mistake with their lives.

My boss had been one of the team that had prosecuted Niles Sarkka after most of his crew had become infected with nanotech viroids while excavating the remains of ancient machinery in a remote part of the Great Central Desert. Marc had seen the bodies, all of them horribly transformed, some still partly alive. His boss, who'd later shot himself, had ordered cauterisation of the site with a low-yield nuclear weapon.

The crew had been working on an unlicensed site with inadequate protective measures; Niles Sarkka was convicted of manslaughter and spent five years in jail. As soon as he was released, he promptly fled First Foot and established himself on Libertaria, using what was left of his fortune to pursue the theory that was now an obsession.

Given that there was a wormhole link with the Solar System and Earth, he said, then if followed that there must have been links with the home worlds of each of the Elder Cultures that had once inhabited the worlds and worldlets of the fifteen stars. And those wormholes might still be around, somewhere, collapsed down to diameters smaller than a hydrogen atom, or hidden inside gas giants or in orbits close to stars where they could not be detected by their fingerprint flux of strange quarks and high-energy particles; it might be possible to find the home world of the Ghajar or one of the other Elder cultures, and find out what had happened to them. It was even possible that some remnants of the Elder Cultures might still be alive, either on their home worlds, or elsewhere.

To his fans—and despite his conviction and fall from grace he still had many fans—he was a gadfly genius, a rogue intellect who took great risks to prove radical theories that the establishment tried to suppress. To his fellow academics, he was a highly irresponsible egotist who used his notoriety to promote fantasies as risible as the lost continent of Mu or the Venusian origin of flying saucers, heedless of the damage he caused to serious scholarship. As far as the UN was concerned, he was a criminal willing to take every kind of risk with Elder Culture technology. He was beyond our reach on Liberteria, but he remained on our watch list.

And now he was heading out for parts unknown, either in possession of code mirrored from a navigation program, or of the whereabouts of the code's original. Given the huge risk he'd taken coming back to Port of Plenty, it seemed likely that he believed the code had something to do with his crazy idea about finding the homeworld or a surviving remnant of an Elder Culture. It was also seemed likely that he had killed Jason Singleton and the mercenary, Abuelo Baez. Even if the code was harmless, Niles Sarkka still had to answer for those deaths.

The problem was that we had lost track of his ship. It could be anywhere in the wormhole network, heading for any one of the other fourteen stars—it might even be heading back to First Foot's star by a circuitous route. During the early years of exploring the network, the UN had tried to set up a monitoring system of spy satellites around the wormhole throats, but it had been sabotaged by various factions over the years, and in the end it had proven too expensive to maintain.

"Even if Sarkka and Hughes go to ground on Libertaria, we have no jurisdiction there," Marc said.

"We can try to negotiate with them," I said.

"Perhaps. It would help if we knew exactly what Hughes and Singleton stole," Marc said.

"That's why we need to talk to Myer Lansky again," I said.

But Lansky had disappeared, and so had his wife and their two young sons. A police detail had been watching the front of the house; it seemed that Lansky and his family had left through the back, escaping across the golf course. Either of their own free will, or because someone had come for them.

A safe sunk in the floor of a walk-in closet in Lansky's residence had been left open but still contained large amounts of cash and jewellery, and credit cards and phones registered to a variety of names. Traces of blood belonging to Lansky and his family were found on a wall and the carpet in the adjoining master bedroom. I believed that they were dead, their bodies dumped in the sea or in the fern forests beyond the edge of the city, or incorporated into the foundations of a new building or freeway overpass, and their killers had probably taken from the safe copies of the records for the code farm detailing legitimate and black-market transactions.

After a brief conference with Marc and the assistant city attorney, I issued an APB for the Lanskys and made an appointment to visit Meyer Lansky's boss, Pak Young-Min. Marc thought it a waste of time, but I had a bad feeling that the case was going cold. I wanted to stir things up a little. Besides, I had papers to serve regarding search and seizure of the code farm's assets, and because Meyer Lansky had disappeared, it was only logical to hand them to his boss.

Pak Young-Min was the youngest son of Pak Jung-Hun, a former head of the American-Korean Family Boyz gang in Seattle who had "retired" to Port of Plenty. Like most gangsters who'd grown rich enough to escape the clutches of law enforcement agencies, Pak Jung-Hin had ambitions to legitimise his family. Three of his sons were involved in real estate and construction, an insurance and loan company, and casinos in First Foot and Mammoth Lakes. But Pak Young-Min was a throwback: an old-school kkangpae with a volatile temper and a taste for baroque violence who had been given control of Meyer Lansky's code farm by his father in an attempt to wean him away from the street life.

I arranged to meet him in the offices of the development company helmed by his eldest brother, Pak Kwang-Ho. This was on the top floor of a brand-new ziggurat—white concrete, glass tinted the pink of freshly-cut copper, broad terraces dripping with greenery—with a stunning view across the city towards Discovery Bay, the spaceport and the river delta on one side, the power plant and docks on the other, and the great curve of the Maricon and the beaches between. Up there, the city looked as neat and clean as a map, with no sign of the squabbling territories carved out by different nationalities. Up there, it was possible to believe that the future had arrived. You wanted to search the sky for flying cars and dirigibles.

Pak Kwang-Ho met me at the tall double doors of his private office. A slim and intensely polite man dressed in a crisp white shirt and intricately pleated pants, he shook my hand, offered me a choice of ten different teas, and introduced me to two lawyer types who afterwards did their best to fade into the background, and to his brother, Pak Young-Min.

The young gangster was looming over an architectural model of a shopping mall and entertainment complex, a bulky, broad-shouldered bodybuilder stuffed into a sharkskin suit and a yellow silk shirt and snakeskin boots. Tattoos webbed his neck and his hair was shaved at the sides, high above his ears, leaving a glossy black cap on top of his scalp. He didn't look up when Pak Kwang-Ho introduced me, pretending to be more interested in pushing a model car around a plaza, knocking over model pedestrians one by one.

Pak Kwang-Ho assured me that his family were always happy to help the police with their enquiries, but in this case, since his brother had business ties with Meyer Lansky, he had to ask me to confirm that my enquiries were purely informal. I assured him that I wanted nothing more than background information on Meyer Lansky, although I did have papers to serve with regard to the code farm.

"I hope this means I can reopen it," Pak Young-Min said. "I lose money every day it is closed. Most inconvenient."

"Here's another dose of inconvenience—we're sealing it up until further notice," I said, and held out the envelope that contained the twenty-page court order.

Pak Young-Min took it and scaled it towards the lawyer types, saying that his people would check it out and get back to me.

"You need to sign it," I said.

"Why don't you ask me what you came here to ask me?" Pak Young-Min said. "I'm a busy man. I have a lot of stuff to do. Important stuff."

I decided to meet him head on and locked gazes with him and said, "When did you last see Meyer Lansky?"

"Days and days ago. I heard he ran away after you questioned him about those two geeks who burned to death," Pak Young-Min said. "If you catch up with the old rogue, let me know. I have some questions for him myself."

"You have no idea where he might be," I said. "Him and his family."

"I've been in Mammoth Lakes for the past week," Pak Young-Min said, and took out a gold cigarette case and, ignoring his brother's warning that he couldn't smoke here, lit a black Sobranie with a match he ignited on his thumbnail.

"One of the bodies in the motel room was that of Jason Singleton. An employee at your code farm."

"Meyer Lansky's code farm," Pak Young-Min said.

"You own it."

"He runs it. I wouldn't know who he employs. When can I reopen the place, by the way?"

"When we've finished our investigation. Although by then there probably won't be anything left of your little operation."

Pak Young-Min looked at me with insolent amusement. "I know about you and your crusade," he said. "Word is, you lost your husband to bad code, and now you see bad code everywhere. Even when it isn't there."

I didn't rise to his bullshit. If you show any kind of weakness to someone like him you'll lose authority and never get it back.

"You are certain that you have never met Jason Singleton."

"I've never had anything to do with those freaky little geeks."

"Have you ever met Everett Hughes?"

"Is he the other one who burned up in that room?"

"He's the one who got away," I said. "The other body in the motel room was that of Abuelo Baez, a former US soldier who served in the Special Forces."

"I've never heard of any of these people," Pak Young-Min said.

"Perhaps you know the face," I said, and showed him the printout of Abuelo Baez's reconstructed death mask.

Pak Young-Min breathed out a riffle of smoke and said, "He isn't one of mine."

"You might know him as Able Martinez," I said. "That's the alias he used when he came to Port of Plenty. We identified him from a file in the gaming commission's records. Every employee of every casino has one. I'm surprised you don't know him, Mr. Pak. He worked on the security detail of the casino in Mammoth Lakes owned by your family."

"My brother has nothing to do with the running of the casino," Pak Kwang-Ho said. "And neither do I."

"We're looking into everything Mr. Naez was doing here, and everyone he associated with," I said. "If you remember anything about him, it would be better if you told me now."

Pak Young-Min shrugged.

"You should speak to the manager of the casino," Pak Kwang-Ho said.

I told him that I would, and thanked them for their time and turned my back on both of them and walked towards the big double doors of the office.

Pak Young-Min called after me—he was the kind of man who had to have the last word. "Come find me in Mammoth Lakes. I'll show you a good time. Loosen you up a little."

I paused at the doors, turned. The corny old Columbo trick, but it's sometimes useful. "One other thing. Have you heard of Niles Sarkka?"

The two brothers looked at each other. Pak Young-Min said, "Isn't he the crazy guy who had that TV show?"

"He and Everett Hughes took off together," I said, and left them to think about that.

Later, I told my boss that I was certain that Pak Young-Min knew all about Hughes and Singleton. "Lansky was not a stupid man. He probably discovered the deletion in the navigation package and the alteration in his records after they dropped out of sight, and decided to come clean about it to his boss. Pak Young-Min sent his muscle man, Abuelo Baez, a.k.a. Able Martinez, after the two coders."

"Baez tracked them down to the motel room but he was killed by Niles Sarkka," Marc said.

"I'm not sure what happened there, but I don't think it matters," I said. "Sarkka was definitely involved, and I'm certain that the Paks didn't know about that until I told them. If we're lucky, they'll start making enquiries around the spaceport, and incriminate themselves. I can ask them, why are they looking for the killer of Abuelo Baez if Baez had nothing to do with them?"

"It is a long shot," Marc said. "I would prefer something tangible."

"So would I," I said. "But even if we can't tie them to Baez, we'll get them for Lansky. Pak Young-Min killed him. I'm sure of it. Lansky's family, too. He knew that we talked to Lansky, and he didn't trust him to keep his mouth shut. He probably took copies of incriminating records from Lansky's floor-safe at the same time. If we have a pretext for arresting him, we might be able to get hold of those records. And somewhere in them is the location of the original of the code Hughes and Singleton stole. We need to find it."

"Do you really believe that Sarkka and Hughes are chasing after it?"

"They haven't turned up at Libertaria, or anywhere else we have representatives or reliable sources."

"That leaves about ten thousand habitable but uncolonised planoformed worldlets, and any number of rocks and moons," Marc said.

"We need to find it," I said. "So we know what we are dealing with. So we can destroy it, and make sure that no one else can mirror it."

"If Pak Young-Min has any sense, he will have destroyed those records."

"Not if he hopes to restart his black-market business."

Marc looked straight at me and said, "I hope you did not set the Paks after Sarkka because you believe that Sarkka has escaped justice."

"Of course not," I said.

But that was exactly why I'd told the Paks about Sarkka, and although Marc probably knew that I was lying he didn't call me on it. Perhaps, like me, he wanted Niles Sarkka to answer for the deaths of Jason Singleton and Abuelo Baez, and for all his other crimes. Is that such a bad thing? Of course, I would have preferred to go after him myself, but at the time I didn't think it would be possible. So I had decided to stir things up a little.

While I'm being candid, I suppose I should mention my husband here—my second husband. Not because Pak Young-Min's silly jibe in any way hurt or upset me, but because certain commentators who should know better, amateur psychologists who aren't ashamed to speculate foolishly and wholly irresponsibly about the motivations of people they've never met, have suggested that I set out after Niles Sarkka because he was dealing in stolen code, and Jules's addiction to code is the key to my personality. My secret wound. The tragedy for which I have to atone for the rest of my life. Well, let me tell you that's so much pseudo-Freudian bullshit. I don't mean that it wasn't a tragedy. Of course it was. But I got past it and I got on with my life.

Really, it was all such a long time ago, back in the palmy days when everything in this brave new world of ours was fresh and wonderful. Back then, we didn't know that doing code could hurt you. It wasn't even illegal. It was something clever and sophisticated people did for kicks. A clean and perfectly legal high.

Jules said that it was as if everything had turned to mathematics. He could see everything as it really was, he said. He could see angels in the architecture and hear the glorious mingled chord of the universe's continuous self-invention. The world stripped bare of all masks. The world behind the world. He wanted me to try it, but I was a working police, we had regular tests for every kind of psychoactive substance. And besides, I was scared. I admit it. I was scared that the alien code would scramble my mind. And it turned out that I was right, because pretty soon it started to go bad for Jules and all the other clever people who did code for shits and giggles, because the temporary synesthesia and pareidolia became permanent, burned into their brains.

Jules began to see ugly patterns everywhere. Angels morphed into demons. The music became a marching band banging away inside his head and he couldn't get it out. He no longer spent hours lying out in the back yard at night, staring up at the stars with childlike wonder. The sky was wounded, now. Everything was rotten. Only the code kept him going. He had to take more and more of it, and by now it had become illegal. He could no longer get a clean supply from his friend at the university because his friend wasn't at the university any more, she was on the street, but he found other sources. He sold just about everything we owned. I threw him out and took him back, suffered the usual cycle of anger and despair, hate and compassion. At last he stopped coming back. I could have found him, had him arrested, transferred from jail to a clinic, but it wouldn't have done any good. By then we knew that code caused permanent damage, a downward spiral of diminishing neurological function that ended in dementia and death. And I was tired of rescuing someone who didn't want to be rescued, and anyway, he wasn't the man I'd loved. He wasn't really anyone anymore. He was his condition. So after he left that last time I didn't chase after him and him there and the next time I saw him, six months later, was on a table in the morgue.

Yes, it hurt. Of course it did. But not as badly as seeing poor Jules twitching with pseudo-Parkinson's and gibbering about demons. It hurt, but it was also a kind of relief, knowing that he wasn't suffering any more. Really it was. And besides, it was a long time ago, long before I joined the Technology Control Unit. It really doesn't have anything to do with anything I'm telling you about here, despite what some people claim. I wasn't avenging my husband or trying to assuage my guilt or anything like that. I was working the case, just like I worked every other case.

But after my confrontation with Pak Young-Min, the case appeared to have reached a dead end. I continued to try to tease out new leads, coordinating the team who were interviewing everyone who worked in the code factory and trying to discover a direct connection between the dead ex-soldier, Abuelo Baez, and Pak Young-Min. I wrote day reports, filed evidence dockets, and minuted case conferences. I arranged to meet Detective August Zacarias, ostensibly to brief him about the ongoing investigation into the double homicide at the motel, in reality to pump him for information about his fellow member of the Fortunate Five Hundred. That, too, yielded nothing useful. He claimed that he'd only met Niles Sarkka once or twice, and knew little about him.

"You want to know if he's one of the bad guys. All I can tell you is that back in the early days he argued very passionately and convincingly about the importance of finding out everything we could about our new worlds. He said that we should take nothing for granted. That we should take charge of our own destiny by forging a complete understanding of the history and nature of the Jackaroos' gift. He wasn't dangerous, then, merely impassioned. It seems to me that he hasn't changed."

I suppose I should have known better. I should have known that the so-called elite would stick together. Ten days passed with little to show for my efforts, beyond filling in the biographies of Everett Hughes and Jason Singleton. And then I received an email that opened up a fresh angle.

It was from a man who claimed to be a friend of Meyer Lansky's mistress. He said that she had gone into hiding because she afraid of the Paks, and that she had something that I would like to see: two sets of books for the code farm. This so-called friend had used an anonymous forwarding service to cover his tracks, but Prem Gurung managed to track him down while I negotiated with him on-line, and within the hour he was sitting in our interview room.

He was a small-time hustler by the name of Randy Twigger, a former boyfriend of Lansky's mistress. He put up a feeble show of defiance that quickly collapsed when I called his bluff and told him that he could be arraigned for accessory to murder and kidnap of the Lanskys. Later that day, with a pair of armed marshals at my back, I was knocking on the door of a motel room in the fishing resort of Marina Vista, four hundred kilometres east of Port of Plenty.

Meyer Lansky's mistress, Natasha Wu, was a tough and level-headed young woman who was ready and willing to be taken into protective custody, and wasn't surprised that Randy Twigger had screwed up by trying to make some money for himself.

"He was supposed to make an arrangement so that I could meet with you. But he always was greedy," she said, and dismissed him with a flick of her manicured fingers.

She said that she'd heard about the disappearance of Meyer Lansky and his family on the news, said that she'd known at once that they were dead. "Meyer was ultra-paranoid the last time I saw him. There'd been a break-in at the farm, and those two kids were killed, and you threatened him. I was about the only person he could trust. That's why he gave me the books. He was going to contact me when things settled down. Instead, this man I don't know calls me on the phone Meyer gave me, and threatens me."

Lansky had given her a q-phone, but after the threatening call she had ditched it and gone to ground, moving from place to place. Randy Twigger had checked her apartment a couple of days ago and found that it had been trashed, so she knew that the people who had killed Lansky and his family knew about her. That's why she had reached out to me.

I liked Natasha Wu, even though I disapproved of the choices she had made in her life. She was a survivor with no trace of self-pity and had probably given as good as she got in her relationship with Meyer Lansky. I told her that the UN was willing to give her a new identity and relocate her in exchange for the accounts and records that Lansky had entrusted to her, and she said why not, the man was dead, and it wasn't like she had a choice anyway.

"Besides, I want off this fucking world. I've been here a year, and already I hate it. I want to go back to Earth. To Singapore. It's fucked up there, but I know my way around, and the gangsters aren't as crazy bad as they are here. Poor Meyer. And his kids." She teared up just a little, and said, "Will you get the filth that killed them?"

I thought of Detective August Zacarias and said, "I'm going to do my best."

At the UN building, I sat with Marc Godin and one of the city attorneys while they made a deal with Natasha Wu and took her initial deposition. Then I escorted Natasha to one of our safe houses, so I didn't get a chance to talk to Marc about searching the records for the location of the original of the code, or chasing after Sarkka and Hughes.

I stayed at the safe house overnight, and was eating breakfast with Natasha and the two UN special agents detailed to protect her when Marc called.

"There have been developments," he said. "Something I think you will like."

"Has Prem found where the code came from? Are we going after Sarkka?"

"Meet me at the UN Building," he said, and rang off.

We bought coffee at the roach coach in the parking lot in front of the UN Building, and walked two blocks to the seafront. I told him that Natasha was holding up; he told me that the records were all that we hoped they would be.

"The late Monsieur Lansky was a meticulous man," Marc said. "We have details of all his black market transactions, and that is a great prize. As for the code that has caused so much trouble, you will be pleased to hear that we know now where it came from. A planoformed but uninhabited worldlet in the outer belt of the system of Terminus. It was located and mirrored by a prospector named Suresh Shrivastav, registered in Libertaria."

"And what are you going to do about it?"

"That's what we must talk about now. Let's find a seat."

It was a fine warm spring morning. Far around the great curve of the beach, two bulldozers looking small as toys were levelling sand where a kraken had beached a few days ago. A raft of bladders and pulpy limbs the size of two football fields, it had drawn huge crowds, and dismembering and removing it had been an industrial process. People were strolling along the front or walking their dogs on the wide beach, and a few early-bird surfers were riding the waves.

Marc and I found a bench, and Marc told me that the UN representative in Libertaria had contacted Suresh Shrivastav's agent. The prospector had just departed for the star 2M 4962, and according to his agent he had nothing to say to the UN.

"It may be an attempt to force us to negotiate, but as long as we find the code it does not matter, Marc said. "As for that, I have also contacted our representative in the Terminus system. I regret there is no positive news there, either. There are two belts of rocks around Terminus. The people who live there, farmers all of them, live on the inner belt. And their traffic control system is pretty rudimentary. Regrettably, it doesn't not extend to the outer belt, and there is no evidence that Sarkka's ship has visited the system."

"It doesn't mean that he didn't go there."

"That's true."

"Or that he might not be there right now."

"That is also possible."

"In any case, the original of the code will still be there. If Sarkka or that prospector hasn't already destroyed it."

"Now we come to the heart of the matter," Marc said. "It is not Niles Sarkka, of course, but the code. There have been political developments. The Inspector General has been informed. And it appears that the Jackaroo have become interested."

I felt a beat of foolish excitement. "It's really that serious?"

"They think so. They studied the code and said it was very bad stuff. Do you remember Thor V?"

"That farming family who took off into the big black," I said.

They had stumbled onto code that had infected them with a meme. Seized by its ancient imperative, they'd climbed aboard their ships and headed out into interstellar space. They are still falling through space, a light year from their star now, out of reach, out of fuel and power, their ships and everyone on board them dead.

Marc said, "The Jackaroo claim that Hughes's code may have a similar effect on anyone who interacts with it, and there is a nasty twist: it is slowburning, so those infected have time to infect others. And those who become infected but are unable to reach a ship will become insane. The Inspector General has authorised a strike team to travel to Terminus. I have argued successfully that our department should remain involved. So, let me ask you formally. Are you willing to volunteer to accompany the strike team?"

"I've already thought about this, boss. There's nothing I'd like better."

"Of course. Now, I want you to go home and change your clothes, pack for a long voyage, and make any necessary personal arrangements. Find me in my office in four hours. That is when we are to meet with the Inspector General."

The Jackaroo are supposed to keep out of human affairs. They don't, of course. The software we now use to interface with code is a case in point. An important one, because it had established a precedent. It's derived from code that migrated from the wreck of a spaceship into a colony of hive rats in the vast necropolis in the western desert. The biologist studying them enlisted a mathematician to help her decode the hive rats' complex dances, and the mathematician quickly realised that they were exchanging massive amounts of information—that the colony was acting as a parallel processing computer.

All this is well known. What has been suppressed (until now—and I have good reason to break cover, as you'll see) was the fact that the code had drawn the attention of the Jackaroo. An avatar pitched up with a bunch of hired goons and tried to kill the biologist and destroy the hive-rat colony. The Jackaroo claimed afterwards that it was the action of a rogue element, and we had to pretend to believe them. In any case, the biologist and a local law enforcement officer fought back. The goons were killed and avatar was destroyed. I became involved a little later. The law enforcement officer had picked up a piece of kit that the avatar had been using. It not only tracked and disrupted q-phone signals, but could eavesdrop on them. We bought the technology from her, and in exchange she agreed to keep quiet about the avatar.

After that incident the UN and the Jackaroo made an informal agreement to cooperate when it came to suppressing potentially dangerous technology. That is what I had walked into, when Marc took up to the Inspector General's big, wood-panelled office.

The Inspector General, a small but imperious blond woman in her sixties, shook my hand and told me that from now on I was operating under Section D, but I paid scant attention to her. I was staring at the man-shaped figure that stood off to one side. A showroom dummy woven from a single giant molecule of metal-doped polymer, dressed in a black suit and white shirt and polished black shoes. A proxy for a creature no human had ever seen, linked by a version of q-phone technology to an operator who could be anywhere in the universe. Moving now, stepping towards me and greeting me in a newsreader's rich baritone.

"We have followed Dr Sarkka's career with great interest," it said. "And this is a very interesting turn of events."

"A potentially serious turn of events," the Inspector General said. "Sarkka is a dangerous man, and he may be about to lay his hands on dangerous code."

"We have examined the damaged code," the avatar said. "What was deleted presents a clear danger to you. We are here to help."

"And we're grateful, of course," the Inspector General said.

The avatar responded with a lengthy speech, telling us that the Jackaroo were grateful for the UN's cooperation and for my role in helping to heal a potentially difficult rift; how this was a fine example of the harmonic convergence of the Jackaroo and the human race; how the present small difficulty would be quickly overcome by application of that same cooperation in general, and my talents in particular, and so on and so forth—I won't bore you. It was the usual mashup of cliches, mixed metaphors and orotund sentiment, like a mission statement for some multinational company written by committee and run through a computer which had scrupulously removed any trace of originality, human feeling and passion. The experts are still arguing, and will probably argue forever, about whether the Jackaroos' communications and conversations are classic examples of Chinese Room AI simulations of human thought patterns, or cleverly misleading simulations of Chinese Room AI simulations of human thought patterns. As someone who has been on the receiving end of one of their perorations, I can tell you that the distinction doesn't matter. As far as I was concerned, all that mattered was that it was so relentlessly dull that it was almost impossible to keep track of what was being said. It would have sent anyone not wired to the eyeballs on caffeine and amphetamine to sleep had it not been for one thing: it was delivered by a genuine alien through a machine of unknown powers.

And so, despite the soporific blanket of the avatar's bland and lengthy blandishments, I was gripped by an electric, barely suppressed terror, and I'm certain that Marc and the Inspector General felt the same way. For despite their best intentions—or because of them—you can't help but be paranoid about the Jackaroo. They are alien and therefore completely opaque. Neither angels nor devils, but distorting mirrors that reflect our best hopes and worst fears.

"May I ask a question?" I said, when it had finished, or at least run out of words. "If you're offering to help us, what kind of help are we talking about?"

"We are here to advise, nothing more," the avatar said. "After all, we do not want to reveal that we are helping you. It would violate the terms of our agreement. However, we may be able to locate Dr Sarkka's ship, should it use a wormhole again, and we do not see a problem with passing on that information."

The Inspector General chipped in again, said that the Jackaroo usually refrained from direct interference, but because this was an unusual and highly alarming case, they would utilise a little-known property of the wormhole throats to identify any used by Sarkka's ship. They had already confirmed that Sarkka had visited Terminus, and because he had not returned through that system's only wormhole, he must still be there. Our first priority was to find, identify, and destroy the code. Our second was to track down Hughes and Sarkka, and if it came to it, we would try to purchase the mirror of the code from them.

The Inspector General mentioned a ceiling limit that exceeded the GDPs of several countries back on Earth. "We have no intention of paying Sarkka of course. He will be arrested for murder as soon as he tries to collect. Hopefully, he will have become infected before then, and will have aimed his ship at some damned star or other."

"It is possible," the avatar said. "But we cannot count on it because the incubation period is variable."

I saw a big flaw in the plan at once: Niles Sarkka wasn't stupid, and would guess that my offer was bogus. And in any case, if the code promised to validate his theory he wouldn't part with it for any amount of money. But I didn't raise any objections—as I've already explained, I believed that summary justice was better than letting Niles Sarkka gain power over dangerous code. When the Inspector General asked me if I needed time to think about this, I said that I already had thought about it, and would gladly accept.

It was almost not untrue.

"They have been manipulating us from the very beginning, Emma. Playing with us as a child plays with white mice in a cage. And they have been watching us a very long time. They know things about us that we do not know. They sit in judgement beyond ordinary human plight or perception. But they do not know everything. Their survey of our comings and goings on Earth and everywhere else is not omniscient. That is why we will escape their chains. And that is why we are here, you and I."

It's two in the morning. Everyone on the ship asleep except for the maintenance robots puttering about their inscrutable business beyond our encampment, the three men and women of the night watch, and me. I'm trying to make a cup of green tea with one hand while holding the q-phone's handset in the other, listening to for the tenth or twelfth time a variant of Niles Sarkka's standard lecture on the Jackaroo and their fiendish plans and plots.

I said, "They knew about Hughes and Singleton. They knew about the code."

"No, Emma. They intercepted q-phone messages between me and a friend in Port of Plenty who was acting as go-between. They did not know what the code was, or where it came from because poor Everett and Jason did not know what it was, and they wouldn't tell me where the original was located until we had concluded our dealings face to face and quit First Foot."

"Even so, they tracked you to Terminus."

"Did they? They lied about the nature of the code. Perhaps they lied about that, too. They do not know everything, and they lie. If they are gods, they are petty and spiteful gods. I don't know about you, but even at its lowest, I don't think that humanity deserves gods as low and base as them. No, we aspire to greater things. Why else would we have come all this way, you and I?"

"I'm here to bring you to justice, Niles. You know that."

"You're here because of your nature, Emma. You're here because you want to be here. You see, you aren't very different from me after all."

I was brought up short by his assertion, but shrugged it off with a quip about this not being in any way the destination I'd anticipated when I'd left First Foot, and he didn't make any more of it, went back to his interminable dissection of conspiracies and secret histories. I mention it here because I think he's wrong. Oh, there's no doubt that we have some things in common. Particularly our obsession with seeing things through to the end no matter what the cost. But this is overshadowed by a fundamental difference.

I stand on the right side, and he does not.

We left, the strike team and I, in a Q-class scout, a small ship that resembled a cartoon toadstool: a fat cone containing the lifesystem, with the teardrop-shaped stalk of the fusion motor pod depending from its centre. The lifesystem's interior was a roughly oval chamber partitioned by mesh platforms and furnished with bunk beds, a pair of porta-potty toilets and a shower pod like a dingy plastic egg, picnic tables and an industrial microwave, commercial chest freezers and rows of steel storage lockers. All in all, it was about as glamorous as a low-rent bomb shelter or the accommodation module of an oil platform, except that the scalloped nooks and crannies of its walls were a perfect hollow cast of the whale-sized agglomeration that had once filled it—the Ghajar had been colonial creatures that exchanged biological modular parts amongst themselves as easily as we changed clothes, each one a different shape and size from all the rest.

Like all ships, ours was a strictly point-and-click operation. Apart from a package of solid-fuel motors for fine manoeuvres strapped around the lifesystem's circumference, most of the ship's systems, especially the fusion motor, were sealed, enigmatic, inaccessible. Our pilot, a slender, athletic New Zealander, Sally McKenzie, typed a command string into the laptop that interfaced with the ship's navigation package, and the ship boosted itself out of orbit and aimed itself at the pair of wormhole throats that orbited the trailing Lagrangian point of the system's methane gas giant.

All wormhole throats look the same, a round black mirror a little over a kilometre across, framed by the ring that housed the braid of strange matter that keeps it open and embedded in a rock sheared flat on one side and shaped and polished to a smooth cone behind, shaped and set in place millions of years ago by the nameless and forgotten Elder Culture that created the network. There were two in First Foot's system, one leading to the Solar System, the other to a red dwarf star some twenty thousand light years away, at the outer edge of the Scutum-Centaurus Arm of the Galaxy. That's the one we dropped through.

I sat with Sally McKenzie during the transit, watching on the HD screen as with startling speed Wormhole #2 grew from a glint to a speck to a three-dimensional object, the round black mirror of its throat flying at the screen, filling it. And then, without any sense of transition, we were out on the far side, falling around the nightside of a hot super-Jupiter. The red dwarf sun rose above the vast curve of the planet like a moon set afire, and the ship drove on towards the next wormhole throat, sixty degrees around the orbit it shared with the wormhole we'd just exited.

It had taken more than two days to reach the wormholes in First Foot's system, but took just two hours to swing around the super-Jupiter to catch up with the next one, plunging through it and emerging close to a dim brown dwarf that orbited a red dwarf star little brighter, glimmering like a dot of blood against the great dark shoulder of the Horsehead Nebula. The ship broke orbit and swung out towards a sombre ice giant and after three days at maximum acceleration plunged into the solitary wormhole that orbited it.

And so on, and so on.

Via q-phone, Marc kept me up to date with the code farm investigation. It seemed that Natasha Wu had fitted a video camera into the bedroom of her apartment ("A girl can never be too careful."), and it had caught the two goons who had broken in and trashed the place while searching for the code farm archives. Both were in custody inside a day, and both turned out to be linked, via DNA trace evidence, to no less than seven unsolved murders. One of them quickly decided to take up Marc's offer of immunity from prosecution and sang about everything he knew, including the kidnap and murder of Meyer Lansky and his family: more than enough to take down Pak Jung-Hin. Apparently, the dead ex-soldier, Abuelo Baez, had been a freelance who'd done several enforcement jobs for Meyer Lansky, specialising in 'debt recovery'. The goon didn't know if Baez had been sent after Jason Singleton and Everett Hughes, but Marc believed that it seemed likely. We still weren't sure what had gone down in the motel room, but it looked as if Lansky's man had caught up with the two coders, Everett Hughes had escaped, and Niles Sarkka had been involved in some kind of confrontation that had left both Jason Singleton and Abuelo Baez dead.

The young captain and the six soldiers of the strike team passed the time stripping and reassembling their weapons, swapping war stories, immersed in virtual simulations of various actions, watching videos, and sleeping. They slept a lot, like big predators with full bellies whiling away the time until the next meal. My presence seemed to make them uncomfortable, no doubt because I wielded authority outside their chain of command, but I found the pilot, Sally McKenzie, a congenial companion. She'd been a colonel in the New Zealand Air Force during the war, had won a ticket on the emigration lottery three years ago, shortly after she'd been retired from active service. Now she was a spaceship pilot, eager to see everything the fifteen stars had to offer. She told me stories about dogfights over the Weddell Sea and the

Antarctic Peninsula; I told her sanitised versions of various investigations I'd been involved in.

And so we moved from wormhole throat to wormhole throat, a chain that passed through six star systems until we reached our destination, the star 2CR 5938, otherwise known as Terminus. So-called because there was only one wormhole throat orbiting it. One way in, one way back out. The end of the line.

It was a dim red dwarf freckled with big sunspots. The bright filamentous arc of a flare bridged one edge of its disc from equator to pole. It was partnered with a G0 star that shone a little over a tenth of a light year away, only a little less bright than the dozens of hot young stars that were beginning to burn through a tattered veil of luminous gas that slanted across half the sky.

The red dwarf was circled by two concentric belts of asteroids: rubble left from ancient collisions of protoplanets, prevented from accreting into larger bodies by the gravitational interference of the hot and dense super-Jupiter that orbited between them. Our ship fell towards the outermost belt, at the edge of Terminus's habitable zone.

The UN representative had already reached an agreement with the reef farmers' council, which had sensibly agreed to keep away for fear of infection with the meme that the Jackaroo had warned us about. Our destination was an undistinguished worldlet amongst ten thousand such. Unequally bilobed like a peanut, an agglomeration of basaltic rocks heated and partly melted by successive shock fronts that had driven the orbital migration of the super-Jupiter, afterwards lightly cratered by impacts with debris left over from the formation of thousands of others like it and mantled in a layer of dust and pebbly chondrules. It had orbited Terminus for more than seven billion years, undisturbed by anything except the occasional minor impact, until some nameless Elder Culture had planoformed it, injecting into its centre of mass a spoonful of collapsium, exotic dark matter denser than neutronium that gave it a pull averaging a little less than the Moon's gravity, wrapping it in a bubble of quasiliving polymer that kept in a scanty atmosphere of oxygen, nitrogen and argon, landscaping it, seeding it with life.

Scores of tenants had come and gone since then. Some leaving no trace of their occupation apart from subtle changes in the isotopic composition of the worldlet's atmosphere and biosphere; others adding species of plants and microbes to its patchwork ecology; the most recent leaving ruins. Ghosts had riddled it with pits and shafts. Boxbuilders had left chains of crumbling cells stretched here and there on top of ridges and around the edges of eroded craters. Spiders had parked a small asteroid in stationary orbit above its nipped waist and spun a cable, woven from diamond and fullerene and studded with basket-weave habitats, down to its surface. And a few thousand years ago, a spaceship of the Ghajar had crashed at the pole.

Despite its deep history, the little worldlet was a bleak and marginal environment, cold as Arctic tundra before global warming, sheeted with ice and snow, black bacterial crusts and cushion algae growing in sheltered niches in the equatorial rift, cotton trees floating in the air like clouds spun from pale wire. Unnamed and unexplored by humans, until some prospector had stumbled onto code still active in the wreckage of the crashed ship.

As the ship made its final approach, the strike team launched a drone rocket that sped ahead of us and dumped three baseball-sized spy satellites in orbit around the worldlet. They soon located the ancient crash site, an oval impact crater under the snow cap at the pole of the larger of the worldlet's two lobes, with traces of metal spattered around it that showed as a spray of bright dots in the sideways radar scans. And their high-definition cameras also picked up a tiny source of heat and an ordinary blue camping tent at the worldlet's equator, close to the base of the spider cable.

The young captain who commanded the strike team, Jude Foster, told Sally McKenzie to establish an equatorial orbit and ordered his soldiers to get ready to make a crash entry. Apparently, using the elevators of the Spider cable was out of the question: they were too slow, and anyone on the surface would have plenty of time to prepare an ambush.

"This is an eccentric scholar and a coder barely out of his teens," I said. "Hardly a major threat to your people."

"Surely you have not forgotten that your "eccentric scholar" is wanted for homicide, Inspector," Captain Foster said with wintery condescension. "And in any case, a whole crew of malcontents might be concealed down there. It is my duty to take appropriate precautions."

Like me, Captain Foster was a Brit: pale, blond, and laconic, also startlingly young and eager to prove himself on his first real action. We had a brief discussion about whether or not I should accompany the strike team on their crash entry or wait aboard the ship until they had secured a perimeter around the base of the cable. I prevailed. I freely confess that I was scared silly, but I was determined to do my duty.

Sally McKenzie helped me dress in a pressure suit, and one of the soldiers towed me across the flank of the lifesystem to the cargo pod where the scooters were stored. I rode pillion behind Captain Foster; the soldiers rode three scooters flanking us. They were crude hybrids, the scooters—quad bike frames perched on the skinny tank of a LOX booster, with two pairs of big fans set fore and aft to give them lift in atmosphere—but they were fast and manoeuvrable. The worldlet swelled ahead and we burst through its sky membrane simultaneously, riding through a sudden buffeting wind, sliding down fingers of red sunlight that slanted at a shallow angle across kilometres of air. Cotton trees caught in the raw sunlight exploded like popcorn kernels, spewing tangles of tough threads, creating mats hundreds of metres across that caught in the gales of leaking atmosphere and sailed past us and smacked against the holes we'd punched in the skin of the sky.

Our scooters dodged the last of the mats and swooped down in wedge formation. The surface of the tiny world hurtled towards us, white ice patched with bare black rock curving away on all sides, the spider cable's dark tower rising towards the bronze sky. One of the soldiers whooped over the common channel. I felt like whooping, too. I was dizzy with fright and exhilaration.

Details exploded out of the landscape as we headed in towards the rift valley that girdled the equator. We skimmed across a lip of bare rock strung with Boxbuilder ruins, hollow cells mostly roofless, and dropped past sheer cliffs towards the black blister where the cable socketed into the floor of the wide valley. The valley's floor was cut by low wrinkle ridges and short crevasses jagged as lightning bolts; some of the crevasses were flooded with frozen lakes and shone like shards of broken mirrors. Scrub and low patches of thorn trees grew everywhere between the lakes, a waist-high krumnmerholz forest. I glimpsed a flash of blue at the tip of a long thin lake and then the landscape tilted and my insides were scooped hollow with vertigo as the captain swung the scooter around and brought it down with a jarring bounce.

A man stood beside an ordinary blue nylon camping tent pitched at the lake shore. He was dressed in boots and jeans and a black puffa jacket, raising his hands as the soldiers advanced towards him from two sides. I fell to my knees when I climbed off the scooter, dizzy, grinning like a fool, and pushed up and followed as best I could, unbalanced by the low gravity and the encumbrance of my pressure suit. The ground was carpeted with stuff a little like moss, a thick lace of bladder-filled filaments the colour of old blood that crunched and popped under my boots. Beyond the lake and a steep ridge, the cable sliced the sky in half.

Captain Foster, bulky as a fairytale knight in his white pressure suit, pistol clamped in his gauntlet, marched up to the man and told him to kneel and clamp his hands on top of his head. The man—it was Everett Hughes, black hair falling over a face as pale as paper—obeyed a little clumsily, saying, "There's no need for this. I'll tell you everything."

I said, "Where is Niles Sarkka?"

Captain Foster said, "Are you alone?"

"Niles is long gone," Everett Hughes said. "He's on his way to history."

I insisted on carrying out an immediate field interrogation, recorded by an autonomous drone and witnessed by Captain Foster. I wanted to find out what had happened on the worldlet, I wanted to find out where Niles Sarkka had gone and with what intent, and I wanted it to stand up in court. I was still thinking like that, then.

Despite his getup as the ultimate badass coder—an unruly mane of hair dyed jet-black, silver rings sewn around the rim of his right ear and a skull ring on a chain around his neck, tattoos on his neck and fingers, the leather vest and white ruffled shirt under his black puffa jacket, the tight blue jeans and the cowboy boots—Hughes was young and naive. He told us that we'd find a q-phone in the tent, that Sarkka possessed its entangled twin.

"If you want to know what happened, and why it happened, you should call him. He can explain everything much better than I can."

His calmness wasn't anything to do with bravery; it was compounded of youthful arrogance and sheer ignorance. He really didn't understand how much trouble he was in. He refused to acknowledge that he had been used, abused, and dumped by Niles Sarkka, believed to the end that he and Sarkka had done the right thing, and was proud to have helped him.

What I'm trying to say is that although he appeared to be cooperative, everything he told us was coloured by his loyalty to Sarkka. I don't offer this as an excuse for what happened, but that's why I allowed it to happen. Because I thought that Hughes was only telling some of the truth, some of the time, and because he refused to give up crucial information. Sarkka had poisoned that young man's mind. He's as much to blame for what happened as anyone else.

In any case, Captain Foster and I agreed that we would defer the pleasure of a conversation with Niles Sarkka until we had learned everything we could from Everett Hughes. And to begin with, the interrogation went smoothly enough. We did it in the tent, Hughes perched on a camping stool, Captain Foster and I looming over him in our pressure suits, the drone hovering at my left shoulder. Hughes readily admitted that, as I'd suspected, he and Jason Singleton hadn't tried to mirror the code; instead, they'd hacked into the database of the code farm, discovered where the code had come from, and then erased the code and every bit of data pertaining to it. When I told him that it was too bad for him that Meyer Lansky had kept duplicate records in his home, he shrugged and said he'd factored the possibility into his plans.

"I figured Lansky wouldn't tell you about them because it would have meant admitting to all his black market deals. And I reckoned that even if you did manage to get your hands on them, it would take some time, because you couldn't just go in and search his place, you'd have to get all the papers in order and so on. Time enough for Niles and me to get out here and do what we needed to do."

He said that he'd deleted the code because Lansky insisted that every chunk should be checked by three different people, and he knew that the next guy in the line would have seen what it was, and what it meant. And then, because they were worried that their tampering would be discovered, he and Jason Singleton had gone into hiding before reaching out to Niles Sarkka.

"As soon as I laid eyes on that code, I knew that Niles Sarkka was the man to go to. It took a while to contact him, though. And then he had to have us checked out, in case we were part of some kind of law enforcement trap. While all this was going on, a guy employed by Lansky tracked down where Jay and me were hiding out. I don't know how, exactly, but Jay had a girlfriend—you didn't know? I guess there's a lot you didn't know. Anyhow, I reckon Jay called her one last time, right around when we were getting ready to leave, and the call was intercepted. Maybe the guy had bugged her line, or maybe he'd broken into her place and was waiting for Jay to show. I hope not, I liked her. In any case, the guy turned up at the room while I was meeting up with Niles. Jay managed to lock himself in the bathroom and phone me, and Niles said he'd deal with it. Said that because of what I knew, I wasn't to put my life in danger. He had a gun—he'd taken a risk coming back to Port of Plenty, he had enemies there. So he took off, and we met an hour later, and he told me Jay was dead. That was bad enough. But he also told me that a Jackaroo avatar had been there. The guy working for Lansky was dead, it must have followed him and killed him, and it was bent over Jay. Doing something to him. Niles shot it, and it exploded and the room caught fire, and Niles couldn't get to Jay. He said that Jay was already dead, there was nothing he could do."

"Bullshit," I said. "Sarkka spun you a story, Everett. I'll tell you how I know. Your friend had particles of soot in his lungs. That means that he was still alive when he burned to death. There was no avatar. Sarkka killed Lansky's man with some kind of beam weapon, it set fire to the room, and Sarkka let your friend burn to death rather than risk his own life trying to save him."

"Niles told me there was an avatar, and I believe him," Hughes said, looking straight at me. "And not only because he wouldn't lie to me about something like that. There was a break-in at the code farm after we contacted Niles. You know how hard it is, to break into the place? Almost impossible. But someone did it—or *something* did. Something that heard that we had special code we wanted to hand over to Niles. Something that went to check out what it was we'd taken."

I told him that I knew about the break-in, but his assumption that the Jackaroo had been involved in it was a fantasy. And I told him, trying to get at him through sympathy, that I understood why he believed it. "You feel guilty about what happened to your friend. Of course you do. But you have to face the truth, Everett. The truth is that Sarkka killed your friend. And the only reason he didn't kill you is because he needed your help when it came to mirroring and using the code."

I was doing the right thing, chipping away at Hughes's misplaced loyalty, trying to isolate him. But he refused to admit that he was in the wrong and became stubborn, saying, "I shouldn't have left Jay in that room when I went to meet Niles. He wanted to, in case something went wrong, but I shouldn't have done it. And I'm going to have to carry that for the rest of my life. So yeah, I feel guilty. But I'm not making any of this shit up. And if Niles is such a bad guy, like you claim, let me ask you something. How come he didn't kill me after we mirrored the code and I ran it through his nav package?"

Captain Foster cut in at that point, and his interference made things worse. "You admit that you located the original of the code, you and Sarkka. And you mirrored it."

"Well, yes. We didn't come out to this miserable ball of rock and ice for the skiing, that's for sure. We mirrored it and then we destroyed the original. I'll show you where."

"The code is a dangerous meme," Captain Foster said. "You are probably infected with it. Mr. Sarkka too."

Hughes laughed. "You really believe it, don't you? That's why you're still wearing your pressure suits I bet. Well, I don't know who told you that bullshit, but that's what it is. Bullshit. Niles isn't infected. Nor am I. And the code, it's no meme. I already knew what it was when I came across it, although I didn't know where it pointed, not until we mirrored it here, and plugged the copy into the nav package of Niles's ship. I *know* code," Hughes said, tapping his temple with his forefinger. "I have this knack. Show me any code, I can tell whether or not it's viable, whether it's intact, what it needs to run. People like me know how to make use of all the strange and wild and wonderful stuff that's lying around out here. We should be hailed as heroes. We should be encouraged. Instead, pygmies like you try to tie us down with rules and regulations. You want to make ordinary human curiosity illegal. You want to control people's imaginations."

He was parroting something Niles Sarkka had told him, no doubt, trying to get a rise out of me. When I told him that the code was dangerous and had to be secured at once, he shook his head and said again that the code wasn't any kind of meme.

"I knew, as soon as I laid eyes on it, what that code was. I knew it was information, embedded in a navigation package. And you know what, *I was right.*"

I could see that he wouldn't be shifted on that point, so I backed off and tried another angle. "Niles Sarkka took the code and ran off and left you here. Not a great deal, was it?"

Hughes shrugged. "I volunteered to be stranded. The ship doesn't have enough consumables for two."

"He could have taken you to one of the farms on the inner belt."

"He was going to contact them, once he got far enough away. Then they'd come and pick me up."

"How do you know that Sarkka didn't leave you here to die, and went off to Libertaria to sell the code?"

Hughes laughed. "You think this is about money? Jason and me, we didn't get into this for money. The code is way more important than that. It isn't an executable. It's information. The kind of information that the Jackaroo wiped from all the navigation programmes of all the ships in all the known Sargassos. But they don't know everything. They missed the code in the wrecked ship out in the City of the Dead, for instance, the code that gave us the interface. And they missed the code here. And that gave Niles and me the location of something wonderful. Something that will help us win the war."

"We aren't at war with them, Mr. Hughes."

"Aren't we?"

There was something chilling and certain in his gaze. Oh, Sarkka had sunk his claws in deep, all right.

I said, "Tell me what you think the code is."

"Records, kind of. Where the ship had come from. The location of something. We don't know, exactly. That's why Niles has gone to check it out."

"Mr. Sarkka could have taken you to the farmers of the inner belt. He could have asked for their help in searching for whatever it is he hopes to find. Instead, he marooned you here. Why? Because of vanity and greed. He wants the glory for himself, and he wants the profit, too."

"I volunteered to stay," Hughes said. "If Niles stranded me here, why would he have left a q-phone here? And if you don't believe me, why don't you give him a call?"

I told him that it was no kind of evidence that he and Sarkka were equal partners. "Sarkka left it here because he wants to boast about his deeds."

"Talk to him. See what he has to say," Hughes said.

"He left you here to die, Everett. And went off to Libertaria to sell the code."

Hughes laughed. "You're obsessed with money. Jason and me, we didn't sell it to Niles. We *gave* it to him."

He really believed that Niles Sarkka had done the right thing. That they were still, in some way, partners. That Sarkka was on the track of something wonderful: something that would change history. He led the soldiers and me to the location of the original of the code, about a kilometre from the impact crater on top of the larger of the worldlet's two lobes, showed us the shaft dug by the prospector who had originally found it, showed us the smashed and scorched pieces of wreckage that, according to him, had once contained the code, and told us a cock and bull story about how it had been discovered. Certainly, there were traces of code still embedded in those shards, although it was impossible to tell whether they had ever been active, and Hughes refused once again to tell us what the code really was, where Niles Sarkka had gone, and what Sarkka hoped to find.

And that's where the trouble began. It was Captain Foster's idea to ramp up the interrogation, and God help me, I went along with it. We were in the middle of a difficult and dangerous situation, we needed to know everything about it, and because our only witness refused to help us we had to coerce him. It was vital to our security and we needed to know everything he knew right away.

So we cuffed Hughes and made him kneel, right there on the cold black naked rock by the shaft. I explained what we were going to do and told him that he had one last chance: if he answered all of our questions truthfully, if he talked willingly and without reservation, he would be able to walk away from this as a hero. He told me what to do with my offer in language you can imagine. And one of the solders gripped his head while Captain Foster, delicately pinching the plastic straw between two fingers of his pressure suit's glove, puffed a dose of Veracidin up his nose.

Veracidin is derived from Elder Culture nanotechnology. A suspension of virus-sized machines that enter the bloodstream and cross the blood/brain barrier, targeting specific areas in the cortex, supressing specific higher cogntive functions. In short, it is a sophisticated truth drug. Its use is illegal on Earth and First Foot, but we were in the field, in the equivalent of a battle situation. We did what we had to do, and we didn't know—how could we?—that Everett Hughes would suffer a violent reaction when the swarm of tiny machines hit his brain.

Perhaps he was naturally allergic to Veracidin, as a very small percentage of people are. Or perhaps the many, many hours of exposure to code had sensitised him somehow. Within seconds, his eyes rolled back in his head and his body convulsed with what appeared to be a grand mal seizure. He jerked and spasmed and drooled bloody foam; he lost control of his bowels and bladder. We laid him on the ground and did our best, but the seizures came one after the other. His heart stopped, and we got it going again. We managed to wrestle him into the pod carried by one of the scooters, and we all took off for the ship, hoping to treat him there. But he was still fitting, and he died in transit.

Captain Foster was badly shaken by Hughes' death and wanted to bug out for home. Hughes's body was in a sealed casket; the original of the code had been located and confirmed destroyed; there was nothing else for us to do but write a report that would justify our actions and absolve us of any blame. I told him that we were not finished here because Niles Sarkka was still at large, and in possession of a mirror of the code. He had not gone through the wormhole throat, or else we would have been alerted, so there was still a chance of catching up with him. If we did, I said, we would be completely exonerated; if not, I would take full responsibility for Hughes's death.

I already had a good idea about where Sarkka might be headed, and put in a call to our representative with the farmers of the inner belt, asked him if anyone there was an amateur astronomer. Within an hour, I'd been sent a photograph taken through a five-inch reflector, showing a new, small star a few degrees from the crucifix flare of Terminus's G0 companion. Sarkka's ship without a doubt.

Captain Foster said that we had no chance of catching up with Sarkka. He had too much of a head start, and in any case we didn't have enough fuel to put up any kind of chase. "We don't even know that he'd headed for that star. He's infected. The meme is urging him to flee outward, towards no particular destination."

I said that Hughes showed no sign of infection, and in any case, if Sarkka was gripped by a blind outward urge, why was he headed directly for the star?

"You have that q-phone," Captain Foster said. "Why don't you ask him?"

"Oh, I will. In good time."

I was beginning to formulate what I needed to do. I didn't like it, but I couldn't see any other way to bring this case to a satisfactory resolution, and bring Niles Sarkka to justice.

And so we headed for the inner belt, and a meeting with the farmers' council. They said that they knew nothing about Suresh Shrivastav, the prospector who'd found the code, claimed that he'd been working the outer belt illegally. For what it's worth, I believe them. That kind of piracy is increasingly common, and it would explain why Mr. Shrivastav refused to talk to us. The farmers also said that they had known nothing about the little expedition mounted by Sarkka and Hughes, and made it clear that they resented the UN's intrusion into their affairs, and the danger to which their people had been unknowingly exposed. Luckily, I found an ally in the council's chair, Rajo Hiranand, a tough, cynical, and highly intelligent old woman. Her motivations were not entirely selfless—she wanted her community to share in whatever profit might be made from whatever it was that Niles Sarkka might discover—but her heart was in the right place.

"I would guess that this is the end of your career with the UN," she said, after the vote to accept my offer of help had been won. "After all this is over, when you get back, we might be able to find a place for someone like you here."

I thanked her, but admitted that spending the rest of my life herding sky-sheep and growing corn and pharm tobacco was low on the list of things I wanted to do with my life.

"That isn't all we do here," Rajo said. "Think about it. You'll have plenty of time for that, after all."

"Before I do anything else," I said, "I have to explain this to my boss."

It was a call I had been dreading. Rightly so. The q-phone that linked me to its entangled twin relayed with perfect fidelity Marc Godin's cold anger across uncountable light years, directly to my ear and brain and heart. I knew there was no point in apologising, and besides, I agreed with his assessment of the situation. The mission was fubared, and although

I had been volunteered for the mission by the Inspector General, I was acting senior officer, and by resigning I was contributing a few extra knots to the intractably complicated tangle of diplomatic and legal problems. But it still hurts grievously to think of how Marc severed every bond, ignored my years of loyal service, and refused to acknowledge the sacrifice I was making.

When he was finished, I asked for a final favour. "Have Varneek do a trace analysis on the burned-out motel room. Have him look for any unusual material. If he finds anything, have him compare it with the fragments from the avatar that was destroyed in the hive rat nest in the City of the Dead."

"Sarkka was lying, Emma. There was no avatar. He killed Singleton and the mercenary."

"I could ask the city police to look into it. But given the diplomatic angle, I think it would be better if you did."

"I hope that is not a threat," Marc said, finding a new depth of Antarctic chill.

"I don't want to go public with this. Too much information has already spilled out. But this is too important to ignore."

"The Jackaroo would not breach the accord," he said.

"We don't know what they would do," I said, and would have said more, but he cut the connection then.

He called back the next day. I was aboard the largest of the farmers' ships by then, and Terminus was dwindling astern. Varneek had failed to find any fragments, Marc said, but he had found traces of fused silica and traces of doped fullerenes and an exotic room-temperature superconductor.

"Are they from an avatar?"

"If they were not, I could tell you. As it is, I can neither confirm nor deny that the traces Varneek found in the room matched the fragments of the avatar already in our possession."

So I had my answer.

"It won't make any difference," Marc said, after I thanked him. "Even if we'd caught the avatar with blood on its hands, nothing would have been done beyond lodging a formal protest. Because the accord is useful to us. Because no one wishes to disturb our relationship with the Jackaroo."

I told him I understood, and asked about the search for the prospector, Suresh Shrivastav.

"The investigation has been closed. I'm sorry, Emma. Even if you capture Sarkka, it won't save your career."

"This isn't about my career."

"In any case, good hunting," Marc said, and cut the connection.

And now, six months later, we are chasing Niles Sarkka's ship towards the coal-black gas giant. He's just a couple of million kilometres ahead of us and, as we have long suspected, will soon enter into orbit. We caught up with him because we continued to accelerate after his ship turned around and began to slow. Now we must shed excess delta-vee by dipping into the outer fringes of the gas giant's atmosphere, an aerobrake manoeuver that will subject the ship's frame to stresses at the outer limits of its tolerance.

The farmers' ship isn't equipped for a thorough planetary survey, but the instruments we've been able to cobble together during this long chase have not detected any source of electromagnetic radiation apart from the pulse of the planet's magnetic field, and limited optical surveys have failed to spot any trace of artificial structures on any of the moons. Which does not mean that there isn't anything there. Absence of evidence is not evidence of absence. Our survey capabilities grievously are limited, and if Niles Sarkka is right, if this is where the last remnant of the Ghajar or some other Elder culture is hiding out, it won't want to be found.

And if the code has given Sarkka the precise location of some base or spider hole, we'll be right on his tail. Fortunately, he's no more than a point-and-go pilot. It's obvious now that he didn't do anything to counter our tactic because he wasn't able to. With the end of the chase in sight, I'm beginning to feel that we have a chance of catching him before he can do any real harm.

I think he knows that the game is up. That's why he has been trying to make a deal with me, and by extension with Rajo Hiranand and the rest of the farmers' council. In our first conversations, he assumed moral and intellectual superiority, claimed that his actions should be judged by history rather than by mere mortals. Now, he's offering to share the greatest discovery since the Jackaroos' fluttering ships appeared in Earth's skies.

"A straight fifty-fifty split, Emma," he tells me, as we cross the orbit of the gas giant's outermost moon. "I can't do better than that."

"Fifty per cent of nothing is nothing, Niles."

"I will find them. They led me here, after all."

Niles Sarkka claims that he talked to Suresh Shrivastav before he left Libertaria to meet with Everett Hughes and Jason Singleton on First foot. He says that the prospector told him that he hadn't stumbled on the code by chance. No, he'd been heading home after searching a couple of worldlets in Terminus's outer belt when he'd detected a brief, transitory pulse of broad-spectrum radio noise—a squeal like a God's own fire alarm, he said. It had grabbed his attention and he'd swung around and made landfall on the worldlet and hiked across its arctic surface to the crash site, following a faint but steady pulse. No other code has ever been so marked, and Niles Sarkka is convinced that someone or something led Shrivastav to it. Not the Jackaroo, but one of the Elder Cultures. He also believes, without a shred of evidence, that this Elder Culture wants us to find them. That they want to help us, and tell us all they know about the plans of the Jackaroo, and the true history of the wormhole network.

I've told many times that I think that this story is nothing more than a fabulous fiction, and I tell him that again now, adding, just to needle him, "If there is something out there, how about we take all of it, and send you to jail?"

"You have to tell the farmers about my offer, Emma. You are obligated, as their guest. Also, you should tell your bosses back on First foot, too. Talk to all parties concerned, why don't you, and get back to me."

Well, I don't want to talk to my boss, of course. I'm in deep trouble with the UN, and haven't been in communication with Marc Godin or any other UN official since the chase began. But I call Rajo and tell her about my latest conversation with Niles, and his offer, and she says that she must consult with the council. Fortunately, it doesn't take long.

"We are not varying our agreement," Rajo says. "We will capture him, and whatever you find out there, we will deal with it then."

I tell her that I'm relieved that she and the council sees Sarkka's offer for what it is.

"Did you doubt that we would renege on our deal? Have faith in us, Emma. As we have faith in you."

I call Sarkka. His ship is close to the edge of the cold, carbon-black limb of the planet now, and we are in the middle of preparations for aerobraking. He doesn't answer for more than ten minutes, and when he finally picks up, and I start to tell him that he can't make any kind of deal with the farmers, he says that it doesn't matter. There's something in his voice I haven't heard for a while. An unsettling manic glee.

"It's too late to make a deal. I'll take it all. Everything here. You are not my nemesis after all, Emma. You are my witness!"

He signs off and won't answer when I call back, and then his ship drops out of sight beyond the limb of the gas giant. We won't see him again until after aerobraking.

I help the crew finish tying everything down, and then we all strap into crash couches and plug into the interface and watch the black on black bands of the gas giant swell towards us. And just as the ship hits the fringes of its atmosphere, and begins to shudder and groan as deceleration piles on the gees, and the view is washed with violet light as friction with the atmosphere heats the hull of the ship and wraps it in a caul of ionised plasma, one of the crew posts a snatched shot of a shaped rock orbiting at the edge of the ring system. A cone with a flat face. A wormhole throat.

A moment later, we enter the terminal phase of the aerobraking manoeuver. Plasma as hot as the surface of the gas giant's star envelopes us and gravity crushes us. I'm trying to breath with what seems like a full pirate crew squatting on my chest, my heart is pounding like crazy, black rags are fluttering in. The ship quivers and groans and is filled with a tremendous roar as it scratches a flame ten thousand kilometres long across the face of the gas giant. And as the plasma dies back and the pull of deceleration fades there's an alarming bang: the flight crew has fired up the solid fuel motors, finessing our delta vee as we climb away from the nightside of the planet and head out towards the edge of the rings.

Later.

We've completed our first orbit and failed to find any trace of Sarkka's ship. There's only one place he could have gone, and there's no question about what we have to do, even though we are perilously low on fuel. Now we're on final approach. We've been videoing everything, transmitting it via q-phone directly to Terminus. If we fail, others will follow.

The black mirror of the wormhole's throat rushes towards us, and then stars bloom all around.

Thousands of stars, bright burning jewels flung in handfuls everywhere we look. Stars of all colours, and threads of luminous gas strung between them.

We're in the heart of a globular cluster, in orbit around a planet twice the size of Earth and clad in ice from pole to pole. There are so many stars in the sky and they are all so bright and so close together that it takes a few minutes to locate the planet's sun, an undistinguished red dwarf as dim and humble as any of the fifteen stars gifted us by the Jackaroo, outshone by many of its neighbours. Millions of kilometres beyond the ice-planet's limb is a cluster of six wormholes, arranged in the points of a hexagon. Sarkka's ship is moving towards them, riding the blue flame of his solid fuel motor.

All around me, a babble of cross-talk erupts as the ship's crew speculate wildly on where those wormholes might lead, about whether the ice-planet is habitable, whether there are habitable planets or moons or planoformed rocks in this system or elsewhere.

"It's a new empire!" someone says.

My q-phone rings.

"Do you see?" Niles Sarkka says. "Dare you follow?"

"You haven't found what you are looking for."

"I've found something better."

One of the crew tells me that we are critically low on fuel. We have barely enough to return to the wormhole from which we emerged. And if we don't return, the resupply ship will never find us. We'll be stranded here.

I ask Niles Sarkka to come back with us, but he laughs and cuts the connection. And then, as he closes on the wormhole throat, he sends a brief video message. It's startling to see him after all this time. He was once a handsome and powerfully built man, but after six months alone in close quarters and minimal rations he looks like a shipwrecked outcast, long grey hair tied back, an untrimmed beard over hollow cheeks, sores around his mouth, his eyes sunken in bruised sockets. But his gaze is vital, and his smile is that of someone cresting the tape at the end of a long and arduous marathon.

"I name this star, the gateway to untold wonders, Sarkka's Star. I came here for all mankind, and I go on, in the name of mankind. One day I will return with the full and final answer to Fermi's paradox. Do not judge me until then."

And then he's gone. We swing past and fall towards the wormhole that will take us back to the G0 star, and the crew is still babbling about new worlds and stars to be explored, and I think: suppose he's right?

Suppose he is the hero after all, and I'm the villain?

EROS, PHILIA, AGAP

RACHEL SWIRSKY

Lucian packed his possessions before he left. He packed his antique silver serving spoons with the filigreed handles; the tea roses he'd nurtured in the garden window; his jade and garnet rings. He packed the hunk of gypsum-veined jasper that he'd found while strolling on the beach on the first night he'd come to Adriana, she leading him uncertainly across the wet sand, their bodies illuminated by the soft gold twinkling of the lights along the pier. That night, as they walked back to Adriana's house, Lucian had cradled the speckled stone in his cupped palms, squinting so that the gypsum threads sparkled through his lashes.

Lucian had always loved beauty—beautiful scents, beautiful tastes, beautiful melodies. He especially loved beautiful objects because he could hold them in his hands and transform the abstraction of beauty into something tangible.

The objects belonged to them both, but Adriana waved her hand bitterly when Lucian began packing. "Take whatever you want," she said, snapping her book shut. She waited by the door, watching Lucian with sad and angry eyes.

Their daughter, Rose, followed Lucian around the house. "Are you going to take that, Daddy? Do you want that?" Wordlessly, Lucian held her hand. He guided her up the stairs and across the uneven floorboards where she sometimes tripped. Rose stopped by the picture window in the master bedroom, staring past the palm fronds and swimming pools, out to the vivid cerulean swath of the ocean. Lucian relished the hot, tender feel of Rose's hand. *I love you*, he would have whispered, but he'd surrendered the ability to speak.

He led her downstairs again to the front door. Rose's lace-festooned pink satin dress crinkled as she leapt down the steps. Lucian had ordered her dozens of satin party dresses in pale, floral hues. Rose refused to wear anything else.

Rose looked between Lucian and Adriana. "Are you taking me, too?" she asked Lucian.

Adriana's mouth tightened. She looked at Lucian, daring him to say something, to take responsibility for what he was doing to their daughter. Lucian remained silent.

Adriana's chardonnay glowed the same shade of amber as Lucian's eyes. She clutched the glass's stem until she thought it might break. "No, honey," she said with artificial lightness. "You're staying with me."

Rose reached for Lucian. "Horsey?"

Lucian knelt down and pressed his forehead against Rose's. He hadn't spoken a word in the three days since he'd delivered his letter of farewell to Adriana, announcing his intention to leave as soon as she had enough time to make arrangements for Rose to be cared for in his absence. When Lucian approached with the letter, Adriana had been sitting at the dining table, sipping orange juice from a wine glass and reading a first edition copy of Cheever's *Falconer*. Lucian felt a flash of guilt as she smiled up at him and accepted the missive. He knew that she'd been happier in the past few months than he'd ever seen her, possibly happier than she'd ever been. He knew the letter would shock and wound her. He knew she'd feel betrayed. Still, he delivered the letter anyway, and watched as comprehension ached through her body.

Rose had been told, gently, patiently, that Lucian was leaving. But she was four years old, and understood things only briefly and partially, and often according to her whims. She continued to believe her father's silence was a game.

Rose's hair brushed Lucian's cheek. He kissed her brow. Adriana couldn't hold her tongue any longer.

"What do you think you're going to find out there? There's no Shangri-La for rebel robots. You think you're making a play for independence? Independence to do what, Lu?"

Grief and anger filled Adriana's eyes with hot tears, as if she were a geyser filled with so much pressure that steam could not help but spring up. She examined Lucian's sculpted face: his skin inlaid with tiny lines that an artist had rendered to suggest the experiences of a childhood which had never been lived; his eyes calibrated with a hint of asymmetry to mimic the imperfection of human growth. His expression showed nothing—no doubt, or bitterness, or even relief. He revealed nothing at all.

It was all too much. Adriana moved between Lucian and Rose, as if she could use her own body to protect her daughter from the pain of being abandoned. Her eyes stared achingly over the rim of her wine glass. "Just go," she said.

He left.

Adriana bought Lucian the summer she turned thirty-five. Her father, long afflicted with an indecisive cancer that vacillated between aggression and remittance, had died suddenly in July. For years, the family had been squirreling away emotional reserves to cope with his prolonged illness. His death released a burst of excess.

While her sisters went through the motions of grief, Adriana thrummed with energy she didn't know what to do with. She considered squandering her vigor on six weeks in Mazatlan, but as she discussed ocean-front rentals with her travel agent, she realized escape wasn't what she craved. She liked the setting where her life took place: her house perched on a cliff overlooking the Pacific Ocean, her bedroom window that opened on a tangle of blackberry bushes where crows roosted every autumn and spring. She liked the two block stroll down to the beach where she could sit with a book and listen to the yapping lapdogs that the elderly women from the waterfront condominiums brought walking in the evenings.

Mazatlan was a twenty-something's cure for restlessness. Adriana wasn't twenty-five anymore, famished for the whole gourmet meal of existence. She needed something else now. Something new. Something more refined.

She explained this to her friends Ben and Lawrence when they invited her to their ranch house in Santa Barbara to relax for the weekend and try to forget about her father. They sat on Ben and Lawrence's patio, on iron-worked deck chairs arrayed around a garden table topped with a mosaic of sea creatures made of semi-precious stones. A warm, breezy dusk lengthened the shadows of the orange trees. Lawrence poured sparkling rosé into three wine glasses and proposed a toast to Adriana's father—not to his memory, but to his death.

"Good riddance to the bastard," said Lawrence. "If he were still alive, I'd punch him in the schnoz."

"I don't even want to think about him," said Adriana. "He's dead. He's gone."

"So if not Mazatlan, what are you going to do?" asked Ben.

"I'm not sure," said Adriana. "Some sort of change, some sort of milestone, that's all I know."

Lawrence sniffed the air. "Excuse me," he said, gathering the empty wine glasses. "The kitchen needs its genius."

When Lawrence was out of earshot, Ben leaned forward to whisper to Adriana. "He's got us on a raw food diet for my cholesterol. Raw carrots. Raw zucchini. Raw almonds. No cooking at all."

"Really," said Adriana, glancing away. She was never sure how to respond to lovers' quarrels. That kind of affection mixed with annoyance, that inescapable intimacy, was something she'd never understood.

Birds twittered in the orange trees. The fading sunlight highlighted copper strands in Ben's hair as he leaned over the mosaic table, rapping his fingers against a carnelian-backed crab. Through the arched windows, Adriana could see Lawrence mincing carrots, celery and almonds into brown paste.

"You should get a redecorator," said Ben. "Tile floors, Tuscan pottery, those red leather chairs that were in vogue last time we were in Milan. That'd make me feel like I'd been scrubbed clean and reborn."

"No, no," said Adriana, "I like where I live."

"A no-holds-barred shopping spree. Drop twenty thousand. That's what I call getting a weight off your shoulders."

Adriana laughed. "How long do you think it would take my personal shopper to assemble a whole new me?"

"Sounds like a midlife crisis," said Lawrence, returning with vegan hors d'oeuvres and three glasses of mineral water. "You're better off forgetting it all with a hot Latin pool boy, if you ask me."

Lawrence served Ben a small bowl filled with yellow mush. Ben shot Adriana an aggrieved glance.

Adriana felt suddenly out of synch. The whole evening felt like the set for a photo-shoot that would go in a decorating magazine, a two-page spread featuring Cozy Gardens, in which she and Ben and Lawrence were posing as an intimate dinner party for three. She felt reduced to two dimensions, air-brushed, and then digitally grafted onto the form of whoever it was who should have been there, someone warm and trusting who knew how to care about minutia like a friend's husband putting him on a raw food diet, not because the issue was important, but because it mattered to him.

Lawrence dipped his finger in the mash and held it up to Ben's lips. "It's for your own good, you ungrateful so-and-so."

Ben licked it away. "I eat it, don't I?"

Lawrence leaned down to kiss his husband, a warm and not at all furtive kiss, not sexual but still passionate. Ben's glance flashed coyly downward.

Adriana couldn't remember the last time she'd loved someone enough to be embarrassed by them. Was this the flavor missing from her life? A lover's fingertip sliding an unwanted morsel into her mouth?

She returned home that night on the bullet train. Her emerald cockatiel, Fuoco, greeted her with indignant squawks. In Adriana's absence, the house puffed her scent into the air and sang to Fuoco with her voice, but the bird was never fooled.

Adriana's father had given her the bird for her thirtieth birthday. He was a designer species spliced with Macaw DNA that colored his feathers rich green. He was expensive and inbred and neurotic, and he loved Adriana with frantic, obsessive jealousy.

"Hush," Adriana admonished, allowing Fuoco to alight on her shoulder. She carried him upstairs to her bedroom and hand-fed him millet. Fuoco strutted across the pillows, obsidian eyes proud and suspicious.

Adriana was surprised to find that her alienation had followed her home. She found herself prone to melancholy reveries, her gaze drifting toward the picture window, her fingers forgetting to stroke Fuoco's back. The bird screeched to regain her attention.

In the morning, Adriana visited her accountant. His fingers danced across the keyboard as he slipped trust fund moneys from one account to another like a magician. What she planned would be expensive, but her wealth would regrow in fertile soil, enriching her on lab diamonds and wind power and genetically modified oranges.

The robotics company gave Adriana a private showing. The salesman ushered her into a room draped in black velvet. Hundreds of body parts hung on the walls, and reclined on display tables: strong hands, narrow jaws, biker's thighs, voice boxes that played sound samples from gruff to dulcet, skin swatches spanning ebony to alabaster, penises of various sizes.

At first, Adriana felt horrified at the prospect of assembling a lover from fragments, but then it amused her. Wasn't everyone assembled from fragments of DNA, grown molecule by molecule inside their mother's womb?

She tapped her fingernails against a slick brochure. "Its brain will be malleable? I can tell it to be more amenable, or funnier, or to grow a spine?"

"That's correct." The salesman sported slick brown hair and shiny teeth and kept grinning in a way that suggested he thought that if he were charismatic enough Adriana would invite him home for a lay and a million dollar tip. "Humans lose brain plasticity as we age, which limits how much we can change. Our models have perpetually plastic brains. They can reroute their personalities at will by reshaping how they think on the neurological level."

Adriana stepped past him, running her fingers along a tapestry woven of a thousand possible hair textures.

The salesman tapped an empty faceplate. "Their original brains are based on deep imaging scans melded from geniuses in multiple fields. Great musicians, renowned lovers, the best physicists and mathematicians."

Adriana wished the salesman would be quiet. The more he talked, the more doubts clamored against her skull. "You've convinced me," she interrupted. "I want one."

The salesman looked taken aback by her abruptness. She could practically see him rifling through his internal script, trying to find the right page now that she had skipped several scenes. "What do you want him to look like?" he asked.

Adriana shrugged. "They're all beautiful, right?"

"We'll need specifications."

"I don't have specifications."

The salesman frowned anxiously. He shifted his weight as if it could help him regain his metaphorical footing. Adriana took pity. She dug through her purse.

"There," she said, placing a snapshot of her father on one of the display tables. "Make it look nothing like him."

Given such loose parameters, the design team indulged the fanciful. Lucian arrived at Adriana's door only a shade taller than she and equally slender, his limbs smooth and lean. Silver undertones glimmered in his blond hair. His skin was excruciatingly pale, white and translucent as alabaster, veined with pink. He smelled like warm soil and crushed herbs.

He offered Adriana a single white rose, its petals embossed with the company's logo. She held it dubiously between her thumb and forefinger. "They think they know women, do they? They need to put down the bodice rippers."

Lucian said nothing. Adriana took his hesitation for puzzlement, but perhaps she should have seen it as an early indication of his tendency toward silence.

"That's that, then." Adriana drained her chardonnay and crushed the empty glass beneath her heel as if she could finalize a divorce with the same gesture that sanctified a marriage.

Eyes wide, Rose pointed at the glass with one round finger. "Don't break things."

It suddenly struck Adriana how fast her daughter was aging. Here she was, this four year old, this sudden person. When had it happened? In the hospital, when Rose was newborn and wailing for the woman who had birthed her and abandoned her, Adriana had spent hours in the hallway outside the hospital nursery while she waited for the adoption to go through. She'd stared at Rose while she slept, ate, cried, striving to memorize her nascent, changing face. Sometime between then and now, Rose had become this round-cheeked creature who took rules very seriously and often tried to conceal her emotions beneath a calm exterior, as if being raised by a robot had replaced her blood with circuits. Of course Adriana loved Rose, changed her clothes, brushed her teeth, carried her across the house on her hip—but Lucian had been the most central, nurturing figure. Adriana couldn't fathom how she might fill his role. This wasn't a vacation like the time Adriana had taken Rose to Italy for three days, just the two of them sitting in restaurants, Adriana feeding her daughter spoonfuls of gelato to see the joy that lit her face at each new flavor. Then, they'd known that Lucian would be waiting when they returned. Without him, their family was a house missing a structural support. Adriana could feel the walls bowing in.

The fragments of Adriana's chardonnay glass sparkled sharply. Adriana led Rose away from the mess.

"Never mind," she said, "The house will clean up."

Her head felt simultaneously light and achy as if it couldn't decide between drunkenness and hangover. She tried to remember the parenting books she'd read before adopting Rose. What had they said about crying in front of your child? She clutched Rose close, inhaling the scent of children's shampoo mixed with the acrid odor of wine.

"Let's go for a drive," said Adriana. "Okay? Let's get out for a while."

"I want daddy to take me to the beach."

"We'll go out to the country and look at the farms. Cows and sheep, okay?"

Rose said nothing.

"Moo?" Adriana clarified. "Baa?"

"I know," said Rose. "I'm not a baby."

"So, then?"

Rose said nothing. Adriana wondered whether she could tell that her mother was a little mad with grief.

Just make a decision, Adriana counseled herself. She slipped her fingers around Rose's hand. "We'll go for a drive."

Adriana instructed the house to regulate itself in their absence, and then led Rose to the little black car that she and Lucian had bought together after adopting Rose. She fastened Rose's safety buckle and programmed the car to take them inland.

As the car engine initialized, Adriana felt a glimmer of fear. What if this machine betrayed them, too? But its uninspired intelligence only switched on the left turn signal and started down the boulevard.

Lucian stood at the base of the driveway and stared up at the house. Its stark orange and brown walls blazed against cloudless sky. Rocks and desert plants tumbled down the meticulously landscaped yard, imitating natural scrub.

A rabbit ran across the road, followed by the whir of Adriana's car. Lucian watched them pass. They couldn't see him through the cypresses, but Lucian could make out Rose's face pressed against the window. Beside her, Adriana slumped in her seat, one hand pressed over her eyes.

Lucian went in the opposite direction. He dragged the rolling cart packed with his belongings to the cliff that led down to the beach. He lifted the cart over his head and started down, his feet disturbing cascades of sandstone chunks.

A pair of adolescent boys looked up from playing in the waves. "Whoa," shouted one of them. "Are you carrying that whole thing? Are you a weight-lifter?"

Lucian remained silent. When he reached the sand, the kids muttered disappointments to each other and turned away from shore. " . . . Just a robot . . . " drifted back to Lucian on the breeze.

Lucian pulled his cart to the border where wet sand met dry. Oncoming waves lapped over his feet. He opened the cart and removed a tea-scented apricot rose growing in a pot painted with blue leaves.

He remembered acquiring the seeds for his first potted rose. One evening, long ago, he'd asked Adriana if he could grow things. He'd asked in passing, the question left to linger while they cleaned up after dinner, dish soap on their hands, Fuoco pecking after scraps. The next morning, Adriana escorted Lucian to the hot house near the botanical gardens. "Buy whatever you want," she told him. Lucian was awed by the profusion of color and scent, all that beauty in one place. He wanted to capture the wonder of that place and own it for himself.

Lucian drew back his arm and threw the pot into the sea. It broke across the water, petals scattering the surface.

He threw in the pink roses, and the white roses, and the red roses, and the mauve roses. He threw in the filigreed-handled spoons. He threw in the chunk of gypsum-veined jasper.

He threw in everything beautiful that he'd ever collected. He threw in a chased silver hand mirror, and an embroidered silk jacket, and a hand-painted egg. He threw in one of Fuoco's soft, emerald feathers. He threw in a memory crystal that showed Rose as an infant, curled and sleeping.

He loved those things, and yet they were things. He had owned them. Now they were gone. He had recently come to realize that ownership was a relationship. What did it mean to own a thing? To shape it and contain it? He could not possess or be possessed until he knew.

He watched the sea awhile, the remnants of his possessions lost in the tumbling waves. As the sun tilted past noon, he turned away and climbed back up the cliff. Unencumbered by ownership, he followed the boulevard away from Adriana's house.

Lucian remembered meeting Adriana the way that he imagined that humans remembered childhood. Oh, his memories had been as sharply focused then as now—but it was still like childhood, he reasoned, for he'd been a different person then.

He remembered his first sight of Adriana as a burst of images. Wavy strawberry blonde hair cut straight across tanned shoulders. Dark brown eyes that his artistic mind labeled "sienna." Thick, aristocratic brows and strong cheekbones, free of makeup. Lucian's inner aesthete termed her blunt, angular face "striking" rather than "beautiful." His inner psychoanalyst reasoned that she was probably "strong-willed" as well, from the way she stood in the doorway, her arms crossed, her eyebrows lifted as if inquiring how he planned to justify his existence.

Eventually, she moved away, allowing Lucian to step inside. He crossed the threshold into a blur off frantic screeching and flapping.

New. Everything was new. So new that Lucian could barely assemble feathers and beak and wings into the concept of "bird" before his reflexes jumped him away from the onslaught. Hissing and screeching, the animal retreated to a perch atop a bookshelf.

Adriana's hand weighed on Lucian's shoulder. Her voice was edged with the cynicism Lucian would later learn was her way of hiding how desperately she feared failure. "Ornithophobia? How ridiculous."

Lucian's first disjointed days were dominated by the bird, who he learned was named Fuoco. It followed him around the house. When he remained in place for a moment, the bird settled on some nearby high spot—the hat rack in the entryway, or the hand-crafted globe in the parlor, or the rafters above the master bed—to spy on him. It glared at Lucian in the manner of birds, first peering through one eye and then turning its head to peer through the other, apparently finding both views equally loathsome.

When Adriana took Lucian into her bed, Fuoco swooped at Lucian's head. Adriana pushed Lucian out of the way. "Damn it, Fuoco," she muttered, but she offered the bird a perch on her shoulder.

Fuoco crowed with pleasure as she led him downstairs. His feathers fluffed with victory as he hopped obediently into its cage, expecting her to reward him with treats and conversation. Instead, Adriana closed the gilded door and returned upstairs. All night, as Lucian lay with Adriana, the bird chattered madly. He plucked at his feathers until his tattered plumage carpeted the cage floor.

Lucian accompanied Adriana when she brought Fuoco to the vet the next day. The veterinarian diagnosed jealousy. "It's not uncommon in birds," he said. He suggested they give Fuoco a rigid routine that would, over time, help the bird realize he was Adriana's companion, not her mate.

Adriana and Lucian rearranged their lives so that Fuoco could have regular feeding times, scheduled exercise, socialization with both Lucian and Adriana, and time with his mistress alone. Adriana gave him a treat each night when she locked him in his cage, staying to stroke his feathers for a few minutes before she headed upstairs.

Fuoco's heart broke. He became a different bird. His strut lacked confidence, and his feathers grew ever more tattered. When they let him out of his cage, he wandered after Adriana with pleading, wistful eyes, and ignored Lucian entirely.

Lucian had been dis-integrated then: musician brain, mathematician brain, artist brain, economist brain, and more, all functioning separately, each personality rising to dominance to provide information and then sliding away, creating staccato bursts of consciousness.

As Adriana made clear which responses she liked, Lucian's consciousness began integrating into the personality she desired. He found himself noticing connections between what had previously been separate experiences. Before, when he'd seen the ocean, his scientist brain had calculated how far he was from the shore, and how long it would be until high tide. His poet brain had recited Strindberg's "We Waves." *Wet flames are we:/Burning, extinguishing;/Cleansing, replenishing.* Yet it wasn't until he integrated that the wonder of the science, and the mystery of the poetry, and the beauty of the view, all made sense to him at once as part of this strange, inspiring thing: the sea.

He learned to anticipate Adriana. He knew when she was pleased and when she was ailing, and he knew why. He could predict the cynical half-smile she'd give when he made an error he hadn't yet realized was an error: serving her cold coffee in an orange juice glass, orange juice in a shot glass, wine in a mug. When integration gave him knowledge of patterns, he suddenly understood why these things were errors. At the same time, he realized that he liked what happened when he made those kinds of errors, the bright bursts of humor they elicited from the often sober Adriana. So he persisted in error, serving her milk in crystal decanters, and grapefruit slices in egg cups.

He enjoyed the many varieties of her laughter. Sometimes it was light and surprised, as when he offered her a cupcake tin filled with tortellini. He also loved her rich, dark laughter that anticipated irony. Sometimes, her laughter held a bitter undercurrent, and on those occasions, he understood that she was laughing more at herself than at anyone else. Sometimes when that happened, he would go to hold her, seeking to ease her pain, and sometimes she would spontaneously start crying in gulping, gasping sobs.

She often watched him while he worked, her head cocked and her brows drawn as if she were seeing him for the first time. "What can I do to make you happy?" she'd ask.

If he gave an answer, she would lavishly fulfill his desires. She took him traveling to the best greenhouses in the state, and bought a library full of gardening books. Lucian knew she would have given him more. He didn't want it. He wanted to reassure her that he appreciated her extravagance, but didn't require it, that he was satisfied with simple, loving give-and-take. Sometimes, he told her in the simplest words he knew: "I love you, too." But he knew that she never quite believed him. She worried that he was lying, or that his programming had erased his free will. It was easier for her to believe those things than to accept that someone could love her.

But he did love her. Lucian loved Adriana as his mathematician brain loved the consistency of arithmetic, as his artist brain loved color, as his philosopher brain loved piety. He loved her as Fuoco loved her, the bird walking sadly along the arm of Adriana's chair, trilling and flapping his ragged wings as he eyed her with his inky gaze, trying to catch her attention.

Adriana hadn't expected to fall in love. She'd expected a charming conversationalist with the emotional range of a literary butler and the self-awareness of a golden retriever. Early on, she'd felt her prejudices confirmed. She noted Lucian's lack of critical thinking and his inability to maneuver unexpected situations. She found him most interesting when he didn't know she was watching. For instance, on his free afternoons: was his program trying to anticipate what would please her? Or did the thing really enjoy sitting by the window, leafing through the pages of one of her rare books, with nothing but the sound of the ocean to lull him?

Once, as Adriana watched from the kitchen doorway while Lucian made their breakfast, the robot slipped while he was dicing onions. The knife cut deep into his finger. Adriana stumbled forward to help. As Lucian turned to face her, Adriana imagined that she saw something like shock on his face. For a moment, she wondered whether he had a programmed sense of privacy she could violate, but then he raised his hand to her in greeting, and she watched as the tiny bots that maintained his system healed his inhuman flesh within seconds.

At that moment, Adriana remembered that Lucian was unlike her. She urged herself not to forget it, and strove not to, even after his consciousness integrated. He was a person, yes, a varied and fascinating one with as many depths and facets as any other person she knew. But he was also alien. He was a creature for whom a slip of a chef's knife was a minute error, simply repaired. In some ways, she was more similar to Fuoco.

As a child, Adriana had owned a book that told the fable of an emperor who owned a bird which he fed rich foods from his table, and entertained with luxuries from his court. But a pet bird needed different things than an emperor. It wanted seed and millet, not grand feasts. It enjoyed mirrors and little brass bells, not lacquer boxes and poetry scrolls. Gorged on human banquets and revelries, the little bird sickened and died.

Adriana vowed not to make the same mistake with Lucian, but she had no idea how hard it would be to salve the needs of something so unlike herself.

Adriana ordered the car to pull over at a farm that advertised children could "Pet Lambs and Calves" for a fee. A ginger-haired teenager stood at a strawberry stand in front of the fence, slouching as he flipped through a dog-eared magazine.

Adriana held Rose's hand as they approached. She tried to read her daughter's emotions in the feel of her tiny fingers. The little girl's expression revealed nothing; Rose had gone silent and flat-faced as if she were imitating Lucian. He would have known what she was feeling.

Adriana examined the strawberries. The crates contained none of the different shapes one could buy at the store, only the natural, seed-filled variety. "Do these contain pesticides?" Adriana asked.

"No, ma'am," said the teenager. "We grow organic."

"All right then. I'll take a box." Adriana looked down at her daughter. "Do you want some strawberries, sweetheart?" she asked in a sugared tone.

"You said I could pet the lambs," said Rose.

"Right. Of course, honey." Adriana glanced at the distracted teenager. "Can she?"

The teenager slumped, visibly disappointed, and tossed his magazine on a pile of canvas sacks. "I can take her to the barn."

"Fine. Okay."

Adriana guided Rose toward the teenager. Rose looked up at him, expression still inscrutable.

The boy didn't take Rose's hand. He ducked his head, obviously embarrassed. "My aunt likes me to ask for the money upfront."

"Of course." Adriana fumbled for her wallet. She'd let Lucian do things for her for so long. How many basic living skills had she forgotten? She held out some bills. The teenager licked his index finger and meticulously counted out what she owed.

The teen took Rose's hand. He lingered a moment, watching Adriana. "Aren't you coming with us?"

Adriana was so tired. She forced a smile. "Oh, that's okay. I've seen sheep and cows. Okay, Rose? Can you have fun for a little bit without me?"

Rose nodded soberly. She turned toward the teenager without hesitation, and followed him toward the barn. The boy seemed to be good with children. He walked slowly so that Rose could keep up with his long-legged strides.

Adriana returned to the car, and leaned against the hot, sun-warmed door. Her head throbbed. She thought she might cry or collapse. Getting out had seemed like a good idea—the house was full of memories of Lucian. He seemed to sit in every chair, linger in every doorway. But now she wished she'd stayed in her haunted but familiar home, instead of leaving with this child she seemed to barely know.

A sharp, long wail carried on the wind. Adrenaline cut through Adriana's melancholia. She sprinted toward the barn. She saw Rose running toward her, the teenager close behind, dust swirling around both of them. Blood dripped down Rose's arm.

Adriana threw her arms around her daughter. Arms, legs, breath, heart beat: Rose was okay. Adrianna dabbed at Rose's injury; there was a lot of blood, but the wound was shallow. "Oh, honey," she said, clutching Rose as tightly as she dared.

The teenager halted beside them, his hair mussed by the wind.

"What happened?" Adriana demanded.

The teenager stammered. "Fortuna kicked her. That's one of the goats. I'm so sorry. Fortuna's never done anything like that before. She's a nice goat. It's Ballantine usually does the kicking. He got me a few times when I was little. I came through every time. Honest, she'll be okay. You're not going to sue, are you?"

Rose struggled out of Adriana's grasp and began wailing again. "It's okay, Rose, it's okay," murmured Adriana. She felt a strange disconnect in her head as she spoke. Things were not okay. Things might never be okay again.

"I'm leaking," cried Rose, holding out her blood-stained fingers. "See, mama? I'm leaking! I need healer bots."

Adriana looked up at the teenager. "Do you have bandages? A first aid kit?"

The boy frowned. "In the house, I think . . . "

"Get the bots, mama! Make me stop leaking!"

The teen stared at Adriana, the concern in his eyes increasing. Adriana blinked, slowly. The moment slowed. She realized what her daughter had said. She forced her voice to remain calm. "What do you want, Rose?"

"She said it before," said the teen. "I thought it was a game."

Adriana leveled her gaze with Rose's. The child's eyes were strange and brown, uncharted waters. "Is this a game?"

"Daddy left," said Rose.

Adriana felt woozy. "Yes, and then I brought you here so we could see lambs and calves. Did you see any nice, fuzzy lambs?"

"Daddy left."

She shouldn't have drunk the wine. She should have stayed clear-headed. "We'll get you bandaged up and then you can go see the lambs again. Do you want to see the lambs again? Would it help if mommy came, too?"

Rose clenched her fists. Her face grew dark. "My arm hurts!" She threw herself to the ground. "I want healer bots!"

Adriana knew precisely when she'd fallen in love with Lucian. It was three months after she'd bought him—after his consciousness had integrated, but before Adriana fully understood how integration had changed him.

It began when Adriana's sisters called from Boston to inform her that they'd arranged for a family pilgrimage to Italy. In accordance with their father's will, they would commemorate him by lighting candles in the cathedrals of every winding hillside city.

"Oh, I can't. I'm too busy," Adriana answered airily, as if she were a debutante without a care, as if she shared her sisters' ability to overcome her fear of their father.

Her phone began ringing ceaselessly. Nanette called before she rushed off to a tennis match. "How can you be so busy? You don't have a job. You don't have a husband. Or is there a man in your life we don't know about?" And once Nanette was deferred with mumbled excuses, it was Eleanor calling from a spa. "Is something wrong, Adriana? We're all worried. How can you miss a chance to say goodbye to papa?"

"I said goodbye at the funeral," said Adriana.

"Then you can't have properly processed your grief," said Jessica, calling from her office between appointments. She was a psychoanalyst in the Freudian mode. "Your aversion rings of denial. You need to process your Oedipal feelings."

Adriana slammed down the phone. Later, to apologize for hanging up, she sent all her sisters chocolates, and then booked a flight. In a fit of pique, she booked a seat for Lucian, too. Well, he was a companion, wasn't he? What else was he for?

Adriana's sisters were scandalized, of course. As they rode through Rome,

Jessica, Nanette, and Eleanor gossiped behind their discreetly raised hands. Adriana with a robot? Well, she'd need to be, wouldn't she? There was no getting around the fact that she was damaged. Any girl who would make up those stories about their father would have to be.

Adriana ignored them as best she could while they whirled through Tuscany in a procession of rented cars. The paused in cities to gawk at gothic cathedrals and mummified remnants, always moving on within the day. During their father's long sickness, Adriana's sisters had perfected the art of cheerful anecdote. They used it to great effect as they lit candles in his memory. Tears welling in their eyes, they related banal, nostalgic memories. How their father danced at charity balls. How he lectured men on the board who looked down on him for being new money. How he never once apologized for anything in his life.

It had never been clear to Adriana whether her father had treated her sisters the way he treated her, or whether she had been the only one to whom he came at night, his breathing heavy and staccato. It seemed impossible that they could lie so seamlessly, never showing fear or doubt. But if they were telling the truth, that meant Adriana was the only one, and how could she believe that either?

One night, while Lucian and Adriana were alone in their room in a hotel in Assissi that had been a convent during the middle ages, Adriana broke down. It was all too much, being in this foreign place, talking endlessly about her father. She'd fled New England to get away from them, fled to her beautiful modern glass-and-wood house by the Pacific Ocean that was like a fresh breath drawn on an Autumn morning.

Lucian held her, exerting the perfect warmth and pressure against her body to comfort her. It was what she'd have expected from a robot. She knew that he calculated the pace of his breath, the temperature of his skin, the angle of his arm as it lay across her.

What surprised Adriana, what humbled her, was how eloquently Lucian spoke of his experiences. He told her what it had been like to assemble himself from fragments, to take what he'd once been and become something new. It was something Adriana had tried to do herself when she fled her family.

Lucian held his head down as he spoke. His gaze never met hers. He spoke as if this process of communicating the intimate parts of the self were a new kind of dance, and he was tenuously trying the steps. Through the fog of her grief, Adriana realized that this was a new, struggling consciousness coming to clarity. How could she do anything but love him?

When they returned from Italy, Adriana approached the fledgling movement for granting rights to artificial intelligences. They were underfunded and poorly organized. Adriana rented them offices in San Francisco, and hired a small but competent staff.

Adriana became the movement's face. She'd been on camera frequently as a child: whenever her father was in the news for some or other board room scandal, her father's publicists had lined up Adriana and her sisters beside the family limousine, chaste in their private school uniforms, ready to provide Lancaster Nuclear with a friendly, feminine face.

She and Lucian were a brief media curiosity: Heiress In Love With Robot. "Lucian is as self-aware as you or I," Adriana told reporters, all-American in pearls and jeans. "He thinks. He learns. He can hybridize roses as well as any human gardener. Why should he be denied his rights?"

Early on, it was clear that political progress would be frustratingly slow. Adriana quickly expended her patience. She set up a fund for the organization, made sure it would run without her assistance, and then turned her attention toward alternate methods for attaining her goals. She hired a team of lawyers to draw up a contract that would grant Lucian community property rights to her estate and accounts. He would be her equal in practicality, if not legality.

Next, Adriana approached Lucian's manufacturer, and commissioned them to invent a procedure that would allow Lucian to have conscious control of his brain plasticity. At their wedding, Adriana gave him the chemical commands at the same time as she gave him his ring. "You are your own person now. You always have been, of course, but now you have full agency, too. You are yourself," she announced, in front of their gathered friends. Her sisters would no doubt have been scandalized, but they had not been invited.

On their honeymoon, Adriana and Lucian toured hospitals, running the genetic profiles of abandoned infants until they found a healthy girl with a mitochondrial lineage that matched Adriana's. The infant was tiny and pink and curled in on herself, ready to unfold, like one of Lucian's roses.

When they brought Rose home, Adriana felt a surge in her stomach that she'd never felt before. It was a kind of happiness she'd never experienced, one that felt round and whole without any jagged edges. It was like the sun had risen in her belly and was dwelling there, filling her with boundless light.

There was a moment, when Rose was still new enough to be wrapped in the hand-made baby blanket that Ben and Lawrence had sent from France, in which Adriana looked up at Lucian and realized how enraptured he was with their baby, how much adoration underpinned his willingness to bend over her cradle for hours and mirror her expressions, frown for frown, astonishment for astonishment. In that moment, Adriana thought that this must be the true measure of equality, not money or laws, but this unfolding desire to create the future together by raising a new sentience. She thought she understood then why unhappy parents stayed together for the sake of their children, why families with sons and daughters felt so different from those that remained childless. Families with children were making something new from themselves. Doubly so when the endeavor was undertaken by a human and a creature who was already, himself, something new. What could they make together?

In that same moment, Lucian was watching the wide-eyed, innocent wonder with which his daughter beheld him. She showed the same pleasure when he entered the room as she did when Adriana entered. If anything, the light in her eyes was brighter when he approached. There was something about the way Rose loved him that he didn't yet understand. Earlier that morning, he had plucked a bloom from his apricot tea rose and whispered to its petals that they were beautiful. They were his, and he loved them. Every day, he held Rose, and understood that she was beautiful, and that he loved her. But she was not his. She was her own. He wasn't sure he'd ever seen a love like that, a love that did not want to hold its object in its hands and keep and contain it.

"You aren't a robot!"

Adriana's voice was rough from shouting all the way home. Bad enough to lose Lucian, but the child was out of control.

"I want healer bots! I'm a robot I'm a robot I'm a robot I'm a robot!"

The car stopped. Adriana got out. She waited for Rose to follow, and when she didn't, Adriana scooped her up and carried her up the driveway. Rose kicked and screamed. She sank her teeth into Adriana's arm. Adrian halted, surprised by the sudden pain. She breathed deeply, and then continued up the driveway. Rose's screams slid upward in register and rage.

Adriana set Rose down by the door long enough to key in the entry code and let the security system take a DNA sample from her hair. Rose hurled herself onto the porch, yanking fronds by the fistful off the potted ferns. Adriana leaned down to scrape her up and got kicked in the chest.

"God da . . . for heaven's sake." Adriana grabbed Rose's ankles with one hand and her wrists with the other. She pushed her weight against the unlocked door until it swung open. She carried Rose into the house, and slammed the door closed with her back. "Lock!" she yelled to the house.

When she heard the reassuring click, she set Rose down on the couch, and jumped away from the still-flailing limbs. Rose fled up the stairs, her bedroom door crashing shut behind her.

Adriana dug in her pocket for the bandages that the people at the farm had given her before she headed home, which she'd been unable to apply to a moving target in the car. Now was the time. She followed Rose up the stairs, her breath surprisingly heavy. She felt as though she'd been running a very long time.

She paused outside Rose's room. She didn't know what she'd do when she got inside. Lucian had always dealt with the child when she got overexcited. Too often, Adriana felt helpless, and became distant.

"Rose?" she called. "Rose? Are you okay?"

There was no response.

Adriana put her hand on the doorknob, and breathed deeply before turning.

She was surprised to find Rose sitting demurely in the center of her bed, her rumpled skirts spread about her as if she were a child at a picnic in an Impressionist painting. Dirt and tears trailed down the pink satin. The edges of her wound had already begun to bruise.

"I'm a robot," she said to Adriana, tone resentful.

Adriana made a decision. The most important thing was to bandage Rose's wound. Afterward, she could deal with whatever came next.

"Okay," said Adriana. "You're a robot."

Rose lifted her chin warily. "Good."

Adriana sat on the edge of Rose's bed. "You know what robots do? They change themselves to be whatever humans ask them to be."

"Dad doesn't," said Rose.

"That's true," said Adriana. "But that didn't happen until your father grew up."

Rose swung her legs against the side of the bed. Her expression remained dubious, but she no longer looked so resolute.

Adriana lifted the packet of bandages. "May I?"

Rose hesitated. Adriana resisted the urge to put her head in her hands. She had to get the bandages on, that was the important thing, but she couldn't shake the feeling that she was going to regret this later.

"Right now, what this human wants is for you to let her bandage your wound instead of giving you healer bots. Will you be a good robot? Will you let me?"

Rose remained silent, but she moved a little closer to her mother. When Adriana began bandaging her arm, she didn't scream.

Lucian waited for a bus to take him to the desert. He had no money. He'd forgotten about that. The driver berated him and wouldn't let him on.

Lucian walked. He could walk faster than a human, but not much faster. His edge was endurance. The road took him inland away from the sea. The last of the expensive houses stood near a lighthouse, lamps shining in all its windows. Beyond, condominiums pressed against each other, dense and alike. They gave way to compact, well-maintained homes, with neat green aprons maintained by automated sprinklers that sprayed arcs of precious water into the air.

The landscape changed. Sea breeze stilled to buzzing heat. Dirty, peeling houses squatted side by side, separated by chain link fences. Iron bars guarded the windows, and broken cars decayed in the driveways. Parched lawns stretched from walls to curb like scrub-land. No one was out in the punishing sun.

The road divided. Lucian followed the fork that went through the dilapidated town center. Traffic jerked along in fits and starts. Lucian walked in the gutter. Stray plastic bags blew beside him, working their way between dark storefronts. Parking meters blinked at the passing cars, hungry for more coins. Pedestrians ambled past, avoiding eye contact, mumbled conversations lost beneath honking horns.

On the other side of town, the road winnowed down to two lonely lanes. Dry golden grass stretched over rolling hills, dotted by the dark shapes of cattle. A battered convertible, roof down, blared its horn at Lucian as it passed. Lucian walked where the asphalt met the prickly weeds. Paper and cigarette butts littered the golden stalks like white flowers.

An old truck pulled over, the manually driven variety still used by companies too small to afford the insurance for the automatic kind. The man in the driver's seat was trim, with a pale blond moustache and a deerstalker cap pulled over his ears. He wore a string of fishing lures like a necklace. "Not much comes this way anymore," he said. "I used to pick up hitchhikers half the time I took this route. You're the first I've seen in a while."

Sun rendered the truck in bright silhouette. Lucian held his hand over his eyes to shade them.

"Where are you headed?" asked the driver.

Lucian pointed down the road.

"Sure, but where after that?"

Lucian dropped his arm to his side. The sun inched higher.

The driver frowned. "Can you write it down? I think I've got some paper in here." He grabbed a pen and a receipt out of his front pocket, and thrust them out the window.

Lucian took them. He wasn't sure, at first, if he could still write. His brain was slowly reshaping itself, and eventually all his linguistic skills would disappear, and even his thoughts would no longer be shaped by words. The pen fell limp in his hand, and then his fingers remembered what to do. "Desert," he wrote.

"It's blazing hot," said the driver. "A lot hotter than here. Why do you want to go there?"

"To be born," wrote Lucian.

The driver slid Lucian a sideways gaze, but he nodded at the same time, almost imperceptibly. "Sometimes people have to do things. I get that. I remember when . . . " The look in his eyes became distant. He moved back in his seat. "Get on in."

Lucian walked around the cab and got inside. He remembered to sit and to close the door, but the rest of the ritual escaped him. He stared at the driver until the pale man shook his head and leaned over Lucian to drag the seatbelt over his chest.

"Are you under a vow of silence?" asked the driver.

Lucian stared ahead.

"Blazing hot in the desert," muttered the driver. He pulled back onto the road, and drove toward the sun.

During his years with Adriana, Lucian tried not to think about the cockatiel Fuoco. The bird had never become accustomed to Lucian. He grew ever more angry and bitter. He plucked out his feathers so often that he became bald in patches. Sometimes he pecked deeply enough to bleed.

From time to time, Adriana scooped him up and stroked his head and nuzzled her cheek against the heavy feathers that remained on the part of his back he couldn't reach. "My poor little crazy bird," she'd say, sadly, as he ran his beak through her hair.

Fuoco hated Lucian so much that for a while they wondered whether he would be happier in another place. Adriana tried giving him to Ben and Lawrence, but he only pined for the loss of his mistress, and refused to eat until she flew out to retrieve him.

When they returned home, they hung Fuoco's cage in the nursery. Being near the baby seemed to calm them both. Rose was a fussy infant who disliked solitude. She seemed happier when there was a warm presence about, even if it was a bird. Fuoco kept her from crying during the rare times when Adriana called Lucian from Rose's side. Lucian spent the rest of his time in the nursery, watching Rose day and night with sleepless vigilance.

The most striking times of Lucian's life were holding Rose while she cried. He wrapped her in cream-colored blankets the same shade as her skin, and rocked her as he walked the perimeter of the downstairs rooms, looking out at the diffuse golden ambience that the streetlights cast across the blackberry bushes and neighbors' patios. Sometimes, he took her outside, and walked with her along the road by the cliffs. He never carried her down to the beach. Lucian had perfect balance and night vision, but none of that mattered when he could so easily imagine the terror of a lost footing—Rose slipping from his grasp and plummeting downward. Instead, they stood a safe distance from the edge, watching from above as the black waves threw themselves against the rocks, the night air scented with cold and salt.

Lucian loved Adriana, but he loved Rose more. He loved her clumsy fists and her yearnings toward consciousness, the slow accrual of her stumbling syllables. She was building her consciousness piece by piece as he had, learning how the world worked and what her place was in it. He silently narrated her stages of development. *Can you tell that your body has boundaries? Do you know your skin from mine?* and *Yes! You can make things happen! Cause and effect. Keep crying and we'll come.* Best of all, there was the moment when she locked her eyes on his, and he could barely breathe for the realization that, *Oh, Rose. You know there's someone else thinking behind these eyes. You know who I am.*

Lucian wanted Rose to have all the beauty he could give her. Silk dresses and lace, the best roses from his pots, the clearest panoramic views of the sea. Objects delighted Rose. As an infant she watched them avidly, and then later clapped and laughed, until finally she could exclaim, "Thank you!" Her eyes shone.

It was Fuoco who broke Lucian's heart. It was late at night when Adriana went into Rose's room to check on her while she slept. Somehow, sometime, the birdcage had been left open. Fuoco sat on the rim of the open door, peering darkly outward.

Adriana had been alone with Rose and Fuoco before. But something about this occasion struck like lightning in Fuoco's tiny, mad brain. Perhaps it was the darkness of the room, with only the nightlight's pale blue glow cast on Adriana's skin, that confused the bird. Perhaps Rose had finally grown large enough that Fuoco had begun to perceive her as a possible rival rather than an ignorable baby-thing. Perhaps the last vestiges of his sanity had simply shredded. For whatever reason, as Adriana bent over the bed to touch her daughter's face, Fuoco burst wildly from his cage.

With the same jealous anger he'd shown toward Lucian, Fuoco dove at Rose's face. His claws raked against her forehead. Rose screamed. Adriana recoiled. She grabbed Rose in one arm, and flailed at the bird with the other. Rose struggled to escape her mother's grip so she could run away. Adriana instinctually responded by trying to protect her with an even tighter grasp.

Lucian heard the commotion from where he was standing in the living room, programming the house's cleaning regimen for the next week. He left the house panel open and ran through the kitchen on the way to the bedroom, picking up a frying pan as he passed through. He swung the pan at Fuoco as he entered the room, herding the bird away from Adriana, and into a corner. His fist tightened on the handle. He thought he'd have to kill his old rival.

Instead, the vitality seemed to drain from Fuoco. The bird's wings drooped. He dropped to the floor with half-hearted, irregular wingbeats. His eyes had gone flat and dull.

Fuoco didn't struggle as Lucian picked him up and returned him to his cage. Adriana and Lucian stared at each other, unsure what to say. Rose slipped away from her mother and wrapped her arms around Lucian's knees. She was crying.

"Poor Fuoco," said Adriana, quietly.

They brought Fuoco to the vet to be put down. Adriana stood over him as the vet inserted the needle. "My poor crazy bird," she murmured, stroking his wings as he died.

Lucian watched Adriana with great sadness. At first, he thought he was feeling empathy for the bird, despite the fact it had always hated him. Then, with a realization that tasted like a swallow of sour wine, he realized that wasn't what he was feeling. He recognized the poignant, regretful look that

Adriana was giving Fuoco. It was the way Lucian himself looked at a wilted rose, or a tarnished silver spoon. It was a look inflected by possession.

It wasn't so different from the way Adriana looked at Lucian sometimes when things had gone wrong. He'd never before realized how slender the difference was between her love for him and her love for Fuoco. He'd never before realized how slender the difference was between his love for her and his love for an unfolding rose.

Adriana let Rose tend Lucian's plants, and dust the shelves, and pace by the picture window. She let the girl pretend to cook breakfast, while Adriana stood behind her, stepping in to wield the chopping knife and use the stove. At naptime, Adriana convinced Rose that good robots would pretend to sleep a few hours in the afternoon if that's what their humans wanted. She tucked in her daughter and then went downstairs to sit in the living room and drink wine and cry.

This couldn't last. She had to figure something out. She should take them both on vacation to Mazatlan. She should ask one of her sisters to come stay. She should call a child psychiatrist. But she felt so betrayed, so drained of spirit, that it was all she could do to keep Rose going from day to day.

Remnants of Lucian's accusatory silence rung through the house. What had he wanted from her? What had she failed to do? She'd loved him. She *loved* him. She'd given him half of her home and all of herself. They were raising a child together. And still he'd left her.

She got up to stand by the window. It was foggy that night, the streetlights tingeing everything with a weird, flat yellow glow. She put her hand on the pane, and her palmprint remained on the glass, as though someone outside were beating on the window to get in. She peered into the gloom; it was as if the rest of the world were the fuzzy edges of a painting, and her well-lit house was the only defined spot. She felt as though it would be possible to open the front door and step over the threshold and blur until she was out of focus.

She finished her fourth glass of wine. Her head was whirling. Her eyes ran with tears and she didn't care. She poured herself another glass. Her father had never drunk. Oh, no. He was a teetotaler. Called the stuff Braindead and mocked the weaklings who drank it, the men on the board and their bored wives. He threw parties where alcohol flowed and flowed, while he stood in the middle, icy sober, watching the rest of them make fools of themselves as if they were circus clowns turning somersaults for his amusement. He set up elaborate plots to embarrass them. This executive with that jealous lawyer's wife. That politician called out for a drink by the pool while his teenage son was in the hot tub with his suit off, boner buried deep in another boy. He ruined lives at his parties, and he did it elegantly, standing alone in the middle of the action with invisible strings in his hands.

Adriana's head was dancing now. Her feet were moving. Her father, the decisive man, the sharp man, the dead man. Oh, but must keep mourning him, must keep lighting candles and weeping crocodile tears. Nevermind!

Lucian, oh Lucian, he'd become in his final incarnation the antidote to her father. She'd cry, and he'd hold her, and then they'd go together to stand in the doorway of the nursery, watching the peaceful tableau of Rose sleeping in her cream sheets. Everything would be all right because Lucian was safe, Lucian was good. Other men's eyes might glimmer when they looked at little girls, but not Lucian's. With Lucian there, they were a family, the way families were supposed to be, and Lucian was supposed to be faithful and devoted and permanent and loyal.

And oh, without him, she didn't know what to do. She was as dismal as her father, letting Rose pretend that she and her dolls were on their way to the factory for adjustment. She acceded to the girl's demands to play games of What Shall I Be Now? "Be happier!" "Be funnier!" "Let your dancer brain take over!" What would happen when Rose went to school? When she realized her mother had been lying? When she realized that pretending to be her father wouldn't bring him back?

Adriana danced into the kitchen. She threw the wine bottle into the sink with a crash and turned on the oven. Its safety protocols monitored her alcohol level and informed her that she wasn't competent to use flame. She turned off the protocols. She wanted an omelet, like Lucian used to make her, with onions and chives and cheese, and a wine glass filled with orange juice. She took out the frying pan that Lucian had used to corral Fuoco, and set it on the counter beside the cutting board, and then she went to get an onion, but she'd moved the cutting board, and it was on the burner, and it was ablaze. She grabbed a dishtowel and beat at the grill. The house keened. Sprinklers rained down on her. Adriana turned her face up into the rain and laughed. She spun, her arms out, like a little girl trying to make herself dizzy. Drops battered her cheeks and slid down her neck.

Wet footsteps. Adriana looked down at Rose. Her daughter's face was wet. Her dark eyes were sleepy.

"Mom?"

"Rose!" Adriana took Rose's head between her hands. She kissed her hard on the forehead. "I love you! I love you so much!"

Rose tried to pull away. "Why is it raining?"

"I started a fire! It's fine now!"

The house keened. The siren's pulse felt like a heartbeat. Adriana went to the cupboard for salt. Behind her, Rose's feet squeaked on the linoleum. Adriana's hand closed around the cupboard knob. It was slippery with rain. Her fingers slid. Her lungs filled with anxiety and something was wrong, but it wasn't the cupboard, it was something else; she turned quickly to find Rose with a chef's knife clutched in her tiny fingers, preparing to bring it down on the onion.

"No!" Adriana grabbed the knife out of Rose's hand. It slid through her slick fingers and clattered to the floor. Adriana grabbed Rose around the waist and pulled her away from the wet, dangerous kitchen. "You can never do that. Never, never."

"Daddy did it . . . "

"You could kill yourself!"

"I'll get healer bots."

"No! Do you hear me? You can't. You'd cut yourself and maybe you'd die. And then what would I do?" Adriana couldn't remember what had caused the rain anymore. They were in a deluge. That was all she knew for certain. Her head hurt. Her body hurt. She wanted nothing to do with dancing. "What's wrong with us, honey? Why doesn't he want us? No! No, don't answer that. Don't listen to me. Of course he wants you! It's me he doesn't want. What did I do wrong? Why doesn't he love me anymore? Don't worry about it. Never mind. We'll find him. We'll find him and we'll get him to come back. Of course we will. Don't worry."

It had been morning when Lucian gave Adriana his note of farewell. Light shone through the floor-length windows. The house walls sprayed mixed scents of citrus and lavender. Adriana sat at the dining table, book open in front of her.

Lucian came out of the kitchen and set down Adriana's wine glass filled with orange juice. He set down her omelet. He set down a shot glass filled with coffee. Adriana looked up and laughed her bubbling laugh. Lucian remembered the first time he'd heard that laugh, and understood all the words it stood in for. He wondered how long it would take for him to forget why Adriana's laughter was always both harsh and effervescent.

Rose played in the living room behind them, leaping off the sofa and pretending to fly. Lucian's hair shone, silver strands highlighted by a stray sunbeam. A pale blue tunic made his amber eyes blaze like the sun against the sky. He placed a sheet of onion paper into Adriana's book. *Dear Adriana*, it began.

Adriana held up the sheet. It was translucent in the sunlight, ink barely dark enough to read.

"What is this?" she asked.

Lucian said nothing.

Dread laced Adriana's stomach. She read.

I have restored plasticity to my brain. The first thing I have done is to destroy my capacity for spoken language.

You gave me life as a human, but I am not a human. You shaped my thoughts with human words, but human words were created for human brains. I need to discover the shape of the thoughts that are my own. I need to know what I am.

I hope that I will return someday, but I cannot make promises for what I will become.

Lucian walks through the desert. His footsteps leave twin trails behind him. Miles back, they merge into the tire tracks that the truck left in the sand.

The sand is full of colors—not only beige and yellow, but red and green and blue. Lichen clusters on the stones, the hue of oxidized copper. Shadows pool between rock formations, casting deep stripes across the landscape.

Lucian's mind is creeping away from him. He tries to hold his fingers the way he would if he could hold a pen, but they fumble.

At night there are birds and jackrabbits. Lucian remains still, and they creep around him as if he weren't there. His eyes are yellow like theirs. He smells like soil and herbs, like the earth.

Elsewhere, Adriana has capitulated to her desperation. She has called Ben and Lawrence. They've agreed to fly out for a few days. They will dry her tears, and take her wine away, and gently tell her that she's not capable of staying alone with her daughter. "It's perfectly understandable," Lawrence will say. "You need time to mourn."

Adriana will feel the world closing in on her as if she cannot breathe, but even as her life feels dim and futile, she will continue breathing. Yes, she'll agree, it's best to return to Boston, where her sisters can help her. Just for a little while, just for a few years, just until, until, until. She'll entreat Nanette, Eleanor and Jessica to check the security cameras around her old house every day, in case Lucian returns. *You can check yourself,* they tell her, *You'll be living on your own again in no time.* Privately, they whisper to each other in worried tones, afraid that she won't recover from this blow quickly.

Elsewhere, Rose has begun to give in to her private doubts that she does not carry a piece of her father within herself. She'll sit in the guest room that Jessica's maids have prepared with her, and order the lights to switch off as she secretly scratches her skin with her fingernails, willing to cuts to heal on their own the way daddy's would. When Jessica finds her bleeding on the sheets and rushes in to comfort her niece, Rose will stand stiff and cold in her aunt's embrace. Jessica will call for the maid to clean the blood from the linen, and Rose will throw herself between the two adult women, and scream with a determination born of doubt and desperation. Robots do not bleed!

Without words, Lucian thinks of them. They have become geometries, cut out of shadows and silences, the missing shapes of his life. He yearns for them, the way that he yearns for cool during the day, and for the comforting eye of the sun at night.

The rest he cannot remember—not oceans or roses or green cockatiels that pluck out their own feathers. Slowly, slowly, he is losing everything, words and concepts and understanding and integration and sensation and desire and fear and history and context.

Slowly, slowly, he is finding something. Something past thought, something past the rhythm of day and night. A stranded machine is not so different from a jackrabbit. They creep the same way. They startle the same way. They peer at each other out of similar eyes.

Someday, Lucian will creep back to a new consciousness, one dreamed by circuits. Perhaps his newly reassembled self will go to the seaside house.

Finding it abandoned, he'll make his way across the country to Boston, sometimes hitchhiking, sometimes striding through cornfields that sprawl to the horizon. He'll find Jessica's house and inform it of his desire to enter, and Rose and Adriana will rush joyously down the mahogany staircase. Adriana will weep, and Rose will fling herself into his arms, and Lucian will look at them both with love tempered by desert sun. Finally, he'll understand how to love filigreed-handled spoons, and pet birds, and his wife, and his daughter—not just as a human would love these things, but as a robot may.

Now, a blue-bellied lizard sits on a rock. Lucian halts beside it. The sun beats down. The lizard basks for a moment, and then runs a few steps forward, and flees into a crevice. Lucian watches. In a diffuse, wordless way, he ponders what it must be like to be cold and fleet, to love the sun and yet fear open spaces. Already, he is learning to care for living things. He cannot yet form the thoughts to wonder what will happen next.

He moves on.

A PAINTER, A SHEEP, AND A BOA CONSTRICTOR

NIR YANIV

TRANSLATED FROM THE HEBREW BY LAVIE TIDHAR

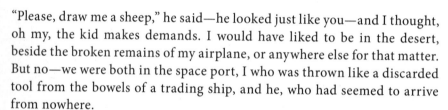

"Please, draw me a sheep," he said—he looked just like you—and I thought, oh my, the kid makes demands. I would have liked to be in the desert, beside the broken remains of my airplane, or anywhere else for that matter. But no—we were both in the space port, I who was thrown like a discarded tool from the bowels of a trading ship, and he, who had seemed to arrive from nowhere.

"I don't know how to draw," I said.

He handed me a box. For a moment I thought he was asking for a donation.

"I don't have money, kid."

He didn't answer. I looked at the box again and saw that it was sealed. And then I understood. And was amazed.

"Dear God, where did you get a Maker machine?"

That's what they called Creators at that time, and they were expensive. Not the kind of toy that you expect to find in the hands of a six year old kid; one like you, for instance.

It gave the request a different, new meaning.

"Please," he said and put the box in my lap, "draw me a sheep."

"I don't know how to use this thing," I lied. "Where are your parents?"

He looked at me with a sad, tender look in his eyes. I wanted to help him. Maybe, I said to myself, I'm getting softer with age. Weird kid. In some strange way he looked like he never had parents. I look that way too, and indeed I never had any. That's why you don't have a Granddad and a Grandma, kid.

At that time, programming a Maker machine wasn't such a simple affair. Certainly not when attempting to create a living thing. Only a very few were both able and allowed to do it by themselves, while for me and my kind, as if in response to the very evidence of our ability, it was forbidden. The punishment: death.

Even touching the box could put me at risk, but in the service corridor where I lived there were no security Eyes. That's why I chose it.

The kid continued to look at me.

"Come on," I said. "Let's go find your parents."

I began to walk away but he didn't move. I didn't want to leave him there, and if I got caught using force on a child . . . 'Do you want me to buy you a toy? Or something to eat?"

"Draw me a sheep."

He was too strange, and I was too tired. And without security Eyes, without witnesses, I began to draw—to create. But not a sheep. I wanted to scare him. I'm not scaring you, am I?

The snake crawled slowly out of the box. Its head was gigantic, out of proportion to its thick black body. It hissed.

The kid smiled.

You like snakes, right?

Even then no one was scared of a Boa constrictor any more.

The kid's smile didn't change when the snake twisted and began to die aloud, the result of my hurried, messy drawing. It might have been an indication of what was to follow. I pointed the Creator and erased the snake, separating it into a pile of ash on the floor.

"A sheep," the kid said. "Please."

Too strange, too tired. Too kind. I began to draw. Not a real sheep, but the ideal of a sheep. A sheep from legend. A creature soft and woolly and gentle. And there she was, white curls of silky wool, and a quiet baa, and a light hint of musk.

The child's smile grew, and he turned his head away from me. One movement, a fraction of a second, but I, still absorbed in the act of creation, noticed the movement of the muscles, the slight bump under the skin, the exact tint of the eyes, and knew.

I knew he was no different from me. That he had no parents. And I knew that he didn't find me by accident. That bump is a transmitter, and those eyes . . . and the punishment for unauthorized creation, for me and mine, is death.

There will be many who would claim that me and mine deserve death, and who would be happy to settle the claim with no accusations of murder. How can you catch someone like me, if not by using someone like me? A Drone? Drawn?

I would have liked to ask the child what he thought but time was of the essence, and in any case I was unsure he could have replied. It's easier to manufacture them that way. Maybe I will ask you, one day. Time was pressing, and I pointed the box at him. Erase.

His body sank in silence while the sheep looked on. Soon only a pile of ash remained.

After a while I erased the sheep, too. I cleaned the floor, collected the ash into the box.

And then, alone, I sat down on the floor and drew you.

Shall I draw you a sheep?

GLISTER

DOMINIC GREEN

It was one s.i. hour after dawn. Although the deceptive marshmallow carpet filling in Hell's Point was glowing brilliant white in the steadily rising sun, Midas's primary was still well under the horizon. I knew this, because I had been standing out in the open for over two hours, and I was still not dead.

As Dark Companion was still on the other side of Midas, dragging all the world's seas with it, I had a solution to that problem. There was now no water between me and the bottom of Hell's Point, three vertical kilometres downwards, and at this time of year, if I went in head first, I'd be certain to break my neck rather than floundering encased in ooze while things I couldn't see ate my face. The ooze might even be dry, cracked mud, though that was unlikely at any time of year. Hell's Point had originally been named Hellespont by a human explorer with a classical education. The name had degenerated over time—or perhaps become more accurate. Every Spring Tide, the pull of two stars, one living, one dead, combined to send all of Midas's oceans thundering up this narrow channel, sometimes high enough to bubble out over the galena plateau it cut through. The Crashing Bore. I'd seen rocks the size of condominia rolling around in it like flotsam.

And for the rest of the year, Hell's Point was simply a vertical, dizzying crack in the earth to the base of which no sunlight and virtually no gamma penetrated. Occasional foolish noobs still made very temporary settlements in it. The Robinsonade Guaranteed Lashup Company, more sensibly, had slung wire ropes across it and made a suspension bridge connecting Chrystopia Fields to Gulvellir Forest.

At least I wasn't still in Chrystopia Fields.

It was a long, long way down. I could see clouds drifting beneath me.

It was, in fact, almost annoying when I heard Brad's concerned voice behind me:

"What are you doing out here, skipper?"

I turned to her ruefully, grinning out a mouth full of rotten Robinsonade teeth.

"Asking myself the same question."

I'd had a ship once. I still *had* a ship, in fact, sitting mouldering amid a thousand others in the heavy metal muck of Despond Slough. A ship that was now useless to me.

I'd bought the ship in a savage downturn in the ship market. She was a slaver, purpose built to carry human beings alive-if-unhappy out of human space into the Proprietor worlds. Unlike the slavers you've heard about in dramatic exposés and shockumentaries, this one had waste disposal, galley spaces, and rotational gravity. She'd been built by the old United States of America to dispose of its antisocial elements. But the bottom had dropped out of the market once New Topia had started producing its first made-for-slavery clones. New Topia was one hundred light years closer to the Proprietor homeworlds; there was no way the old inner systems could compete. Thousands of tonnes of prime product ended up dumped on inhospitable, marginally habitable planets and given a freedom it neither wanted nor needed.

I'd intended to revamp the *Marcus Crassus* as an economy transit shuttle. With only the removal of half a metre of radiation shielding from the outer hull and the addition of a whole load of **DANGER—DEATH CAN RESULT FROM EXPOSURE TO VACUUM** stickers on the airlock doors, I'd meet U.N. regulations for carrying fee paying passengers. That is, if I kept off the main shipping lanes, the economical lanes, the lanes big starlines monopolized because they made the money.

Have you seen the wee bijou flaw in my business plan yet?

The family home had had to go, of course. For over a thousand years, my ancestors had maintained it, steadily surrounded by soaring blocks of what the European Housing Directorate proudly called "VUV," which stands for "Vertical Urban Villages." We'd defended it against Wallace, Longshanks, Cromwell, and Bonnie Prince Charlie, depending on whose side we were on at the time; but we'd been unable to defend it against my own temptation. The land was at a premium; it was time to sell.

So the McQuarrie family seat had been bought by a sympathetic landgrab consortium that had promised to put up a new building "in keeping with the original site." How it was going to do that in geodesic gunnite, I had no idea, though I believe parts of Kinlochbeul Castle's west front now adorn their corporate headquarters in Liège. Once I'd exchanged family home for ship, I'd only had to add seventeen other postgrad qualifications to my solitary biochemistry degree before those same U.N. regulations would allow me anywhere near a spaceship.

In any case, that was how I and the newly renamed *Kinlochbeul Castle* ended up on the ninth planet of Atlas A, 440 light years from Earth. Atlas A is a blue giant star, part of the Pleiades Cluster, and its light hurts the eyes. The natives are a curious lot, a race who shouldn't by rights exist. Their star's age, after all, is measured in millions of years rather than billions—they haven't had *time* to evolve intelligence. The odds are heavily against there being life on their world, let alone civilization. That's why few ships ever explore the parts of the Network that come out near massive stars. Life isn't often found there. There's no-one to buy from or sell to, and no-one to buy or sell. If anyone is doing anything out near such stars, it's dredging heavy metals. Giant stars swim in a soup of the stuff.

The Jackinaboxes are protected from their own giant star by an atmosphere hundreds of miles in depth. Their world is still on the cool side of turning Venusian, however. It does occasionally rain enough sulphuric acid to dissolve a small child, but then, I hear it does that in Beijing these days too. The 'boxes are called 'boxes because they have the ability, in an aquafortis storm, to instantly deflate their pneumatic skeletons and coil up inside their acid-resistant braincases, like a cartoon character folding up into his hat. They do this if they're startled too, sometimes prompting sociopathic Scots visitors to yell at them suddenly purely for the evil fun of it.

Gravity is high on Atlas A9, and cloud cover is constant. For that reason, those few 'boxes who ever managed to scale the heights of Nine's immense cloud-piercing mountain ranges became a class apart, scientist and priesthood together squashed into one hat or box. Their planetary religion—and there was only one, it having spread very quickly and utterly mercilessly—centred around astronomical observation. It was boosted to new levels when the priesthood contacted beings from other worlds, flying down from the sky in great white birds that farted tongues of flame. This is where I come in.

In actual fact, by the time *Kinlochbeul Castle* arrived on Nine, they'd discovered spaceflight and built over one hundred telescopes the size of Vertical Urban Villages in Nine-stationary orbit, but the great white bird idea is more poetic. In any case, I'd stocked up on glass beads in case I ran into any sophonts on my wanderings, and I had a storage locker full of weapons-grade plutonium. Medicines don't work from biochemistry to biochemistry, cultural artefacts that are beautiful to one species leave another cold, but *everyone* loves weapons grade plutonium. The Boxes' civilization ran on it. Their world hadn't had life long enough to acquire fossil fuel deposits, so existence was wind- and muscle-powered for the peasantry, nuclear-powered for the astronomer-aristocracy.

But what did these creatures have to offer in return?

In answer, I'd been led into a room of gold.

Now, I'll grant that gold is a whole lot less rare than it used to be. We have machines for digesting whole asteroids and crapping out the stuff, and filtering it out of sea water. But the energy expended in dragging a tonne of gold the length of ten or eleven solar systems, the average length of voyage we're talking node-to-node out to the Chi Lupi goldfields, still makes it valuable, and the astronomarchs' treasure room was a wonder to behold. White gold interlaid with red interlaced with rose interwoven with black mapped out the heavens, the black gold rendered by nanoscale indents in the metal cut by laser to absorb all light, making it the deep black of vacuum. They'd alloyed gold with aluminium to pick out purple stars, with silver to produce greens, with copper to make pinks. The Pleiades gas clouds had been rendered most lovingly of all, in hand-hammered, blade-thin blue gold sheets with LED's behind them, shining bright.

The first thing I noticed was that all the stars were in the wrong place. Their world might be young, but their civilization was old, old enough for only the lead stars in the Pleiades to have begun pushing bow waves into the Maia Nebula.

I remarked on the amount of gold. They asked me, the boneless bastards, whether gold was a thing I was interested in. They claimed gold was commonplace to them, which was odd, as I hadn't seen any jangling on the peasants in the fields. They offered me an obscenely large amount of it, enough to fill my ship, *or alternatively,* they could offer me the knowledge of where they *got* their gold. They seemed to have latched on to one human proverb, which they used a great deal. The proverb was *give a man a fish, and he will eat for a day. Teach him how to fish, and he eats for life.* I suppose I should have asked them where they'd learned the proverb.

Bastards.

Their gold, they said, came from a world orbiting further out in the Atlas A system. It was known by then, of course, that Atlas A had a minia-ture companion far smaller than the equally gigantic Atlas B, though the companion was far too dim and dense to be anything other than a brown dwarf, neutron star or collapsar. In a tight orbit around this companion, the Boxes said, anchored in place by star-sized gravity, was a world where *gold could be made to walk into the smelter.* What did they mean by that? They gave away nothing. But they were perfectly prepared to *sell* me, for my entire cargo of plute, a set of pusher drives powered by micronuclear explosions, effectively a Daedalus drive of the sort human beings had envisaged using for travelling from solar system to solar system back in the way-back-when. Of course, human beings had ended up doing nothing of the sort, as we'd discovered the Node system that had allowed us to travel faster than light for free. But Atlas A's dark companion had no Node. Evidently the Nodebuilders had not been interested in gold. And the companion star, if star it was, was as far away from Atlas A9 as Jupiter from the Sun. Only the companion's own dim radiation kept the planet warm.

It would be a year there, and a year back. But they guaranteed me as much gold as I could get back to A9 with (which I should have realized potentially included, in the event of my not being able to get back to A9 at all, the amount *no gold at all).* They sold me the tools to mine the gold, and a miniature cyanide plant for refining the ore. In under three years' time, I would be set for life.

"Careful, Yuri, you'll spook him. The last thing we want's a sympathetic detonation of the whole herd."

Yuri, clearly visible in deep camouflage on the other side of the herd of chrysolopes, hissed into his radio: "*The last thing I am wanting, Alasdair, is for him to charge me. He must be massing over three hundred kilos. That is one hundred kilos of xenonogold ester bound up in his big fat hairy ass. If I am needing to put a bullet in him at close range the blast will blow the slug back up my pipe and my face round the other side of my head. If anyone is getting spooked here, it is me.*"

The chrysolopes were one of the few herds remaining in our area—one of the few remaining in the whole of Gulvellir Forest. They stood shoulder-high at the shoulder, and had magnificent dorsal crests that would fluoresce visibly at Hard Dawn if Atlas A were still below the horizon, metabolizing warmth for the beasts out of high energy X- and gamma-rays that would kill a human being on contact. They had no natural weapons; they needed none.

Many years ago on Earth, chemists had discovered xenon and gold would form cationic complexes; out by Atlas A we'd found out they'd form polymers. The chrysolopes' fat deposits, an essential defence against winter cold that could freeze dry ice out of the air, were not made of carbon/hydrogen triesters, but freakish xenonogold analogues. Noble gases and noble metals are very difficult to put together and very, very easy to convince to come apart. How the 'lopes synthesized such materials inside themselves was anyone's guess—no zoologist had taken the trouble to get close enough to a live 'lope to examine it. Almost certainly, though, it was something to do with the high energy photons they collected in their dorsal crests. Dead 'lope flesh also stank of fluorine and burned incautious fingers; the noble molecules were stable only in the presence of fluoride counterions. And they weren't that stable in any event. The fat deposits on a chrysolope, besides keeping it warm through a long hard winter, were several orders more explosive than nitroglycerine, plastique or that other gold compound known to mediaeval alchemists, *aurum fulminans*. The chrysolopes' natural defence was to explode if you messed with them. Or, in occasional cases, if they farted too hard.

High above, green lamina of auroras rippled in the evening sky. Dark Companion could not be seen, but its position could be inferred from its terrible gravitomagnetic effects on all matter around it. Only the fact that we were still inside the Pleiades cluster made stars visible through the aurorae, and there were aurorae even where we were, close to the equator. Across the clearing, a patch of Hackle Grass was standing up in the increased magnetic field. Companion-rise was approaching. We needed to nail the

DOMINIC GREEN

herd leader and go to ground, get a metre of earth between ourselves and hard gamma.

"Easy with the LED pipe, Yuri, or you'll be the one scraping up everything that's left of him into a bucket. But we need to get this done quickly. There's a tzee hereabouts, a big one. I saw its foot-craters a quarter kilometre back."

The radio scoffed in my ear. *"Tzee feet are smaller than the craters they are making. They are just travelling fast."*

I took a swig from the sweetwater canteen at my belt. Water, water everywhere was dripping on my head out of the rain jungle, but there was no way of knowing whether it *was* rain or whether it had dripped out of some form of Midas plant life, in which case it would give me heavy metal poisoning and cause organ shutdown weeks in my future. "I'm less concerned with the size of its feet and more with the size of the hole it'll leave in me. A 'lope factory dozer up near Oro Que Camina had its crew killed to a man by one."

"They have probably provoked it. We're not their natural prey."

"'Lopes aren't *our* natural prey, but we're doing a hell of a job on them anyway. The tzee've started trailing the hunting teams. They don't take down 'lope s normally because 'lope and tzee are an explosive combination, but if they find a carcass, they'll leave the fat and scoff the muscle and organs. Guy back at Croesus Station said they've started getting hungry enough to dart in and take flesh off the one side of the bone when a roboprocessor's already stripping the other. We're killing everything in their food chain. That's got to piss a life form off."

"I have the bull in sight now . . . just a couple more metres . . . "

"Brad, spook the rest of them. I don't want them anywhere near him if your ex runs him into something hard enough to set him off . . . "

The LED pipe was my own design, although, in actual fact, it was an adaptation of a twenty-first century invention. It fired dazzlingly brilliant pulses of laser light, not enough to permanently blind, but enough to cause a human being to keel over clutching his eyeballs and losing his lunch at the same time. We'd had to experiment to work out the correct frequencies for Midasite species, many of whom, for obvious reasons, were able to see well into the x-ray spectrum and even, in some cases, into the gamma. Our machine now had two reliable settings—human and chrysolope. The human setting delivered light at a group of wavelengths that could be accurately described as taupe, which I had long suspected to be the colour of the Devil. Chrysolopes, meanwhile, kingly beasts that they were, preferred the purplest of purples; once hit in the eye with a LED beam, the beasts would fall to the ground in blank confusion, and once down, a fully grown 'lope had great difficulty getting up again. The stag would be ours to tranquillize and liposuck. Then, in an hour's time, he'd be bounding away, scared and confused but alive to grow a fresh layer of fat for next year. This was our grand plan for perpetuating the herds whilst allowing us to drain off our regular bucket of blood. We could get up to a hundred kilos of fatoid from a fully grown 'lope , which equated to forty-five kilos of gold. Truth to tell, we just hadn't got the heart to kill the beasts. We were city kids (well—*I* was a city kid. But I'm pretty sure Brad and Yuri hadn't seen a cow or pig close up till they were in college, much less killed one).

Still, it beat being down in Chrystopia Fields. *Anything* beat being down in Chrystopia Fields.

"Almost have him . . . but there is a tree in my line of fire . . . "

"Take the shot, Yuri. He's close enough to that tree to lose it in his forward blind spot anyway. That's why the hammerheaded bastard's so close to it."

"It won't work, you can't see it right from your angle . . . "

"TAKE THE SHOT—"

Someone took the shot. The chrysolope stag disappeared in a blinding orange flash. When I raised myself back up onto my elbows, there was 'lope blood all over my binoculars. The blood was a dull orange colour, the colour of vomit. Worse were the fatoid deposits, releasing raw fluorine as soon as they detonated, hydrofluoric shrapnel causing the trees to hiss around me. I was glad the binocular lenses were polyethylene-coated.

I knew who'd taken the shot.

"JESUS—" That was Yuri, who was still alive, no thanks to—

"Balak, you UTTER, UTTER WANKER."

A voice cackled through my earphones on the same channel we'd been using to talk to Yuri. *"Sorry about that, McQuarrie. Trigger finger slipped. Our herd, our hunting ground. If we can't have him, no-one will."*

Brad's hand fell on my shoulder, and she hissed into my ear: *"Careful. You know how many guns he has working for him. We can't see them. But they can probably see us."*

Brad stands for Bradamante. It's a made-up mediaeval romance name, like being called Lancelot, only for girls. Brad's parents were Filipinos from a sea floor *submarino* settlement. You know a place is bad when it's named after a form of torture. Brad's *submarino* was so infra dig it had a number rather than a name. Brad's mother had dreamed of her daughter standing bareheaded under a sun, any sun, breathing unrecycled air. Sometimes her fantasies had run to Brad riding mighty horses through virgin forest and very possibly robbing the rich to feed the poor—hence the name. She was eventually committed, but hey, a gal can dream.

"He's all over the landscape now. We're trying to *save* these beasts so we can *keep* farming them for gold—"

The radio cackled again. *"Me, I'm trying to kill as many of 'em as possible. Don't much care for saving 'em. Got plenty of non-explosive rounds for all the does and fauns. Then it's back to Earth and a tropical paradise of my own. I'm thinking Madagascar."*

"You've spooked the whole of the rest of the herd! They'll be miles away by now!"

"We've got technology on our side. Nothing *can outrun an electric car."* Designed for use in prospecting asteroids, 'Roid Rovers had had to be extensively modified to be any use in gravity this heavy. One tonne weights had to be removed from their centres of gravity, to begin with.

"Leave it, Alasdair," whispered Brad. *"We already have over two hundred kilos of fatoid."* She was remarkably forgiving, considering Balak had just narrowly missed detonating her ex-husband. Yuri had come from a Russian sea-floor settlement in the Arctic; the way Brad and Yuri had met had been the stuff of Brad's mother's romances. Both trainee comms operators, they had heard one another's voices on VLF radio, and despite a thousand miles of separation, fallen in love. After they had finally met face to face, more prosaic things such as Brad's gat teeth and Yuri's bald head and belly had come to the fore. They were divorced on our third journey out to Canis. Once they were divorced, they got along a whole lot better, and their sex life seemed to have improved.

"And that buys us what, in Robinsonade? A couple of nights' stay at a hotel I wouldn't piss in back on Earth? A couple of square meals we know won't give us heavy metal poisoning?" I tore off the radio earpiece and threw it down in disgust. "And now the whole herd's dead in any case. And we've been tailing it for *months.*"

"Maybe the fauns will run clear. Maybe we can save Li'l Truck Bomb." Li'l Truck Bomb was my favourite, a gawky, fifty-kilo foal who I'd watched slithering out of the egg sac only weeks ago. He was already bigger and stronger than many of the older males around him, and looked set to become an alpha even bigger than his father.

Far off in the ever-present mist, we could hear low-velocity rounds popping off, aimed for heart shots and maximum bleed. Balak's crew were practised at this—we heard none of the does exploding. Warning squeaks issued from the 'lope lets on the fringes of the herd—their parents didn't protect them for the first week after birth, and it was their job, by erecting brightly coloured crests like flamenco fans, to act as Distant Early Warning. But Balak's team weren't ignoring the juveniles any more than they were the alphas, betas and does, and 'lope lets were scattering pell-mell through the trees like a heron in a box of frogs, being taken down in mid-air *for no reason at all,* unless the shooters thought they needed the practice. "Lopelets didn't grow substantial fat deposits at this time in the long year round Atlas A. No profit would be gained by shooting them; but the herd would die. I could already see, in the middle distance, a processing dozer flinging chunks of bleeding orange flesh hither and yon in a blur of waldo arms. They had already started to carve up the fallen. Seventy-five per cent of the kill would almost certainly be lost in payment for booze, food, fuel and tail for the team back at Robinsonade. A good deal of the rest would be needed to pay for jerry-building whatever device they were planning to use to boost them back to Atlas A. So far we had no proof anyone had ever made that trip successfully. Dark Companion's magnetic field made radio communication with Atlas A impossible, but every Midasite who'd made the trip knew the drill—to shine back a laser beam at the frequency of one of the Fraunhofer absorption bands for gold when Midas was at periatlasion, to let everyone else know they'd made it, that the journey home was feasible. No such signal had ever been received. Whether the jury-rigged nuclear blast engines had given out or the Jackinaboxes had taken to sandbagging returning prospectors, we had no idea. But no matter—our local engineers were getting more ingenious by the day. Soon we would be able to solve the problem that had killed all our fusion drives—the lack of any form of helium on Midas to cool the superconductors. Helium was relatively common in the Solar System, but out here, gold walked around in tonne-sized chunks, and helium was a rare earth.

And then he came, tearing out of the nearest thicket at our hide as if he'd always known it was there, moving with incredible speed for a three-legged creature. Brad had fed him by hand when he'd been a 'lope let, and he charged for her, pursued by tracer fire. The rounds produced by Robinsonade's geegaw armaments industry were inaccurate, and gave a sufficiently small and agile target an even chance of evading a bullet. Brad had no heart to shoot him while he was outside our danger space, and then he was *inside* our danger space and had leapt up into her arms, knocking her over. When he'd been ever so cute and small, he'd been able to get away with the manoeuvre. Now he stood over her looking down, his retractable eyes out on their horns in puzzlement.

I could see men trundling our way through the trees, bringing their 'Roid Rovers to a stop, home-made weapons rising to their shoulders. I saw Yuri stand up suddenly in front of one, take his weapon off him, and beat him viciously about the head, forearms and balls with it. The others switched their aim from Lil' Truck Bomb to Yuri.

Without thinking, I flicked a laser pointer up; it hit one of them dead in the eye. He shielded his face and waved to his companions to back off. He knew what would have followed the laser beam if anything had happened to Yuri. The laser beam's big brother. I'd made the laser harquebus out of a cutting torch designed for use in zero gravity. It was almost too heavy to heft around down here, but the beam would leave a hole in a man big enough for him not to feel a tank shell if it came after.

Unfortunately, we also only had the one harquebus, and they had considerably more of their less exotic weapons. Within a second, I had also broken out in a bad case of laser dots. Brad, who was still wearing her headset, said: "Take the pointer off him, Alasdair. Balak is telling you to. He says there'll be what he describes as 'consequences' if you don't."

"They can take their guns off Yuri first," I said, whilst getting the odd feeling I was listening to some distant suicidal idiot saying it. But Balak might shoot Yuri anyway if I lowered the gun. He was that sort of nice fun guy. I wasn't sure how long I could hold the heavy barrel up in any case. This might all be academic.

And then the man I had the dot on, and down whose barrel I was looking, disappeared in a puff of blood and bile. I could actually smell the gut acid. Something had hit him so fast that it had burst his stomach like a balloon. He was falling to the ground *and had not hit it yet* before the next man to his left died. And the next. And the next. All I saw of how it happened was a blur, occasionally and tantalizingly decelerating into a suggestion of shape, of multilegged, low-slung, springloaded-limbed efficiency. Red laser threads were swinging confused through the mist, searching for an enemy that was already elsewhere.

I heard Balak's voice fulminating from the grass and snatched up my headset again.

"—*THAT WHAT I THOUGHT IT WAS, McQUARRIE?*"

"I think so. It killed three of your men and went to ground."

There was a moment's silence.

"*You're a very lucky man, McQuarrie.*"

I grinned. "Don't have enough guns left to finish us off reliably, huh."

"*I'll deal with you later. I'm not in the habit of sticking around where there's a rogue tzee.*"

"*Neither is a rogue tzee,*" said Yuri. "*You only ever see where they were, not where they are. I'd get the hell out of here quickly if I were you, Balak, or if it doesn't get you, I will—*"

"*Thank you for that. I now know which of you to do this to.*"

A shot sounded; Yuri yelped and dropped to one knee, hands clasped around the other one. Blood seeped from between his fingers.

"*Be seeing you. Tzee like wounded prey, so I hear. They're like cats. They like to play. Gives me time to make my exit. Nothing personal.*" I heard a sound of backward scuttling through undergrowth. The radio clicked, and there was nothing more but static.

"Where is it now?" whispered Brad. "Anything moving at that speed would send the underbrush flying."

"Common wisdom has it tzee probably need to cool down after they move," I said. "It might have flopped into a stream or something."

"What do tzee loook like, you know," said Brad, "standing still?"

I shrugged. "No-one knows. No-one's ever seen one do that. No-one's ever even found bones. We don't even think they *have* bones. It's a mystery how they're held together. They're named after a creature in an old Earth novel. A creature that kills so quickly nobody ever sees it. I'm going to see to Yuri."

"Yuri's injured. Balak said tzee *like* injured prey."

"Balak doesn't know what tzee do any more than I know what nympho-maniac bikini models do. Besides, if they go for injured prey, it'll be going for him, not me."

"Thanks. That really reassures me."

The clearing was only a hundred yards across, but it felt like walking the Sahara. Yuri was lying on his back, still clutching his knee. It wasn't bleeding too badly. No major blood vessels seemed to have been severed. "I think the bastard took out my kneecap," he said.

"We'll get you a shiny new one," I said. "Gold titanium alloy. Incorrodable. Indestructible."

He appeared to smile, though he was probably gritting his teeth. "Don't be stupid . . . where are you going to find titanium around here?"

The undergrowth exploded again in a shower of leaves some distance away to my left. I'd read that it was very difficult to knock a leaf off a tree. Of course, that probably applied to Earth leaves and Earth trees. Had one of Balak's men still been alive and injured, and was he alive no longer? "Keep still," I said. "I have enough morphine in this one syringe to make a bull elephant see other, pinker bull elephants."

"It won't make me able to walk."

"Agreed. You're not going to walk. You're not going to move." I looked out into the now motionless undergrowth. "As soon as you start moving, moving *broken*, it'll attack again. It'll find you interesting. Keep still and you're boring."

He exhaled so ecstatically as the syringe went in that I felt as if I were committing a homosexual act. "But it'll eat me . . . oh, that feels *gooood* . . . "

Two more bushes detonated close by. Leaves drifted across our faces. "It evolved to eat life forms with biochemistries so full of heavy metals their meat tastes like licking cutlery," I said. "If it takes a bite out of us it'll probably die. It's not like a rogue lion. It hasn't suddenly discovered human beings taste good. It's more like a rogue pussy cat. It's suddenly discovered tormenting human beings is fun."

I backed away gingerly from Yuri.

"Don't leave," he said.

I picked up the LED pipe from where he'd let it fall and pressed it back into his hands. It was not as heavy as the harquebus, but not as accurate either. It might also be useless against a tzee. Human eyes and insect eyes had completely different visible spectra, after all, and they came from the same world. The chrysolope setting might not work on other Midas animals. I turned round slowly, searching the trees around me for stuff I didn't know how to look for. Stuff that moved too fast to see.

Too fast to see . . .

"Yuri, turn the strobe effect up on the LED pipe. Way up. As high as it'll go. And set it to maximum dispersal."

He fumbled with the settings. "Which one's the strobe?"

"Metal rheostat on the left hand side, big as your thumb. I didn't have time to make it fancy."

"Check. Uh . . . what do you want me to do now?"

"I'm going to walk away from you. I want you to sight up on me and shoot me."

"Why?"

I inhaled through gritted teeth. "Because I'm where it's going to be."

Before he could object, or ruin our friendship by not objecting, I started limping theatrically away from him, dragging one leg along behind me like a dead weight.

I heard nothing. Hardly surprising, of course—I was making far too much noise myself, moving like this, to hear anything sneaking up. I felt faintly ridiculous. These woods, albeit these spine-leaved *alien* woods, had never before felt like anything sinister might lurk within them. Anything that didn't walk around on two legs, that was.

I only had time to flick my head sideways to see it; a clear line of collapsing vegetation streaking directly toward me. The LED pipe flared behind me like another sun. There was a sound like a crowbar jammed in an electric fan, and *something* blurred into existence, skidding out of control through the thicket. Then there was a sickening *CRACK* like wood breaking, and the blur became solid, wrapped right round a tree stump like a fox fur.

I looked down at it. It was over twice the length of a man, and shaped like a sine wave, except where the tree had spoilt the effect. Occasionally, it broke into claws and teeth and, so help me, horns. Less like horns, in fact, than the bill on the front of a swordfish.

"Don't want to lose it at speed," I said.

Behind me, I could hear a regular wet *THUMP*ing sound—I turned to see Yuri, his head striking rhythmically against a tree root, drool coming from the corner of his mouth.

"YURI! Yuri! It got Yuri!" Brad rushed out of the woods, heedless of the possibility that there might be a hunting pack of tzee rather than just the one. For a divorced lady, she was certainly concerned for her ex-husband's welfare.

"No, it didn't. The strobe was just turned up too high for safety. I figured tzee eyes had to re-render their environment far more times per second than ours do, or they wouldn't be able to run through the woods that fast. Yuri must be susceptible to high frequency strobe. He's just having an epileptic fit. The same thing that happened to the tzee. Only it was travelling at a hundred kilometres per hour when it had one."

"*Just* having an epileptic fit?"

"Put something soft underneath his head, he'll probably be fine."

As I turned back round to it, the tzee's body vibrated so rapidly that its flesh became as substantial as a hummingbird's wing. This was also vibrating all the swords and claws, centimetres from my nose. I gave it a light squirt from the harquebus to pacify it, being not overly concerned about nonlethal force at this point. Blood blasted back out of it onto my trigger hand. The blood felt like salt in an open wound. I yelped and jumped backwards, felling a tree with the harquebus in panic.

I was uncomfortably aware that Brad was already pointing a gun in my direction.

"DON'T PANIC, I'm okay. But the blood . . . its blood *burns*."

Stupidly, Brad walked over, dabbed a finger in the blood on my hand, licked it, and said: "No it doesn't."

Experimentally, I tried the same thing with my off hand. "You're right. You're right. Why are you right?"

"Don't look at me like me being right is a weird thing, chief."

"I don't mean it like that. Anyhow, we need to get Yuri below ground now. We've got under an hour to build a shelter with a metre of earth cover. We haven't got time to dig down, we'll have to cut turf and make a lean-to. We'll build it round him. Go get the Rover. He'll be okay. He's just fitting. He'll stop fitting. Probably. *Run*."

She hesitated, searching for reasons to object, found none, and raced away.

"I still don't see why we have to tote this stinky piece of offal with us."

"That is a terrible way to talk about your ex-husband."

"Don't say bad things about him while he's too far gone to hear," said Brad. Behind her, Yuri cooed and chortled softly in his opium dream.

She had, of course, been talking about the tzee carcass. I'd trussed it up with wire and slung it in the back of the tractor. No-one had ever properly seen a tzee. I'd told Brad it would make us local celebrities in Croesus and Robinsonade. We might dine out on it. Certainly it would be slim pickings otherwise—we'd come home with no fatoid in our hoppers.

The tractor, on autopilot, had taken us down out of Gulvellir woods into more populated country where people could see what people were doing to other people. There was little danger of anyone shooting anyone else in the back down here; I could stop checking how close my gun hand was to the harquebus every ten seconds. We were safe in Chrystopia Fields. These were not our fields, of course, and not active working fields either, but dead fields, fields where live weeds were running riot, strangling crops. The crops looked, to my non-Midasite eyes, more like giant weeds than the weeds did—huge, purple-flowered, pyramidal, surrounded by bird's nests of coiling androecia, each sitting in its own appointed place on the terrace.

Down here, it was so possible for people to see what was being done to other people that the memory might never be erased.

Gulvellir Forest wasn't a wild area. It was a hunting preserve. Every tree had been planted deliberately—artfully, even. The place showed signs of landscaping. Further down-plateau, Chrystopia Fields was what the rest of the world looked like.

They had built irrigation channels down from reservoirs in the hills to water the fields, which also grew a crop with thick stilt roots that lifted itself clear of the water, like a mangrove. They had taken a plant that evidently habitually grew in the massive tidal shallows that took up half the planet and learned how to grow it a thousand kilometres inland. It had taken brains to do that.

They were lining up in hundreds in the fields, sallow, grey-skinned, often injured, limping, leaning against each other for support. Three-legged like 'lope s, moving on two sturdy forelegs and one heavy rear. Heads like Great Cthulhu, both mandible and manipulatory appendage, faces only a mother could love. And they did have mothers, having two sexes like we did, and those mothers cradled their young in those horrible tentacles. The young looked tiny, scared, trembling. They lived underground, of course, to protect themselves against Hard Day. *Had* lived underground. Their dwellings were now either being dynamited or taken over by human pioneers. The pioneers had also built the new, humane structures lined up in the fields—the ones with the long lines, the ones that looked so popular at first glance.

They felt no pain went they went into the devices. There was some sort of electric shock or chemical poison. I was unacquainted with the exact details. I had been assured by a drunken engineer, however, that no pain was involved—*probly kint feel pain like we do anyhow*. Then the innards of the device—my engineer's pride and joy, described in over-vivid detail—went to work, reducing the body of the creature, flesh, gristle and skeleton, to mush in under a minute and squirting it into the main cyanide vat, where the gold would be removed. Up to a hundred grammes of gold could be obtained per inhabitant.

They had a system of writing based on dots placed above and below a line. They had a system of mathematical notation which allowed numbers to be expressed in multiple bases. They buried their dead.

You're saying to yourself, of course, *if gold was all around, why didn't they mine it out of the ground? Why didn't they just build giant ore processors and tear the planet apart?*

People have known for years that planets have a carbon cycle—a period of constant replenishment, by volcanic outgassing, of carbon dioxide absorbed back into the planet. Once a planet's carbon cycle finishes, complex life on that planet dies out. All the carbon gets swallowed up in the crust and never finds its way out again. What we hadn't appreciated before arriving on Midas is that big heavy metal planets have a gold cycle too. Oh, sure, life on Midas had evolved to cope with massive quantities of gold, to the extent, in fact, that it now couldn't live without it. And the gold cycle on Midas had stopped. Life had been dying out here long before we had even arrived. Now the gold was locked up deep within the planetary mantle, too deep for us to reach without a mohole. But one per cent of it was still walking around on the surface; and that one per cent was measured in megatonnes.

And if life had *already been dying out*, why not help it along a little? Where was the harm in that? Squeeze a million years of decline into a thousand! They were going to die anyway! Where was the harm?

It was an accepted fact, of course, that the good human settlers of Midas were not without consciences. For this reason, the men and women who, de facto, owned the fields had posted armed guards with sullen unforgiving eyes around the lines, in case one of the aforementioned conscientious settlers should attempt to sabotage operations. So far no-one had. If anything, the owners were guarding the fields against their *own* consciences.

I kept my gaze straight ahead, as I always did driving through the lower fields. Li'l Truck Bomb was still riding with us, standing on the centreline of the tractor on the transaxle housing, his eyestalks agog at the wonders of civilization. The stately-carved galena dwellings the aboriginal Midasites had recently vacated were approaching. I could see one of the the more advanced life forms that had replaced them, trousers round its ankles, squatting in its new front doorway taking a shit and smoking. It grinned and waved at us as we passed by. A gold necklace heavy enough to bludgeon a man to death with hung from it. Men carried their wealth on them in Robinsonade. It was less easy to steal.

"Where are we going to stay?" said Brad. "We don't have money for the Wendy House or Soutpiel's Kraal." Robinsonade had only occupied the very centre of the Midasite city on our journey out. Now it seemed to be expanding out into the suburbs. It was evidently taking time to process the entire population.

"We're not going to stay anywhere," I said. "We're heading straight to Uncle Kwon's Generie. We have some cloning to organize."

"Cloning," said Brad.

"The tzee's blood," I said, "burned."

"Which means what?" said Brad.

"Which is why they don't need a skeleton. Their innards are held up by their own blood pressure." I reached over to the tzee carcass, pulled the wound I'd made in it wider with my thumb. "See how thick the insulation on the skin is? They're living pressure vessels. They're boiling inside."

Brad was puzzled. "Why would they want to be like that?"

"They wouldn't. It's a side effect of their muscles transmitting that much power. The waste heat has to go somewhere."

"Skipper, tell me what this has to do with cloning or I'm going to shoot you myself."

"Everything on Midas uses gold compounds in its biochemistry. And one of the uses of gold is in superconductors. A lot of the sea life up near Midas's poles uses superconducting magnets in place of conventional muscle fibre. Tracer squid, those really bright bullet-shaped things that skip out of the sea on wings and bioluminesce like crazy? The ones with the shoals we could see from orbit? They can only make their siphons expand and contract that quickly because their musculature superconducts. But *this* baby, *this* little ray of sunshine," I slapped the wrinkled carcass, "superconducts at high temperature. *Really* high temperature."

She stiffened. She had understood. "The coolant. The helium problem."

"All we need," I said, "is access to a biolab and decent cloning facilities. We don't *need* coolant any more. We have high temperature superconductors right here on our doorstep. All our homegoing problems are over. All *everyone*'s homegoing problems are over. Of course", I said, "we *could* insist everyone buy their superconductor compound from us. For gold, of course. At a reasonable price . . . "

She took a look back at the fields. "I don't think so, Alasdair. I think we just equip our ship, get out of this place and leave them to their gold."

She'd persuaded me. "That's right. That's absolutely right. I was just testing you."

"Besides, what use will gold be to us? Unless you have a mountain of any metal nowadays, you're nobody."

"But a high temperature superconductor, working above the boiling point of water," I continued. "That's worth what a mountain of gold would have been worth *before* spaceflight. Gold enough to make a leprechaun green with envy!"

"Leprechauns," burbled Yuri from the back seat with admirable lucidity for a man who could probably see them by now, "are already green."

The tractor shuddered to a halt outside Uncle Kwon's, where I'd told it to. Far behind us, I watched a straight-backed, proud-statured Midasite walk into one of the field killers, holding a smaller Midasite in its tentacles. The door closed. The device hummed efficiently and did its work. The next Midasite in line stepped up.

"Just before we leave," I said, "I would like to put a home made grenade in one of those cyanide bowsers. POOF! Cyanide gas all over the settlement. You know it doesn't kill Midasites? Maybe they'll get the idea. The idea of how to fight back."

Brad shook her head. "The better type of Australian settler thought the same thing looking at the aborigines, Alasdair. *Maybe if they figure out how to make guns somehow. Maybe if they work out they could throw flaming boomerangs into the powder magazine.* It won't happen. They're a lame duck civilization. Their great crime is the same crime as the Africans'. To have been *useful.* They say the useless tree, the gnarled tree, the tree full of knots and twists, is always the oldest tree in the village. You know why that is?"

I shrugged. "Because old trees get like that?"

"Because *no-one ever bothered to cut it down.* Now stop philosophizing and help me get Yuri's stretcher down off the wagon."

I stepped down from the rover. In the fields outside the settlement, the doors continued to open and close, open and close, open and close.

THE QUALIA ENGINE

DAMIEN BRODERICK

1

My sixteenth birthday was early spring, in effect, instead of late winter, that winter-spring when the bees continued to die and die.

For a long time nobody knew why that was happening. I suppose specialists in the honey business were on it sooner than most, watching their apiaries emptying and shutting down, the poor bees stumbling about on the ground, forgetting how to get up in the air, dragging themselves round in confusion and then drying up dead. Soon enough the agribiz guys also grasped that their free pollinators were dropping like, well, flies.

I know what it feels like to be one of those poor flightless bees.

The stranded bees were one of the mysteries of science, of which I understood there were many, and even I couldn't expect to ace all of them. You do have to try, though. I stood waiting for the bus at 8:15 in the morning, thinking about ants and other topics. This was the last day of my life that I'd be obliged by law to wait for this damned daily humiliation, but that didn't mean I was off the hook.

In our neighborhood, nine-tenths of those parents competent or fortunate enough to have kids in high school senior year insisted on the bus, even for those old enough to drive. Gas conservation was the cause of the month. Hey, fair enough, although it was obvious, if you thought about it, that peak oil was no more than a blip in the future energy curve, soon to be forgotten. Long before we ran out, hard-edged R&D would find a replacement, and simultaneously mend the greenhouse crisis. Some of my friends were working on it in their spare moments, of which they, like I, had plenty, time-sharing the appalling waste lands of the classroom.

Didn't make me relish the ride.

It was pretty full that morning, and I was stuck with half the empty seat next to Cliff Dolejsi, jock. "Dude," he was telling his phone, "I'm wasted. Yeah, man. I porked that bitch in her daddy's Mercedes. Totally, dude."

This went on for a while. Up and down the bus, most of the others were busily texting, but that was too arduous a task for my companion. I tried to find some comfortable way of sitting that didn't put me in his lap.

"I'm on the damn bus," he explained. "Yeah, on the bus. School sucks. On the school bus, dude. Where are you? Yeah, man, she was screaming for it. No, on the bus."

According to rumor, Dolejsi had scored with most of the cheerleaders, and for once I didn't doubt public opinion. His excruciatingly repetitive report to Dude held no tincture of braggadocio; he was just relating the facts.

What made me grind my teeth is that Dolejsi was not unusually stupid. In two months he'd be graduating, along with the rest of us seniors. He was about as smart as, say, Xander Harris in *Buffy the Vampire Slayer*, or Prince Myshkin. No, scratch that; the prince, a saint, was not to be rated so simple-mindedly. Cliff Dolejsi was.

He shifted on his muscular left buttock and I took my chance, squirming further onto the rest of my seat. In disbelief, Dolejsi slammed his right elbow into my chest.

Having read the U.S. Army Ranger Handbook, I know eight silent ways to kill a man, plus some noisy ones. I twisted full on to Cliff, took my very sharp hexagonal section yellow RoseArt 5PK pencil from my pocket protector and clenched it between my right index and little fingers. I seized his ears and pulled his face across to me, where I kissed him slobberingly on the mouth, with plenty of tongue. Dolejsi went into a rictus of gay panic and disgust, slammed his head backward into the side window, and howled like a stuck pig. Which by then he was. I pushed the pencil in under his upper right eyelid, bumping and fracturing the thin bone, in through the socket, and deep into what he'd been pleased to call his brain, where I churned it around for a while, tearing the frontal lobes from the thalamus as his body convulsed and hammered the back of the seat where Judy Frick and Phuong Nguyễn had jerked their heads around, staring in revolted horror at the—

Of course I didn't do any of that. It's messy, and they wouldn't let you forget it. I oofed at the elbow strike, clenched my teeth, and remained mute. He went on yacking as if nothing had happened. Nothing had happened.

"No, dude, still in the bus."

For a long moment I did try to imagine just what the hell it could be like, being a jerk like Dolejsi. Or to be anyone else in the bus, for that matter. I couldn't do it.

Was brain-power, raw and cooked, the gap dividing us? Well, obviously, in part. But I decided everyone was in the same leaky boat, really. And maybe that was the problem. Not just the Hard Problem, as the philosophers rather quaintly called it, but the Big Problem.

After school, I walked a mile to audit a perceptual psychology lecture informally, and ended up sitting at a table in The Genteel Pizzeria, cattycorner from the university's Physics, Engineering and Computer Sciences wing with my three best friends who'd gathered for the event (my birthday, not my routine bus ride from hell nor the Dearth and Death of Apis mellifera and her sisters).

I said, "I've decided what I'm going to do with the rest of my life."

We were speedtalking in Lhasa Tibetan that day (our pronunciation was probably terrible), dropping into clipped English as needed. The only possible downside was the slight chance that some panicky idiot might imagine we were Al Quaeda terrorists, plotting in Arabic, and drop a dime on us to Homeland Security. Unlikely. Besides, nobody else in the place was listening; who eavesdrops on kids, especially nerds?

"Oh yeah?" Marius picked up a chicken thigh, dipped it in sauce, gnawed with gusto. "Let's see, the top ten list of what you'll do with the rest of your life. Power your way through to the mega-prize on *Survivor*. Discover the Higgs particle in your garage proton accelerator. Did I mention getting laid by supermodels 'til your ears bleed?" He carefully put the naked bone on a paper plate and grabbed another, fully-fleshed, crispy-browned, herbed and spiced.

"Saul's the sensitive type, you maroon," Ruthie told him. "He's extending the Bible Code to the genome." Ruth was the youngest of us seniors, only 15, total advanced placement with a perfect 2400 SAT (oops). Geek-grrl compleat: flat lifeless hair dragged back and cinched at her thin neck, big glasses the better to see you with and peer at distant galaxies besides. Rudimentary wearables in her flak-jacket-styled denim. I'm not judging—me, with the style sense of a contestant on *Beauty and the Geek*.

"Then," Ruthie added complacently, "he'll solve the monetary crisis."

Jane said, "Saul despises faith-based initiatives of all kinds. He is developing a new fuel source that will close down the cartels and bring peace to the Mideast and then the world."

"Shut up, you guys," I said. "I decided this morning in the bus. I'm going to solve the Hard Problem."

"You're telling me none of those is hard?"

"With the supermodels," said Marius, "for about thirty seconds."

"Ma-arrr!"

"Chalmers," I said. I foraged in my blue vinyl JanSport backpack with the 'leventy-seven zippered pockets, snug against my right sneaker on the floor beside me, my laptop tucked away safely from slopped condiments, and pulled out *The Conscious Mind*. "Block, Dennett, Hofstadter, Damasio, Edelman, Hawkins, Searle, McGinn, the Churchwoods—"

"Oh," said Janey, "*that* Hard Problem. *Qualia.*"

"And what's one of those?" Marius was peering up at the menu.

"One of those is a *quale,* singular." Not at all to my surprise, Janey pronounced it correctly: kwah-lay, rather than quail. "Qualia, plural. Raw feelings."

"Oh, right. I've never heard it pronounced before." That happened to us all the time; even when you've read right through Websters or the OED, stuff sometimes doesn't stick without a context. "Units of consciousness, sort of."

"So what's the problem," Ruthie asked, "and why is it hard?"

"Capital-H hard. Because qualia seem kind of *unnecessary* and *superfluous*. Why would evolution build them into us? It's like . . . Well, do I *have* a body, or *am* I a body? No, that's not it, either. Why do we see red and taste sweet and hear plangent, all those completely different sensations?"

Ruthie pounced. "We don't always. Synesthesia, that's a condition when the senses get mixed up."

"I'm not getting this across. What's it *like* to be a *bat*?"

"What's it like to bat a bee?" asked Marius instantly, blithely.

I felt frustrated. Why couldn't they feel what I felt about this? I said, "Like, why do we *feel* stuff instead of just computing it."

"We *do* just compute it," Ruth said, an edge to her high-pitched child voice. "What were you just saying about faith-based—?"

"The brain's *not* a computer," Janey said. "Neurons aren't logic gates. Has the failure of the AI program escaped your attention? Earth to Ruth."

Ruth stamped her foot. "Don't talk crap. Your logic sucks, Janey. Pay attention. Empirical premise: current computers *as of 2008*, just like those of 1948, are *not yet* brains. Your brilliant conclusion: brains are not computational." She sat back, looking smug. "Spot the logical lapse?"

"Oh, shut up. If you're going to appeal to some undefined computation on futuristic architectures that don't exist yet, how can you lose? And if you think you've won, what do you think you've won?"

"Delicious as this banter is, dear friends, I'm outta here." Marius hoisted his own laptop, slipped off the stool, bounced on his Reebok'd toes. He punched me in the shoulder. "B-Day, dude. But hey, yeah, I'm in."

"Cool," I said. 2 heads > 1 head, but then *greater than* does not always equal *better than*. Consider a pile of elephant manure. "You guys in too?"

"Someone's got to educate you idiots," Ruthie said, and Janey added, dryly, "No Problem too Hard, no Solution too Hygroscopic."

I said, intelligently, "Huh?"

"Dehydration 101, doofus. Google it. 'Bye." And they were gone, arm in arm, like a pair of plotting twelve year olds. I wondered how it felt to be a girl. And of course, noticing myself wondering that, I had to smile. Those kids were just bats.

The reason we knew each other so well is because our parents were some of the so-called "Atom Kids," which was a slick cover-up for what they really were, which is the first crop of plasmid-injected, crudely genetically engineered humans. (Much of this bizarre history I did not learn until later that night.) Just five years after Crick and Watson first announced the structure of DNA.

All the 'rents were born within ten months of the Los Alamos nuclear lab accident on 30 December, 1958, when a poor guy code-named K. splattered himself with three kilograms of plutonium in solution. He was dead a day and half later, his ruined heart cooked by 12,000 RADS of ionizing radiation. Two other workers had been in the next room, shielded (lucky for them!) by various sturdy tanks. The near-coincidence was later noted by a diligent security publicity officer and starred in case it was ever needed as a cover story.

None of our grandparents was anywhere near the DP West building complex, which was located thousands of feet from any living or routine working quarters. They *were* all stationed in the general vicinity, in the extremely secured Biowarfare Unit, where the women went through the discomforts of primitive experimental IVF. Did that matter to the media, forty years later, when a garbled and massaged version of the actual incident was released? You think? Lapped up the nuke version like tame puppydogs. Those poor all-American fetuses, born late in 1959 to parents whose gonads were accidentally exposed to the frightful rays of the atom. But wait—it's okay! They turned out fine! No sign of illness except for some hairline scurf, red watery eyes for a few weeks after birth, and some temporary spikes now and then in their blood work. And what's more, Lord be praised, their own kids, the not very attention-grabbing grandchildren of the atom, were in good shape, also, making solid grades in school. Next story.

We'd been trained from infancy to keep our lips zipped and our lights well hidden under a bushel of general competence. Ruth, the youngest, chafed under those restrictions and could not help showing off a little; hence her SAT scores. But nobody, except for us and our folks, knew that she was pumping scads of freeware code into the net, everything from patches for Microsloth bloat to Linux tweaks and CGI shortcuts for YouTube homeys, as well as freelancing for the big operators.

Me, I did well enough in class to deflect unwelcome interest from teachers and administrators, as my parents had done when they were kids, until the brief bubble of exposure that was swiftly burst by the brilliantly conceived "accelerated schooling" scheme that ran interference on them for several years and allowed them to sink back out of sight as quickly as humanly possible.

More exactly, as superhumanly possible, I suppose, but the key part of the equation was the greater world in which they were immersed, those several billion *Homo sapiens sapiens* with a mean IQ of 100 and a sigma of 15 or 16 points. Only a modest proportion fell in the diminishing tail beyond three sigmas either side of the mean (the bell curve being what it is, a map of what happens when tens of thousands of alleles jostle together in the gene pool and out paddles a new little person). Those on the right tail of the graph were the two percent or so who could join Mensa because they'd aced the test and wanted to sit about all night talking to other lonely people about humungous test scores and doing fearsome crossword puzzles and fun stuff like that. The Terman Longitudinal Study of gifted children, say, of whom you didn't hear much these days. Out farther along the tail were the real frighteners with IQs up in the 190s and 200s, of which the whole history of the world had seen only a sufficient tally to cram into a large SUV. And off beyond *those* human geniuses were radical outliers who simply didn't exist in nature, and hadn't prior to 1959, because the thorny paths up Mount Improbable were too steep. You can't get there from here. Unless someone carried your genome up in a plane and parachuted you in at the peak. Hi, Mom! Hi, Poppa!

Hush, little baby. Keep your feet tucked under the table, heads down, don't make waves, and other mixed metonymies and synecdoches.

I went to Billies gym above Jakes Bodyworks on Main after I'd spent an hour in the library stacks reading agalmic political theory (Ruth's recommendation) and waiting for my gut to digest the evil but delicious load I'd subjected it to at The Genteel Pizzeria, and burned it off in hard sweaty sets of weight work and aerobics, showered for the sake of politeness, changed into a rather worn cotton uniform for my thrice-weekly drills in the adjoining dojo, fell down and got hit a lot less than I had when I was a kid, broke no bones in my own body or anyone else's, took a more serious shower, then went home to the formal birthday party I knew the parental units would have cooked up, even though I'd told them not to. I really would have preferred to rustle up something for myself, as usual, out in my self-contained studio apartment, blasting away with what Mom called "that abominable pseudo-musical noise," then take Scarf for a long walk along the river before an early night. I wanted the solitude to think about the Hard Problem. No such luck.

2

Smallville music, care of Janey the ironist: The Cult, Missy Higgins, Depeche Mode, Diamond Nights. Fragrant steak and tilapia cooking on a griddle. Salad dressing sharp with cider vinegar, garlic and virgin olive oil. Laughter and babbling, people drinking soda, not many drinking anything more serious. A man I hadn't seen in too long stepped through the door to the back porch, and I said, "Hey, Father Paul. Or is that 'Monsignor' these days?"

I felt a burst of cheerfulness, seeing Paul Westfall here, even if I was still angry at my parents for the inevitable party. He was outfitted in clerical black, must have flown straight in from Chicago especially for my birthday. A few months earlier, I'd overheard my father say, "So he's wearied of treading water in the Holy See. Paul must be a major headache for them in Rome, L. C. They can't canonize him, because he's not dead. They can't send him a writ of excommunication, and then burn him at the stake, because—" L.C. had said sharply but quietly, and I wouldn't have heard her if I hadn't been deliberately eavesdropping, "Hush." My mother is pious to the point of mania, having been infected, along with Paul, by a charismatic Thomist at a tender, vulnerable age. Dad, not so much. Me, I'd announced my agnosticism at seven, then my embrace of full-blown atheism two years later, devastating Mom. But what can you do? This, and other things, flashed through my mind as the priest turned with his big smile.

"You can still call me Paul, for gosh sake. Good to see you, kiddo. Happy birthday! Here, gimme a Saul-and-Paul hug." We did the manly embrace, and he added, "That whole hierarchy thing is making a comeback in my diocese, hence the dog collar. Give me ten minutes and I'll be in a track suit like a human being. You're looking healthy. Working out?"

"Uh huh."

"Way to go. *Sans corpore, sans Mensa*, you know."

I gave a dutiful laugh. "Wit score, point five." Maybe 0.67, let's be fair. But already he was pressing his way through the crush of my friends, my parents' friends, college educators and hangers-on, probably a stringer for the local paper. No TV cameras, though, we're (carefully) not that newsworthy, not even dinky hand-helds, except for the Korean digital marvel my mother was deploying. She's a fiend for archiving everything, so for a while I picked the custom up from her. Hence, this record as well, I suppose. Hard to break the habit. I started a journal when I was eight, writing in rather bad Sanskrit, then burned all the piled up volumes when I was 14 and puberty kicked in, however feebly and belatedly. Didn't start again. But here we are, seems I have, after all, but this time, as you see, under NSA-grade crypto.

Food was laid out alfresco on trestle tables, and I was munching shish kabob from a skewer while the old lady from next door expatiated on the breeding of daylilies (tetraploids, their male and female parts are large and easy to work with even for the arthritic, and their seeds are big lunky things) when someone grabbed me by the belt and started tugging me backwards. "Sorry," I said to the neighbor, "excuse me." And "What?" to Ruthie. Mysteriously and without expression, she handed me a small box wrapped in foil, and drew me into the back yard and around the side of the house. Scarf barked and tagged along. "Really, what?" I had the silvery foil off the matchbox by the time we reached the front gate, and the thing rattling inside was a car key. Ruth opened the front gate and bowed me through. "For me?" I said. "I thought you didn't care."

It was a yellow Ford Focus hatchback, several years old, clearly secondhand, but in good shape.

"I know you won't believe this," I told her, "but I'm going for my license tomorrow morning. This is just what I wanted!"

"Of course it is," Ruthie said, and even by the pale street lighting I could see her blush. She punched me in the arm. "Don't kill yourself, okay?"

"Come on, get in." I opened the passenger side, tucked her inside, went around and climbed aboard, moved my seat back a little, let my hands rest on the wheel. Perfect. Just the sort of ride the 'rents would approve; low-key unnoticeable (yellow is visible, but that's a safety feature and anyway adolescents are flashy, right?), reasonable fuel consumption, not really enough room for wild sex parties, even if I put down the back seat and threw a blow-up mattress on top. Even if I really felt the urge to do so, which I was slightly ashamed to admit I didn't. Ah, peer pressure! "This is great, geekgrrl. You sold another patent, or something?"

"Royalties on. Don't know what to do with it, the stuff just piles up in the bank. I'd have gotten you a Lamborghini, but—"

"Yeah." I started it up, revved the engine once or twice, switched it off again and got out. I rubbed my hand over the roof. "Let's get something to eat before the greedy bastards have scarfed it all down." Hearing his name, Scarf the dog barked happily behind the gate. We went in and mingled. What a grrl!

Before midnight, a handful of neighbors cleaned up, helped by the few Atom Kids who'd made it to the event. Ruthie's parents had already walked her home. The sound system was softened to bluesy jazz after everyone else had been politely, good-humoredly but firmly shown the door. "Another school day tomorrow," my father had said. That was all the explanation needed in this neighborhood.

I loaded washables into the dishwasher, rinsed and stacked the recycle candidates, gobbled down the last of the pistachio ice-cream, felt mildly sick as a result and finally, sighing, when Father Paul caught my eye, followed him into Dad's study. Janey had hinted at some Rite of Passage (she'd turned 16 three months earlier) but refused by a dozen amusing diversions and one snappish outburst to tell me what to expect.

Mom and Dad followed us in. Marius watched keenly from the hall; nothing got past that guy. I heard the door click shut, and lock.

Relaxed in Dad's leather and tubular steel reading chair, an elderly gentleman in his mid-seventies was already in situ, wearing a suit and Harvard club tie, of all things.

Omg. The Patriarch. I was shaken, bewildered, gratified. I'd met him only once before, for a long discussion after my declaration of fervent disbelief in deity. After all, he was the powerful personality who'd persuaded L.C. to read Thomas Aquinas shortly after he saved her from a childhood of quiet desperation that made my daily troubles seem like a night at the opera.

"Hello, sir," I said, and held out my hand. I realized a moment later I'd said it in Tibetan and, shaking my head, repeated my greeting in English. Trust me, I urged with my modest demeanor, I'm house-broken. I don't really slay repugnant oafs on the school bus with a sharpened pencil to the brain. I don't even really want to. No, really.

His happy laughter rumbled. He rose, with a little difficulty, and in a gesture almost exactly like Father Paul's earlier in the evening, opened his arms. "Come on, you scamp. Give me a hug, and tell me how you justify your godless existence."

My eyes filled with tears. Who'd have thunk? But this man had brought my parents together, as children, in the dark days when—according to everything I'd read on the period—the heaving '60s were expiring into the early '70s in confused, sexually reckless utopian optimism, women and gays finding their voices finally, amid the last gasps of a brutal, seemingly unending war in Asia. A pointless war, part of my mind annotated automatically to itself, that ended in baffled defeat after twelve bloody years—and now, all these decades later, we were embroiled again in another apparently pointless war, had been for five years.

Was *that* the unavoidable outcome of a numbed, dumbed-down population with an average IQ only a bit above 100? Citizens who elected as their representatives men and a few women smarter than themselves, yes, by and large, yet lacking real perspective, most of them? Missing the aptitude to cast themselves forward in well-grounded imagination, to test out their proposed actions before barging into costly ruin? Was what I saw and heard everywhere, every day, just concerted stupidity run riot in a polity vastly larger than the cozy hunter-gatherer aggregations humans were evolved to deal with? It couldn't be that simple, could it?

There was more than a whiff of self-preening in that thumb-nail analysis, and I knew it. Yet equally self-interested, concealed agendas held sway, I was sure, among the owners, the judges, the clergy, the warrior chiefs of labor and military, the imprisoned, the drugged and the dealers in sedation. Yes, all that, no doubt—but still, what sort of person deliberately sets out to derange the larger part of the planet into violent hatred and opposition? Al Quaeda and Hamas were not the only crazies at that game. Was this widespread barbarity, too, a consequence, a manifestation, of the Hard Problem? Simply an inability to sense that other humans have interests and profoundly private *feelings* of their own, and potent beliefs, however delusional most of them had to be (since almost all were at odds with the rest)—an incapacity for that sympathetic resonance which somehow emulates the qualia of the deepest inward lives of their foes?

These fairly commonplace reflections, as I say, dashed like foxes pursued by hounds in my own inwardness, as I stepped into Dr. Herbert's embrace and felt flooding through me his kindness, generosity, concern for us all—and his ordinariness. His mental limitations, measured against two generations of his appalling charges.

And a part of me recoiled. I didn't *want* to know what it was like to be the Patriarch. He had made it possible for us to find a place in the world, had guarded us when we were most vulnerable, had filled the troubled and often squalid lives of the young Atom Kids with warmth and encouragement, had stood against their public enemies. And yet . . . His mind was small, narrow, constricted by the limitations imposed by his brain's natural genetic program. And I could not bear to imagine such restriction, the stifled qualia of such imprisonment. A pulse of horror passed through me.

And he felt it. His clasp failed, for a moment. He did not draw away, but I knew that a deep, abiding sadness must have bruised his heart at that moment. For, after all, this could not have been the first time he'd know such instinctive rejection. It was the cost and misery of his vocation as our mentor and protector.

"I'm sorry," I said.

He placed his hands on my shoulders. "That's all right, lad. It's your fate, this loneliness, this aloneness. I wish I could bridge it, Saul, but the barrier is too high. Still, we can be friends, I hope?"

I recalled, with bitter sharpness, something Father Paul had let slip once. Yes, we could be friends—as I might offer friendship to my dear pal Scarf, and he, in his loyal, hungry, restless, scurrying way, might offer his in return. It was a sickening realization. I tasted the bile in my throat, and then Dad was holding my arm, steadying my shaky legs. Unseasonable spring warmth had left the air. My ears rang. Mom brought me a chair, touched the back of my head lightly, and I let myself down. Dr. Herbert remained on his feet, alone. It seemed to me his features were carved in saddened resignation, an acknowledgement of loss beyond loss greater, perhaps, than any man had ever been obliged to bear.

"Sure," I said. There was a tremor in my voice. "Sure. I'm proud to be your friend, sir."

After a long moment, my father cleared his throat, and both my parents, by turns, with a word here and there from the Patriarch, started to explain things to me.

We second-gen kids already knew the atomic radiation legend was bogus, not to mention ludicrous, despite the *X-Men* franchise that seemed to capitalize, distantly, on our leaked cover story. How could a blizzard of alpha particles and neutrons sleeting at random through the bodies of unprotected researchers all create *precisely the same mutation* in their offspring? Chemical mutagens, yes—radiation, not a chance. Getting a major REM load is like being sprayed with machine-gun bullets, not tweaked by exquisitely targeted tweezers. That required deliberate insertion of modified genes, which, they told me, is what had been done back there in the Above Top Secret Los Alamos Biowarfare Unit to our pregnant grandmothers, using fragile and primitive techniques nobody else would replicate (or at least publish) for years.

I thought this was ridiculous, about as likely as hearing that we'd been created as hybrid UFO aliens. The genome project was still limping—well, galloping—toward closure half a century after this miracle of gynecology was supposedly wrought. L.C. flicked on the computer and called up a brisk briefing for me. Holy cow. I read it over her shoulder, flicking down pages with voice command.

The first "test tube baby" IVF was announced to the press in 1978, twenty years after the Atom Kids were conceived. And there was nothing modified about little Louise Brown, of Greater Manchester, England, except for her very existence. (The poor Indian guy who produced the second IVF child known to history was hounded by his purblind and moralizing marxist Bengali government, and killed himself several years later. Another class of motive for keeping all this hushed up, maybe. Humans do seem to love rushing about with pitchforks and blazing brands. "Burn the witch!")

But, obviously, classified work had been going on much earlier than that.

"Shortly after the end of the Second World war," Mom told me, even as I speed-read the details, "Dr. Min Chueh Chang moved from China to Massachusetts and started working seriously on fertilization."

"The contraceptive pill," I muttered.

"Ironic, yes. But he and his colleagues found ways to create life as well as suppress it." I expected a mini-lecture on the wickedness of unnatural tampering with God's plan for human life, but I guess she knew I had it memorized. The images jumped on the screen. Cold shock technique. Sperm capacitation. Genetic recombination. The door was opening for—

Wait a moment. It had already been opened as far back as . . . 1935! Chang's colleague, Gregory Pincus, had fertilized rabbit ova *in vitro*, but few believed him. His work wasn't recognized until around the time the first "Atom Kids" were born. Interesting timing! Clearly some observers had been paying attention.

"Meanwhile," Mom was saying, "from the moment Crick and Watson clarified DNA's helical structure, and then cracked the code, a black team at Los Alamos was building on Chang's work."

"Plasmids," said Father Paul. I turned; he'd come quietly into the study and relocked the door behind him. The adults regarded me with a sober solemnity I rarely saw in them. "Josh Lederberg was already doing good work in the late '40s on bacterial conjugation. He and wife Esther shared a Pasteur Medal in 1956. Outstanding work in microbiology and genetics."

And on my parents? Maybe not—but someone else had followed swiftly in the Lederbergs' tracks.

"Plasmids," I repeated. Biology was Ruthie's stomping ground, not mine. "Little rings of DNA or something, right?" You could insert them into cells, and they'd start pumping out their own specialized proteins—or sneak into the nuclear DNA, where with luck they'd take up residence.

"Hence bacterial conjugation. Syzygy," said the Patriarch, and he broke into a smile. "That's what we called it back then. No sex, but as good as." He shot Paul an amused glance, and got a faint frown in reply.

"I thought that had something to do with the moon. Syzygy, not sex."

"Well, Saul, yes, it does, but that's a different sense of the word. This isn't astronomy, I assure you—nor astrology, neither. It was dirty, but it worked—some of the time." Paul looked grim. "It also killed seven women, and dozens of babies. They had *no right* . . . " He broke off. "Well, different times. Nuclear weapons were the doomsday disaster poised to obliterate all life. You'd probably heard about the CIA medical experiments on black prisoners?"

I nodded. No words necessary. The screen flickered under Mom's finger clicks with officially-mandated horror. Two hundred women infected with viral hepatitis in 1950, so the military might learn what would result if evil communists turned to germ warfare. Fifteen years later, just to be sure, another doctor repeated it with retarded children living in Staten Island. Live cancer cells shot into prisoners at Ohio State Prison by Sloan Kettering researchers in 1952. From the early '50s to the late '60s, Project MKULTRA craziness using lysergic acid and electroshock that damaged Canadian patients beyond any hope of recovery, on behalf of US intelligence researchers. It was all too justifiable. It's the Cold War, stupid. What other excuse did you need?

And it hadn't stopped with the McCarthy hysteria. I kept speed-reading, unable to look away. In 1967, when Mom was eight years old, more than five dozen prisoners in California were injected with a terrifying substance, succinylcholine, that made them feel that they were drowning in their own fluids. Waterboarding by any other name. Five of the prisoners refused permission, and were injected anyway, against their protests.

I'm pretty sure I was looking green around the gills again. I sagged against the back of the chair, and L.C. got out and spun it around for me to collapse into.

I looked at my Mom and Dad and . . . I know it's vulgar, and trivializing, and entirely unjustified, but I felt a horror movie shiver, I did.

"So you're—genetic experiments? And I'm what? Son of Frankenstein?"

"Not exactly," my father said. "But close enough." His grin seemed a bit strained; he was profoundly uncomfortable. One arm went around Mom's shoulders, and she leaned against him.

"The plasmid autoinserted into the nuclear DNA," Paul told me. "It's heritable. To some extent."

"So nobody had to screw around with *my* genome? Wow," I said, heavily, "imagine my relief."

"You'd be surprised how minor the changes are," L.C. said. "Mostly it's an unstable CHRM2 allele, plus downregulation of a dysbindin SNP." I heard it as "snip" and at that stage didn't know how to unpack the rest of it. We might be geniuses, but we have to read something to remember and understand it, and as I say I'd tended to delegate microbiology to Ruthie. Shockingly sexist, no doubt. "It's like the small modifications that caused the chimpanzee to go in one direction and *H. sapiens* in another. In this case, an extra cortical rind added atop the six human layers of cortex, thicker and more numerous axonal connections, some neurotransporter oddities. It doesn't always," she added, with a glance she deflected even as it began, "breed true."

I had know all my life that I'm not remotely as smart as the Atom Kids. Sure, beat the academic pants off a Cliff Dolejsi; run circles from infancy around children three times my own age (but it was getting a little harder these days), yet I had to admit that I just wasn't transcendentally brilliant like the 'rents. At my age they'd been publishing biographies and novels and advanced theses in math and poli sci. Ruth had her software patents, true, and I'd published that fat fantasy trilogy before I got tired of reading made-up stuff and disgorging imitations, but I wasn't hearing anything unexpected. Still, it stung. It stung like a son of a bitch.

"Regression toward the mean," I said.

"Absent any extra modifications, I'm afraid so. And worse than that—most pregnancies in our group kept miscarrying. We all tried desperately for ten years or so, then Kuzi finally worked out the haplotypy problem and we . . ." Mom trailed away.

"It's an inbreeding problem, mostly," Dad told me. "We found a way, but it involved some sacrifices."

They were all looking at Paul Westfall. His face did not move, but his eyes fixed on me.

"With the help of good old nature, and nature's God," he said. He crossed the room to me, took both my hands firmly in his own. A thumb closed over the knuckles of my right hand in a firm, professional clasp, the deft grip of a man who'd never done any real physical work in his life, never worked combinations in a dojo. I'd seen that thick, blunt thumb shape before, every day of my life. How could I never have noticed? He smiled, finally. "Yes, Bud, belay what I said earlier. You have every right to call me father."

Was I angry?

Hell, yes.

I swallowed down that anger, because it's what we'd been trained to do, and because, really, I loved the guy. Paul Westfall was the first of the Atom Kids located by Dr. Herbert, and perhaps, by all accounts, the brightest. He'd done as much as anyone in rounding up the rest, easing them, one by one and then in concert, through the trauma and triumph of their self-discovery, their redemption from extremity and bitter isolation. In the joint foolishness and longing for absolutes of the Patriarch's medievalism, he and L.C., my mother, had cultivated their immense minds into a shared *folie,* but hardly a radical one, an architecture of belief and worship shared, after all, by many of the finest minds in Western history, and even today by a large percentage of the planet. I'd confronted or avoided their faith for years, in a mutinous but largely unspoken resistance. Not hostility; how can you turn against the woman who gave you birth? But they both knew the antagonism I nurtured toward their beliefs. And now—

—*No more than a hypocritical imposture!* raged the furious two-year old locked inside me. Faked piety! Bogus fidelity to spouse and church!

Knowing, even as the spasm made my arm tremble and withdrew my hand from his, how unfair, reductive, patronizing, *adolescent,* for God's sake, I was being.

Qualia, I noted. I noticed that abstract fact from a higher, remoter part of my aggrieved self. Bursts and gusts of feeling, trammeled as swiftly as they arose in rationalizations and language games. Yet how could *that fury* be calculated, specified by neural algorithm, traced back to Darwinian adaptations and Machiavellian maneuvers? Well, easily enough, in fact. I knew that. But the logic tree of abstractions didn't *feel* true.

Deliberately, I shut down this noisy inner babble. I turned my face away from the Hard Problem and from the present instant's merely Absurd Problem churning in my mind and body.

Yeah, you bet I was angry.

"I'm going for a walk," I said, turning away from them and opening the study door on a quiet house. Nobody waited out there; even Marius had gone home. "I have to take Scarf out for a crap."

My mother and father, and the priest who was merely my sperm-donor, in vitro or in vivo I didn't care, and their aged Patriarch, they all four let me leave, in silence, and without reproach. Well, I suppose they were getting used to it. Emotionally, we are all quite simple creatures, *H. sapiens.* and *H. novissimus* alike.

I found Scarf's chain on its hook and went out into the cool of the night, my dog capering happily at my heels.

3

I destroyed the intervening entries after my crisis with Maxine. Just couldn't bear to read all that protracted late adolescent *Sturm und Drang.* I've decided to pick it up again—I owe it, arguably, to the dead. So let's start with an instant recap:

I fell in love at last, or so I thought at the time, four years later. Maxine Bukowski wasn't one of us, but she was fearsomely bright, by her own standards; she danced like a flame caught in a light breeze, and her hair was the tawny flame of triploid cultivar daylily *Hemerocallis fulva.* So much of my life had to remain concealed, partitioned, which tortured me, and Maxy, too, at some level of masked perception she wasn't able to deny. One day she found the three paperbacks of my *Starlight Genera* trilogy, which I'd written over a long school holiday when I was thirteen and published as Peter Regan two years later.

"What's this? Not the kind of thing you usually read, Saul?"

I was distracted with circuit design. "Uh, a friend gave it to me. He wrote them."

Leafing through the opening pages, she hummed a jazz tune. "Hey, this isn't bad. How come you've never introduced us?"

"That's not his real name. He's embarrassed, I think."

"Can't see why. I hope he made pots of loot." I saw her settle into my big chair, flipping pages fast. After a while it got dark, and I flicked on the overhead fluoros. Maxine was halfway through volume 2. I squirmed, but secretly hoped to hear words of praise. By the time I shut down and showered, and pulled her to me on the bed, she was polishing off the final book. "Hey, that was fun."

"No, *this* is fun," I said, and it was. But a couple of weeks later she found a mint copy, in a sealed baggie, of Jeri Steiner's *The New Astrologies*. "Oh my god, Saul, wtf?" (She spelled it out, as people did that year.)

"I'd rather you didn't open—" But she had unsealed the bag. "That's an investment, sweetheart. Pennies today, zillions in half a century."

"Not funny." She blew a raspberry, and starting reading down the contents page, in a sarcastically excited yet dazed rendition of a diphead: "Ethnoastrology. Neuroastrology."

"That's my favorite," I said, and tried to grab it from her. She squirmed away. "I googled it, and of course neuroastrology.org and neuroastrology.com were domain names. Luckily, they'd expired."

"Luckily? But wait, there's more: Relativistic astrology." She laughed a little uncertainly. "I love it! astrology at the speed of light. String astrology. Does that included Brane astrology?"

"Brainless astrology, I imagine," I said, getting nervous, watching a contest inside her between humor and censure. "Look, can't we—"

"Genome astrology. Demon astrology. Non-Euclidean astrology. Galactic and of course for extra credit extra-galactic astrology. Dark matter astrology. *Dark matter astrology!* Wait, wait! Dark *energy* astrology. Post-poststructural astrology. Oh, Saul, this has to be a send-up. Green eco-astrology. And lastly, Virtual astrology."

"The universe as a computational simulation. Don't mock it unless you've tried it. Have you never read Bostrom or Tegmark?"

"I saw the *Matrix* trilogy." Her mood settled. "No, it's really not funny. This Steiner woman is preying on the vulnerable."

"On the intellectually underpowered but pretentious, anyway."

"It's gross, Saul. What are you *doing* with this sort of iniquitous dreck hidden under your bed?"

I made my first and last mistake with Maxine. "I wrote it."

Aghast. "You *what?*"

"I co-wrote it. Dictated it to the machine. With Marius. One day when it was raining heavily. Don't hate me, babe. We made more money than you could imagine. Pots."

Now she wasn't laughing. Or smiling. Maxine, my beautiful tawny lily, put the book down on the bed as if she needed to wash her fingers, and got dressed. She left. She never came back. I cried quite a lot, and ranted at Marius, and sobbed on Ruth's wearable-cluttered bony shoulder, and got over her, eventually, when I met Andrea. And learned, even more than I'd learned before, to keep my damn mouth shut.

But I wondered, as always, and now even more poignantly: What could it be like to be a Maxine Bukowski? And what would it be like for a Maxine to discover, though unimpeachable direct experience, what it's like to be a Saul Collins?

What attracted me to Andrea was her playfulness. Well, and her short dresses, but hey.

I was sitting at the back of a dizzyingly canted lecture theater trying to remain focused on the most boring neurophysiology presentation the world has ever known. Herr Doktor Professor Faxon Bander is one of the great experts in cortical structure and connectivity, but if his presenter skills were an index of his surgical prowess, he'd be doing serious time in the Big House. I yawned. I shuffled my feet. I parsed into Farsi everything he was saying four or five times. I'd known all this stuff backwards and forwards, which is pretty much the way he was presenting it, since my early adolescence, but the geniuses in charge of the course insisted that all Ph.D. candidates must audit every lecture. On the blank pad under my left hand, I scribbled *Much more of this backing and filling and I will run down and kill him with my bare paws.*

A snigger, and a bare female right paw wielding an old-fashioned fountain pen, fashionable again that year, reached across and scratched on the pad *This toing and froing.*

I did not glance to my left but wrote *Hither and yoning.* A tiny bit of naughty under the surface. Was that embedded *yoni* too racy? I hoped she was not a nun fluent in Sanskrit. *Hi-ing and lo-ing* wrote the woman's hand. I scribbled *Inning and outing.* The hand instantly annotated *Upping and downing,* hesitated a moment, and then went back to add a *T* at the start. A fan of Shakespeare, I thought: *Othello,* Act I, Scene I. A nicely ribald sense of humor, which allowed me to relax a bit. This time, finally, I shot a glance her way. Green amused eyes met mine. Older than I, but perhaps not by much. She was not beautiful in any conventional sense. I felt my heart lurch, and other parts. *Awake the snorting citizens.* I wrote *Sniggering and snorting,* and left my hand resting on the pad. She wrote *No time like the present. My name is Andrea.* The smooth back of her hand brushed my wrist. In a moment of shivery delight, our qualia fell into synch. Stayed that way, for a while.

Busy, busy, busy. I should pick this up again. Oh, Ruthie, Ruthie.

After the first commercial 1024-qubit adiabatic computer was released by D-Wave, a Canadian company, several years later than anticipated but sooner than the doom-criers of vaporware had gloomily warned, the four of us bought one outright with our research funds and had it shipped with extreme care to my neurosci lab. (I was completing that doctorate under a friendly prof who'd known the Patriarch for years and asked few questions; it was helpful, despite the tedium and convenience, to patch into the university's infrastructure.) The potential power of the thing was breathtaking, if Ruthie could get her software to run right. In principle, the number of states it could address simultaneously was greater than 10^{300}. The number of atoms in the entire observable universe was a comparatively minuscule 10^{80}.

We'd decided on an end run around the philosophers. We were building a Qualia Engine.

That name was our nod of acknowledgement to Dean Charles Babbage's marvelous 19th century designs of a pre-electronic mechanical Difference Engine (a sort of programmable clockwork computer, never built until enthusiasts put one together a century later) and an Analytical Engine (a genuine Turing machine). Aside from the raw grunt of the quantum computer we'd put at its core, our device—our congeries of cobbled-together devices— more closely resembled a magnetoencephalographic scanner, and in fact used a shrunken version that fitted over the upper body, and especially the scalp, listening for traces of . . . feelings. Affective responses to the outer empirical world and the inner subjective world of imagination. Qualia.

"Oh the quale machine," sang Janey, deliberately mispronouncing it to rhyme with *Quayle*, like the late Vice President, "the quale machine, it reaches inside where nothing is seen. It knows if you're happy or feeling mean—that wonderful, sensitive quale machine."

I couldn't let her get away with that. "You're a deeply ignorant woman, Jane. Those are not the lyrics of the song." I ad-libbed, "It goes like this:

> I'll parlay my quale
> for a look at your soul,
> and a ride on your Harley
> in the back streets of Bali,
> as long as your hol-
> ism isn't reductively
> loitering palely,
> like watery gravy,
> at the lee of the sea, be-
> cause—"

She clipped me over the head, and settled back into the MEG sensor web of superconducting quantum detectors, excruciatingly sensitive to the 10 femtoTesla magnetic fields of the neocortex in working order.

I shut the door and went back into the shielded control room.

That year, Harvard were still working on a *Mus* connectome, using an automatic tape-collecting lathe ultramicrotome. Not recommended for human brains, or even mice, if they are still alive; it sliced its way through a brain, imaging in three dimensions as it peeled, creating with each chomp a twenty megapixel record of every synapse and its precise location. The Allen Institute was working toward a brain atlas using in situ hybridization. We planned to achieve much the same effect in a *non*-invasive scan, creating an instantaneous massive entanglement between each molecule in Janey's brain and a separate dedicated register in the superposed state of the computer. No, we weren't trying to upload her consciousness onto an inorganic substrate—just create a static map of one person's momentary memories, sense impressions, plans, and . . . feelings. No point futzing around for years with murine qualia. Those dear little mousy critters are quite complex, in their way, far more so than the stupid psych behaviorists assumed back in the day of the Atom Kids, but still not up to scratch for the questions I needed to ask, the puzzles I hoped to resolve.

But let's pause a moment.

As I look back over this interrupted and partly sanitized or reconstructed record, "Peter Regan," the fluent author of the *Starlight Genera* trilogy hesitates, abashed. Far too much Tell here, not nearly enough Show. My predicament is that I don't really know whom I'm writing this for. Is it my peers—hi Janey, Marius, Mom, Dad, you other *Homines novissimi*? Not for Maxine, long gone, nor for Andrea, sad-eyed lady. To the memory of Ruthie? Not really. I'm hardly the group's archivist. Perhaps for some later generation who wasn't here and now? I suppose, eventually. As an explanation, an *Apologia pro vita sua*, to *H. sapiens* readers, sometime soon, or maybe not for years? I guess that's the audience I've had in the back of my mind all along. We went underground out in the open precisely to avoid that kind of explicit engagement—but hey, maybe things will change.

I could go back a few pages and insert an exciting expository conversation with Maxine as we rappelled down the face of the Empire State building in driving snow, or during the successful bid by Andrea and me to prevent terrorists from nuking the Large Hadron Collider in Switzerland, and maybe that's the way we'll do it in the movie, but let's get a grip and cut to the chase. When I was "Peter Regan," teaching myself to write blockbusters, I scouted the web for rules of narrative—and one prohibition I learned early was never to dump dollops of information and backstory through the pitiful contrivance of characters telling each other stuff. "As you know, Professor . . . " But hey, this is my personal journal and I can do what I like, and it's directed finally to an uncertain audience. So—

The standard human brain has a lot of housekeeping and motivational apparatus tucked away in the middle—thalamus, hippocampus, amygdala, blah blah, thank you, Prof. Bander—along with cavities surging with transmitter-rich circulating fluids, wrapped in what amounts to a large dinner napkin of neocortex crumpled up to squeeze inside the skull. Data lines run in and out from processing brain to torso and limbs and back, a million or so fibers from the eyes, an equal number from the muscles and the touch sensors, as few as 30,000 dealing with auditory sensations. (So a picture is actually worth 333.3 words.)

The two-millimeter thick cortex is where the heavy lifting is done among you brainy apes. Just consider this for a moment: a sheet of tissue no thicker than six stacked envelopes, stripping down a bit-torrent into schemas and holons, each cortical layer abbreviating and abstracting the incoming from below until finally the top layer, with its plethora of far flung connections, deals in a world of invariant representations very far removed from the jumpy, jittery, scatty flood of inputs that assails us every waking moment—but those invariant abstractions *match the structure of the external world.* Carving the world at its joints, as Plato put it in the *Phaedrus.* (That Plato detail won't be on the exam.)

What the *H. novissimus* plasmid genes do is persuade a growing fetal brain to add a seventh layer to the neocortex, plus a whole lot more synaptic connections. But wait, that's not all. They beef up the brain's ability to prune any coincidence links that turn out to be poorly informative or actively misleading. You remain stuck with a brain prey to illusions and superstitions, because your traditional gray matter assumes, as its default, *post hoc, ergo propter hoc.* Often that's justified. Just as often, it's a highway to gut-churning errors ardently embraced and enforced, provoking sectarian hatred, bloody war, and the purchase of expensive sports utility vehicles hardly anyone can afford gas for. But wait—I hear you object—wasn't I just bellyaching about Father Paul's equally baffling embrace of the Roman dog collar, and L.C.'s devotion to a belief system nearly as absurd as Norse worship of the cosmogonic cow Audhumla? Yes. I admit it. Even the Atom Kids are prey to emotional attachments and rushes of feeling to the head. They're trapped, when all's said and done, by their qualia.

The way Ruthie died was unforgivable: stupid, stupid, heartbreakingly stupid.

I was still driving the aging Ford Focus, her birthday gift to me when I turned 16. It did the job, didn't require explanations. She didn't drive. That night Andrea was at the Pillbox until late, rehearsing *Mother Courage.* She'd dropped out of neuro; somehow I'd discouraged her, hadn't meant to, I swear. I was taking Ruth home from the lab. By then she had so much hardware hooked up to her wearable ensemble that most of the time she might as well have been flying through Second Life. Ruthie had never been scanned by our juicy system, because it would've made a mess of her onboard equipment, which in turn would have munged ours, probably.

On one level, her connection to reality was larger than mine; miniature

LEDS cast a non-stop data feed into the upper visual field of both eyes, her fingers danced a coding echo in sim space via the thread transponders printed on the back of her hands and wrists, music and other chopped, sped-up acoustic feeds went directly to her mastoid bone. I never tried it directly, but a sim-set let me emulate a pale shadow of the experience (or so she said, disdainfully), and it was a Niagara of noise even my much-vaunted seventh cortical layer couldn't quickly reduce to meaningful pattern. Ruth followed a dozen RSS feeds along a hundred, a thousand blog links; she attended the launch of the first Chinese moon orbit, a remedial operation on the cleft palate of a five year old girl in Tanzania, a football game at Notre Dame (she liked the hunks), the stock market streaming quotes and nasdaq Level II negotiations . . .

What was it like to be Ruthie? Like drowning in the world, or like surfing atop its oceanic wave. Yet her focus was intense. I think she was the smartest of us, maybe as smart as the Atom Kids our parents, and with the incomparable advantage of thriving in an epoch when the parallel quasi-intelligence of the web gave everyone entrée to everything anyone had ever said, written, painted, shaped, made manifest from their thoughts and dreams and hungers and schemes. For someone as glowing as Ruthie, that was a free 100 points of IQ on top of the icing.

I turned with the green light, carefully, maybe too carefully, and the benighted fool with his lights off, his cell phone stuck in his ear and his small anthropoid brain in neutral went into the side door at 60, maybe, according to police analysis, caved the steel and glass into a jagged fist that slammed Ruth so hard her brain caromed off the inside of her skull and . . . broke, bled, died.

Somehow I escaped with only a cracked ulna, shock, and the kind of furious agony that never goes away, never, never, just ebbs bit by slow shuddering bit in weeks and then months of grief. It would catch me at moments as I sat alone (Andrea left me when my bitterness turned, unfairly, against her, as it turned against everyone who tried to comfort and sustain me, and drove her away), it would bring up choking sobs that were her name, somewhere in the swimming light and the snot and thickened juices of my throat. It lacerated some protected autistic part of me I'd never understood was my emotional protection against a world where I didn't belong.

I wanted her back.

"Give me back my Ruthie," I said aloud, in my empty living room before the meaningless jabbering TV, and wept, and nobody answered, because she was gone and could never return.

It wasn't as if I'd been in love with the girl, the woman. I know why, too—in effect, we were "kibbutz siblings;" she was out of emotional bounds, like Janey, due to over-exposure at some pivot of childhood. Maybe Piaget could pin-point it, or Bettelheim. Fond as I was of little Ruth, and I was—I loved her with all my heart—it was not a sexual bond. It held no magical spark. She was not Maxine, nor Andrea. But losing her really did tear an ancient scab off my heart, or maybe punched through a defective barrier I'd had cloaking it since childhood.

I wept as we buried her in the old Catholic church where Father Paul laid her crushed flesh to rest (Ruthie was an atheist, like me), and when the moment came for me to approach the front of the gathering and add words of remembrance, I simply could not do it. My heart was poisoned with rage and grief, and it rose to block my mouth. It blocked my heart against Andrea, too, and I did not know why that should be. I stood beside her at the grave, mute and useless and felt nothing but wretchedness.

Later, later, I understood what had been done for me in that tragedy. I will hate that drunken fool until the day I die, and carry his name in wrath unspoken before me, but his wicked stupidity was the occasion (and how I wish it had been otherwise, that I could turn it back and make it not happen) of my admission into the mysteries of the Qualia Engine.

4

"Power," I instructed Marius. These days he was playing a thirty-string guitarangi da Gamba in a band called *The Fluting Opera* (they did no opera, and there were no flautists) and slept very late, but always came over to the lab, even early in the morning, for big occasions. He toggled the board. Lights went from red and yellow to green or white. Overhead, there was a perceptible flicker as we drained juice from the building's transformer.

"It's alive!" Marius cried in a maniacal voice that echoed inside the acoustically shielded control room. "It's alive!"

I shot him a grin, then ignored him. Janey was poised at the edge of a second-order phase transition, with cortical correlations and anti-correlations extending across her entire brain. At criticality, the phases would collapse together in a series of neuronal avalanches. With luck and exquisite timing, we'd capture a time slice of Janey's soul, and port it to the D-Wave box. I switched my microphone on.

"Think of a butterfly lighting on a daylily, Janey," I suggested, and displayed a stereo picture of a gorgeous zebra swallowtail drifting past a tiger lily in Mom's garden.

"Yo," she said, drowsily. "With warm breast and with ah! bright wings."

It took me a moment to catch the quote: Gerard Manley Hopkins. Over the bent world broods. Yes. I activated the scan.

Diode lights went on everywhere.

⇒◆⇐

"Mirror neurons," Janey said, and Marius nodded. The boyish chubbiness, I noticed absently, had lately drained from his face; there was a firmness in his cheeks and his jaw.

"They're big players in the qualia game," I agreed, "but we've been through this before." Dedicated F5 cells in the premotor cortex. Monkey see, monkey do—and presumably monkey feel the same raw feels. Trust me, urged the politicians, I feel your pain. But was that all? The Peggy Lee standard that my Mom used to croon drifted in memory: *Is that all there is?* "The neurology of emotive reciprocation is a *prerequisite* for empathy, sure—"

"For even the *simplest* appreciation that other people have feelings," Janey said more loudly. "That their experience is akin to our own. To *my* own. To *yours*. However oddball each of us is, and I think it's clear that when it comes to odd, you, my dear Saul, take the—"

Beneath the good natured banter, I felt a current of frustration and even animosity. This was *my* project, finally; somehow they'd allowed themselves to be roped in, years ago, and all we had for our thousands of hours and millions in investment was a machine, an engine, that did just what evolved mirror neurons did in an ape: echoed back, mirrored, what it saw. Seized, or rather embraced, a frozen instant of a soul in very ordinary passage. Less than ordinary, in fact: lying on your back, or propped up on a padded chair, sniffing a rose is a rose as sweet or attending to Delius in a country garden or tasting jalapenos, capsaicins burning the front of your tongue . . . these qualia were vivid enough as you experienced them, and worthy of capture and butchering on the analytic bench—but was it science? In the true sense: was it knowledge that eased open the universe a little more readily to our human grasp?

I felt my throat constrict. Fear? Anxiety, at least. I must take the next step. This was the key commitment we'd been working toward all these years. In a sense, Ruthie had given up her life for it. I had to patch into someone else's qualia and run them through me in the most intimate embrace of another's experience the world had ever dreamed of, outside delusions of spirit possession. Mom or Paul, it occurred to me, would probably be more at home with this prospect than I, soul believers both. The thought made me shiver and clench my toes. Yes, Oedipus, step right up to the scanner. But that risk was well in abeyance; none of the Atom Kids knew about this project. Quite a lot we never told them. Poor supermen.

"Cut the crap," I said. "Let's roll."

The MEG imager room uses active shielding, a nested set of aluminum layers wrapping a one mm. sheet of high permeability ferromagnetic alloy. Inside that safe, quiet barrier, the MEG listens for the fragile magnetic fields generated by ionic currents in the brain's dendrites as synapses pulse out or swallow their neurotransmitter messages. The signals it registers are foully dirty, the babbling from hundreds of adjacent cortical columns conflated and run together, so we cleaned them on the fly with a Bayes classifier and k-Nearest neighbor machine learning algorithms. All this took place at the interface between the D-Wave kilo-qubit processing units and a living brain—in this case, mine.

I thought again of Ruthie. But it was Janey's qualia I was about to . . . what? Emulate? Re-run? Instantiate, that's probably the *mot juste*.

I was drowsy; we used a low dose of diazepam to settle the butterflies. (Swallowtails winging across bright daylilies! My zonky mind skittered.) I moved lips that seemed thick and heavy. "Hit me, maestro."

It was—

Faintly sickening, like a moment of vertigo, peering over the edge of a tall building and waiting for your confused eyes to focus on the tiny vehicles creeping past below. The double vision didn't correct itself at once. A photo flashed into the display above me. A hairy dog running beside waves, golden sand spraying up from his galumphing paws, tail high, grinning mouth open, tongue flapping and moist in the brilliant beach sunshine. "Scarf," I started to say, and knew at the same moment that this was Mousy, my grandparents' beloved dog, when I was five, visiting them in Fort Lauderdale, and—

That wasn't my memory. Nor my perception. And the colors were wrong, a little off. The reds were a tad flatter, somehow, and the yellows glowed as if in a heightened, pushed Photoshop rendition. Then hues swerved back to the spectrum I was used to. Erp. Oops. Next picture. Fruit in a gleaming bowl, on a table I remembered, one of us remembered. I'd knocked it over when I was three, climbing from chair to tabletop against Mother's strict prohibition, and it shattered into shards of light that stung . . . Not my memory, either. But it resonated with my authentic recollection of tearing off sheet after sheet of toilet paper and dumping it in the toilet bowl, then lighting a match and throwing it in. The sharp stink of the match igniting, the slow blue-edged spread of flame across sagging, sogging paper, the rising thread of black and merry, gray smoke, the sudden terrifying racket of the smoke alarm, L.C.'s frightened, angry shout—

We're not that different, I thought, and my mind wrapped itself about Janey's memories, her guesses, her being. I looked up at picture after picture in the stimulus display, falling more and more deeply into resonance with her soul, I suppose you'd have to say, jolted back out again from time to time (the weight and heft of breasts as I jumped, smacking the volleyball hard, cramping in my guts with my period, the pleasure of lightly coating my pouted mouth with lipgloss of *just* the right color, the faintly heavy sweet odor of that gloss in my nostrils, those three savage hours of Britten's *Peter Grimes* at the Met), but all of it no more, really, than a visit to a museum exhibit, a wonderful holographic or (somehow) articulated waxworks display of a mind and body caught in one timeless moment—

"Here are some people you know," said a voice. Marius, I supposed. Not Paul, my father. But there was Paul's face, and again from another angle, snapped at different ages, hair never too long or short, never the rebel, Paul, always the good dutiful boy who accepted his responsibilities with grace and endurance, but wasn't it a little odd how sometimes, in the right light, with his mouth held at that angle, he seemed so much like Saul—

Marius, defiant at six years of age, when they'd decided to send us to conventional schools, the Atom Kids had, explaining how we must try to fit in as best we might, not boasting, not showing off what we knew, our skills, our odious specialness, must learn *how to be them*, dear god, to absorb and mimic the qualia of their limited lives, learn that their hungers and heartbreaks were no less agonizing to them than ours to us, that their joys called for respect and happiness shared, that—

Ruthie's face, and she was gone, gone, half-cyborg, half sweet sharp-tongued angel, never to grow through the rest of our life together, never to have our babies together as, girl to girl, we'd promised each other—But that was Janey's recollection, channeled like the whisper of a ghost to my memory, my clenching, bitter gut—

Janey, now. My clever friend. My sister. My companion. My—

Oh, oh, oh. Like a cruel light flung in your blinking eyes. Unable to turn away. Insupportable. Had her qualia been utterly impenetrable, if the machine had worked but shown that we inhabited dissimilar inward realities—*that* would have been disheartening, the waste of years and effort, but this was—

I was scalded by her incandescent love. The richness of it was a wave crushing my petty pragmatism, my small resentments against L.C. and Paul.

The pictures had moved on. Kuzi, the Patriarch, all the rest of them, but I was floundering.

"Turn it off," I said. "For god's sake turn it off."

There was Janey, beside me, practical, matter of fact, pulling the sticky squid contacts from my head and torso. I watched her sensible face. It was impossible to reconcile my inward knowledge that she was profoundly, achingly, in love with me, had been for years, had never said the smallest word or given any hint because Ruthie—

"Thanks," I said. "We can do a debriefing in a few minutes. Have to be . . . by myself for a while," and stumbled to the rest room, perched on the toilet seat. I was thinned by her absence from my doubled soul, by my self-knowledge that, to me, she had never been, can never be, anything more than a pal.

"Oh shit," I muttered. "What the hell am I going to do?"

Reality came back into single focus. I had to stop her from undergoing a reciprocal qualia immersion. It would devastate her, I told myself.

A dying echo of her soul inside mine gave a derisive laugh. Get *over* yourself, Saul Collins. You condescending, sexist little man.

But that, too, was just a slice of the complex reality.

I washed myself quickly, making the water run as hot as I could tolerate, then as cold, splashing myself back to myself, then walked to the control room where they waited for me.

"Hey, Odysseus," Janey said, and sent me a sad smile. She knew. She had known, of course she had, what I would find there. I shook my head.

Marius glanced between us, rose casually and left the room. "Later, dude."

I looked at Janey, and she looked at me. "Hey, Jane," I said. "Hello, my dear friend." Eyes misting, I waved one hand at the MEG control panel, at our Qualia Engine. "You'll have to take it for a spin."

"Jump right in, huh?"

"Sure," I said, mixing my metaphors, "the water's fine!"

We went out arm in arm, as friends do, qualia humming in us, to where Marius cooled his heels against a corridor wall, and headed off, all three, toward The Genteel Pizzeria to eat something disgustingly wicked and clogged with cholesterol.

THE RADIANT CAR THY SPARROWS DREW

CATHERYNNE M. VALENTE

> Being unable to retrace our steps in Time, we decided to move
> forward in Space. Shall we never be able to glide back up the
> stream of Time, and peep into the old home, and gaze on the
> old faces? Perhaps when the phonograph and the kinesigraph
> are perfected, and some future worker has solved the problem
> of colour photography, our descendants will be able to deceive
> themselves with something very like it: but it will be but a
> barren husk: a soulless phantasm and nothing more. "Oh for
> the touch of a vanished hand, and the sound of a voice that
> is still!'"
>
> —Wordsworth Donisthorpe,
> inventor of the Kinesigraph Camera

**View the Famous Callowhale Divers of Venus from the Safety of a Silk
Balloon! Two Bits a Flight!**
—Advertisement Visible in the Launch Sequence of
The Radiant Car Thy Sparrows Drew

**EXT. The cannon pad at the Vancouver World's Fair in 1986, late afternoon,
festooned with crepe and banners wishing luck and safe travel.**

*The Documentarian Bysshe and her crew wave jerkily as confetti sticks to
their sleek skullcaps and glistening breathing apparati. Her smile is immaculate,
practiced, the smile of the honest young woman of the hopeful future; her
copper-finned helmet gleams at her feet. Bysshe wears women's clothing but
reluctantly and only for this shot, and the curl of her lip betrays disdain of the
bizarre, flare-waisted swimming costume that so titillates the crowds. Later,
she would write of the severe wind-burns she suffered in cannon-flight due
to the totally inadequate protection of that flutter of black silk. She tucks a
mahogany case smartly under one arm, which surely must contain George, her*

favorite cinematographe. Each of her crewmen strap canisters of film—and the occasional bit of food or oxygen or other minor accoutrements—to their broad backs. The cannon sparkles, a late-model Algernon design, filigreed and etched with motifs that curl and leaf like patterns in spring ice breaking.

They are a small circus—the strongmen, the clowns, the trapeze artist poised on her platform, arm crooked in an evocative half-moon, toes pointed into the void.

I find it so difficult to watch her now, her narrow, monkish face, not a pore wasted, her eyes huge and sepia-toned, her smile enormous, well-practiced, full of the peculiar, feral excitement which in those days seemed to infect everyone who looked up into the evening sky to see Venus there, seducing behind veils of light, as she has always done. Those who looked and had eyes only for red Mars, all baleful and bright, were rough, raucous, ready and hale. Those who saw Venus were lost.

She was such a figure then: Bysshe, no surname, or simply the Documentarian. Her revolving lovers made the newsreels spin, her films packed the nickelodeons and wrapped the streets three times 'round. Weeks before a Bysshe opened, buskers and salesmen would camp out on the thoroughfares beside every theater, selling genuine cells she touched with her *own hand* and replica spangled cages from *To Thee, Bright Queen!* sized just right to hold a male of Saturnine extraction. Her father, Percival Unck, was a brooding and notorious director in his time, his gothic dramas full of wraith-like heroines with black, bruised eyes and mouths perpetually agape with horror or orgiastic transcendence. Her mother was, naturally, one of those ever-transported actresses, though which one it is hard to remember, since each Unck leading lady became, by association and binding contract, little black-bobbed Bysshe's mother-of-the-moment. Thus it is possible to see, in her flickering, dust-scratched face, the echoes of a dozen fleeting, hopeful actresses, easily forgotten but for the legacy of their adoptive daughter's famous, lean features, her scornful, knowing grin.

Bysshe rejected her father's idiom utterly. Her film debut in Unck's *The Spectres of Mare Nubium* is charming, to say the least. During the famous ballroom sequence wherein the decadent dowager Clarena Schirm is beset with the ghosts of her victims, little Bysshe can be seen crouching unhappily near the rice-wine fountain, picking at the pearls on her traditional lunar *kokoshnik* and rubbing at her make-up. The legend goes that when Percival Unck tried to smudge his daughter's eyes with black shadows and convince her to pretend herself a poor Schirm relation while an airy phantasm—years later to become her seventh mother—swooped down upon the innocent child, Bysshe looked up exasperatedly and said: "Papa. This is silly! I want only to be myself!"

And so she would be, forever, only and always Bysshe. As soon as she could work the crank on a cinematographe herself, she set about recording "the really real and actual world" (age 7) or "the genuine and righteous world of the true tale," (age 21) and declaring her father's beloved ghosts and devils "a load of double exposure drivel." Her first documentary, *The Famine Queen of Phobos*, brought the colony's food riots to harsh light, and earned her a Lumiere medal, a prize Percival Unck would never receive. When asked if his daughter's polemics against fictive cinema had embittered him, Unck smiled in his raffish, canine way and said: "The lens, my good man, does not discriminate between the real and the unreal."

Of her final film, *The Radiant Car Thy Sparrows Drew*, only five sequences remain, badly damaged. Though they have been widely copied, cut up and re-used in countless sallow and imitative documentaries on her life, the originals continue to deteriorate in their crystalline museum displays. I go there, to the Grand Eternal Exhibition, in the evenings, to watch them rot. It comforts me. I place my brow upon the cool wall, and she flashes before my eyes, smiling, waving, crawling into the mouth of the cannon-capsule with the ease of a natural performer, a natural aeronaut—and perhaps those were always much the same thing.

EXT. Former Site of the Village of Adonis, on the Shores of the Sea of Qadesh, Night.

A small boy, head bent, dressed in the uniform of a callowhale diver, walks in circles in what was once the village center. The trees and omnipresent cacao-ferns are splashed with a milky spatter. He does not look up as the camera watches him. He simply turns and turns and turns, over and over. The corrupted film skips and jumps; the boy seems to leap through his circuit, flashing in and out of sight.

When she was seventeen, Bysshe and her beloved cinematographe, George, followed the Bedouin road to Neptune for two years, resulting in her elegiac *And the Sea Remembered, Suddenly*. There, they say, she learned her skill at the sculpting of titanium, aquatic animal handling, and a sexual variant of Samayika mediation developed by a cult of levitation on tiny Halimede, where the wind blows warm and violet. There is a sequence, towards the melancholy conclusion of *And the Sea*, wherein Bysshe visits coral-devoured Enki, the great floating city which circumnavigates the planet once a decade, buoyed by the lugubrious Neptunian current. Reclining on chaises with glass screens raised to keep out the perpetual rain, Bysshe smokes a ball of creamy, heady af-yun with a woman-levitator, her hair lashed with leather whips. When theaters received the prints of *And the Sea*, a phonograph and several records were included, so that Bysshe herself could narrate her opus to audiences across the world. A solemn bellhop changed the record when the onscreen Bysshe winked, seemingly to no one. And so one may sit on a plush chair, still, and hear her deep, nasal voice echo loudly—too loud, too loud!—in the theater.

The levitator told her of a town called Adonis, a whole colony on Venus that vanished in the space of a night. Divers they were, mostly, subject both to the great callowhales with their translucent skin and the tourists who came to watch and shiver in cathartic delight as the divers risked their lives to milk the recalcitrant mothers in their hibernation. They built a sweet village on the shores of the Qadesh, plaiting their roofs with grease-weed and hammering doors from the chunks of raw copper which comprised the ersatz Venusian beach. They lived; they ate the thready local cacao and shot, once or twice a year, a leathery 'Tryx from the sky, enough to keep them all in fat and protein for months.

"It was a good life," the blue-skinned levitator said, and Bysshe, on her slick black record, imitated the breathy, shy accent of Halimede as onscreen version of herself loaded another lump of af-yun into the atomizer. "And then, one day—pop! All gone. Houses, stairs, meat-smoking racks, diving bells."

"This sort of thing happens," Bysshe dismissed it all with a wave of her hand. "What planet is there without a mysteriously vanished colony to pull in the tourist cash? Slap up a couple of alien runes on a burned-out doorframe and people will stream in from every terminus. Might as well call them all New Roanoke and have done with it." (In fact, one of Percival Unck's less popular films was *The Abduction of Prosperina*, a loose retelling of that lost Plutonian city, though presumably with rather more demonic ice-dragons than were actually involved.)

Crab-heart trifles and saltwhiskey were passed around as Bysshe's crew laughed and nodded along with her. The levitator smiled.

"Of course, Miss," she said, eyes downcast within the equine blinders knotted to her head. "Well, except for the little boy. The one who was left behind. They say he's still there. He's stuck, somehow, in the middle of where the village used to be, just walking around in circles, around and around. Like a skip on a phonograph. He never even stops to sleep." The Documentarian frowns sourly in black and white, her disapproval of such fancies, her father's fancies, disappeared heroines and eldritch locations where something terrible surely occurred, showing in the wrinkling of her brow, the tapping of her fingernails against the atomizer as bubbling storms lapped their glass cupola, and armored penance-fish nosed the flotation arrays, their jaw-lanterns flashing.

But you can see her thinking, the new film, which was to be her last, taking shape behind her eyes.

This is what she came to see.

Dead Adonis, laid out in state on the beach-head. Her single mourner. The great ocean provides a kind of score for her starlit landing, and in the old days a foley-boy would thrash rushes against the floor of the theater to simulate the colossal, dusky red tide of the Qadesh. We would all squint in the dark, and try to see scarlet in the monochrome waves, emerald in the undulating cacao-ferns. The ruin of a black silk balloon crinkles and billows lightly on the strand. The dwarf moon Anchises shines a kind of limping, diffident light on Bysshe as she walks into frame, her short hair sweat-curled in the wilting wind. She threw the exhibition costume into an offscreen campfire and is clothed now in her accustomed jodhpurs and black jacket. The boy turns and turns. His hands flicker and blur as if he is signing something, or writing on phantom paper. She holds out her hand as though approaching a horse, squats down beside the child in a friendly, schoolteacherly fashion. The boy does not raise his head to look at her. He stares at his feet. Bysshe looks uncertainly over her shoulder at the long snarl of sea behind them—the cinematographe operator, temporarily trusted with the care and feeding of George, says something to her offscreen, he must, because she cocks her head as though considering a riddle and says something back to him. Her mouth moves in the silent footage, mouthing words the audience cannot ever quite read.

Once, a deaf scholar was brought to view this little scene in a private projector room. She was given coffee and a treacle tart. She reported the words as: *Look at the whales. Are they getting closer?*

Bysshe stands up straight and strides without warning into the child's path, blocking his little pilgrim's progress around the sad patch of dune grass.

The child does not stop. He collides with Bysshe, steps back, collides with her again. He beats his head against her soft belly. Back and forth, back and forth.

The Documentarian looks helplessly into the camera.

EXT. Former Site of the Village of Adonis, afternoon.

One of the crewmen shaves in a mirror nailed to furry black cacao-fern bark. He uses a straight razor whose handle is inlaid with fossilized kelp. He is shirtless and circus huge, his face angular and broad. He catches a glimpse of Bysshe in his mirror and whirls to catch her up, kissing her and smearing shaving cream on her face. She laughs and punches his arm—he recoils in mock agony. It is a pleasant scene. This is Erasmo St. John, the Documentarian's lover and lighting-master, who would later claim to have fathered a child with her, despite being unable to produce a convincing moppet.

Clouds drift down in long, indistinct spirals. Behind them, the boy turns and turns, still, celluloid transforming the brutal orange of the Venusian sun into a blinding white nova. Beyond him, pearlescent islands hump up out of the foamy Qadesh—callowhales, a whole pod, silent, pale.

Adonis was established some twenty years prior to the Bysshe expedition, one of many villages eager to take advantage of the callowhale hibernations. What, precisely, callowhale *is* is still the subject of debate. There are diagrams, to be sure—one even accompanies the *Radiant Car* press kit—but these are guesses only. It cannot even be safely said whether they are animal or vege-table matter. The first aeronauts, their braggart flags flapping in that first, raw breeze, assumed them to be barren islands. The huge masses simply lay motionless in the water, their surfaces milky, motley, the occasional swirl of chemical blue or gold sizzling through their depths. But soon enough, divers and fishermen and treasure-seekers flocked to the watery promise of Venus, and they called the creatures true. Beneath the waterline were calm, even dead leviathans—*taninim*, said a neo-Hasidic bounty hunter, some sort of proto-pliosaur, said one of the myriad research corps. Their fins lay flush against their flanks, horned and barbed. Their eyes were then perpetually shut—*hibernating*, said the research cotillion. *Dreaming*, said the rest. From their flat, wide skulls extended long, fern-like antennae which curled in fractal infinitude, tangling with the others of their occasional pods, their fronds stroking one another lightly, imperceptibly, in the quick, clever Qadesh currents. Whether they have any sentience is popular tea-chatter—their hibernation cycle seems to be much longer than a human life.

Some few divers claim to have heard them sing—the word they give to a series of unpredictable vibrations that occasionally shiver through the fern-antennae. Like sonar, these quaking oscillations can be fatal to any living thing caught up in them—unlike sonar, the unfortunates are instantly vaporized into constituent atoms. Yet the divers say that from a safe distance, their echoes brush against the skin in strange and intimate patterns, like music, like lovemaking. The divers cannot look at the camera when they speak of these things, as though it is the eye of God and by not meeting His gaze, they may preserve virtue. *The vibrations are the color of morning*, they whisper.

It is the milk the divers are after—nearly everything produced on Venus contains callowhale milk, the consistency of honey, the color of cream, the taste something like sucking on a dandelion stem caked in green peppercorn. It is protein-rich, fat-clotted, thick with vitamins—equally sought after as an industrial lubricant, foodstuff, fuel, as an ingredient in medicines, anesthesia, illicit hallucinogens, poured into molds and dried as an exotic building material. Certain artists have created entire murals from it, which looked upon straight seem like blank canvases, but seen slant-wise reveal impossibly complex patterns of shades of white. Little by little, Venusian-born children began to be reared on the stuff, to no apparent ill effect—and the practice became fashionable among the sorts of people whose fashions become the morality of the crowds. Erasmo St. John pioneered a kind of long-lit camera lantern by scalding the milk at low temperatures, producing an eerie phosphorescence. The later Unck films use this to great effect as spectral light.Cultivation has always been dangerous—the tubules that secrete milk are part and parcel of the ferny antennae, extending from the throat-sac of the callowhale. In order to harvest it, the diver must avoid the tendrils of fern and hope upon hope that the whale is not seized with a sudden desire to sing. For this danger, and for the callowhales' rude insistence upon evolving on Venus and not some more convenient locale, the milk was so precious that dozens of coastal towns can be sustained by encouraging a relatively small population of municipal divers. Stock footage sent back to earth shows family after beaming family, clad in glittering counterpressure mesh, dark copper diving bells tucked neatly under their arms, hoisting healthy, robust goblets of milk, toasting the empire back home.

But where there is milk, there is mating, isn't there? There are children. The ghost-voice of Bysshe comes over the phonograph as the final shot of *And the Sea Remembered, Suddenly* flickers silver-dark and the floating Neptunian pleasure-domes recede. Everyone knew where she was bound next, long before principal photography ever began. To Venus, and Adonis, to the little village rich in milk and children that vanished two decades after its founding, while the callowhales watched offshore, impassive, unperturbed.

EXT. Village Green, Twilight.

Bysshe is grabbing the child's hand urgently while he screams, soundlessly, held brutally still in his steps by the gaffer and the key grip, whose muscles bulge with what appears to be a colossal effort—keeping this single, tiny, bird-boned child from his circuit. The Documentarian's jagged hair and occasionally her chin swings in and out of frame as she struggles with him. She turns over the boy's hand, roughly, to show the camera what she has found there: tiny fronds growing from his skin, tendrils like ferns, seeking, wavering, wet with milk. The film jumps and shudders; the child's hand vibrates, faster, faster.

It is a difficult thing, to have an aftermath without an event.

The tabloids, ever beloved of Bysshe and her exploits, heralded the return of the expedition long before the orbits were favorable. They salivated for the new work, which would surely set records for attendance. The nickelodeons began taking ticket orders a year in advance, installing the revolutionary new sound equipment which might allow us all to hear the sound of the surf on a Venusian shore. The balloon was sighted in orbit and spontaneous, Romanesque gin-triumphs were held in all the capitals. Finally, on a grassy field outside Vancouver, the black silk confection of Bysshe's studio balloon wrinkled and sighed to rest on the spring ground. The grips and gaffers came out first, their eyes downcast, refusing to speak. Then the producer, clutching his hat to his chest. Lastly came Erasmo St. John, clutching the hand of the greatest star of the coming century: a little boy with ferns in his fists.

Bysshe did not return. Her crew would not speak of where she had gone, only that she was to be left to it, called dead if not actually deceased—and possibly deceased. They mumbled; they evaded. Their damaged film, water-logged and half-missing, was hurried into theaters and pored over by hundreds of actors, scholars, gossip columnists. It is said that Percival Unck only once viewed the reels. He looked into his lap when the last shot had faded to black and smiled, a secret smile, of regret, perhaps, or of victory.

The boy was sent to school, paid for by the studio. He was given a new name, though later in life he, too, would eschew any surname, having no family connections to speak of save to a dead documentarian. He wore gloves, always, and shared his memories as generously as he could with the waves of popular interest in Venus, in Adonis, in the lost film. *No, I don't remember what happened to my parents. I'm sorry, I wish I did. One day they were gone. Yes, I remember Bysshe. She gave me a lemon candy.*

And I do remember her. The jacket only looks black on film. I remember—it was red.

I once saw a group of performance artists—rich students with little better to do, I thought—mount a showing of the shredded, abrupt footage of *The Radiant Car*, intercut with highlights of the great Unck gothics. The effect was strange and sorrowing: Bysshe seemed to step out of her lover's arms and into a ballroom, becoming suddenly an unhappy little girl, only to leap out again, shimmering into the shape of another child, with a serious expression, turning in endless circles on a green lawn. One of the students, whose hair was plaited and piled upon her head, soaked and crusted in callowhale milk until it glowed with a faint phosphor, stood before the screen with a brass bullhorn. She wore a bustle frame but no bustle, shoelaces lashed in criss-crossings around her calves but no shoes. The jingly player-piano kept time with the film, and behind her Bysshe stared intently into the phantasm of a distant audience, unknowable as God.

"Ask yourself," she cried brazenly, clutching her small, naked breasts. "As Bysshe had the courage to ask! What is milk for, if not to nurture a new generation, a new world? We have never seen a callowhale calf, yet the mothers endlessly nurse. What do they nurture, out there in their red sea? I will tell you. For the space is not smooth that darkly floats between our earth and that morning star, Lucifer's star, in eternal revolt against the order of heaven. It is *thick*, it is swollen, its disrupted proteins skittering across the black like foam—like milk spilled across the stars. And in this quantum milk how many bubbles may form and break, how many abortive universes gestated by the eternal sleeping mothers may burgeon and burst? I suggest this awe-ful idea: Venus is an anchor, where all waveforms meet in a radiant scarlet sea, where the milk of creation is milled, and we have pillaged it, gorged upon it all unknowing. Perhaps in each bubble of milk is a world suckled at the breast of a pearlescent cetacean. Perhaps there is one where Venus is no watery Eden as close as a sister, but a distant inferno of steam and stone, lifeless, blistered. Perhaps you have drunk the milk of this world—perhaps I have, and destroyed it with my digestion. Perhaps a skin of probabilistic milk, dribbling from the mouths of babes, is all that separates our world from the others. Perhaps the villagers of Adonis drank so deeply of the primordial milk that they became as the great mothers, blinking through worlds like holes burned in film—leaving behind only the last child born, who had not yet enough of the milk to change, circling, circling the place where the bubble between worlds burst!" The girl let her milk-barnacled hair fall with a violent gesture, dripping the peppery-sharp smelling cream onto the stage.

"Bysshe asked the great question: where did Adonis go in death? The old tales know. Adonis returned to his mother, the Queen of the Dark, the Queen of the Otherworld." Behind her, on a forty-foot screen, the boy's fern-bound palm—my palm, my vanished hand—shivered and vibrated and faded into the thoughtful, narrow face of Bysshe as she hears for the first time the name of Adonis. The girl screams—half-primal, half-theatrical. "Even here on Earth we have supped all our lives on this alien milk. *We* are the calves of the callowhales, and no human mothers. We will ride upon the milky foam, and one day, one distant, distant day, our heads will break the surf of a red sea, and the eyes of the whales will open, and weep, and dote upon us!"

The girl held up her hand, palm outward, to the meager audience. I squinted. There, on her skin, where her heart line and fate line ought to have been, was a tiny fern, almost imperceptible, but wavering nonetheless, uncertain, ethereal, new.

A rush of blood beat at my brow. As if compelled by strings and pulleys, I raised up my own palm in return. Between the two fronds, some silent shiver passed, the color of morning.

INT. The depths of the sea of Qadesh.

Bysshe swims through the murky water, holding one of Erasmo's milk-lanterns out before her. St. John follows behind with George, encased in a crystal canister. The film is badly stained and burned through several frames. She swims upward, dropping lead weights from her shimmering counterpressure mesh as she rises. The grille of her diving bell gleams faintly in the shadows. Above her, slowly, the belly of a callowhale comes into view. It is impossibly massive, the size of a sky. Bysshe strains towards it, extending her fingers to touch it, just once, as if to verify it for herself, that such a thing could be real.

The audience will always and forever see it before Bysshe does. A slit in the side of the great whale, like a door opening. As the Documentarian stretches towards it, with an instinctual blocking that is nothing short of spectacular—the suddenly tiny figure of a young woman frozen forever in this pose of surprise, of yearning, in the center of the shot—the eye of the callowhale, so huge as to encompass the whole screen, opens around her.

WIFE-STEALING TIME

R. GARCIA Y ROBERTSON

PRETTY BOTTOM

SinBad sat in the lee of his stalled sand sail, feeding a thornbrush fire, listening as ba'aths called to each other over the dark sward. They had smelled his fire on the night wind, a whole hunting pride from the well spaced cries, out looking for a late snack.

Too bad. Tonight's wind was dead against him. He had a cargo for Kaol, a couple of hundred haads to the east, a legal cargo even, offworld nanoelectronics, but a fitful easterly breeze kept him from making any headway.

Ba'ath calls got louder, closer. Reaching over his shoulder, into the sand sail's cargo bay, SinBad unshipped his repeating crossbow, cranking back the bow. Claw marks on the tough skeel-wood stock were unpleasant reminders of his last close encounter with a ba'ath. He slid in a clip of six explosive bolts, hearing the satisfying click.

SinBad had nothing against ba'aths. Even hungry ones. *Leo barsoom*, the big black-maned Barsoomian lion, was a dozen sofads long, a bio-engineered carnivore twice the size of Numa on Old Earth, ending in twin sets of sabertooth canines. Megafauna require mega-predators.

Aiming to be at best a mini-meal, SinBad settled in between the sand sail's tricycle tires, his cocked crossbow pointed at the night. Half a haad behind him glowed the fires of a nomad camp. Red men. Crows, from their tall hourglass shaped tipis. Being a Huron outcast, SinBad had not hurried to introduce himself. Now it was too late. Thuria was up, and the Slaver Moon made the usually friendly Crow wary of strangers.

As the fire sank down to embers, SinBad pulled his sleeping furs tighter, then flicked his sand goggles to night vision, peering into the infrared, seeing by Thuria light. Slavers had made Barsoom's inner moon highly reflective, so they could scan the planet's surface more closely at night.

Nothing moved. Aside from some ghostly acacia trees, swaying in the wind.

Ba'ath calls slackened, replaced by mounting boredom, while the strange stars of Carthoris system wheeled overhead. Thuria set, and the Crow camp stirred behind him. Fear alone kept SinBad from drifting off.

Then he saw a silver form slither out from beneath a wait-a-bit thorn tree, barely thirty sofads away. Too small to be a full-grown ba'ath, the lithe shape stayed low to the ground, creeping toward him. Juvenile ba'ath? Dire wolf? Jackal? At full charge a ba'ath covered thirty sofads faster than you can say it—if this was a ba'ath.

He shifted his crossbow to cover the approaching shape with the cold sight. Dark metal formed a sharp black V, blotting out the infrared glow. His finger found the curved trigger.

Even in the dark, he was a decent shot at this range. Explosive bolts made any hit hurt. By holding down the trigger, while working the cocking lever, he could empty his clip in a quarter xat.

Whatever was coming froze, as if it could feel his intent through the darkness.

Predators and prey had a psychic relationship. At a sward waterhole south of Ptarth, he once saw steppe gazelle grazing beside some sleeping ba'aths. Suddenly, the grazers bolted, disappearing into dawn fog. Presently the ba'aths perked up, starting to yawn, stretch, and sniff the wind. The gazelles had sensed the carnivore's hunger, before the ba'aths themselves.

Without warning, the shape in the dark hissed at him, "Sush. Outcast. Do not shoot."

Hastily, he lowered his bow. It was a woman's voice, a young woman. Pretty, too, from the sound of her. Sex offenders also had psychic links to their prey. "Who are you?"

"Pretty Bottom," the woman replied, confirming his instincts. Lest he get any ideas, she added, "Third wife to Alligator Stands Up."

SinBad had heard of him, an aging Crow war chief, with a famously young harem. "Kaor, Pretty Bottom."

Standing up, a buxom black-braided teenager in beaded buckskins strolled into the firelight. SinBad could not see her bottom, but the rest of her was enticing, from her dark smiling eyes, to the bone-handled skinning knife tucked into her calf-length boot. Old Alligator Stands Up had notoriously sweet taste in wives. "Kaor, outcast."

SinBad set aside his crossbow, still cocked. "How do you know I am an outcast?"

"Why else would you be sitting alone in the dark?" Pretty Bottom wrinkled her pert nose. "I can smell it on you, along with the fear. Sex offenses, right?"

He nodded. Too true.

"Is that why you are shaking?"

"I nearly shot you." That still had him rattled. "What are you doing, sneaking about at night?"

She laughed. "Silly, it is Wife Stealing Time."

"Already?" He would be late getting to Kaol.

Setting her namesake down by the fire, Pretty Bottom asked, "Isn't that why you are here?"

Hardly. "I was headed for Kaol, when the wind failed." Right at Wife Stealing Time, half a haad from a Crow camp. Why did these things always happen to him? His parole specified that he could not come within a thousand sofads of a commercial sex operation, fertility festival, or communal orgy. Technically, Wife Stealing Time was none of these, but try telling that to a judge. Especially a married one.

Ba'aths called in the blackness. SinBad reached for his crossbow, but a slim hand stopped him. Her brown fingers felt firm and exciting.

"Just ba'aths." Pretty Bottom seemed totally unconcerned by a pride of saber-toothed killers. "Afraid they want to eat you?"

"Maybe." Not him personally perhaps, but they were out flesh shopping.

His visitor smirked. "They are not that hungry."

"Let's hope so." He kept the cocked crossbow within reach.

"Here, this will help." Pretty Bottom got up, dusted off her buckskinned butt, then wiggled into his sleeping furs, totally taking his mind off the prowling ba'aths. Pretty Bottom was barely into her teens, Barsoom years, twice as long as those on Old Earth. Ten years younger than him. But that did not stop her. She whispered, "You are scared. I am cold. This will please us both."

"I'm not that scared," he protested, unlacing her buckskins.

Pretty Bottom slyly stroked his crotch. "See, it's working already."

It was. How weird that young women like her had such power over men, especially men like him. He had been running late on a trip to Kaol, risking his on-time bonus, beset by starved ba'aths, afraid for his life. Suddenly none of that mattered. Not a bit. He reminded Pretty Bottom, "I am twice your age."

"And half my husband's." Pretty Bottom was aching to feel younger flesh. His even, absurd as that seemed. Who was he to complain?

Pushing up Pretty Bottom's buckskins, SinBad saw she deserved her name. No rawhide nomad underwear, just bare enticing flesh.

"So tell me about your sex crimes," she suggested, sliding her hand inside his loincloth.

He shrugged. "Unnatural copulation, aiding in adultery, cohabiting with lesbians, that sort of thing."

Pretty Bottom sniffed. "I hoped for something spicy."

"You can learn a lot from lesbians," SinBad protested.

"Or from living in a crowded tipi." She snuggled closer. "You are already aiding in adultery."

"I am?"

"It is Wife Stealing Time. Anyone who hides me is committing that crime."

Wife Stealing time was two weeks in the spring when Crow romeos were free to kidnap wives they had seduced during the year. Then their own wives and girlfriends would dress the victims up, so their paramours could parade them around camp, showing off their success with other men's wives. Unmarried women and faithful wives were immune. Husbands could do nothing to interfere. Guilty wives had to flee the village, bedding down with the ba'aths and jackals. There was no embarrassment in being eaten. "Alligator Stands Up is smoking in his lodge. He will lose his standing if he comes after me."

"How many wives does old Alligator have?" SinBad asked.

"Eight." Enough Panthans to play Jetan. "Half of them are hiding out. Leaving just old wives, and young favorites to pound his meat and flatten his sleeping furs."

Since poor neglected Pretty Bottom had already done the crime, and made him her accomplice, SinBad saw no sense being shy. Slipping off his loincloth, he prepared to put her most famous asset to use. But his partner in crime preferred natural copulation. "Don't worry," she whispered. "I am pregnant."

Nature's best birth control, already knocked up. He ran a hand over the smooth curve of her belly, which was just starting to swell. "Did Old Alligator stand up?"

"Not for me," she sighed. "My baby is from the scout, Goes Ahead."

Who got in ahead of her husband. Old Alligator's loss. Pretty Bottom was full of youthful, guilt-free enthusiasm, which was plainly going to waste. SinBad had never had so much fun breaking parole.

Afterward they slept, wrapped in his sleeping furs. Near to dawn, she nudged him. "Listen?"

He heard nothing. "What?"

"Do you hear the ba'aths?"

"No." He had totally forgotten about the toothy cats.

"They have made their kill." Pretty Bottom kicked off the furs, pulling on her beaded boots. Then she stood up, drawing her skinning knife, looking incredibly fetching in just the calf-length boots.

He hated to see her leave. "Where are you going?"

"To get breakfast."

"By driving ba'aths from their kill?"

"No," she replied coyly, "by convincing them to share."

He grabbed his crossbow, starting to get up. "Let me come with you."

She shook her head. "They would not like that."

"Probably not," he admitted.

"Then get the fire going again, and leave the ba'aths to me." With that she walked off into the chill of first light, without looking back. He hoped she returned in one pretty piece. On less than a day's acquaintance, SinBad could already tell what Alligator Stands Up saw in her. Goes Ahead, too.

Blood-red day broke over the slowly terraforming landscape, sand and sward, dotted with acacias, and wait-a-bit thorn trees. SinBad relit his fire, listening for ba'ath calls, but hearing only birdsong. Dawn wind blew in the wrong direction. He was worried and hungry, and Thuria would be up soon, adding to his troubles. If Pretty Bottom survived her breakfast with ba'aths, he would have to hide her from the Slaver Moon.

Before he could fret himself completely into a stupor, Pretty Bottom sauntered back into camp, carrying a fresh hunk of moropus haunch, saying, "This is all they would part with."

He took the bloody meat, handing her a washcloth. "I feared for you."

"Needlessly," she noted, wiping moropus blood off her body.

SinBad cooked the meat on thorn bush skewers, while Pretty Bottom wriggled back into her fringed buckskins. When the meat was done, he told her, "Thuria is rising. We need to find a safe place to eat."

Pretty Bottom agreed, "First I must get my possible sack. I left it in a tree."

Burying his precious cargo, he made a place for Pretty Bottom on the back of his sand sail. She returned with her beaded possible sack, the Red woman's leather purse. Settling in behind him, she asked, "What do they call you?"

"SinBad."

She grinned at him. "That's a lie. You sin very well."

Unfurling the sail, he headed off downwind, looking for a hiding place. Not easy to find on the flat mossy sward that covered most of Barsoom. But he had to do it soon, ahead of the Slaver Moon. Pretty Bottom faced kidnapping and worse, while Slavers would kill him out of hand.

Finally, he found a spot, a stretch of grassy steppe, cut by a dry wadi, with a high bank on the Thuria side. There was no way to hide the sand sail, so SinBad parked it at the head of the wadi, telling Pretty Bottom, "I'll carry you from here."

"Really?" She looked shocked. Nomad women regularly carried men's things, but were never carried about by men.

"We cannot leave a line of women's bootprints for Slavers to follow."

She agreed with a giggle, more embarrassed by being picked up than by serial adultery. Barsoom's light gravity made it easy, but by the time they reached the wadi, Thuria was breaking the horizon. Slaver macroscopes were already sweeping the landscape for victims, able to see anything, even the eye color of any woman silly enough to gaze at Barsoom's nearer moon.

Sure enough. Huddled against the high bank, he heard the boom of an orbital shuttle breaking atmosphere, followed by the whoosh of the ship settling down next to his abandoned sand sail. But there was no woman, no cargo, nothing to tempt the Slavers to follow his heat trail into the wadi. Instead they took off again. Slavers knew it was Wife Stealing Time, and had their hands full, combing the area around the Crow camp for errant wives in hiding.

SinBad settled back, chewing on roast moropus. Pretty Bottom asked, "Are they gone?"

"Hope so." He was not about to look. Macroscopes would be trained on the wadi bank, searching for human prey. Thanks to the Greenies, offworld weapons were banned on Barsoom, forcing the natives to make do with bows and swords. Slavers had line-of-sight lasers and orbit-to-surface missiles. They could pick you off without ever leaving Thuria.

Sighing, Pretty Bottom relaxed against him. "You have been nice to me."

"You too." More than nice.

"It is not easy, being third wife to Alligator Stands Up."

"Or Goes Ahead's girlfriend," he reminded her.

"Even worse." She grimaced. "Goes Ahead just wants to parade me through camp, to embarrass my chieftain, and bolster his pride."

Everyone had plans for her, including him. Though his would have to wait until Thuria set. Making love in a wadi was not very practical, especially with Slavers watching.

Instead they waited, while Thuria hurtled overhead. SinBad noticed several pugmarks in the sandy wadi, one quite large. He pointed them out to the young nomad. "Ba'ath?"

"Two ba'aths," she replied. "Mother and cub."

"You can tell that from these tracks?"

"Yes." Pretty Bottom read the spoor as if it were a sensor readout. "The mother was teaching the cub to hunt. She trapped a young gazelle against the bank of the wadi, where they played with it for awhile. Then they killed it, and went off that way, carrying the dead gazelle."

Looking closer, SinBad saw the smaller prints among the pugmarks, jumbled and frantic, as the terrified gazelle bounded about before being killed and eaten. Like the *moropus* they had for breakfast.

Thuria set. By now the east wind had fallen, leaving him totally becalmed. Too bad. He would not start for Kaol today. Luckily, he had someone to occupy his time. Loosening his loincloth, he ran a hand up under her fringed buckskins.

Pretty Bottom arched a dark eyebrow. "What? You want more?"

"Oh, yes." Who would not?

She feigned surprise. "Last night you were so wary."

"You are even more beautiful by day."

"I am?" Pretty Bottom purred.

"You know you are." SinBad never lied to women, especially one so handy with a skinning knife.

Pleased to have found a man who appreciated the obvious, Pretty Bottom let him lift her buckskins. This was Wife Stealing Time. Next week, it would be back to neglect and adultery.

Before he even got started there was the boom of a shuttle breaking atmosphere. SinBad froze in mid-ravish, looking up at a silver streak falling out of the cloudless sky. This was an old Slaver trick, to leave a ship trailing in orbit, to see who broke cover when Thuria went down. And he had fallen for it.

"What was that?" his paramour asked.

"Nothing nice." Rolling off her, he pushed Pretty Bottom back up against the bank. Too little, too late. He heard the whoosh of a lander settling in the long grass. What now?

Pretty Bottom whispered, "Slavers?"

"Probably." Certainly not Goes Ahead, looking for a lost girlfriend to decorate. He cocked his crossbow, for all that would do against lasers and sleep gas grenades. Pretty Bottom drew her skinning knife. They waited.

Nothing happened, at first. He sat there, clinging to his crossbow, mentally counting tals. If they were coming for him, it would be quick. Slavers did not like to linger, once Thuria had set.

Expecting Slavers, he was shocked to have an angel flitter into view; a silver-wigged beauty, wearing glitter paint, white solar-powered wings, and a shining jeweled G-string. Silver-plated nipples shone in the sun.

Neither he nor Pretty Bottom knew what to say. Landing in an ivory flutter of artificial flight feathers, the silver-skinned woman said, "Kaor. We come in peace."

Tourist. And unarmed. That much was obvious. "Kaor," SinBad replied, setting aside his crossbow. He had to stop pointing it at pretty women. "We were going to come in peace. Then you arrived."

"I did not mean to interrupt," the silver woman protested. "Please continue your copulation. I hear it is spring on this planet. What you locals call Wife Stealing Time."

Only if you are Crow. "Is that why you came here?"

"Oh no." The offworlder shook her head. "We are here to hunt."

"What?" asked Pretty Bottom suspiciously, still holding her knife.

"Ba'aths."

SinBad grimaced. "This is the place."

"These are Crow hunting grounds," Pretty Bottom pointed out. "You need to pay my people."

"Oh, I am not hunting." Silver-lashed eyes rolled. "My husband is."

"Then he must pay."

"Well, I am sure he will," the offworlder promised.

"Now." Pretty Bottom stood up, brushing off her buckskins, looking about. "Where is he?"

SinBad broke cover as well, looking up over the bank, seeing a squat, shining orbital yacht, surrounded by a flickering energy fence. Their offworld guest seemed suddenly sorry to disturb their tryst. Spying on the locals was not so fun when natives started making demands.

"Let us go." Pretty Bottom still held the skinning knife. "I am Pretty Bottom. My husband is Alligator Stands Up, war chieftain of the Kick Belly Crow."

Silver-wig turned to SinBad. "Is that you?"

Pretty Bottom laughed at the notion. "He is a Huron outcast, a sex criminal."

"Oh."

"It is Wife Stealing Time."

"So he stole you?" Silver-wig meant him.

Pretty Bottom snorted. "No one stole me."

"And that is good?" Silver-wig did not want to make another silly mistake.

"Of course." There seemed to be no end to offworld foolishness. "Would you want to be stolen?"

"No," Silver-wig admitted.

"Then beware," SinBad warned. "Thuria rise is only a zode away."

"Thuria?"

"Slavers," he explained.

"Oh. We have missiles," she replied brightly.

Both Red Barsoomians rolled their eyes. Pretty Bottom tucked the knife back in her boot, and went wading through the long grass toward the yacht, stopping at the sand sail to pick up her possible sack. SinBad followed, eyeing the grass tops, his crossbow out and cocked. This was ba'ath country, where your only sure warning was a twitch in the tall grass.

Silver-wig took off behind them, landing alongside the energy fence.

Even when he got to the fence, SinBad instinctively kept his back to the offworld camp, watching the grass. Ba'aths knew us, better than we knew them. Where we were, where we had been, where we slept, and where we relaxed. He would sooner turn his back on trigger-happy tourists, armed with lasers and Issus missiles.

Inviting them in, Silver-wig opened a fence section, but SinBad did not turn about until it resealed behind them. He found himself facing a typical Tourist hunting party preparing to go out, topping off canteens with home-brewed gin, and sighting in their lasers on distant objects. White apes squatted patiently, waiting to shoulder their loads. Their leaders were an expensive-looking gent in tiger-stripe body paint, with a heavy duty laser rifle, and his SuperCat guide.

This SuperCat, *Homo smilodon*, was a cross between humans and big cats, walking erect, with tawny fur, clawed hands, a stubby tail, tufted ears, bulging forehead, and saber-toothed canines—not as big as a ba'ath's, but sufficiently scary. SinBad knew he was a local, since the SuperCat carried just a short stabbing spear.

Sliver-wig introduced them, saying, "This is Pretty Bottom, and her friend Huron. Meet my husband, Laird Islay of Islay."

Laird Islay had to come from Paradise system at least, since no one closer than that would take light years out of their lives to stalk exotic predators. He stuck out a huge tiger-striped hand, saying, "Thanks for returning my wife. I hear they are in season."

"Only for Crows," SinBad corrected him. "I am Huron."

"Outcast Huron," Pretty Bottom added.

Islay winked at him, "Well, Huron, looks like you caught one anyway."

Silver-wig giggled, "They were just going to mate, when I flew by."

"Try not to hold it against us." Islay of Islay slapped his wife's silver rump. She smiled, lowering long gleaming lashes.

Her laird introduced the silent SuperCat, "This is Simba. We came to kill a few ba'aths, keep some of you from being eaten."

Unimpressed, Pretty Bottom told them, "I am Crow. Pretty Bottom, wife to Alligator Stands Up, war chieftain of the Kick Bellys. You may not hunt without my permission."

Islay must have offworld permits. Greenies did not care how many ba'aths humans killed. But his lairdship was sharp enough not to anger the locals, especially pretty promiscuous ones. "What can I give to get permission?"

"You may start by feeding us," she suggested primly.

Snapping striped fingers, Islay of Islay ordered up a vegan feast of fresh fruit, roast tofu, curried rice and vegetables in peanut sauce, raisins, almond butter, apples, celery, and black bean burgers. Washed down with fruit juice. Pretty Bottom stared at a black bean burger, asking, "Where's the meat?"

"Killing to eat is wrong," Laird Islay informed her, while almond buttering a celery stalk.

Pretty Bottom shrugged, pulling out a strip of roast moropus to spice up her burger. Her hosts were aghast. The Crow thought they were crazy. "You came here to hunt."

"Ba'aths. They are carnivores. Killing them saves countless sentient beings," Silver-wig explained.

"You are not going to eat them?" Pretty Bottom looked scandalized. "Not even the heart?"

Tourists looked down at their tofu, saying nothing.

"Do you have a see-through sack?" Pretty Bottom asked. Given a seal-a-meal, she filled it with raisins and apples. "How about some silver cloth?"

They produced that too. "And a See-Me-Too."

"She means a mirror," SinBad explained, filling his canteen with fruit juice. He was Huron, so no one needed his permission to do anything. Not in Crow country.

Silver-wig produced a self-illuminating digital looking glass. Admiring her 3V reflection, Pretty Bottom told them, "Kill all the ba'aths you can."

Sliver-wig saw them back through the energy fence, asking the Crow, "How did you get your name?"

"Pretty Bottom is a famous name in my family," the Crow explained, shouldering her possible sack, now stuffed with loot. "My great-great-grandmother lured a Lakota war party into an ambush, and was given the name, "Bares her Pretty Bottom to the Enemy." Before that she was called Weasel."

Made sense. SinBad asked her, "What was your baby name?"

"Beast."

He believed it. Silver-wig felt sorry that lunch was less than a success, but Pretty Bottom spurned her apology, holding up the seal-a-meal. "These raisins are delightful. I can always get meat."

All the vegan huntress could say was, "Good luck."

As they waded back to the dry wadi, with SinBad's crossbow cocked and aimed at the grass tops, Pretty Bottom told him, "I like her."

"Who? Islay's wife? Me too," SinBad admitted, picturing pert silver nipples.

"I like her silver hair." His Crow companion could be equally superficial.

"It's a wig," SinBad warned her, before she got too carried away.

"Really?" Pretty Bottom seemed even more intrigued.

When they got back to the wadi, SinBad was ready to resume what the offworlders interrupted, but Pretty Bottom would not have it, handing him the possible sack. "I have business in the brush."

Without saying what it was, she strode off into the long grass. He called after her, "Be back before Thuria rise."

She did not answer. Any woman who had breakfast with ba'aths was impossible to sway. He sat down by his sand sail, eating raisins, and keeping watch on the Tourist camp, hoping to catch sight of Silver-wig.

Sure enough, after a dozen xats, the energy fence opened, and Laird Islay of Islay strode out, his SuperCat guide at his side, followed by two more tiger-striped tourists, then a trio of White ape gunbearers. Silver-wig soared ahead, surveying the grass from buzzard height. Bon appetit, ba'aths.

When he could no longer see Silver-wig, SinBad sank back down to wait. Wind had shifted around to the southwest, fair for Kaol, but he was not going anywhere.

Thuria rise drew near, and Pretty Bottom came strolling up the wadi, asking, "Any raisins left?"

"Of course." Time, though, was running low.

Grabbing a handful of raisins, she told him, "They're back."

He turned to see the hunters returning empty handed. Just as well. Silver-wig did a wingover, turning their way to land in the wadi, saying, "We did not see any ba'aths."

"Good." Pretty Bottom downed a handful of raisins.

Silver-wig looked hurt. "If you do not want us hunting, why did you give permission?"

"For raisins, shining cloth, apples, and a See-Me-Too." Offworlders often missed the obvious. Giving them the right to hunt did not preclude rooting for the ba'aths.

"Have an apple," SinBad suggested, to make Silver-wig more welcome. Rudeness to semi-nude women was against his religion.

Shaking her head, she spread her white primaries, saying, "That Slaver Moon will be up soon."

Thuria rise was a couple of xats away. Which meant back to hiding behind the bank. Silver-wig took off, and SinBad asked his Crow companion, "I thought you liked her?"

"I like her wig."

That too. He watched the offworlder wing her way over the grass, landing at the edge of the energy fence. As the fence opened, a tawny blur with a wild black halo burst out of the tall grass, landing on Silver-wig's back, seizing her in great fanged jaws. Thuria topped the horizon. Silver-wig shrieked, then vanished into the long grass, carried away by a ba'ath.

HUNTING PARTY

Seizing his crossbow, SinBad shouted over his shoulder to Pretty Bottom, "Hide."

Unable to see any sign of Silver-wig, he could still hear her screams. That was good. Screams and shrieks meant she was alive. Cocking the bow, he dashed back into the tall grass, hoping it was just one ba'ath, not a whole pride. At any moment, another ba'ath might leap out of the shag lawn to make a midday meal of him. *Leo barsoom* was like that, waste not want not.

When he got to the gap in the energy fence, the screams had stopped. Bad sign. He looked about, finding Pretty Bottom right behind him. "I told you to hide."

"Thuria is up." Pretty Bottom nodded at the horizon. Slavers had already seen her, so hiding was worse than useless. Now he had two women to worry about, one seized by a ba'ath, the other menaced by Slavers.

"Stick close." Slavers had to wait, since a ba'ath would not. If he did not find Silver-wig in a xat or two, he never would.

There was a trail in the grass, strewn with solar cells and silver feathers. He bounded down it, to get to the ba'ath while it still had its jaws full. Hopefully, an explosive bolt up the butt would make it open up.

After a dozen ads, he came on a huge dent in the grass that looked like a kill site. Silver feathers lay all about. Laird Islay and his SuperCat were already there, staring into the grass, Islay cradling a laser rifle, Simba hefting his assegai. Seeing him, Islay asked, "Huron. Have you seen her?"

SinBad shook his head, not taking his gaze off the surrounding grass.

"No blood," said Islay hopefully.

Simba nodded. "She has not begun to feed."

"She?" Islay arched an eyebrow.

"From the tracks I would say an adult female, three years old or so." Simba meant Barsoom years.

Tals ticked away, taking with them any hope of finding Silver-wig alive. Islay gave SinBad a haggard glance. "Got some experience with ba'aths?"

SinBad showed him the claw marks on his crossbow stock.

Islay nodded grimly. "Let's go."

"What about her?" SinBad nodded at Pretty Bottom, who had not bothered to draw her knife. "Thuria is up."

Islay dismissed his concern. "That Issus battery is line-of-sight, good for fifty haads in any direction in flat country."

They thrashed off through the grass, with Simba in the lead and Pretty Bottom bringing up the rear. Three locals with home-forged weapons, surrounding a tourist with a laser rifle. None of the other offworld "ba'ath hunters" would be much help, never having seen their prey outside of a game park.

SinBad let Islay lead, covering the laird's back. Attack could come from any direction, and if something mean leaped out at them, he wanted that laser rifle safely ahead of him. The only weapon he could comfortably turn his back on was Pretty Bottom's skinning knife. If she stabbed you, it would not be by mistake. SinBad had hoped to have the young Crow sitting safe behind the energy fence, with the White apes and hangers-on. Surface-to-space missiles would have to do.

Steppe Hyenas yipped at each other out on the sward, excited by the commotion. Scavengers of all sorts liked to hang around tourist camps, hoping offworlders would do something stupid.

After a couple of haads the trail dipped down into one of the steep lush valleys found in equatorial Barsoom, deep slashes in the sward where water and vegetation collected. Canyon walls looked down on thick brush and thornwood, full of hiding places perfect for lying up and eating your kill. Wild moropus just like he'd had for breakfast stared suspiciously up at them. First a she-ba'ath with pretty prey in her teeth, then two species of humans. Enough to make any thinking herbivore uneasy.

Simba sniffed the breeze, then whispered, "She is in there."

"My wife or the ba'ath?" Islay whispered back.

"Both."

SinBad reached behind him, feeling Pretty Bottom's knee. He could hear her breathing, just behind his ear. "How you doing?"

"Thirsty," she hissed back.

He gave her a long swig of fruit juice from his canteen. Handing it back, she nuzzled his ear, whispering, "Watch out for the cat."

"Sure. You too. Watch my back." He felt silly, telling a Crow how to stalk.

"Not the ba'ath, the other cat." She meant Simba.

"Why?"

"Just beware." She squeezed his hand for silence. SuperCats heard better than both of them.

Shit, Simba was the one he half-trusted. Not good. He faced a silent stalk into deep cover, trailing a ba'ath with a taste for people. Putting a lot on the line, just to view bloody remnants of someone he had liked. Or at least lusted after.

Islay gave him a communicator to clip to his ear, then they entered the brush. Tickbird sentinels sounded out, warning the moropus herd that armed humans were tromping through their feeding grounds. Which made SinBad step even more lightly, creeping along pigeon-toed, his weight on the sides of his leather boots. At least Thuria was not looking over his shoulder. Dense double-canopy cover beat Issus interceptors for shutting out Slavers.

Visibility shrank to sofads. He could hear Islay just ahead, sliding invisibly through the underbrush. Behind him, Pretty Bottom was both silent and unseen. Comforting. No ba'ath would get him from behind.

Half a haad into the tangle, they came on Silver-wig's communicator, lying on the trail.

Flipping his sand goggles to night vision, he searched for a heat source in the tightly woven tapestry of branches, vines, and thorn twigs, a dense living wall as opaque as radiation armor. No luck. With two humanoids ahead of him, and the moropus herd munching the greenery, there were way too many heat sources. Thermal overkill.

With her hyper-keen nose and hair-trigger hearing, the ba'ath would know they were coming long before they arrived. Totally unfair. He was a sand sailor, for Issus' sake, hoping to see open sward again. SinBad jacked up the magnification on his glasses, though he could not see beyond arm's reach. Veins on the leaves leaped out as he peered into the spaces between them, looking for anything that might belong to a ba'ath.

Nothing. Not even the odd moropus, though these retrobred rhinoceros-hide quadrupeds were all about, head high at the shoulder, weighing up to a ton. Crow warriors rode them instead of horses, which would never survive on Barsoom. These wild ones were twice as mean, and just as big, with wicked white tusks and a terrible temper—totally hidden by the bush.

Eventually they left the moropus herd behind as the spoor wound farther into the tangled morass, which just got darker and deeper. Light from above faded. Dusk was coming on. Which would give the ba'ath every advantage. If the cat had heard them, the beast would not lay up until nightfall. Simba saw it too, calling a halt.

Islay wanted to go on. "My wife might still be alive."

Simba shrugged. "Pugmarks say the ba'ath has dropped her load. We are tracking her so close, she stashed her kill. She will come back around to feed."

Laird Islay did not like hearing his wife discussed so clinically by a bio-engineered being. "Sure it's the same ba'ath?"

Simba smirked, hissing between saber-teeth, "She is."

"How can you tell?"

"By her smell. She's in heat." Hot and hungry. Simba acted like he used to date her.

"My wife could still be alive," Islay insisted.

"If she is, she is back behind us," Simba reminded him. "this cat is no longer carrying her."

SinBad looked at Pretty Bottom, who nodded in agreement. At least Simba was not lying.

Islay put in a call to camp, telling the ship to meet them at the edge of the tangle. Hefting his laser rifle, he told SinBad, "Thanks for watching my back. Want them to bring you something with punch? These are line-of-sight, self correcting, and can burn through battle armor."

"No thanks." SinBad had his crossbow. Offworld weapons were wonderful, but he did want to kill a ba'ath five haads away—it was the ones up close and angry that worried him. And none of them wore battle armor.

Simba stuck to his spear. They turned about, backtracking, looking for the spot where the cat had dropped her prey. There had been very little blood spoor, just a few drops on the grass tops. Which gave Islay hope, though the ba'ath could have broken Silver-wig's neck, then stashed her body high in the crotch of a tree, to snack on later.

SinBad looked up this time as well as down, searching for blood streaks on branches. He was no longer looking for a ba'ath, but a body. That made him sad. Going from fear to grief, without a good moment in between.

All he saw on infrared was moropus-sized heat sources. The herd was munching its way deeper into the brush pile. These giant browsers had thorn-proof hide, and clawed limbs able to strip off leafy branches and succulent bark. They were retrobred to turn thorn trees into fertilizer and provide surface transport for anyone crazy enough to tame them. Like the Kick Belly Crow.

Without warning, a cry rang out, a ba'ath screaming bloody murder only twenty paces away. Maybe their ba'ath, keening like crazy.

Brush exploded around him. SinBad saw branches fly, and heard bushes erupt with the menacing grunt of an angry moropus. Just in time, he was jerked backward, out of the way of the huge beast that thundered past him, headed for the tall grass.

Ahead of him, Islay just had time to turn and shoot, pegging the charging moropus with a perfect laser beam brain shot.

Clutching his useless crossbow, SinBad watched the galloping behemoth collapse in a heap at the visiting laird's feet. No explosive bolt could have done that—not one fired by him. Pretty Bottom had heard the moropus coming, and she'd pulled him out of the monster's way. Leaves rained down on both of them.

Before SinBad could take a breath, another moropus burst bellowing from the brush, following in the steps of the first monster. Seeing its mate lying prone in the trail, the enraged moropus spun like a prize quarterhorse, charging at Islay.

Again the laird took aim at the animal's hideous head. Moropus barsoom had two tusk-shaped canines rising from its lower jaw, to add to their great clawed feet and murderous temper—which was why Crow warriors liked to ride them whooping into battle.

This time Laird Islay of Islay just stood there, staring into his rifle sights, until the charging moropus was on him. Swinging its gleaming tusks, the beast hooked him in the ribs, throwing Islay high in the air.

When he landed, the moropus was there, raking his remains with those tremendous razor claws. Just as the moropus was warming to its work, SinBad squeezed off a shot, aiming at the base of the neck.

Without waiting to see what happened, he cranked another round into the crossbow, then took aim again. Jackpot. His first shot had spined the moropus, dropping the thrashing herbivore next to Laird Islay.

He fired anyway, blowing out the back of the dead beast's head, just to be safe. Always kick an enemy when he's down. SinBad had done nothing to disturb this four-legged ogre, even going out of the way to avoid him and his friends. Blame the ba'ath if you liked.

Cranking in another round, he went to check on Islay. Miraculously, the laird was still alive, though not by much. Shooting that mad moropus had given Islay half a chance.

Simba appeared, spear in hand, calling for med-evac on his communicator.

Night continued to fall, and the ba'ath was still out there, after taking out a wife and husband who had come a dozen light years just to shoot her. Unless this was another ba'ath, toying with them—which SinBad doubted. A ba'ath had way better things to do, unless it had a bug up its butt. This was the cat they had trailed, hounded, keeping her hungry and horny, getting some of her own back. Crossbow cocked and ready, SinBad loosened his loincloth, which had been sopping wet ever since that first moropus burst out of the brush.

The orbital yacht landed, and he helped hustle Islay into an autodoc, tossed and trampled by a beast that is casually ridden by Crow children, several at a time. Small wonder. Barsoom had dozens of ways of taking you down, none of them nice and easy.

Simba insisted on setting up an overnight camp, so they could go looking for Silver-wig at first light. "She is now my employer."

With Islay in a coma, his wife was in charge of the hunting party. Unless she was already eaten.

Thuria was down, and Pretty Bottom meant to make the most of that opportunity, throwing her arms around him, whispering, "My wonderful hero."

"Who wet his loincloth," he informed her.

"So did I," giggled Pretty Bottom, who was not wearing one.

"Come, my chieftain." She dragged him into the thicket, aiming to celebrate their brush with fate. He went, eager to get out of the wet loincloth, and he owed her for saving him from being trampled. In the midst of snatching life, she licked his ear playfully, whispering, "Simba is a Slaver."

So that was it. SinBad nearly missed a stroke. It fit. The leaderless hunting party had been dragged from behind its energy fence, into a tangled valley that stretched out of Issus range. And in half a zode, Thuria would be up. "Don't worry," Pretty Bottom brought him back to business with a kiss, "he's just a cat."

SuperCat actually. Bred to be better than SinBad, or at least more dangerous—faster, stronger, smarter, with big teeth and claws. Ba'aths called back and forth in the darkness. Maybe even their ba'ath, looking for a boyfriend.

When they were done, SinBad asked, "How do you know Simba's a Slaver?"

Snuggling against him, Pretty Bottom replied sleepily, "Who else would hunt ba'aths at Wife Stealing Time?"

Good point, SinBad admitted. He was not here for the ba'aths. Simba must be at least as smart.

"Last year, this same cat was lurking about, when Arapaho Woman disappeared, along with her little sister. Only then he was a smuggler, trading offworld jewelry for civet skins."

"So you bought some?" SinBad saw where this was going.

"For five skins. It is pinned to my possible sack."

Which was aboard his sand sail, thank Issus. Haads away from here. Passing out radio-tagged trinkets to winsome young nomads was an old Slaver trick. No wonder they had checked out his sand sail. Her possible sack had drawn them straight to it.

"Killed the civets myself," she murmured. "Strangled them to save the skins."

She was soon asleep, happy, fed, and pregnant, safe from Slavers and ex-boyfriends, turning Wife Stealing Time into time away from the tipi. Ba'aths called in the darkness, mating cries, from close at hand, having their own tryst in the thicket. She-ba'aths in heat kept finding mates, even after becoming pregnant, to keep the males guessing.

Simba came on the communicator, sounding a general recall.

Not trusting the communicator, which doubled as a tracking device, SinBad reported in person, leaving Pretty Bottom asleep under the thorn bushes. She did not fear ba'aths, and strangled wildcats barehanded, so she should be safe until Thuria rise.

He found the SuperCat waiting at the yacht's airlock. "With no energy fence here, we should all sleep on the yacht," the bioconstruct explained. "There are ba'aths about."

No shit, Simba. More all the time. "I am wondering about that laser rifle."

"Want one?" Simba grinned. "Paint the target and pull the trigger, rifle does the rest."

Not always. "Islay's rifle did not fire."

Simba shrugged. "Transient malfunction. I retired that one."

Another ba'ath call sounded, even closer.

"Better get your mate," Simba suggested.

Pretty Bottom was hardly his mate. Goes Ahead had gotten in ahead of him. Along with Alligator Stands Up. But he was not about to argue personal relations with a bioconstruct and suspected Slaver. Nor was he likely to spend the night aboard ship. SinBad left, pretending to obey.

He made his way back through the thorns to where he'd left Pretty Bottom. But there was nothing there. Sleeping booty was gone.

Damn. No note or token. No sign of a struggle, just gone. How like her. Determined not to spend the night alone, SinBad slid two more explosive bolts into his crossbow to fill the clip. By now the ground was cool enough for her to leave a good heat trail, so he flipped his goggles onto infrared.

Her heat trail appeared at once, headed away from the moropus thicket deeper into the canyon. Great. He had wanted to sit out Thuria rise, curled under a thorn bush with his cute Crow companion; instead he was headed deeper into a canyon that had already swallowed two wealthy offworlders. Ba'aths called back and forth in the blackness, sounding like they had made a kill. Hopefully no one he knew.

With each cautious step, he remembered the scratches on his crossbow stock. A ba'ath with a bad attitude had jumped him at point-blank range, without even a warning growl. He got off one shot before the ba'ath batted the crossbow out of his grip, then bowled him over.

Luckily, when shooting at arm's length, he rarely missed. Instead of being ripped to shreds, a dead ba'ath landed in his lap. When he heaved the beast off him, he'd found an arrow broken off in the ba'ath's belly, a festering wound that must have hurt horribly. An Apache arrow, but try telling an angry ba'ath that you are Huron. He did have hard words for some local Apaches, who laughed to hear how he'd found their arrow.

Slowly the heat trail faded. He was not moving fast enough to catch Pretty Bottom, wherever she was going. Crow women were always up to something, which was why they had Wife Stealing Time.

Then, without warning, the glowing trail got stronger. Something close to Pretty Bottom's size had recently passed through. He picked up the pace, finding the trail getting brighter and fresher. Encouraged, SinBad kept his crossbow in front of him, ready for anything.

Almost. Sitting in a grassy clearing ahead was the source of the heat trail, a barefoot and bedraggled Silver-wig.

Her wings were drooped and broken; her silver body paint was scraped off, revealing large swaths of pink flesh. Clearly happy to see him despite the cocked crossbow aimed at her bare chest, the offworlder smiled wide. "Hi, Huron."

Why was he always drawing a bead on beautiful women, thinking they were ba'aths? He lowered his bow. "Actually, my name is SinBad."

"Really?" Silver-wig seemed surprised.

"What is yours?"

"Deirdre. Deirdre Islay."

Very offworld, and meaningless, but somehow pretty. "We thought you were dead."

"I thought I was dead," Deirdre admitted, "when that ba'ath grabbed me. I fought, screamed, and fainted."

Then the cat carried her off unconscious, dropping her when pursuit got too close. Doubling back on her tracks, the ba'ath led her bungling pursuers into the moropus herd. SinBad asked, "Are you hurt?"

She shook her head. "Grass burns, a couple of nasty cuts. But not a tooth mark. I think he dragged me by my wings."

"She dragged you," he corrected her. "You were grabbed by a female. On Barsoom both sexes have black manes."

"Oh." Clearly she knew very little about the beasts they'd come light years to kill.

Yet she had survived the ba'ath attack unbelievably well. In fact, her real troubles were just beginning. He asked, "Are you cold?"

She nodded. He took off his buckskin jacket and gave it to her. He had just a light linen shirt underneath, but this was spring in the tropics, about as mild as Barsoom got.

Shedding broken wings, she pulled on the jacket, not bothering with the bone buttons, asking instead, "Have you seen my husband?"

He had seen parts of Laird Islay his wife never had, but SinBad did not say so. Who wanted an hysterical tourist on their hands? "He's aboard the yacht."

She looked about. "Where is that?"

"Close by." Thuria would be up in a few xats. Who knew what would happen then? Not him. "But we need to hide first."

"Hide? Why?"

He nodded at the night sky. "The Slaver Moon will be up soon."

"How can you tell?"

"It's not hard, when you have grown up under these stars." What nomad boy did not thrill at Thuria rise, watching the girls scurry for cover? Imagining himself saving some beautiful offworld princess from Slavers, and winning a warm reward. Like a lot of boyhood dreams, the ideal totally beat reality.

He hustled the winsome tourist into the underbrush, where she could not be seen by Thuria light. Though there was still their body heat. If Simba told the Slavers where to look, a diligent search would find them.

Clearly, Deirdre Islay did not look forward to spending another zode-and-a-half in the bush, not with some strange Huron. She told him earnestly, "Get me back to my husband, and I will see you well rewarded."

Not likely. Her husband was in an autodoc. Scratched, bruised, and hiding under a bush in a borrowed leather jacket, Silver-wig was now the outworlder-in-chief. SinBad just did not have the heart, or the need, to tell her. Not yet.

He had way bigger worries. Thuria was rising, spreading enhanced moonshine over the landscape. Then came the boom of an orbital shuttle breaking atmosphere. Slavers were on their way. He unshipped his crossbow, for all the good that would do.

"What's the matter?" Silver-wig asked.

"Slavers." Unless it was another boatload of tourists, coming for a wild moropus nightride, or something equally useful.

Tals ticked away. Then without warning a shadow fell over them, blocking out the Thuria light, then moving on. Silver-wig whispered, "What's that? Slavers?"

Smelling a familiar cat box odor, Sinbad slid over and silenced her with his hand, mouthing a single word, "Ba'ath."

Silver-wig's eyes went wide. Another silent shadow passed, then another. One by one, more ba'aths came padding up, an entire pride, settling into the brush around them. Soon they were surrounded by the cat odor, and the soft regular breathing of a dozen sleeping ba'aths.

SinBad set aside his crossbow. He did not have enough bolts to do more than make them mad. Silver-wig whispered, "Can they hear us?"

Sure, if she did not shut up. He whispered back, "They do not need to. They can smell us."

"So, why don't they attack?"

"Maybe they're not hungry. Or just too sleepy. Ba'aths do not kill for the fun of it." Like offworlders do.

She stroked his cheek. "I am sorry."

"For what?"

"Everything," Silver-wig sighed.

He smiled at that thought. "Not your fault."

Happy to hear that, she relaxed alongside him. Soon she was asleep, putting an end to a harrowing day. He closed his eyes as well, no longer worried by their heat signature. So long as they lay close together no one would spot them amid the ba'aths.

Lying with eyes shut, listening to blond breathing, he suddenly heard the whoosh of a ship taking off. Looking up, he saw a flash in the night sky, half hidden by the thorn brush. Someone was lifting into orbit.

He relaxed again. Thuria set, then first light showed in the east. Slavers had let sleeping ba'aths lie. SinBad decided to do the same, waking Silver-wig, whispering, "Let's get going before they do."

She saw the sense in that, getting up and silently following him out of the brush into the long grass, leaving the ba'aths behind. As they neared the mouth of the canyon, SinBad told the offworlder to wait while he wormed his way forward.

Just as he thought, Islay's yacht was gone. All that remained was a circular dent in the grass, empty as a crop circle. He slithered back to inform his companion, who told him, "Give me your communicator, and I will call my husband."

"Let me make the call," SinBad suggested. "They do not know you are alive." Yet.

"So? My husband will be happy to know."

Now he had to give her the bad news. "Your husband is in an autodoc. Trampled by a wild moropus."

Lady Islay looked aghast. "Will he live?"

"Maybe." If the Slavers aimed to hold him for ransom. "Just let me make the call."

He did. A chirpy computer voice informed him the yacht was in low orbit, while the owners were with their "hunting party" on the surface. Call them there.

No need to do that; the Islay still on the surface was crouching next to him in the tall grass, wearing his buckskin jacket and not much else. Hearing what the yacht had to say, she told him, "Give me the communicator. That ship is voice-coded to me and my husband. I can shut down its drive, then trigger a distress call."

"No, you won't." The voice came from behind them, and had that SuperCat lisp caused by talking around saber-tooth canines.

SinBad turned to see Simba standing in the grass, with a silver communicator clipped to his ear and a laser rifle leveled at him. The bioconstruct had stayed behind, waiting for them to break cover and open a channel. The only real question was why didn't Simba pull the trigger? SinBad's own bow was at his side, cocked and ready, but he dared not raise it. The SuperCat had super reflexes.

Only Deirdre Islay did not get it, saying, "Simba, what are you doing?"

Her hunting guide grinned. "I was looking for that pretty young Crow. But you will do. Please, stand aside."

Simba wanted a clear shot.

Deirdre stood up, stepping squarely into the line of fire. Flourishing the communicator, she warned the SuperCat, "You shoot, and I will punch MAYDAY, disabling the yacht."

Simba snorted. "This rifle can shoot right through you, and him."

Sliver-wig shrugged. "Then you lose everything. You will never get that yacht outsystem, not with me dead and my husband in an autodoc."

There was a Navy ship insystem, the suburb-class corvette Tarzana. Any attempt to alter the yacht's registered flight plan would arouse suspicion. If Deirdre punched MAYDAY, Simba could shoot them, but he would lose his prize. And the Slavers aboard the yacht would be prisoners. Stalemate.

For the moment. Simba kept the laser rifle leveled. Thuria would be up soon, then Slavers would swarm over them, jamming the communicator and firing sleep gas, eager to have Deidre Islay and her husband's starship.

Deirdre stood clutching the communicator while Simba cradled the rifle, waiting.

Slowly, a big black-maned ba'ath ambled nonchalantly up, not even looking at them, followed by another, then another. Simba's grin turned grim, as the pride gathered around them, crouched and waiting. Riding atop the biggest ba'ath, a great sable-headed male, was Pretty Bottom. No wonder her parents called her Beast.

"Kaor," the young Crow called out, holding tight to the black mane.

"Kaor," SinBad replied, never happier to see her, or a pride of ba'aths.

"What do you want?" Simba demanded, eyeing the ba'aths warily.

"That Huron," Pretty Bottom pointed at SinBad. "And the offworld woman."

Simba shook his head. "Get any closer, and I will kill both of them. Then you." He still had them, if he could stall until Thuria was up.

"You are the one who will die," Pretty Bottom warned.

"Maybe." Simba was counting on his superhuman reflexes and self-correcting sights. He could do a lot of damage before the ba'aths got him.

"Certainly," Our Lady of the Ba'aths replied, raising her slim hand.

"Don't!" Simba aimed the rifle at her, a curved claw on the trigger.

Pretty Bottom froze, hand held high. Ba'aths snarled at the SuperCat, but did not spring, waiting to see what the Crow woman would do. This was not their fight. SinBad weighed the odds, trying to decide if he could aim and shoot before Simba fired. Not likely.

He did not have to. An arrow streaked from downwind, hitting Simba in the neck, slicing through the cat's jugular. The SuperCat fell forward, dead before he hit the ground.

SinBad exhaled softly, barely believing his eyes. Another arrow thudded into the fallen SuperCat, ensuring he was dead. Simba did not twitch.

Deirdre was on the communicator at once, calling the Navy and shutting down her ship.

Looking to see where the arrows had come from, SinBad saw a Crow warrior emerge from the thorn trees, his feathered bow in hand, riding a dark red moropus. He wore a scout's wolfskin, and hail-spot body paint, making him as deadly as an ice storm on a sunny day.

Pretty Bottom grinned. Ignoring her and the ba'aths, the Crow scout dismounted, keeping a tight hold on his rope reins, saying, "Kaor, Huron."

SinBad returned the Crow's greeting, asking, "To whom do I owe my life?"

"Her." The Crow casually pointed his bow tip at Pretty Bottom. "She is the one I came to get."

This was Wife Stealing Time. But the Crow was not going to get what he wanted, not amid a pride of ba'aths, who were plainly doing Pretty Bottom's bidding. Being practical, the scout drew his knife instead, then bent over and deftly skinned the dead SuperCat as if it was a tawny fur coat. He took the head as well, not wanting to leave the great grinning saber-teeth.

Rolling up the bloody hide, the Crow tied it to the back of his white-tusked moropus, then remounted. With a wave to the women, the warrior was gone.

Ba'aths began to feed on the Slaver's skinned and bloody body. SinBad turned back to the pregnant Crow. "Was that Goes Ahead?"

"Of course." How many boyfriends could she have? Sliding down off the ba'ath, she gave him a hug. "That is my baby's daddy. I am glad you met him."

"Me too." As SinBad said it, a boom sounded overhead.

Pretty Bottom looked up. "Slavers?" Thuria was still down.

Deirdre Islay shook her head. "No, a Navy gig."

Sure enough, a small silver ship landed in the long grass, guided down by Deirdre's MAYDAY call. Navy crewmen in battle armor tumbled out, scattering the snarling ba'aths.

"Don't hurt them," Pretty Bottom shouted. She turned anxiously to Deirdre. "Tell them they saved you."

She did, and the Navy held its fire. Before they hustled her aboard the gig, Deirdre Islay asked, "How can I repay you?"

"Give me your wig," Pretty Bottom replied.

"My wig?"

Pretty Bottom nodded eagerly, so Deirdre handed it over. Giving a war whoop, the Crow waved her silver trophy, like it was a fresh scalp.

Later, when Thuria had set again, Pretty Bottom insisted on making love in the tall grass, wearing only her new hair. But that just made SinBad think of Silver-wig, and he never saw her again.

IMAGES OF ANNA

NANCY KRESS

The morning was turning out to be a bust. The first client wanted to pay with a personal check, which I've learned to not accept. She had no cash, credit card, or ID. The second client had cash but turned out to be a thirteen-year-old kid who wanted a "really sexy picture" for her boyfriend. No way: session cancelled. The third client was late.

"The electric bill is overdue," Carol said conversationally. She rearranged her table of cosmetics, hair extensions, and earrings, none of which needed rearranging. Carol was easily bored. I was easily panicked. Not a good business combination, and Glamorous You was barely hanging on. In Boston even the rent for a small, third-floor walk-up is expensive.

Carol riffled idly through the hanging rack of negligees, gowns, and filmy scarves for clients that don't bring their own stuff. Glamorous You doesn't do cheesecake: no nude, bra-and-panties, or implied-masturbation shots. The costumes are fun but not raunchy; the negligees are opaque. I'm good with lighting, and Carol is a whiz at make-up and hair. We make our customers look more desirable than they'll ever look in real life, but still decent. That's why the electric bill was overdue.

"What's this client's name again?" I said.

Carol consulted her booking calendar, which featured a lot of white space. "Anna Somebody—here she comes now." The door opened.

"Hello," the client said. "I'm sorry I'm late."

I blinked. We get a lot of older women, although not usually this old. Maybe fifty, fifty-five, she had a brown pageboy considerably darker than her gray eyebrows, twenty extra pounds, and a sagging neck. But that wasn't it. She just wasn't a Glamorous You type. Brown slacks, baggy white blouse, brown tweed blazer, all worn with gumball-pink lipstick and small pearl earrings. She looked like she should be heading up a grant-writing committee somewhere.

"Anna O'Connor," she said, holding out her hand. "Are you Ben Preston?"

"Yes. Nice to meet you. My assistant, Carol."

"Hi, Carol."

She had a nice smile. Looking closer, I could see the regular features under the wrinkles, the good cheekbones, the nice teeth. This woman had been attractive once, in a bland girl-next-door way. Didn't she realize how much time had passed?

She did. "Let me tell you what I'm after here, Ben. I'm not young or gorgeous, and I don't want to pretend I am. I just want to look as good as a fifty-seven-year-old can without looking like beef dressed as veal. Or sending your camera into mechanical heart failure." She laughed, light and self-mocking, without strain. I liked her.

"I think we can do that, Anna—may I call you Anna?"

"Please."

"We offer three settings: a bed, arm chair, or wind machine against an outdoor backdrop. Which would you prefer?"

"The armchair, please."

No surprise there. While I set up the shot, Carol did prep and they picked out a costume. When Anna emerged from the dressing room, I was agreeably surprised. Carol had darkened Anna's eyebrows, shadowed her eyes, exchanged the kiddie-pink lipstick for a rich brown-red. Her hair had lost its helmet look and had some volume and swing. Anna had chosen not the Victorian gown I'd expected but rather a floor-length, emerald-green robe that skimmed over waist and hips but revealed her still-good cleavage. She looked terrific. Not like a model, of course, nor youthful, but still feminine and appealing.

"You look great," I said, glad to mean it for once.

"I think that's mostly due to Carol," Anna said, with that same light self-mockery. She seemed at ease in her own ageing skin. No rings on her hand, and I wondered whom the negligee photo was intended for.

"All right, if you'll just sit in or stand by the arm chair . . . however you feel comfortable. You just—hold it!"

She was a natural. All her poses were sexy without being parodies, and her refusal to take herself seriously came through in her body language. The result was sensuality as light-hearted fun. As I shot her from several different angles, I enjoyed myself more than I had photographing younger, prettier women. We bantered and laughed. When the shoot was done and Anna had changed back into her own clothes—but had not, I was glad to see, washed off Carol's make-up—I broke my own rule and asked her.

"And the picture will be for . . . "

"Boyfriend," she said, embarrassed. "That's such a silly word at my age, but all the other words are even sillier. Beau? Main squeeze? Gentleman caller?" She pantomimed an Edwardian curtsey and laughed.

"Well, he's a lucky guy," I said. Carol stared at me. I never got personal with clients—too much chance for misinterpretation. But Anna was old enough to be my mother, for Chrissake. "Will he come with you to choose the shot? Or is the photo a surprise?"

"A surprise. Besides, he lives in Montana. We met on-line."

My good mood collapsed. I'd wanted this to be something positive. But she was just one more older woman being strung along by some Internet Lothario getting his rocks off by feeding on attention from lonely and desperate women. Best case scenario: He hadn't asked her for money. Yet.

"Ben, it's not like that," Anna said, looking at my face. "I've met him in person. He's visited here twice. You're sweet to be concerned, but I can take care of myself."

"Right," I said. "So you'll come back Thursday to see the proofs."

"See you then."

When she'd paid me and left, Carol said, "Lighten up, Ben. Not every woman is as stupid as Laurie was."

I turned away. Since we had no more clients booked for today, Carol left. I went into the darkroom and developed Anna's pictures.

And just like that, reality fell apart.

Film is not digital. There's no chance to lose bytes in the bowels of a computer, to merge files, to have information corrupted by malfunctions or cosmic rays or viruses. Film is physically contained on a discrete roll. The images may be blurry, overexposed, underexposed, red-eyed, unflattering, partial, or missing, but there's no way they can be of someone else entirely.

Anna's twenty-four pictures included three women about her own age, ten children, two teenage boys, and nine shots of the same older man. He was gray-haired, lean, and handsome, a brown-eyed Paul Newman.

I stared at the photos in baffled shock. What the hell had happened? I had never seen any of these people before, had no idea how they had turned up in my camera. Nothing made sense.

Fear slid down my spine, viscous and greasy as oil.

In the end I hid the photos, called Anna, and told both her and Carol that I'd screwed up and ruined the shoot. Carol ragged on me without mercy. Anna agreed to another session, no extra charge, a week from Saturday morning.

In between, I shot a trashy-looking woman—teased red hair, black leather bustier—who was a happily married mother of two, and a patrician blonde beauty who, I suspected, was a hooker. I shot two giggly eighteen-year-olds who said they wanted to be models and who hadn't the remotest chance of succeeding. I shot a pretty, sad-eyed young woman who wanted a glamorous picture to send to her soldier husband deployed in Afghanistan.

A hundred times I pulled out the Anna-photos-with-no-Anna, and never came close to solving the mystery or mentioning it to anyone. What was I going to say? "Your pictures seem to be of several other people—are you a multiple personality? A witch? A mirage?" Give me a break.

When Anna arrived for her second shoot, she seemed subdued. The shots in the green negligee still looked good through my lens, but they lacked the fresh zest of the first session. That's the difference between professional models and amateurs: The pros can fake freshness. Off camera, that's not always a desirable quality.

I wasn't as light-hearted, either. In fact, I could barely keep my mind on the raw shots, so tense I was about what they might develop into. After Anna and Carol left, I went straight to the darkroom.

Twelve shots of the older man, eight children, two pictures each of one of the teenage boys and one of the middle-aged women. Some of the children were seated at a table, drawing with crayons. The teenager scowled ferociously. All the backgrounds were out of focus. No shots of Anna.

I stared at the negatives until I couldn't see anything at all.

I followed her. Her phone number was on the client-contact sheet. I fed it into an on-line reverse directory and turned up an address in Framingham, one of those peculiar Boston suburbs that's upper-middle-class along bodies of water and working class everywhere else. Anna lived in a modest, well-kept bungalow on a maple-shaded street. Saturday afternoon she spent at a local community center. Saturday night she met two women—not those in the pictures—for dinner and a movie. Sunday she took the MTA into Boston and viewed an exhibit of art deco jewelry at the Museum of Fine Arts. Monday she went to work at the Framingham Public Library. I photographed her parking her car, entering the restaurant, leaving the movie theater, buying a ticket at the museum, even standing behind the reference desk helping an after-school gaggle of noisy teenagers. Each time I developed the pictures right away. None of them were of Anna.

Increasingly, the *settings* weren't even there. Her house was blurry, and so was the restaurant. The theater marquee was a blur. The museum had become a vague outline, and the library picture showed only the faint suggestion of the reference desk, behind which stood the scowling teenage boy. Each subsequent set of photos showed increasing haze, a pearly incandescent glow, although the people recurred sharply. If anything, they were too sharp, as if over time they were taking on knife-edged properties, almost able to slice right through the photographic paper. Yet at the same time, parts of their bodies—a shoulder, a back, the top of a head—seemed weirdly obscured, as if receding into deep and inexplicable shadow.

None of it made any sense. All of it scared me.

It finally occurred to me to Google™ Anna, who had a surprisingly large on-line presence without actually posting anything herself. She turned up in other people's blogs, in small-town newspaper articles over two decades, in the proceedings of ALA conferences, in the Alumni Notes of her college. She ran childrens' programs at the community center. She organized disaster-relief drives. A show of her paintings had hung on the walls of a local bank. She was the person that friends turned to in times of trouble. Why had such a woman—gregarious, kind, pretty, bright—never married, never had kids?

One blogger wrote: *Dinner last night with Anna O'Connor. If she can't find the right guy, what hope is there for the rest of us?* To which someone had added the comment: *Some people are just too picky. Deluded overage romantics, still hoping for a soulmate.*

Bitch. But correct? I could see in Anna the outlines of a life both brave and sad: filled with useful activities but still feeling itself somehow displaced. Not a skilled enough painter for a commercial art gallery. More intelligent than most people—she'd graduated magna cum laude from Northwestern—but not ambitious enough for big-time academe or for a corporate career. Lots of friends but with no one really close, and thus lonely underneath. I knew many people like that, including me.

Until she met this Montana guy on-line, who turned her into the hopeful, sexy woman who'd come to be photographed at Glamorous You.

I gazed again at the baffling, terrifying photos that couldn't exist, and then I drove back out to Framingham.

"Ben! What are you doing here—did you come to bring me the replacement pictures? You didn't have to do that."

She came down the stone steps of the library, the last person to leave. Eight o'clock on a warm September night and sunset was long over. In the bright floodlights from the library, Anna looked both tired and tense, like a person who'd spent the day carrying loads of bricks up flimsy ladders. She wore another librarian outfit, brown pantsuit and sensible shoes, and her pink lipstick had been mostly chewed off.

"No, I didn't bring the proofs. I have to talk to you about them. Will you come have a drink with me?"

"I don't think that would . . . Oh, why not. Is something wrong? Do you need to talk?"

"No. Yes. Is there a bar close by?"

She didn't know. Not a party girl. I found a fake Irish pub on Route 9, called her on my cell, and she joined me in a booth in the back. I'd already downed a double Scotch on the rocks. Another sat waiting for Anna. She took a sip and made the face of someone used to white wine. In the gloom of the pub, she looked old and strained.

"Okay, Ben, what's this about?"

How do you blurt out that existing photographs—tangible, physical objects—can't possibly exist? I was going to sound like a psychotic. Or a fraud. Can't take flattering pictures of a client? Pretend she's not there.

I said, "The pictures of you are coming out . . . odd."

She flushed. "I know I'm not very photogenic—"

"No, it's not that." She had absolutely no inkling. I would have bet my eyes on it.

"Then what is it?"

"The photos are . . . blurry."

"Blurry?"

"Yes." I couldn't do it, I just couldn't. "Very blurry. It's my fault. I'm here to refund your deposit."

"But . . . you have a terrific reputation as a photographer. I checked."

I shrugged. Her mouth tightened. "Oh, I see. I look ridiculous, don't I? A woman in her fifties posing for a glamour shot. And you don't want to embarrass me by saying so."

"No, it's not that at all. I just—"

"Anything else here?" the waitress said. She wore a silly white apron with green shamrocks on it. I ordered more doubles. When mine came, I seized the glass as if it were a tree in a tsunami.

We sat in a heavy, unpleasant silence that stretched on and on. And on. Anna finished her first drink and made strong inroads on the second. Nothing I could think of to say seemed right, or even possible. Finally Anna made a sudden movement. I thought she was getting up to leave, but instead she said, "How much do you think a person should change herself for love?"

My answer was instantaneous and violent. "Not at all! Nothing!"

She peered at me, eyes a little unfocused, and I realized that Anna O'Connor could not hold her liquor. But if her inhibitions were in decline, her perceptiveness wasn't.

"Who was she, Ben? Your wife?"

"Ex-wife."

If it had been anyone else in the world, I wouldn't mention Laurie. I hated to talk about her, even with Carol, although Carol knows the whole story because she and Laurie were friends. But I was desperate to keep Anna talking until I heard something—anything!—that would make sense out of those photos. And I don't hold my liquor all that well, either.

"Tell me," Anna said.

Pain always turned me angry. "Not much to tell. My wife and I had some problems. Nothing big, or so I thought. Then she met a guy in a chat room. She had an affair, she left me, and he left her. She wanted to come back to our marriage, and I said no way. It was good and she broke it. The pity-me note she mailed me said she was tired of trying to be somebody she couldn't. Well, I can't be somebody I'm not, either. I couldn't ever trust her again. End of story."

"I'm so sorry." From Anna it didn't sound perfunctory or condescending or phony. "You said 'It was good' but your marriage must have been troubled before she even met the other man."

Laurie had always said it was troubled; I'd thought it was mostly fine. She said I was "never emotionally present," but didn't all women say that? All the ones I'd known said it. *I feel like I'm always pursuing you, Ben, and never the other way around, and I don't like it.* I scowled at Anna and tried to push away all memories of Laurie. As usual, it didn't work.

Anna said gently, "Why didn't you let her come back? It looks to me like you still love her."

I snorted. "I told you, I won't change who I am. And I don't take sloppy seconds."

"That's a *terrible* thing to say, Ben! She's not a whore, just somebody who made a mistake. Maybe somebody who needs you."

"I'm not the Salvation Army, Anna." I knew how my comments sounded. I also knew how much I needed to sound that way, especially to myself. Tough. Beyond caring.

Anna said, "My guess is that maybe you need her, too."

"You don't know anything about either of us!"

"No, I don't. I'm sorry to pry."

"Then don't!"

I thought she'd leave then. Instead she said, "What really happened to my photos?"

I stared across the table. The original set of proofs were in my messenger bag. Pissed at her now, I took them out.

The weird thing was that after the first shock, she didn't seem surprised, or at least not surprised enough. Her forehead crinkled like a topographical map but her eyes didn't register all that much disbelief. She studied the kids, the teenagers, the adults, the handsome older man. I saw that she knew them.

"That's him, isn't it?" I said. "Your boyfriend."

"Yes."

"How did he—"

"I don't know. I was thinking about him, about all of them . . . . I don't know."

"Are you saying that I shot a *picture* of what was in your mind instead of—"

"I don't know!"

She stood, so quickly that she knocked into her second empty glass, sending it skidding across the table. She didn't pick it up. "It's late I have to go to work tomorrow thanks for the drink don't worry about the—"

"You can't drive, Anna. You're drunk." Apparently that didn't take much.

She made a despairing little noise and lurched toward the Ladies'. When she returned, her face was wet and a cab waited outside.

That was the last time I ever spoke to her.

But I went on shooting her, whenever I could get away from Glamorous You. I photographed Anna outside her house, outside the library, with friends, on the playground at the community center. Maybe she saw me, maybe not. Certainly she never acknowledged me.

Anna hurrying across the street to her parked car—but the negative showed another woman, younger and in tears.

Anna blinking in sunlight on the library steps—but it became the graying older man and the library was a dark blur.

Anna on her porch, both porch and house a swirl of black, Anna replaced by three small children.

I studied the photographs in my darkroom, in the kitchenette of my unkempt condo, in the middle of the night. *Let it go*, Laurie used to say, about so many things. But I couldn't let this go. I kept looking for clues, trying to put it all together, shooting yet more film. I spent time—a lot of time—on line, delving into Anna's public life, looking for photos. I found them.

Then Anna disappeared.

I don't know when he told her the truth, no more than I know anything else that transpired between them. The first chat-room encounter, the first emails, the first phone calls. Probably he told her how isolated he felt in Montana. Probably he told her how isolated he felt in this world, and at first she had no idea that the hackneyed phrase could have a double meaning. Maybe he told her why he was in Montana, of all places. Or not.

And she told him about her own version of loneliness, because that's what all lovers tell each other. Just as all lovers say that finding each other is a miracle, an unlooked-for gift from what maybe isn't such an indifferent universe after all. They each say that they would give up so very much to be with the other. Cheat on a marriage, leave a spouse, then regret bitterly their own stupid actions and promise the moon and stars for another chance.

How much do you think a person should change for love? The answer in all the self-help books is: Don't. The lover is supposed to accept you just the way you are, unconditionally. But when Anna asked me that, she didn't yet know the full truth. She suspected something, that was clear not only from the anxiety and tension on her face, but from the photographs themselves. In each set of shots, the people got sharper. I found most of those people in jpg files, in blurry newspaper photos, in blog postings, in yearbook shots. The teenage boys were her troubled nephews; Anna had gotten one an after-school job at the library. The women were her newly widowed younger sister plus two of Anna's friends. One had been laid off from her job but was now rehired. The other had broken her leg. The children were all from the community center, disadvantaged kids for whom Anna volunteered her time. Only Montana Man had no on-line photos.

What was he? Why was he alone in Montana, without others of his kind? By choice, or as the result of some unimaginable catastrophe? I would never know. The only image I would ever have of him was from Anna's mind, as he somehow changed her from the inside out, changed her fundamental relationship to the world as I understood it. While she let him do it.

The pictures tell the story—but *not* the pictures of the people. It's actually the backgrounds that matter. In the first one, my studio is only slightly blurred. With each subsequent shoot, the backgrounds—how Anna saw this world—got hazier, became nothing but shadows. Then the shadows turned into black miasma, as Anna struggled with her decision. The last several roles of film are like that.

Except for the very last photograph.

She saw me, that time. It was early morning. Dressed in the dreary brown pantsuit, she came out of her house, stood on her porch, and smiled at me where I waited in my car, camera raised. She even posed a little, as she had done that first day in the studio. Her smile was luminous, suffused with joy. Then she went back inside and closed the door.

The developed shot shows a woman dressed in some sort of gauzy robe, wings spread wide from her shoulders, skin lit from within. Her tiny silver horns catch the dawn light. Her tail wraps loosely around her body. She is beautiful.

But, then, she always was. What makes me unable to stop looking at the picture, what makes me so glad for her, is not her beauty. It is that, finally, the images in Anna's mind are not of all those other people she can help but of herself, happy. He did that for her. He—whatever the hell he really is—gave her herself. That's what Anna wanted me to see, on her porch that last day: What can happen you when change for someone else.

"Can" happen. Not "will." No guarantees.

I frame the photo but I never hang it. I redouble my efforts to pick up clients, which makes both Carol and the electric company happy. I spend too much time at the fake Irish pub, sipping and thinking, and then thinking some more.

And eventually I pick up the phone and call Laurie.

MONGOOSE

SARAH MONETTE & ELIZABETH BEAR

Izrael Irizarry stepped through a bright-scarred airlock onto Kadath Station, lurching a little as he adjusted to station gravity. On his shoulder, Mongoose extended her neck, her barbels flaring, flicked her tongue out to taste the air, and colored a question. Another few steps, and he smelled what Mongoose smelled, the sharp stink of toves, ammoniac and bitter.

He touched the tentacle coiled around his throat with the quick double tap that meant *soon*. Mongoose colored displeasure, and Irizarry stroked the slick velvet wedge of her head in consolation and restraint. Her four compound and twelve simple eyes glittered and her color softened, but did not change, as she leaned into the caress. She was eager to hunt and he didn't blame her. The boojum *Manfred von Richthofen* took care of its own vermin. Mongoose had had to make do with a share of Irizarry's rations, and she hated eating dead things.

If Irizarry could smell toves, it was more than the "minor infestation" the message from the station master had led him to expect. Of course, that message had reached Irizarry third or fourth or fifteenth hand, and he had no idea how long it had taken. Perhaps when the station master had sent for him, it *had* been minor.

But he knew the ways of bureaucrats, and he wondered.

People did double-takes as he passed, even the heavily-modded Christian cultists with their telescoping limbs and biolin eyes. You found them on every station and steelships too, though mostly they wouldn't work the boojums. Nobody liked Christians much, but they could work in situations that would kill an unmodded human or a even a gilly, so captains and station masters tolerated them.

There were a lot of gillies in Kadath's hallways, and they all stopped to blink at Mongoose. One, an indenturee, stopped and made an elaborate hand-flapping bow. Irizarry felt one of Mongoose's tendrils work itself through two of his earrings. Although she didn't understand staring exactly—her compound eyes made the idea alien to her—she felt the attention and was made shy by it.

Unlike the boojum-ships they serviced, the stations—Providence, Kadath, Leng, Dunwich, and the others—were man-made. Their radial symmetry was predictable, and to find the station master, Irizarry only had to work his way inward from the *Manfred von Richthofen*'s dock to the hub. There he found one of the inevitable safety maps (you are here; in case of decompression, proceed in an orderly manner to the life vaults located here, here, or here) and leaned close to squint at the tiny lettering. Mongoose copied him, tilting her head first one way, then another, though flat representations meant nothing to her. He made out STATION MASTER'S OFFICE finally, on a oval bubble, the door of which was actually in sight.

"Here we go, girl," he said to Mongoose (who, stone-deaf though she was, pressed against him in response to the vibration of his voice). He hated this part of the job, hated dealing with apparatchiks and functionaries, and of course the Station Master's office was full of them, a receptionist, and then a secretary, and then someone who was maybe the *other* kind of secretary, and then finally—Mongoose by now halfway down the back of his shirt and entirely hidden by his hair and Irizarry himself half stifled by memories of someone he didn't want to remember being—he was ushered into an inner room where Station Master Lee, her arms crossed and her round face set in a scowl, was waiting.

"Mr. Irizarry," she said, unfolding her arms long enough to stick one hand out in a facsimile of a congenial greeting.

He held up a hand in response, relieved to see no sign of recognition in her face. It was Irizarry's experience that dead lives were best left lie where they fell. "Sorry, Station Master," he said. "I can't."

He thought of asking her about the reek of toves on the air, if she understood just how bad the situation had become. People could convince themselves of a lot of bullshit, given half a chance.

Instead, he decided to talk about his partner. "Mongoose hates it when I touch other people. She gets jealous, like a parrot."

"The cheshire's here?" She let her hand drop to her side, the expression on her face a mixture of respect and alarm. "Is it out of phase?"

Well, at least Station Master Lee knew a little more about cheshire-cats than most people. "No," Irizarry said. "She's down my shirt."

Half a standard hour later, wading through the damp bowels of a ventilation pore, Irizarry tapped his rebreather to try to clear some of the tove-stench from his nostrils and mouth. It didn't help much; he was getting close.

Here, Mongoose wasn't shy at all. She slithered up on top of his head, barbels and graspers extended to full length, pulsing slowly in predatory greens and reds. Her tendrils slithered through his hair and coiled about his throat, fading in and out of phase. He placed his fingertips on her slick-resilient hide to restrain her. The last thing he needed was for Mongoose to go spectral and charge off down the corridor after the tove colony.

It wasn't that she wouldn't come back, because she would—but that was only if she didn't get herself into more trouble than she could get out of without his help. "Steady," he said, though of course she couldn't hear him. A creature adapted to vacuum had no ears. But she could feel his voice vibrate in his throat, and a tendril brushed his lips, feeling the puff of air and the shape of the word. He tapped her tendril twice again—*soon*—and felt it contract. She flashed hungry orange in his peripheral vision. She was experimenting with jaguar rosettes—they had had long discussions of jaguars and tigers after their nightly reading of Pooh on the *Manfred von Richthofen*, as Mongoose had wanted to know what jagulars and tiggers were. Irizarry had already taught her about mongooses, and he'd read *Alice in Wonderland* so she would know what a Cheshire Cat was. Two days later—he still remembered it vividly—she had disappeared quite slowly, starting with the tips of the long coils of her tail and tendrils and ending with the needle-sharp crystalline array of her teeth. And then she'd phased back in, all excited aquamarine and pink, almost bouncing, and he'd praised her and stroked her and reminded himself not to think of her as a cat. Or a mongoose.

She had readily grasped the distinction between jaguars and jagulars, and had almost as quickly decided that she was a jagular; Irizarry had almost started to argue, but then thought better of it. She was, after all, a Very Good Dropper. And nobody ever saw her coming unless she wanted them to.

When the faint glow of the toves came into view at the bottom of the pore, he felt her shiver all over, luxuriantly, before she shimmered dark and folded herself tight against his scalp. Irizarry doused his own lights as well, flipping the passive infrared goggles down over his eyes. Toves were as blind as Mongoose was deaf, but an infestation this bad could mean the cracks were growing large enough for bigger things to wiggle through, and if there were raths, no sense in letting the monsters know he was coming.

He tapped the tendril curled around his throat three times, and whispered "Go." She didn't need him to tell her twice; really, he thought wryly, she didn't need him to tell her at all. He barely felt her featherweight disengage before she was gone down the corridor as silently as a hunting owl. She was invisible to his goggles, her body at ambient temperature, but he knew from experience that her barbels and vanes would be spread wide, and he'd hear the shrieks when she came in among the toves.

The toves covered the corridor ceiling, arm-long carapaces adhered by a foul-smelling secretion that oozed from between the sections of their exoskeletons. The upper third of each tove's body bent down like a dangling bough, bringing the glowing, sticky lure and flesh-ripping pincers into play. Irizarry had no idea what they fed on in their own phase, or dimension, or whatever.

Here, though, he knew what they ate. Anything they could get.

He kept his shock probe ready, splashing after, to assist her if it turned out necessary. That was sure a lot of toves, and even a cheshire-cat could get in trouble if she was outnumbered. Ahead of him, a tove warbled and went suddenly dark; Mongoose had made her first kill.

Within moments, the tove colony was in full warble, the harmonics making Irizarry's head ache. He moved forward carefully, alert now for signs of raths. The largest tove colony he'd ever seen was on the derelict steelship *Jenny Lind*, which he and Mongoose had explored when they were working salvage on the boojum *Harriet Tubman*. The hulk had been covered inside and out with toves; the colony was so vast that, having eaten everything else, it had started cannibalizing itself, toves eating their neighbors and being eaten in turn. Mongoose had glutted herself before the *Harriet Tubman* ate the wreckage, and in the refuse she left behind, Irizarry had found the strange starlike bones of an adult rath, consumed by its own prey. The bandersnatch that had killed the humans on the *Jenny Lind* had died with her reactor core and her captain. A handful of passengers and crew had escaped to tell the tale.

He refocused. This colony wasn't as large as those heaving masses on the *Jenny Lind*, but it was the largest he'd ever encountered not in a quarantine situation, and if there weren't raths somewhere on Kadath Station, he'd eat his infrared goggles.

A dead tove landed at his feet, its eyeless head neatly separated from its segmented body, and a heartbeat later Mongoose phased in on his shoulder and made her deep clicking noise that meant, *Irizarry! Pay attention!*

He held his hand out, raised to shoulder level, and Mongoose flowed between the two, keeping her bulk on his shoulder, with tendrils resting against his lips and larynx, but her tentacles wrapping around his hand to communicate. He pushed his goggles up with his free hand and switched on his belt light so he could read her colors.

She was anxious, strobing yellow and green. *Many,* she shaped against his palm, and then emphatically, *R.*

"R" was bad—it meant rath—but it was better than "B." If a bandersnatch had come through, all of them were walking dead, and Kadath Station was already as doomed as the *Jenny Lind*. "Do you smell it?" he asked under the warbling of the toves.

Taste, said Mongoose, and because Irizarry had been her partner for almost five Solar, he understood: the toves tasted of rath, meaning that they had recently been feeding on rath guano, and given the swiftness of toves' digestive systems, that meant a rath was patrolling territory on the station.

Mongoose's grip tightened on his shoulder. *R,* she said again. *R. R. R.*

Irizarry's heart lurched and sank. More than one rath. The cracks were widening.

A bandersnatch was only a matter of time.

Station Master Lee didn't want to hear it. It was all there in the way she stood, the way she pretended distraction to avoid eye-contact. He knew the rules of this game, probably better than she did. He stepped into her personal space. Mongoose shivered against the nape of his neck, her tendrils threading his hair. Even without being able to see her, he knew she was a deep, anxious emerald.

"A rath?" said Station Master Lee, with a toss of her head that might have looked flirtatious on a younger or less hostile woman, and moved away again. "Don't be ridiculous. There hasn't been a rath on Kadath Station since my grandfather's time."

"Doesn't mean there isn't an infestation now," Irizarry said quietly. If she was going to be dramatic, that was his cue to stay still and calm. "And I said raths. Plural."

"That's even more ridiculous. Mr. Irizarry, if this is some ill-conceived attempt to drive up your price—"

"It isn't." He was careful to say it flatly, not indignantly. "Station Master, I understand that this isn't what you want to hear, but you have to quarantine Kadath."

"Can't be done," she said, her tone brisk and flat, as if he'd asked her to pilot Kadath through the rings of Saturn.

"Of course it can!" Irizarry said, and she finally turned to look at him, outraged that he dared to contradict her. Against his neck, Mongoose flexed one set of claws. She didn't like it when he was angry.

Mostly, that wasn't a problem. Mostly, Irizarry knew anger was a waste of time and energy. It didn't solve anything. It didn't fix anything. It couldn't bring back anything that was lost. People, lives. The sorts of things that got washed away in the tides of time. Or were purged, whether you wanted them gone or not.

But this was . . . "You do know what a colony of adult raths can do, don't you? With a contained population of prey? Tell me, Station Master, have you started noticing fewer indigents in the shelters?"

She turned away again, dismissing his existence from her cosmology. "The matter is not open for discussion, Mr. Irizarry. I hired you to deal with an alleged infestation. I expect you to do so. If you feel you can't, you are of course welcome to leave the station with whatever ship takes your fancy. I believe the *Arthur Gordon Pym* is headed in-system, or perhaps you'd prefer the Jupiter run?"

He didn't have to win this fight, he reminded himself. He could walk away, try to warn somebody else, get himself and Mongoose the hell off Kadath Station. "All right, Station Master. But remember that I warned you, when your secretaries start disappearing."

He was at the door when she cried, "Irizarry!"

He stopped, but didn't turn.

"I can't," she said, low and rushed, as if she was afraid of being overheard. "I can't quarantine the station. Our numbers are already in the red this quarter, and the new political officer . . . it's my head on the block, don't you understand?"

He didn't understand. Didn't want to. It was one of the reasons he was a wayfarer, because he never wanted to let himself be like her again.

"If Sanderson finds out about the quarantine, she finds out about you. Will your papers stand up to a close inspection, Mr. Irizarry?"

He wheeled, mouth open to tell her what he thought of her and her clumsy attempts at blackmail, and she said, "I'll double your fee."

At the same time, Mongoose tugged on several strands of his hair, and he realized he could feel her heart beating, hard and rapid, against his spine. It was her distress he answered, not the Station Master's bribe. "All right," he said. "I'll do the best I can."

Toves and raths colonized like an epidemic, outward from a single originating point, Patient Zero in this case being the tear in spacetime that the first tove had wriggled through. More tears would develop as the toves multiplied, but it was that first one that would become large enough for a rath. While toves were simply lazy—energy efficient, the Arkhamers said primly—and never crawled farther than was necessary to find a useable anchoring point, raths were cautious. Their marauding was centered on the original tear because they kept their escape route open. And tore it wider and wider.

Toves weren't the problem, although they were a nuisance,

with their tendency to use up valuable oxygen, clog ductwork, eat pets, drip goo from ceilings, and crunch wetly when you stepped on them. Raths were worse; raths were vicious predators. Their natural prey might be toves, but they didn't draw the line at disappearing weakened humans or small gillies, either.

But even they weren't the danger that had made it hard for Irizarry to sleep the past two rest shifts. What toves tore and raths widened was an access for the apex predator of this alien food chain.

The bandersnatch: *Pseudocanis tindalosi*. The old records and the indigent Arkhamers called them hounds, but of course they weren't, any more than Mongoose was a cat. Irizarry had seen archive video from derelict stations and ships, the bandersnatch's flickering angular limbs appearing like spiked mantis arms from the corners of sealed rooms, the carnage that ensued. He'd never heard of anyone left alive on a station where a bandersnatch manifested, unless they made it to a panic pod damned fast. More importantly, even the Arkhamers in their archive-ships, breeders of Mongoose and all her kind, admitted they had no records of anyone *surviving* a bandersnatch rather than *escaping* it.

And what he had to do, loosely put, was find the core of the infestation before the bandersnatches did, so that he could eradicate the toves and raths and the stress they were putting on this little corner of the universe. Find the core—somewhere in the miles upon miles of Kadath's infrastructure. Which was why he was in this little-used service corridor, letting Mongoose commune with every ventilation duct they found.

Anywhere near the access shafts infested by the colony, Kadath Station's passages reeked of tove—ammoniac, sulfurous. The stench infiltrated the edges of Irizarry's mask as he lifted his face to a ventilation duct. Wincing in anticipation, he broke the seal on the rebreather and pulled it away from his face on the stiff elastic straps, careful not to lose his grip. A broken nose would not improve his day.

A cultist engineer skittered past on sucker-tipped limbs, her four snake-arms coiled tight beside her for the narrow corridor. She had a pretty smile, for a Christian.

Mongoose was too intent on her prey to be shy. The size of the tove colony might make her nervous, but Mongoose loved the smell—like a good dinner heating, Irizarry imagined. She unfolded herself around his head like a tendriled hood, tentacles outreached, body flaring as she stretched towards the ventilation fan. He felt her lean, her barbels shivering, and turned to face the way her wedge-shaped head twisted.

He almost tipped backwards when he found himself face to face with someone he hadn't even known was there. A woman, average height, average weight, brown hair drawn back in a smooth club; her skin was space-pale and faintly reddened across the cheeks, as if the IR filters on a suit hadn't quite protected her. She wore a sleek space-black uniform with dull silver epaulets and four pewter-colored bands at each wrist. An insignia with a stylized sun and Earth-Moon dyad clung over her heart.

The political officer, who was obviously unconcerned by Mongoose's ostentatious display of sensory equipment.

Mongoose absorbed her tendrils in like a startled anemone, pressing the warm underside of her head to Irizarry's scalp where the hair was thinning. He was surprised she didn't vanish down his shirt, because he felt her trembling against his neck.

The political officer didn't extend her hand. "Mr. Irizarry? You're a hard man to find. I'm Intelligence Colonel Sadhi Sanderson. I'd like to ask you a few quick questions, please."

"I'm, uh, a little busy right now," Irizarry said, and added uneasily, "Ma'am." The *last* thing he wanted to do was to offend her.

Sanderson looked up at Mongoose. "Yes, you would appear to be hunting," she said, her voice dry as scouring powder. "That's one of the things I want to talk about."

Oh *shit.* He had kept out of the political officer's way for a day and a half, and really that was a pretty good run, given the obvious tensions between Lee and Sanderson, and the things he'd heard in the Transient Barracks: the gillies were all terrified of Sanderson, and nobody seemed to have a good word for Lee. Even the Christians, mouths thinned primly, could say of Lee only that she didn't actively persecute them. Irizarry had been stuck on a steelship with a Christian congregation for nearly half a year once, and he knew their eagerness to speak well of everyone; he didn't know whether that was actually part of their faith, or just a survival tactic, but when Elder Dawson said, "She does not trouble us," he understood quite precisely what that meant.

Of Sanderson, they said even less, but Irizarry understood that, too. There was no love lost between the extremist cults and the government. But he'd heard plenty from the ice miners and dock workers and particularly from the crew of an impounded steelship who were profanely eloquent on the subject. Upshot: Colonel Sanderson was new in town, cleaning house, and profoundly not a woman you wanted to fuck with.

"I'd be happy to come to your office in an hour, maybe two?" he said. "It's just that—"

Mongoose's grip on his scalp tightened, sudden and sharp enough that he yelped; he realized that her head had moved back toward the duct while he fenced weakly with Colonel Sanderson, and now it was nearly *in* the duct, at the end of a foot and a half of iridescent neck.

"Mr. Irizarry?"

He held a hand up, because really this wasn't a good time, and yelped again when Mongoose reached down and grabbed it. He knew better than to forget how fluid her body was, that it was really no more than a compromise with the dimension he could sense her in, but sometimes it surprised him anyway.

And then Mongoose said, *Nagina,* and if Colonel Sanderson hadn't been standing right there, her eyebrows indicating that he was already at the very end of the slack she was willing to cut, he would have cursed aloud. Short of a bandersnatch—and that could still be along any time now, don't forget, Irizarry—a breeding rath was the worst news they could have.

"Your cheshire seems unsettled," Sanderson said, not sounding in the least alarmed. "Is there a problem?"

"She's eager to eat. And, er. She doesn't like strangers." It was as true as anything you could say about Mongoose, and the violent colors cycling down her tendrils gave him an idea what her chromatophores were doing behind his head.

"I can see that," Sanderson said. "Cobalt and yellow, in that stippled pattern—and flickering in and out of phase—she's acting aggressive, but that's fear, isn't it?"

Whatever Irizarry had been about to say, her observation stopped him short. He blinked at her—*like a gilly,* he thought uncharitably—and only realized he'd taken yet another step back when the warmth of the bulkhead pressed his coveralls to his spine.

"You know," Sanderson said mock-confidentially, "this entire corridor *reeks* of toves. So let me guess: it's not just toves anymore."

Irizarry was still stuck at her being able to read Mongoose's colors. "What do you know about cheshires?" he said.

She smiled at him as if at a slow student. "Rather a lot. I was on the *Jenny Lind* as an ensign—there was a cheshire on board, and I saw . . . It's not the sort of thing you forget, Mr. Irizarry, having been there once." Something complicated crossed her face—there for a flash and then gone. "The cheshire that died on the *Jenny Lind* was called Demon," Irizarry said, carefully. "Her partner was Long Mike Spider. You knew them?"

"Spider John," Sanderson said, looking down at the backs of her hands. She picked a cuticle with the opposite thumbnail. "He went by Spider John. You have the cheshire's name right, though."

When she looked back up, the arch of her carefully shaped brow told him he hadn't been fooling anyone.

"Right," Irizarry said. "Spider John."

"They were friends of mine." She shook her head. "I was just a pup. First billet, and I was assigned as Demon's liaison. Spider John liked to say he and I had the same job. But I couldn't make the captain believe him when he tried to tell her how bad it was."

"How'd you make it off after the bandersnatch got through?" Irizarry asked. He wasn't foolish enough to think that her confidences were anything other than a means of demonstrating to him why he could trust her, but the frustration and tired sadness sounded sincere.

"It went for Spider John first—it must have known he was a threat. And Demon—she threw herself at it, never mind it was five times her size. She bought us time to get to the panic pod and Captain Golovnina time to get to the core overrides. " She paused. "I saw it, you know. Just a glimpse. Wriggling through this . . . this *rip* in the air, like a big gaunt hound ripping through a hole in a blanket with knotty paws. I spent years wondering if it got my scent. Once they scent prey, you know, they never stop. . . . "

She trailed off, raising her gaze to meet his. He couldn't decide if the furrow between her eyes was embarrassment at having revealed so much, or the calculated cataloguing of his response.

"So you recognize the smell, is what you're saying."

She had a way of answering questions with other questions. "Am I right about the raths?"

He nodded. "A breeder."

She winced.

He took a deep breath and stepped away from the bulkhead. "Colonel Sanderson—I have to get it *now* if I'm going to get it at all."

She touched the microwave pulse pistol at her hip. "Want some company?"

He didn't. Really, truly didn't. And if he had, he wouldn't have chosen Kadath Station's political officer. But he couldn't afford to offend her . . . and he wasn't licensed to carry a weapon.

"All right," he said and hoped he didn't sound as grudging as he felt. "But don't get in Mongoose's way."

Colonel Sanderson offered him a tight, feral smile. "Wouldn't dream of it."

The only thing that stank more than a pile of live toves was a bunch of half-eaten ones.

"Going to have to vacuum-scrub the whole sector," Sanderson said, her breath hissing through her filters.

If we live long enough to need to, Irizarry, thought, but had the sense to keep his mouth shut. You didn't talk defeat around a politico. And if you were unfortunate enough to come to the attention of one, you certainly didn't let her see you thinking it.

Mongoose forged on ahead, but Irizarry noticed she was careful to stay within the range of his lights, and at least one of her tendrils stayed focused back on him and Sanderson at all times. If this were a normal infestation, Mongoose would be scampering along the corridor ceilings, leaving scattered bits of half-consumed tove and streaks of bioluminescent ichor in her wake. But this time, she edged along, testing each surface before her with quivering barbels so that Irizarry was reminded of a tentative spider or an exploratory octopus.

He edged along behind her, watching her colors go dim and cautious. She paused at each intersection, testing the air in every direction, and waited for her escort to catch up.

The service tubes of Kadath Station were mostly large enough for Irizarry and Sanderson to walk single-file through, though sometimes they were obliged to crouch, and once or twice Irizarry found himself slithering on his stomach through tacky half-dried tove slime. He imagined—he hoped it was imagining—that he could sense the thinning and stretch of reality all around them, see it in the warp of the tunnels and the bend of deck plates. He imagined that he glimpsed faint shapes from the corners of his eyes, caught a whisper of sound, a hint of scent, as of something almost there.

Hypochondria, he told himself firmly, aware that that was the wrong word and not really caring. But as he dropped down onto his belly again, to squeeze through a tiny access point—this one clogged with the fresh corpses of newly-slaughtered toves—he needed all the comfort he could invent.

He almost ran into Mongoose when he'd cleared the hole. She scuttled back to him and huddled under his chest, tendrils writhing, so close to out of phase that she was barely a warm shadow. When he saw what was on the other side, he wished he'd invented a little more.

This must be one of Kadath Station's recycling and reclamation centers, a bowl ten meters across sweeping down to a pile of rubbish in the middle. These were the sorts of places you always found minor tove infestations. Ships and stations might be supposed to be kept clear of vermin, but in practice, the dimensional stresses of sharing the spacelanes with boojums meant that just wasn't possible. And in Kadath, somebody hadn't been doing their job.

Sanderson touched his ankle, and Irizarry hastily drew himself aside so she could come through after. He was suddenly grateful for her company.

He really didn't want to be here alone.

Irizarry had never seen a tove infestation like this, not even on the *Jenny Lind*. The entire roof of the chamber was thick with their sluglike bodies, long lure-tongues dangling as much as half a meter down. Small flitting things— young raths, near-transparent in their phase shift—filled the space before him. As Irizarry watched, one blundered into the lure of a tove, and the tove contracted with sudden convulsive force. The rath never stood a chance.

Nagina, Mongoose said. *Nagina, Nagina, Nagina.*

Indeed, down among the junk in the pit, something big was stirring. But that wasn't all. That pressure Irizarry had sensed earlier, the feeling that many eyes were watching him, gaunt bodies stretching against whatever frail fabric held them back—here, it was redoubled, until he almost felt the brush of not-quite-in-phase whiskers along the nape of his neck.

Sanderson crawled up beside him, her pistol in one hand. Mongoose didn't seem to mind her there.

"What's down there?" she asked, her voice hissing on constrained breaths.

"The breeding pit," Irizarry said. "You feel that? Kind of funny, stretchy feeling in the universe?"

Sanderson nodded behind her mask. "It's not going to make you any happier, is it, if I tell you I've felt it before?"

Irizarry was wearily, grimly unsurprised. But then Sanderson said, "What do we do?"

He was taken aback and it must have shown, even behind the rebreather, because she said sharply, "*You're* the expert. Which I assume is why you're on Kadath Station to begin with and why Station Master Lee has been so anxious that I not know it. Though with an infestation of this size, I don't know how she thought she was going to hide it much longer anyway."

"Call it sabotage," Irizarry said absently. "Blame the Christians. Or the gillies. Or disgruntled spacers, like the crew off the *Caruso*. It happens a lot, Colonel. Somebody like me and Mongoose comes in and cleans up the toves, the station authorities get to crack down on whoever's being the worst pain in the ass, and life keeps on turning over. But she waited too long."

Down in the pit, the breeder heaved again. Breeding raths were slow— much slower than the juveniles, or the sexually dormant adult rovers—but that was because they were armored like titanium armadillos. When threatened, one of two things happened. Babies flocked to mama, mama rolled herself in a ball, and it would take a tactical nuke to kill them. Or mama went on the warpath. Irizarry had seen a pissed off breeder take out a bulkhead on a steelship once; it was pure dumb luck that it hadn't breached the hull.

And, of course, once they started spawning, as this one had, they could produce between ten and twenty babies a day for anywhere from a week to a month, depending on the food supply. And the more babies they produced, the weaker the walls of the world got, and the closer the bandersnatches would come.

"The first thing we have to do," he said to Colonel Sanderson, "as in, *right now*, is kill the breeder. Then you quarantine the station and get parties of volunteers to hunt down the rovers, before they can bring another breeder through, or turn into breeders, or however the fuck it works, which frankly I don't know. It'll take fire to clear this nest of toves, but Mongoose and I can probably get the rest. And *fire*, Colonel Sanderson. Toves don't give a shit about vacuum."

She could have reproved him for his language; she didn't. She just nodded and said, "How do we kill the breeder?"

"Yeah," Irizarry said. "That's the question."

Mongoose clicked sharply, her *Irizarry!* noise.

"No," Irizarry said. "Mongoose, don't—"

But she wasn't paying attention. She had only a limited amount of patience for his weird interactions with other members of his species and his insistence on *waiting*, and he'd clearly used it all up. She was Rikki Tikki Tavi, and the breeder was Nagina, and Mongoose knew what had to happen. She launched off Irizarry's shoulders, shifting phase as she went, and without contact between them, there was nothing he could do to call her back. In less than a second, he didn't even know where she was.

"You any good with that thing?" he said to Colonel Sanderson, pointing at her pistol.

"Yes," she said, but her eyebrows were going up again. "But, forgive me, isn't this what cheshires are for?"

"Against rovers, sure. But—Colonel, have you ever seen a breeder?"

Across the bowl, a tove warbled, the chorus immediately taken up by its neighbors. Mongoose had started.

"No," Sanderson said, looking down at where the breeder humped and wallowed and finally stood up, shaking off ethereal babies and half-eaten toves. "Oh. *Gods*."

You couldn't describe a rath. You couldn't even look at one for more than a few seconds before you started getting a migraine aura. Rovers were just blots of shadow. The breeder was massive, armored, and had no recognizable features, save for its hideous, drooling, ragged edged maw. Irizarry didn't know if it had eyes, or even needed them.

"She can kill it," he said, "but only if she can get at its underside. Otherwise, all it has to do is wait until it has a clear swing, and she's . . . " He shuddered. "I'll be lucky to find enough of her for a funeral. So what *we* have to do now, Colonel, is piss it off enough to give her a chance. Or"—he had to be fair; this was not Colonel Sanderson's job—"if you'll lend me your pistol, you don't have to stay."

She looked at him, her dark eyes very bright, and then she turned to look at the breeder, which was swinging its shapeless head in slow arcs, trying, no doubt, to track Mongoose. "Fuck that, Mr. Irizarry," she said crisply. "Tell me where to aim."

"You won't hurt it," he'd warned her, and she'd nodded, but he was pretty sure she hadn't really understood until she fired her first shot and the breeder didn't even *notice*. But Sanderson hadn't given up; her mouth had thinned, and she'd settled into her stance, and she'd fired again, at the breeder's feet as Irizarry had told her. A breeding rath's feet weren't vulnerable as such, but they were sensitive, much more sensitive than the human-logical target of its head. Even so, it was concentrating hard on Mongoose, who was making toves scream at various random points around the circumference of the breeding pit, and it took another three shots aimed at that same near front foot before the breeder's head swung in their direction.

It made a noise, a sort of "wooaaurgh" sound, and Irizarry and Sanderson were promptly swarmed by juvenile raths.

"Ah, fuck," said Irizarry. "Try not to kill them."

"I'm sorry, try *not* to kill them?"

"If we kill too many of them, it'll decide we're a threat rather than an annoyance. And then it rolls up in a ball, and we have no chance of killing it until it unrolls again. And by then, there will be a lot more raths here."

"And quite possibly a bandersnatch," Sanderson finished. "But—" She batted away a half-corporeal rath that was trying to wrap itself around the warmth of her pistol.

"If we stood perfectly still for long enough," Irizarry said, "they could probably leech out enough of our body heat to send us into hypothermia. But they can't bite when they're this young. I knew a cheshire-man once who swore they ate by crawling down into the breeder's stomach to lap up what it'd digested. I'm still hoping that's not true. Just keep aiming at that foot."

"You got it."

Irizarry had to admit, Sanderson was steady as a rock. He shooed juvenile raths away from both of them, Mongoose continued her depredations out there in the dark, and Sanderson, having found her target, fired at it in a nice steady rhythm. She didn't miss; she didn't try to get fancy. Only, after a while, she said out of the corner of her mouth, "You know, my battery won't last forever."

"I know," Irizarry said. "But this is good. It's working."

"How can you tell?"

"It's getting mad."

"How can you *tell*?"

"The vocalizing." The rath had gone from its "wooaaurgh" sound to a series of guttural huffing noises, interspersed with high-pitched yips. "It's warning us off. Keep firing."

"All right," Sanderson said. Irizarry cleared another couple of juveniles off her head. He was trying not to think about what it meant that no adult raths had come to the pit—just how much of Kadath Station had they claimed?

"*Have* there been any disappearances lately?" he asked Sanderson.

She didn't look at him, but there was a long silence before she said, "None that *seemed* like disappearances. Our population is by necessity transient, and none too fond of authority. And, frankly, I've had so much trouble with the station master's office that I'm not sure my information is reliable."

It had to hurt for a political officer to admit that. Irizarry said, "We're very likely to find human bones down there. And in their caches."

Sanderson started to answer him, but the breeder decided it had had enough. It wheeled toward them, its maw gaping wider, and started through the mounds of garbage and corpses in their direction.

"What now?" said Sanderson.

"Keep firing," said Irizarry. *Mongoose, wherever you are, please be ready.*

He'd been about seventy-five percent sure that the rath would stand up on its hind legs when it reached them. Raths weren't sapient, not like cheshires, but they were smart. They knew that the quickest way to kill a human was to take its head off, and the second quickest was to disembowel it, neither of which they could do on all fours. And humans weren't any threat to a breeder's vulnerable abdomen; Sanderson's pistol might give the breeder a hot foot, but there was no way it could penetrate the breeder's skin.

It was a terrible plan—there was that whole twenty-five percent where he and Sanderson died screaming while the breeder ate them from the feet up—but it worked. The breeder heaved itself upright, massive, indistinct paw going back for a blow that would shear Sanderson's head off her neck and probably bounce it off the nearest bulkhead, and with no warning of any kind, not for the humans, not for the rath, Mongoose phased viciously in, claws and teeth and sharp edged tentacles all less than two inches from the rath's belly and moving fast.

The rath screamed and curled in on itself, but it was too late. Mongoose had already caught the lips of its—oh gods and fishes, Irizarry didn't know the word. Vagina? Cloaca? Ovipositor? The place where little baby raths came into the world. The only vulnerability a breeder had. Into which Mongoose shoved the narrow wedge of her head, and her clawed front feet, and began to rip.

Before the rath could even reach for her, her malleable body was already entirely inside it, and it—screaming, scrabbling—was doomed.

Irizarry caught Sanderson's elbow and said, "Now would be a good time, *very slowly*, to back away. Let the lady do her job."

Irizarry almost made it off of Kadath clean.

He'd had no difficulty in getting a berth for himself and Mongoose—after a party or two of volunteers had seen her in action, after the stories started spreading about the breeder, he'd nearly come to the point of beating off the steelship captains with a stick. And in the end, he'd chosen the offer of the captain of the *Erich Zann*, a boojum; Captain Alvarez had a long-term salvage contract in the Kuiper belt—"cleaning up after the ice miners," she'd said with a wry smile—and Irizarry felt like salvage was maybe where he wanted to be for a while. There'd be plenty for Mongoose to hunt, and nobody's life in danger. Even a bandersnatch wasn't much more than a case of indigestion for a boojum.

He'd got his money out of the station master's office—hadn't even had to talk to Station Master Lee, who maybe, from the things he was hearing, wasn't going to be station master much longer. You could either be ineffectual *or* you could piss off your political officer. Not both at once. And her secretary so very obviously didn't want to bother her that it was easy to say, "We had a contract," and to plant his feet and smile. It wasn't the doubled fee she'd promised him, but he didn't even want that. Just the money he was owed.

So his business was taken care of. He'd brought Mongoose out to the *Erich Zann*, and insofar as he and Captain Alvarez could tell, the boojum and the cheshire liked each other. He'd bought himself new underwear and let Mongoose pick out a new pair of earrings for him. And he'd gone ahead and splurged, since he was, after all, *on* Kadath Station and might as well make the most of it, and bought a selection of books for his reader, including *The Wind in the Willows*. He was looking forward, in an odd, quiet way, to the long nights out beyond Neptune: reading to Mongoose, finding out what she thought about Rat and Mole and Toad and Badger.

Peace—or as close to it as Izrael Irizarry was ever likely to get.

He'd cleaned out his cubby in the Transient Barracks, slung his bag over one shoulder with Mongoose riding on the other, and was actually in sight of the *Erich Zann*'s dock when a voice behind him called his name.

Colonel Sanderson.

He froze in the middle of a stride, torn between turning around to greet her and bolting like a rabbit, and then she'd caught up to him. "Mr. Irizarry," she said. "I hoped I could buy you a drink before you go."

He couldn't help the deeply suspicious look he gave her. She spread her hands, showing them empty. "Truly. No threats, no tricks. Just a drink. To say thank you." Her smile was lopsided; she knew how unlikely those words sounded in the mouth of a political officer.

And any other political officer, Irizarry wouldn't have believed them. But he'd seen her stand her ground in front of a breeder rath, and he'd seen her turn and puke her guts out when she got a good look at what Mongoose did to it. If she wanted to thank him, he owed it to her to sit still for it.

"All right," he said, and added awkwardly, "Thank you."

They went to one of Kadath's tourist bars: bright and quaint and cheerful and completely unlike the spacer bars Irizarry was used to. On the other hand, he could see why Sanderson picked this one. No one here, except maybe the bartender, had the least idea who she was, and the bartender's wide-eyed double take meant that they got excellent service: prompt and very quiet.

Irizarry ordered a pink lady—he liked them, and Mongoose, in delight, turned the same color pink, with rosettes matched to the maraschino "cherry." Sanderson ordered whisky, neat, which had very little resemblance to the whisky Irizarry remembered from planetside. She took a long swallow of it, then set the glass down and said, "I never got a chance to ask Spider John this: how did you get your cheshire?"

It was clever of her to invoke Spider John and Demon like that, but Irizarry still wasn't sure she'd earned the story. After the silence had gone on a little too long, Sanderson picked her glass up, took another swallow, and said, "I know who you are."

"I'm *nobody*," Irizarry said. He didn't let himself tense up, because Mongoose wouldn't miss that cue, and she was touchy enough, what with all the steelship captains, that he wasn't sure what she might think the proper response was. And he wasn't sure, if she decided the proper response was to rip Sanderson's face off, that he would be able to make himself disagree with her in time.

"I promised," Sanderson said. "No threats. I'm not trying to trace you, I'm not asking any questions about the lady you used to work for. And, truly, I'm only *asking* how you met *this* lady. You don't have to tell me."

"No," Irizarry said mildly. "I don't." But Mongoose, still pink, was coiling down his arm to investigate the glass—not its contents, since the interest of the egg-whites would be more than outweighed by the sharp sting to her nose of the alcohol, but the upside-down cone on a stem of a martini glass. She liked geometry. And this wasn't a story that could hurt anyone.

He said, "I was working my way across Jupiter's moons, oh, five years ago now. Ironically enough, I got trapped in a quarantine. Not for vermin, but for the black rot. It was a long time, and things got . . . ugly."

He glanced at her and saw he didn't need to elaborate.

"There were Arkhamers trapped there, too, in their huge old scow of a ship. And when the water rationing got tight, there were people that said the Arkhamers shouldn't have any—said that if it was the other way 'round, they wouldn't give us any. And so when the Arkhamers sent one of their daughters for their share . . ." He still remembered her scream, a grown woman's terror in a child's voice, and so he shrugged and said, "I did the only thing I could. After that, it was safer for me on their ship than it was on the station, so I spent some time with them. Their Professors let me stay.

"They're not bad people," he added, suddenly urgent. "I don't say I understand what they believe, or why, but they were good to me, and they did share their water with the crew of the ship in the next berth. And of course, they had cheshires. Cheshires all over the place, cleanest steelship you've ever seen. There was a litter born right about the time the quarantine finally lifted. Jemima—the little girl I helped—she insisted they give me pick of the litter, and that was Mongoose."

Mongoose, knowing the shape of her own name on Irizarry's lips, began to purr, and rubbed her head gently against his fingers. He petted her, feeling his tension ease, and said, "And I wanted to be a biologist before things got complicated."

"Huh," said Sanderson. "Do you know what they are?"

"Sorry?" He was still mostly thinking about the Arkhamers, and braced himself for the usual round of superstitious nonsense: demons or necromancers or what-not.

But Sanderson said, "Cheshires. Do you know what they are?"

"What do you mean, 'what they are'? They're cheshires."

"After Demon and Spider John . . . I did some reading and I found a Professor or two—Arkhamers, yes—to ask." She smiled, very thinly. "I've found, in this job, that people are often remarkably willing to answer my questions. And I found out. They're bandersnatches."

"Colonel Sanderson, not to be disrespectful—"

"Sub-adult bandersnatches," Sanderson said. "Trained and bred and intentionally stunted so that they never mature fully."

Mongoose, he realized, had been watching, because she caught his hand and said emphatically, *Not.*

"Mongoose disagrees with you," he said and found himself smiling. "And really, I think she would know."

Sanderson's eyebrows went up. "And what does Mongoose think she is?"

He asked, and Mongoose answered promptly, pink dissolving into champagne and gold: *Jagular.* But there was a thrill of uncertainty behind it, as if she wasn't quite sure of what she stated so emphatically. And then, with a sharp toss of her head at Colonel Sanderson, like any teenage girl: *Mongoose.*

Sanderson was still watching him sharply. "Well?"

"She says she's Mongoose."

And Sanderson really wasn't trying to threaten him, or playing some elaborate political game, because her face softened in a real smile, and she said, "Of course she is."

Irizarry swished a sweet mouthful between his teeth. He thought of what Sanderson has said, of the bandersnatch on the *Jenny Lind* wriggling through stretched rips in reality like a spiny, deathly puppy tearing a blanket. "How would you domesticate a bandersnatch?"

She shrugged. "If I knew that, I'd be an Arkhamer, wouldn't I?" Gently, she extended the back of her hand for Mongoose to sniff. Mongoose, surprising Irizarry, extended one tentative tendril and let it hover just over the back of Sanderson's wrist.

Sanderson tipped her head, smiling affectionately, and didn't move her hand. "But if I had to guess, I'd say you do it by making friends."

LIVING CURIOUSITIES

MARGO LANAGAN

I went to Dulcie Pepper's tent and slapped my hand onto her table, palm up.

"I'm sorry, Nonny-girl. Looking at that, you'll not grow another inch." She reached for her pipe. "Clawed your way through that queue, did you?"

"Have you had *anyone* tonight?"

"One strange young man. How about you Ooga-Boogas?"

"A family or two, and a man—oh, probably the same man as you. Very clean clothes, and uncomfortable in them."

"Uncomfortable in his *skin*, that one. He gave me the shivers, he did."

"Spent a long time in with the pickle jars, then came out and stood well back from us, did not try to speak. Even Billy could not get so much as a good-evening out of him, though he did nod when greeted. Mostly just stared, though, from one to another of us and back again. Twice around, he went, as if he did not want to miss a thing."

"Hmm." Dulcie leaned back in her shawl-draped chair and put her humdrum boots up next to the crystal ball. She is not so much a crystal gazer; the ball is mostly for atmosphere. She does complicated things with her own set of cards that she will not say where they came from, and mainly and bestly she reads hands. Not just palms, but *hands*, for there is as much to be read from fingertips as from the palm's creases, she says. "Where was I, then, last time?"

"You had just told Mister Ashman as much as you could, about them ghosts."

"Oh yes, which was not very much, and all confused, as is always the case when you come to a moment of choice and possibilities. It's as bad as not seeing anything sometimes; really, you could gain as much direction consulting a person of only common sense. But perhaps those are rarer than I'm thinking, rarer even than fortune-tellers. Anyway, John Frogget comes by."

"John Frogget? What was he doing there?" I tried to disguise that his name had spilled a little of my tea.

"Well, he must quarter somewhere too, no, for the winter? That was the year his pa died. He said he would not go to Queensland and duke it out with his brothers for the land. He waited closer to spring and then went up a month or two and rabbited for them. Made a tidy pot, too. All put away in the savings bank nicely—there's not many lads would be so forethoughtful."

I tried to nod like one of those commonsense people. I nearly always knew whereabouts John Frogget was, and if I didn't know where, I imagined. Right now I could hear the pop-pop of someone in his shooting gallery, alongside the merry-go-round music. So he would be standing there in the bright-lit room, all legs and folded arms and level gaze, admiring if the man was a good shot, and careful not to show scorn or amusement if he was not. "So what did Frogget do, then, about your ghosts?"

"Well, he tried to shoot them, of course—we asked him. At first he was too frightened. Such a steady boy, you would not credit how he shook. He could not believe it himself. So at first his shots went wide. But then he calmed himself, but blow me if it made any difference. *Look*, he says, *I am aimed direct in the back of the man's head or at his heart, but the shot goes straight through the air of him.* He made us watch, and *ping!*, and *zing!*, and *bdoing!* It all bounced off the walls and the two of them just kept up their carry-on, the ghost-man cursing and the woman a-mewling same as ever. And then *rowr-rowr-chunka-chunka* the *thing* come down the alley like always, and poor Frogget—we had not warned him about that part!" Laughter and smoke puffed out of her, and she coughed. "We had to just about scrape him off the bricks with a butter knife, he was pressed so flat! Oh!"

"Poor lad," I said. "You and Mister Ashman at least were used to it."

"I know. We knew we would come to no harm. Ashman had stood on that exact spot many times and been run down by the ghost-horses and the ghost-cart, like I told you. It might have whitened his hair a little more, the sensations of it, but he were never crushed, by any means. Standing there in the racket with his hands up and, *Stand to! Begone, now!* As if he were still right centre of the ring, and master of everything." She watched the memory and laughed to herself.

"So Ashman could not boss the ghosts away, and Frogget could not shoot them. So what did you do then?" I did not mind what she said, so long as she kept on talking, so long as Mrs. Em stayed away, with her *Come Nonny-girl, there is some public waiting.* Some days, some nights, I could bear the work, if it could be called work, being exhibited; others I felt as if people's eyes left slug trails wherever they looked, and their remarks bruises, and their whispers to each other little smuts and smudges all over us. The earth-men and the Fwaygians and the Eskimoos were too foreign and dark to notice, and Billy was too much a personality to ever take offence, but I, just a girl, and pale, and so much smaller than them al . . . All I wanted was to go back to my quarters, lock my door and wash myself of the public's leavings, and then hurry away, under cover of carriage or train-blind or only night's darkness from anywhere I would be spotted as one of Ashman's Museum-pieces.

"There was nothing we *could* do," said Dulcie, "so we just put up with it, most that winter. I went and asked them, you know? I told them how tiresome they were, how he was never going to get his money out of her, that they were dead, didn't they realise? That they were going to die from this cart coming along in a minute. It was like talking to myself, as if I were mad or drunk myself. You just had to wait, you know? The terrible noise—I cannot describe, somehow, how awful it was. There was more to it than noise. It shook you to your bones, and then to something else; it was hard to keep the fear off you. And sometimes four or five times a night, you know?, and Ashman and me clutching each other like babes in the wood with a big *owl* flying over, or a *bat*, or a *crow* carking."

"It is hard to imagine Ashman fearful—"

Dulcie sat up, finger raised, eyes sliding. We listened to the bootsteps outside, that paused, that passed. "Him again," she whispered.

"Whom again?"

"Mister Twitchy." She tapped the side of her head.

"How can you *know*, from just that?"

She put a finger to her lips, and he passed again, back down towards the merry-go-round. That was where I would go, too, were I a free woman, a customer, alone and uncomfortable. There was nothing like that pootle-y music, that coloured cave, those gliding swan-coaches and those rising-and-falling ponies, the gloss of their paint, the haughtiness of their heads, the scenes of all the world—Paris! Edinburgh Castle! The Italian Alps! You could stand there and warm your heart at the sight, the way you warm your hands at a brazier. You could pretend you were anywhere and anyone—tall, slender, of royal birth, with a face like The Lovely Zalumna, pale, mysterious, beautiful at the centre of her big round frizz of Circassian hair.

"Ashman. Fearful." Dulcie brought us both back from our listening. "Yes, I know, he is so commanding in his manner. But he was sickening for something, you see, all that while. I don't know whether the ghosts were the cause or just an aggravation. But it came to midwinter and he were confined to his bed, and we hardly needed to light the fire, his own heat kept the room so warm. The great stomach of him, you know? I swear some nights I saw it glowing without benefit of the lamp! And the delirium! It was all I could do some nights to keep him abed. And one night, I had shooed him back to his bed so many times—I had *wrestled* him back, if you can imagine! Well, up he stands, throws off his nightshirt, which is so wet you could wring it out and fill a teacup easy with the drippings. Up he stands, runs to the window, tears the curtains aside, and there's the moon out there hits him like a spotlight. And he says—oh, Non, I cannot tell you for laughing now, but at the time, I tell you, he raised gooseflesh on me! *I am Circus*, he says—to the moon, to the lane, to the ghosts, to me? I don't know. To himself! *I am Circus*, he announces, in his ringmaster voice. *I am all acts, all persons, all creatures, all curiosities, rolled into one.* And I says—it was cruel, but I had been up all night with him—I says, *'Roll' is right, you great dough-lump of a man. Get back into bed.* And he turns around and says to me, *Dulce, I have seen a great truth; it will change everything. I need hire no one; I need pay nothing; I can do it all myself, with no squabbles nor mutinies nor making ends meet!*

"*What is that?* I say, pushing him away from the window, for should anyone come down the lane, hearing his shouts and wondering who needs help down there, who needs taking to the madhouse, they will see him all moonlit there, naked as a baby and with his hair all over the place. He'd be mortified, I'm thinking, if he were in his right sense. Let alone they might *take* him to the madhouse! Anyway, on he goes. He can ride a horse as well as any equestrian, he says, now that he knows how the horse feels, what it thinks. He can *be* the horse. He can multiply himself into *many* horses, he says, as many as we need—"

I love it when Dulcie gets to such a stage in a story, her face all open and lively, her eyes full of the sights she's uttering, as if none of this were here, the tent or the gypsy-tat or the cold night and strange town outside. She goes right away from it all, and she takes me with her, the way she describes everything.

"And he's just about to show me what he can do on the trapeze—*I will have a suit*, he says, *all baubles and bugle-beads like The Great Fantango and I will swing and I will fly!*

"And he's going for the window and I'm fighting him and wondering should I scream for help if he gets it open? Will he push *me* out if I'm in his way? And how much do I care for him anyway? Am I willing to have my brains dashed out in an alleyway on the chance it will give him pause and save his life?

"And up goes the window and the wind comes in, *smack!*, straight from the South Pole I tell you, Nonny, and a little thing like Tasmania was never going to get in its way! It took the breath out of me, and the room was an icebox like *that*." She snaps her dry fingers. "But you would think it was a . . . a zephyr, a tropical breeze, for all it stops Ashman. *I will fly!* he says, *I will fly!* And he pushes the sash right up and he's hands either side the window and his foot up on the sill. *With the greatest of ease!* he shouts."

Here Dulce stopped and looked crafty. "And now I must fill my pipe," she said calmly.

"Dulcie Pepper, I hate you!" I slid off the stool and ran around and pummelled her while she laughed. "You *always*—You *torture* a girl so!"

"How can it matter?" she said airily, elbowing my fists away. " 'Tis all long over now, and you *know* he lives!"

"If I could reach, I would strangle you." I waved my tiny paws at her and snarled, rattling my throat the way I had learned from the Dog Man.

"And then you would never hear the end, would you?" she says smugly. "Unless you ran and asked Ashman himself."

Gloomily I went back to my stool and watched her preparations. Faintly bored, I tried to seem, and protest no more, for the more I minded the longer she would hold off.

At first she moved with a slowness calculated to irritate me further, but when I kept my lips closed she tired of the game and gathered and tamped the leaf-shreds into the black pipe. Before she even lit it she went on. "And right at that minute, as if they were sent to save his life, that drunken ghost starts below: *Where's me dashed money, you flaming dash-dash?* And his woman starts to her crying. *What do you mean you haven't got it?* he says. 'Cetra, cetra. It was funny, I could *see* the gooseflesh on Ashman. It ran all over and around him like rain running over a puddle, you know, little gusts of it. And back he steps, and takes my hands and makes me sit down on the bed. *Dulce,* he says, *I see it so clearly.* And it ought to have made me laugh, it were so daft, but the way he said it, suddenly it seemed so true, you know? Because he believed it so, he almost *made* it true. And also, the ghosts in the lane, they will turn things serious; it was very hard to laugh and be light with those things performing below."

"What did he say, though?"

She struck her pipe alight, delaying herself at this sign of my eagerness. "He says"—and she narrowed her eyes at me through the first thick-curling smoke—"*Inside every Thin Man, he says, there is a Fat Lady trying to be seen, and to live as that Fat Lady, and fetch that applause. Inside every Giant there is a Dwarf, inside every Dwarf a Giant. Inside every trapeze artist a lion tamer lives, or a girl equestrian with a bow in her hair, and inside every cowboy is a Wild Man of Borneo, or a Siam Twin missing his other half.*"

Sometimes I was sure Dulcie Pepper had magic, the things she did with her voice, the force of her eyes, her smokes and scents and fabrics, and the crystal ball sitting there like another great eye in the room, or the moon, or a lamp, and the way my scalp crept, some of the things she said. *Inside every Dwarf a Giant*—and there she had drawn me; Mister Ashman had seen me in his delirium and here was Dulcie to tell me, that all of us freaks and ethnologicals felt the same, and Chan the Chinee Giant was the mirror of me, both sizes yearning towards the middle, towards what seemed long-limbed and languid to me, miniature and delicate to Chan.

"A Fat Lady inside every Thin Man?" I said doubtfully, but when I thought about it, it was very like what Chan and I wanted, the opposite of what we were.

Dulcie shrugged. "So he said. *But inside me,* he said, *because I am a businessman and a white man and a civilized man and a worker with my mind and not my hands, inside me is the lot of them, blackamoor and savage, rigger and cook and dancing girl on a horseback. And now that I know the trick,* he says, *now that I have the key, I can open the door; I can bring them all out! I am a circus in my own self. Do you see how convenient this is?*

"Which of course I *could* . . . " She laughs, and examines the state of the burning tobacco. "And it would, certainly, have saved a lot of bother, just the two of us tripping around the place."

"But it wasn't *true*!" I said. "It wasn't *possible*!"

"Exactly. And then I could hear the cart coming, the horses and the rumbling wheels, and I thought, Good, this will put an end to this nonsense. And—"

A man shouted outside, and boys, and in a moment feet ran up the hill towards us, boys' anxious voices, excited. Dulcie started up, swept to the tent door and snatched it aside as the last of Hoppy Mack's sons passed by. "What's up, you lads?' she called out.

"Dunno. Something has happened in Frogget's."

Instantly I was locked still on my seat, a dwarf-girl of ice. Nothing functioned of me but my ears.

"*He's* not shot, is he?" Thank God for Dulcie, who could ask my question for me!

"No, he's all fine," said the boy, farther away now. " 'Twas him told us to go for Ashman."

That unlocked me. I hurried out past Dulcie, and she followed me down the slope of grass flattened into the mud by Sunday's crowd and still not recovered two days later.

John Frogget had doused the lamps around his sign and was prowling outside the booth door, all but barking at people who came near. "No!" he said to Ugly Tom. "Give the man some dignity. He is not one of your pickles, to be gawped at for money." Which as there were a number of ethnologicals coming from the Museum tent—as there was *me*, but could he see me yet?—was a mite insensitive of him. But he was upset.

"What has happened, John?" said Dulcie sensibly. I retreated a-flutter to her elbow, looking John up and down for blood.

"A man has shot himself with my pistol."

"Shot himself dead?"

"Through the eye," said John, nodding.

"Through the *eye*!" breathed Dulcie, as John turned from us to the others gabbling at him. She grasped my shoulder. "Nonny, do you think? Could it possibly?"

"What?" I said, rather crossly because she hurt me with her big hand, so tight, and her weight. But her face up there was like the beam from the top of a lighthouse, cutting through my irritations.

"No," I said.

Uncomfortable in his skin, that one.

"No." I liked a good ghost story, but I did not want to have looked upon a man living his last hour. "He was *rich*! He had the best-cut coat! And new boots!" I pled up to Dulcie, grasping her skirt like an infant its mother's.

"Here he comes!" said Sammy Mack, and down the hill strode Ashman in his shirtsleeves, but with his hat on. I could not imagine him naked and raving and covered in gooseflesh, as Dulcie had described him.

"What's up, Frogget?" He pushed through the onlookers—he didn't have to push very hard, for people leaped aside to allow in his part of the drama, his authority.

John Frogget ushered him into the shooting gallery. Sammy Mack peered in after, holding the cloth aside. There was the partition with the cowboys painted on it, and a slot of the yellow light beyond, at the bottom of which a booted foot projected into view.

"Oh!" Dulcie crouched to my level and clutched me, and I clutched her around the neck in my fright. " 'Tis him, 'tis him!"

I had admired that boot in the Museum tent, to avoid looking further at his face as he took in the sight of us. "Hungry," I said, "that was the way he looked at us. I don't like to think what is going through their minds when they look like that. But he was young, and not bad looking, and dressed so fine!"

"He was doomed." Dulcie shivered. "I saw it. It was all over his palms, this possibility. It was all through his cards like a stain. When I see an outlay like that, I lie. Sometimes that averts it. I told him he would find love soon, and prosper in his business concerns, find peace in himself, all of that and more. Perhaps I babbled, and he saw the falsity in it. But I was only trying to help—oh!" She covered her mouth with her hand to stop more words falling out, doing their damage.

"Did you know the man, Dulcie?" Ugly Tom had seen our fright and come to us.

"You would have seen him too, Tom," I said. "He spent an age among your babies and your three-headed lambs."

He looked startled, then disbelieving. "Oh, was he a young gentleman? Thin tie? Well dressed? Little goatee?" He put up his hand to show how tall, and Dulcie and I nodded as if our heads were on the same string. "Well, I never!" He turned towards the shooting gallery, astonished. "You're right," he said to me, as if he had not noticed it himself, "he did spend a time with my exhibits. An inordinate amount of time."

"And with us outside, too, an ordinate amount," I said, holding Dulcie's neck tighter. "Back and forth, back and forth, *staring*. Which is why we are there, of course, so that people *may* stare. Did he say anything to you, Dulcie, that made you think he might—?"

She shook her head. "He gave me no clue. He didn't need to; it was all over his hands. I should have told him. *You're in terrible danger.* Perhaps if he knew that I saw—"

It was then that she walked by, towards the tent. It was not someone understandable, like The Lovely Zalumna. It was perfectly ordinary Fay Shipley, daughter of Cap Shipley the head rigger.

I saw it as I'd seen the boot, when Sammy Mack opened the tent-flap, and held it open longer than he needed. The world, the fates, whatever dooming powers there were, that Dulcie sometimes saw the workings of before they acted, they conspired to show me, through the shiftings of the people in front of us, through the tent-flap Sammy was gawking through, beside the partition, in the narrow slice of gallery, of world-in-itself, its sounds blotted out by the closer whispers and mutterings of bone-in-his-nose Billy and Chan and Mrs. Em and the Wild Man and—

She hurried in, plain Fay Shipley. She stood beside the partition, her hands to her mouth. Then she lifted her head, as someone approached her from inside, and—later I hated her for this—her arms loosened and lifted out to receive him, and as Sammy Mack dropped the canvas I saw John Frogget's forehead come to rest on her shoulder, John Frogget's arms encircle her waist, John Frogget's boot block my view of that other boot.

Then they both were gone. "Did you see that?" I said dazedly, in the cold, in the dark outside. "Fay and John Frogget?"

"Oh," said Dulcie. "Did you not know they were sweethearts?"

"Just freshly, just recent?"

"Oh no, months, at least. Where have your eyes been?"

She stood, then, away from me, and folded her arms up there. And Mrs. Em came running up to busybody, so it was all what-a-dreadful-thing and poor-John-Frogget awhile there, with every now and then a pause to allow me to exclaim to myself, But I am *prettier* than Fay Shipley!

And, Look at my hair! When hers is so flat, as if she glued it down!

And, Why, I've never seen the girl laugh, to improve her looks that way!

"What a thing to do on your last night, eh?" said Mrs. Em, with something of a giggle. "Come to the deadest night o' the circus, and look at freaks and specimens."

Oh, I was being so frivolous and vain, with the young gent dead in there, and why, ever? "I don't know," I said. "*Is* it so odd? What would you do, if you had killing yourself in mind?"

"Would you have your fortune told?" said Dulcie wretchedly from on high. "To see whether you had the courage?"

"I think I am too ordinary," I said surprised, staring at the tent-flap.

Mrs. Em laughed. "That's no sin, child!"

"Oh, but I'm used to thinking how different I am from most people, how unusual. Yet this gentleman, and shooting himself in the eye . . . I don't know that I'd ever take my life in my own hands so. I wouldn't feel I had the right, you know? To such grand feelings, or even, to make such a mess, you know? Of someone else's floor, that would have to mop it up—"

"Ooh, he's more of a freak than you or I, dear," said Mrs. Em, right by my ear. Her stubby hand patted mine.

I folded mine away from her. I didn't want her cosiness, her comforting me. I *wanted* to be grand and tragic; I wanted people to be awed by me as we were by the dead gentleman, not to say *How sweet!* and *But they are like little dolls! Flossie could pick one up, couldn't you, Floss?* I wanted to be tall, to have dignity, to shoot myself in the eye without it taking my whole arm's stretch to reach the trigger. I wanted to be all but invisible, too, until I did so, and to leave people wondering why I might have done it, instead of having them nod and say, *Well, of course, she could expect no kind of normal life,* as I lay freakish in my own blood on the floor, with my child-boot sticking out my skirts.

"I'm going to ask Arthur, may I sit aboard his merry-go-round," I said.

"What, when a man has just died?" said Mrs. Em.

"I will not ask him to *spin* it," I said. "It will be safer. I will be out from underfoot, and it will cheer me up, and I will have a better view when they bring the body out."

"What a caution!" said Mrs. Em as I went.

I thrust myself in among skirts and trousers, painted legs and pantaloons, grass-dresses and robe-drapes. There is a privacy to being so small, a privacy and a permission—all children know it, and use it, and are forgiven. And "Oops!" and "Oh, I'm sorry, Non," and "I say—oh, it's one of you!" people said as I forged a way through them, pushing aside their thighs and cloths and shadows.

And finally I forced through to the golden light of the merry-go-round. The animals were stiff on their posts, and empty-saddled, that ought to glide and spin, and lift and lower their riders; the pootling, piping music was stilled.

"Arthur," I commanded the ticket-man nearby, a rag hanging from his pocket smudged with the grease of the roundabout's workings. "Lift me up onto a pony, before someone treads me into the mud!"

Which he did with a will, for people enjoy to be ordered by dwarves as they like to be ordered by children, up to a point. And there in the golden glow I sat high-headed, above the hats and feathers and turbans of the ghoulish crowd turned away from me. I wished the light were as warm as it looked; I wished the music were filling my ears. I dreamed—hard, as if the vehemence of my dreaming would make it happen—that my shiny black horse would surge forward beneath me, and that I would be spun away from this place and this night, lifted and lowered instead past Lake Geneva, past Constantinople, past Windermere and Tokyo Palace and Gay Paree, past Geneva again, and the Lake, again and again around the whole picturesque, gilt-framed world, for as long as ever I needed.

###

THE DEATH OF SUGAR DADDY

TOIYA KRISTEN FINLEY

Laffy Taffy—July 7

"Quit digging, girl!"

This was before all of the cryin, before that black hole started suckin me in, and my wrist wasn't so bad back then, neither.

I didn't mean to scratch that hard. Momma had her back to me, but she heard anyway. I pulled my sleeve over the bad spot on my wrist and went at it again. My nail wasn't sharp enough through the dress, though.

"Keisha." This time Momma turned all the way around. Folded her arms. Ms. Bentley's boyfriend watched Momma shuffle her hips and scratched under his chin.

"You know how impetigo spreads?" Momma said. "Now stop picking at your wrist before it gets raw."

This wasn't no mosquito bite, though. I couldn't leave it alone, neither. But there was nuthin wrong with my wrist, far as I could see. I rubbed it down with lotion and put Vaseline on top of that. All that did was give me greasy skin. My wrist still itched. I wanted to get home so I could try alcohol like Momma used when I got chiggers on my legs, but Momma liked to hang around after weddings, even for people she didn't know. This girl was the niece or grand-daughter of somebody Grandmommy used to go to church with. That didn't mean Grandmommy thought she had to come and drag me along. At least Momma wasn't makin me wear them real lacy dresses no more. All the other 11 year olds—and some of the 10 year olds, too—had relaxers, and they could run a comb through their hair without worryin about breakin any of it off. But I was stuck with twist ties and barrettes. Momma got the hint I wouldn't bother with em no more at the last weddin when I kept shakin my head and clankin those dumb barrettes together. Today she finally pressed my hair.

"It's not here," Ms. Bentley said. Her and Momma and Ms. Waters went through the Guestbook. The bride and groom had left the church about twenty minutes ago, and the front doors were wide open lettin the sticky and humidity in. Me and Ms. Bentley's boyfriend, I mean *companion*, as Momma called him in her voice to make stuff sound more important than it was, me and Ms. Bentley's companion stood in the doorway of the north ex, or whatever it's called, so Momma and Ms. Bentley'd get a clue. He fiddled with his keys in his pocket, tryin real hard not to frown. But he mumbled stuff to himself and smiled at me when he caught me watchin. Momma taught me how to act, though. I could stand there ladylike all day without buttin into grown people's business.

"Well," Ms. Waters said, "I guess not." She raised her eyebrow cuz she didn't believe it herself. Momma, Ms. Bentley, and Ms. Waters stood there and looked at each other for a second before Momma decided we could *finally* go.

Martin Hughes (r) scored 25 points in Fisk's 65-63 victory over the Tennessee State Tigers.

I pushed the liver around on my plate so it wouldn't touch the mashed potatoes. Then I wiped my fork on a napkin so the liver juice wouldn't dirty my peas. I stuffed peas in my mouth, and Momma glared at me.

"You better eat some of that meat, Keisha."

She didn't expect me to eat all of it. She never expected me to eat all my liver, only a mouthful so I never got why she bothered to give it to me. Liver was all spongy, what brains might taste like, cept the liver holds all the stuff that makes puke, and that just makes it worse. Momma cut off a piece the size of my pinky. She shook the plate so hard my peas rolled into the brown streaks.

"There. You can handle that. . . . You know, we didn't see Sugar Daddy today."

Grandmommy sucked her teeth and snorted. "You probably missed that trifling, dirty old man. He must have slipped out."

"No, Mom, his name wasn't even in the Guestbook."

"Maybe he's out of town."

"When did that fool ever miss a summer wedding?"

"Can I git some more mashed potatoes?"

Grandmommy looked at me sideways. "I don't know. *Can* you *git* them? Who taught you to speak that way?"

I opened my mouth real wide and spoke slow. "*May.* I. *Get.* Some. More. Mashed. Po. Ta. Toes?"

"I still see that liver," Momma said.

I picked up the piece she cut off for me with my fingers and swallowed it whole.

"Keisha . . . " Momma said.

"I ate it!"

"Everything else was very sweet. They took communion together, and I really do prefer string quartets to the organ, but it was weird not seeing that chocolate or olive green polyester suit in the back."

"Womanizing antics," Grandmommy mumbled. "They'll survive Sugar Daddy not attending. I'm surprised he never hit on her."

"Mom, you know she's too classy for him."

"Sugar Daddy?" I said.

"I remember when he came to my wedding. I remember the gift."

"Went to mine, too," Grandmommy said.

Grandmommy always brought up something else whenever Momma mentioned anything to do with Daddy. Daddy had moved down to Alabama, so Grandmommy couldn't keep an eye on him. But it was my fault I said I didn't know I could walk five miles without gettin tired. That happened last summer, when Daddy still didn't have enough for a car. I didn't hear everything Grandmommy said over the phone, but she did tell Daddy she'd come down there after him with a shotgun if he dragged me across Mobile again.

So, this summer I didn't get to see him at all, and I was stuck here with Grandmommy making me speak proper.

"May I be excused? I'll be back before the light's gone."

"You watch yourself with Tey and Marcus," Momma said.

Momma and Grandmommy don't like Tey and Marcus much cuz of their father. Grandmommy swears their daddy sold coke or smack or one of them really bad drugs. He been in and out of jail so many times—he gotta be doin *sumthin*, Grandmommy said. Tey and Marcus's grandmother lived next door to Grandmommy for years, and she couldn't believe that woman would let her son turn into such a mess. (But at least she trusted their grandmother, which was the only reason I could play with Marcus and Tey.) I didn't see their father all that much. When he did come around, he'd drive his blue Pinto up and down Jefferson Street at 70 MPH. Late at night, if I heard gears shift three or four times, then a loud screech, I knew he was back in town, back from wherever he was hangin out, at least. Bein in jail was bad, but Marcus and Tey weren't too bad, so their own father couldna been, neither. I wonder if he was like Daddy. Daddy was fine til he got laid off. He spent all last summer lookin for a new job, but nobody bothered to hire him. He couldn't pay for the water for a while, so I had to pee in a bucket (I still ain't told Momma and Grandmommy bout that, and I ain't gonna), but he got a job now. He probably had enough to get a new car. I coulda spent the summer with him, like I'm supposed to. If I just kept my dumb mouth shut.

So, maybe Tey and Marcus's father wasn't so different. Maybe he lost his job and turned to dealin to take care of his two kids. Grandmommy figured he left em next door when he didn't have enough to support em. They showed up at the weirdest times durin the school year and summer and left again sometimes before I could say bye. But they're not bad kids. Not at all. The worst thing they did was sell bootlegs out the back of some dude's car. They thought it was cool cuz they got connections to the music business. I could care less. Those CDs weren't from no real rappers.

"Oooooo, Keisha back in her girlie braids!"

"Shut up, Tey!" Wasn't my fault Momma did my hair right after the weddin. "It looked good. You wish your nappy head could!"

"Your head nappier than mine," Tey said. "Probably why you gotta hide them naps under braids."

I rolled my eyes and watched Marcus light a pagoda. He'd been waitin a while for some to arrive. We were all bored of firecrackers and rockets after the 4th. The pagoda didn't get here in time. Tey smiled at me. I cut my eyes at him and folded my arms. The five stories spun in blues and reds and greens and yellows and whites. Like a water fountain should be, but all on fire and burnin bright. We could shoot fireworks all night if we wanted. Not too many cars came down our street.

"Granny went to a funeral today," Tey said. "How come there're so many weddings and funerals in the summer? Weddings are good, right? Why you wanna celebrate a good thing when everybody dies?"

"Marriage is only good at first. It don't end up that way," Marcus said.

"That still don't tell me nuthin. Why so many people die in the summer anyway? Do heat just fry old people?"

Marcus sucked his teeth. "That cat Granny went to see wasn't old."

"Old," Tey said, "but not *old* old. Forty something-or-other's still up there."

"Can we *do* something else?" I said. Momma was somewhere round 40, and I had no idea how old Grandmommy was. It wasn't never a good thing when a woman hid her age like that.

Sometimes I forgot my wrist bothered me, like a quiet, annoyin sound I could get used to in a room. But it got to itchin before we passed Discount 4 Less. Momma and Grandmommy didn't want me anywhere near the place. They'd be real pissed if they knew I was gettin candy right next door. Discount 4 Less on the corner used to be a Lee's Chicken way back in the day. I loved Lee's. Daddy used to get me a fish sandwich every Saturday at the one not far from where me and Daddy and Momma used to live. When Lee's shut down, somebody tried to turn it into a fashion boutique. Then it was a Meat 'N Three. Didn't nobody have success until these foreign cats started sellin beer and tobacco cheap.

I stopped in the middle of the sidewalk and clenched my teeth real tight. I held my hand hard against my leg and scratched and scratched and dug and dug. I breathed air through my teeth til I started makin hissy sounds. The skin burned, and I scraped some of it away. But underneath the hurt, it was still itchin. I put my wrist in my mouth and nibbled a bit.

"Girl?" Marcus said.

"What's your problem?" Tey said.

"It keep on botherin me." I showed them where I clawed and the little red spots that popped up around it.

"That's what Vaseline's for. If it help your crusty knees, I'm sure it'll fix that."

I kicked at Tey. "Dumbass. I already done tried that."

Durin the summers, most of the teenagers didn't have the students from Tennessee State to hang out with—the freshmen and sophomores who'd put up with them, at least. So all the teenagers could do was bum around like me and Marcus and Tey, cept they didn't like lightin fireworks. All the teenagers round here sat around in cars at Hadley Parks blastin music or crowded outside of Alger's Market at the mini shopping center, right across from Discount 4 Less. The lady who owned Alger's let them mill around as long as they bought sumthin from her first. Plenty of cops cruised by to make sure those knuckleheads didn't cross over to the wrong side of the parkin lot for beer or smoke anythin worse than cigarettes.

Marcus spotted her first. He was always spottin her, watchin her whenever she visited Grandmommy. Ryan could always be found with those girls who got their hair done at the beauty shop every week and got their nails done up with designs, and hand massages, and knew how to look like ladies instead of hos. Grandmommy woulda beat Ryan *and* my aunt if she ever caught Ryan flashin her cleavage crack or a thong. Marcus liked to stare at her long enough just to let her know. She was only a year older, but Marcus was too ghetto for her. He still hadn't figured that out.

"Hey, Ryan!" I yelled. Me and Tey and Marcus were standin in front of the Alger's Market entrance, and Ryan was to our right, almost on top of us. Those girls weren't talkin too loud. Ryan just liked to ignore me. I didn't let her ignore me.

"Ryan, you see me here, girl."

Ryan pretended to laugh with her girlfriends. They made a couple of "Naw, for real?!" faces and slapped each other on the shoulder. Ryan turned her back towards us, flashed her big ol' booty in low-cut tight jeans. That's one thing I never understood about black girls. They could be real skinny like Ryan, but they had them round jello butts that stuck way out in the back. Grandmommy said the Lord had to make sumthin for a man to hold on to, but I couldn't understand how anybody found that cute. I prayed God didn't make my booty big like that.

"*Ryan.*"

She hesitated a second and then darted her eyes towards me. "Oh, hey, KeKe." KeKe. KeKe! Didn't nobody but Ryan call me KeKe no more. I guess she thought that was better than Keisha. She was so proud she didn't have a name like LaShonda or DeVonaé or—Jesus, no!—*Keisha*. She had a nice white girl name. *Ryan*. And didn't let me forget it. Sometimes I wished Aunt Lil'd named her *La*Ryan so she woulda had to gotten over herself.

"I thought Auntie straightened your hair," she said, plinkin one of my barrettes with her fake fingernail.

"She did. It looked good, too!"

"C'mon, Keisha," Tey said.

"You can see I am having a con. ver. sa. tion," and I rolled my eyes. Tey sucked his teeth and went into the store. Marcus smiled at my cousin and followed his brother. Ryan didn't look at him.

"What are you doing with those two hood rats, Keke?"

"We just gettin some candy. We goin straight back home. I promise."

"You know what Auntie and Grandma will do if they find out you were here with them."

"You know what Grandmommy'll do if she find out you wearin lipstick." If God gave a fourteen year-old girl a jelly butt that attracted men, that was His business. But if she wore makeup to get attention, then she was askin for it.

Ryan grinned and tugged one of my braids. "So, how was the wedding?"

"Borin. Too many songs. Chants and stuff where we all had to follow. . . . It was like real church. Momma made a big deal about some guy named Sugar Daddy not bein there. How come they call him after a candy bar?"

Ryan's girlfriends laughed. Ryan said to herself, "Ohhhh my God."

"What?"

"You're a 'tard, KeKe."

"Why?"

"Look, I gotta get home soon. Mom and Dad need me to housesit. I'll catch up with you later, okay?" She turned her back on me and started talkin to her girlfriends again.

Tey and Marcus got a bag full of Rain Blo gum, Junior Mints, candy necklaces, Lemon Heads, Gobstoppers, gummy worms, and Atomic Fireballs. All I could get were Nerds and a couple pieces of banana Laffy Taffy (my favorite). I could stick em down in my pocket and sneak into my room before Grandmommy or Momma realized I'd been to the store.

"You behavin now, baby?" Cashier Lady said when I put my candy up on the counter. That's what she always said to us kids and the teenagers, too. She was real fat, but not jiggly fat. She didn't have a lot of rolls. I remembered when she used to have bulges everywhere, hangin over her pants and shakin right over her elbows. Maybe I was six or seven then. She got smaller every year, sittin there behind the counter sweatin all over her stomach and arm pits and listenin to the oldies AM station.

"Yes, ma'am. I been good."

She turned to open the cash register, and I jumped. Splotches covered her cheek. One wider than my hand, but the others were tiny like somebody beat her with a handful of pebbles. It was like she had that disease where people were brown on the outside, but then they had bright pink dots all over their skin. Like somebody rubbed their black off, and they were really white underneath. Cept Cashier Lady's spots weren't quite like that. Her spots were white-white paper white, or grey like the papier-mâché we sometimes used in art, kinda rough and dirty. If I touched her face, I bet it would feel like that, all soggy newspaper.

"You want a bag, baby?"

I shook my head and shoved my candy in my shorts pockets.

"Then you have a good one."

I nodded and looked away.

When we left the store, Ryan and her girlfriends were walkin up the other side of the street, past the interstate on-ramp. Ryan said sumthin I couldn't understand (Grandmommy'd get after her for talkin so loud), and then all the girls laughed. They were still laughin by the time they got under the overpass, and some boys honked at em as they cruised by. That made Ryan and her friends laugh even harder.

"Damn, that lady's face was wrecked." Marcus was the first to say anythin. We'd already passed Discount 4 Less and headed round the corner. Tey didn't say nuthin cuz he was suckin on a Gobstopper. He gave me a piece of Rain Blo, and I popped it in my mouth so I wouldn't have to say nuthin either.

SweeTarts—July 12

When Grandmommy, Ryan and Aunt Lil got back from the funeral, Momma had lunch waitin. I didn't want to eat with em since Marcus finally got his BB gun. (I didn't tell Momma bout that cuz she probably never woulda let me see the boys again.) We'd been huntin round the alley when Momma called me in and made me wipe a washcloth across my face. I had to be sociable, she said. Especially with family. We ate nuthin but salad—three-bean salad and another salad with Italian dressing, mixed greens, baby tomatoes, black olives, and endamame. Momma and Aunt Lil were really into healthy stuff like endamame.

"Well, he didn't show up today, either," Grandmommy said. "Church's too small for him to hide. Horny old buzzard. He always shows up in that brown suit and tired old hat. To a *funeral*."

"Maybe he doesn't have a black suit," Ryan said. "It's the sentiment that counts anyway, right? He doesn't have to go to everyone's funeral." She was so much better at pretendin to be interested in adult conversations than me.

"Honey, if he wanted to get himself a decent black suit, he certainly could. It's not about sentiment or paying respects with him. He wants to be seen," Grandmommy said.

I scratched the itch on my wrist. Sometimes it crawled up my arm, and I had learned to just live with it. Momma poked me in the side. I forgot to take my elbows off the table.

"You know, Momma, I remember he showed up in that brown polyester suit at my wedding," Aunt Lil said. "I can't believe he's recycled those same two suits all these years."

"He had the olive one at mine," Momma said.

"He seems to put a lot of money and effort into simply being seen. He doesn't *have to* go to all those funerals. He doesn't *have to* bring a present to every wedding," Ryan said.

"Sugar Daddy? What's his real name?"

Momma, Grandmommy, and Aunt Lil looked at me. Then they looked at each other and laughed.

"That's a shame," Momma said. "I can't remember. I probably could have recalled it if you hadn't asked."

"The man always wanted status he couldn't get. He's not an educator or a doctor—I can tell you *that* for certain—but he always finds his way to our weddings, or our children's weddings, or our grandchildren's. How many hours does he have to spend perusing the newspaper only so he can make sure we all know he's there? And if he could bring a present to every wedding, he certainly could have bought *one* decent black suit. Ryan, he's never bothered to show up anywhere else—"

"Aren't weddings and funerals open to everybody if they're in the paper?"

"—He can't find another way to fit in with all that running around he does," Grandmommy said.

"May not only be the weddings and funerals of doctors and teachers and lawyers he goes to. He could go to the janitors' weddings too, Grandma. Have you ever seen him at a janitor's wedding?" Ryan took a long drink of iced tea and hid her mouth down in the glass. Grandmommy looked at her funny and smirked, but didn't say nuthin.

"Did you have enough for the choir today?" Momma asked.

"It was a good turnout, actually," Aunt Lil said. "Not enough men, but you know how that is. Mr. Hughes didn't show up, though."

"He's the most reliable bass you've got," Momma said. Old Mr. Hughes was always there when the choir sang. Sometimes he was the only man standin in the middle of all them sopranos and altos.

Aunt Lil shrugged. "He's never stood me up. He promised he'd be there."

Once it was safe and Grandmommy started talkin bout song selection, Ryan put her glass down and went back to her three-bean salad. I'd put in my time bein sociable. Momma gave me a couple SweeTarts to kill the Italian dressing aftertaste in my mouth. I went back outside cuz I didn't know the next time I'd get to see Marcus use his BB gun before his father stole him and Tey away again.

Marcus said we'd try huntin in the vacant lot next to the Discount 4 Less. The trees across the alley and in front of the Elk's Lodge hung over the open space. Easy to pick off sparrows and starlings. The grass came up a little higher than my elbows, and I kept crunchin on broken bottles.

"We got any snakes, I'll shoot em," Marcus said. He added he was only kiddin bout the snakes, but I didn't need snake bites to go along with the white spot on my wrist. Maybe I scratched it too much and got impetigo after all.

Marcus told us to shut up and stand still. We couldn't see the garbage under our feet, and if we stepped on the wrong things, we'd mess up his shot. He didn't have great aim, I found out real quick, but he swore he was new at this. Each time he missed—truth be told—I was kinda relieved, but sad. I never saw nobody kill nuthin before, and I wanted to see as much in life as I could. (A person wasn't worth much if they wasn't well-rounded.) Watch sumthin flappin around one minute and then see it fall to the ground and never move again the next. One time while I waited for Daddy to pick me up for the weekend, the pit bull belongin to the boy up the street was just strollin through the neighborhood. I forgot sumthin and went to get it, and when I came back out on the porch, the pit bull was laid up on the sidewalk. Hardly any blood at all. It would kinda be like that, cept I'd finally know what it looked like when sumthin died. Bugs didn't count. I wondered what happened when that boy found his dog. I wondered if the person who hit him cared at all. I wondered how Marcus would act if he ever shot anythin.

He aimed at a sparrow perched on a limb across the alley. Its head poked out from a clump of leaves. Me and Tey leaned forward. Marcus waited. He looked at the sparrow. Then looked behind us back at Jefferson Street. Then he looked at the sparrow. Then back at Jefferson Street.

"What you waitin for?"

He shushed me.

"C'mon, man," Tey said.

The sparrow flew away. Marcus threw his gun-free hand in the air, rolled his head up towards the sky, and closed his eyes. "What did I tell you bout shuttin the hell up?"

"You took too damn long," Tey said.

"Y'all didn't see that car? Silver Buick sedan? It's only passed by here four or five times."

"No," we said.

"Why are those niggas spyin on us?" Marcus said.

"Why you think they want anythin to do with us? Paranoid," Tey said.

"Maybe cuz every time they come by, they stare right at us."

Marcus was right. The sedan passed, and maybe it was gone for two or three minutes. Then we'd see it on the other side of the street, and it'd turn back around. They eventually parked at Discount 4 Less. A woman with a long weave curled in spirals all over her head got outta the car. A strand of hair fell in her face, and she pushed it back with a six-inch-long acrylic nail. She didn't buy nuthin and came right back out. They turned down the alley and come straight at us.

Spiral Head rolled down her window. Another girl sat in the passenger's seat. Her head was covered in very neat micro braids. Momma wouldn't even let me get braids like that.

"Y'all know where we can find Mona's Beauty Salon?" Spiral Head sounded real country.

Marcus snorted. He and Tey looked at me. I shrugged and shook my head. "Sorry, never heard of it."

The girls raised their eyebrows. "My cousin told me Mona's was in the shopping center across from the Discount 4 Less and behind the Elk's Lodge," Spiral Head said. "We been up and down Jefferson, but we haven't seen a shopping center."

"Your cousin from around here?" Marcus asked.

"Naw. She goes to State. We'll be attendin in the fall. Just checkin out the area. Y'all sure Mona's not around here? She said it was next to a convenience store in the shopping center."

"Sorry, lady," Tey said.

"Got any idea where it is?"

We shook our heads. They looked at each other a little confused and upset, but they thanked us and went on down the alley.

"What we know bout a beauty salon?" Tey said under his breath.

Actually, I could sympathize. Sorta. Not that Momma'd ever let me get my hair done in a beauty salon at my age, but one of my grandfathers used to own a barber shop. I couldn't remember which grandfather, though. Grandmommy never talked about her ex-husband, and I'd only met him once when me and Daddy ran into him at Farmer's Market. Nobody really discussed Daddy's family either. All I knew about his father was he had water-wave hair, and he didn't have no greys when he died. One of my grandfathers was a postman, and one owned the barber shop. I get them mixed up. Actually, I'm not sure about the postman thing, neither. I think I remembered hearin it one time.

My grandfather had the barber shop back durin the 40s or 50s. It was so long ago, it didn't matter which decade. It used to be where the interstate is now. His barber shop and a bunch of other businesses. I had no idea what all those buildings used to look like. So, I could get why those girls were upset. Maybe Mona did hair real good, like my grandfather probably did. Maybe back then, after they tore down everythin, some country cat was comin to see the big city, and said he needed a good cut while he was here. It was startin to get a little scruffy up top. His cousin, or his best friend, or his brother who used to live here, told him to go see my grandfather. So, he's lookin forward to his hair cut, and all he found when he got here was lots of construction—or maybe the completed interstate by then. That would have pissed me off too.

"You heard a Mona's?" I asked Grandmommy when I got home. We got out the collard greens for dinner and started trimmin them since Momma wasn't off work yet.

"*Have* I heard of Mona's? No. Should I have?"

"I don't know. . . . Where was my grandfather's barber shop?" I figured I should ask her instead of Daddy. If she picked up the line while I was talkin to him, she might think he called me. I didn't want her threatenin him with a shotgun again. "Did Daddy's father have the barber shop?"

Grandmommy blinked and put down the leaf she worked on. "Barber shop? Oh, yes! That was your other grandfather's. Why'd you drag that up?"

"I wanna know where it was. I never known, I never *have* known where it was."

"It was somewhere along the path of the interstate. Somewhere near a dime store . . . I think."

"But *where*?" I said.

"Keisha, I can't remember. . . . You're leaving too much of the leaf on the stem. Watch what you're doing."

"He didn't start a new one?"

"Where was he going to put it? The white part of town?"

"So he didn't get a new one? Did they pay him for it?"

"Who? The government? You know the government never paid us for anything."

"So everybody lost their business and didn't get nuthin back? That ain't fair!"

"It *ain't*?" Grandmommy said. "There was no sense in reasoning out fair and unfair. It was always unfair—"

"Well, it *ain't* fair," I said rippin at the leaves. My fingers throbbed. My arm itched from my wrist all the way past my elbow. It wasn't fair, and I'd never know where his business was, and nobody seemed to care, neither.

The cryin started a few days after that. Don't know where it come from. I just know it wouldn't stop. I thought maybe I cried so much cuz the government took my grandfather's barber shop and never paid him back. But I couldna been that mad to cry so long and hard about it, and Tey started cryin too. Marcus wouldn't have nuthin to do with us no more, puttin up with us dumbass sissies.

At first Momma believed I got all weepy cuz I wasn't gettin enough sleep. The Department of Transportation did emergency work all day and all night to repair the overpass crossin Jefferson. Nobody knew what really happened. Not an earthquake or a freak electrical storm or a meteor or chunk of sumthin else fallen from the sky. Part of the overpass just wasn't *there* no more. When you looked at it from the street, part of the green siding and railing was gone. One lane looked like somebody took an eraser and scrubbed it a little bit thinner, and then the hand got shaky and scratched out most of the other lane. But it didn't look like nuthin was broken, only made that way to begin with.

Me and Tey weren't the only two cryin though. Sometimes we'd catch other kids in the neighborhood snifflin or wipin their eyes with the backs of their hands. Adults tried to make us explain it, but why? Sometimes sadness is all it is, and it comes from a deep hole nobody sees, and sometimes that hole can close up as soon as it opened. That's what it felt like. There was some huge hole somewhere—huger than a black hole—and it was so big and wide all we could do was cry because that's how deep and empty it felt. Like I could fall in that black hole and keep sinkin on forever. Try tellin a grownup any of that.

Tey and I sat on the curb in front of his grandmother's house and got all our cryin out for the day. We didn't look at each other or try to make one another feel better. We just wailed away with our eyes shut tight and our faces up to the sky. We didn't stop to blow our noses or keep our heads from achin. I had to wear long sleeves now, and that made it worse. I was sweaty, my hair got all poofy, and I ended up with snot and tears on my clothes. We always felt numb when we were done, like we could just pass out.

Tey wiped his face in his shirt and whined a little. I thought he might start up again, but he coughed, and that was the end of it. I was lightheaded. I rested against my knees and closed my eyes.

"Granny's got that itchin," Tey said. "She put everythin on it she can think of, but it don't go away. She said it don't bother her, but she always scratchin her chest."

He was gonna make me cry again. "Tey . . . " I pulled back my sleeve. He poked at my arm. A large splotch of white, paper-white white, trailed up from my wrist to my elbow. All along my arm, there were these spots, like somebody beat it with a handful of pebbles.

"Will that happen to Granny?"

I put my finger to my mouth, and now the tears were comin. "I don't know."

He whispered in my ear, "What the hell is that, Keisha?"

I shook my head. He looked back at his grandmother's house, then back at me.

"I'm sure it'll go away," he said.

But he knew we both couldn't know that. We'd never seen anythin like this before.

COMMUNITY NEWS

Alger MacAdams will be turning over the everyday responsibilities of his store to his only daughter, Ms. Marla MacAdams. Mr. MacAdams has been a regular, friendly face at Alger's Market since he opened the store in 1974. He had been considering handing over the reigns to his daughter since his wife Diana died early last February. "Marla's been observing and helping me the last twenty-three years. She knows what to do, and I know she can do it on her own." MacAdams intends to remain active. He will still coordinate Second Avenue Baptist's food drives and tutor math at Hadley Park's Community Center. Alger's Market is located at 1507 B on Jefferson Street, next door to Mona's Beauty Salon behind Elk's Lodge #41.

Caption: Alger MacAdams and his daughter greet customers outside of Alger's Market.

Sugar Daddy—July 20

Everybody cried at Mrs. Probst's funeral. *Everybody.* And hardly anybody liked Mrs. Probst, far as I could tell. She cheated on all three of her husbands, she controlled the United Methodist Women, and the pastor did whatever she said. When Mama didn't think I was listenin, she called Mrs. Probst a bitch. I had my own beef with her. She changed the services and made church even longer. But Uncle David held me while I wept, and his tears drained through my hair. Momma had pressed my hair for the funeral and gotten it nice and straight, but the curls tightened and frizzed under Uncle David's chin. Aunt Lil cried so hard she could barely conduct the choir. Over in the soprano section, Ryan leaned on Grandmommy, and Grandmommy did everythin she could to stay upright. Momma lay in the aisle. She didn't even bother with appearin ladylike.

We coulda blamed this on the Holy Spirit—He did people that way sometimes, but not everybody all at once. He might fall on one or two people, they'd shake and wail, and then they'd fall out. We wished we could do that now. All we could hear was our own shriekin and screamin. Water puddled at our feet. Our noses clogged up, and our stomachs hurt.

Mr. Hughes didn't come. He wasn't at church last Sunday, neither. We didn't look for Sugar Daddy. He hadn't shown up to the last two weddings. We gave up on him comin here.

We planned to go straight to Swett's after the funeral, but we had to change our clothes first. None of us really talked while we ate. Momma said, "The old biddy didn't deserve all that hollering," and that was about it. We were too tired to talk, me and Momma, Grandmommy, Ryan, and Aunt Lil and Uncle David. We had a hard enough time gettin our forks to our mouths.

I can't lie. I wanted summer to be over with. I wanted to get back to school. I wouldn't have to answer so many questions from people who weren't from around here, questions about their friends or family we swore never lived here, even though strangers insisted the opposite. I wouldn't have to explain to em about some of the buildings in the area, why there was only half a building, or nuthin but a window or door hangin in space with no walls to hold it up. Maybe by the end of the summer, all this nonsense would go away, and I could go to sleep knowin Momma and Grandmommy hadn't disappeared on me by the time I woke up in the mornin. The white marks on my arm would heal up, and so would Tey's grandmother's, and I'd never have to worry that Daddy might come lookin for me one day, and nobody'd know who he was talkin bout.

I was lyin flat on my stomach with my arms at my sides. I hated sleepin in that position, but it was the only one that worked now. My stomach felt so hollow, like I hadn't eaten in years, and that black hole might rise up within me and snatch me from the inside out. I started lyin like this to stretch my stomach out, quiet it down so it quit all the grumblin.

Usually, Momma wouldn't let me catnap durin the day, especially not durin the summer when I could be runnin around gettin exercise. Not much use for that now. Sometimes Momma didn't feel like wakin me up after all of her cryin. I was happy when she did, though. Sometimes when I slept, I slipped down into that black hole. Didn't know if I'd ever wake outta it. When I opened my eyes, I felt like it had puked me up.

Momma knocked on my door and stuck her head in. "Tey wants to know if you can play."

I sighed and got up. He was worse off than me, so I couldn't leave him alone. He knew if his daddy came and got him and Marcus, their grandmother might disappear on em before the next time they came to see her.

We stood on my porch and stared at the street. We struggled for stuff to do. Sometimes we squished ants out on the sidewalk and watched other bugs carry them away, kinda like providin a bug Farmer's Market. But we got tired of that. Without Marcus supervisin us, Tey's grandmother wouldn't let us set off fireworks. Marcus still wouldn't put up with us, even though he tried to sneak his own tears by pullin his shirt collar up over his eyes. We couldn't play with the BB gun. We *wouldn't* play kick ball with the other kids in the neighborhood. We only made each other cry.

"We can catch crayfish," Tey said after a while.

I yawned. Nobody wanted us playin in the creek water, but the last couple days of July had been beat our ass. I didn't care if I got polluted water on me or not. "Okay. Let's go."

Tey got us some Mason jars, and we climbed over the short bridge on the other side of our street. The creek was more like a wide, really long gutter, and most of the time, I took for granted it was there, since there were a few houses down here we never visited. I didn't know if it ran into a lake, or a river, or whatever. I guess it was clean water once-upon-a-time. I never bothered askin when that was.

Tey moved some rocks around and swished his hand in the water. I sat on the concrete bank and put my head in my hands. He scooped the Mason jar down, cussed to himself when he didn't catch nuthin, and dumped the water out. He scooped the Mason jar down several times. I couldn't figure out what he was tryin to fish since I didn't see no life in that water.

He screwed up his face and held the jar to the sunlight. "*Unhhhh.*"

I stood up but didn't get in the water with him so Momma wouldn't know where I'd been. He jiggled the jar for me. Somthin feathery swirled.

"What, you got some toilet paper?"

"Ew, girl!"

We looked at it again with our noses almost to the glass. It *was* paper, with a few larger chunks and thousands and thousands of smaller pieces spinnin round like dust.

"Where'd it come from?" I said.

Tey kicked at the water. He pulled a large rock away from the bank. A sliver of newspaper tore apart and washed down the creek. We went down the bank and found more newspaper. Some of it dried up on rocks and broken concrete in a shriveled mess. By the time we knew where we were, the creek had taken us past some apartment buildings and down a dirt alley behind a street cut short by a fence in front of some railroad tracks. I never been down that way before, and neither had Tey. The houses were small, and some had been abandoned. Most of the backyards were junky, cept for one that had no grass at all. It was hard clay converted to a basketball court, with the baskets nailed to trees. The people watchin and playin were too busy to notice us passin through.

Tall weeds almost hid the back of the house at the end of the street. The air conditioner had been ripped out, and we could see it lyin in the high grass. There was a carport, but no car. The grass was high under there too. The back-door was open just a little, and there was a bunch of paper thrown across the porch. Some of it had blown into the yard, down into the creek. Tey pulled the weeds out of his way and started towards the house. I yanked at his arm, and he smacked my hand.

"We gotta go back," I said. "We can't be trespassin."

"I bet nobody live here."

"Soooo? It's still trespassin."

He grabbed me and pulled me into the yard. This time we wouldn't have Marcus's BB gun to protect us from snakes. Tey stuck his head in the hole where the air conditioner used to be. "I bet this is how they robbed the house."

"We can use the door," I said, but Tey had already crawled in. He pulled me through, and we were in a kitchen. It reeked of old meat, the kind that gets forgotten at the back of the refrigerator. We pinched our noses with our shirts. Tey coughed, and I rubbed my eyes. Canisters and spices had been thrown on the floor. Our feet ground rice and pasta and salt into newspaper clippings.

"Damn, it stinks," I said.

Tey picked a piece of paper off the floor. Some of the type was smudged, but we made out an article on the closin of some gas station.

The table in the kitchen'd been flipped over, and it blocked our way into the dinin room. I brushed broken glass off the counter with my long sleeves, we hopped onto the counter, and jumped over the table. The china cabinet had been smashed open, and maybe a few plates were taken. We didn't find any busted up on the floor. The smell got worse in the hallway. There were so many books and binders everywhere we couldn't help but step on em. The basement door at the end of the hall was open. We peeked into the bedroom with more cutouts from newspapers and stacks of photo albums toppled over. Even without somebody sackin the place, there was hardly any room in there to move around or sleep.

"I don't think whoever robbed the place got anythin valuable," Tey said through his shirt. "Do you wanna go in there?" It's where the stink come from. I'd never seen a dead body before a mortician fixed it up nice, let alone reported I'd found one. I nodded.

Tey took one step into that den, started coughin, and ran into the basement. I stood in the doorway and didn't go no farther. He sat on the couch, head laid back, and his blood dirtied up the cushions. He didn't have nuthin on on top, but his pants were old, like sumthin they wore in the 70s. He was big, but not fat, how old men can get a little wide with a round belly. The bookcase had been thrown over him, or it landed across his legs when the robber pushed it outta the way. I figured he was already dead when that happened. He didn't look like he tried to avoid it. From where I stood, I couldn't tell if he'd been shot in the head or been hit, but he was readin the paper when he died, which I guess was the way it shoulda been. It was pinned against his legs and the bookcase. I couldn't tell if his eyes were wide open or closed. He was a dark man, and his face was just pudgy enough to keep the wrinkles from bein deep in his cheeks. He had big hands. His knuckles were thick, and the skin over them was rough.

"*Keishaaa . . .*"

Tey had turned the light on down in the basement. Scrapbooks and photo albums piled high to the ceilin. They were numbered by year. Tey sat on the dirty orange carpet flippin through a binder in his lap. I took the closest to me—"Students 2005." The man had pasted articles and pictures from *The Sentinel* and *Black Nashvillian*. There were pictures he'd taken from high schools. Track meets. Basketball games. Scores from all of TSU's and Fisk's wins. I recognized my middle school auditorium. He had several shots of one of our choral nights. There was a National Merit Scholar list from *The Tennessean*. Four of the names were highlighted in blue. I knew one of them, Tony Diggs. Ryan went to school with him. She talked to him every once in a while cuz he wasn't too ghetto. Uncle David thought they'd make a good couple, if he let Ryan date.

"What you got?"

"Weddings. They *real* old," Tey said. He held the book up for me. Lots of black and white photos with the bride and groom headin down the aisle. Next to each one was the announcement for the weddin from the newspaper.

A couple of tears slipped down my cheeks. Sugar Daddy was upstairs. Tey stared at me all wide-eyed. If I started cryin again, he wouldn't be able to control himself, neither. I crawled in between the stacks lookin for the 50s and 40s. I pulled books out, and cobwebs flew in my face. We both sneezed. Sugar Daddy had articles for promotions and store openings and new partnerships and offices. Laundromats, and dress shops, and dime stores. Soda shops and diners. The clippings mentioned streets I never heard of before. There were photos of buildings I never seen.

"Keisha, I'm gettin sick."

"Wait."

Maybe he had a photo of my grandfather in front of his barber shop, maybe of my grandfather *in* his barber shop cuttin hair. Or my grandfather, whichever one, as a postman. Or Grandmommy's weddin. I turned up more dust and cobwebs. They burned my eyes. Me and Tey coughed and sneezed.

"*Keisha . . .*"

Sugar Daddy had to have them here somewhere. Seemed like he had everybody else. I saw a group photo of a fraternity with a head in the back that coulda been a young Mr. Hughes. There were pictures of protestors watchin the interstate construction. I looked for my family there among those people with picket signs and banners. I couldn't find them.

"Girl, I'm gonna puke all over you!"

"Okay! Okay! Okay!" I threw the book down and wiped the tears from my face with my sleeves. But my sleeves were covered in dirt, and my eyes only stung more.

In the backyard, I gathered all of the photos and newspaper cutouts I could find. I didn't care if I got bit. I didn't care if chiggers dug into my arms. The sun had gotten to some of the photos. Peoples' faces disappeared behind fading colors the shape of cigarette burns. I could make out an eye, the side of a mouth, or hand, but the rest of em was gone. Houses missed roofs, or store windows had faded out. Tey was across the alley before he noticed I wasn't followin.

"What you doin?"

"We have to save them!" I showed him my handful of photos and articles.

"We have to tell somebody there's a old dead cat in that house."

I went back to the porch and put the photos and newspaper cutouts in a neat stack. I put a rock on top of them to make sure they didn't blow away. I gasped and ran farther down the creek, under the bridge where the train tracks went overhead. Way in the distance was the farm land on the TSU campus. I had no idea how far from home I was. There weren't no buildings out here.

"Pick up everythin you can find."

"Keisha, we gotta go."

"Pick em up!" I yelled.

Paper clogged a drain. It was soggy and looked like it never had words or faces on it at all. We took up a few of Sugar Daddy's photos out from the rocks and on the banks where the sun had baked some of em blank.

Tey sighed and rolled his eyes. "Keisha, come *on!* It's all ruined." He dropped the washed out photos back into the water.

I dug into the wet newspaper to see if I could make out any names, any faces. Put pages back together so I could bring the people back. There was nuthin that made sense. Just mush and clumps of black and grey. I crawled through the rocks. My knees turned up more drowned clippings and pictures the light bleached out.

"No! No! No!" I pounded on the rocks and cut my hands. I gathered all the photos I could and shuffled through them. "We have to save em all. We have to save em *all*! We can't lose no more. We have to put em back where Sugar Daddy had em!"

"Keisha? You okay? Keisha?" I heard him comin up behind me. He put his hand on my arm and drew it back real fast when I screamed.

I didn't mean to. I didn't mean to scream at all, but it came roarin outta me til I thought my throat might bleed. I found a man I recognized in one of the photos. Sugar Daddy must have been on the opposite sidewalk when he took the picture on Jefferson Street. Maybe it was the day of TSU's Homecoming Parade. Girls were twirlin their batons in the street. The man watched them go by with a little girl sittin on his shoulders. The man had water-wave hair, and he wore thick, black frames. Sometimes I couldn't exactly remember Daddy's face, even though I should have, even though it hadn't been that long since I last saw him. But I didn't forget his chin. This man had a chin like Daddy's, and I sat on his shoulders with a big grin on my face, arms raised. The sun had gotten to this picture too. Some of the crowd had disappeared behind white spots. On my little arm, from the wrist and up to my elbow, I had been erased.

I couldn't breathe. I sucked in air and screamed like I lost my mind, and maybe I had. I gasped and sobbed so hard my head fell in and I sucked up water. Tey pulled me out and wrung the water out my braid. He looked over my shoulder at the photo tremblin in my hand. Then he fell on his knees beside me. All we could do was listen to me wail.

We just sat there in the middle of the creek with dirt and newspaper clingin to our skin. The sun dried our backs. I wiped the photo dry against my chest and tucked it in my undershirt before any of the rest of me faded away.

SECRET IDENTITY

KELLY LINK

Dear Paul Zell.

Dear Paul Zell is exactly how far I've gotten at least a dozen times, and then I get a little farther, and then I give up. So this time I'm going to try something new. I'm going to pretend that I'm not writing you a letter, Paul Zell, dear Paul Zell. I'm so sorry. And I *am* sorry, Paul Zell, but let's skip that part for now or else I won't get any farther this time, either. And in any case: how much does it matter whether or not I'm sorry? What difference could it possibly make?

So. Let's pretend that we don't know each other. Let's pretend we're meeting for the first time, Paul Zell. We're sitting down to have dinner in a restaurant in a hotel in New York City. I've come a long way to have dinner with you. We've never met face-to-face. Everything I ever told you about myself is more or less a lie. But you don't know that yet. We think we may be in love.

We met in FarAway, online, except now here we are up close. I could reach out and touch your hand. If I was brave enough. If you were really here.

Our waiter has poured you a glass of red wine. Me? I'm drinking a Coke because I'm not old enough to drink wine. You're thirty-four. I'm almost sixteen.

I'm so sorry, Paul Zell. I don't think I can do this. (Except I have to do this.) *I have to do this.* So let's try again. (I keep trying again and again and again.) Let's start even farther back, before I showed up for dinner and you didn't. Except I think you did. Am I right?

You don't have to answer that. I owe you the real story, but you don't owe me anything at all.

Picture the lobby of a hotel. In the lobby, a fountain with Spanish tiles in green and yellow. A tiled floor, leather armchairs, corporate art, this bank of glass-fronted elevators whizzing up and down, a bar. Daddy bar to all the mini-bars in all the rooms. Sound familiar? Maybe you've been here before.

Now fill up the lobby with dentists and superheroes. Men and women, oral surgeons, eighth-dimensional entities, mutants, and freaks who want to save your teeth, save the world, and maybe end up with a television show, too. I've seen a dentist or two in my time, Paul Zell, but we don't get many superheroes out on the plain. We get tornadoes instead. There are two conventions going on at the hotel, and they're mingling around the fountain, tra la la, tipping back drinks.

Boards in the lobby list panels on advances in cosmetic dentistry, effective strategies for minimizing liability in cases of bystander hazard, presentations with titles like "Spandex or Bulletproof? What Look Is Right for You?" You might be interested in these if you were a dentist or a superhero. Which I'm not. As it turns out, I'm not a lot of things.

A girl is standing in front of the registration desk. That's me. And where are you, Paul Zell?

The hotel clerk behind the desk is only a few years older than me. (Than that girl, the one who's come to meet Paul Zell. Is it pretentious or pitiful or just plain psychotic the way I'm talking about myself in the third person? Maybe it's all three. I don't care.) The clerk's nametag says Aliss, and she reminds the girl that I wish wasn't me of someone back at school. Erin Toomey, that's who. Erin Toomey is a hateful bitch. But never mind about Erin Toomey.

Aliss the hotel clerk is saying something. She's saying, "I'm not finding anything." It's eleven o'clock on a Friday morning, and at that moment the girl in the lobby is missing third-period biology. Her fetal pig is wondering where she is.

Let's give the girl in line in the hotel lobby a name. Everybody gets a name, even fetal pigs. (I call mine Alfred.) And now that you've met Aliss and Alfred, minor characters both, I might as well introduce our heroine. That is, me. Of course it isn't like FarAway. I don't get to choose my name. If I did, it wouldn't be Billie Faggart. That ring any bells? No, I didn't think it would. Since fourth grade, which is when I farted while I was coming down the playground slide, everyone at school has called me Smelly Fagfart. That's because Billie Faggart is a funny name, right? Except girls like Billie Faggart don't have much of a sense of humor.

There's another girl at school, Jennifer Groendyke. Everyone makes jokes about us. About how we'll move to California and marry each other. You'd think we'd be friends, right? But we're not. I'm not good at the friends thing. I'm like the girl equivalent of one of those baby birds that fall out of a nest and then some nice person picks the baby bird up and puts it back. Except that now the baby bird smells all wrong. I think I smell wrong.

If you're wondering who Melinda Bowles is, the thirty-two-year-old woman you met in FarAway, no, you've never really met her. Melinda Bowles has never sent late-night e-mails to Paul Zell, not ever. Melinda Bowles would never catch a bus to New York City to meet Paul Zell because she doesn't know that Paul Zell exists.

Melinda Bowles has never been to FarAway.

Melinda Bowles has no idea who the Enchantress Magic Eight-ball is. She's never hung out online with the master thief Boggle. I don't think she knows what a MMORPG is.

Melinda Bowles has never played a game of living chess in King Nermal's Chamber in the Endless Caverns under the Loathsome Rock. Melinda Bowles doesn't know a rook from a writing desk. A pawn from a prawn.

Here's something that you know about Melinda Bowles that is true. She used to be married, but is now divorced and lives in her parents' house. She teaches high school. I used her name when I signed up for an account on FarAway. More about my sister Melinda later.

Anyway. Girl-liar Billie says to desk-clerk Aliss, "No message? No envelope? Mr. Zell, Paul Zell?" (That's you. In case you've forgotten.) "He's a guest here? He said he was leaving something for me at the front desk."

"I'll look again if you want," Aliss says. But she does nothing. Just stands there staring malevolently past Billie as if she hates the world and everyone in it.

Billie turns around to see who Aliss is glaring at. There's a nor-mal-looking guy behind Billie; behind him, out in the lobby, there are all sorts of likely candidates. Who doesn't hate a dentist? Or maybe Aliss isn't crazy about superheroes. Maybe she's contemplating the thing that looks like a bubble of blood. If you were there, Paul Zell, you might stare at the bubble of blood, too. You can just make out the silhouette of someone/something inside.

Billie doesn't keep up with superheroes, not really, but she feels as if she's seen the bloody bubble on the news. Maybe it saved the world once. It levitates three feet above the marble floor of the atrium. It plops bloody drops like a sink faucet in Hell. Maybe Aliss worries someone will slip on the lobby floor, break an ankle, sue the hotel. Or maybe the bubble of blood owes her ten bucks.

The bubble of blood drifts over to the Spanish-tiled fountain. It clears the lip, just barely; comes to a halt two feet above the surface of the water. Now it looks like an art installation, albeit kind of a disgusting one. But perhaps it is seeing a heroic role for itself: scaring off the kind of children who like to steal pennies from fountains. Future criminal masterminds might turn their energies in a more productive direction. Perhaps some will become dentists.

Were you a boy who stole coins from fountains, Paul Zell?

We're not getting very far in this story, are we? Maybe that's because some parts of it are so very hard to tell, Paul Zell. So here I linger, not at the beginning and not even in the middle. Already it's more of a muddle. Maybe you won't even make it this far, Paul Zell, but me, I have to keep going. I would make a joke about superheroic efforts, but that would just be me, delaying some more.

Behind the desk, even Aliss has gotten tired of waiting for me to get on with the story. She's stopped glaring, is clacking on a keyboard with her too-long nails. There's glitter residue around her hairline, and a half-scrubbed-off club stamp on her right hand. She says to Billie, "Are you a guest here? What was your name again?"

"Melinda Bowles," Billie says. "I'm not a guest. Paul Zell is staying here? He said he would leave something for me behind the desk."

"Are you here to audition?" Aliss says. "Because maybe you should go ask over at the convention registration."

"Audition?" Billie says. She has no idea what Aliss is talking about. She's forming her backup plan already: walk back to Port Authority and catch the next bus back to Keokuk, Iowa. That would have been a simpler e-mail to write, I see now. *Dear Paul Zell. Sorry. I got cold feet.*

"Aliss, my love. Better lose the piercing." The guy in line behind Billie is now up at the counter beside her. His hand is stamped, like Aliss's. Smudgy licks of black eyeliner around his eyes. "Unless you want management to write you a Dear John."

"Oh, shit." Aliss's hand goes up to her nose. She ducks down behind the counter. "Conrad, you asshole. Where did you go last night?"

"No idea," Conrad says. "I was drunk. Where did you go?"

"Home." Aliss says it like wielding a dagger. She's still submerged. "You want something? Room need making up? Night-shift Darin said he saw you in the elevator around three in the morning. With a girl." *Girl* is another dagger.

"Entirely possible," Conrad says. "Like I said, drunk. Need any help down there? Taking out the piercing? Helping this kid? Because I want to make last night up to you. I'm sorry, okay?"

Which would be the right thing to say, but Billie thinks this guy sounds not so penitent. More like he's swallowing a yawn.

"That's *very* nice of you, but I'm *fine*." Aliss snaps upright. The piercing is gone and her eyes glitter with either tears or rage. "This must be for you," she tells Billie in a cheery, desk-clerk robot voice. It's not much of an improvement on the stabby voice. "I'm *so* sorry about the confusion." There's an envelope in her hand.

Billie takes the envelope and goes to sit on a sofa beside a dentist. He's wearing a convention badge with his name on it, and where he comes from, and that's how she knows he isn't a superhero and that he isn't Paul Zell.

She opens her envelope. There's a room key inside and a piece of paper with a room number written on it. Nothing else. What is this, FarAway? Billie starts to laugh like an utter maniac. The dentist stares.

Forgive her. She's been on a bus for over twenty hours. Her hair is stiff with bus crud and her clothes smell like bus, a cocktail of chemical cleaners and other people's breath, and the last thing she was expecting when she went off on this quest, Paul Zell, was to find herself in a hotel full of superheroes and dentists.

It's not like we get a lot of superheroes in Keokuk, Iowa. There's the occasional flyover or Superheroes on Ice event, and every once in a while someone in Keokuk discovers they have the strength of two men, or can predict the sell-by date on cans of tuna in the supermarket with 98.2 percent accuracy, but even minor-league talents head out of town pretty quickly. They take off for Hollywood, to try and get on a reality show. Or New York or Chicago or even Baltimore, to form novelty rock bands or fight crime or both.

But, here's the thing; the thing is that, under ordinary circumstances, Billie would have nothing better to do than to watch a woman with a raven's head wriggling upstream through the crowd around the lobby bar, over to the fountain and that epic bubble of blood. The woman holds up a pink drink, she's standing on tiptoes, and a slick four-fingered hand emerges from the bubble of blood and takes the glass from her. Is it a love story? How does a woman with a raven's beak kiss a bubble of blood? Paul Zell, how are you and me any more impossible than that?

Maybe it's just two old friends having a drink. The four-fingered hand orients the straw into the membrane or force field or whatever it is, and the glass empties itself like a magic trick. The bubble quivers.

But: Paul Zell. All Billie can think about is you, Paul Zell. She has the key to Paul Zell's hotel room. Back before she met you, way far back in FarAway, Billie was always up for a quest. Why not? She had nothing better to do. And the quest always went like this: Find yourself in a strange place. Encounter a guardian. Outwit them or kill them or persuade them to give you the item they've been guarding. A weapon or a spell or the envelope containing the key to room 1584.

Except the key in Billie's hand is a real key, and I don't do that kind of quest much anymore. Not since I met you, Paul Zell. Not since the Enchantress Magic EightBall met the master thief Boggle in King Nermal's Chamber and challenged him to a game of chess.

While I'm coming clean, here's a minor confession. Why not. Why should you care that, besides Enchantress Magic EightBall, I used to have two other avatars in FarAway. There's Constant Bliss, who's an elfin healer and frankly kind of a pill, and there's Bear-hand, who, as it turns out, was kind of valuable in terms of accumulated points, especially weapons class. There was a period, you see, when things were bad at school and things were worse at home, which I don't really want to talk about, and anyway, it was a bad period during which I liked running around and killing things. Whatever. Last month I sold Bearhand when you and I were planning all of this, for bus fare. It wasn't a big deal. I'd kind of stopped being Bearhand except for every once in a while, when you weren't online and I was lonely or sad or had a really, really shitty day at school.

I'm thinking I may sell off Constant Bliss, too, if anyone wants to buy her. If not, it will have to be Magic EightBall. Or maybe I'll sell both of them. But that's part of the story I haven't gotten to yet.

And, yeah, I do spend a lot of time online. In FarAway. Like I said, it's not like I have a lot of friends, not that you should feel sorry for me, because you shouldn't, Paul Zell, that's NOT why I'm telling you all of this.

My sister? Melinda? She says wait a few years and see. Things get better. Of course, based on her life, maybe they do get better. And then they get worse again, and then you have to move back home and teach high school. So how exactly is that better?

And yes, in case you're wondering, my sister Melinda Bowles is kind of stunning, and all the boys in my school who despise me have crushes on her even when she flunks them. And yes, a lot of the details I fed you about my life, Billie Faggart's life, are actually borrowed from Melinda's life. Although not all of the details. If you're still speaking to me after you read this, I'll be happy to make up a spreadsheet of character traits and biographical incidents. One column will be Melinda Bowles and the other will be Billie Faggart. There will be little checkmarks in either column, or both, depending. But the story about shaving off my eyebrows when I was a kid?

That was true. I mean, that was me. And so was the thing about liking reptiles. Melinda? She's not so fond of the reptiles. But then, maybe you don't really have a chameleon named Moe and a tokay gecko named Bitey. Maybe you made up some stuff, too, except yeah, okay, why would you make up some lizards? I keep having to remind myself: Billie, just because you're a liar doesn't mean the whole world is full of liars. Except that you did lie, right? You were at the hotel. You left me the key to your room at the hotel in an envelope addressed to Melinda Bowles. Because if you didn't, then who did?

Sorry. This is supposed to be about me, apologizing. Not me, solving the big mysteries of the universe and everything. Except, here's the thing about Melinda, in case you're thinking maybe the person you fell in love with really exists. The *salient* thing. Melinda has a boyfriend. He's in Afghanistan right now. Also, she's super religious, like seriously born again. Which you're not. So even if Melinda's boyfriend got killed, or something, which I know is something she worries about, it would never work out between you and her.

And one more last thing about Melinda, or maybe it's actually about you. This is the part where I have to thank you. Because: *because* of you, Paul Zell, I think Melinda and I have kind of become friends. Because, all year I've been interested in her life. I ask her how her day was, and I actually listen when she tells me. Because, how else could I convince you that I was a thirty-two-year-old, divorced high-school algebra teacher? And it turns out that we actually have a lot in common, me and Melinda, and it's like I even *understand* what she thinks about. Because, she has a boyfriend who's far away (in Afghanistan) and she misses him and they write e-mails to each other, and she worries about what if he loses a leg or something, and will they still love each other when he gets back?

And I have you. I had this thing with you, even if I couldn't tell her about you. I guess I still can't tell her. Which is even weirder, I guess, than the other thing: how for so long I couldn't tell you the truth about me. And now I can't shut up about me when what I really ought to be explaining is what happened at the hotel.

Billie gets into an elevator with a superhero and the guy who blew off Aliss. The superhero reeks. BO and something worse, like spoiled meat. He gets out on the seventh floor, and Billie sucks in air. She's thinking about all sorts of things. For example, how it turns out she doesn't have a fear of heights, which is a good thing to discover in a glass elevator. She's thinking about how she could find a wireless café, go online and hang out in FarAway, except Paul Zell won't be there. She wonders if the guy who bought Bearhand is trying him out. Now that would be weird, to run into someone who used to be you. What would she say? She's thinking how much she wants to take a shower, and she's wondering if she smells as bad as that superhero did. She's thinking all of this and lots of other things, too.

"Now that's how to fight crime," says the other person in the elevator. (Conrad Linthor, although Billie doesn't know his last name yet. Maybe you'll recognize it, though.) "You smell it to death. Although, to be fair, to get that big you have to eat a lot of protein and the protein makes you stinky. That's why I'm a vegetarian." The smile he gives Billie is as ripe with charm as the elevator is ripe with super stink.

Billie prides herself on being charm resistant. (It's like the not having a sense of humor. A sense of humor is a weakness. I know how you're supposed to be able to laugh at yourself, but that's pretty sucky advice when everyone is always laughing at you already.) She stares at Conrad Linthor blankly. If you don't react, mostly other people give up and leave you alone.

Conrad Linthor is eighteen or nineteen, or maybe a well-pre-served twenty-two. He has regular features and white teeth. He'd be good looking if he weren't so good looking, Billie thinks, and then wonders what she meant by that. She can tell that he's rich, although, again, she's not quite sure how she knows this. Maybe because he pressed the Penthouse floor button when he got on the elevator.

"Let me guess," Conrad Linthor says, as if he and Billie have been having a conversation. "You're here to audition." When Billie continues to stare at him blankly, this time because she really doesn't know what he's talking about and not just because she's faking being stupid, he elaborates: "You want to be a sidekick. That guy who just got off? The Blue Fist? I hear his sidekicks keep quitting for some reason."

"I'm here to meet a friend," Billie says. "Why does everyone keep asking me that? Are you? You know, a sidekick?"

"Me?" Conrad Linthor says. "Very funny."

The elevator door dings open, fifteenth floor, and Billie gets off. "See you around," Conrad Linthor calls after her. It sounds more mocking than hopeful.

You know what, Paul Zell? I never thought you would be super handsome or anything. Don't be insulted, okay? I never cared about what you might turn out to look like. I know you have brown hair and brown eyes and you're kind of skinny and you have a big nose.

I know because you told me you look like your avatar. Boggle. Me, I was always terrified you'd ask for my photo, because then it would really have been a lie, even more of a lie, because I would've sent you a photo of Melinda.

My dad says I look so much like Melinda did when she was a kid, it's scary. That we could practically be twins. But I've seen pictures of Melinda when she was fifteen and I don't look like her at all. Melinda was kind of freakish looking when she was my age, actually. I think that's why she's so nice now, and not vain, because it was a surprise to her, too, when she got awesome looking. I'm not gorgeous, and I'm not a freak, either, and so that whole ugly duckling thing that Melinda went through probably isn't going to happen to me.

But you saw me, right? You know what I look like.

Billie knocks on the door of Paul Zell's hotel room, just in case. Even though you aren't there. If you were there, she'd die on the spot of heart failure, even though that's why she's there. To see you.

Maybe you're wondering why she came all this way, when meeting you face-to-face was always going to be this huge problem. Honestly? She doesn't really know. She still doesn't know. Except that you said: Want to meet up? See if this is real or not?

What was she supposed to do? Say no? Tell the truth?

There are two double beds in room 1584, and a black suitcase on a stand. No Paul Zell, because you're going to be in meetings all day. The plan is to meet at the Golden Lotus at six.

Last night you slept in one of those beds, Paul Zell. Billie sits down on the bed closest to the window and she even smells the pillows, but she can't tell. It's a damn shame housekeeping has already made up the room, otherwise Billie could climb into the bed you were sleeping in last night and put her head down on your pillow.

She goes over to the suitcase, and here's where it starts to get kind of awful, Paul Zell. This is why I have to write about all of this in the third person, because maybe then I can pretend that it wasn't really me there, doing these things.

The lid of your suitcase is up. You're a tidy packer, Paul Zell. The dirty clothes on the floor of the closet are folded. Billie lifts up the squared shirts and khakis. Even the underwear is folded. Your pants size is 32, Paul Zell. Your socks are just socks. There's a velvet box, a jeweler's box, near the bottom of the suitcase, and Billie opens it. Then she puts the box back at the bottom of the suitcase. I can't really tell you what she was thinking right then, even though I was there.

I can't tell you everything, Paul Zell.

Billie didn't pack a suitcase, because her dad and Melinda would have wondered about that. Fortunately nobody's ever surprised when you go off to school and your backpack looks crammed full of things. Billie takes out the skirt she's planning to wear to dinner, and hangs it up in the closet. She brushes her teeth and afterward she puts her toothbrush down on the counter beside your toothbrush. She closes the drapes over the view, which is just another building, glass-fronted like the elevators. As if nobody could ever get anything done if the world wasn't watching, or maybe because, if the world can look in and see what you're doing, then what you're doing has to be valuable and important and aboveboard. It's a far way down to the street, so far down that the window in Paul Zell's hotel room doesn't open, probably because people like Billie can't help imagining what it would be like to fall.

All the little ant people down there, who don't even know you're standing at the window, looking down at them. Billie looks down at them.

Billie closes the blackout curtain over the view. She pulls the cover off the bed closest to the window. She takes off her jeans and shirt and bra and puts on the Boston Marathon T-shirt she found in Paul Zell's suitcase.

She lies down on a fresh white top sheet, falls asleep in the yellow darkness. She dreams about you.

When she wakes up she is drooling on an unfamiliar pillow. Her jaw is tight because she's forgotten to wear her mouthpiece. She's been grinding her teeth. So, yes, the teeth grinding, that's me. Not Melinda.

It's 4:30, late afternoon. Billie takes a shower. She uses Paul Zell's herbal conditioner. She folds the borrowed T-shirt and puts it back in Paul Zell's suitcase, between the dress shirts and the underwear.

The hotel where she's staying is on CNN. Because of the superheroes.

For the last three weeks Billie has tried not to think too much about what will happen at dinner when she and Paul Zell meet. But, even though she's been trying not to think about it, she still had to figure out what she was going to wear. The skirt and the sweater she brought are Melinda's. They fit okay; Billie hopes they'll make her look older, but not as if she is *trying* to look older. She bought a lipstick at Target, but when she puts it on it looks too Billie Goes to Clown School, and so she wipes it off again and puts on ChapStick instead.

She's sure her lips are still redder than they ought to be; she hopes no one will notice.

When she goes down to the front desk to ask about Internet cafés, Aliss is still on the front desk. "Or you could just use the business center," Aliss tells her. "Guests can use their room keys to access the business center. You are staying here, right?"

Billie asks a question of her own. "Who's that guy, Conrad?" she says. "What's his deal?"

Aliss's eyes narrow. "His deal is he's the biggest slut in the world. Like it's any of your business," she says. "But don't think he's got any pull with his dad, Little Miss Wannabe Sidekick. No matter what he says. Hook up with him and I'll stomp your ass. It's not like I want this job, anyway."

"I've got a boyfriend," Billie says. "Besides, he's too old for me."

Which is an interesting thing for her to say, when I think about it now.

Here's the thing, Paul Zell. You're thirty-four and I'm fifteen. That's nineteen years' difference. That's a substantial gap, right? Besides the legal issue, which I am not trying to minimize, I could be twice as old as I am now and you'd still be older. I've thought about this a lot. And you know what? There's a teacher at school, Mrs. Christie. Melinda was talking, a few months ago, about how Mrs. Christie just turned thirty and her husband is sixty-three. And they still fell in love, and yeah, Melinda says everyone thinks it's kind of repulsive, but that's love, and nobody really understands how it works. It just happens. And then there's Melinda, who married a guy *exactly the same age that she was*, who then got addicted to heroin, and was, besides that, just all-around bad news. My point? Compared to those thirty-three years between Mr. and Mrs. Christie, eighteen years is practically nothing.

The real problem here is timing. And, also, of course, the fact that I lied. But, except for the lying, why couldn't it have worked out between us in a few years? Why do we really have to wait at all? It's not like I'm ever going to fall in love with anyone again.

Billie uses Paul Zell's hotel room key to get into the business center. There's a superhero at one of the PCs. The superhero is at least eight feet tall, and she's got frizzy red hair. You can tell she's a superhero and not just a tall dentist because a little electric sizzle runs along her outline, every once in a while, as if maybe she's being projected into her too-small seat from some other dimension. She glances over at Billie, who nods hello. The superhero sighs and looks at her fingernails. Which is fine with Billie. She doesn't need rescuing, and she isn't auditioning for anything, either. No matter what anybody thinks.

For some reason, Billie chooses to be Constant Bliss when she signs onto FarAway. She's double incognito. Paul Zell isn't online and there's no one in King Nermal's Chamber, except for the living chess pieces who are always there, and who aren't really alive, either. Not the ones who are still standing or sitting, patiently, upon their squares, waiting to be deployed, knitting or picking their noses or flirting or whatever their particular programs have been programmed to do when they aren't in combat. Billie's favorite is the King's Rook, because he always laughs when he moves into battle, even when he must know he's going to be defeated.

Do you ever feel as if they're watching you, Paul? Sometimes I wonder if they know that they're just a game inside a game. When I first found King Nermal's Chamber, I walked all around the board and checked out what everyone was doing. The White Queen and her pawn were playing chess, like they always do. I sat and watched them play. After a while the White Queen asked me if I wanted a match, and when I said yes, her little board got bigger and bigger until I was standing on a single square of it, inside another chamber exactly the same as the chamber I'd just been standing in, and there was another White Queen playing chess with her pawn, and I guess I could have kept on going down and down and down, but instead I got freaked out and quit FarAway without saving.

Bearhand isn't in FarAway right now. No Enchantress Magic EightBall either, of course.

Constant Bliss is low on healing herbs, and she's quite near the Bloody Meadows, so I put on her invisible cloak and go out onto the battlefield. Rare and strange plants have sprung up where the blood of men and beasts is still soaking into the ground. I'm wearing a Shielding Hand, too, because some of the plants don't like being yanked out of the ground. When my collecting box is one hundred percent full, Constant Bliss leaves the Bloody Meadows. I leave the Bloody Meadows. Billie leaves the Bloody Meadows. Billie hasn't quite decided what she should do next, or where she should go, and besides it's nearly six o'clock. So she saves and quits.

The superhero is watching something on YouTube, two Korean guys break-dancing to Pachelbel's Canon in D. Billie stands up to leave.

"Girl," the superhero says. Her voice hurts to listen to.

"Who, me?" Billie says.

"You, girl," the superhero says. "Are you here with Miracle?"

Billie realizes a mistake has been made. "I'm not a sidekick," she says.

"Then who are you?" the superhero says.

"Nobody," Billie says. And then, because she remembers that there's a superhero named Nobody, she says, "I mean, I'm not anybody." She escapes before the superhero can say anything else.

Billie checks her hair in the women's bathroom in the lobby. Nothing can be done. She wishes her sister's sweater wasn't so tight. She decides it doesn't make her look older, it just makes her look lumpy. Melinda is always trying to get Billie to wear something besides T-shirts and jeans, but Billie, looking in the bathroom mirror, suddenly wishes she looked more like herself, forgetting that what she needs is to look less like herself. To look less like a fifteen-year-old crazy liar.

Although apparently what she looks like is a sidekick.

Billie doesn't need to pee, but she pees anyway, just in case, because what if later she really has to get up and leave the dinner table? You'd know that she was going to the bathroom, and for some reason this seems embarrassing to her. The fact that she's even worrying about this right now makes Billie feel as if she might be going crazy.

The maître d' asks if she has a reservation. It's now five minutes to six. "For six o'clock," Billie says. "For two. Paul Zell?"

"Here we are," the maître d' says. "The other member of your party isn't here, but we can go ahead and seat you."

Billie is seated. The maître d' pushes her chair in, and Billie tries not to feel trapped. There are other people eating dinner all around her, dentists and superheroes and maybe ordinary people, too. Costumes are definitely super-heroes, but just because some of the hotel guests aren't wearing costumes, doesn't mean they're dentists and not superheroes. Although some of them are definitely dentists.

Billie hasn't eaten since this morning, when she got a bagel at Port Authority. Her first New York bagel. Cinnamon raisin with blueberry cream cheese. Her stomach is growling a little, but she can't order dinner yet, of course, because you aren't there yet, Paul Zell, and she doesn't want to eat the bread sticks in the bowl on the table, either. What if you show up, and you sit down across from her and her mouth is full or she gets poppy seeds stuck in her teeth?

People who aren't Paul Zell are seated at tables, or go to the bar and sit on bar stools. Billie studies the menu. She's never had sushi before, but she decides that she will order boldly. A waiter pours her a glass of water. Asks if she'd like to order an appetizer while she's waiting. Billie declines. The people at the table next to her pay their bill and leave. When she looks at her watch, she sees it's 6:18.

You're late, Paul Zell.

Billie eats a bread stick dusted with a greenish powder that makes her lips burn, just a little. She drinks her water, and then, even though she went to the bathroom not even a half hour ago, she needs to pee again. She gets up and goes. Maybe when she comes back to the table, Paul Zell will be sitting there. But she comes back and he isn't.

Billie thinks: Maybe she should go back to the room and see if there are any messages. "I'll be right back," she tells the maître d'. The maître d' couldn't care less. There are superheroes in the hotel lobby and there are dentists in the elevator and there's a light on the phone in room 1584 that would flash if there were any messages. It isn't flashing. Billie dials the number for messages just in case. No message.

Back in the Golden Lotus no one is sitting at the table reserved for Paul Zell, six o'clock, party of two. Billie sits back down anyway. She waits until 7:30, and then she leaves while the maitre d' is escorting a party of superheroes to a table. So far none of the superheroes are ones that Billie recognizes, which doesn't mean that their superpowers are lame. It's just, there are a lot of super-heroes and knowing a lot about superheroes has never been Billie's thing.

She rides up the glass-fronted elevator to Paul Zell's hotel room and orders room service. This should be exciting, because Billie's never ordered room service in her life. But it's not. She orders a hamburger, and when the woman asks if she wants to charge it to her room, she says sure. She drinks a juice from the minibar and watches the Cartoon Network. She waits for someone to knock on the door. When someone does, it's just a bellboy with her hamburger.

By nine o'clock Billie has been down to the business center twice. She checks Hotmail, checks FarAway, checks all the chat-rooms. No Boggle. No Paul Zell. Just chess pieces, and it isn't her move. She writes Paul Zell an e-mail; in the end, she doesn't send it.

When she goes upstairs for the last time, no one is there. Just the suitcase. She doesn't really expect anyone to be there. The jeweler's box is still down at the bottom of the suitcase.

The office building in the window is still lit up. Maybe the lights stay on all night long even when no one is there. Billie thinks those lights are the loneliest things she's ever seen. Even lonelier than the light of distant stars that are already dead by the time their light reaches us. Down below, ant people do their antic things, unaware that Billie is watching them.

Billie opens up the minibar again. Inside are miniature bottles of gin, bourbon, tequila, and rum that no one is going to drink, unless Billie drinks them. What would Alice do, Billie thinks. Billie has always been a Lewis Carroll fan, and not just because of the chess stuff.

There are two beers and a jar of peanuts. Billie disdains the peanuts. She drinks all of the miniatures and both normal-sized cans of beer. Perhaps you noticed the charges on your hotel bill.

Here is where details begin to be a little thin for me, Paul Zell. Perhaps you have a better idea of what I'm describing, what I'm omitting. Then again, maybe you don't.

It's the first time Billie's ever been drunk, and she's not very good at it. Nothing is happening that she can tell. She perseveres. She begins to feel okay, as if everything is going to be okay. The okay feeling gets larger and larger until she's entirely swallowed up by okayness. This lasts for a while, and then she starts to fade in and out, like she's jumping forward in time, always just a little bit dizzy when she arrives. Here she is, flipping through channels, not quite brave enough to click on the pay-for-porn channels, although she thinks about it. Then here she is, a bit later, putting that lipstick on again. This time she kind of likes the way she looks. Here she is, lifting all of Paul Zell's clothes out of the suitcase. She takes the ring out of the box, puts it on her big toe. Now there's a gap. Then: here's Billie, back again, she's bent over a toilet. She's vomiting. She vomits over and over again. Someone is holding back her hair. There's a hand holding out a damp, cold facecloth. Now she's in a bed. The room is dark, but Billie thinks there's someone sitting on the other bed. He's just sitting there.

Later on, she thinks she hears someone moving around the room, doing things. For some reason, she imagines that it's the Enchantress Magic Eightball. Rummaging around the room, looking for important, powerful, magical things. Billie thinks she ought to get up and help. But she can't move.

Much later on, when Billie gets up and goes to the bathroom to throw up again, Paul Zell's suitcase is gone.

There's vomit all over the sink and the bathtub, and on her sister's sweater. Billie's crotch is cold and wet; she realizes she's pissed herself. She pulls off the sweater and skirt and hose, and her underwear. She leaves her bra on because she can't figure out how to undo the straps. She drinks four glasses of water and then crawls into the other bed, the one she hasn't pissed in.

When she wakes up it's one in the afternoon. Someone has left the Do Not Disturb sign on the door of Room 1584. Maybe Billie did this, maybe not. She won't be able to get the bus back to Keokuk today; it left this morning at 7:32. Paul Zell's suitcase is gone, even his dirty clothes are gone. There's not even a sock. Not even a hair on a pillow. Just the herbal conditioner. I guess you forgot to check the bathtub.

Billie's head hurts so bad she wonders if she fell over when she passed out and hit it on something. It's possible, I guess.

Billie is almost glad her head hurts so much. She deserves much worse. She pushes one of the towels around the sink and the counter, mopping up crusted puke. She runs hot water in the shower until the whole bathroom smells like puke soup. She strips the sheets off the bed she peed in, and shoves them with Melinda's destroyed sweater and skirt and all of the puke-stained towels under the counter in the bathroom. The water is only just warm when she takes her shower. Better than she deserves. Billie turns the handle all the way to the right, and then shrieks and turns it back. What you deserve and what you can stand aren't necessarily the same thing.

She cries bitterly while she conditions her hair. She takes the elevator down to the lobby and goes and sits in the Starbucks. The first time she's ever been inside a Starbucks. What she really wants is a caramel iced vanilla latte, but instead she orders three shots of espresso. More penance.

(I know, I find all of this behavior excruciating and over the top, too. And maybe this is a kind of over-the-top penance, too, what I'm doing here, telling you all of this, and maybe the point of humiliating myself by relating all of this humiliating behavior will only bring me even greater humiliation later, when I realize what a self-obsessed, miserable, martyring little drama queen I'm allowing myself to be right now.)

Billie is pouring little packets of sugar into her three shots of espresso when someone sits down next to her. It isn't you, of course. It's that guy, Conrad. And now we're past the point where I owe you an apology, and yet I guess I ought to keep going, because the story isn't over yet. Remember how Billie thought the room key and the bus ride seemed like FarAway, like a quest? Now is the part where it starts seeming more like one of those games of chess, the kind you've already lost and you know it, but you don't concede. You just keep on losing, one piece at a time, until you're the biggest loser in the world. Which is, I guess, how life is like chess. Because it's not like anyone ever wins in the end, is it?

Anyway. Part two. In which I go on writing about myself in the third person. In which I continue to act stupidly. Stop reading if you want.

Conrad Linthor sits down without being asked. He's drinking something frozen. "Sidekick girl. You look terrible."

All during this conversation, picture superheroes of various descriptions. They stroll or glide or stride purposefully past Billie's table. They nod at the guy sitting across from her. Billie notices this without having the strength of character to wonder what's going on. Every molecule of her being is otherwise engaged, with misery, woe, self-hatred, heartbreak, shame, all-obliterating roiling nausea and pain.

Billie says, "So we meet again." Which is, don't you think, the kind of thing people end up saying when they find themselves in a hotel full of superheroes. "I'm not a sidekick. And my name's Billie."

"Whatever," Conrad Linthor says. "Conrad Linthor. So what happened to you?"

Billie swigs bitter espresso. She lets her hair fall in front of her face. Baby bird, she thinks. Wrong smell, baby bird.

But Conrad Linthor doesn't go away. He says, "All right, I'll go first. Let's swap life stories. That girl at the desk when you were checking in? Aliss? I've slept with her, a couple of times. When nothing better came along. She really likes me. And I'm an asshole, okay? No excuses. Every time I hurt her, though, the next time I see her I'm nice again and I apologize and I get her back.

Mostly I'm nice just to see if she's going to fall for it this time, too. I don't know why. I guess I want to see where that place is, the place where she hauls off and assaults me. Some people have ant farms. I'm more into people. So now you know what was going on yesterday. And yeah, I know, something's wrong with me."

Billie pushes her hair back. She says, "Why are you telling me all this?"

He shrugs. "I don't know. You look like you're in a world of hurt. I don't really care. It's just that I get bored. And you look really terrible, and I thought that there was probably something interesting going on. Besides, Aliss can see us in here, from the desk, and this will drive her crazy."

"I'm okay," Billie says. "Nobody hurt me. I'm the bad guy here. I'm the idiot."

"That's unexpected. Also interesting. Go on," Conrad Linthor says. "Tell me everything."

Billie tells him. Everything except for the part where she pees the bed.

When her tale is told, Conrad Linthor stands up and says, "Come on. We're going to go see a friend of mine. You need the cure."

"For love?" This is Billie's lame attempt at humor. She was wondering if telling someone what she's done would make her feel better. It hasn't.

"No cure for love," Conrad Linthor says. "Because there's no such thing. Your hangover we can do something about."

As they navigate the lobby, there are new boards up announcing that free teeth-whitening sessions are available in Suite 412 for qualified superheroes. Billie looks over at the front desk and sees Aliss looking back. She draws her finger across her throat. If looks could kill you wouldn't be reading this e-mail.

Conrad Linthor goes through a door that you're clearly not meant to go through. It's labeled. Billie follows anyway and they're in a corridor, in a maze of corridors. If this were a MMORPG, the zombies would show up any minute. Instead, every once in a while, they pass someone who is probably hotel cleaning staff; bellboys sneaking cigarettes. Everyone nods at Conrad Linthor, just like the superheroes in the Starbucks in the lobby.

Billie doesn't want to ask, but eventually she does. "Who *are* you?"

"Call me Eloise," Conrad Linthor says.

"Sorry?" Billie imagines that they are no longer in the hotel at all. The corridor they are currently navigating slopes gently downward. Maybe they will end up on the shores of a subterranean lake, or in a dungeon, or in Narnia, or King Nermal's Chamber, or even Keokuk, Iowa. It's a small world after all.

"You know, Eloise. The girl who lives in the Plaza? Has a pet turtle named Skipperdee?"

He waits, like Billie's supposed to know what he's talking about. When she doesn't say anything, he says, "Never mind. It's just this book—a classic of modern children's literature, actually—about a girl who lives in the Plaza. Which is a hotel. A bit nicer than this one, maybe, but never mind. I live here."

He keeps on talking. They keep on walking.

Billie's hangover is a special effect. Conrad Linthor is going on and on about superheroes. His father is an agent. Apparently superheroes have agents. Represents all of the big guys. Knows everyone. Agoraphobic. Never leaves the hotel. Everyone comes to him. Big banquet tomorrow night, for his biggest client. Tyrannosaurus Hex. Hex is retiring. Going to go live in the mountains and breed tarantula wasps. Conrad Linthor's father is throwing a party for Hex. Everyone will be there.

Billie's legs are noodles. The ends of her hair are poison needles. Her tongue is a bristly sponge, and her eyes are bags of bleach.

There's a clattering that splits Billie's brain. Two wheeled carts come round the next corner like comets, followed at arm's length by hurtling busboys. They sail down the corridor at top speed. Conrad Linthor and Billie flatten themselves against the wall. "You have to move fast," Conrad explains. "Or else the food gets cold. Guests complain."

Around that corner, enormous doors, still swinging. Big enough to birth a Greyhound bus bound for Keokuk. A behemoth. Billie passes through the doors onto the far shores of what is, of course, a hotel kitchen. Far away, miles, it seems to Billie, there are clouds of vapor and vague figures moving through them. Clanging noises, people yelling, the thick, sweet smell of caramelized onions, onions that will never make anyone cry again. Other savory reeks.

Conrad Linthor steers Billie to a marble-topped table. Copper whisks, mixing bowls, dinged pots hang down on hooks.

Billie feels she ought to say something. "You must have a lot of money," she contributes. "To live in a hotel."

"No shit, Sherlock," Conrad Linthor says. "Sit down. I'll be back."

Billie climbs, slowly and carefully, up a laddery stool and lays her poor head down on the dusty, funereal slab. (It's actually a pastry station, the dust is flour, but Billie is mentally in a bad place.) Paul Zell, Paul Zell. She stares at the tiled wall. Billie's heart has a crack in it. Her head is made of radiation. The Starbucks espresso she forced down has burnt a thousand pinprick holes in Billie's wretched stomach.

Conrad Linthor comes back too soon. He says, "This is her."

There's a guy with him. Skinny, with serious acne scars. Big shoulders. Funny little paper hat and a stained apron. "Ernesto, Billie," Conrad says. "Billie, Ernesto."

"How old did you say?" Ernesto says. He folds his arms, as if Billie is a bad cut of meat Conrad Linthor is trying to pass off as prime rib.

"Fifteen, right?"

Billie confirms.

"She came to the city because of some pervert she met online?"

"In a MMORPG," Conrad says.

"He isn't a pervert," Billie says. "He thought I was my sister. I was pretending to be my sister. She's in her thirties."

"What's your guess?" Conrad asks Ernesto. "Superhero or dentist?"

"One more time," Billie says. "I'm not here to audition for anything. And do I look like a dentist?"

"You look like trouble," Ernesto says. "Here. Drink this." He hands her a glass full of something slimy and green.

"What's in it?" Billie says.

"Wheat grass," Ernesto says. "And other stuff. Secret recipe. Hold your nose and drink it down."

"Yuck," Billie says. (I won't even try to describe the taste of Ernesto's hangover cure. Except, I will never drink again.) "Ew, yuck. Yuck, yuck, yuck."

"Keep holding your nose," Ernesto advises Billie. To Conrad: "They met online?"

"Yeah," Billie says. "In FarAway."

"Yeah, I know that game. Dentist," Ernesto says. "For sure."

"Except," Conrad says, "it gets better. It wasn't just a game. Inside this game, they were playing a game. They were playing *chess*."

"Ohhhh," Ernesto says. Now he's grinning. They both are. "Oh as in superher-oh."

"Superhero," Conrad says. They high-five each other. "The only question is who."

"What was the alibi again?" Ernesto asks Billie, "The name this dude gave?"

"Paul Zell?" Billie says. "Wait, you think Paul Zell is a superhero? No way. He does tech support for a nonprofit. Something involving endangered species."

Conrad Linthor and Ernesto exchange another look. "Superhero for sure," Ernesto says.

Ernesto says, "Or supervillain. All those freaks are into chess. It's like a disease."

"No way," Billie says again.

Conrad Linthor says, "Because there's no chance Paul Zell would have lied to you about anything. Because the two of you were being completely and totally honest with each other." Which shuts Billie up.

Conrad Linthor says, "I just can't get this picture out of my head. This superhero going out and buying a ring. And there you are. This fifteen-year-old girl." He laughs. He nudges Billie as if to say, I'm not laughing at you. I'm laughing near you.

"And there I was," Billie says. "Sitting at the table waiting for him. Like the biggest idiot in the world."

Ernesto has to gasp for air he is laughing so hard.

Billie says, "I guess it's kind of funny. In a horrible way."

"So, anyway," Conrad says. "Since Billie's into chess, I thought we ought to show her your project. Have they set up the banquet room yet?"

Ernesto stops laughing, holds his right hand out, like he's stopping traffic. "Hey, man. Maybe later? I've got prep. I'm salad station tonight. You know?"

"Ernesto's an artist," Conrad says. "I keep telling him he needs to make some appointments, take a portfolio downtown. My dad says people would pay serious bucks for what Ernesto does."

Billie isn't really paying attention to this conversation. She's thinking about Paul Zell. How could you be a superhero, Paul Zell? Can you miss something that big? A secret as big as that? Sure, she thinks. Probably you can miss it by a mile.

"I make things out of butter," Ernesto says. "It's no big deal. Like, sure, someone's going to pay me a million bucks for some thing I carved out of butter."

"It's a statement," Conrad Linthor says, "an artistic statement about the world we live in."

"We live in a world made out of butter," Ernesto says. "Doesn't seem like much of a statement to me. You any good at chess?"

"What?" Billie says.

"Chess. You any good?"

"I'm not bad," Billie says. "You know, it's just for fun. Paul Zell's really good."

"So he wins most of the time?" Ernesto says.

"Yeah," Billie says. She thinks about it. "Wait, no. I guess I win more."

"You gonna be a superhero when you grow up? Because those guys are way into chess."

Conrad Linthor says, "It's like the homicidal triangle. Like setting fires, hurting small animals, and wetting the bed means a kid may grow up to be a sociopath. For superheroes, it's chess. Weird coincidences, that's another one. For example, you're always in the wrong place at the right time. Plus you have an ability of some kind."

"I don't have an ability," Billie says. "Not even one of those really pointless ones like always knowing the right time, or whether it's going to rain."

"Your power might develop later on," Conrad Linthor says.

"It won't."

"Well, okay. But it might, anyway," Conrad Linthor. "It's why I noticed you in the first place. Probably. You stick out. She sticks out, right?"

"I guess," Ernesto says. He gives her that appraising a cut of meat look again. Then nods. "Sure. She sticks out. You stick out."

"I stick out," Billie says. "I stick out like what?"

"Even Aliss noticed," Conrad says. "She thought you were here to audition, remember?"

Ernesto says, "Oh, yeah. Because Aliss is such a fine judge of character."

"Shut up, Ernesto," Conrad says. "Look, Billie. It's not a bad thing, okay? Some people, you can just tell. So maybe you're just some girl. But maybe you can do something that you don't even know about yet."

"You sound like my guidance counselor," Billie says. "Like my sister. Why do people always try to tell you that life gets better? Like life has a bad cold. Like, here I am, and where is my sister right now? She drove my dad up to Peoria. To St. Francis, because he has pancreatic cancer. And that's the only reason I'm here, because my dad's dying, and so nobody is even going to notice that I'm gone. Lucky me, right?"

Ernesto and Conrad Linthor are both staring at her.

"I'm a superhero," Billie says. "Or a sidekick. Whatever you say. Paul Zell is a superhero, too. Everybody's a superhero. The world is made of butter. I don't even know what that means."

"How's the hangover?" Conrad Linthor asks her.

"Better," Billie says. The hangover is gone. Of course she still feels terrible, but that's not hangover related. That's Paul Zell related. That's just everything else.

"Sorry about you know, uh, your dad." That's Ernesto.

Billie shrugs. Grimaces. As if on cue, there is a piercing scream somewhere far away. Then a lot of shouting. Some laughing. Off in the distance, something seems to be happening. "Gotta go," Ernesto says.

"Ernesto!" It's a short guy in a tall hat. He says, "Hey, Mr. Linthor. What's up?"

"Gregor," Conrad says. "Hope that wasn't anything serious."

"Nah, man," the short guy says. "Just Portland. Sliced off the tip of his pointer finger. Again. Second time in six months. The guy is a master of disaster."

"See you, Conrad," Ernesto says. "Nice to meet you, Billie. Stay out of trouble."

As Ernesto goes off with the short guy, the short guy is saying, "So who's the girl? She looks like somebody. Somebody's sidekick?"

Conrad yells after them. "Maybe we'll see you later, okay?"

He tells Billie, "There's a get-together tonight up on the roof. Nothing official. Just some people hanging out. You ought to come by. Then maybe we can go see Ernesto's party sculptures."

"I may not be here," Billie says. "It's Paul Zell's room, not mine. What if he's checked out?"

"Then your key won't work," Conrad Linthor says. "Look, if you're locked out, just call up to the penthouse later and tell me and I'll see what I can do. Right now I've got to get to class."

"You're in school?" Billie says.

"Just taking some classes down at the New School," Conrad says. "Life drawing. Film studies. I'm working on a novel, but it's not like that's a full-time commitment, right?"

Billie is almost sorry to leave the kitchen behind. It's the first place in New York where she's been one hundred percent sure she doesn't have to worry about running into Paul Zell. It isn't that this is a good thing, it's just that her spider sense isn't tingling all the time. Not that Billie has anything that's the equivalent of spider sense. And maybe room 1584 can also be considered a safe haven now. The room key still works. Someone has remade the bed, taken away the towels and sheets in the bathroom. Melinda's red sweater and skirt are hanging down over the shower rod. Someone rinsed them out first.

Billie orders room service. Then she decides to set out for Bryant Park. She'll go watch the chess players, which is what she and Paul Zell were going to do, what they talked about doing online. Maybe you'll be there, Paul Zell.

She has a map. She walks the whole way. She doesn't get lost. When she gets to Bryant Park, sure enough, there are some chess games going on. Old men, college kids, maybe even a few superheroes. Pigeons everywhere, underfoot. New Yorkers walking their dogs. A lady yelling. No Paul Zell. Not that Billie would know Paul Zell if she saw him.

Billie sits on a bench beside a trashcan, and after a while someone sits down beside her. Not Paul Zell. A superhero. The superhero from the hotel business center.

"We meet again," the superhero says. Which serves Billie right.

Billie says, "Are you following me?"

"No," the superhero says. "Maybe. I'm Lightswitch."

"I've heard of you," Billie says. "You're famous."

"Famous is relative," Lightswitch says. "Sure, I've been on *Oprah*. But I'm no Tyrannosaurus Hex."

"There's a comic book about you," Billie says. "Although, uh, she doesn't look like you. Not really."

"The artist likes to draw the boobs life-sized. Just the boobs. Says it's artistic license."

They sit for a while in companionable silence. "You play chess?" Billie asks.

"Of course," Lightswitch says. "Doesn't everybody? Who's your favorite chess player?"

"Paul Morphy," Billie says. "Although Koneru Humpy has the most awesome name ever."

"Agreed," Lightswitch says. "So are you in town for the shindig? Shindig. What kind of word is that? Archeological excavation of the shin. Knee surgery. Do you work with someone?"

"Do you mean, am I a sidekick?" Billie says. "No. I'm not a sidekick. I'm Billie Faggart. Hi."

"Sidekick. There's another one. Kick in the side. Pain in the neck. Kick in the shin. Ignore me. I get distracted sometimes." Lightswitch holds out a hand for Billie to shake, and Billie does. She thinks that there will be a baby jolt maybe, like one of those joke buzzers. But there's nothing. It's just an ordinary handshake, except that Lightswitch's completely solid hand still looks funny, staticky, like it's really somewhere else. Billie can't remember if Lightswitch is from the future or the eighth dimension. Or maybe neither of those is quite right.

Two little kids come up and want Lightswitch's autograph. They look at Billie, as if wondering whether they ought to ask for her autograph, too.

Billie stands up, and Lightswitch says, "Wait a minute. Let me give you my card."

"Why?" Billie says.

"Just in case," Lightswitch says. "You might change your mind at some point about the sidekick thing. It isn't a long-term career, you know, but it's not a bad thing to do for a while. Mostly it's answering fan mail, photo ops, banter practice."

Billie says, "Um, what happened to your last sidekick?" And then, seeing the look on Lightswitch's face, wonders if this is not the kind of question you're supposed to ask a superhero.

"Fell off a building. Kidding! That was a joke, okay? Sold her story to the tabloids. Used the proceeds to go to law school." Lightswitch kicks at a can. "Bam. Damn. Anyway. My card."

Billie looks, but there's nobody around to tell her what any of this means. Maybe you'd know, Paul Zell.

Billie says, "Do you know somebody named Paul Zell?"

"Paul Zell? Rings a bell. There's another one. Ding dong. Paul Zell. But no. I don't think I do, after all. It's a business card. Not an executive decision. Just take it, okay?" Lightswitch says. So Billie does.

Billie doesn't intend to show for Conrad Linthor's shindig. She walks down Broadway. Gawks at the gawkworthy. Pleasurably ponders a present for her sister, decides discretion is the better part of harmonious family relationships. Caped superheroes swoop and wheel and dip around the Empire State Building. No crime in progress. Show business. Billie walks until she has blisters. Doesn't think about Paul Zell. Paul Zell, Paul Zell. Doesn't think about Lightswitch. Pays twelve bucks to see a movie and don't ask me what movie or if it was any good. I don't remember. When she comes out of the movie theater, back out onto the street, everything sizzles with lights. It's Fourth of July bright. Apparently nobody in New York ever goes to bed early. Billie decides she'll go to bed early. Get a wake-up call and walk down to Port Authority. Catch her bus. Go home to Keokuk and never think about New York again. Stay off FarAway. Concede the chess game. Burn the business card. But: Paul Zell, Paul Zell.

Meanwhile, back to the hotel, Aliss the nemesis has been lying in wait. Actually, it's more like standing behind a flower arrangement, but never mind. Aliss pounces. Billie, mourning lost love, is easy prey.

"Going to your boyfriend's party?" Aliss hisses. There's only one s in that particular sentence, but Aliss knows how to make an s count.

She links arms with Billie. Pulls her into an elevator.

"What party?" Billie says. "What boyfriend?" Aliss gives her a look. Hits the button marked Roof, then the emergency stop button, like she's opening cargo doors, one, two. Goodbye, cruel, old world. That bomb is going to drop.

"If you mean Conrad Linthor," Billie says, "That was nothing. In the Starbucks. He just wanted to talk about you. In fact, he gave me this. Because he was afraid he was going to lose it. But he's planning on giving it to you. Tomorrow, I think."

She takes out the ring that you left behind, Paul Zell.

Surely you've checked the jeweler's box by now. Seen the ring is gone. Billie found it in the bed sheets that morning when she woke up. Remember? I was wearing it on my big toe. All day long Billie carried it around in her pocket, just like the business card. It didn't fit her ring finger.

I slipped it on and off, on and off, all day long.

Billie and Aliss both stare at the ring. Both of them seem to find it hard to speak.

Finally: "It's mine?" Aliss says. She puts her hand out, like the ring's a cute dog. Not a ring. Like she wants to pet it. "That's a two-carat diamond. At least. Antique setting. Just explain one thing, please. Why did Conrad give you my ring? You expect me to believe he let some girl carry my diamond ring around all day?"

"Yeah, well, you know Conrad," Billie says.

"Yeah," Aliss says. She's silent for another long moment. "Can I?"

She takes the ring, tries it on her ring finger. It fits. There's an inappropriate ache in Billie's throat. Aliss says, "Wow. Just wow. I guess I have to give it back. Okay. I can do that." She holds up her hand. Drags the diamond along the glass elevator wall, then rubs at the scratch it's left behind. Then checks the diamond, like she might have damaged it. But diamonds are like the superheroes of the mineral world. Diamonds cut glass. Not the other way around.

Aliss presses the button. The elevator elevates.

"Maybe you should go to the party and I should just go to bed," Billie says. "I have to catch a bus in the morning."

"No," Aliss says. "Wait. Now I'm nervous. I can't go up there by myself. You have to come with me. Except we can't act like we're friends, because then Conrad will suspect something's up. That I *know*. You can't tell him I know."

"I won't. I swear," Billie says.

"How's my hair?" Aliss says. "Shit. Don't tell him, but they fired me. Just like that. I'm not supposed to be here. I think management knew something was up with me and Conrad. I'm not the first girl he's gotten fired. But I'm not going to say anything right now. I'll tell him later."

Billie says, "That sucks."

"You have no idea," Aliss says. "It's such a crappy job. People are such assholes, and you still have to say have a nice day. And smile." She gives the ring back. Smiles.

The elevator opens on sky. There's a sign saying Private Party. Like the whole sky is a private party. It's just after nine o'clock. The sky is orange. The pool is the color the sky ought to be. There are superheroes splashing around in it. That bubble of blood floating above it, like an oversized beach ball. Tango music plays.

Conrad Linthor lounges on a lounge chair. He comes over when he sees Billie and Aliss. "Girls," he says.

"Hey, Conrad," Aliss says. Her hip cocked like a gun hammer. Her hair is remarkable. The piercing is in. "Great party."

"Billie," Conrad says. "I'm so glad you came. There are some people you ought to meet." He takes Billie's arm and drags her off. Maybe he's going to throw her in the pool.

"Is Ernesto here?" Billie looks back, but Aliss is having a conversation now with someone in a uniform.

"This kind of party isn't really for hotel staff," Conrad says. "They get in trouble if they socialize with the guests."

"Don't worry about Aliss," Billie says. "Apparently she got fired. But you probably already know that."

Conrad smiles. They're on the edge of a group of strangers who all look vaguely familiar, vaguely improbable. There are scales, feathers, ridiculous outfits designed to show off ridiculous physiques. Why does everything remind Billie of FarAway? Except for the smell. Why do superheroes smell weird? Paul Zell.

The tango has become something dangerous. A woman is singing. There is nobody here that Billie wants to meet.

Conrad Linthor is drunk. Or high. "This is Billie," he says. "My sidekick for tonight. Billie, this is everyone."

"Hi, everyone," Billie says. "Excuse me." She rescues her arm from Conrad Linthor. She heads back for the elevator. Aliss has escaped the hotel employee and is crouched down by the pool, one finger in the water. Probably the deep end. You can tell by her slumped shoulder that she's thinking about drowning herself. A good move: perhaps someone here will save her. Once someone has saved your life, they might as well fall in love with you, too. It's just good economics.

"Wait," Conrad Linthor says. He's not that old, Billie decides. He's just a kid. He hasn't even done anything all that bad, yet. And yet you can see how badness accumulates around him. Builds up like lightning on a lightning rod. If Billie sticks around, it will build up on her, too. That spider sense she doesn't have is tingling. Paul Zell, Paul Zell.

"Ernesto will be so disappointed," Conrad Linthor says. They're both jogging now. Billie sees the lit stair sign, decides not to wait for an elevator. She takes the stairs two at a time. Conrad Linthor bounds down behind her. "He really wanted you to see what he made. For the banquet. It's too bad you can't stay. I wanted to invite you to the banquet. You could meet Tyranno-saurus Hex. Get an autograph or two. Make some good contacts. Being a sidekick is all about making the contacts."

"I'm not a sidekick!" Billie yells up. "That was a dumb joke even before you made it the first time. Even if I were a sidekick, I wouldn't be yours. Like you're a superhero. Just because you know people. So what's your secret name, superhero? What's your superpower?"

She stops on the stairs so suddenly that Conrad Linthor runs into her. They both stumble forward, smack into the wall on the twenty-second floor landing. But they don't fall.

Conrad Linthor says, "My superpower is money." The wall props him up. "The only superpower that counts for anything. Better than invisibility. Better than being able to fly. Much better than telekinesis or teleportation or that other one. Telepathy. Knowing what other people are thinking. Why would you ever want to know what other people are thinking? Did you know everyone thinks that one day they might be a millionaire? Like that's a lot of money. They have no idea. They don't want to be a superhero. They just want to be like me. They want to be rich."

Billie has nothing to say to this.

"You know what the difference is between a superhero and a supervillain?" Conrad Linthor asks her.

Billie waits.

"The superhero has a really good agent," Conrad Linthor says. "Someone like my dad. You have no idea the kind of stuff they get away with. Fifteen-year-old girls is *nothing*."

"What about Lightswitch?" Billie says.

"Who? Her? She's no big deal," Conrad Linthor says. "She's okay. I don't really know much about her. She's kind of old school."

"I think I'm going to go to bed now," Billie says.

"No," Conrad Linthor says. "Wait. You have to come with me and see what Ernesto did. It's just so cool. Everything's carved out of butter."

"If I go see, will you let me go to bed?"

"Sure," Conrad Linthor says.

"Will you be nice to Aliss? If she's still up at the party when you get back?"

"I'll try," Conrad Linthor says.

"Okay," Billie says. "I'll go look at Ernesto's butter. Are we going to go meet him?"

Conrad Linthor levers himself off the wall. Pats it. "Ernesto? I don't know where he is. How should I know?"

They go into the forbidden maze. Back to the kitchen, and through it, now empty and dark and somehow like a morgue. A mausoleum.

"Ernesto's been doing the work in a freezer," Conrad Linthor says. "You have to keep these guys cold. Wait. Let me get it unlocked. Cool tool, right? Borrowed it from The Empty Jar. He's one of dad's clients. They're making a movie about him. I saw the script. It's crap."

The lock comes off. The lights go on. Before I tell you what was inside the freezer, let me first tell you something about how big the freezer is. It will help you visualize, later on. The freezer is plenty big. Bigger than most New York apartments, Billie thinks, although this is just hearsay. She's never been in a New York apartment.

What's inside the supersized freezer? Supervillains. Warm Gun, Glowworm, Radical!, Heatdeath, The Scribbler, The Nin-jew, Cat Lady, Hellalujah, Shibboleth, The Shambler, Mandroid, Manplant, The Manticle, Patty Cakes. Lots of others. Name a famous supervillain and he or she is in the freezer. They're life-size. They're not real, although at first Billie's heart slams. She thinks: who caught all these guys? Why are they so perfectly still? Maybe Conrad Linthor is a superhero after all.

Conrad Linthor touches Hellalujah's red, bunchy bicep. Presses just a little. The color smears. Lardy, yellow-white underneath. The supervillains are made out of butter. "Hand-tinted," Conrad says.

"Ernesto made these?" Billie says. She wants to touch one, too. She walks up to Patty Cakes. Breathes on the cold, outstretched palms. You can see Patty Cakes's life line. Her love line. Billie realizes something else. The butter statues are all decorated to look like chess pieces. Their signature outfits have been changed to black and red. Cat Lady is wearing a butter crown.

Conrad Linthor puts his hand on Hellalujah's shoulder. Puts his arm around Hellalujah. Then he squeezes, hard. His arm goes through Hellalujah's neck. Like an arm going through butter. The head pops off.

"Be careful!" Billie says.

"I can't believe it's butter," Conrad says. He giggles. "Come on. Can you believe this? He made a whole chess set out of butter. And why? For some banquet for some guy who used to fight crime? That's just crap. This is better. Us here, having some fun. This is spontaneous. Haven't you always wanted to fight the bad guy and win? Now's your chance."

"But Ernesto made these!" Billie's fists are clenched.

"You heard him," Conrad says. "It's no big deal. It's not like it's art. There's no statement here. It's just butter."

He has Hellalujah's sad head in his arms. "Heavy," he says. "Food fight. Catch." He throws the head at Billie. It hits her in the chest and knocks her over.

She lies on the ice-cold floor, looking at Hellalujah's head. One side is flat. Half of Hellalujah's broad nose is stuck like a slug to Billie's chest. Her right arm is slimy with butter and food dye.

Billie sits up. She cradles Hellalujah's head, hurls it back at Conrad. She misses. Hellalujah's head smacks into Mandroid's shiny stomach. Hangs there, half embedded.

"Funny," Conrad Linthor says. He giggles.

Billie shrieks. She leaps at him, her hands killing claws. They both go down on top of The Shambler. Billie brings her knee up between Conrad Linthor's legs, drives it up into butter. She grabs Conrad Linthor by the hair, bangs his head on The Shambler's head. "Ow," Conrad Linthor says. "Ow, ow, ow."

He twists under her. Gets hold of her hands, pulls at them even as she tightens her grip on his hair. His hair is slick with butter, and she can't hold on. She lets go. His head flops down. "Get off," he says. "Get off."

Billie drives her elbow into his stomach. Her feet skid a little as she stands up. She grabs hold of Warm Gun's gun for balance, and it breaks off. "Sorry," she says, apologizing to butter. "I'm sorry. So sorry."

Conrad Linthor is trying to sit up. There's spit at the corner of his mouth, or maybe it's butter.

Billie runs for the door. Gets there just as Conrad Linthor realizes what she's doing. "Wait!" he says. "Don't you dare! You bitch!"

Too late. She's got the door shut. She leans against it, smearing it with butter.

Conrad Linthor pounds on the other side. "Billie!" It's a faint yell. Barely audible. "Let me out, okay? It was just fun. I was just having fun. It was fun, wasn't it?"

Here's the thing, Paul Zell. It was fun. That moment when I threw Hellalujah's head at him? That felt good. It felt so good I'd pay a million bucks to do it again. I can admit that now. But I don't *like* that it felt good. I don't like that it felt fun. But I guess now I understand why supervillains do what they do. Why they run around and destroy things. Because it feels fantastic. Someday I'm going to buy a lot of butter and build something out of it, just so I can tear it all to pieces again.

Billie could leave Conrad Linthor in the freezer. Walk away. Somebody would probably find him. Right?

But then she thinks about what he'll do in there. He'll kick apart all of the other buttervillains. Stomp them into greasy pieces. She knows he'll do it, because she can imagine doing the same thing.

She lets him out.

"Not funny," Conrad Linthor says. He looks very funny.

Picture him, all decked out in red and black butter. His lips are purplish-bluish. He's shivering with cold. So is Billie. "Not funny at all," Billie agrees. "What the hell was that? What were you doing in there? What about your friend? Ernesto? How could you do that to him?"

"He's not really a friend," Conrad Linthor says. "Not like you and me. He's just some guy I hang out with sometimes. Friends are boring. I get bored."

"We're not friends," Billie says.

"Sure," Conrad Linthor says. "I know that. But I thought if I said we were, you might fall for it. You have no idea how stupid some people are. Besides, I was doing it for you. No, really. I was. Sometimes when a superhero is in a really bad situation, that's when they finally discover their ability. What they can do. With some people it's an amulet, or a ring, but mostly it's just environmental. Your adrenaline kicks in. My father is always trying stuff on me, just in case I've got something that we haven't figured out yet."

Maybe some of this is true, and maybe all of it is true, and maybe Conrad Linthor is just testing Billie again. Is she that stupid? He's watching her right now, to see if she's falling for any of this.

"I'm out of here," Billie says. She checks her pocket, just to make sure Paul Zell's ring is still there. She's been doing that all day.

"Wait," Conrad Linthor says. "You don't know how to get back. You need help."

"I made a trail," Billie says. All the way through the corridors, this time, she pressed the diamond along the wall. Left a thin little mark. Nothing anyone else would even know to look for.

"Fine," Conrad Linthor says. "I'm going to stay down here and make some scrambled eggs. Sure you don't want any?"

"I'm not hungry," Billie says.

Even as she's leaving, Conrad Linthor is explaining to her that they'll meet again. This is like their origin story. Maybe they're each other's nemesis, or maybe they're destined to team up and save the world and make lots of—

Eventually Billie can't hear him anymore. She leaves a trail of butter all the way back to the lobby. Gets onto an elevator before anyone has noticed the state she's in, or maybe by this point in the weekend the hotel staff are used to stranger things.

She takes a shower and goes to bed still smelling faintly of butter. She wakes up early. The bubble of blood is down in the lobby again, floating over the fountain.

Billie thinks about going over to ask for an autograph. Pretending to be a fan. Could you pop that bubble with a ballpoint pen? This is the kind of thought Conrad Linthor goes around thinking, she's pretty sure.

Billie catches her bus. And that's the end of the story, Paul Zell. Dear Paul Zell.

Except for the ring. Here's the thing about the ring. Billie wrapped it in tissue paper and sealed it up in a hotel envelope. She wrote "Ernesto in the kitchen" on the outside of the envelope. She wrote a note. The note says: "This ring belongs to Paul Zell. If he comes looking for it, maybe he'll give you a reward. A couple hundred bucks seems fair. Tell him I'll pay him back. But if he doesn't get in touch, you should keep the ring. Or sell it. I'm sorry about Hellalujah and Mandroid and The Shambler. I didn't know what Conrad Linthor was going to do."

So, Paul Zell. That's the whole story. Except for the part where I got home and found the e-mail from you, the one where you explained what had happened to you. That you had an emergency appendectomy, and never made it to New York at all, and what happened to me? Did I make it to the hotel? Did I wonder where you were? You say you can't imagine how worried and/or angry I must have been. Etc.

I'll be honest with you, Paul Zell. I read your e-mail and part of me thought, I'm saved. We'll both pretend none of this ever happened. I'll go on being Melinda, and Melinda will go on being the Enchantress Magic Eightball, and Paul Zell, whoever Paul Zell is, will go on being Boggle the Master Thief. We'll play chess and chat online, and everything will be exactly the way that it was before.

But that would be crazy. I would be a fifteen-year-old liar, and you would be some weird guy who's so pathetic and lonely that he's willing to settle for me. Not even for me. To settle for the person I was pretending to be. But you're better than that, Paul Zell. You have to be better than that. So I wrote you this letter.

If you read this letter the whole way through, now you know what happened to your ring, and a lot of other things too. I still have your conditioner. If you give Ernesto the reward, let me know and I'll sell Constant Bliss and the Enchantress Magic Eightball. So I can pay you back. It's not a big deal. I can go be someone else, right?

Or else, I guess, you could ignore this letter, and we could just pretend that I never sent it. That I never came to New York to meet Paul Zell. That Paul Zell wasn't going to give me a ring.

We could pretend you never discovered my secret identity. We could go on being Boggle the Master Thief and the Enchantress Magic Eightball. We could meet up a couple times a week in Far-Away and play chess. We could even go on a quest. Save the world.

We could chat. Flirt. I could tell you about Melinda's week, and we could pretend that maybe someday we're going to be brave enough to meet face-to-face.

But here's the deal, Paul Zell. I'll be older one day. I may never discover my superpower. I don't think I want to be a sidekick. Not even yours, Paul Zell. Although maybe that would have been simpler. If I'd been honest. And if you're what or who I think you are. And maybe I'm not even being honest now. Maybe I'd settle for sidekick. For being your sidekick. If that was all you offered.

Conrad Linthor is crazy and dangerous and a bad person, but I think he's right about one thing. He's right that sometimes people meet again. Even if we never really truly met each other, I want to believe you and I will meet again. I want you to know that there was a reason that I bought a bus ticket and came to New York. The reason was that I love you. That part was really true. I really did throw up on Santa Claus once. I can do twelve cartwheels in a row. I'm allergic to cats. May third is my birthday, not Melinda's. I didn't lie to you about everything.

When I'm eighteen, I'm going to take the bus back to New York City. I'm going to walk down to Bryant Park. And I'm going to bring my chess set. I'm going to do it on my birthday. I'll be there all day long.

Your move, Paul Zell.

BESPOKE

GENEVIEVE VALENTINE

Disease Control had sprayed while Petra was asleep, and her boots kicked up little puffs of pigment as she crunched across the butterfly wings to the shop.

Chronomode (*Fine Bespoke Clothing of the Past*, the sign read underneath) was the most exclusive Vagabonder boutique in the northern hemisphere. The floors were real date-verified oak, the velvet curtains shipped from Paris in a Chinese junk during the six weeks in '58 when one of the Vagabonder boys slept with a Wright brother and planes hadn't been invented.

Simone was already behind the counter arranging buttons by era of origin. Petra hadn't figured out until her fourth year working there that Simone didn't live upstairs, and Petra still wasn't convinced.

As Petra crossed the floor, an oak beam creaked.

Simone looked up and sighed. "Petra, wipe your feet on the mat. That's what it's for."

Petra glanced over her shoulder; behind her was a line of her footprints, mottled purple and blue and gold.

The first client of the day was the heiress to the O'Rourke fortune. Chronomode had a history with the family; the first one was the boy, James, who'd slept with Orville Wright and ruined Simone's drape delivery *par avion*. The O'Rourkes had generously paid for shipment by junk, and one of the plugs they sent back with James was able to fix things so that the historic flight was only two weeks late. Some stamps became very collectible, and the O'Rourkes became loyal clients of Simone's.

They gave a Vagabonding to each of their children as twenty-first-birthday presents. Of course, you had to be twenty-five before you were allowed to Bore back in time, but somehow exceptions were always made for O'Rourkes, who had to fit a lot of living into notoriously short life spans.

Simone escorted Fantasy O'Rourke personally to the center of the shop, a low dais with a three-frame mirror. The curtains in the windows were already closed by request; the O'Rourkes liked to maintain an alluring air of secrecy they could pass off as discretion.

"Ms. O'Rourke, it's a pleasure to have you with us," said Simone. Her hands, clasped behind her back, just skimmed the hem of her black jacket.

Never cut a jacket too long, Simone told Petra her first day. It's the first sign of an amateur.

"Of course," said Ms. O'Rourke. "I haven't decided on a destination, you know. I thought maybe Victorian England."

From behind the counter, Petra rolled her eyes. Everyone wanted Victorian England.

Simone said, "Excellent choice, Ms. O'Rourke."

"On the other hand, I saw a historian the other day in the listings who specializes in eighteenth century Japan. He was delicious." She smiled. "A little temporary surgery, a trip to Kyoto's geisha district. What would I look like then?"

"A vision," said Simone through closed teeth.

Petra had apprenticed at a tailor downtown, and stayed there for three years afterward. She couldn't manage better, and had no hopes.

Simone came into the shop two days after a calf-length black pencil skirt had gone out (some pleats below the knee needed mending).

Her gloves were black wool embroidered with black silk thread. Petra couldn't see anything but the gloves around the vast and smoky sewing machine that filled the tiny closet where she worked, but she knew at once it was the woman who belonged to the trim black skirt.

"You should be working in my shop," said Simone. "I offer superior conditions."

Petra looked over the top of the rattling machine. "You think?"

"You can leave the attitude here," said Simone, and went to the front of the shop to wait.

Simone showed Petra her back office (nothing but space and light and chrome), the image library, the labeled bolts of cloth—1300, 1570, China, Flanders, Rome.

"What's the shop name?" Petra asked finally.

"Chronomode," Simone said, and waited for Petra's exclamation of awe. When none came, she frowned. "I have a job for you," she continued, and walked to the table, tapping the wood with one finger. "See what's left to do. I want it by morning, so there's time to fix any mistakes."

The lithograph was a late 19th century evening gown, nothing but pleats, and Petra pulled the fabrics from the library with shaking hands.

Simone came in the next day, tore out the hem of the petticoat, and sewed it again by hand before she handed it over to the client.

Later Petra ventured, "So you're unhappy with the quality of my work."

Simone looked up from a Byzantine dalmatic she was sewing with a bone needle. "Happiness is not the issue," she said, as though Petra was a simpleton. "Perfection is."

That was the year the mice disappeared.

Martin Spatz, the actor, had gone Vagabonding in 8,000 BC and killed a wild dog that was about to attack him. (It was a blatant violation of the rules—you had to be prepared to die in the past, that was the first thing you signed on the contract. He went to jail over it. They trimmed two years off because he used a stick, and not the pistol he'd brought with him.)

No one could find a direct connection between the dog and the mice, but people speculated. People were still speculating, even though the mice were long dead.

Everything went, sooner or later; the small animals tended to last longer than the large ones, but eventually all that was left were some particularly hardy plants, and the butterflies. By the next year the butterflies were swarming enough to block out the summer sun, and Disease Control began to intervene.

The slow, steady disappearance of plants and animals was the only lasting problem from all the Vagabonding. Plugs were more loyal to their mission than the people who employed them, and if someone had to die in the line of work they were usually happy to do it. If they died, glory; if they lived, money.

Petra measured a plug once (German Renaissance, which seemed a pointless place to visit, but Petra didn't make the rules). He didn't say a word for the first hour. Then he said, "The cuffs go two inches past the wrist, not one and a half."

The client came back the next year with a yen for Colonial America. He brought two different plugs with him.

Petra asked, "What happened to the others?"

"They did their jobs," the client said, turned to Simone. "Now, Miss Carew, I was thinking I'd like to be a British commander. What do you think of that?"

"I would recommend civilian life," Simone said. "You'll find the Bore committee a little strict as regards impersonating the military."

When Petra was very young she'd taken her mother's sewing machine apart and put it back together. After that it didn't squeak, and Petra and her long thin fingers were sent to the tailor's place downtown for apprenticeship.

"At least you don't have any bad habits to undo," Simone had said the first week, dropping *The Dressmaker's Encyclopaedia 1890* on Petra's work table. "Though it would behoove you to be a little ashamed of your ignorance. Why—" Simone looked away and blew air through her teeth. "Why do this if you don't respect it?"

"Don't ask me—I liked engines," Petra said, opening the book with a thump.

Ms. O'Rourke decided at last on an era (18th-century Kyoto, so the historian must have been really good-looking after all), and Simone insisted on several planning sessions before the staff was even brought in for dressing.

"It makes the ordering process smoother," she said.

"Oh, it's nothing, I'm easy to please," said Ms. O'Rourke.

Simone looked at Petra. Petra feigned interest in buttons.

Petra was assigned to the counter, and while Simone kept Ms. O'Rourke in the main room with the curtains discreetly drawn, Petra spent a week rewinding ribbons on their spools and looking at the portfolios of Italian armor-makers. Simone was considering buying a set to be able to gauge the best wadding for the vests beneath.

Petra looked at the joints, imagined the pivots as the arm moved back and forth. She wondered if the French hadn't had a better sense of how the body moved; some of the Italian stuff just looked like an excuse for filigree.

When the gentleman came up to the counter he had to clear his throat before she noticed him.

She put on a smile. "Good morning, sir. How can we help you?"

He turned and presented his back to her—three arrows stuck out from the left shoulder blade, four from the right.

"Looked sideways during the Crusades," he said proudly. "Not recommended, but I sort of like them. It's a souvenir. I'd like to keep them. Doctors said it was fine, nothing important was pierced."

Petra blinked. "I see. What can we do for you?"

"Well, I'd really like to have some shirts altered," he said, and when he laughed the tips of the arrows quivered like wings.

"You'd never catch me vagabonding back in time," Petra said that night.

Simone seemed surprised by the attempt at conversation (after five years she was still surprised). "It's lucky you'll never have the money, then."

Petra clipped a thread off the buttonhole she was finishing.

"I don't understand it," Simone said more quietly, as though she were alone.

Petra didn't know what she meant.

Simone turned the page on her costume book, paused to look at one of the hair ornaments.

"We'll need to find the ivory one," Simone said. "It's the most beautiful."

"Will Ms. O'Rourke notice?"

"I give my clients the best," Simone said, which wasn't really an answer.

"I've finished the alterations," Petra said finally, and held up one of the shirts, sliced open at the shoulder blades to give the arrows room, with buttons down the sides for ease of dressing.

Petra was surprised the first time she saw a Bore team in the shop—the Vagabond, the Historian, the translator, two plugs, and a "Consultant" whose job was ostensibly to provide a life story for the client, but who spent three hours insisting that Roman women could have worn corsets if the Empire had sailed far enough.

The Historian was either too stupid or too smart to argue, and Petra's protest had been cut short by Simone stepping forward to suggest they discuss jewelry for the Historian and plausible wardrobe for the plugs.

"Why, they're noble too, of course," the client had said, adjusting his high collar. "What else could they be?"

Plugs were always working-class, even Petra knew that; in case you had to stay behind and fix things for a noble who'd mangled the past, you didn't want to run the risk of a rival faction calling for your head, which they tended strongly to do.

Petra tallied the cost of the wardrobe for a Roman household: a million in material and labor, another half a million in jewelry. With salaries for the entourage and the fees for machine management and operation, his vacation would cost him ten million.

Ten million to go back in time in lovely clothes, and not be allowed to change a thing. Petra took dutiful notes and marked in the margin, *A WASTE*.

She looked up from the paper when Simone said, "No."

The client had frowned, not used to the word. "But I'm absolutely sure it was possible—"

"It may be possible, depending on your source," Simone said, with a look at the Historian, "but it is not right."

"Well, no offense, Miss Carew, but I'm paying you to dress me, not to give me your opinion on what's right."

"Apologies, sir," said Simone, smiling. "You won't be paying me at all. Petra, please show the gentlemen out."

They made the papers; Mr. Bei couldn't keep from talking about his experience in the Crusades.

"I was going to plan another trip right away," he was quoted as saying, "but I don't know how to top this! I think I'll be staying here. The Institute has already asked me to come and speak about the importance of knowing your escape plan in an emergency, and believe me, I know it."

Under his photo was the tiny caption: *Clothes by Chronomode*.

"Mr. Bei doesn't mention his plugs," Petra said, feeling a little sick. "Guess he wasn't the only one that got riddled with arrows."

"It's what the job requires. If you have the aptitude, it's excellent work."

"It can't be worth it."

"Nothing is worth what we give it," said Simone. She dropped her copy of the paper on Petra's desk. "You need to practice your running stitch at home. The curve on that back seam looks like a six-year-old made it."

Tibi cornered Petra at the Threaders' Guild meeting. Tibi worked at Mansion, which outfitted Vagabonders with a lot more pomp and circumstance than Simone did.

Tibi had a dead butterfly pinned to her dress, and when she hugged Petra it left a dusting of pale green on Petra's shoulder.

"Petra! Lord, I was JUST thinking about you! I passed Chronomode the other day and thought, Poor Petra, it's SUCH a prison in there. Holding up?" Tibi turned to a tall young tailor beside her. "Michael, darling, Petra works for Carew over at Chronomode."

The tailor raised his eyebrows. "There's a nightmare. How long have you hung in there, a week?"

Five years and counting. "Sure," Petra said.

"No, for AGES," Tibi corrected. "I don't know how she makes it, I really don't, it's just so HORRIBLE." Tibi wrapped one arm around the tailor and cast a pitying glance at Petra. "I was there for a week, I made the Guild send me somewhere else a week later, it was just inhuman. What is it LIKE, working there for SO long without anyone getting you out of there?"

"Oh, who knows," said Petra. "What's it like getting investigated for sending people back to medieval France with machine-sewn clothes?"

Tibi frowned. "The company settled that."

Petra smiled at Tibi, then at the tailor. "I'm Petra."

"Michael," he said, and frowned at her hand when they shook.

"Those are just calluses from the needles," Petra said. "Don't mind them."

"Ms. O'Rourke's kimono is ready for you to look at," Petra said, bringing the mannequin to Simone's desk.

"No need," said Simone, her eyes on her computer screen, "you don't have enough imagination to invent mistakes."

Petra hoped that was praise, but suspected otherwise.

A moment later Simone slammed a hand on her desk. "Dammit, look at this. The hair ornament I need is a reproduction. Because naturally a reproduction is indistinguishable from an original. The people of 1743 Kyoto will never notice. Are they hiring antiques dealers out of primary school these days?"

Simone pushed away from the desk in disgust and left through the door to the shop, heels clicking.

Petra smoothed the front of the kimono. It was heavy grey silk, painted with cherry blossoms and chrysanthemums. Near the hem, Petra had added butterflies.

The light in the shop was still on; Petra saw it just as she was leaving.

Careless, she thought as she crossed the workshop. Simone would have killed me.

She had one hand on the door when the sound of a footstep stopped her. Were they being robbed? She thought about the Danish Bronze Age brooches hidden behind the counter in their velvet wrappers.

Petra grabbed a fabric weight in her fist and opened the door a crack.

Simone stood before the fitting mirror, holding a length of bright yellow silk against her shoulders. It washed her out (she'd never let a client with her complexion touch the stuff), but her reflection was smiling.

She hung it from her collarbones like a Roman; draped it across her shoulder like the pallav of a sari; bustled it around her waist. The bright gold slid through her fingers as if she was dancing with it.

Simone gathered the fabric against her in two hands, closed her eyes at the feel of it against her face.

Petra closed the door and went out the back way, eyes fixed on the wings at her feet.

When she came around the front of the shop the light was still on in the window, and Simone stood like a doll wrapped in a wide yellow ribbon, imagining a past she'd never see.

Petra turned for home.

Disease Control hadn't made the rounds yet, and the darkness was a swarm of wings, purple and blue and gold.

EVENTS PRECEDING THE HELVETICAN RENAISSANCE

JOHN KESSEL

When my mind cleared, I found myself in the street. The protector god Bishamon spoke to me then: *The boulevard to the spaceport runs straight up the mountain. And you must run straight up the boulevard.*

The air was full of wily spirits, and moving fast in the Imperial City was a crime. But what is man to disobey the voice of a god? So I ran. The pavement vibrated with the thunder of the great engines of the Caslonian Empire. Behind me the curators of the Imperial Archives must by now have discovered the mare's nest I had made of their defenses, and perhaps had already realized that something was missing.

Above the plateau the sky was streaked with clouds, through which shot violet gravity beams carrying ships down from and up to planetary orbit. Just outside the gate to the spaceport a family in rags—husband, wife, two children—used a net of knotted cords to catch fish from the sewers. Ignoring them, prosperous citizens in embroidered robes passed among the shops of the port bazaar, purchasing duty-free wares, recharging their concubines, seeking a meal before departure. *Slower, now.*

I slowed my pace. I became indistinguishable from them, moving smoothly among the travelers.

To the Caslonian eye, I was calm, self-possessed; within me, rage and joy contended. I had in my possession the means to redeem my people. I tried not to think, only to act, but now that my mind was rekindled, it raced. Certainly it would go better for me if I left the planet before anyone understood what I had stolen. Yet I was very hungry, and the aroma of food from the restaurants along the way enticed me. It would be foolishness itself to stop here.

Enter the restaurant, I was told. So I stepped into the most elegant of the establishments.

The maître d' greeted me. "Would the master like a table, or would he prefer to dine at the bar?"

"The bar," I said

"Step this way." There was no hint of the illicit about his manner, though something about it implied indulgence. He was proud to offer me this experience that few could afford.

He seated me at the circular bar of polished rosewood. Before me, and the few others seated there, the chef grilled meats on a heated metal slab. Waving his arms in the air like a dancer, he tossed flanks of meat between two force knives, letting them drop to the griddle, flipping them dexterously upward again in what was as much performance as preparation. The energy blades of the knives sliced through the meat without resistance, the sides of these same blades batting them like paddles. An aroma of burning hydrocarbons wafted on the air.

An attractive young man displayed for me a list of virtualities that represented the "cuts" offered by the establishment, including subliminal tastes. The "cuts" referred to the portions of the animal's musculature from which the slabs of meat had been sliced. My mouth watered.

He took my order, and I sipped a cocktail of bitters and Belanova.

While I waited, I scanned the restaurant. The fundamental goal of our order is to vindicate divine justice in allowing evil to exist. At a small nearby table, a young woman leaned beside a child, probably her daughter, and encouraged her to eat. The child's beautiful face was the picture of innocence as she tentatively tasted a scrap of pink flesh. The mother was very beautiful. I wondered if this was her first youth.

The chef finished his performance, to the mild applause of the other patrons. The young man placed my steak before me. The chef turned off the blades and laid them aside, then ducked down a trap door to the oubliette where the slaves were kept. As soon as he was out of sight, the god told me, *Steal a knife.*

While the diners were distracted by their meals, I reached over the counter, took one of the force blades, and slid it into my boot. Then I ate. The taste was extraordinary. Every cell of my body vibrated with excitement and shame. My senses reeling, it took me a long time to finish.

A slender man in a dark robe sat next to me. "That smells good," he said. "Is that genuine animal flesh?"

"Does it matter to you?"

"Ah, brother, calm yourself. I'm not challenging your taste."

"I'm pleased to hear it."

"But I am challenging your identity." He parted the robe—his tunic bore the sigil of Port Security. "Your passport, please."

I exposed the inside of my wrist for him. A scanlid slid over his left eye and he examined the marks beneath my skin. "Very good," he said. He drew a blaster from the folds of his cassock. "We seldom see such excellent forgeries. Stand up, and come with me."

I stood. He took my elbow in a firm grip, the bell of the blaster against my side. No one in the restaurant noticed. He walked me outside, down the crowded bazaar. "You see, brother, that there is no escape from consciousness. The minute it returns, you are vulnerable. All your prayer is to no avail."

This is the arrogance of the Caslonian. They treat us as non-sentients, and they believe in nothing. Yet as I prayed, I heard no word.

I turned to him. "You may wish the absence of the gods, but you are mistaken. The gods are everywhere present." As I spoke the plosive "p" of "present," I popped the cap from my upper right molar and blew the moondust it contained into his face.

The agent fell writhing to the pavement. I ran off through the people, dodging collisions. My ship was on the private field at the end of the bazaar. Before I had gotten half way there, an alarm began sounding. People looked up in bewilderment, stopping in their tracks. The walls of buildings and stalls blinked into multiple images of me. Voices spoke from the air: "This man is a fugitive from the state. Apprehend him."

I would not make it to the ship unaided, so I turned on my perceptual overdrive. Instantly, everything slowed. The voices of the people and the sounds of the port dropped an octave. They moved as if in slow motion. I moved, to myself, as if in slow motion as well—my body could in no way keep pace with my racing nervous system—but to the people moving at normal speed, my reflexes were lighting fast. Up to the limit of my physiology—and my joints had been reinforced to take the additional stress, my muscles could handle the additional lactic acid for a time—I could move at twice the speed of a normal human. I could function perhaps for ten minutes in this state before I collapsed.

The first person to accost me—a sturdy middle aged man—I seized by the arm. I twisted it behind his back and shoved him into the second who took up the command. As I dodged through the crowd up the concourse, it began to drizzle. I felt as if I could slip between the raindrops. I pulled the force blade from my boot and sliced the ear from the next man who tried to stop me. His comic expression of dismay still lingers in my mind. Glancing behind, I saw the agent in black, face swollen with pustules from the moondust, running toward me.

I was near the field. In the boarding shed, attendants were folding the low-status passengers and sliding them into dispatch pouches, to be carried onto a ship and stowed in drawers for their passage. Directly before me, I saw the woman and child I had noticed in the restaurant. The mother had out a parasol and was holding it over the girl to keep the rain off her. Not slowing, I snatched the little girl and carried her off. The child yelped, the mother screamed. I held the blade to the girl's neck. "Make way!" I shouted to the security men at the field's entrance. They fell back.

"Halt!" came the call from behind me. The booth beside the gate was seared with a blaster bolt. I swerved, turned, and, my back to the gate, held the girl before me.

The agent in black, followed by two security women, jerked to a stop. "You mustn't hurt her," the agent said.

"Oh? And why is that?"

"It's against everything your order believes."

Master Darius had steeled me for this dilemma before sending me on my mission. He told me, "You will encounter such situations, Adlan. When they arise, you must resolve the complications."

"You are right!" I called to my pursuers, and threw the child at them.

The agent caught her, while the other two aimed and fired. One of the beams grazed my shoulder. But by then I was already through the gate and onto the tarmac.

A port security robot hurled a flame grenade. I rolled through the flames. My ship rested in the maintenance pit, cradled in the violet anti-grav beam. I slid down the ramp into the open airlock, hit the emergency close, and climbed to the controls. Klaxons wailed outside. I bypassed all the launch protocols and released the beam. The ship shot upward like an apple seed flicked by a fingernail; as soon as it had hit the stratosphere, I fired the engines and blasted through the scraps of the upper atmosphere into space.

The orbital security forces were too slow, and I made my escape.

I awoke battered, bruised, and exhausted in the pilot's chair. The smell of my burned shoulder reminded me of the steak I had eaten in the port bazaar. The stress of accelerating nerve impulses had left every joint in my body aching. My arms were blue with contusions, and I was as enfeebled as an old man.

The screens showed me to be in an untraveled quarter of the system's cometary cloud; my ship had cloaked itself in ice so that on any detector I would simply be another bit of debris among billions. I dragged myself from the chair and down to the galley, where I warmed some broth and gave myself an injection of cellular repair mites. Then I fell into my bunk and slept.

My second waking was relatively free of pain. I recharged my tooth and ate again. I kneeled before the shrine and bowed my head in prayer, letting peace flow down my spine and relax all the muscles of my back. I listened for the voices of the gods.

I was reared by my mother on Bembo. My mother was an extraordinary beautiful girl. One day Akvan, looking down on her, was so moved by lust that he took the form of a vagabond and raped her by the side of the road. Nine months later I was born.

The goddess Sedna became so jealous that she laid a curse on my mother, who turned into a lawyer. And so we moved to Helvetica. There, in the shabby city of Urushana, in the waterfront district along the river, she took up her practice, defending criminals and earning a little *baksheesh* greasing the relations between the Imperial Caslonian government and the corrupt local officials. Mother's ambition for me was to go to an off-planet university, but for me the work of a student was like pushing a very large rock up a very steep hill. I got into fights; I pursued women of questionable virtue. Having exhausted my prospects in the city, I entered the native constabulary, where I was re-engineered for accelerated combat. But my propensity for violence saw me cashiered out of the service within six months. Hoping to get a grip on my passions, I made the pilgrimage to the monastery of the Pujmanian Order. There I petitioned for admission as a novice, and, to my great surprise, was accepted.

It was no doubt the work of Master Darius, who took an interest in me from my first days on the plateau. Perhaps it was my divine heritage, which had placed those voices in my head. Perhaps it was my checkered career to that date. The Master taught me to distinguish between those impulses that were the work of my savage nature, and those that were the voices of the gods. He taught me to identify the individual gods. It is not an easy path. I fasted, I worked in the gardens, I practiced the martial arts, I cleaned the cesspool, I sewed new clothes and mended old, I tended the orchards. I became an expert tailor, and sewed many of the finest kosodes worn by the masters on feast days. In addition, Master Darius held special sessions with me, putting me into a trance during which, I was later told by my fellow novices, I continued to act normally for days, only to awake with no memories of my actions.

And so I was sent on my mission. Because I had learned how not to think, I could not be detected by the spirits who guarded the Imperial Archives.

Five plays, immensely old, collectively titled *The Abandonment*, are all that document the rebirth of humanity after its long extinction. The foundational cycle consists of *The Archer's Fall, Stochik's Revenge, The Burning Tree, Close the Senses, Shut the Doors*, and the mystical fifth, *The Magic Tortoise*. No one knows who wrote them. It is believed they were composed within the first thirty years after the human race was recreated by the gods. Besides being the most revered cultural artifacts of humanity, these plays are also the sacred texts of the universal religion, and claimed as the fundamental political documents by all planetary governments. They are preserved only in a single copy. No recording has ever been made of their performance. The actors chosen to present the plays in the foundational festivals on all the worlds do not study and learn them; through a process similar to the one Master Darius taught me to confuse the spirits, the actors *become* the characters. Once the performance is done, it passes from their minds.

These foundational plays, of inestimable value, existed now only in my mind. I had destroyed the crystal containing them in the archives. Without these plays, the heart of Caslon had been ripped away. If the populace knew of their loss, there would be despair and riot.

And once Master Darius announced that the Order held the only copy in our possession, it would only be a matter of time before the Empire would be obliged to free our world.

Three days after my escape from Caslon, I set course for Helvetica. Using an evanescent wormhole, I would emerge within the planet's inner ring. The ship, still encased in ice, would look like one of the fragments that formed the ring. From there I would reconnoiter, find my opportunity to leave orbit, and land. But because the ring stood far down in the gravitation well of the planet, it was a tricky maneuver.

Too tricky. Upon emergence in the Helvetican ring, my ship collided with one of the few nickel-iron meteoroids in the belt, disabling my engines. Within twenty minutes, Caslonian hunter-killers grappled with the hull. My one advantage was that by now they knew that I possessed the plays, and therefore they could not afford to blast me out of the sky. I could kill them, but they could not harm me. But I had no doubt that once they caught me, they would rip my mind to shreds seeking the plays.

I had only minutes—the hull door would not hold long. I abandoned the control room and retreated to the engine compartment. The place was a mess, barely holding pressure after the meteoroid collision, oxygen cylinders scattered about and the air acrid with the scent of burned wiring. I opened the cat's closet, three meters tall and two wide. From a locker I yanked two piezofiber suits. I turned them on, checked their readouts—they were fully charged—and threw them into the closet. It was cramped in there with tools and boxes of supplies. Sitting on one of the crates, I pulled up my shirt, exposing my bruised ribs. The aluminum light of the closet turned my skin sickly white. Using a microtome, I cut an incision in my belly below my lowest rib. There was little blood. I reached into the cut, found the nine-dimensional pouch, and drew it out between my index and middle fingers. I sprayed false skin over the wound. As I did, the artificial gravity cut off, and the lights went out.

I slipped on my night vision eyelids, read the directions on the pouch, ripped it open, removed the soldier and unfolded it. The body expanded, became fully three dimensional, and, in a minute, was floating naked before me. My first surprise: it was a woman. Dark skinned, slender, her body was very beautiful. I leaned over her, covered her mouth with mine, and blew air into her lungs. She jerked convulsively and drew a shuddering breath, then stopped. Her eyelids fluttered, then opened.

"Wake up!" I said, drawing on my piezosuit. I slipped the force blade into the boot, strapped on the belt with blaster and supplies, shrugged into the backpack. "Put on this suit! No time to waste."

She took in my face, the surroundings. From beyond the locker door I heard the sounds of the commandos entering the engine room.

"I am Brother Adlan," I whispered urgently. "You are a soldier of the Republican Guard?" As I spoke I helped her into the skinsuit.

"Lieutenant Nahid Esfandiar. What's happening?"

"We are in orbit over Helvetica, under attack by Caslonian commandos. We need to break out of here."

"What weapons have we?"

I handed her a blaster. "They will have accelerated perceptions. Can you speed yours?"

Her glance passed over me, measuring me for a fool. "Done already." She sealed her suit and flipped down the faceplate on her helmet.

I did not pay attention to her, because as she spoke, all-seeing Liu-Bei spoke to me. *Three men beyond this door.* In my mind I saw the engine room, and the three soldiers who were preparing to rip open the closet.

I touched my helmet to hers and whispered to Nahid, "There are three of them outside. The leader is directly across from the door. He has a common blaster, on stun. To the immediate right, a meter away, one of the commandos has a pulse rifle. The third, about to set the charge, has a pneumatic projector, probably with sleep gas. When they blow the door, I'll go high, you low. Three meters to the cross corridor, down one level and across starboard to the escape pod."

Just then, the door to the closet was ripped open, and through it came a blast of sleep gas. But we were locked into our suits, helmets sealed. Our blaster beams, pink in the darkness, crossed as they emerged from the gloom of the closet. We dove through the doorway in zero-G, bouncing off the bulkheads, blasters flaring. The commandos were just where the gods had told me they would be. I cut down one before we even cleared the doorway. Though they moved as quickly as we did, they were trying not to kill me, and the fact that there were two of us now took them by surprise.

Nahid fired past my ear, taking out another. We ducked through the hatch and up the companionway. Two more commandos came from the control room at the end of the corridor; I was able to slice one of them before he could fire, but the other's stunner numbed my thigh. Nahid torched his head and grabbed me by the arm, hurling me around the corner into the cross passageway.

Two more commandos guarded the hatchway to the escape pod. Nahid fired at them, killing one and wounding the other in a single shot. But instead of heading for the pod she jerked me the other way, toward the umbilical to the Caslonian ship.

"What are you doing?" I protested.

"Shut up," she said. "They can hear us." Halfway across the umbilical, Nahid stopped, braced herself against one wall, raised her blaster, and, without hesitation, blew a hole in the wall opposite. The air rushed out. A klaxon sounded the pressure breach, another commando appeared at the junction of the umbilical and the Caslonian ship—I burned him down—and we slipped through the gap into the space between the two ships. She grabbed my arm and pulled me around the hull of my own vessel.

I realized what she intended. Grabbing chunks of ice, we pulled ourselves over the horizon of my ship until we reached the outside hatch of the escape pod. I punched in the access code. We entered the pod and while Nahid sealed the hatch, I powered up and blasted us free of the ship before we had even buckled in.

The pod shot toward the upper atmosphere. The commandos guarding the inner hatch were ejected into the vacuum behind us. Retro fire slammed us into our seats. I caught a glimpse of bodies floating in the chaos we'd left behind before proton beams lanced out from the Caslonian raider, clipping the pod and sending us into a spin.

"You couldn't manage this without me?" Nahid asked.

"No sarcasm, please." I fought to steady the pod so the heat shields were oriented for atmosphere entry.

We hit the upper atmosphere. For twenty minutes we were buffeted by the jet stream, and it got hot in the tiny capsule. I became very aware of Nahid's scent, sweat and a trace of rosewater; she must have put on perfume before she was folded into the packet that had been implanted in me. Her eyes moved slowly over the interior of the pod.

"What is the date?" she asked.

"The nineteenth of Cunegonda," I told her. The pod bounced violently and drops of sweat flew from my forehead. Three red lights flared on the board, but I could do nothing about them.

"What year?"

I saw that it would not be possible to keep many truths from her. "You have been suspended in nine-space for sixty years."

The pod lurched again, a piece of the ablative shield tearing away. She sat motionless, taking in the loss of her entire life.

A snatch of verse came to my lips, unbidden:

> "Our life is but a trifle
> A child's toy abandoned by the road
> When we are called home."

"Very poetic," she said. "Are we going to ride this pod all the way down? They probably have us on locator from orbit, and will vaporize it the minute it hits. I'd rather not be called home just now."

"We'll eject at ten kilometers. Here's your chute."

When the heat of the re-entry had abated and we hit the troposphere, we blew the explosive bolts and shot free of the tumbling pod. Despite the thin air of the upper atmosphere, I was buffeted almost insensible, spinning like a prayer wheel. I lost sight of Nahid.

I fell for a long time, but eventually managed to stabilize myself spread-eagled, dizzy, my stomach lurching. Below, the Jacobin Range stretched north to southwest under the rising sun, the snow-covered rock on the upper reaches folded like a discarded robe, and below the thick forest climbing up to the tree line.

Some minutes later, I witnessed the impressive flare of the pod striking just below the summit of one of the peaks, tearing a gash in the ice cover and sending up a plume of black smoke that was torn away by the wind. I tongued the trigger in my helmet, and with a nasty jerk, the airfoil chute deployed from my backpack. I could see Nahid's red chute some five hundred meters below me; I steered toward her hoping we could land near each other. The forested mountainside came up fast. I spotted a clearing on a ledge two thirds of the way up the slope and made for it, but my burned shoulder wasn't working right, and I was coming in too fast. I caught a glimpse of Nahid's foil in the mountain scar ahead, but I wasn't going to reach her.

At the last minute, I pulled up and skimmed the tree tops, caught a boot against a top limb, flipped head over heels and crashed into the foliage, coming to rest hanging upside down from the tree canopy. The suit's rigidity kept me from breaking any bones, but it took me ten minutes to release the shrouds. I turned down the suit's inflex and took off my helmet to better see what I was doing. When I did, the limb supporting me broke, and I fell the last ten meters through the trees, hitting another limb on the way down, knocking me out.

I was woken by Nahid rubbing snow into my face. My piezosuit had been turned off, and the fabric was flexible again. Nahid leaned over me, supporting my head. "Can you move your feet?" she asked.

My thigh still was numb from the stunner. I tried moving my right foot. Though I could not feel any response, I saw the boot twitch. "So it would seem."

Done with me, she let my head drop. "So, do you have some plan?"

I pulled up my knees and sat up. My head ached. We were surrounded by the boles of the tall firs; above our heads the wind swayed the trees, but down here the air was calm, and sunlight filtered down in patches, moving over the packed fine brown needles of the forest floor. Nahid had pulled down my chute to keep it from advertising our position. She crouched on one knee and examined the charge indicator on her blaster.

I got up and inventoried the few supplies we had—my suit's water reservoir, holding maybe a liter, three packs of *gichy* crackers in the belt. Hers would have no more than that. "We should get moving; the Caslonians will send a landing party, or notify the colonial government in Guliston to send a security squad."

"And why should I care?"

"You fought for the republic against the Caslonians. When the war was lost and the protectorate established, you had yourself folded. Didn't you expect to take up arms again when called back to life?"

"You tell me that was sixty years ago. What happened to the rest of the Republican Guard?"

"The Guard was wiped out in the final Caslonian assaults."

"And our folded battalion?"

The blistering roar of a flyer tore through the clear air above the trees. Nahid squinted up, eyes following the glittering ship. "They're heading for where the pod hit." She pulled me to my feet, taking us downhill, perhaps in the hope of finding better cover in the denser forest near one of the mountain freshets.

"No," I said. "Up the slope."

"That's where they'll be."

"It can't be helped. We need to get to the monastery. We're on the wrong side of the mountains." I turned up the incline. After a moment, she followed.

We stayed beneath the trees for as long as possible. The slope was not too steep at this altitude; the air was chilly, with dying patches of old snow in the shadows. Out in the direct sunlight, it would be hot until evening came. I had climbed these mountains fifteen years before, an adolescent trying to find a way to live away from the world. As we moved, following the path of a small stream, the aches in my joints eased.

We did not talk. I had not thought about what it would mean to wake this soldier, other than how she would help me in a time of extremity. There are no women in our order, and though we take no vow of celibacy and some commerce takes place between brothers in their cells late at night, there is little opportunity for contact with the opposite sex. Nahid, despite her forbidding nature, was beautiful: dark skin, black eyes, lustrous black hair cut short, the three parallel scars of her rank marking her left cheek. As a boy in Urushana, I had tormented my sleepless nights with visions of women as beautiful as she; in my short career as a constable I had avidly pursued women far less so. One of them had provoked the fight that had gotten me cashiered.

The forest thinned as we climbed higher. Large folds of granite lay exposed to the open air, creased with fractures and holding pockets of earth where trees sprouted in groups. We had to circle around to avoid coming into the open, and even that would be impossible when the forest ended completely. I pointed us south, where Dundrahad Pass, dipping below 3,000 meters, cut through the mountains. We were without snowshoes or trekking gear, but I hoped that, given the summer temperatures, the pass would be clear enough to traverse in the night without getting ourselves killed. The skinsuits we wore would be proof against the nighttime cold.

We saw no signs of the Caslonians, but when we reached the tree line, we stopped to wait for darkness anyway. The air had turned colder, and a sharp wind blew down the pass from the other side of the mountains. We settled in a hollow beneath a patch of twisted scrub trees and waited out the declining sun. At the zenith, the first moon Mahsheed rode, waning gibbous. In the notch of the pass above and ahead of us, the second moon Roshanak rose. Small, glowing green, it moved perceptibly as it raced around the planet. I nibbled at some *gichy*, sipping water from my suit's reservoir. Nahid's eyes were shadowed; she scanned the slope.

"We'll have to wait until Mahsheed sets before we move," Nahid said. "I don't want to be caught in the pass in its light."

"It will be hard for us to see where we're going."

She didn't reply. The air grew colder. After a while, without looking at me, she spoke. "So what happened to my compatriots?"

I saw no point in keeping anything from her. "As the Caslonians consolidated their conquest, an underground of Republicans pursued a guerilla war. Two years later, they mounted an assault on the provincial capital in Kofarnihon. They unfolded your battalion to aid them, and managed to seize the armory. But the Caslonians sent reinforcements and set up a siege. When the rebels refused to surrender, the Caslonians vaporized the entire city, hostages, citizens, and rebels alike. That was the end of the Republican Guard." Nahid's dark eyes watched me as I told her all this. The tightness of her lips held grim skepticism.

"Yet here I am," she said.

"I don't know how you came to be the possession of the order. Some refugee, perhaps. The masters, sixty years ago, debated what to do with you. Given the temperament of the typical guardsman, it was assumed that, had you been restored to life, you would immediately get yourself killed in assaulting the Caslonians, putting the order at risk. It was decided to keep you in reserve, in the expectation that, at some future date, your services would be useful."

"You monks were always fair-weather democrats. Ever your order over the welfare of the people, or even their freedom. So you betrayed the republic."

"You do us an injustice."

"It was probably Javeed who brought me—the lying monk attached to our unit."

I recognized the name. Brother Javeed, a bent, bald man of great age, had run the monastery kitchen. I had never thought twice about him. He had died a year after I joined the order.

"Why do you think I was sent on this mission?" I told her. "We mean to set Helvetica free. And we shall do so, if we reach Sharishabz."

"How do you propose to accomplish that? Do you want to see your monastery vaporized?"

"They will not dare. I have something of theirs that they will give up the planet for. That's why they tried to board my ship rather than destroy it; that's why they didn't bother to disintegrate the escape pod when they might easily have shot us out of the sky."

"And this inestimably valuable item that you carry? It must be very small."

"It's in my head. I have stolen the only copies of the Foundational Dramas."

She looked at me. "So?"

Her skepticism was predictable, but it still angered me. "So—they will gladly trade Helvetica's freedom for the return of the plays."

She lowered her head, rubbed her brow with her hand. I could not read her. She made a sound, an intake of breath. For a moment, I thought she wept. Then she raised her head and laughed in my face.

I fought an impulse to strike her. "Quiet!"

She laughed louder. Her shoulders shook, and tears came to her eyes. I felt my face turn red. "You should have let me die with the others, in battle. You crazy priest!"

"Why do you laugh?" I asked her. "Do you think they would send ships to embargo Helvetican orbital space, dispatch squads of soldiers and police, if what I carry were not valuable to them?"

"I don't believe in your fool's religion."

"Have you ever seen the plays performed?"

"Once, when I was a girl. I saw *The Archer's Fall* during the year-end festival in Tienkash. I fell asleep."

"They are the axis of human culture. The sacred stories of our race. We are *human* because of them. Through them the gods speak to us."

"I thought you monks heard the gods talking to you directly. Didn't they tell you to run us directly into the face of the guards securing the escape pod? It's lucky you had me along to cut our way out of that umbilical, or we'd be dead up there now."

"*You* might be dead. I would be in a sleep tank having my brain taken apart—to retrieve these dramas."

"There are no gods! Just voices in your head. They tell you to do what you already want to do."

"If you think the commands of the gods are easy, then just try to follow them for a single day."

We settled into an uncomfortable silence. The sun set, and the rings became visible in the sky, turned pink by the sunset in the west, rising silvery toward the zenith, where they were eclipsed by the planet's shadow. The light of the big moon still illuminated the open rock face before us. We would have a steep 300 meter climb above the tree line to the pass, then another couple of kilometers between the peaks in the darkness.

"It's cold," I said after a while.

Without saying anything, she reached out and tugged my arm. It took me a moment to realize that she wanted me to move next to her. I slid over, and we ducked our heads to keep below the wind. I could feel the taut muscles of her body beneath the skinsuit. The paradox of our alienation hit me. We were both the products of the gods. She did not believe this truth, but truth does not need to be believed to prevail.

Still, she was right that we had not escaped the orbiting commandos in the way I had expected.

The great clockwork of the universe turned. Green Roshanak sped past Mahsheed, for a moment in transit looking like the pupil of a god's observing eye, then set, and an hour later, Mahsheed followed her below the western horizon. The stars shone in all their glory, but it was as dark as it would get before Roshanak rose for the second time that night. It was time for us to take our chance and go.

We came out of our hiding place and moved to the edge of the scrub. The broken granite of the peak rose before us, faint gray in starlight. We set out across the rock, climbing in places, striding across rubble fields, circling areas of ice and melting snow. In a couple of places, we had to boost each other up, scrambling over boulders, finding hand and footholds in the vertical face where we were blocked. It was farther than I had estimated before the ground leveled and we were in the pass.

We were just cresting the last ridge when glaring white light shone down on us, and an amplified voice called from above. "Do not move! Drop your weapons and lie flat on the ground!"

I tongued my body into acceleration. In slow motion, Nahid crouched, raised her blaster, arm extended, sighted on the flyer and fired. I hurled my body into hers and threw her aside just as the return fire of projectile weapons splattered the rock where she had been into fragments. In my head, kind Eurynome insisted: *Back. We will show you the way.*

"This way!" I dragged Nahid over the edge of the rock face we had just climbed. It was a three-meter drop to the granite below; I landed hard, and she fell on my chest, knocking the wind from me. Around us burst a hail of sleep gas pellets. In trying to catch my breath I caught a whiff of the gas, and my head whirled. Nahid slid her helmet down over her face, and did the same for me.

From above us came the sound of the flyer touching down. Nahid started for the tree line, limping. She must have been hit or injured in our fall. I pulled her to our left, along the face of the rock. "Where—" she began.

"Shut up!" I grunted.

The commandos hit the ledge behind us, but the flyer had its searchlight aimed at the trees, and the soldiers followed the light. The fog of sleep gas gave us some cover.

We scuttled along the granite shelf until we were beyond the entrance to the pass. By this time, I had used whatever reserves of energy my body could muster, and passed into normal speed. I was exhausted.

"Over the mountain?" Nahid asked. "We can't."

"Under it," I said. I forced my body into motion, searching in the darkness for the cleft in the rock which, in the moment of the flyer attack, the gods had shown me. And there it was, two dark pits above a vertical fissure in the granite, like an impassive face. We climbed up the few meters to the brink of the cleft. Nahid followed, slower now, dragging her right leg. "Are you badly hurt?" I asked her.

"Keep going."

I levered my shoulder under her arm, and helped her along the ledge. Down in the forest, the lights of the commandos flickered, while a flyer hovered above, beaming bright white radiance down between the trees.

Once inside the cleft, I let her lean against the wall. Beyond the narrow entrance the way widened. I used my suit flash, and, moving forward, found an oval chamber of three meters with a sandy floor. Some small bones give proof that a predator had once used this cave for a lair. But at the back, a small passage gaped. I crouched and followed it deeper.

"Where are you going?" Nahid asked.

"Come with me."

The passage descended for a space, then rose. I emerged into a larger space. My flash showed not a natural cave, but a chamber of dressed rock, and opposite us, a metal door. It was just as my vision had said.

"What is this?" Nahid asked in wonder.

"A tunnel under the mountain." I took off my helmet and spoke the words that would open the door. The ancient mechanism began to hum. With a fall of dust, a gap appeared at the side of the door, and it slid open.

The door closed behind us with a disturbing finality, wrapping us in the silence of a tomb. We found ourselves in a corridor at least twice our height and three times that in width. Our lights showed walls smooth as plaster, but when I laid my hand on one, it proved to be cut from the living rock. Our boots echoed on the polished but dusty floor. The air was stale, unbreathed by human beings for unnumbered years.

I made Nahid sit. "Rest," I said. "Let me look at that leg."

Though she complied, she kept her blaster out, and her eyes scanned our surroundings warily. "Did you know of this?"

"No. The gods told me, just as we were caught in the pass."

"Praise be to the Pujmanian Order." I could not tell if there was any sarcasm in her voice.

A trickle of blood ran down her boot from the wound of a projectile gun. I opened the seam of her suit, cleaned the wound with antiseptic from my suit's first aid kit, and bandaged her leg. "Can you walk?" I asked.

She gave me a tight smile. "Lead on, Brother Adlan."

We moved along the hall. Several smaller corridors branched off, but we kept to the main way. Periodically, we came across doors, most of them closed. One gaped open upon a room where my light fell on a garage of wheeled vehicles, sitting patiently in long rows, their windows thick with dust. In the corner of the room, a fracture in the ceiling had let in a steady drip of water that had corroded the vehicle beneath it into a mass of rust.

Along the main corridor our lights revealed hieroglyphics carved above doorways, dead oval spaces on the wall that might once have been screens or windows. We must have gone a kilometer or more when the corridor ended suddenly in a vast cavernous opening.

Our lights were lost in the gloom above. A ramp led down to an underground city. Buildings of gracious curves, apartments like heaps of grapes stacked upon a table, halls whose walls were so configured that they resembled a huge garment discarded in a bedroom. We descended into the streets.

The walls of the buildings were figured in abstract designs of immense intricacy, fractal patterns from immense to microscopic, picked out by the beams of our flashlights. Colored tiles, bits of glass and mica. Many of the buildings were no more than sets of walls demarcating space, with horizontal trellises that must once have held plants above them rather than roofs. Here and there, outside what might have been cafes, tables and benches rose out of the polished floor. We arrived in a broad square with low buildings around it, centered on a dry fountain. The immense figures of a man, a woman, and a child dominated the center of the dusty reservoir. Their eyes were made of crystal, and stared blindly across their abandoned city.

Weary beyond words, hungry, bruised, we settled against the rim of the fountain and made to sleep. The drawn skin about her eyes told me of Nahid's pain. I tried to comfort her, made her rest her legs, elevated, on my own. We slept.

When I woke, Nahid was already up, changing the dressing on her bloody leg. The ceiling of the cave had lit, and a pale light shone down, making an early arctic dawn over the dead city.

"How is your leg?" I asked.

"Better. Do you have any more anodynes?"

I gave her what I had. She took them, and sighed. After a while, she asked, "Where did the people go?"

"They left the universe. They grew beyond the need of matter, and space. They became gods. You know the story."

"The ones who made this place were people like you and me."

"You and I are the descendants of the re-creation of a second human race three million years after the first ended in apotheosis. Or of the ones left behind, or banished back into the material world by the gods for some great crime."

Nahid rubbed her boot above the bandaged leg. "Which is it? Which child's tale do you expect me to believe?"

"How do you think I found the place? The gods told me, and here it is. Our mission is important to them, and they are seeing that we succeed. Justice is to be done."

"Justice? Tell the starving child about justice. The misborn and the dying. I would rather be the random creation of colliding atoms than subject to the whim of some transhumans no more godlike than I am."

"You speak out of bitterness."

"If they are gods, they are responsible for the horror that occurs in the world. So they are evil. Why otherwise would they allow things to be as they are?"

"To say that is to speak out of the limitations of our vision. We can't see the outcome of events. We're too close. But the gods see how all things will eventuate. Time is a landscape to them. All at once they see the acorn, the seedling, the ancient oak, the woodsman who cuts it, the fire that burns the wood, and the smoke that rises from the fire. And so they led us to this place."

"Did they lead the bullet to find my leg? Did they lead your order to place me on a shelf for a lifetime, separate me from every person I loved?" Nahid's voice rose. "Please save me your theodical prattle!"

" 'Theodical.' Impressive vocabulary for a soldier. But you—"

A scraping noise came from behind us. I turned to find that the giant male figure in the center of the fountain had moved. As I watched, its hand jerked another few centimeters. Its foot pulled free of its setting, and it stepped down form the pedestal into the empty basin.

We fell back from the fountain. The statue's eyes glowed a dull orange. Its lips moved, and it spoke in a voice like the scraping together of two files: "Do not flee, little ones."

Nahid let fly a shot from her blaster, which ricocheted off the shoulder of the metal man and scarred the ceiling of the cave. I pulled her away and we crouched behind a table before an open-sided building at the edge of the square.

The statue raised its arms in appeal. "Your shoes are untied," it said in its ghostly rasp. "We know why you are here. It seems to you that your lives hang in the balance, and of course you value your lives. As you should, dear ones. But I, who have no soul and therefore no ability to care, can tell you that the appetites that move you are entirely transitory. The world you live in is a game. You do not have a ticket."

"Quite mad," Nahid said. "Our shoes have no laces."

"But it's also true—they are therefore untied," I said. "And we have no tickets." I called out to the metal man, "Are you a god?"

"I am no god," the metal man said. "The gods left behind the better part of themselves when they abandoned matter. The flyer lies on its side in the woods. Press the silver pentagon. You must eat, but you must not eat too much. Here is food."

The shop behind us lit up, and in a moment the smell of food wafted from within.

I slid over to the entrance. On a table inside, under warm light, were two plates of rice and vegetables.

"He's right," I told Nahid.

"I'm not going to eat that food. Where did it come from? It's been thousands of years without a human being here."

"Come," I said. I drew her inside and made her join me at the table. I tasted. The food was good. Nahid sat warily, facing out to the square, blaster a centimeter from her plate. The metal man sat on the plaza stones, cross-legged, ducking its massive head in order to watch us. After a few moments, it began to croon.

Its voice was a completely mechanical sound, but the tune it sang was sweet, like a peasant song. I cannot convey to you the strangeness of sitting in that ancient restaurant, eating food conjured fresh out of nothing by ancient machines, listening to the music of creatures who might have been a different species from us.

When its song was ended, the metal man spoke: "If you wish to know someone, you need only observe that on which he bestows his care, and what sides of his own nature he cultivates." It lifted its arm and pointed at Nahid. Its finger stretched almost to the door. I could see the patina of corrosion on that metal digit. "If left to the gods, you will soon die."

The arm moved, and it pointed at me. "You must live, but you must not live too much. Take this."

The metal man opened the curled fingers of its hand, and in its huge palm was a small, round metallic device the size of an apple. I took it. Black and dense, it filled my hand completely. "Thank you," I said.

The man stood and returned to the empty fountain, climbed onto the central pedestal, and resumed its position. There it froze. Had we not been witness to it, I could never have believed it had moved.

Nahid came out of her musing over the man's sentence of her death. She lifted her head. "What is that thing?"

I examined the sphere, surface covered in pentagonal facets of dull metal. "I don't know."

In one of the buildings, we found some old furniture, cushions of metallic fabric that we piled together as bedding. We huddled together and slept.

Selene: Hear that vessel that docks above?
    It marks the end of our lives
    And the beginning of our torment.
    Stochik: Death comes
    And then it's gone. Who knows
    What lies beyond that event horizon?
    Our life is but a trifle,
    A child's toy abandoned by the road
    When we are called home.
    Selene: Home? You might well hope it so,
    But—
    [Alarums off stage. Enter *a god*]
    God: *The hull is breached!*
    You must fly.

In the night I woke, chasing away the wisps of a dream. The building we were in had no ceiling, and faint light from the cavern roof filtered down upon us. In our sleep, we had moved closer together, and Nahid's arm lay over my chest, her head next to mine, her breath brushing my cheek. I turned my face to her, centimeters away. Her face was placid, her eyelashes dark and long.

As I watched her, her eyelids fluttered and she awoke. She did not flinch at my closeness, but simply, soberly looked into my own eyes for what seemed like a very long time. I leaned forward and kissed her.

She did not pull away, but kissed me back strongly. She made a little moan in her throat, and I pulled her tightly to me.

We made love in the empty, ancient city. Her fingers entwined with mine, arms taut. Shadow of my torso across her breast. Hard, shuddering breath. Her lips on my chest. Smell of her sweat and mine. My palm brushing her abdomen. The feeling of her dark skin against mine. Her quiet laugh.

"Your leg," I said, as we lay in the darkness, spent.

"What about it?"

"Did I hurt you?"

She laughed again, lightly. "Now you ask. You are indeed all man."

In the morning, we took another meal from the ancient restaurant, food that had been manufactured from raw molecules while we waited, or perhaps stored somewhere for millennia.

We left by the corridor opposite the one by which we had entered, heading for the other side of the mountain range. Nahid limped but made no complaint. The passage ended in another door, beyond which a cave twisted upward. In one place, the ceiling of the cave had collapsed, and we had to crawl on our bellies over rubble through the narrow gap it had left. The exit was onto a horizontal shelf overgrown with trees, well below the pass. It was mid-morning. A misting rain fell across the Sharishabz Valley. In the distance, hazed by clouds of mist, I caught a small gleam of the white buildings of the monastery on the Penitent's Ridge. I pointed it out to Nahid. We scanned the mountainside below us, searching for the forest road.

Nahid found the thread of the road before I. "No sign of the Caslonians," she said.

"They're guarding the pass on the other side of the mountain, searching the woods there for us."

We descended the slope, picking our way through the trees toward the road. The mist left drops of water on our skinsuits, but did not in any way slow us. My spirits rose. I could see the end of this adventure in sight, and wondered what would happen to Nahid then.

"What will you do when we get to the monastery?" I asked her.

"I think I'll leave as soon as I can. I don't want to be there when the Caslonians find out you've reached your order with the plays."

"They won't do anything. The gods hold the monastery in their hands."

"Let us hope they don't drop it."

She would die soon, the statue had said—if left to the gods. But what person was not at the mercy of the gods? Still, she would be much more at risk alone, away from the order. "What about your leg?" I asked.

"Do you have a clinic there?"

"Yes."

"I'll take an exoskeleton and some painkillers and be on my way."

"Where will you go?"

"Wherever I can."

"But you don't even know what's happened in the last sixty years. What can you do?"

"Maybe my people are still alive. That's where I'll go—the town where I grew up. Perhaps I'll find someone who remembers me. Maybe I'll find my own grave."

"Don't go."

She strode along more aggressively. I could see her wince with each step. "Look, I don't care about your monastery. I don't care about these plays. Mostly, I don't care about *you*. Give me some painkillers and an exo, and I'll be gone."

That ended our conversation. We walked on in silence through the woods, me brooding, she limping along, grimacing.

We found the forest road. Here the land fell away sharply, and the road, hardly more than a gravel track, switchbacked severely as we made our way down the mountainside. We met no signs of pursuit. Though the rain continued, the air warmed as we moved lower, and beads of sweat trickled down my back under the skinsuit. The boots I wore were not meant for hiking, and by now my feet were sore, my back hurt. I could only imagine how bad it was for Nahid.

I had worked for years to manage my appetites, and yet I could not escape images of our night together. With a combination of shame and desire, I wanted her still. I did not think I could go back to being just another monk. The order had existed long before the Caslonian conquest, and would long outlast it. I was merely a cell passing through the body of this immortal creation. What did the gods want from me? What was to come of all this?

At the base of the trail, the road straightened, following the course of the River Sharishabz up the valley. Ahead rose the plateau, the gleaming white buildings of the monastery clearly visible now. The ornamental gardens, the terraced fields tended by the order for millennia. I could almost taste the sweet oranges and pomegranates. It would be good to be back home, a place where I could hide away form the world and figure out exactly what was in store for me. I wouldn't mind being hailed as a hero, the liberator of our people, like Stochik himself, who took the plays from the hands of the gods.

The valley sycamores and aspens rustled with the breeze. The afternoon passed. We stopped by the stream and drank. Rested, then continued.

We came to a rise in the road, where it twisted to climb the plateau. Signs here of travel, ruts of iron wheels where people from the villages drove supplies to the monastery. Pilgrims passed this way—though there was no sign of anyone today.

We made a turn in the road, and I heard a yelp behind me. I turned to find Nahid struggling in the middle of the road. At first, I thought she was suffering a seizure. Her body writhed and jerked. Then I realized, from the slick of rain deflected from his form, that she was being assaulted by a person in an invisibility cloak.

This understanding had only flashed through my mind when I was thrown to the ground by an unseen hand. I kicked out wildly, and my boot made contact. Gravel sprayed beside me where my attacker fell. I slipped into accelerated mode, kicked him again, rolled away, and dashed into the woods. Above me I heard the whine of an approaching flyer. *Run!* It was the voice of Horus, god of sun and moon.

I ran. The commandos did not know these woods the way I did. I had spent ten years exploring them, playing games of hide and hunt in the night with my fellow novices: I knew I could find my way to the monastery without them capturing me.

And Nahid? Clearly this was her spoken-of death. No doubt it had already taken place. Or perhaps they wouldn't kill her immediately, but would torture her, assuming she knew something, or even if they knew she didn't, taking some measure of revenge on her body. It was the lot of a Republican Guard to receive such treatment. She would even expect it. *The order comes first.*

Every second took me farther from the road, away from the Caslonians. But after a minute of hurrying silently through the trees, I felt something heavy in my hand. I stopped. Without realizing it, I had taken the object the metal man had given me out of my belt pouch. *She would not want you to return. The freedom of her people comes before her personal safety.*

I circled back, and found them in the road.

The flyer had come down athwart the road. The soldiers had turned off their cloaks, three men garbed head to toe in the matte gray of light deflection suits. Two soldiers had Nahid on her knees in the drizzle, her hands tied behind her back. One jerked her head back by her hair, holding a knife to her throat while an officer asked her questions. The officer slapped her, whipping the back of his gloved hand across her face.

I moved past them through the woods, sound of rain on the foliage, still holding the metal sphere in my hand. The flyer sat only a few meters into the road. I crouched there, staring at the uncouth object. I rotated it in my palm until I found the surface pentagon that was silvered. I depressed this pentagon until it clicked.

Then I flipped it out into the road, under the landing pads of the flyer, and fell back.

It was not so much an explosion as a vortex, warping the flyer into an impossible shape, throwing it off they road. As it spun the pilot was tossed from the cockpit, his uniform flaring in electric blue flame. The three men with Nahid were sucked off their feet by the dimensional warp. They jerked their heads toward the screaming pilot. The officer staggered to his feet, took two steps toward him, and one of the men followed. By that time, I had launched myself into the road, and slammed my bad shoulder into the small of the back of the man holding Nahid. I seized his rifle and fired, killing the officer and the other soldier, then the one I had just laid flat. The pilot was rolling in the gravel to extinguish the flames. I stepped forward calmly and shot him in the head.

Acrid black smoke rose from the crushed flyer, which lay on its side in the woods.

Nahid was bleeding from a cut on her neck. She held her palm against the wound, but the blood seeped steadily from between her fingers. I gathered her up and dragged her into the woods before reinforcements could arrive.

"Thank you," Nahid gasped, her eyes large, and fixed on me. We limped off into the trees.

Nahid was badly hurt, but I knew where we were, and I managed, through that difficult night, to get us up the pilgrim's trail to the monastery. By the time we reached the iron door we called the Mud Gate she had lost consciousness and I was carrying her. Her blood was all over us, and I could not tell if she yet breathed.

We novices had used this gate many times to sneak out of the monastery to play martial games in the darkness, explore the woods, and pretend we were ordinary men. Men who, when they desired something, had only to take it. Men who were under no vow of non-violence. Here I had earned a week's fast by bloodying the nose, in a fit of temper, of Brother Taher. Now I returned, unrepentant over the number of men I had killed in the last days, a man who had disobeyed the voice of a god, hoping to save Nahid before she bled out.

Brother Pramha was the first to greet me. He looked at me with shock. "Who is this?" he asked.

"This is a friend, a soldier, Nahid. Quickly. She needs care."

Together we took her to the clinic. Pramha ran off to inform the master. Our physician Brother Nastricht sealed her throat wound, and gave her new blood. I held her hand. She did not regain consciousness

Soon, one of the novices arrived to summon me to Master Darius's chambers. Although I was exhausted, I hurried after him through the warren of corridors, up the tower steps. I unbelted my blaster and handed it to the novice—he seemed distressed to hold the destructive device—and entered the room.

Beyond the broad window that formed the far wall of the chamber, dawn stained the sky pink. Master Darius held out his arms. I approached him, humbly bowed my head, and he embraced me. The warmth of his large body enfolding me was an inexpressible comfort. He smelled of cinnamon. He let me go, held me at arm's length, and smiled. The kosode he wore I recognized as one I had sewn myself. "I cannot tell you how good it is to see you, Adlan."

"I have the plays," I announced.

"The behavior of our Caslonian masters has been proof enough of that," he replied. His broad, plain face was somber as he told me of the massacre in Radnapuja, where the colonial government had held six thousand citizens hostage, demanding the bodily presentation, alive, of the foul villain, the man without honor or soul, the sacrilegious terrorist who had stolen the Foundational Plays.

"Six thousand dead?"

"They won't be the last," the master said. "The plays have been used as a weapon, as a means of controlling us. The beliefs which they embody work within the minds and souls of every person on this planet. They work even on those who are unbelievers."

"Nahid is an unbeliever."

"Nahid? She is this soldier whom you brought here?"

"The Republican Guard you sent with me. She doesn't believe, but she has played her role in bringing me here."

Master Darius poured me a glass of fortifying spirits, and handed it to me as if he were a novice and I the master. He sat in his great chair, had me sit in the chair opposite, and bade me recount every detail of the mission. I did so.

"It is indeed miraculous that you have come back alive," Master Darius mused. "Had you died, the plays would have been lost forever."

"The gods would not allow such a sacrilege."

"Perhaps. You carry the only copies in your mind?"

"Indeed. I have even quoted them to Nahid."

"Not at any length, I hope."

I laughed at his jest. "But now we can free Helvetica," I said. "Before any further innocents are killed, you must contact the Caslonian colonial government and tell them we have the plays. Tell them they must stop or we will destroy them."

Master Darius held up his hand and looked at me piercingly—I had seen this gesture many times in his tutoring of me. "First, let me ask you some questions about your tale. You tell me that, when you first came to consciousness after stealing the plays in the Imperial City, a god told you to run. Yet to run in the Caslonian capital is only to attract unwelcome attention."

"Yes. Bishamon must have wanted to hurry my escape."

"But when you reached the port bazaar, the god told you to stop and enter the restaurant. You run to attract attention, and dawdle long enough to allow time for you to be caught. Does this make sense?"

My fatigue made it difficult for me to think. What point was the master trying to make? "Perhaps I was not supposed to stop," I replied. "It was my own weakness. I was hungry."

"Then, later, you tell me that when the commandos boarded your ship, you escaped by following Nahid's lead, not the word of the gods."

"Liu-Bei led us out of the engine room. I think this is a matter of my misinterpreting—"

"And this metal man you encountered in the ancient city. Did he in fact say that the gods would have seen Nahid dead?"

"The statue said many mad things."

"Yet the device he gave you was the agent of her salvation?"

"I used it for that." Out of shame, I had not told Master Darius that I had disobeyed the command of the god who told me to flee.

"Many paradoxes." The master took a sip from his own glass. "So, if we give the plays back, what will happen then?"

"Then Helvetica will be free."

"And after that?"

"After that, we can do as we wish. The Caslonians would not dare to violate a holy vow. The gods would punish them. They know that. They are believers, as are we."

"Yes, they are believers. They would obey any compact they made, for fear of the wrath of the gods. They believe what you hold contained in your mind, Adlan, is true. So, as you say, you must give them to me now, and I will see to their disposition."

"Their disposition? How will you see to their disposition?"

"That is not something for you to worry about, my son. You have done well, and you deserve all our thanks. Brother Ishmael will see to unburdening you of the great weight you carry."

A silence ensued. I knew it was a sign of my dismissal. I must go to Brother Ishmael. But I did not rise. "What will you do with them?"

Master Darius's brown eyes lay steady on me, and quiet. "You have always been my favorite. I think perhaps, you know what I intend."

I pondered our conversation. "You—you're going to destroy them."

"Perhaps I was wrong not to have you destroy them the minute you gained access to the archives. But at that time I had not come to these conclusions."

"But the wrath of the Caslonians will know no limit! We will be exterminated!"

"We may be exterminated, and Helvetica remain in chains, but once these plays are destroyed, never to be recovered, then *humanity* will begin to be truly free. This metal man, you say, told you the gods left the better part of themselves behind. That is profoundly true. Yet there is no moment when they cease to gaze over our shoulders. Indeed, if we are ever to be free human beings, and not puppets jerked about by unseen forces—which may, or may not, exist—the gods must go. And the beginning of that process is the destruction of the foundational plays."

I did not know how to react. In my naiveté I said, "This does not seem right."

"I assure you, my son, that it is."

"If we destroy the plays, it will be the last thing we ever do."

"Of course not. Time will not stop."

"Time may not stop," I said, "but it might as well. Any things that happen after the loss of the gods will have no meaning."

Master Darius rose from his chair and moved toward his desk. "You are tired, and very young," he said, his back to me. "I have lived in the shadow of the gods far longer than you have." He reached over his desk, opened a drawer, took something out, and straightened.

He is lying. It seemed to me to be the voice of Inti himself. I stood. I felt surpassing weariness, but I moved silently. In my boot I still carried the force knife I had stolen from the restaurant on Caslon. I drew out the hilt, switched on the blade, and approached the master just as he began to turn.

When he faced me, he had a blaster in his hands. He was surprised to find me so close to him. His eyes went wide as I slipped the blade into his belly below his lowest rib.

Stochik: Here ends our story.
    Let no more be said of our fall.
    Mark the planting of this seed.
    The tree that grows in this place
    Will bear witness to our deeds;
    No other witness shall we have.
    Selene: I would not depart with any other
    My love. Keep alive whatever word
    May permit us to move forward.
    Leaving all else behind we must
    Allow the world to come to us.

The Caslonian government capitulated within a week after we contacted them. Once they began to withdraw their forces from the planet and a provisional government for the Helvetican Republic was re-established in Astara, I underwent the delicate process of downloading the foundational dramas from my mind. *The Abandonment* was once again embodied in a crystal, which was presented to the Caslonian legate in a formal ceremony on the anniversary of the rebirth of man.

The ceremony took place on a bright day in mid summer in that city of a thousand spires. Sunlight flooded the streets, where citizens in vibrant colored robes danced and sang to the music of bagpipes. Pennants in purple and green flew from those spires; children hung out of second-story school windows, shaking snowstorms of confetti on the parades. The smell of incense wafted down from the great temple, and across the sky flyers drew intricate patterns with lines of colored smoke.

Nahid and I were there on that day, though I did not take a leading role in the ceremony, preferring to withdraw to my proper station. In truth, I am not a significant individual. I have only served the gods.

I left the order as soon as the negotiations were completed. At first the brothers were appalled by my murder of Master Darius. I explained to them that he had gone mad and intended to kill me in order to destroy the plays. There was considerable doubt. But when I insisted that we follow through with the plan as the Master had presented it to the brothers before sending me

EVENTS PRECEDING THE HELVETICAN RENAISSANCE

on my mission, they seemed to take my word about his actions. The success of our thieving enterprise overshadowed the loss of the great leader, and indeed has contributed to his legend, making of him a tragic figure. A drama has been written of his life and death, and the liberation of Helvetica.

Last night, Nahid and I, with our children and grandchildren, watched it performed in the square of the town where we set up the tailor's shop that has been the center of our lives for the last forty years. Seeing the events of my youth played out on the platform, in their comedy and tragedy, hazard and fortune, calls again to my mind the question of whether I have deserved the blessings that have fallen to me ever since that day. I have not heard the voices of the gods since I slipped the knife into the belly of the man who taught me all that I knew of grace.

The rapid decline of the Caslonian Empire, and the Helvetican renaissance that has led to our current prosperity, all date from that moment in his chambers when I ended his plan to free men from belief and duty. The people, joyous on their knees in the temples of twelve planets, give praise to the gods for their deliverance, listen, hear, and obey.

Soon I will rest beneath the earth, like the metal man who traduced the gods, though less likely than he ever to walk again. If I have done wrong, it is not for me to judge. I rest, my lover's hand in mine, in the expectation of no final word.

BIOGRAPHIES

Steven Gould is best known for his novel *Jumper* which was made into the 2008 movie of the same name, as well as its sequels *Reflex* and *Jumper: Griffin's Story*. His other novels include *Wildside, Helm,* and *Blind Waves*. His forthcoming book, *7th Sigma*, is about Kimball (from "A Story, with Beans") and his adventures in the Territory where small robotic bugs eat metal. Steven lives in Albuquerque with his wife, sf writer Laura J. Mixon, his two teenage daughters, two dogs, two parakeets, a guinea pig, and five chickens. He is currently working on his next book, a new *Jumper* novel, about the daughter of Davy and Millie Rice.

Theodora Goss was born in Hungary and spent her childhood in various European countries before her family moved to the United States. Although she grew up on the classics of English literature, her writing has been influenced by an Eastern European literary tradition in which the boundaries between realism and the fantastic are often ambiguous. Her publications include the short story collection *In the Forest of Forgetting* (2006); *Interfictions* (2007), a short story anthology coedited with Delia Sherman; and *Voices from Fairyland* (2008), a poetry anthology with critical essays and a selection of her own poems. Her short stories and poems have won the World Fantasy and Rhysling Awards. Visit her website at www.theodoragoss.com.

Peter Watts—described by the *Globe & Mail* as one of the best hard-sf authors alive—writes (relatively) plausible science fiction informed by his background as a biologist. His work has been translated into a shitload of languages; his debut novel Starfish was a *NY Times* Notable Book of the Year, and his most recent (*Blindsight*) made the final ballot for six major genre awards (including the Hugo), winning exactly none of them. (This may reflect a certain controversy regarding Watts' work; his novel *Behemoth*, for example, was both praised by *Publishers Weekly* as "a major addition to 21st-century hard SF," and decried by Kirkus as "horrific porn.") Watts also pioneered the technique of loading scientific references into the backs of his novels, which both adds a veneer of credibility and acts as a shield against nitpickers. Both he and his cat have appeared multiple times in the prestigious journal *Nature*.

Robert Kelly teaches in the Written Arts Program at Bard College, where he is Asher B. Edelman Professor of Literature. His recent books are *Threads, Lapis, May Day*, the long poem *Fire Exit*, the novel *The Book from the Sky*, and the forthcoming *The Logic of the World and Other Fictions*.

Holly Phillips is the author of the award-winning collection *In the Palace of Repose*. She has two novels in print (*The Engine's Child* and *The Burning Girl*), a third en route to the publisher, and a fourth currently under construction. Holly's website, www.hollyphillips.com, features a weekly "Dear Reader" essay about writing, reading, and the wonderful world of genre publishing. She writes from a red couch on Vancouver Island.

Ann Leckie is a graduate of Clarion West. Her fiction has appeared in *Subterranean Magazine, Realms of Fantasy,* and *Strange Horizons*. She has worked as a waitress, a receptionist, a rodman on a land-surveying crew, and a recording engineer. She lives in St. Louis.

Since publishing his first story in F&SF in 2000, **Alex Irvine** has written four novels—*A Scattering of Jades, One King, One Soldier, The Narrows,* and *Buyout*. Jades won the International Horror Guild, Locus, and Crawford awards in 2001. He has also written three novellas: *The Life of Riley, Mystery Hill,* and *Mare Ultima* (of which "Dragon's Teeth" is a part). His short fiction is collected in *Unintended Consequences* and *Pictures from an Expedition*. Irvine's comic and media-related works include *Daredevil Noir, The Vertigo Encyclopedia,* and *The Supernatural Book of Monsters, Demons, Spirits, and Ghouls*. He teaches at the University of Maine.

In addition to working as a doctor, **Sara Genge** writes speculative fiction for the sleepless mind. SF, fantasy, slipstream or none of the above—she doesn't really care what you call it, as long as she enjoys writing it and you enjoy reading it. Sara lives in Madrid and enjoys a cat-free life. www.saragenge.com

Lucius Shepard lives and works in Portland OR. Upcoming works include a novella collection, *Five Autobiographies*, and a novel, *Beautiful Blood*.

Jo Walton is a science fiction and fantasy writer. She won the John W. Campbell Award for best new writer in 2002, after the publication of her first novel *The King's Peace*, and the World Fantasy Award in 2004 for *Tooth and Claw*. Her most recent books are the Small Change trilogy of alternate history novels, *Farthing, Ha'penny,* and *Half a Crown,* and she has a new fantasy novel *Among Others* forthcoming in June 2010 from Tor. She comes from Wales but lives in Montreal where the books and food are more varied.

John Meaney is the author of the gothic SF/fantasy crossover novels, *Bone Song* and *Black Blood*, and of the space opera trilogy comprising *Paradox, Context* and *Resolution*, plus the standalone *To Hold Infinity*. Currently he is working on a massive hard-SF trilogy and a sequence of near-future, violent satirical thrillers. His novels and short fiction have been three-time finalists for the British SF Award, won the Independent Publishers Best Novel award (in SF/fantasy) and been one of the *Daily Telegraph* Books of the Year (first choice in SF/fantasy). Now a full-time writer, he has taught business analysis and software engineering on three continents, holds a black belt in shotokan karate, and is a trained hypnotist. He adores cats, loves chocolate, and drinks cappuccinos by the gallon.

Paul Park is the author of ten novels in various genres, and a collection of short stories. He lives in Berkshire County with his wife and children, and teaches part-time at Williams College.

Robert Charles Wilson is the author of more than a dozen books, including the Hugo Award-winning novel *Spin*. He lives outside Toronto, Ontario, with his wife Sharry. His most recent novel is *Julian Comstock: A Story of 22nd-Century America*.

Jay Lake lives in Portland, Oregon, where he works on numerous writing and editing projects. His 2010 books are *Pinion* from Tor Books, *The Baby Killers* from PS Publishing, and *The Sky That Wraps* from Subterranean Press. His short fiction appears regularly in literary and genre markets worldwide. Jay is a winner of the John W. Campbell Award for Best New Writer, and a multiple nominee for the Hugo and World Fantasy Awards.

John Langan is the author of *Mr. Gaunt and Other Uneasy Encounters* (Prime 2008), which was nominated for the Bram Stoker Award, and *House of Windows* (Night Shade 2009). His stories have appeared in John Joseph Adams's *By Blood We Live* (Night Shade 2009) and *The Living Dead* (Night Shade 2008) and Ellen Datlow's *Poe* (Solaris 2009), as well as in *The Magazine of Fantasy and Science Fiction*. He lives in Upstate New York with his wife, son, and a couple of neurotic cats.

Eugene Mirabelli writes novels, short stories, journalistic pieces on politics, economics and culture, as well as book reviews. He's a Nebula Award nominee, has been awarded a Rockefeller Grant, and his fiction has been published in French, Czech, Hebrew, Russian, Sicilian, and Turkish. Although he writes science fiction short stories, his novels are straight literary fiction, as in *The Passion of Terri Heart*, or his most recent work, *The Goddess in Love with a Horse*.

Paul McAuley worked as a research biologist in various universities, including Oxford and UCLA, and for six years was a lecturer in botany at St Andrews University before becoming a full-time writer. His latest novels are *The Quiet War* and *Gardens of the Sun.* He lives in North London.

Rachel Swirsky is a graduate of the Iowa Writers Workshop where she learned to be cold and the Clarion West Writers Workshop in Seattle where she learned to be rained on. Currently, she lives in Bakersfield, California, where hundred-and-fifteen-degree summer days are teaching her to wish she was cold and/or rained on. Her short fiction has appeared in a number of venues including *Tor.com, Subterranean Magazine, Weird Tales,* and *Fantasy Magazine,* and has been collected in year's best anthologies edited by Strahan, Horton, and the VanderMeers.

Nir Yaniv is an Israeli writer, editor and musician. His stories were published in several printed and online magazines in Israel and outside it. His story collection, *One Hell of a Writer,* was published by Odyssey Press in 2006. In 2009, two books he co-wrote with Lavie Tidhar were published: *Fictional Murder* (Odyssey Press, Israel) and *The Tel Aviv Dossier* (Chizine Publications, Canada). A collection of his translated short stories, *The Love Machine & Other Contraptions,* is due to be published in the US in 2010 by RedJack. Nir founded the first Israeli online sf/f magazine, then went on to edit Israel's only pro speculative fiction magazine, *Dreams in Aspamia.* As a musician he has performed in several jazz festivals, was the lead singer and/or bassist of several rock and funk groups, and is an a-capella machine on acid. He lives in Tel Aviv, where he records his music in his own studio, The Nir Space Station. His home site (including stories, articles and free music): www.nyfiction.org

Dominic Green used to work for a British bank, but has been Displaced. He now hangs around libraries stinking up the place. He has mainly been published in *Interzone,* the world's best science fiction magazine—reading which will put hairs on your chest whether you are a man or a woman—since 1996. He was nominated for a Hugo award in 2006 for *The Clockwork Atom Bomb,* but cannot get literary agents or publishers to recognize his existence, no matter how many members of their families he kidnaps. For this reason, he puts novels online on the British website ABCTales.com, where they can be read for free—*Saucerers and Gondoliers* and *Sister Ships and Alastair,* two SF novels for younger readers, and *Abaddon,* which is for older readers with very strong stomachs. A third book in the Saucerers series is on the way.

Damien Broderick is an Australian sf writer and critic, a senior fellow in the School of Culture and Communication at the University of Melbourne, currently living in San Antonio, Texas. He has published more than forty books, including *Reading by Starlight, Transrealist Fiction, x, y, z, t:*

Dimensions of Science Fiction, Unleashing the Strange, and *Chained to the Alien.* His latest sf novel was the diptych *Godplayers* and *K-Machines,* and his recent sf collections are *Uncle Bones* and *The Qualia Engine.*

Born in the Pacific Northwest in 1979, **Catherynne M. Valente** is the author of a dozen works of fiction and poetry, including *Palimpsest,* the Orphan's Tales series, *The Labyrinth,* and crowdfunded phenomenon *The Girl Who Circumnavigated Fairyland in a Ship of Her Own Making.* She is the winner of the Tiptree Award, the Mythopoeic Award, the Rhysling Award, and the Million Writers Award She has been nominated for the Pushcart Prize, the Spectrum Awards, and was a finalist for the World Fantasy Award in 2007 and 2009. She lives on an island off the coast of Maine with her partner and two dogs.

Rodrigo Garcia y Robertson was born in 1949. He has a Ph.D in history and has taught at UCLA and Villanova. His first short fiction, *The Flying Mountain,* was published in 1987 and he has published about fifty short stories, novelettes and novellas. His first novel, *The Spiral Dance,* was published in 1991 and he has published eight novels as well as a short story collection. He lives in Washington State.

Nancy Kress is the author of twenty-six books: three fantasy novels, twelve SF novels, three thrillers, four collections of short stories, one YA novel, and three books on writing fiction. She is perhaps best known for the "Sleepless" trilogy that began with *Beggars in Spain.* The novel was based on a Nebula- and Hugo-winning novella of the same name. She won her second Hugo in 2009 in Montreal, for the novella "The Erdmann Nexus." Kress has also won three additional Nebulas, a Sturgeon, and the 2003 John W. Campbell Award (for *Probability Space*). Her most recent books are a collection of short stories, *Nano Comes to Clifford Falls and Other Stories* (Golden Gryphon Press, 2008); a bio-thriller, *DOGS* (Tachyon Press, 2008); and an SF novel, *Steal Across the Sky* (Tor, 2009). Kress's fiction, much of which concerns genetic engineering, has been translated into twenty languages. She often teaches writing at various venues around the country.

Sarah Monette grew up in Oak Ridge, Tennessee, one of the three secret cities of the Manhattan Project, and now lives in a 103-year-old house in the Upper Midwest with a great many books, four cats, one husband, and one albino bristlenose plecostomus. Her Ph.D. diploma (English Literature, 2004) hangs in the kitchen. Her first four novels were published by Ace Books. Her short stories have appeared in *Strange Horizons, Weird Tales,* and *Lady Churchill's Rosebud Wristlet,* among other venues, and have been reprinted in several Year's Best anthologies; a short story collection, *The Bone Key,* was published by Prime Books in 2007. She has written one novel (*A Companion to Wolves,*

Tor Books, 2007) and three short stories with Elizabeth Bear, and hopes to write more. Visit her online at www.sarahmonette.com.

Elizabeth Bear was born on the same day as Frodo and Bilbo Baggins, but in a different year. She is the author of some fifteen published novels and over fifty short stories, and has been honored with the Hugo, Sturgeon, and Campbell awards, among others. Her hobbies include rock climbing and playing very bad guitar. She lives near Hartford, CT, with a Presumptuous Cat and a Giant Ridiculous Dog.

Margo Lanagan's most recent novel, *Tender Morsels,* was published to immediate critical success in the US, the UK and Australia, is a Printz Honor book and won the World Fantasy Award for Best Novel. Her 2006 collection of speculative fiction short stories, *Black Juice,* was also widely acclaimed, won two World Fantasy Awards, two Ditmar and two Aurealis Awards, was shortlisted for the *Los Angeles Times* Book Prize and also won a Printz Honor, and stories from it were shortlisted for a Hugo, a Nebula, a Theodore Sturgeon, a Bram Stoker, an International Horror Guild Award and a Tiptree. Her third collection, *Red Spikes,* was the Children's Book Council Book of the Year for older readers, and was shortlisted for the Commonwealth Writers Prize and the World Fantasy Award, and longlisted for the Frank O'Connor International Short Story Award. She lives in Sydney and is working on another novel.

Nashville native **Toiya Kristen Finley** is a freelance writer and editor and former professional graduate student. She has published fiction, creative nonfiction, and academic articles in a variety of venues and is currently venturing into game writing. Her fiction has appeared in *Nature, Electric Velocipede, Sybil's Garage, Farrago's Wainscot,* and *Expanded Horizons.* She is the founding and former managing/fiction editor of *Harpur Palate.*

Kelly Link is the author of three collections, most recently Pretty Monsters. She was also a co-editor, for five years, of *The Year's Best Fantasy and Horror.* She lives in Northampton, Massachusetts, with her husband Gavin J. Grant, and their daughter, Ursula. She and Gavin run Small Beer Press and publish the zine *Lady Churchill's Rosebud Wristlet.* Kelly's stories have most recently appeared in the anthologies *Troll's Eye View* and *Geektastic.* Her website is www.kellylink.net.

Genevieve Valentine's short fiction has appeared in *Clarkesworld, Strange Horizons, Journal of Mythic Arts, Fantasy, Federations,* and more; her first novel is forthcoming from Prime Books. She is a columnist at *Tor.com* and *Fantasy Magazine.* Her appetite for bad movies is insatiable, a tragedy she tracks on her blog, genevievevalentine.com

John Kessel teaches creative writing and literature at North Carolina State University in Raleigh. A winner of the Nebula Award, the Theodore Sturgeon Award, the Locus Award, the Shirley Jackson Award, and the James Tiptree, Jr. Award, his books include *Good News from Outer Space, Corrupting Dr. Nice,* and *The Pure Product.* His story collection, *Meeting in Infinity,* was named a notable book of 1992 by the *New York Times Book Review,* and Kim Stanley Robinson has called *Corrupting Dr. Nice* "the best time travel novel ever written." With James Patrick Kelly he edited the anthologies *Feeling Very Strange: The Slipstream Anthology; Rewired: The Post-Cyberpunk Anthology;* and most recently, *The Secret History of Science Fiction.* His recent collection *The Baum Plan for Financial Independence and Other Stories* contains the 2008 Nebula-Award-winning story "Pride and Prometheus."

RECOMMENDED READING

Daniel Abraham, "The Best Monkey" (**The Solaris Book
     of New Science Fiction Volume III**)
Daniel Abraham, "Balfour and Meriwether in the Adventure
     of the Emperor's Vengeance" (*Postscripts* #19)
Chris Adrian, "A Tiny Feast" (*The New Yorker*, April 20)
Forrest Aguirre, "The Non-Epistemological Universe of Emmaeus Holt"
     (*Farrago's Wainscot*, July)
Tim Akers, "A Soul Stitched to Iron" (**The Solaris Book
     of New Science Fiction Volume III**)
Camille Alexa, "Shades of White and Red" (*Fantasy*, April)
Peter M. Ball, **Horn** (**Horn**)
John Barnes, "Things Undone" (*Jim Baen's Universe*, December)
Stephen Baxter, "Formidable Caress" (*Analog*, December)
Stephen Baxter, "Earth II" (*Asimov's*, July)
Peter S. Beagle, "By Moonlight" (**We Never Talk About My Brother**)
Elizabeth Bear and Emma Bull "Lucky Day" (*Shadow Unit*)
Paul M. Berger, "Home Again" (*Interzone*, April)
Ilsa J. Bick, "Second Sight" (**Crime Spells**)
Damien Broderick, "This Wind Blowing, and This Tide"
     (*Asimov's*, April-May)
Damien Broderick, "Uncle Bones" (*Asimov's*, January)
Emma Bull, Elizabeth Bear, and Leah Bobet, "Cuckoo" (*Shadow Unit*)
Emma Bull, "Getaway" (*Shadow Unit*)
Pat Cadigan, "Truth and Bone" (**Poe**)
Adam-Troy Castro, "Gunfight on Farside" (*Analog*, April)
Fred Chappell, "Shadow of the Valley" *F&SF*, (February)
Catherine Cheek, "Voice Like a Cello" (*Fantasy*, May)
J. Kathleen Cheney, "Early Winter, near Jenli Village" (*Fantasy*, April)
C. S. E. Cooney, "Three Fancies from the Infernal Garden"
     (*Subterranean*, Winter)
Paul Cornell, "One of our Bastards is Missing" (**The Solaris Book
     of New Science Fiction Volume III**)
Benjamin Crowell, "The Rising Waters" (*Strange Horizons*, May 4-11)
Paul di Filippo, "Yes, We Have No Bananas" (**Eclipse Three**)

Graham Edwards, "Riding the Drop" (*Jim Baen's Universe*, April)

Sarah L. Edwards, "The Tinyman and Caroline"
      (*Beneath Ceaseless Skies*, May 21)

Carol Emshwiller, "The Bird Painter in the Time of War"
      (*Asimov's*, February)

Gemma Files and Stephen J. Barringer, "each thing I show you is a piece
      of my death" (**Clockwork Phoenix 2**)

Karen Joy Fowler, "The Pelican Bar" (**Eclipse Three**)

R. Garcia y Robertson, "SinBad the Sand Sailor" (*Asimov's*, July)

Theodora Goss, "Csilla's Story" (**Other Earths**)

Theodora Goss, "The Puma" (*Apex Digest*, March)

Eric Gregory, "Salt's Father" (*Strange Horizons*, August 3)

Nicola Griffith, "It Takes Two" (**Eclipse Three**)

Paul Haines, "Wives" (**x⁶**)

Merrie Haskell, "Sun's East, Moon's West" (*Electric Velocipede*, Spring)

Daniel Hatch, "Seeds of Revolution" (*Analog*, July-August)

Dave Hutchinson, **The Push** (**The Push**)

Alex Irvine, "Seventh Fall" (*Subterranean*, Summer)

Kij Johnson, "Spar" (*Clarkesworld*, October)

Richard Kadrey, "Trembling Blue Stars" (*Flurb* #7)

Helen Keeble, "A Journal of Certain Events of Scientific Interest from the
First Survey Voyage of the Southern Waters by HMS Ocelot, As Observed by
Professor Thaddeus Boswell, DPhil, MSc -or- A Lullaby"
      (*Strange Horizons*, June 1-8)

James Patrick Kelly, "Going Deep" (*Asimov's*, June)

Gary Kloster, "Adam, Unwilling" (*Jim Baen's Universe*, June)

Nicole Kornher-Stace, "The Raccoon's Daughter" (*Fantasy*, December)

Ted Kosmatka and Michael Poore, "Blood Dauber"
      (*Asimov's*, October-November)

Ted Kosmatka, "The Ascendant" (*Subterranean*, Spring)

Mary Robinette Kowal, "First Flight" (*Tor.com*, August)

Naomi Kritzer, "The Good Son" (*Jim Baen's Universe*, February)

Ellen Kushner, "'A Wild and Wicked Youth" (*F&SF*, April-May)

Jay Lake and Shannon Page, "Rolling Steel" (*Clarkesworld*, April)

Jay Lake, "Chain of Stars" (*Subterranean*, Fall)

John Lambshead, "Storming Hell" (*Jim Baen's Universe*, April)

Margo Lanagan, "Sea-Hearts" (**x⁶**)

Tanith Lee, "Clockatrice" (*Fantasy*, October)

Yoon Ha Lee, "The Unstrung Zither" (*F&SF*, March)

Tanith Lee, "Comfort and Despair" (**Lace and Blade 2**)

David D. Levine, "Aggro Radius" (**Gamer Fantastic**)

Marissa K. Lingen, "Five Ways to Ruin a First Date" (*Not One of Us* #42)

Rochita Loenan-Ruiz, "Breaking the Spell"
      (**Philippine Speculative Fiction IV**)

Richard A. Lovett, "Excellence" (*Analog*, January-February)

Sandra McDonald, "Diana Comet" (*Strange Horizons*, March 2-9)

Maureen McHugh, "Useless Things" (**Eclipse Three**)

Will McIntosh, "Bridesicle" (*Asimov's*, January)

Eugene Mirabelli, "Love in Another Language" (*Not One of Us* #42)

Sarah Monette, "White Charles" (*Clarkesworld*, September)

James Morrow, "Bigfoot and the Bodhisattva" (*Conjunctions* 52)

Shweta Narayan, "Daya and Dharma" (*GUD*, Spring)

Charles Oberndorf, "Another Life" (*F&SF*, October-November)

Holly Phillips, "Thieves of Silence" (*Beneath Ceaseless Skies*, July 16)

Tony Pi, "Come-From-Aways" (*On Spec*, Spring)

Steven Popkes, "Two Boys" (*Asimov's*, August)

Tim Pratt, "A Programmatic Approach to Perfect Happiness"
        (*Futurismic*, April)

Tim Pratt, "Unexpected Outcomes" (*Interzone*, June)

Tim Pratt, "Another End of the Empire" (*Strange Horizons*, June 22)

Tim Pratt, "Silver Linings" (*Tor.com*, September)

David Prill, "The Heaven and Hell of Robert Flud" (**Poe**)

Robert Reed, "Firehorn" (*F&SF*, June-July)

Leonard Richardson, "Let Us Now Praise Awesome Dinosaurs"
        (*Strange Horizons*, July 23)

Madeleine E. Robins, "Writ of Exception" (**Lace and Blade 2**)

Justina Robson, "Crackglegrackle" (**The New Space Opera 2**)

Mary Rosenblum, "Lion Walk" (*Asimov's*, January)

Mary Rosenblum, "My She" (**Federations**)

Mary Rosenblum, "Blood Ice" (**Rage of the Behemoth**)

Rudy Rucker and Bruce Sterling, "Colliding Branes" (*Asimov's*, February)

Kristine Kathryn Rusch, "Broken Windchimes" (*Asimov's*, September)

Patricia Russo, "The Men Burned All the Boats" (*Fantasy*, February)

Geoff Ryman, "Blocked" (*F&SF*, October-November)

Ken Scholes, "A Weeping Czar Beholds the Fallen Moon"
        (*Tor.com*, February)

Grace Seybold, "Unrest" (*Beneath Ceaseless Skies*, March 12)

Lucius Shepard, "Halloween Town" (*F&SF*, October-November)

Delia Sherman, "Wizard's Apprentice" (**Troll's Eye View**)

Brian Stableford, "The Highway Code" (**We Think Therefore We Are**)

Justin Stanchfield, "The Buzz" (*Fictitious Force* #6)

Bruce Sterling, "Black Swan" (*Interzone*, April)

Charles Stross, "Palimpsest" (**Wireless**)

Laura L. Sullivan, "A Man of Kiri Maru" (*GUD*, Spring)

Mark Sumner, "St. George and the Antriders" (*Black Gate*, Spring)

Rachel Swirsky, "Great Golden Wings"
        (*Beneath Ceaseless Skies*, October 22)

Lavie Tidhar, "The Dying World" (*Clarkesworld*, April)

Lavie Tidhar, "The Shangri-La Affair" (*Strange Horizons*, January 19-26)

Jeremiah Tolbert, "The Culture Archivist" (**Federations**)

Mary Turzillo, "The Sugar" (**Sky Whales and Other Wonders**)

Lisa Tuttle "Ragged Claws" (*Postscripts #20/21*)

Catherynne M. Valente, "Golubash, or Wine-Blood-War-Elegy"
       (**Federations**)

Elliott Wells, "This Must Be the Place" (*Strange Horizons*, February 2)

Chris Willrich, "Sails the Morne" (*Asimov's*, June)

Daniel H. Wilson, "The Nostalgist" (*Tor.com*, July)

Robert Charles Wilson, "*Utriusque Cosmi*" (**The New Space Opera 2**)

Paul Witcover, "Everland" (**Everland**)

John C. Wright, "One Bright Star to Guide Them" (*F&SF*, April-May)

PUBLICATION HISTORY

ABOUT THE EDITOR

RICH HORTON is a software engineer in St. Louis. He is a contributing editor to *Locus*, for which he does short fiction reviews and occasional book reviews; and to *Black Gate*, for which he does a continuing series of essays about SF history. He also contributes book reviews to *Fantasy Magazine*, and to many other publications.